"ROBUST, RAMBUNCTIOUS . . . AN INTRICATELY WROUGHT BOOK REPLETE WITH PEOPLE, PLACES, AND EVENTS THAT ARE UNIQUELY CALIFORNIAN."

St. Louis Post-Dispatch

"Readers who like a multiplicity of characters, a colorful historical backdrop, and plenty of romance should enjoy this sweeping three-generational saga of Old California."

Publishers Weekly

"THE PROUD BREED brings to vivid life the landscape, the people, the difficulties, the torments, the joys, and victories of a unique section of America . . . a potent, volatile love story."

Deborah Hill, author of
This Is the House

THE
PROUD
BREED

a novel by

Celeste De Blasis

FAWCETT CREST • NEW YORK

THE PROUD BREED

THIS BOOK CONTAINS THE COMPLETE TEXT OF THE
ORIGINAL HARDCOVER EDITION.

Published by Fawcett Crest Books, a unit of CBS Publications,
the Consumer Publishing Division of CBS Inc., by arrangement
with Coward, McCann & Geoghegan, Inc.

ISBN: 0-449-23905-5

Printed in the United States of America

10 9 8 7 6 5 4 3 2 1

ACKNOWLEDGMENTS

Many people located books for me or loaned precious volumes from their private libraries, and many tracked down information I sorely needed. The following is only a sketchy accounting, and I ask pardon for any omissions: Joyce Anderson, Craig and Joseph Campbell, Lyn Coffman, Betty Coon, Harry Cross, Susan Dailey, Emil and Mary Ann Danenberg, Raymond De Blasis, Corki Goble, Dorothy Henderson, Aurora Martinez, Bonnie McRae, Mae Nassif, Mildred Packer, Petra Ramirez, Charlotte Sheward, Katie Taylor, and Nancy Young.

Some of the librarians at the Victorville branch of the San Bernardino County system did their utmost and used many alternate and time-consuming methods to circumvent rules which seemed designed to hinder research; without their assistance, the bibliography would be much the poorer. And while the officials at the Bancroft Library at Berkeley confiscated my folder before I entered the inner sanctum and followed me with cameras thereafter, they were unfailingly polite and even allowed me to handle original documents.

The Roman Catholic pastors of St. Joan of Arc, Victorville, St. David's, Apple Valley, Christ the Good Shepherd, Adelanto, and San Juan Capistrano Mission, and a noted historian of the Archdiocese of Los Angeles were generous with their knowledge of early California's church ritual.

Special people helped with the tedious task of preparing the final manuscript. My aunt, Donna Campbell, served as proofreader and gave me the gift of her involvement in the story despite the hours of careful reading her job demanded. My mother, Jean De Blasis, and my friends, Leonard Henderson and Michael Lowe, provided the necessary copies of the original.

As would be expected, most of the time involved in writing *The Proud Breed* was spent seated at my desk surrounded by a sea of papers and books, but there was one blissful interlude which was spent on the road. My mother drove, stopping whenever I thought there was something I ought to see. My grandmother, Litta Belle Campbell, kept us informed of the changing flora and fauna. Our friend, Trudi Jackson, added much to each day with her unfailing good humor and keen interest. We never had a disagreement; we were the best of traveling companions. Laughter sang through all our days and made my task much easier than it would otherwise have been. And my companions' willingness to join my fantasy made it possible for me to know my characters were only one day's ride away. Sometimes they were even closer—clear silhouettes at dusk.

We followed El Camino Real north to Monterey and then traveled east to Mariposa, tracing the Forty-Niners' trail backwards, heading north to Nevada City before I ended my quest in San Francisco. And in those old mining towns in the foothills of the great Sierras, I found people who possessed what I had lacked when I began this saga—a strong, sure sense of California's history. It was not something they had been formally taught, it was something they had experienced in the roughhewn texture of their towns and the vivid recollections of older generations. And without exception, the people I met were proud and eager to share what they knew.

To everyone, named and unnamed, who helped me in my quest, my deepest gratitude.

California
May 1977

CHAPTER I

She awakened as the first light touched the wall of the house and fell in ruby patterns on the tile of her bedroom floor. "I am sixteen years old today," she whispered, and then she laughed aloud. *"Feliz cumpleaños,* Tessa. On this twenty-fourth day of April in the year of our Lord eighteen hundred and forty-four, you are exactly sixteen years old."

She lay still for a moment thinking about what she might do with the day, and then her excitement got the better of her, and she was out of bed in one lithe movement.

She washed and dressed hurriedly in a simple blouse, skirt, and sash and ran a brush through the heavy length of her hair before she tied it back with a ribbon. There wasn't much chance her father would awaken from his drunken stupor this early, but she didn't want to risk it. Better to be gone than to listen to his remorseful explanations.

María was already busy in the kitchen when Tessa walked in, and the old woman scolded, "Look at you, dressed no better than a peasant. And I was going to spoil my little one with a late sleep and the breakfast in your bed."

Tessa held out the soft muslin of her skirt as she pirouetted around the room. "Don't I look a proper lady?" she giggled as she hugged María's short, stout body against her own slender form. María's broad, callused hands reached up to stroke the dark head before she pushed Tessa away with a small clucking sound. "It is not my birthday. There is work to be done, and you must eat before you go wandering."

"No, I must not. I'm too excited," Tessa protested, and María intoned solemnly, *"Tripa vacía, corazón sin alegría."* "Empty belly, unhappy heart." And Tessa shot back, *"A palabras necias, oidos sordos."* "To foolish words, deaf
10

ears." "You should know better, you and your sayings, I've learned them too well."

"Your clever tongue will lead you to trouble one of these days," María warned, but her scowl changed to a grin that lighted her brown face. "Before you go, you will look under the cloth there."

Tessa did as she was told and gasped with pleasure. She needed no labels to tell her who had made the gifts. The creamy white shawl, embroidered with silken flowers in all colors of the rainbow, could only have been made by María, and the halter and reins skillfully braided from the hair of the mares' manes, the many shades worked into a wondrously complicated pattern, were the work of María's husband Ramón, undoubtedly with the help of their two sons, Juan and Julio, who had learned the art from their father from cradle age.

Tessa kissed María soundly and exclaimed, "I would be lost without you, without all of the Ramirez family, my family."

"I want no other daughter," the old woman said softly before she thrust a packet of food tied in cloth into Tessa's hands. "Go now and have a beautiful day, my child, but take care."

Tessa stopped back in her room only long enough to pick up her knife, tying its leather scabbard to her sash— had María seen it, it would have told her that her darling planned to roam beyond call of the *vaqueros*. She worried enough as it was.

Neither of them had mentioned Tessa's father, and she gave only a cursory glance toward his quarters as she left the house. There was no sound of movement; it had been silly to worry. He would not be up for hours. Her unconscious sound of angry disgust died abruptly as she stepped outside. The day was already full of the sounds of the army of servants setting about their tasks, and the milling pack of dogs added their voices to the general clamor. She knew it was Ramón who had done yet another thing for her. Amordoro's coat had been brushed to the gleaming metal of his name, *Amor de oro*, love of gold, long since made one fond word by Tessa. His mane and tail shone like spun silver, and he had been saddled. Though he was not tied, he waited patiently for his mis-

11

tress, nickering softly at the sight of her. She rubbed the soft muzzle and spoke to the animal in Spanish and English as she slipped the new halter on. Horses were no rarity in California; tales were still told of the thousands that had been driven into the sea years before to rid the land of surplus. But a great golden stallion that needed neither bit nor spurs was a treasure indeed, not even matched by the fine chestnuts or dappled grays which many favored. A gift from her great-grandfather. She wondered what he would send this year. She did not wonder out of greed, but out of curiosity and the sure knowledge that he would send something extravagant and beautiful. It had been the same for the past six years, ever since her first sight of him at her mother's funeral. Her father had sent word by Ramón, and her great-grandfather had come. Other relatives she had never seen before had come also, but it was the lean old man dressed in black velvet whom she remembered.

Though his hair was white, his eyes were fierce and black with no shadow of age in them. His face was thin, arrogant, and hawk-nosed. He had stood looking down at her, and she had stared back and spoken first. "You look like an eagle. I like eagles." The old man had glared at her for a moment, and then he had thrown back his head and howled with laughter, rich and true, a sound oddly at variance with his stern aspect and the sadness of the occasion.

Tessa had liked him, and she had sensed that he liked her. He had held her hand tightly through the long drone of Latin poured over the still form of her mother and the tiny body of the infant son who had died with his mother in the ordeal of birth. She had seen death before in slaughtered bullocks, in all the casualties of life on the land, but she had not connected it to her own mortality and certainly not to her parents'. Parents lived forever. She had pressed tightly against the old man, whispering, "Soon she will wake up, won't she, and then all these people can go home."

"She will wake to God, no more to us," Don Esteban had said, but the fearsome words had been softened by the arms which had come around her, holding her close, and the tears which had fallen from the dark eyes. Tessa
12

had been astonished that someone who looked so much like God himself should cry, but she had been strangely comforted too.

Only once more had she seen Don Esteban, though she knew now that he had kept careful track of her and knew much of her life. And she knew the Ramirez family had been the ones to give him the answers to his questions. She was not resentful; as they had served her mother, now they served her in their way. In their hearts, Don Esteban, not her father, was *el patrón*, and as close to God as Tessa had judged him when she was ten years old.

Her father had died with her mother. Only his shell remained to drink up much of their hide and tallow profits in endless draughts of brandywine. Young as she was, she had begun to pick up the reins one by one as he dropped them. All on the rancho looked to her for decisions, and she made them. The normal order of things broke down. María could hardly claim the power of *dueña* over her, and she gave up the attempt when she discovered that Tessa's bright, quick mind was matched by an iron will that had been strengthened by the death of her mother. Tessa ran wild, and Don Esteban heard of it. His summons came, and for once her father showed the strength he had once had. As much as he and Don Esteban hated each other, they agreed on this.

Tessa made the long journey southward to the house of an aunt and an uncle she had never seen. They lived near the pueblo of Santa Barbara. Unlike hers, their blood was untainted by foreign influence. They were pure Spanish and proud of it. They had three daughters and two sons. The girls all looked forward to the prospect of good marriages. The sons planned to follow their father into the lucrative service to the government. They went to mass every morning, the girls wearing ugly dresses of cheap material, both *rebozo* and petticoat black, to show their humility and the equality of all in the eyes of God, and carrying embroidered rugs to kneel on. And when they returned from church, they donned rich fabrics and jewelry and spent the day gossiping and sewing. The only thing Tessa enjoyed was the musical sessions in the evening. Her mother had taught her to play the guitar, and she

13

knew she played it well though her relatives said the fire of her music was more suitable for a gypsy than a lady.

On the eve of Lent they had had a *Cascarone* Ball, and though Tessa had been told she was too young to attend, she had slipped out to the patio to dance. Her aunt had found her dancing with one of her daughters' suitors while some of the other young men looked on. Though the accepted style of dance demanded arms at one's side, feet demurely hidden under a circle of skirt, Tessa was holding her skirt well above her knees with one hand while the other arm was raised in a graceful arch above her head. Her hair had come down; her eyes were flashing, her feet keeping perfect, wild time to the music. Her aunt called her a foreign whore among other things and sent for Don Esteban to come in from his rancho.

She had expected an ugly scene with her great-grandfather, and she had gone before him with her head held defiantly high. She had no way of knowing she had won as soon as the old man saw her, no way of knowing she looked so much like his dead granddaughter that he was helpless against his memories of love. He looked at her a long time, and when he spoke, his voice was soft. "It is too late?"

She understood. "Far too late. I could not be like these people, not in a thousand years. They are as simple and stupid as cattle. Someday someone may sell their hides to the Boston trade. I want to go home."

"Your aunt will undoubtedly be happy to hear that," Don Esteban commented drily. "Be ready to leave tomorrow." His face creased suddenly in a rueful smile. "I have spent much of my life regretting the new blood that came into my family. Now I am not so sure my shame was justified. I fear you are correct. The old way is too easy; it will be swept away. And you, Teresa María Julietta Margarita Macleod y Amarista—my God, that such a name as Macleod should come into my family!—you, Tessa Macleod" (his lips twisted wryly at the Anglo name) "will of a certainty be there to sell our hides." The words were bitter, but they carried pride and paid her tribute.

He was true to his word. She left for home the next day.

And a short time later, on her fourteenth birthday, the golden two-year-old Amordoro arrived. There could have been no clearer assurance of the old man's acceptance. Even her father had roused himself enough to take notice of the gift and to rage that it was too late for his wife. And finally Tessa had heard the story of her family from María.

She sighed. It seemed to her that people were too quick to complicate their lives for foolish reasons, worrying about bloodlines as if they were breeding horses. Even the people most dear to her, the Ramirez family, thought she would be doing well for herself to marry Don Luis Estudillo y Bolado. His family believed he would be marrying beneath his station, but they would bear it because of the connection with Don Esteban Amarista y Amarista. Surely two lines of pure Spanish blood would be enough to remove the taint. No one seemed to care about how Tessa felt, and she herself wasn't sure. There was so little choice. Even for Luis, it was a good day's ride to pay a visit, and because of the strangeness of her family life, Tessa wasn't part of the society which made elaborate advance plans and traveled great distances to attend parties at each other's ranchos.

Only lately had she become increasingly aware of her isolation, and since the alternative would be life as it was at her aunt's and uncle's house, she did not mourn. But Luis made her uncomfortable. Fear was so rare a part of Tessa, she had some difficulty recognizing it, but she knew she was growing ever more fearful of Luis.

Outwardly he was everything a Spanish gentleman should be: courtly in speech, magnificent in dress, aristocratic in every bone and muscle, pale-skinned in winter's soft light, thick black hair and flashing dark eyes emphasizing his high-bridged nose and thin-lipped mouth. He was well known for his daring horsemanship, a reputation worth having since Californios almost without exception rode as if born to the saddle. He was known for doing everything well, but Tessa knew one additional thing about him, and it was becoming more important than all the rest.

Luis was cruel. It was a basic part of his nature, and she no longer believed it would change. She had met him

15

as a child, only five years older than she, and even then she had seen it. He enjoyed pain in other creatures; he enjoyed causing it. María had dismissed it as a part of every boy's nature at one time or another, and for a while Tessa had been lulled by the explanation, but now she knew it wasn't true. It was a native sport enjoyed by many to risk the danger of roping a grizzly bear with the *reata* and bringing it in to tie it to a wild bullock and watch the two animals fight to the death in the ring. And many men shot the poor wild Indians whenever they could find them. But Luis enjoyed both sports and others like them with a fierce passion which frightened Tessa. He only seemed fully alive when something was suffering. She did not think it possible that he would make a kind husband. She hoped he would not visit today; she didn't want to number him among her birthday gifts.

She paused to look back at the house as she rode off. She never tired of its beauty. A small, pure stream nearby provided water, and like the houses of most ranchos, it was set in a clearing so that enemies of all sorts could be easily seen before they were too close. The house ran long and low, its smooth adobe walls brilliant with whitewash, its graceful tile roof deep red softened by moss, the line interrupted here and there by chimneys. The house was divided into two basic wings—one for sleeping quarters and one for kitchen and common rooms, each wing having a right angle which made the house form part of a rectangle, a rectangle finished by the wall which enclosed the patio and the separate space of the garden. Even here, out of sight of it, Tessa could see every plant in her mother's garden. It was a fine thing to have such a place of flowers with no value save beauty. The overhang of porch roof supported by graceful white posts cast some shadow, but not enough to obscure the diamond reflections of the sun on the small panes of real glass. Heavy shutters could be closed from the inside in case of attack, but they had had no threat from Indians for some years now.

It was a spacious, lovely house, built for love and beauty and a large family. Tessa remembered with a sudden sharp pain the longing of her mother for more children.

In back of the main house ran the long, low *Indiada*, quarters of the Indian *vaqueros*, a strange wild lot but

16

marvelous with the livestock. The Ramirez family had their own small adobe a short distance away, near the corrals. Ramón's passion for the animals in his care had not diminished with the years, and his sons were cast in the same mold as their father.

Tessa never ceased to joy in the Rancho Valle del Mar, and she never ceased to feel the weight of it either. She was responsible for all of the people and all of the animals; it was like being the queen of a small kingdom, and with the privilege went the task. But not today.

Valle del Mar was one of the oldest land grants claimed under rule of the Mexican government. Tessa's father had acquired the rancho in 1826, early indeed since most of the grants had been patented after 1834. Don Esteban had helped, and Michael Macleod had not been hurt by the fact that the land lay in a sparsely populated region. Perhaps the climate was easier where there was more sun and less interference from the whims of the sea, but Tessa could not believe there was a more beautiful place anywhere.

The generous leagues of land lay roughly in a triangle with the buildings near the center, the apex formed by the closure of hills behind to the east, the broad base to the west made absolute by the Pacific. The countryside boasted everything from deep grass in gentle valleys to rolling hills to sudden outcroppings of rock, small mountains clothed in twisted oak and singing pine. Tessa thought she would never tire of riding the land; there was so much to see and so much that changed with the seasons. But she had a favorite place, even more beloved than the rocky shore with its constant surf sound. She ordered the dogs to stay behind as she always did, not wanting their noise and scent to send the wildlife fleeing, and she rode southward.

She was not surprised to see Ramón and some of his *vaqueros* on her way. Where the beasts had most need of him was always where he would be found, and in his hollow of grass were some of their prize horses, some mares already accompanied by new foals, others ready to give birth at any time. Within her vision, she counted four *manadas*, each having twenty-five mares and a stallion. To form each small herd, Ramón and the *vaqueros* at first kept them together by day and corralled them together at night. Soon enough the mares and their stallion became a closely knit unit and did not wander or interfere with other families. The mares were unbroken and used only for breeding; it was considered undignified for a lady or gentleman to ride a mare, though Tessa considered that unfair to the mares, as unfair as their close-cropped manes and tails in comparison to the flowing locks of the stallions. The poor mares gave up their adornment for the ropes woven by Ramón and his sons while the stallions remained untouched. She smiled to herself, remembering what Ramón had told her when she had questioned the justice of this as a small child.

"Las yeguas los aborrecen," he had said in all seriousness. "The mares would no longer love or respect their stallions."

Ramón caught sight of her, and she waved and put Amordoro into a canter to meet him. "Ramón, my gifts are beautiful! See how well Amordoro looks in his new halter and reins!" She reached across and took his hand. "I do love you and your family so much. I don't know what I'd do without you."

The old man's weather-lined skin went even darker than it was, and Tessa took pity on his embarrassment and laughed. "And now I'm off for a swim, and no one is to follow me."

"You have no rifle," Ramón said, his face deadly serious now.

"No, but I have my knife, and there is nothing to interest the bears where I am going. I am not going to swim in *los calaveras*," she said, making a face at him. *Los calaveras* was "the place of the skulls," a slaughter corral where cattle and sheep, if you had them, were killed by the Indian *vaquero* butchers to supply meat for the rancho. The offal was a sure lure for grizzly bears.

Ramón was still not easy about her going alone, but he had been through this too many times to think he could change her mind. His smile was reluctant. "Go then. And pray God you do not find a bear who is fond of peaceful waters."

"I'll be fine. You promise, you will not waste your day by following me?"

18

The old man nodded. "I think the mares have more need of me than you do. Such fine colts we have this year."

She tarried a while longer to exclaim over the long-legged, if wobbly, appeal of the foals. Many of the horses had the finely chiseled heads and sculptured bodies of their Arabian ancestors, and she never ceased to marvel at their beauty.

After she left Ramón, she came soon to the rising of the land, a place where a strange rocky jumble had erupted millions of years before to form something more than a hill, less than a mountain. The pine scent was strong, and birds sang rapturously with the joy of a day that truly felt like spring. She scarcely had to guide Amordoro; he was used to her preference for this place and picked his way carefully up the narrow trail until she dismounted. On this slope there was sweet grass in a clearing, a good place for Amordoro to pass the day while she did as she wished.

She took the package of food María had given her and began the climb on foot. It was not a hard trail, just narrow and slippery where pine needles lay in a thick carpet. She came over a little rise and drew in her breath at the beauty as she always did. The natural hollow in the rocks was fed by a soft ripple from a small waterfall running down the back cliff from a spring, and the hollow was large enough to form a fair-sized pool before the overflow continued its secret way down the forest to the valley. Tree branches overhung the water casting dappled patterns, and wildflowers were beginning to bloom. It was soft and green and secret. If you stood on the rise and peered intently until you found an opening in the trees, you could see the ocean far in the distance. There was no place on the rancho Tessa loved as much as this one. It was the one place she felt totally free. She laughed aloud for the sheer joy of it, and a squirrel chattered at her from the safety of a branch. She had surprised deer drinking here, but she was the only human who visited regularly. Only rarely had the spell been broken, when she had fallen asleep on the rock near the water's edge or forgotten the time in daydreams and stayed too long, and Ramón had come to find her. He himself had shown her the place when she was a young child. It was a ritual between them for her to tell him where she was going and

19

warn him not to follow. He obeyed to a point, his sense of what was late and what was not as absolute as God's.

She stripped and piled her clothes on the rock, and then she held her breath against the sudden shock of the cold water as she slipped into the pool. She swam and floated and gloried in it, and soon the cold changed to a sensuous warmth touching her body gently, everywhere, making her as weightless as the leaves drifting with her.

CHAPTER II

He was tired and hungry, and he forgot both when he saw the girl in the pool. He rubbed his eyes; the figure remained, black hair spreading out on the water, slender brown arms cutting the surface with long, easy strokes as she swam. He stared harder. Her body beneath the water gleamed whitely, many shades lighter than the tan of her arms. He could not see her face, but he could imagine it—long slanting dark eyes and the high cheekbones set in the wide face of mixed Indian-Spanish heritage, light and dark which came in countless combinations. She could be nothing else. Daughters of the ruling class did not swim nude and unattended anywhere, anytime.

He smiled to himself. He would be willing to pay just about any price she asked. From what he'd seen so far, she would be worth it. He hadn't had a woman since he'd left Soledad at San Diego. His eyes searched the surrounding area intently. He was sure no one was with her. He began to move quietly down the bank toward her clothes.

Tessa had seen the man when his shadow had fallen briefly across the water before he had stepped into the broken shade. She had thought with sudden terror that it was Luis come to spy upon her, but it was not Luis; the man's build was wrong, wrong for any man on the rancho. A stranger, a man who carried a rifle as though it were an extension of his arm, a man who did not call out reassurance or turn away to allow her to reach her clothes, a man who was coming stealthily down the bank intending harm. She had killed rattlesnakes before, and once a puma which had killed a promising colt. She had no gun now, but the knife would do if she could reach it. Her fear was fast becoming white-hot rage. Her strong strokes carried her to the ledge, her feet found it, and she was out of the pool.

He saw her sudden swiftness, and he increased his own pace. He called to her in Spanish, his laughter making his words nonsensical. Indian would never believe he had seen such a creature in the wilderness of California. He was still thinking about Indian's reaction when he caught up with the girl. She whirled around, and he had only a split second to see she had a lethal-looking knife and eyes the color of wild violets before the blade flashed, aimed to gouge between his ribs and find his heart. He ducked, trying to avoid it, and it plunged deep into his shoulder.

The pain surprised him. It burned down his arm, and when the arm went numb, the pain stayed alive, spreading down his chest into his vitals. The quick warm blood flowing over his skin was a different sensation. He found himself sinking slowly to his knees, and then the girl pushed him backwards and he was lying flat on the ground. He saw her hands moving toward the knife, and he tried to roll away, but she was too quick, and he swore violently as she jerked the knife from his shoulder, using both hands. He tried to get his legs under him, knowing she could slit his throat easily as he lay there, but his limbs seemed incapable of responding.

Her voice rang out, sharp and commanding. "Lie still. You are bleeding badly. I won't kill you now."

A rueful grin touched his drawn face. "I don't think you'll have to. I can do this on my own. Perfect English, eyes like flowers, lady, why didn't you just say No?"

"Because I had no way of knowing whether you are a reasonable man or not. What would you have done in my place?"

"Same thin'." His words were slurring, and his eyes were closed.

"You will let me touch you, let me stop the bleeding?" She took his silence for affirmation and knew he was too weak to resist anyway. She worked quickly, tearing a strip from her petticoat and dipping it into the cool water of

21

the pool, returning to the man to pull the blood-soaked shirt away from the wound and to press the cold dressing against the ugly gash. He came to with a groan when she touched him, but then his jaw clamped shut, and he bore her ministrations in silence. She found the vessel in his neck and pressed down on it with the thumb of her free hand, feeling the hard ridge of his collar bone and the pulsing of his blood, María's voice telling her, "You can stop the bleeding in this way," María's hands showing her how.

She didn't know how long she stayed like that, crouched over him, blood flowing through the cloth beneath her hand while the other hand used fierce pressure to stop the flow. She became aware of separate and strange things. She had an instant's vision of herself clothed only in the man's blood, nearly impossible to explain to Ramón or any of the *vaqueros* without hastening the man's death. Yet she would give almost anything to have Ramón find her now. There was no way for her to get the man down the hill and home without help. But if the whole episode were to happen again, she would do the same thing. She had had only the advantages of her speed and the knife he hadn't seen. He had had a rifle and far superior strength. She had been taught from childhood that while survival was not always beautiful, it was always desirable. Now the advantage was hers, and it made perfect sense to her that she should be working as fiercely to save his life as she had to take it. Of the man himself she knew nothing except that by his speech he was a Yankee and he had blue eyes. She had only become aware of the blueness after she had stabbed him and he had fallen. They were such a dark blue, they looked black. Strangers passed through so seldom, foreigners even less often; what was he doing here?

Her attention focused again on the wound. The bleeding seemed to have stopped, and she moved her hands away carefully, watching intently. She gave a sigh of satisfaction; there was no new stream of crimson.

His eyes opened slowly. They were very, very blue, but the light was gone from them, and the pupils were enormous. And not even the weathered brown of his skin could hide the pallor beneath. The shadows around his mouth were faint echoes of the color of his eyes. His skin was beaded with sweat, and though the day was warm, his face was cold and clammy to her touch. She could barely find the faint race of his pulse. He moved restlessly and seemed to be making an effort to focus on her. She didn't think he was having much success, and she spoke to him as though he were a small child. "You musn't move. You must stay very still. Do you hear me?"

The blue gaze sharpened for an instant before his eyes closed again, and he was still save for the small shivers which shook his body involuntarily. She emptied the deer-skin pouch he carried, praying she would find more than ammunition there; otherwise, it would take so long. She found it—the flint and steel any good traveler carried. She found something else too, a small package bearing her name and her great-grandfather's seal. She dropped it as though it were the fire she sought, but her mind kept on carrying it as she collected the best tinder and driest wood she could find and lined the soon crackling heap with stones. The package was her birthday gift, but why had it come with this man? Perhaps he had stolen it—and left it unopened with her name on it? No sense in that. There was only one explanation—Don Esteban had trusted the man to carry the package for him. She closed her eyes and shuddered, imagining what her great-grandfather would think if he could see the outcome.

She had built the fire as close to the man as she dared, and she used his buckskin pouch to protect her hands as she lifted the hot stones and placed them around him, hoping they would give him some warmth. She worked hard, finding additional stones, reheating the original ones as they cooled. She gathered moss from the pool and carried it swiftly to the man, dripping the water on his mouth, watching in relief as his mouth opened and he swallowed thirstily.

His color was better, his pulse stronger; his breathing was deep and he was no longer shivering when she ceased her labors. Her skin was slick with her sweat and his blood, and she couldn't stand either. The icy water of the pool felt heavenly even for the brief time of bathing. When she emerged she put on her clothes before she picked

23

up the package from Don Esteban. Even in this secluded place, she could feel his presence.

Her hands were shaking as she unwrapped it. The collar of emeralds set in gold smoldered with green embers even in the half light of the glade, another world, another time. The beautiful Spanish script spanned past and present. "This was your grandmother's. It should have been your mother's. Now it is yours." No words of love, all words of love. Tears pricked her eyelids, and she looked up to find the blue eyes watching her.

"Please," he said, "whatever else, that must be delivered to the right person. Her name is there." His voice was stronger than it had been.

"It has been delivered. Don Esteban is my great-grandfather," Tessa said.

"I thought it would be an older woman . . . Oh, my God!" the man groaned, and Tessa couldn't tell whether it was curse or prayer, but she knew how the man felt; she felt the same. She tried to stifle it; the circumstances were all wrong, but she couldn't. Her laughter rang out suddenly, filling the quiet place, soaring above the water sound.

She clapped her hands over her mouth, trying like a small child to muffle the noise, gasping, "I'm sorry! I really am," but when she looked at him, he was smiling, and he admonished her, "Hell, I can't laugh, don't make me laugh. You're related to the old tyrant, I'm not. He'll finish your work." If he ever saw Indian again, he wouldn't bother to explain. There wasn't any way to make it believable. He couldn't believe it himself. Everything had been mad from the time he had seen the girl in the pool. The only thing he could believe was the throbbing in his shoulder.

She could see him fading in and out from the present, and it hit her suddenly. She had wounded him grievously with that first and only thrust, but he was a big man, and by the look of his muscles a strong one.

She bent over him again and asked sharply, "How long since you've eaten?"

He looked up at her. "I like you better with no clothes," he said hazily.

24

"You will bleed to death for pride," she said to Gavin. "If that is what you wish, we will leave you here."

They carried him down the hill as carefully as they could, watching their footing against a sliding fall, Tessa doggedly holding up her corner of the blanket. There wasn't a sound from Gavin, and Tessa thought he had fainted until his eyes opened under the intensity of her gaze. She realized suddenly how much it hurt his pride to be so helpless, a hurt worse than the physical, which was something he could bear. This man was not used to being at the mercy of others. She smiled at him and turned her attention back to the ground.

Jesus! he thought, it's a good thing I didn't see that smile before, I might have raped her after all. His idea that she was a child was forgotten. The smile had transformed her face, making it luminous, ageless, and more beautiful than any face he had ever seen. He knew she had not lied about the fever; he could feel it taking him beyond reason on endless waves of warmth. He was only sorry the pain followed him. He concentrated on Tessa until he saw nothing but her smile, felt nothing except the slender body cradling him against the jolts, her hands touching, holding him, heard nothing save the comfort of her voice.

The *carreta,* a rough wooden cart slung on an axle hewn from a single tree with great wheels of wood which groaned and squeaked with every turn as the oxen pulled it, was practical and durable for the hauling of supplies or for taking a load of laundry to the nearest stream, and it was the only vehicle available; but for transporting an injured man, it was only slightly less excruciating than slinging him over a horse. None of the men had objected when Tessa got in the *carreta* with the man. Even had they wanted to, they would not have dared; they had seen the look on her face. Julio went meekly to find the two horses on the hill while Ramón and Juan handled the oxen and the cart.

She lay along his good side, holding him, trying to cushion him against the rough progress. She felt the growing heat of his skin, and before they were home, she felt the warm spreading stream of his blood. The journey

29

seemed interminable and so was her fierce, primitive need to keep the man alive.

María screamed when she saw Tessa, bloodstained and staggering from cramped muscles when she got out of the *carreta*, but Tessa brushed her aside with brusque assurance that she was not injured but the man in the cart was. And none of María's scolding could make her leave the man's side as they carried him into the house.

María gave up, knowing it was no use, and the two women worked side by side to stop the bleeding and bandage the wound. Only when it was done and the man lay still and unknowing did Tessa give in to María long enough to eat something and bathe and change, but when the old woman would have made her go to bed, she refused. "No. I will watch beside him. Don't tire me further with useless words."

María loved her too much to be offended, and her heart ached for the girl. "There is little you can do, *niña*. He has lost much blood. It is in the hands of God now."

"Then God should be grateful for an extra pair of hands to help him," Tessa snapped, and María left her, mourning because her child was gone, a woman in her place.

CHAPTER III

Tessa watched over the man all night, sponging him down with cool cloths, giving him water drop by drop, refusing to leave him until morning when his fever was down and he was no longer hitching his shoulder restlessly. He was sleeping deeply when she left him in María's care, but she made María promise to come for her if there was any change.

Food had been left for her, and she found she was hungry, as well as tired. Her father came in while she was eating, and she eyed him warily, but he seemed fairly sober this morning.

"Tessa, I'm . . . I'm sorry. I knew it was your birthday yesterday. I had this for you, but . . ." His hands shook as he held the package awkwardly, and Tessa felt a wave of pity and compassion for him. He looked so miserable, as though he feared she would refuse his present and order him to get out.

She took the package from him and her voice was gentle. "I know, things were very confused here last night, but the man is better this morning. And your present has just made my birthday happen all over again. Shall I say I am seventeen now?" She smiled at him, and he smiled back gratefully, but he was not to be deterred. "Ramón told me about the man, but it is strange no one saw the one who stabbed him, isn't it?"

Tessa used her struggle with the heavy covering as an excuse not to look at him—sometimes he emerged from his stupor to be sharper than was comfortable. "Well, no," she mumbled, "there are a thousand places a man could ride through without ever being seen."

"And I have seen the horse he was riding, a splendid animal, from the rancho of Don Esteban I think. He breeds them as he does the golden horses."

"Yes, it is probably one of great-grandfather's horses. The man, his name is Gavin Ramsay. He brought my birthday gift." Her crow of delight as she discovered what her father had given her stopped the conversation. It was the most precious of all things and hard to obtain, a book, and in English besides. Its stained and worn condition showed it must have come from a sailor, undoubtedly after being read and reread by all hands aboard ship who cared for such pleasure, but it was still intact and legible. It was called *Oliver Twist* and was by a man named Charles Dickens. It made no difference to Tessa that she had never heard of either. A new book, a new adventure even if a dull one, was beyond price.

"Thank you, Father, thank you very much," she said softly. "Nothing could have pleased me more." The "nothing" told him clearly that she found his gift even more dear than Don Esteban's, and his face reflected his pleasure that it was so, but his last words as he left her were, "A knife is a dangerous weapon in the hands of those who know how to use one. A gift from Don Esteban."

She sighed in exasperation. The two of them could never

31

just talk, could never meet each other head on. All their loving and all their hating had to be done with words and gestures so twisted and subtle that misunderstandings and the widening gulf between them were inevitable. And nothing would help it. He had never ceased mourning the death of her mother, and she knew each day she grew to look more like her. Even his drinking could not obliterate the pain in his eyes when he looked at her. Her own marriage to Luis would be a way to make things better for her father. But for her? She was suddenly so weary it was an effort just to get up and go to her room.

She did not awaken until late afternoon. Since María had not called her, the man Gavin's condition must be about the same. She hummed as she splashed water on her face. It would take time for his body to replace all the blood it had lost, but now the man would live; she was sure of it.

When she went into the room, María smiled at her. "He still has some fever, but he is resting peacefully. Soon I think he will awaken. Then he should eat. I will have a strong soup ready." She left the room quietly and Tessa took her place by the bed. She touched Gavin's forehead; he was much cooler than he had been. And she found his pulse with ease because the beat was so much stronger. She settled down to read the book her father had given her, smiling with pleasure as Mr. Dickens's fine prose drew a world foreign to her with perfect clarity.

"Who taught you to read?" His voice startled her so, she nearly dropped the book. His eyes were just as blue as she remembered them.

"My father. But I have not read so much, you understand. Books are rare in California. Here we have the Bible, the works of Mr. Shakespeare—those I like very much—but for the rest a book on mathematics, some history, and many on how to live a saintly life." She wrinkled her nose. "To be a saint would be most boring, I think."

"I agree completely," Gavin said, his eyes twinkling. His type or not, this creature was fascinating, and he found he was curious about what other unorthodox views

32

she might hold. But he frowned suddenly. "How long has it been?"

"We brought you in last night. It has not been long."

"But you stayed with me all night, didn't you? I remember you being here. You must be very tired."

"I am not tired. I have slept all day. I was responsible, so it was just for me to watch the night," she said quietly. "And now you must eat something better than talk of books and saints."

When she returned with the soup, he made an effort to rise, but she forestalled him. "No, still for a while you must be a child. All you must do is swallow María's magic. She is a very good cook."

He found it wasn't hard to obey. She fed him skillfully, no messy spilling or trembling hands, and the soup tasted delicious, strongly flavored with beef. She had nearly finished her task when she heard voices—María's raised in protest and Luis's in demand. Her hands which had been so steady shook suddenly, and the spoon clattered in the bowl.

Gavin saw her eyes widen and darken to deep purple. He would not have thought she was afraid of anything, but now he saw she was. "What is it?" he asked urgently, but all her concentration was fixed on the voices, and she did not hear him.

Luis came into the room, María trailing behind him, still protesting. Tessa put the bowl down with extravagant care, and when she turned to face the man, Gavin could see her hands clasped tightly behind her back.

The man spoke first, launching into a stream of abuse. Gavin's Spanish was good enough to follow the words. "You go too far, Teresa María. This is not fitting, that you should be alone with this man. If you do not care about your own name, think of mine. It is noble and you must not disgrace it."

Tessa's voice was calm, but Gavin could see she was shaking. "The man is gravely injured. He can do me no harm. Would you have me deny my Christian duty to care for him? My name is my own; I do not yet bear yours." Anger began to creep into her voice, and Gavin applauded it silently. He had a sudden fierce urge to plant his fist right on that aristocratic nose.

Luis did a swift about-face, reaching out to take Tessa's resistant body into his arms, crooning, "My darling, I am sorry for my temper. I am too possessive, I know, but I care for you, *mi alma.*" The lie was in his eyes, still black and cold with anger, and Gavin saw it.

Tessa pulled away, and with stiff, mechanical gestures and voice, she introduced the two men. Gavin was amazed by the change; it was incredible that anything could so rob her of her supple grace, but this Don Luis had. He hated having to meet the man lying flat on his back—Don Luis was not the sort of man he wanted to give any advantage. Though each acknowledged the other with cold formality, their eyes were not so polite. The best there could ever be between them was icy dislike; if they saw much of each other, it would be worse than that. Gavin wondered why he was even considering it; he would soon be on his way and would not see the man again nor Tessa.

Tessa had had all she could bear of the tension in the room, and her anger gave her courage. "Luis, please leave this room. María will give you something to eat, and she will prepare a place for you to sleep if you wish to stay, but I have no time for visitors now."

Luis glared at her for a moment, and then he said deliberately, "The next time you go hunting, take a rifle; the kill will be cleaner."

He turned to go, but Tessa's hand on his arm stopped him. "But Luis, it is you who taught me that slow death is so much more entertaining."

Gavin thought the man might strike her, and he rolled to his good side and pushed himself up to a sitting position. Tessa heard the movement, and she cried, "No!" even as she screamed at Luis, "Get out! Leave me alone!" and pushed him toward the door. Only the heavy wood slamming shut told her he had obeyed, for all of her attention was focused on Gavin. "Please, please lie down," she implored him, trying to ease him back on the pillows.

"I'm stronger than you think," he protested, knowing it was true. The world was swinging around a bit, but he knew he could stand and walk if he had to.

"I know that!" Tessa snapped. "It is the edges of the wound which are not strong enough. If you make it split and bleed again, I wash my hands of you."

María returned a short while later to tell Tessa that Luis had left, and though it troubled María, it was good news to Tessa.

Gavin's voice broke the silence after María left. "Maybe you will be lucky. It should be dark soon; maybe he'll break his neck."

The obvious appeal the idea had for him startled her, and she stared at him for a moment before she smiled grimly and shook her head. "Not that one. He is one of the best *caballeros* in all of California." She slumped in the chair suddenly, covering her face with her hands. "I should not have behaved so badly. I seem to go out of my way to make Luis angry."

"You are afraid of him," Gavin stated quietly, not asking a question.

"No, I'm not, I . . ." The blue eyes caught and held the violet ones, and Tessa swallowed hard. "All right, yes, I do fear him but it is foolish of me, and I must learn. We have known each other since we were children."

"Rattlesnakes and grizzly bears and blizzards in winter are familiar too, but that doesn't make them any less dangerous, just makes you careful where you travel. The only thing that man is ever going to love is Don Luis, and I'm not sure he feels too kindly toward him. You'd be a fool to marry him."

"You are the only one who thinks that."

"Besides yourself, you mean. Can't say I've ever claimed to think like everyone else. And it doesn't appear to me you make a habit of it either. What could you possibly gain by marrying him?"

Her laugh was sharp and bitter, completely unlike the melodious sound he had heard hours that seemed like years ago by the pool. "I have much to gain: vast leagues of land and uncounted thousands of cattle and horses, perhaps children of my own, but most of all his name. It is as noble as he claims."

"Seems to me you've got names enough, if that package was really for you," he teased, wishing he could ease the white misery from her face, but she would not be charmed.

"You met my great-grandfather, and even you, a foreigner, must be able to see he is of noble blood. Perhaps where you come from this does not matter so much, but to Californios, the degree of pure Spanish heritage is of the greatest importance. And though many claim it, there are few who are truly pure. But Don Esteban is, and it is a great sorrow to him that there is a line in his family that is not, as mine is not."

She paused, and her eyes looked curiously blind with the effort to see into the past. "Don Esteban and his wife, my great-grandmother, were cousins and carried the same name, Amarista. They were married in Spain with great ceremony marking the joining of two parts of the same powerful family who had served their kings well. They had four sons and finally a daughter, and then no more children. The daughter was a favored child, spoilt and protected. Her name was Julieta. Great plans were made even when she was an infant for the fine marriage she would make.

"No one ever knew how she managed it, she was so closely watched by her parents and her *dueña*, but Julieta fell in love with an English soldier. He was of high birth in his own country, but he was a younger son with no prospects beyond his life in the army. When Don Esteban learned of the romance, he was in a fury and forbade Julieta ever to see the man again. Julieta was more determined and more in love than he knew. She ran away with the soldier and married him. She returned to her parents two years later. Her husband was dead, and she was without money and heavy with child. Don Esteban took her back, but the name of the Englishman was stricken from the family, and he only waited until Julieta had had her baby and was well enough to travel before he moved his family to the New World, to Mexico and then to California. Julieta's child was my mother, María Julieta. Julieta sickened and died not long after the family came to California. Perhaps she did not want to live without her Englishman. My mother was raised by Don Esteban, her grandfather. I don't think her grandmother had much to do with it, and in any case, she too died before my mother was fully grown. And the worst Don Esteban could imagine happened again. My mother met a foreigner, Michael Macleod, and fell in love with him. You understand, there are few foreigners in California now, how many less there were nineteen years ago. I think my great-grandfather must believe God has singled him out for special punishment.

"He tried to stop the marriage. He even threatened to have my father put in custody of the government and sent from this country, but my mother won." There was something touching in the way Tessa's head lifted a fraction in pride, and Gavin had to make an effort to concentrate on the story instead of the girl's face.

"Don Esteban gave in, and the wedding was a proper one, my father being baptized as a Catholic and taking Mexican citizenship and my mother. But Don Esteban is a strange, hard man. Though he gave my mother a lavish dowry and wedding gifts and helped to make it easier for my father to acquire this land, he forbade them ever to enter his house again, and he never saw my mother alive again. The first time I ever saw him was at her funeral when he brought the priest to say the words, and I have only seen him once more since then. I have never seen the place where he lives." Her voice trailed away.

"So you, who are only one-quarter Spanish, as I see it, are planning to throw yourself on the fire of honor and marry that questionable gentleman whose blood is so pure. I can see it quite clearly now. You have a lot to make up for what with your grandmother and mother marrying those . . . 'foreigners,'" Gavin sneered. He couldn't understand why, but he was truly angry, and it was making him even more light-headed than he had been.

"It doesn't make a goddamn bit of difference that your grandmother and mother loved their husbands, does it? They tainted the sacred blood. But you'll make it right, won't you, Miss Violet Eyes, and if you're lucky, all your little brats will look just like Luis the Magnificent, cold, black-eyed, and pure, and no one will ever suspect their mother was even less than a half-breed. And you're too stupid to see that the time for people like Luis is coming to an end in this part of the world, that your terrible foreign blood is the only kind that will matter in a few years. Luis and others like him are hundreds, maybe thousands of years behind the times. They are content to graze on the land like so many fat cattle, and there will be little enough work to sell their hides and their fat."

She heard Don Esteban's words clearly, "You, Tessa Macleod, will be there to sell our hides." And she saw how white Gavin's face was and how hard he was breathing, and she didn't understand half of what she was feeling, but her anger dissolved in her concern for him, and she bent over him pleading, "Please, none of it matters now. You have talked too much, and the excitement is bad for you."

Whatever else she meant to say was lost as his good hand came up and pulled her head down. His mouth was hard on hers, and he forced hers open, probing, tasting, demanding. At first she was so stunned, that she did not respond at all, and then she did, not resisting, opening her mouth willingly, her urgency matching his. She was inexperienced, never having known anything like this, and Gavin knew her ignorance, but he knew her promise too, the yielding sweetness of her, the inborn sensuality that taught her, without teaching, how to move, to touch, to kiss just so. It was he who ended it, wrenching his head sideways, gasping, "Enough!"

He expected any reaction save the one she had. Her eyes were enormous, and she touched her bruised mouth before she asked, "Why did you do that?" There was no anger in her voice at all, just a curious wonder about what had happened.

"Because I didn't get the chance yesterday," he said, his smile mocking her. It was partially the truth, but he might as well have told her other parts of the truth— that he wanted her to know the difference between a man and a creature like Luis, that he couldn't stand the idea of Luis possessing her. He resented the conflicting emotions this girl aroused in him, half an urge to master, half an urge to protect. He had no place in his life for emotional complexities. The sooner he left this place, the better off he would be.

Tessa accepted his words at face value, and her smile had no bitter edge. "You are a most persistent man, and you are a weary one also. Go to sleep now."

When Tessa and María changed the bandage, they were pleased to see that the wound was beginning to heal. Flexing his shoulder cautiously and peering down at it, Gavin said with pleasure, "I've had worse than this and never such good care. I'll be able to leave in a few days."

María, her maternal instinct never far from the surface, scolded, "Señor, if you have had worse than this, you have been dead perhaps. If you see the one who did this again, you must be quicker than before." Whatever Ramón believed, María had accepted the story, and a little revenge seemed in order to her.

Gavin agreed with her solemnly, "Don't plan to give him another chance," but his eyes glowed with mischief as he watched Tessa, who was suddenly very busy gathering up used dressings and the basin.

María still did not suspect the truth, but she felt the current between the two, and she was troubled. Lying in her husband's arms late in the night she said, "Ramón, perhaps Don Luis has reason for his anger."

"Don Luis was born with anger," Ramón answered heavily, and would have gone to sleep, but his wife persisted. "You do not think then that his marriage to our little one would be good? You have never said such a thing before."

"Who am I to say such a thing now? You think of her as our child; we have been as parents to her, but it is not the truth. She is the great-granddaughter of Don Esteban. Though twice it has been in his family, such do not often marry for love."

The conversation was finished, and María murmured, "*Si Dios quiere*," and fell asleep, leaving Ramón to wrestle with the knowledge that he did not like Don Luis and never had, and no matter how wealthy the marriage, it would not be a good one for his Tessa. Somehow the stranger's coming had made him think things he had not meant to think. He wished suddenly that Tessa had used the knife with better skill and on Don Luis.

CHAPTER IV

The stronger Gavin grew, the more Tessa retreated into herself. Though she did not know all of the reasons, she knew the man was a danger to her existence. His mere presence made what had been at least partially acceptable, totally unacceptable. Every time she looked at him or talked with him, she drew automatic comparisons with Luis, and Luis was always the loser. In her first hours of knowing the stranger she had been only dimly aware of his power, because of the grave injury she had inflicted on him, but now with healing, his power grew more undeniable each minute. It showed in the way he moved, his long body as strong and quick as the great mountain cat's in spite of the hurt it had suffered. It showed in his eyes, bright and mocking, seeming to know what she was thinking even when she did not give words to her thoughts. It showed in his voice, deep, and not given to needless speech or courtly phrases, always coming to the point of things rather than the politeness of them.

It was Tessa's first real encounter with a Yankee—her father had long since adopted the casual perhaps-tomorrow attitude of most Californios—and she found it difficult to cope. Up until now she had always been the one to make the decisions and act on them with the greatest speed in her world. But now she found herself confronted with one who was even more forceful than she. He made her feel as if she were lost somewhere between the slow pace of the old way and the fast pulse of his. Yet she was hungry for news of all the places he had seen and she had not, hungry for the pattern of what his life had been, what had brought him here. She heard how he had traded on the Santa Fe Trail and how he had first come to California after time spent in Mexico. He had hunted, trapped, traded, done a thousand things since he had first left home as a boy of fourteen, twelve years before. He told the tale of his coming to manhood quietly, emphasizing other

40

people and the places he had seen more than himself. He saw great promise in the land of California, and he and his partner, Indian, had made the trek east to buy goods and secure passage for themselves and their wares on a ship bound for California. Gavin had left the ship at San Diego so that he might explore the country along the coast; Indian had remained aboard to travel north and clear the goods at the Monterey Custom House, the one legal point of entry in California.

"He told me I was crazy. He'll be wondering what the hell happened to me. He's a good man. I've trusted him with my life a good many times, so it's no problem to trust him with my goods."

"Indian is a strange name for a man," Tessa said.

"Indian is a strange man," Gavin answered, but he did not elaborate; his attention was elsewhere, and his eyes glittered. "The Boston trade! It's a fitting name for it. Everything going in and coming out of California has been controlled for so long by so few—Bryant and Sturgis in Boston, a few merchants here. It's ridiculous. A vast land with vast fortunes to be made. I intend to get my share."

Tessa saw it—Don Esteban's vision of destruction. The slow quiet way could not withstand the force of many men such as this one. Even in her limited view, Tessa knew how little support the province of California received from the government in Mexico. Spain had cared, but ever since freedom from her had come to Mexico in 1822, the care had lessened. And the orderly Spanish system had been further weakened in 1834 when the missions had been secularized, their lands taken away to become great ranchos, their function reduced to mere religious observances in the churches. Of course, the original plan had been to hold the land in trust for the Indians, who, as they became civilized, would take it over. So, in fact, only the Indians should have been counted the losers. But the Indians had never been considered civilized enough, and Tessa knew they never would have been, not by Old World standards. Thus, until stripped of their possessions, the missions had been centers of order and wealth, wealth in orchards, vineyards, fields of grain and vegetables, herds of cattle and horses. Now all of that

41

was gone, and the great landowners lacked the initiative for true empire building—why should they, life was pleasant and bounteous in California. They would learn from men like this Gavin Ramsay, but the lesson would come too late. Tessa felt a wave of sadness sweep over her, leaving her weary and afraid. She could even feel compassion for Luis who so hated the foreigners.

Gavin asked the question she had not heard once more. "What's wrong, why do you look like that?"

This time she heard, and her impulse was to scream at him, "Because you mean an end to the life I love," but she changed the subject instead. "You have told me what you did after you left your home, but not why you left. You are a well-educated man; something of that must have come from the home."

His eyes and his voice were suddenly as hard as flint. "You speak of purity of blood; it's something I don't even have to worry about. My mother fell in love with a sailor. Supposedly he promised to marry her, but he never did. He probably had a woman in every port. He died at sea a short while before my mother gave birth to me. She named me for my father, and a short time later she died. Her sister and her sister's husband, my aunt and uncle, took me in. They had no children of their own. It was only one of the many crosses they had to bear that God had given my whorish mother a bastard and kept legitimate sons and daughters from the worthy. The only joy my uncle found in life was in his books, though even that was dim. He could have been a brilliant man, but he was warped and narrow. His scholarship was directed toward finding the exact path to God. The least he and my aunt could do was to guide the bastard on that path.

"My uncle used a cane to encourage scholarship and subdue sin." Gavin's face was so twisted and bitter that Tessa looked away, but not before she saw him touch the scar on his cheek involuntarily. Not a mark like the others, won in battles for survival on his own terms.

"He thought if he could mold me into a schoolmaster or a parson, God would be pleased with him for producing godliness from such sinful material. He was a large, strong man for all his bookish ways, but at fourteen I was finally
42

stronger. I thrashed him before I left the house. I never went back. Maybe I killed him. It's a pleasant possibility."

For the first time since his vitality had begun to return to him, Tessa felt stronger than Gavin. Under the harsh words, she saw a small boy in a house without love, beaten and threatened constantly with the wrath of a God who hated him for his birth. She could imagine clearly how he must have looked, small and slender with enormous blue eyes in a pale face made paler by the frame of black hair. No wonder he had such an ambition to prove himself worthy. His aunt and uncle had left him with more scars than he knew.

"You have told me it is wrong to hold any child responsible for his birth, and it is," she said. "It is terribly, terribly wrong! And surely you must see that perhaps your mother and father were very much in love, perhaps he did intend to marry her. And at the very least your mother must have loved him very much to risk so much. Your aunt and uncle would never have let you believe any of that, but it might have been true." The smile she gave him was twin to the one she had given him on the hill.

He tried to think of Soledad, lush, practiced, easy. He tried to think of Indian, a master of survival, knowledgeable, quiet with words of warning. He tried to think of the cargo—a sampling of everything from nails to ribbons —which must even now be in the Custom House in Monterey. He tried to think of all he had to do, his hurry to be gone. He tried, and all he saw was Tessa's face, Tessa's smile. He could drown in the violet depths of her eyes. He could trace forever the delicate browline and high curving cheekbones, the straight nose with finely flared nostrils, the full mouth and firm chin. His hands flexed with the urge to touch her face and the smooth long line down her neck from jaw to collarbone to. . . . He saw the slender perfection of her body even more clearly than he had seen it by the pool. His manhood stirred and he cursed the girl silently for being able to draw such a response from him with no effort.

Just how unconscious she was of her effect on him was confirmed by her next words, for she saw the change in him and put it to the wrong cause. They were sitting in

43

the coolness of the garden, the scent of first flowers and the hum of early bees around them. She had thought it a restful place for Gavin to be, but when she saw his sudden paleness as he stared at her, her pleasure in their talk vanished. "You are not as strong as I thought. I should not have made you tell so much. You should be resting."

"I should be to hell and gone from here," he corrected harshly, and saw her flinch.

"You will be soon," she said quietly.

His desire to hurt her was strong, to pierce her calm command and make her feel the wild, confusing pain she aroused in him. Instinctively he found her vulnerability. "Yes, I will be gone soon. But I have yet to meet my host. Do you keep your father locked in a hidden room somewhere?"

He succeeded all too well. The color drained from her face and her eyes darkened to the shade he already knew meant pain or fear. Her hands knotted in her lap, and he saw the effort she was making to keep her mouth from trembling. But her head was high when she answered him. "My father is in a prison, Señor Ramsay, but it is not of my making, and I do not hold the key. Only my mother or his own will could release him. But my mother has been dead for six years now, and my father buried his spirit with her."

She rose to leave him, turning her head away, murmuring that María would attend to him if he needed anything, but he saw the sun catching crystal in her tears, and he moved swiftly, taking her in his arms, holding her stiff body against his own, stroking the soft darkness of her hair, offering words of comfort he had not known he could say, trying to explain something to her he himself only half understood.

"My poor girl, I'm sorry. You didn't deserve that. My uncle didn't manage to beat the devil out of me, not in all his years of trying. There, little one, there, Tessa, perhaps it is time you cried."

He felt her body relaxing in his hold, and he drew her back down to the wooden seat and held her as she sobbed. He had heard women cry before, had held more than he could remember while they did, but theirs had been easy, professional tears, sometimes for a favor, sometimes for the pretense of sadness at parting, never like this. Gavin knew Tessa was one who seldom cried. Her body trembled with the violence of her grief, and her sobs were ragged shreds of sound, choking and unfamiliar. He doubted she had ever before cried aloud for the tragedy of her mother's death and the diminishing of her father. He cradled her against him while the storm swept over them both, his passion replaced by a great tenderness.

María came into the garden once and was alarmed by the sound she heard, and when she saw Tessa crying in the Yankee's arms, she knew it was her duty to put a stop to the scene immediately. A small smile curving her lips, she slipped away unseen, thinking how strange it was how one's idea of duty changed with the years.

The shadows lengthened in the garden, and Tessa's crying eased, and still she did not pull away from Gavin, nor did he put her away from him. She felt lightheaded, peaceful, and above all safe. Gavin listened to her voice, low and husky from crying, telling of her mother and father, and he began to understand the forces which had shaped the complex creature he held in his arms.

"My father's people came from Scotland to the New World, to the American colonies before your war with England. They were very poor, but they were strong and willing, and they prospered. And when the war came, they fought against the English king even as they had always done at home. And when the war was over, they continued to prosper, and every child was given as fine an education as could be found. My father was a schoolmaster in Boston. Though he could have enjoyed a richer life by becoming a merchant with his two uncles, he did not do so. He truly loved his books and his pupils, as much as his own father had done before him; they were not like your uncle. But he also loved to learn new things, and finally the call of the ships in the harbor was louder than the call of his work. Though he was not paid much, his wants were few and he had saved some money and had a sum which had been left to him by his grandfather. He could have bought passage on a ship, but instead he signed on to work his way. He used to laugh about it;

45

he was a terrible sailor." Tessa's voice was so wistful, Gavin tightened his arms for a minute and felt her nestle closer.

"By the time the ship reached this coast, Father was full done with life at sea, but what he saw at first of life in California did not seem much better. Wild country, Indians, and dirty little pueblos seemed to be all there were. But then the ship put in at Santa Barbara. If he had been a true sailor, my father would probably not have met my mother, but he was a scholar and somewhat apart from life on the ship. The captain did not like his work, but he enjoyed his conversation, and a friendship that would have been strange and impossible under normal circumstances was helped by the captain knowing my father's uncles. It did not make things better for Father with the crew, but it made things better on shore. There was a ball, and the captain took my father and the ship's officers with him. My father met my mother that night, and California became his home. He did not desert the ship to be hunted as many are; the captain wished him well." Gavin recognized the small rippling sound as laughter, and he smiled in the darkness, glad of the sound.

"It made no difference that Don Esteban was furious and forbade the marriage; it made no more difference than it had when my grandmother had done the same thing. They were married and came north, to this place. They had no wish to be close to the wrath of Don Esteban, and Father was searching for a place green and cool and more like the coast he knew in his homeland. This house he built for Mother with the finest materials he could buy or have made—beautiful wood, fine tile, strong adobes. And Don Esteban helped, in spite of his feelings, even to sending fine cattle and horses, cuttings from his gardens and orchards; even the Ramirez family he sent so that Mother should not want for anything save his company.

"I doubt she missed him as much as he thought she would. My mother and father loved each other very much. Father even used to say he wanted nothing more than a girl who looked like her mother. Certainly I did not lack his attention when I was growing up. He taught me English, Spanish, French, and Latin, mathematics, history, and philosophy, things of the earth and sky, all of the
46

things he had taught his pupils in Boston. And he instructed Ramón to teach me to ride and to shoot as well as any boy, though hunting is still not a thing I like to do. My mother was not so successful, but she tried to teach me the things of her girlhood: to dance, to sing, to play the guitar, to do fine needlework. We were a good family, happy together. There was always talk and music and laughter in our house." Her voice faded for a moment, and Gavin felt the deep breath she took before she went on.

"Then, after so long that she had ceased to hope, my mother found she was with child again. She rejoiced and Father seemed to, but now I know he was afraid—she had had a difficult time bringing me to birth, and she was years older. Father had reason to be afraid. She died giving birth to the son who died with her." Her voice was flat and even, telling the hardest part without faltering. "Father was never the same, never again. He began to drink too much and to gamble recklessly whenever he got the opportunity. Most of the men, they drink, they gamble, but few do it to excess. He stopped riding out to watch the work on the land. We used to have visitors. Travelers knew they would find a warm welcome and a joyful place to be. There would be plentiful food for them, coins on the bureau if they needed them, fresh horses and a *vaquero* to guide them when they went on their way to the next place. But after my mother's death, they learned quickly this was not a good place to rest. Don Luis and the people of his family are the only ones who come often, and I do not believe his family comes willingly. It is the thought of Don Esteban that brings them."

"You give yourself too little credit. You are here, Don Esteban is not," Gavin said gently. He did not want to make matters worse by pointing out that her father was very selfish, something she seemed not to have considered. He felt the heavy weight of the responsibilities she carried, and he felt his own panic. The only solution would be to take her away, and that he was not prepared to do. He had no wish to be encumbered by a woman; there was no place for more than casual encounters in his restless life. Even in so short a time, he had come to care a great deal about Tessa, but he was not prepared to call it love. He wasn't at all sure what love meant; there had been very little in his life. Any man would want this woman. Only a blind man could fail to see the rare beauty she possessed. But wanting and loving were different things entirely.

Tessa felt the change in him, and she pulled away enough to look up into his face. Then she kissed him softly as though he were a brother. "It is not just that my troubles should become yours, but I thank you. You have given me comfort. I did not know how much I needed to say these things until now. You must not feel pity for me. I am strong, and healthy, and my life is a good one. And I must go quickly to see if María needs help with supper."

He watched her go, the faint rose of dusk tinting the white of her dress and making it seem as if she drifted away, insubstantial and ethereal. But she was not so insubstantial; he could feel the warmth and weight of her in his arms. He stirred uneasily. The old tale of Circe the enchantress was not confined to legend. Tessa's father had heeded the siren's call and stayed forever in her kingdom, and now the house built of love had become as lonely and stark for him as any prison.

He flexed his shoulder; it was stiff and sore, but it was workable, and there was no damage to his arm or hand. Tomorrow he would ride, test his strength. By the next day surely, he could be on his way.

He found a change when he sat down to dine. Before he had taken his meals with Tessa alone, though María had always been in the background, waiting on them. Tonight Michael Macleod had joined them.

Gavin cast a quick glance at Tessa as she introduced the two to each other. Her face was pale but composed though her eyes flashed briefly at him as though to say, "This is what you wanted. Make what you will of it."

At first he could not identify the reaction he had to Tessa's father, but then he realized it was anger. As much as she might resemble her mother, she bore the stamp of her father too. It showed in the certain cast of features, heavy in his face, delicate in hers, but the same nonetheless. Their profiles were startlingly alike. But Tessa's face was cleanly chiseled, as strong as it was beautiful, while her father's was blurred and ravaged by six years of
48

desperate waste. Tessa's eyes were shining, alive, and they reflected every mood and thought. Michael Macleod's eyes were the same slightly almond shape and as heavily lashed as his daughter's, gray where hers were violet, but his were glazed and bloodshot, seemingly incapable of looking at anyone directly. It sickened Gavin that there was any resemblance at all between the two. And though he tried to feel compassion for this man who had been destroyed by the death of his love, he could not. He felt contempt for him and the first stirrings of dislike. This man made life harder for Tessa than it needed to be.

For the most part Michael made no attempt to talk, and when he did, his words were jumbles of half-finished sentences that seemed to have nothing to do with anything which had gone before or followed after. But once he focused suddenly on Gavin. "Your name, in the old tongue of Scotland it means falcon. Have you come hunting then, fine bird? Better not, the prey is claimed."

"Father, you go too far!" Tessa snapped, and the man subsided into silence, but the sly smile was slow to leave his face and his eyes glittered.

Gavin himself had never known the origin of his name, and the man's brief display of scholarship turned to malice was unnerving, proving him to be not nearly as unconscious as Gavin had first judged him. But then, this was the same man who had taught Tessa the multitude of things she knew. Gavin was relieved when the meal ended and Tessa's father left them.

Tessa made no mention of what had happened; there was nothing to say. But rather than staying to talk to Gavin, she bid him good night and left him before he could protest. Though the change in her attitude was subtle, it was very real, and he could not mistake it. She understood his need to leave, to continue in freedom, and she accepted it. He knew there would be no tears and no words asking him to stay when the time came. He wondered why he did not feel more thankful about it. He laughed ruefully, guessing the cause. It was damn hard on male pride to know a beautiful woman was willing to let you go without one word of regret.

CHAPTER V

She read a few pages of the new book. Fine as it was, she could not keep her mind on it. She lay down again, willing sleep to come, finding instead that her muscles were so tense it was painful to be still. She gave up the effort and paced her room until her own footsteps made her nervous. And finally she covered her nightgown with a long robe and fled to the garden, taking care to go quietly, wanting no one to know of her flight.

The night air was cool and wet with beginning dew, and moonlight bleached the first roses of their color but took nothing from their sweet fragrance. Tessa drew a deep steadying breath and sank down on the bench where Gavin had held her so comfortably such a short time before. She heard a faraway hunting cry, coyote or wolf she could not tell, and an owl whispered close by. She felt peace begin to flood into her, and she hugged herself for the relief of it.

Things are as they are, how many times had she heard María say that? So many times she had ceased for a while to remember that the words were true. One had to be at least a partial fatalist to survive. Gavin would leave, and she would not see him again. Things are as they are, and there is a certain, even if ugly, rightness about them. Her world and his, they were very different. He would leave, and she would make no plea to stop him. She did not think she could in any case. He was too strong a man. That was one of the many things she loved about him. The knowledge of her love came swiftly, but it brought no sense of shock. He would leave, but she was young, and she would know the feeling when it came again. And she would settle for no less. Gavin had wanted her to see Luis clearly, and now she did. There was no question any more. She would not marry Luis. She returned to her room and slept deeply until she heard the first sounds of morning.

María eyed her so closely that Tessa laughed. "Have I turned into a strange beast to have you stare so, old woman?"

"You have turned into a woman in love," María replied gravely.

"You know me too well. Luckily he does not. He will be going soon, and he will go without knowing. You promise?"

María sputtered in indignation at the thought that any man should be too blind to see the love of her child or that he should not want it, and the scene in the garden was still clear in her mind. "But it makes no sense! You love this man, but he is going. And there is Don Luis."

"No, there is not Luis. María, I will not marry him."

María recognized the determination in Tessa's voice and argued no more, but her confusion did not lessen. She found she was glad Tessa was not to marry Don Luis—she too had been vulnerable to the comparison between him and Gavin—but she was sad things did not seem right between Tessa and the man she wanted.

When Gavin announced his intention to ride, Tessa did not try to dissuade him. She knew he had to test his strength before he left. She simply had his horse and Amordoro saddled and went with him. She had not ridden since they had brought Gavin in, and her horse was as frisky as Gavin's. The palomino danced with his desire to run, and Tessa chided him, "Have patience, you will have your way soon enough, when your muscles are not so stiff from laziness."

Gavin had never seen a woman who sat a horse as well as she did. She was elegantly at ease, her body anticipating every movement of the golden horse, her hands gentle on the reins. She looked superb, and he knew he had been staring when she turned her head to look at him inquiringly.

He used the first excuse he could find. "Your horse, he is from the herds of Don Esteban?"

"Yes, he was a gift for my fourteenth birthday. And the horse you ride, he is also from those herds, is he not? There are many horses in California, but few so fine as these." She had had a curious reluctance to discover what

51

part and why her great-grandfather had played in the chaotic event of Gavin's coming into her life, but now time was short, and she wanted to know.

"Yes, Don Esteban gave him to me. In fact, it was embarrassing. I was a stranger to him. I met him only because he is such an important man in his region, yet he showed me great hospitality. He would take no payment for the horse and was insulted when I offered. He said he would be amply repaid if I would deliver the package on my way north. I was hard pressed to turn down an escort and extra horses."

"And he told you nothing about me?"

"Nothing. He said only that the gift was for a relative."

"How convenient for him you were traveling this way," Tessa observed in a small voice. She knew, she had known since she first saw the package, but she hadn't wanted to admit it. Don Esteban had entrusted this man with a valuable gift, had given him a valuable horse, and had sent him to her. She wondered what freakish notion had made him do it. She had no way of knowing whether he was saying, "Go to the devil with your foreign blood and this foreign man," or "Go with this man and my blessing." It made no difference in any case.

Gavin barely had time to gather his reins and agree to a run before Tessa took off, letting Amordoro show his great speed. She wore no hat, and her hair came loose, streaming behind her in a black veil. At first Gavin wanted to yell at her to slow the breakneck pace, but when he saw she was in perfect control, he grinned and urged his own mount to greater speed. The chestnut was willing and strong, but he could not match Amordoro. They pounded down the grassy valley, jumping small streams and gullies as they came, avoiding knots of cattle, heading toward the sea, Tessa in front the whole way. They were in sight of it and could hear the surf thudding against the rocks before she slowed her horse to a cooling walk.

She searched Gavin's face before she smiled. "You look none the worse for it."

Her face was flushed and her eyes were shining with the joy of the race, and Gavin nearly groaned aloud from the pain of wanting her. Siren, witch, whatever she was, the sooner away, the better.

They stopped to rest near a stand of wind-stunted pines on a bluff overlooking the Pacific. Light glinted and rippled on the water. Gulls wheeled and cried over the rocks where the sea lions were basking in the sun. Tessa stared out over the water, making no attempt at conversation.

Gavin could feel her withdrawal from him even more clearly than he had the day before. "You will be all right?" he asked, unable to stop the dangerous question.

She glanced at him in surprise and then turned her gaze back to the sea. "Of course I will. You are the one who is making a journey. I am at home, safe as I have always been."

"You know I'm talking about Luis."

"You needn't worry. I shan't marry him." The complete certainty in her voice reassured him.

"We should be getting back," she said, and mounted Amordoro before Gavin had a chance to help her up, clearly not wanting him to touch her.

Their ride back was silent and subdued, which was fine with Gavin. He was more tired than he had thought he would be, and his shoulder throbbed from hard usage, but he knew he was strong enough to take up his journey again.

Ramón and Julio were working near the corrals when they arrived, and Gavin settled down on his haunches to talk with them about horses and cattle and the general nonsense of life. Since he had been well enough to be up, he had found Ramón or one of his sons working around the house on several occasions, and he enjoyed talking with them. Once they had gotten over the initial reserve toward him, they had been open and friendly. He resisted the impulse to watch Tessa as she left them and headed for the house, and he saw instead the look of hopeless adoration on Julio's face. My God, he thought, and I worry about her! It's the hapless men who deserve concern. He looked studiously at the ground so the boy wouldn't know he'd been found out.

Tessa didn't even bother to wash her hands and face before she marched into her father's study, and Michael looked surprised and apprehensive to see her where she so seldom ventured.

She noted with disgust her father was already well on

his way to insensibility, before the sun was even fully down. "I have something to tell you, and I want you to listen carefully," she snapped. "I am not going to marry Luis, not ever. I will not commit the rudeness of forbidding him this house and your friendship which you both seem to enjoy so much, but you must forget all ideas of a match between us. And when he comes here again, I will tell him."

"The Yankee?"

"No. He is leaving tomorrow. He has nothing to do with this." Half truth, half lie. "I simply will not marry Luis."

"But you will," her father said, and she felt a jolt of terror at the tone of his voice, dry and dead as old leaves, no anger or demand which could be challenged. He looked far older than his forty-two years, old and crumpled. He fumbled in his desk, and she knew he was going to show her something she had no desire to see. She took the sheaf of papers from him in silence.

At first she did not know what the figures meant, recorded neatly in remembrance of his schoolmaster's hand. And then she understood. It was a record of monies owed to Don Luis. There were some actual loans for small sums, but most of the figures were from gambling debts incurred over the past three years. All those times Luis had come and the two men had played cards. She had been glad her father had seemed to rouse himself enough to enjoy some regular social interchange. It had never occurred to her that they were playing for such sums; the total owed was enormous.

She put the papers back on the desk with extravagant care and held herself rigidly erect. "I fetched a fair price for you, didn't I? Does the sale mean debt canceled when the goods are delivered, or do you gain some additional benefit? Tell me, my loving father, what are the terms?"

He put his head down, and his voice was so strangled by sobs Tessa could hardly understand the words. He had thought she and Luis would marry in any case. It was wrong, he knew it was wrong, but he had thought all along he would win most of it back. But even if he did not, on the day of her marriage, the debt would be forgotten.

Tessa stared at him blankly, and no pity stirred for

him—her own desolation was too great and rage swift and deadly was rising in her, not against her father who was a weak and foolish pawn, but against Luis who had plotted the whole thing to guarantee his will. She would make him pay for it every day of their married life until he would curse the day he had first desired her.

Parents planned marriages of their children more often than the children chose, and debts of honor must be paid even if one of the parties was less than honorable. If she did not fulfill the bargain, everything Michael Macleod owned would be taken from him; she knew Luis would do that. Her father deserved it, but she could not do it to him. The shame it would bring and the last vestiges of love for her father were tangled together. If she moved swiftly and could find buyers for all the herds, the amount might be found, but it was doubtful, and would leave the pastures as bare as if Luis stripped them. She was not even accustomed to thinking in terms of money. She had always been well provided for, but almost every transaction was based on barter; she had seen very little coinage in her life. The gambling debt entries specified that the sums were to be paid in Mexican or Spanish doubloons or some true coinage of gold or silver. And few things were truly hers; the rope of pearls and a few other pieces of jewelry from her mother, the collar of emeralds, and Amordoro were the only things she had of value. Last year's gift of silk and velvet could not even be considered, long since made into dresses. And Don Esteban had not given the emeralds or anything else for ransom even if she could sell them. Don Esteban, he was the only person she knew who might have the actual money, and she would never ask him. She thought of telling Gavin, asking him to take her with him, to leave the whole mess behind, let her father do what he would. She thought of Luis, murderous, and skilled in accomplishing his ends, following them. She thought of the unwelcome burden and the danger she would be to Gavin.

She wanted to lash out from her own hurt, and before she left her father, she chose the words which would wound him the most. "My mother must have been a terrible fool to have loved you," she said and saw his body heave with the agony of it, but he did not lift his bowed head from his arms.

She felt very brittle, as though if anyone were to touch her, she would shatter into a thousand slivers of glass. She felt the urge to scream and to go on screaming in rage until she did break. Instead she sat very quietly in her room, her hands balled into separate fists, and she willed herself to accomplish the one task before her. She must not reveal what had happened, what she knew. Gavin must leave in complete ignorance of the debt to Luis.

Tessa and Gavin shared dinner in their old way without the presence of Michael, and Gavin felt the change in Tessa instantly. Not the cold withdrawal he had sensed before, something quite different. Her eyes were overly bright, her movements were too sharp and quick. She laughed at the right times and answered politely when he asked her something, but everything seemed off key, music played a half note away from the truth.

He asked abruptly, "Has something happened since this afternoon?" and Tessa's heart pounded against her ribs; she had not thought him so aware of her moods. "No," she said, "nothing has happened, nothing at all." She made herself meet his eyes.

And at the earliest opportunity, she excused herself from his company, pleading fatigue from the long ride they'd had. Frowning, he watched her go. He missed the warm Tessa he knew lived beneath this cold control. But then, the cold Tessa would be easier to leave.

Not until he retired to his room, to the wing which held the bedrooms, did he hear the guitar. The strings mourned and raged without discord. Gavin tried to tell himself that all Spanish music had always sounded so to him, but the lie did not stop the misery, and he gave thanks when the last notes died away.

It was as if spring had never been. During the night the fog had rolled into the valley from the sea and probably would not lift at all this day. It swirled and eddied around the house, and any traveling would have to be done slowly and carefully, but Gavin held to his plan to leave, and it was still early when he set out. He would follow the coast until the cliffs became too severe, and then he would cut inland to the easier passage of the valleys.

Tessa insisted on riding partway with him since she was so familiar with the land, but she was no company, aloof and distant, every line of her showing the arrogance of fine breeding, her strange maturity wrapped around her like a protective mantle. Even though it angered Gavin, he realized it might be her way of making the farewell easier.

He was right. Tessa was exercising more control over herself than she had ever done before; her body felt as though every ounce of flesh had been turned to stone. She feared if she let go for a minute, she would be wailing, "I love you, take me with you, don't leave me to Luis!"

The fog was so heavy by the sea that sometimes Gavin could not see Tessa though she rode close beside him. Sounds were separate and distinct, surf rolling in and the slow, steady drum of the horses' hooves; had he not heard them, it would have been like riding with a ghost. Tessa's hair was hidden and her face shadowed by the hood of the dark cloak she wore against the chill and wet, and when the gray mist swirled around her, she seemed to dissolve and become part of it. Gavin wanted to shut out the image, but he could not.

Finally Tessa reined Amordoro to a stop. "This is as far as I go." The mist swirled open for a moment, and the two looked at each other. Tessa's hood had fallen, and the black cloud of her hair, gleaming with tiny beads of moisture, framed the perfect oval of her face. Under the delicate brows, her eyes were enormous pools of violet shadows, and now Gavin could see her mouth trembling as it had in the garden before she cried.

She drank in every detail of his hard, beautiful face. She would not forget anything. Not the faint white scar on his right cheek nor the thick curling darkness of his hair, not the firm mouth, and never the incredibly deep blue of his eyes. She would not forget the broadness of his shoulders nor the long, lean length of his body. She had heard his voice taut with pain, deep with amusement, harsh with anger. She would not forget.

He thought if he had to look at her for a minute longer, he would commit himself forever, asking her to come with him, to leave everything she knew.

It was she who broke the spell. Her mouth curved into a small, brief smile. "Take care in your travels, especially when you come upon girls who swim without clothes. They are the most dangerous of all. You would do well to wear a poncho even on the hottest of days; it makes it harder for the knife to enter. *Vaya con Dios*, Gavin Ramsay."

She wheeled Amordoro around, and the mist swallowed them instantly. The pain in Gavin's throat burst out in one word, in the harsh, angry cry of her name. But there was no answer, and he could not even hear the hoofbeats of Amordoro.

It was what he wanted. Better for him, better for her. He headed north.

CHAPTER VI

Had Gavin been riding a lesser beast than the one given to him by Don Esteban, he would have killed it. He was in the saddle for well over fourteen hours the first day, setting the pattern for the rest of the journey. When the sea cliffs grew impassable, he cut inland cursing the thick brush and steep hills, cursing himself for a fool, cursing Tessa.

He was bone-weary and shaking as though he had the ague when he finally stopped for the first night's rest. His shoulder throbbed as if he had just received the wound. He built a fire only because he didn't want to be attacked and eaten by a grizzly during the night, and he forced himself to eat some of the food María and Tessa had packed in his saddlebags, though he was beyond hunger.

The chestnut looked as tired as Gavin felt, and Gavin stroked his head gently as he fed him some of the grain Ramón had sent. "You poor devil, Don Esteban would kill me if he could see you now."

The horse nickered softly, and Gavin grinned in spite
58

of himself. "Recognize the name? Then Devil it is. No, Diablo for your Californio friends." The grin faded, leaving his face bleak and aged. He saw the great palomino, and he saw Tessa, her black hair streaming behind her as she set the breakneck pace down the valley. "God damn you, woman!" he swore viciously, but he heard the difference in his own voice when he awakened before the dawn. "Tessa, my Tessa."

The pleading sound appalled him. He saddled Diablo and was on his way before first light broke, increasing the pace as the sun rose to illuminate the way.

Once he struck El Camino Real, the going was easier. The King's Highway was well worn now from its use by agents of the hide and tallow trade. Mustard plants marked the trail with pale yellow streaks, legacy of the seeds carried in the wool of the sheep brought by the Franciscans as they carried their creed into the wilderness.

The growing spring color did nothing to improve Gavin's temper. He saw herds of cattle and horses by the thousands and sometimes *vaqueros* and an occasional rancho, and he saw the peeling decay of the missions on the way, but he stopped for nothing short of Diablo's exhaustion.

He arrived in Monterey early on the third day, and at first he was so stunned, he stared like a peasant just in from the farm. He had heard the town was pleasant enough, as would be expected of the main port of entry and the capital of the country, but he hadn't anticipated this.

The adobes sparkled in the light, their walls brilliant with whitewash. Many of the roofs were of tile, some of shakes, but all gave their age away, the older ones sporting the additional colors of moss, the newer ones still bare of growth. Graceful balconies and verandahs and flowers beginning to bloom in patios gave proof that life in the capital was gracious indeed and had moved beyond the first function of a *presidio,* a military outpost. The water of the bay glittered and rolled in the sun, and the back hills were deep green with twisted pine and cypress.

Caballeros rode by outfitted in fine cloth and silver, horses and tack polished to a high gleam. Women dressed

59

in lace and silk eyed the tall Yankee curiously, and Gavin was suddenly aware of how unkempt he and Diablo looked. He wanted nothing more than a hot bath and hours of sleep, but first he'd have to find Indian.

It wasn't difficult to locate the Custom House; the long building was the largest in town. Gavin grimaced when he saw it. It was a good distance from the water where a few ships rolled in the tide, and everything to be sold in California had to be unloaded, brought to the Custom House where duty would be decided. Then anything to be used in the coastal trade would have to be reloaded. He could imagine how Indian felt about that. He could hear the choice words.

He was hearing them. "You son of a bitch, where th' hell you been?" Indian was roaring as he came up beside Gavin and pulled him without ceremony from the saddle.

"God damn it, don't——!" Gavin gasped as Indian gripped him by the shoulders.

Indian steadied him and let go, looking at Gavin's pale face with concern. "What's wrong, little brother? You find a war on your way up here?"

"Something like that," Gavin agreed with a tired grin. "Little brother" was one of the many shared jokes between them. By no common measure could Gavin be called little, yet Indian's bulk made everyone around him seem frail. And no one would ever mistake the two men for brothers, the one blue-eyed and black-haired, the other black-eyed and brown-skinned. But in all things that made brotherhood valuable, they were related. They had saved each other's lives so many times, survived so many things together, shared so much success and failure, there was no debt line between them.

Gavin leaned against Diablo and focused on Indian's face. He saw the strong bones and broad features, mixed heritage of his friend's African and Indian parentage. He saw the huge dark eyes so gentle in contrast with the heavily muscled body. He wondered how Indian and Tessa would get along. He knew he ought to ask about the cargo, and he tried, but the exhaustion he had held off for what seemed an eternity was hitting him with a vengeance.

"It wait till now, can wait some more," he heard Indian

say, and then the whole world was the tide rolling in and out, deep and dark.

"Sweet lord, what you done this time?" Indian asked softly, knowing Gavin was beyond answering.

"Tessa?"

"Ain't nobody here by that name, ain't been since you started askin' two days ago."

Gavin looked around the room. The same, but not the same. Floor boards, not tile, he must be on a second story. He looked at Indian. "Two days. Where am I, and how in the hell did I get here?"

"I brung you here, slung over that fine horse you got, seemed too much work to carry you with him jus' standin' there. This Casa Vargas. Belongs to a widder woman, an' she cain't hardly wait till you wake up. My, my, she got plans for you. Like what she saw even though you a runt an' all. An' here I been tryin' ever since I got here. Here's Monterey in case you don't know that either. An' you clean as a newborn babe, widder woman help me, my yes." The mockery faded because Indian couldn't sustain it any longer. His face was hard, his voice completely changed. "That a bad one. Any fool can see you might a' died. Somebody hurt you real bad an' somebody took good care. Who's Tessa? An' why you ride so hard with time gone anyways? Ain't like you to near kill a horse, 'specially not a horse like that one."

"Diablo, the horse, is he all right?"

"He do, same as you. Both of you jus' needed a little more sleep than you been gettin'. You goin' answer my questions?"

Gavin stared at Indian for a long moment. "No," he said quietly. "I'm not going to answer your questions, not now anyway." He saw the hurt in Indian's face. "If there was a sensible way to tell you, I would, I swear I would. It has nothing to do with trusting you. It has to do with me being a damn fool. The day I can laugh about it, I'll let you know."

"Day you laugh 'bout bein' cut like that, they lock you up for mad," Indian muttered, but there was no longer anger or hurt in his voice, and Gavin knew it was all right between them. There were also many episodes in Indian's life that he would never know about.

An episode, over and done with, it was the only sane way to think about Tessa. Already he suspected his memory was playing tricks on him. No woman could have hair so black, eyes that color, a body so lithe that . . . He looked up to find Indian regarding him with interest. "Mos' men find helps to take a horse when they go travelin', but you put your mind to it, you find all sorts of sin right here, won't have to go nowhere."

Gavin took Indian's suggestion with a vengeance, drowning himself in work and pleasure with equal fervor. With Lent over and each day showing more signs of spring, the social life in Monterey blossomed too. Almost every night there was a ball or a dance somewhere, and within a short period of his arrival, Gavin found himself invited to almost every one. The Californios were basically a very hospitable race, but Gavin was not blind to the additional reasons for the invitations. Though some people had gotten to know Indian fairly well and liked him for himself, most regarded him as something quite exotic and rather dangerous, and to have his vast, dark-skinned bulk among one's guests was counted a social coup, though had he not had the status of a foreign merchant, prejudice would have barred him completely. Indian did not attend half as many parties as Gavin did—he was no more blind to the motives than Gavin was. As for himself, Gavin viewed his own popularity with cynical amusement. Though some of the men and women who were fiery Californios at heart and resented foreigners were cold to the point of rudeness, most people were genuinely warm because they were charmed by the tall Yankee—one of the favored blue-eyed ones, *los ojos azules*—and curious about what he had seen and where he had been. And almost all saw him as marriage bait, sure to make a Californio marriage and live happily ever after as so many of them did. It was not that there were so many Yankee men in California—their numbers were few—it was just that there were even fewer Yankee women. For a long while the wife of Thomas Larkin had been the only one in all of the country. Surely the newcomer with the hard name and the harder blue eyes would find one among their own lovely daughters to soften his nature. There was never an overabundance of young men; the climate of California seemed to encourage the conception of girls. And this Señor Ramsay did not seem disposed to seduce young ladies while he searched for the perfect one, a fact which comforted the parents if not their daughters.

Indian teased Gavin unmercifully about his romantic conquest of Monterey. "Mystery man, they call you, cain't figure how you look so hot-blooded an' act so cold. Guess th' widder Vargas could tell them a thing or two."

Gavin scowled at him so ferociously Indian let the subject drop. The bitterness had nothing to do with Indian; it was self-directed.

Carmelita Vargas wasn't thirty yet and already she had had two husbands and was on the lookout for a third. Her husbands had added generously to her natural talents; she was good in bed and enjoyed every minute of it. And she had a shrewdly practical side that allowed her to accept without too much regret the fact that her Yankee lover was not going to be her third husband. It really was just as well; he did not so much enjoy life as stampede through it. Carmelita knew herself well enough to know that would tire her greatly before too much time had passed; she was addicted to the slow pace of a true Californio. But her sadness for Gavin was genuine. He called out often in the night, called out another woman's name, and the sound was too sorrow-filled for Carmelita to be angry. She was too wise to ask the Yankee about the woman or even to admit she had heard the name.

Gavin understood Carmelita as well as she understood herself, and under normal circumstances, he would have been truly fond of her and appreciative of her honesty and generosity in bed. But nothing had been normal since he'd left Tessa. He seemed incapable of feeling anything except pain at the memory of her; nothing else seemed to touch him at all.

The moonlight fell on the face of the woman beside him, and just for a moment, the gleaming mass of black hair and the moon-chiseled features were Tessa's, and then they were not. The rounded flesh which would betray

63

Carmelita in a few years' time if she were not careful was suddenly repellent to Gavin, and he swung out of bed with a barely suppressed oath.

He stood at the window staring blindly at the white spill of light on the waters of the bay. The same sea touched the land to the south, the same moon was shining where Tessa slept. Did she sleep? Yes, of course she did. Tough and practical and probably totally without memories of him by now, of course she slept. Damn her! He knew he'd said it aloud when he heard Carmelita's voice.

"You will catch a chill there. The nights are not so warm yet. Please, come back to bed; I too am cold."

Carmelita ignored his hesitation and the unyielding stiffness of his body as she put her arms around him.

Gavin drew some small comfort from the fact that while his personal life was a shambles, the business venture was going very well indeed, though he and Indian could not claim all the credit since Thomas Larkin had helped so much to ease the way through the endless bureaucracy of the government. Only a month before, on April 2, Larkin had received formal confirmation of his appointment as the first American consul in California, and now his magnificent house on the Calle Principal was the consulate and had official sanction for the service it had rendered for nearly ten years as a meeting place for both prominent Californios and Yankees.

Thomas Oliver Larkin was a phenomenon. In his early forties, he had already lived for twelve years in Monterey and for some years before to the north in Yerba Buena. Yet for all the time spent in California, he remained a shrewd, brisk Massachusetts man, a true Yankee. Even his marriage was in keeping with his background. Rachel Holmes Larkin was also Massachusetts born and had been the first American wife in California as their oldest son had been the first child with two American parents to be born in the Far West as far as anyone knew.

Larkin had quietly built his own empire in California. He had worked as a bookkeeper and clerk in Yerba Buena, and then he had moved to Monterey and opened a store with borrowed money. Before long he had gone beyond selling the supplies from the Boston ships and had a flour mill, his own lumber and contracts to erect buildings, and many other irons in the fire.

Gavin not only respected the man for his industry and accomplishments, he also liked him personally. Though Larkin's receding hairline had left a threatening expanse of forehead unsoftened by his thin, sharp features, his pale eyes were as friendly as they were shrewd, and he was genuinely interested in people and willing to like them unless something radical was done to change his mind. And he made up for his lack of formal education by native intelligence and great tenacity.

Thomas and Rachel entertained graciously and often, and normally Gavin enjoyed himself, but tonight he found it took great effort to behave with even minimal civility. It had been a week since he had first awakened in the middle of the night to leave Carmelita's bed, and now his sea watch had become a nightly ritual, lengthening each time until Carmelita had lost patience and snapped, "It does not keep me warm to have you stand forever by the window; it keeps me awake." He had moved back into the room he had had when he first came to Monterey.

As he stood in the shadows of the Larkins' verandah, he could hear Carmelita's gay voice and her laughter. He smiled ruefully, wondering idly who the next lucky man would be. He was startled by the voice beside him. In his preoccupation, he hadn't heard Mr. Larkin come out of the house.

"Mrs. Larkin has a bad habit of mothering strays even when they are full grown, Mr. Ramsey. She sent me out to make sure you had not been taken ill. She claims you've been looking off color for some time now. I am not as observant in these matters as my wife is, but I must agree with her in this case. Is there anything we can do?"

"No, sir, there isn't, but I am flattered by your concern and Mrs. Larkin's," Gavin managed to say in spite of his surprise.

"You mustn't worry too much about your cargo. It's coming along nicely, almost all cleared. These things take time in California. I'm not a good example, but I must admit it saves time and costs less if you are married to a native-born woman, especially if she is from one of the

65

more important families. And I haven't noticed too much suffering for those who have followed this course. The women here are quite lovely."

Gavin was thankful it was too dark for Larkin to see his face. Larkin's observations were certainly valid about life in California. The duty charged on goods could be exorbitant, three hundred percent or more, and the delays endless, yet these problems disappeared as if by magic if the trader was married to a Californio woman of high birth. Larkin himself had a half-brother who had settled in Monterey in 1826, married into the Vallejo family, been baptized into the Church, and had been granted Mexican citizenship plus a great deal of land and a mill. Larkin, had he done the same, would have been granted twenty thousand acres of land almost anywhere he wanted it in California. Of course, he hadn't; he'd married Yankee and stayed American and Protestant, and he'd done just as well anyway, but there were few Thomas Larkins in the world.

What bothered Gavin was that while Larkin could be simply commenting on conditions in the country, he could just as easily be talking about specifics, about Tessa. No, that was impossible. He couldn't know about her. But he could sense that Gavin's restlessness was caused by a woman, not my business.

It was embarrassing to discover he was being as obvious as a boy in the throes of first love.

He made an effort to put things back on a businesslike footing. "Indian and I are pleased with your offer," he said, and meant it. Larkin had not only agreed to pay good prices for part of their cargo, he had also volunteered to help them find a coastal vessel at reasonable cost so they could expand their own trade. He had no fear of competition. Gavin was already well acquainted with the older man's belief that there were endless opportunities in California. He also knew that though the consul wanted no bloodshed, he would never be happy until California belonged to the United States.

Larkin dismissed Gavin's thanks as unnecessary, each party standing to gain, and he spoke about what was always closest to his heart. "Have you heard what Micheltorena has done?" he asked.

Gavin knew little about Governor Manuel Micheltorena

66

except that he had been appointed by Mexico in 1842 and was generally respected and well liked personally, though the convict soldiers, the *cholos* who had been sent with him, were terribly unpopular. He admitted his ignorance to Larkin.

The consul's voice was deliberate as he enumerated Micheltorena's recent decrees. "He has ordered public schools to be established all up and down the coast. All children, boys and girls, between the ages of six and eleven must attend or their parents will be fined. He has passed laws curtailing excessive medical fees. He has declared Yerba Buena an official port of entry, and he wants foreign vessels to pay only fair duties and landing fees. He is even going so far as to try to end smuggling and the bribery of officials, and he has ordered that the missions be returned to the *padres*, albeit only for religious use, so that the buildings will not decay and disappear forever. Of course, what he had decreed and what will be done are two different matters."

Gavin was just able to prevent himself from the blunder. Micheltorena's reforms sounded excellent to him, and he suffered a moment's total confusion over the dry, almost grim note in Larkin's voice, made even more incomprehensible by the knowledge that the governor and the consul were fairly good friends. And then suddenly he saw. Mexico and a succession of governors had neglected the affairs of California for a very long time, and such neglect paved the way for a takeover, especially an efficient Yankee takeover. A worthy and hard-working Mexican governor was no asset to Larkin's dream.

Gavin was spared the necessity of comment by the appearance of Mrs. Larkin. She brushed aside the gallantries both men started to offer her. "Mr. Ramsay, there is a young man here to see you. He looks tired to death and just as frightened. He won't come in the house. Would you come with me, please?"

"Yes, of course," Gavin agreed though he was completely at a loss as to who it might be.

Rachel led him to the front door, and when he opened it the light spilled out to illuminate the haggard face of Julio Ramirez.

"My God! Tessa, what's happened to her?" Nearly

67

everyone in the room behind him heard the half-curse, half-prayer, and Carmelita's face was bleak for an instant before she carefully restored her smile, but Gavin was no longer aware of anyone except Julio.

CHAPTER VII

Tessa's defiant courage lasted for nearly a week after Gavin's departure. The idea of tormenting Luis was almost enough to make her resigned to the marriage. And then she was terrified.

The wedding was not to be in some dim unrealized time in the future, some time by which she would have undergone a miraculous change causing her to be able to cope with every aspect of the match. That thought alone had given her the false courage. She knew it to be false when the date for her marriage was set only a little over a month away. No protest to her father or to Luis made any difference; her wishes in the matter were of no account.

Luis was calling in the debt. Perhaps he was afraid the Yankee would come back or another like him. More likely he was simply losing patience. Tessa could sense it in the new way he treated her, seeking every opportunity to touch her, pulling a tendril of her hair just hard enough to hurt or leave a bruise where his hands had held her with sudden brutal pressure. He enjoyed hurting her, enjoyed watching her struggle to control her fear of him, enjoyed warning her of what life with him would be like. She could even sense the perverse joy he got when he pushed her far enough to make her retaliate, once trying to claw his face, another time sinking her teeth into his hand when he cornered her in the garden.

Like a sleek cat lapping cream, Luis licked the blood from the punctures, watching her through narrowed lids, crooning, "That is what my wife must have, some fire, some fear." His hands shot out suddenly to grip her head on either side while he kissed her, bruising her mouth and leaving the taste of his blood on her lips. She heard the
68

sound of his horse pounding away even as she felt the sickness overwhelm her. She retched helplessly, the taste of his blood seeming to grow stronger every second.

He was driving her mad, spending more time here than at his own rancho, always ferreting out her whereabouts, trapping her alone. For the first time in her vital existence, life had lost all pleasure. When she tried to eat, her throat closed and the sickness welled in her. When she tried to escape into sleep, her mind and body refused, leaving her lying rigid while endless images of life with Luis flashed before her. She could see the dreadful changes in herself and could do nothing to stop them. Her laugh was bitter when she thought of how she'd planned to torment him. There had never been the slightest possibility of that. His evil was so inborn, it was as strong as the virtue born in other men.

The only way she could be sure of avoiding him was to be off on Amordoro at dawn, not returning until the sun was nearly down. And even then Luis found her once by the sea, and only Amordoro's speed allowed her to reach home first where she threw herself from the saddle and sought María's presence, hearing Luis laughing behind her about what a good race it had been.

She went often to the pool now, and in this Ramón helped her. She broke down enough to ask him, "Please, if you love me, tell no one where I am. I need these days to myself." She knew he heard many of the words she had not spoken, and she was sorry because it would do no good and only hurt María and Ramón further, emphasizing all they did not know, but she could not bear the idea of Luis invading this one last refuge. Often she wondered dully why, not having the courage to kill him, she did not make an end of herself. Though she could not understand all of it, she realized part of the reason was that it would be Luis's final victory, not her own.

The pool held its own measure of pain now too. Before it had been pure, a place to be alone and peaceful; now it carried the strongest images of Gavin. She could see him nowhere else as clearly as she could see him here. And though this was where he had lain wounded and in pain, she saw him strong and whole, laughing, angry, thoughtful, and a thousand shades between. Gavin. Sometimes she said his name aloud as if to reassure herself that such a man existed. Though she had tried to give it weight, the fact that he had by now most certainly forgotten her in the arms of another woman made no difference. When the day came that she could no longer remember him, then a beautiful part of her life, of herself would be dead.

She heard a fluting whistle and sighed. Poor Ramón, with all his other duties, his worry had driven him to come for her again. The sun was far lower than she'd noticed. Dear old man, they'd scarcely be back before dark. It was so unjust that her trouble should be weighing so heavily on the Ramirezes. She got up wearily and waited for the dizziness to ease. She would have to make herself eat more or she would no longer have the strength to come here.

"I'm coming," she called, and she started down the path.

When Ramón caught sight of her, he set his face in stern, respectful lines, half father, half servant; it was what he had always been to her, and he knew how to play the role well. But his impulse was to take her in his arms and weep. There had been no need for his warning whistle; his little one had not been swimming in the pool. He did not even need her dry hair to tell him that. Though the weather had been warming for days now, he doubted Tessa had even thought of enjoying what had been one of her chief pleasures.

The changes he had been so diligently denying to himself could no longer be ignored. There was almost nothing left of the Tessa he and his wife had helped to raise. This ghostlike being with the dull eyes and slow, unsure movements was a stranger.

"It was kind of you to, come for me, Ramón." The dry whisper of a voice, another thing which had nothing to do with his Tessa.

No one could have been more stunned by his actions than he himself was. He had just reminded himself of his position and had been quite sure he accepted it, but Tessa's voice finished him.

Great storms of the heart he left to María; it was her way to have them often, to weather them, and to find peace afterward. For himself, it was better to be as patient and careful with human beings as he was with the beasts

70

in his charge. And yet now his blood was singing in his ears, he could hear his own voice shouting loud enough to bring fearful silence to the sundown birds, and his hands were holding onto Tessa's shoulders, shaking her. "This is madness! You run and hide, and he looks for you. He was here again today. I lied, telling him I did not know where you had gone, and I sent a *vaquero* to follow him safely, to be sure he would not come back to find my trail and yours. He is evil and you are afraid, yet you are going to marry him in not many days' time. Where will you hide then, where? Those who are married in God's sight share all things. You will share his days and his nights, his house and his bed. Where will you hide then, Teresa María Julieta Margarita Macleod y Amarista who will soon also be Estudillo?"

Tessa stared at him for a moment, her eyes as purple dark as storm clouds; not even seeing Ramón angry for the first time she could remember sparked anything in her. It was just one more example of the disintegration of her world. She was dazed from the rough handling, and her voice was small and flat when she answered him. "I won't hide then. I will be in hell. Youu can't hide there, can you?"

She looked at him and saw the tears begin to roll down the leathery cheeks, and his grief did what his anger could not. Just for an instant, the horrible, dead feeling of terror eased, and Tessa collapsed sobbing against him, her tears staining the rough weave of his serape.

His callused hands stroked her hair as gently as if she were a fragile newborn, but his voice was hard. "If this is the Yankee's doing, I will find him and I will kill him."

Tessa stiffened in his arms and then nestled closer, and he had to believe her labored words. "No, it is none of his doing, except that he is . . . he is the kind of man he is. While Luis, Luis is the kind of man he is."

"Then why, *niñita*, are you marrying him?" Ramón asked softly.

He felt the sudden harsh angling of her body, every muscle tense and hard as bone as she pulled away to look up at him. "If it could be changed," she said slowly, "I would change it or ask you and María to help me change it. But it cannot be. I must marry Luis, and I will. And it is my sorrow that this is something which has caused hurt to you and to María. But it will never change my love for you."

Ramón held her, wordless now with his sorrow and his love for this girl who was, save for actual birth, his daughter. "I am so tired," he heard her murmur as he held her close again. He felt a thousand years old—his Tessa was never tired, but now she sounded like an old woman, not a young girl at all. He vowed to end the silence that had fallen between himself and María over this. Perhaps they would be too late, perhaps they could do nothing—this he knew was more than probable. He was accustomed to being shaped by life and accepting things as they came. But if he did not try to change things for Tessa, he would never sleep easily again.

If Ramón needed anything to strengthen his resolve, the ride home provided it. He himself had taught Tessa to ride almost before she could walk. He had taught her to ride fearlessly and at the same time as gracefully as the highest-born lady anywhere. And now as he watched her, he saw even this had changed. She still rode competently, taking care of the horse because to do otherwise was against all her instincts, but the straight-backed line of grace had blurred. Her whole body proclaimed that this was a wearisome task to be accomplished without joy.

It was the first thing he told María. He rushed through the last chores for the livestock kept close to the houses, startling his sons, who were left with a foal to feed and an injured hoof to tend.

He waited impatiently for his wife to return from the main house. "María, she does not even ride as I taught her anymore," was his only greeting.

María's face fell into such lines of age and sadness that Ramón was stunned. He had not seen her look so since they had lost the twin girls who had been born and died within minutes of each other so many years ago. And not until now had he realized that this woman he had loved since the time he was more boy than man was as marked by the years passing as he was.

She refused to meet his eyes as she spoke. Her hands were knotted so tightly in her lap, Ramón wanted to take them in his own and smooth out the shining white bone marks. He heard the harshness of her voice as his own.

72

"She swore to me she would not marry that one. She swore. She was strong and happy in her word. She was sad, very sad, over the leaving of the Yankee, which she knew must come, but she was not afraid. Now she is only fearful, nothing else. She does not eat. I know she does not sleep. And she is marrying that one."

Her voice died, and she looked fully at her husband before she continued venomously. "You have been blind even as I have been. When Tessa saw the truth, we were blind. Luis is evil. If the devil himself had fathered him, he could be no more evil. And she is not blind, yet she is marrying him. She swore to me she would not, she swore it. She breaks her own word now. And she will not speak to me of it. For the first time since her birth, she reminds me I am her servant, no more." María's anger was nothing to her hurt. She drew a deep breath and went on. "Something has happened, something has changed, something not to do with the Yankee. And I think it is to do with the father." Not for the world would she call him *patrón* at this moment. "He has had too much to do with Luis, and now it is our little one who is paying the price. I know this as surely as if God Himself told me." Only in moments of the greatest stress did María mention God; all other petitions went through the Virgin.

"We have little time. Already the butchering of chosen beasts has begun for meat to feed the guests. Don Esteban and the priest and many relations will soon be here. It is scarcely more than a week's time before Tessa will be wed," Ramón reminded her desperately.

They regarded each other in tense silence, and then Ramón saw the sudden gleam beginning in María's eyes. He knew it well after so many years with his woman. She was planning, and once she had decided her course, nothing would change her mind.

"I will find the cause of this," she announced. "I should have done this long before. I will find out from her father. The drink makes him talk. Tomorrow he will talk to me."

She looked at her husband as though expecting him to challenge her, but instead, Ramón took her hand and patted it before he kissed her. "You are a good woman, my María. I am better at knowing what an animal will do, what must be done for it to live and be strong. I leave to you

73

this knowing of people. I pray only that there is time to change this terrible thing."

María prayed too; she prayed fiercely and slept little, disturbing Ramón often during the night with her twisting and turning, receiving only his loving touch in reassurance and no scolding for the sleep lost.

She barely saw Tessa even though she was early at the house. As was so often the case these days, Tessa gave her no more than a swift kiss before she was off, not once meeting María's eyes, clearly in a frantic hurry to be gone in case Luis came looking for her. The new frail look of this child-woman she loved so much banished the last of María's doubts. Her only agony was the waiting.

She spent the morning cleaning furiously and unnecessarily in the house she and the servants under her always kept spotless, and as the afternoon advanced, she felt no guilt for listening at the door of the study for the first sounds of the clumsiness that came over Tessa's father when he had drunk too much. She added to her list of prayers a plea that Luis would not come to visit this day and Tessa would not return early.

The sound of something falling to the floor was the voice of God to María, and she was in the room before the pile of books had fully settled.

She realized that Michael Macleod was already so hazed by drink, he could make no sense of her being there, if indeed he knew who she was. All her ideas of the subtle words she was going to use fled as she watched his weak, fumbling attempts to pick up the books.

Only briefly did she allow the image of his strong love for Tessa's mother to invade her mind. That time was over. Only Tessa mattered now, and this man was in some way responsible for her destruction.

"Don Miguel, your daughter is soon to marry Don Luis. He is an evil man, and Tessa is afraid, but still she is going to marry him. It is your doing, your fault. I know this. I do not know why. You will tell me."

Michael tried to focus on the woman. Vaguely he knew it was only María Ramirez, reminding himself she was only a servant, and then the picture slipped and she was the woman who had cared for his wife, raised his daughter, and now stood over him blaming him with perfect justice

74

for what he was doing to his only child. Tessa had avoided him more than ever lately, but he had caught glimpses of her, and even in his befuddled state, he had seen the changes.

The pain and pleasure of pouring out his guilt to the woman standing before him were so intertwined he could not differentiate between them, and there was satisfaction in seeing the disbelief on her face replaced by horrified comprehension. He even forgot she could not read and pushed toward her the same papers that had ended Tessa's joy.

María lost all control, screeching at him, "You are a foul thing out of hell!"

She wanted to hurt him as she had never wanted to hurt another living thing. She grabbed the papers and fled, from herself as much as from him. Michael slumped on the desk, moaning with the effort of trying to sort out his mind, knowing for some good reason he did not want to. He was unaware that María had taken the papers.

Tessa had once tried to persuade María to learn to read, offering to teach her. María had refused, and not even now did she regret that decision. Reading was not a thing she wished or needed to do. She could hear well and her mind remembered words exactly. She could still hear every terrible word Don Miguel had uttered. But the papers were important. One did not need to know how to read them to know that papers were the final indisputable weapons in the affairs of men. She clutched them as if they might disappear from her hands.

Both of her sons could read, though Julio was far better at it than Juan. In the long-ago happy days of the rancho, they had often shared lessons with Tessa. If Ramón doubted her word, Julio could read the proof. And the papers would convince the Yankee.

María was decided on this. It was the Yankee, not Don Esteban, who must be told, who must save Tessa. Her mind refused to think of it as buying. Every act of salvation had its price.

Ramón came in early, before she had to return to the main house to fix the evening meal. She greeted him as he had greeted her the day before, pouring out what she had learned about Tessa without preamble.

75

He shook his head as though he had received a physical blow. He wanted to tell her she had heard wrong, but he knew she had not, and he did not need the papers to be read by his son to convince him. He gritted his teeth and called Don Miguel a name so foul María blinked and then smiled in grim agreement. And very quickly she told him what must be done.

Ramón stared at nothing for a long moment before he asked, "What if he does not come? What if he cannot even be found? What if he has left Monterey? What if he does not love her? What if he does not have so much gold?"

"What if the sun does not come up tomorrow?" She snapped at him because the questions were her own, and then she pleaded, "Ramón, it is her only chance. We do not know what Don Esteban wants anymore, but before this he has wished she marry into a noble family. Luis comes from such a family; the Yankee does not. If this fails, then she is lost, but at least we have done all we can to prevent it."

They chose Julio to go, trusting the Yankee would remember him. And they sent with him one of the *vaqueros*, a half-breed Indian named Pedro, a man who said little but knew much of survival and who had once been as far north as Monterey for trading. Ramón selected four of the best horses—the men would travel more swiftly if they had extra mounts to share the work.

Ramón himself wanted to go more than he had wanted to do anything for longer than he could remember, but he could not leave the rancho, and in any case, Tessa, even in her present state, would notice his absence. If any questions were asked about Julio, Ramón and María were quite prepared to tell the same lie—he had gone with one of the *vaqueros* into the back hills in search of some stray horses. Though the trip was dangerous, neither hesitated to send their son, and Julio himself would have walked clear to Mexico if it would have helped Tessa. Even Juan understood the gravity of the situation well enough to yield to the privilege of the older son.

When María returned to the main house, she found Tessa had come home only a short while before to find Luis waiting for her. She looked cowed and miserable and

76

picked at her food while Luis wolfed down everything María grudgingly served him.

She wanted desperately to reassure Tessa, but she had to content herself with playing the unfamiliar role of *dueña*, refusing to leave Tessa alone with Luis. With false politeness she offered him a room for the night, saying it was time for Tessa to retire, so weary was she. Luis muttered something under his breath and left, and María sincerely hoped he would fall over a cliff on the long ride back to his own rancho.

Tessa kissed her in thanks, too tired to speak, and was gone.

In the chill gray mist before full dawn, Ramón, María, and Juan saw Julio and Pedro on their way. And though it was María's plan, it was Ramón who spoke to his son.

"You have the papers?"

Julio nodded gravely.

"Take care, my son. It is not only your life you carry, it is hers also. You must find the Yankee, and you must make him understand."

Julio nodded again, awed by the responsibility made so much heavier by his lifelong devotion to Tessa, equally resolute at this unlooked for chance to aid her, his ardor undiminished by the fact that his mission was to deliver her to another man.

Ramón looked at the other rider, and Pedro met his gaze squarely. There was no need of words here. The *vaquero*'s mind was already miles ahead on the trail he would choose. He would take good care of himself and Julio.

But it was María who had the last word as the figures disappeared into the mist. "*Vaya con Dios,*" she said, her words clear and singing on the cold morning air.

CHAPTER VIII

Tessa would not have believed things could have gotten any worse than they had been, but they did.

It was bad enough when the aunts and uncles and now complacently married cousins arrived from Santa Barbara. They reminded her of her mother's funeral and her own unhappy sojourn with them when they had tried so unsuccessfully to civilize her. She greeted them all with polite distance and left them in María's charge, apologizing as she did so.

"It is not just, but I cannot bear them, any of them. Forgive me for leaving you to take care of them." She paused and added dully, "It will be over soon enough."

She fled to the pool. She understood María's reactions no better than she understood anything that was happening to her now. María seemed to spend her days looking off into the distance, preoccupied but strangely unperturbed. She performed the added chores and marshaled her underlings with a calm air as though none of it made any difference. She was right, Tessa conceded, none of it did make any difference. What would be would be. María had told her that often enough.

She knew it was somehow wrong, damaging, making it harder than ever for her to resign herself to a lifetime with Luis, but she spent the day sitting quietly by the shaded water, ignoring the advancing signs of spring, shutting out the joy of innumerable birds, concentrating until she saw no one, heard no one except Gavin. Only when the shadows were deep and the day nearly closed did she fail, panicking when she could see nothing but Luis's leering face, feel nothing beyond the bruising pressure of his hands. She rode Amordoro as hard as she dared in the fading light, arriving home to the terror of Luis on yet another visit. And the final blow was to learn that Don Esteban and the priest had arrived.

She had known she would have to face her great-grandfather, but knowing had nothing to do with the reality. Now he was waiting for her, and the meeting could not be postponed.

Some last defiance made her seek him out immediately without repairing the ravages of her long outdoor day. She was not even surprised to find him in her father's study. Her father had disappeared to his bedroom with the first influx of relatives. Everyone spoke politely of his "illness" and ignored the full decanters María delivered to his room.

Even her fear of the meeting did not blind Tessa to the changes in the room. María had finally gotten her chance to clean it, and the thick layers of dust were gone. The room smelled of beeswax and damp, scrubbed wood, and the man sitting behind the desk now was as much of a change from the normal occupant as was the absence of clutter.

Don Esteban had aged little in the years since Tessa had seen him. The lines were all sharper drawn, the eyes more piercing than ever, but that was all. He was dressed in black velvet as he had been then, and Tessa was tempted for an instant to reverse the years and tell him again that she liked eagles. Indeed, she felt as young in his presence now as she had those long years before.

The silence stretched taut between them as the dark eyes continued to watch her. Don Esteban was not one to observe normal pleasantries.

When she could bear his scrutiny no longer, she made herself speak, though she was not sure until she heard her first words that her paralyzed throat would work. "Welcome, Great-grandfather, I am honored that you have come to witness my wedding."

Unconsciously she had drawn herself up to the limits of her slender height, and her voice was devoid of any feeling. She saw the anger flash in his eyes to be followed by grudging respect and a small, tight smile.

"I see your manners have not improved since the last time I saw you, Teresa María."

She realized then she had nothing left to lose; nothing could harm her as much as her marriage to Luis would. "Rudeness runs in the blood, Great-grandfather, on both sides," she replied, and was gratified to see two spots of color appear on his white cheeks.

He changed the subject abruptly. "You received your gift? I have had no word," and it was her turn to flush, though embarrassment, not anger, caused it. In all that had happened since Gavin's arrival, she had sent no word to Don Esteban for the magnificent gift.

Her head dropped. "I'm sorry. The collar is most beautiful. I am honored by the gift." This time the word "honored" was spoken truthfully, and they both knew it.

She watched Don Esteban curiously as he hesitated,

choosing his next words with care. "The man who brought it to you, the Yankee, how did you find him?"

She saw Gavin clearly again on that first day when she had nearly killed him; she saw everything she had ever seen of him, and she did not know that Don Esteban was seeing her face drained of all color, dominated by the great shadowed eyes. She ignored the shape of his question. "He found me. He gave me your gift, and he went on his way," she lied, daring him to contradict her.

He deliberately let the silence fall between them again as he studied her. She thought if he asked one more thing about Gavin, she would scream, just stand there and scream until everyone in the house came running.

All rebellious impulses died in her with his next words. "Don Luis comes from a noble family. Your marriage will unite vast leagues of land and pure lines of blood. But even this is not enough."

He held her with his eyes until all she saw was their gleaming blackness.

"It has taken me all these years of living to know this. It is not enough, Teresa María. My marriage to your great-grandmother brought enormous gain to both families, but the value of the marriage was not in this." Still the dark eyes compelled her, and each word dropped another stone onto her burden. "I loved my wife. I loved her from the first moment I saw her when we were no more than children. I will never know why God has decreed that I should live so many years beyond the death of my beloved. Teresa María, Tessa, do you love Don Luis?"

He had been speaking in Spanish though his English was very good, and to hear the beauty of the words, "*mi amado*," and so soon after the name, "Don Luis," was an obscenity which made Tessa feel ill. She was stunned by this change in Don Esteban. She could hardly credit that he was telling her love was more important than anything else, even purity of blood. She looked for a trap and could find none. And for an agonizing space of time, she was tempted to tell him everything, to beg him to pay the debt. Then she remembered Gavin was gone and had been glad of leaving, and she felt again the old loyalty to her father. Whatever had happened and was happening now, she owed him much. He had loved her mother to the point of his own destruction, and she herself could still remember the loving, nourishing years of her childhood. Her debt was greater than the one Don Esteban could pay.

"I am content with the marriage." She couldn't say the word "love," but she trusted Don Esteban's natural restraint to reassert itself; she was sure he would not ask for the word again.

He did not, but she saw its cost. For the first time he looked terribly old, his skin like parchment, even his bright eyes seemed dimmed. His attempt at reassuming his normal brusqueness was so hollow that the lump rose in Tessa's throat until it nearly choked her.

"Knowing you as little and yet as well as I do, Teresa María, I have brought two wedding gowns for you, one the humble black, the other proud. I could not imagine you would take the time to consider such trivial things."

"How well you judge me. I had not thought beyond wearing one of the gowns I possess already." Her laugh was a bad attempt, but they both ignored it.

"María Ramirez assures me she will see they fit well enough," he said. "And now you must go lest you neglect your beloved." He gave no sign he had seen her wince.

She was almost out of the room when his last words stopped her. "I would be pleased if you wore the emeralds to your wedding."

"I will, Great-grandfather," she managed, without turning back to face him. He was not so changed after all—the eagle with far seeing eyes and a fine killing edge. To wear the collar would be to have Gavin beside her even as she pledged her life to Luis. And Don Esteban knew it as well as she did.

She escaped to her room without meeting anyone, and when she saw the gleaming fabrics of the gowns lying on her bed, she did nothing more than hang them out of sight on hooks in her wardrobe. The emeralds would look lovely with the second one. She shuddered at the idea of Luis's appreciation.

She was so late in joining the guests that she received many inquiring glances, but she was beyond caring what anyone thought. She only hoped her relatives were very

81

uncomfortable in the cramped accommodations that were the best that could be offered to so many and included some tents outside.

Luis saw her immediately and kept her pressed close to his side for the rest of the evening. Her arm ached with the tightness of his hold, and her face felt so stiff that she soon lost track of whether she was smiling or not. But no one seemed to care. Everyone was so pleased with the match. Only Don Esteban never appeared. It was easy to understand. He was, after all, an old man, and old men tire easily. Tessa didn't believe that for a minute.

The only benefit she could find in the host of people settled on the household was that even though Luis stayed this night, there were too many people within hearing distance for him to attempt anything. María made sure he had the most awkward accommodation—a makeshift pallet in the kitchen—and Tessa fell in with it, adding her own false apologies for his discomfort in the overcrowding.

She made sure she slipped away before María was finished with the bare courtesies, and she was well aware María was running interference for her. She was also aware that it was next to the last time María would be able to do so. She had one more free day in her life. The day after tomorrow she would become Luis's wife. The round-faced, smilingly vague priest Don Esteban had brought with him would make sure it was done according to God's law in addition to the temporal.

She didn't sleep. It seemed the least important thing now. She was beyond knowing how tired she was. Everything she wanted in her life, her last hope of rejoicing lay in the next few hours.

She performed each act as if it were part of a thousand-year-old ritual. She put her evening dress away carefully, and she dressed in the same blouse, skirt, and sash she had worn then. Not even María's care and labor had removed the stains completely. The faint brown boundaries flowed and changed in the candlelight. Tessa traced each one with careful fingers. And she waited.

She knew it was not so, but she felt as if she could hear every separate breathing rhythm in the house.

She listened for the first sleepy birdcall. She waited patiently to feel the deep night cold in its final strength before the light. She tasted the damp metal of the fog when it began its drift to morning, and she knew the exact minute when the flowers in her mother's garden released the first fragile perfume of the new day.

Amordoro nickered and nuzzled her shoulder, willing yet puzzled at being asked to set out in near darkness. Tessa buried her face in his mane. "One more day, it is all we have, my golden one. But I promise you, he will never ride you. Never!" She knew what the vow entailed. She would kill Amordoro before she would let Luis hurt him.

Her hunger to live this last day to the fullest became Amordoro's, and his stride was long and quick even in the uncertain light. She rode through the half light of her childhood and every memory of the land and its freedom. The palomino was on such good behavior he didn't even shy when the cattle and horses stirred restlessly at their passing.

Tessa feared nothing in their progress. No grizzly, no sudden fault in the land, nothing was as terrifying as the man left sleeping.

The fog grew heavy near the sea, and she could smell the salt and hear the pounding of the surf long before she could distinguish the shape of shore and waves.

Again she waited patiently. It was important. Each leave-taking was important now, and not even a lifetime of familiarity made it less so.

The sun flooded the fog, streaming from the horizon into infinite blue-gray particles turning gold in the instant. Tessa closed her eyes and let the warmth touch her skin.

Even though she knew it would be over in less than twenty-four hours, the knowledge that now she was far ahead of the enemy sleeping at the rancho was intoxicating.

She had seen the sun rise over the sea. She had seen it and felt it in freedom she would never have again.

She turned Amordoro toward their final destination. It seemed a final good omen that though she arrived at the pool long past dawn, she was still in time to see a doe and twin fawns drinking delicately from the clear water. The doe raised her head and stared a long moment at Tessa before she and her fawns faded into the foliage and were gone.

She knew that by now the household must be fully risen.

There would be endless speculation on her rude disappearance this day before the wedding, countless comments on how ill-bred she was to care so little for the preparations. Luis would be furious because of the public insult. She trusted Ramón to keep him from finding her. No one would spoil these hours.

She sat very still by the pool. She could not only smell the pine scent, she could feel its sharp cleanness on her skin. The swell of birdsong separated into a thousand individual voices. A rabbit hopped out and regarded her in alarm, ears and whiskers twitching before he tore back into the underbrush. She gloried in the soft grays and browns blending in his thick fur.

Deliberately she conjured the image of Gavin, tracing every line of him mentally, and then just as deliberately she made the image slip, blur, and disappear. Finally she accepted that the banishment was necessary if she was to have any sanity left at all.

She gave each minute its own life. If she were able, she would spin this day into eternity.

He saw her as he came over the rise. She was sitting by the pool, and nothing was as it had been the first day. She was fully clothed, and her hair showed no damp smoothness of a swim. Her head was bowed, and her shoulders slumped; all the proud fire he remembered had vanished. Had this indeed been the first day, he could have surprised her easily and would not have wanted to. All the vital energy and grace that had made her so compelling were gone.

He called her name with more anguish than he knew, and she started up, eyes wide with shock. She would have fallen had he not reached her so quickly.

He held her, looking down at her, and he moaned, "Oh, my God, Tessa."

He could not credit the change. Her eyes were as beautiful as they had been, but now they were ringed with shadows so dark, they appeared abnormally large in her thin face. She had lost so much weight, he could feel every bone. He was appalled by her fragility; he felt as if she might shatter in his arms. He swore violently at the pain of finding her splendid strength broken. "God damn them all, your father, Luis, Don Esteban, all of them. God damn them to hell!"

"Not Don Esteban," Tessa whispered brokenly. "I don't think he approves any more," and suddenly she was touching his face, her fingers tracing his features as if she were blind, her hands telling her that which could not be true was true. "It can't be. Luis, he owns . . . but I love you, I love you, Gavin Ramsay. Whatever happens, that will never change, *mi amado*."

He forgot the trapped misery that had replaced his anxiety once Julio had told him Tessa was not injured or dead. He forgot the division in himself that had made him resent each minute even as he hurried through the money arrangements with Thomas Larkin and raced south once more, leaving a weary Julio and Pedro in Indian's care. He forgot Indian's accusations that he was an idiot and his own anger at having his life irrevocably changed, his freedom suddenly curtailed without his own volition.

He forgot everything and everyone except Tessa. She was dazed and at the end of her endurance; she loved him; and he knew if he wished he could take her now, and she would offer herself without reservation. But his instinct to protect her was stronger than his will to possess her. Never in his life had he felt this.

Very gently he cupped her face in his hands. She closed her eyes, and he kissed the delicate lids, the smooth skin of brow and cheek, tasting the sun-warm youth of her, smelling the faint, flowery fragrance that seemed always to cling to her. He kissed her soft mouth and felt her lips tremble and open to him. He drew her close against him and stroked the heavy silk of her hair. Tall as she was, she fit perfectly against him, her head against the hollow of his neck. He could feel the quick beat of her heart. "*Mi amado*," he heard her whisper again, and he knew the words meant "my beloved"—he had heard them before but never like this.

He had agreed, many times, to the endearments spoken by women, but he had never himself made the full commitment of words. "You are my beloved, Tessa," he said deliberately. "I love you as I love my life, Teresa María Julieta Margarita Macleod y Amarista." The names came to him with ease, as if the script on the package he had carried had been forever imprinted.

Her head moved against him in denial. "No, just Tessa."

"Tessa Ramsay," he corrected, and he kissed her long and deep for the promise of it.

She was so lost in the wonder of being with him again, of having his warm strength supporting her, of seeing his eyes were bluer than any memory could make them, it took a moment for the words to sink in. Her body shivered suddenly in his arms, and her voice was barely audible. "You don't understand. I am marrying Luis tomorrow. I have been sold for a great sum." The bitter, terrible words were said.

"It's over, my darling. You don't need to fear him any longer. I will pay the debt." He would not say "buy you," though he knew that was the truth of it. "And you will indeed be married tomorrow." Not until she was his wife would he be assured of her safety; it was as if he had never had any reservations about the marriage.

The reality of what had happened was finally beginning to reach her. Gavin really was with her by the pool, holding her, telling her everything would be all right. How had he known?

He saw the question before she asked it, and when he told her of Julio's mad ride and his own, she saw many other things. María's calm pretense and air of waiting; Ramón's abstraction; Juan's mumbled explanation of Julio's absence when she had asked him where his brother was and had been told he had gone with Pedro after strays.

She could guess how María had gotten the information. "What will be will be as I wish it with God's help and a great deal of work." She smiled as she thought of what María really meant when someone she loved was threatened. But then she sobered. "You have been to the rancho? You have seen Don Esteban, all of them?"

"No," he admitted, laughing. "This was a well-planned battle. Ramón was waiting to head me off. I think he'd calculated to the minute when I would ride in. All he needed was a fiery sword, and he could have qualified for the gatekeeper in Paradise."

When her tense expression did not ease, he drew her close again. "Tessa, I know you've been through hell, but
86

you're safe now. Let me do the worrying for a while. I liked Don Esteban, and I think he liked me, and between the two of us, we can manage your father." It was the kindest way he could find to mention the despicably weak character of the man.

She pulled away and the fear was back, draining her skin of all color. "It's Luis, he's the one. He's dangerous."

Gavin's rage at the man returned full force. "So am I," he said.

She saw the truth of it in the change in him, the eyes suddenly cold and deadly under narrowed lids, his face all hard angles that made him look years older.

"Maybe I am not being saved after all," she said, trying to make light of it, but his face was instantly gentle for her again.

"So far I've told you, I haven't yet asked. Will you marry me?" His voice was soft.

"Now, tonight, tomorrow, forever. I love you, Gavin Ramsay, married to you or not." She drew his head down and kissed him.

They stood by the pool for a few minutes longer, and both saw vividly the first violent moments of their knowledge of each other.

Gavin broke the silence when they had walked far enough to be in sight of the horses. "His name is Diablo now," he told her, and he explained.

Neither of them was surprised when Ramón intercepted them before they were in sight of the houses. He needed no words; his eyes told him everything. Tessa still looked apprehensive, but the paralyzing fear had left her. She rode the golden horse as she had been trained to do. And the Yankee looked as a man should look when he has been accepted by the woman he loves. Ramón could see the ghost of himself the day he had asked a very young María to marry him.

He hated having to speak of bad things, but he had no choice. "He is still there," he said quietly to Tessa. "Only Don Esteban prevented him from searching for you." He allowed himself a grim smile. "I think it gives Don Esteban some pleasure to curb Don Luis with polite words."

Gavin laughed and his eyes gleamed. "I can see it quite clearly. I must thank Don Esteban for one more favor."

He was beginning to suspect Tessa was correct in her belief that her great-grandfather did not approve of the match, at least not anymore.

Within seconds of their arrival at the house, the scene was utter chaos. María came running and threw her arms around Gavin, thanking God and him that he had come. He kissed her soundly, and laughingly scolded her for not including her name on the list, then added softly, "Thank you for sending for me."

The swirl of gaping relatives broke apart to reveal the two men walking rapidly toward them, Don Esteban making no attempt to hide his fierce pleasure, Luis equally open in his fury.

Tessa stepped back nervously until she was half sheltered behind Gavin. Gavin ignored Luis, speaking to the older man. "It is good to see you again, Don Esteban. There is a business matter which must be settled, and then I would ask your blessing on my marriage to your great-granddaughter."

Don Esteban took the brief words without blinking, a slow smile curving his thin mouth, but his question about the nature of the business was drowned out in the sudden howl of rage from Luis. "No! She's mine! I own her! I bought her!" he shrieked in Spanish, and a string of obscenities followed. Gavin felt Tessa trembling violently, and he knew the extent of her fear more clearly than ever. The man was quite mad.

The sharp, ringing blow across Luis's face belied Don Esteban's fragile look. "Come, we will discuss this privately," he commanded, and not even Luis dared gainsay him.

Gavin took the heavy saddlebags off Diablo, and Tessa followed him into the house, ignoring the scandalized faces and the swell of whispers around them.

When Don Esteban raised an eyebrow at Tessa's presence in the study, Gavin said, "She has been a pawn for long enough. This concerns her."

Don Esteban nodded curtly and took the documents Gavin handed to him. The crackle of the heavy sheets was the only sound in the room as he read. Tessa saw the grim control of Gavin's face, and in spite of herself, she stole a look at Luis. His face was white and dead

88

looking, a muscle twitched in his cheek, and his mouth was frozen in an ugly, distorted line. Only his eyes were alive, hot and murderous, shifting from one face to the other as if choosing his first victim. Tessa looked away, but his malevolence was tangible, inescapable. She wished as she had countless times that he was dead.

"This is a monstrous thing," Don Esteban growled, and the power of his voice filled the room. "You are less than a man. You should be cut as any bad-blooded stallion is to protect the herds." Even Luis looked cowed by the biblical thunder of the voice.

"But it is a debt that must be paid," the old man continued, and he looked at Tessa. "Child, all you had to do was to ask it of me."

Tessa looked at him helplessly, unable to explain, fearful now of hurting him further.

It was Gavin's quiet words that explained for her. "Sir, I believe you, and I am sure Tessa does also. But she has not always known this. She has believed for a very long time that you and everyone else approved of this cruel match. And there are other reasons. Tessa is as proud and loyal as her great-grandfather." He met the old man's eyes squarely and saw that he understood before he continued. "I appreciate your willingness to help Tessa, but the debt is now mine to pay." He opened the saddlebags and poured the gold and silver coins on the desk. "It's all here. The bastard can count it if he wishes, as long as he signs the papers."

Gavin spoke as if Luis was not there, and whatever protest Don Esteban was going to make about the Yankee's payment of the debt went unuttered. He admitted wryly to himself that the man was an even better choice than he had guessed, with strength and pride no less than his own. He could do no less than abide by his own choice.

Tessa was struggling to control her tears. That Gavin understood her so well already was an unhoped-for gift.

The papers were laid out, Don Esteban was handing Luis the freshly dipped quill, commanding him to sign, and Luis looked completely cowed. The scratch of the point on paper was loud.

The inkpot went flying, and Luis had Tessa in his arms before either of the other men knew what was happening.

89

Tessa screamed Gavin's name and clawed at Luis's face, feeling the flesh under her nails as she raked bloody runnels on his cheeks. He seemed unaware of the pain. His arms were iron around her ribs as he lifted her off her feet; his breath was hot against her face as the foul words telling what he wanted to do to her poured over her.

Gavin lunged, and his blow caught Luis across the back of the neck. Luis let go of Tessa and fell sideways. He lay very still, breathing heavily, and after a brief glance, Gavin ignored him; all of his attention was focused on Tessa, his touch, his voice telling her she was all right.

Watching the fallen man nervously from the corner of her eye, she saw the sudden gleam of metal, and her scream, "Luis, knife!" blended with Don Esteban's warning cry.

Luis had gotten his legs underneath him, and as Gavin swung around toward him, he sprang, the lethal blade flashing with a life of its own. All Tessa and Don Esteban could do was to stay out of the way.

Luis was in superb condition, but so was Gavin, and Gavin outweighed him. But the difference went deeper than that. Eeven in her terror, Tessa could not fail to see it. Luis was fighting in his madness, growing more desperate in every movement, unable to understand why the weapon and his surprise attack were not working to his advantage. Gavin's fury had exactly opposite results. Compared to Luis's wild snarling and contorted face, Gavin moved with the cold precision of a swordsman though he held no weapon, waiting until the last split second each time Luis made a thrust, parrying it by minute turns of his body, dealing sharp blows to Luis with every turn.

Gavin was enjoying it. He could finish Luis easily, but he was drawing out the pleasure. Tessa glanced at Don Esteban and saw the same knowledge, the same savage joy in his face. She could not share it; she felt cold and sick and wanted it over. She saw the force of the blow that brought Luis to his knees, followed swiftly by another that sent the knife flying. Then Gavin wrenched Luis's arm back, shattering the bone outward at the elbow.

The sound of the bone breaking was as loud and ugly as Luis's high-pitched shriek before he slumped unconscious to the floor. Though Tessa was the cause of the battle, Gavin and Don Esteban ignored her as they looked at each other. The old man nodded, eyes as fierce and unblinking as Gavin's, agreeing to the killing if Gavin chose to finish it.

Gavin wanted to kill Luis; the man was cowardly and dangerously insane, but his fury was easing, and he saw the consequences. Despite Don Esteban's support, it would be irreparably damaging to be responsible for the murder of the heir of one of California's prominent families. He had fought and won the most primitive of battles. He had Tessa now; Luis had nothing.

He was suddenly conscious of her again. She was swaying on her feet, her skin bloodless, her eyes dilated and blind. He picked her up. "She has had enough. It is finished. I will have Ramón and his sons send Luis on his way. Perhaps the journey will kill him. Wait for me please, sir. There is still much to plan."

Only after the man had left the room carrying his woman did Don Esteban permit himself to smile.

Even after the rigors of combat, Gavin felt no strain in carrying his burden. She was weightless in his arms. Her eyes were closed and small shivers rippled through her and touched him. He bellowed for María and Ramón and noted with grim amusement that they came immediately, clearly having waited close by. Neither of them questioned or protested his orders.

He carried Tessa to her room and put her down gently on her bed, drawing the coverlet over her, taking her cold hands to warm them in his own. "Tessa, I'm sorry you had to witness that," he apologized.

The huge eyes stared at him without blinking. "No, you must not be sorry. Luis would have killed you. It is just that . . ." she paused, struggling to express the contradiction. "I hated the fighting, it was horrible to watch, to hear. I did not want you to kill him, and yet, I wanted him to die. It is not what you have done, but the feelings in myself I cannot bear." She gave up helplessly, sure he could never understand, but he did.

"It is only people like Luis who don't suffer from the same doubt," he said. He leaned down to kiss her lightly on the forehead, then stood to make way for María, who came bustling in with a tray bearing a steaming cup.

"You must let María pamper you, and then you must sleep. Don Esteban and I will arrange everything for tomorrow."

She giggled at the idea of two men planning a wedding, and Gavin, glad to hear the sound, raised an eyebrow at her. "Just you wait, young woman, we'll show you." And he was gone.

María sighed blissfully. "Such a man, and when he looks at you he is young and happy. It will be a good marriage."

"Because of you," Tessa said. "I will never be able to thank you enough."

"As God wills," María insisted firmly, adding, "as he willed the downfall of Luis. That one has been sent off wounded and in disgrace, as he should be." The question of Luis held no complications for her.

Tessa did as she was bid and drank the warm chocolate laced with brandy, and she felt herself relaxing as she had not done for weeks. When Gavin looked in on her later, she was sound asleep, and he drank in the beauty of her young face, innocent and untroubled in the soft golden candlelight before he snuffed the flame and went to his own rest.

CHAPTER IX

Tessa could believe the day that dawned was a gift of God without María's claim this was so. The valley was bathed in sun without fog or cloud to obscure the brilliant light, and every leaf and blade of grass was etched in silver dew.

Nothing seemed quite real, from María's frequent bouts with happy tears to the priest who heard Tessa's confession and gave her the Sacrament. She was relieved he did not seem overly concerned with sin. She was not accustomed to thinking in those terms any more than she was accus-

92

tomed to priests or the power of the Church. She smiled to herself, wondering what kind of exchange Gavin had had with the man.

The gowns Don Esteban had brought were perfect because María and the seamstress of the household had worked long night hours to take them in. For her devotions with the priest she had worn the black gown, symbolizing the humility and equality of all in God's eyes; but hardly humble in this case, since it was silk brocade. Now she changed into the second one, a magnificent dress not in any of the bright shades normal for such occasions. The heavy satin glowed with its own soft ivory radiance, needing no fussy embroideries to make it richer. The wide, slightly ruffled collar left her shoulders bare, and the bodice of the gown fit her slender figure without a wrinkle before the skirt fell in heavy folds to the floor. Don Esteban had given her the gown to please herself and her man. The emeralds glowed against the skin of her throat. María had dressed her hair high on her head, and now she fixed the intricately carved comb of tortoise shell in place and reverently spread the fragile lace of the creamy mantilla over the gleaming black tresses. The mantilla was nearly floor length. The comb and the lace had belonged to Tessa's mother.

María stepped back and regarded her gravely. "My child, if I did not know your sweetness matches your beauty, I would fear for Don Gavin. Never have I seen so beautiful a bride. Not even your mother."

"May Gavin see with your fond eyes. I have little enough to give him," Tessa said softly, and she followed María down the hall and outside. There were gasps of admiration from the wedding party, but all deferred to Don Esteban, leaving the way clear for her to go to him.

María had been purposely vague about where the wedding would take place, volunteering only that it would not be in the house. Surely no other bride had ever had so little to do with her wedding plans. Tessa had thought Don Esteban and Gavin would favor a simple ceremony, perhaps in the garden since there was no church within easy riding distance, but as soon as she saw Don Esteban, she knew she was wrong—the grandest Californio traditions were to be observed, though tailored to fit the place.

She loved Gavin for it, knowing he was going along with the old way as gift to her and to her great-grandfather.

Don Esteban looked every bit the powerful *ranchero*. His black knee breeches were trimmed at the bottom with gold lace, his leggings were of the finest deerskin richly stamped with ornamental devices, and the silk cord that wound around them and tied at the knee ended in gold tassels. His black vest and jacket bore filigreed gold buttons, and his poncho was trimmed with gold fringe around the edges. His hat was of vicuña, imported from Mexico, as were the rest of his garments.

It was considered a privilege for a male relative to escort the bride to the church, either taking her before him on his saddle or providing protection as she rode beside him. She saw the latter course was to be followed as Amordoro stood saddled beside Don Esteban's own palomino. But never had she seen such saddles. In each the *coraza*, the fine leather covering which extended all around the saddle, and the *anquera*, the half-moon-shaped piece of leather which served as both ornament and convenience should one want to take another rider behind the saddle, were lavishly worked in gold and silver thread. But where Don Esteban's saddle had stirrups and *tapaderas*, the one for Tessa had no stirrups at all. In their place was a piece of blue silk, gathered like a bunch of flowers at the fastening, hanging in a loop from the saddle, for Tessa to rest her foot in as she rode sidesaddle.

She looked up at Don Esteban with awareness and joy beginning to shine in her eyes. "Great-grandfather, they are beautiful! You are beautiful!"

"A strange word for a man so marked with the years passing as I am, more fitting for the loveliest woman I have ever seen," he said, and swept her an extravagant bow to cover the sudden moisture in his eyes.

"In another place it would be my honor to see you safely to the church." For an instant, his eyes were blind, seeing the time long before. He gestured toward Amordoro. "Only your mother graced that saddle until today. She rode to the mission for her marriage." His eyes focused on Tessa again, black and piercing. "It was not all lost. You were born of that union. You are stronger than she was, and Don Gavin is stronger than your father.

So it should be, each generation stronger than the last."
He gestured for her to go to Amordoro, and when Ramón
started forward to help her, Don Esteban waved him
away, cupping his own hands to give Tessa a step up to the
saddle. "So, Great-granddaughter, I will escort you now
not to a church but to a place your intended has chosen.
You know this place?"

Of course Gavin would choose it; so much had happened
to them there, and he knew how she felt about that particular spot. She couldn't help the blush rising in her
cheeks. Don Esteban was in his own saddle in one easy
motion, and Tessa stole a look at him. His eyes were
gleaming.

"He told you!" Tessa accused.

"Indeed he did, but only after I pressed him for details
of his first visit here." He smiled. "He also assured me it
was justly deserved. It is to be hoped your marriage bed
will be softer."

Tessa's eyes widened, and then she smiled back at him,
catching another glimpse of the man Don Esteban must
have been, still in many ways.

The wedding party set out, the gay colors of their clothing marking a trail of brightness, the silver and gold on
bridles, spurs, and saddles flashing in the sun. Now and
then someone started a song, and the chatter and laughter
were constant. Even the relatives who most disapproved
of Tessa recognized the happiness of the day and were
determined to enjoy it. Everyone came along because only
those strong enough to ride had made the long journey,
at Don Esteban's command, from Santa Barbara.

Everyone except Michael Macleod. Tessa and Don Esteban rode a little ahead of the others, and he saw her turn
to look back. His voice was suddenly severe. "He knows
the plans. He will come or not as he decides. Nor must
you think of Luis. No one of his family has come to
question. They must also know he is accursed. You
must not allow either of them to spoil your joy on this
day."

She met his eyes squarely. "No, I will not allow it." She
did not look back again.

"You must not worry any longer about the rancho. Don
Gavin and I have planned well. Your father will be taken

care of, as always, but now Ramón, María, and their sons will wield the power you have had. Ramón has long been *mayordomo* in any case."

"Thank you. I can be more peaceful knowing that." Her tone lightened suddenly, and she grinned at the old man. "How did you make the priest agree to this marriage? It is against Church law, I think. Surely Gavin could not be converted in a single night or change his citizenship so quickly."

"In his own heart he gave up neither his soul nor his citizenship," Don Esteban answered solemnly, but his eyes were twinkling again. "Rather I am careful in my choice of priests. I always have been. I do not care for meddlesome men of God. This one I brought has a sense of the practical, and he is a kindly man. A small fee has been paid, and Don Gavin is now fast made a member of the Church and a citizen of this country. I will see that it is made official. The priest was not charmed by Luis, and he would rather see you married with God's blessing than for you to live without it with your Yankee."

"Which you assured him I would do."

"Yes."

"You know me well."

"I know myself and that part of you which came from me."

It was a tribute from the proud old aristocrat, and Tessa was touched.

They rode on, sometimes talking, most of the time simply enjoying the sun and the merry sounds that followed them, and when they came to the clearing they were greeted by nickers of welcome from Diablo and the priest's horse.

Surefooted even in her wedding finery, Tessa began the walk up the trail, not needing Don Esteban's arm but glad of the warm support anyway. Suddenly her heart was beating so wildly, she could hear it. Gavin was waiting there for her, forever.

Gavin and the priest had spent a pleasant time discussing various subjects, discovering they had more in common than they would have expected, the priest finding particular relief in his liking for this foreigner, feeling his last doubts and pricks of conscience about the ceremony

96

disappearing. But their conversation ceased when the sounds of the approaching crowd reached them.

Gavin watched her as she came over the rise with Don Esteban and stepped into the dappled light, and then he saw no one but Tessa. Her eyes, her hair, her wedding garments all seemed to be shining with their own light. The perfection of her stunned him anew. Fragile and so young, still she radiated a strength which he only now fully realized would be his to share, to depend on from this day forward.

In contrast to the Californios, Gavin was dressed plainly in dark breeches and a white shirt. He looked wonderful to Tessa. She stood before him, and she saw the depth of his feeling in his eyes, younger and more vulnerable than she had ever seen them, yet fierce, resolute, and so very, very blue. His hand was warm on hers; she could feel the two streams pulsing together.

She listened to the music in the glade—the water running into the pool, small silvery notes; the priest's voice, deep chant of ritual; her own voice, Gavin's, both strong and sure, the same song. Ramón, chosen with María as godparents of the marriage, came to bind them together with a silken cord for a moment, performing the ceremony of the lasso, signifying they were henceforth one.

They knelt for the last time on the embroidered material María had provided. The priest gave them the final blessing. And the quiet held while Gavin took Tessa in his arms and kissed her. He meant it to be a gentle kiss acknowledging their marriage, but Tessa's mouth opened under his and the sweet length of her pressed against him, and he forgot his intention and kissed her savagely, proclaiming his right of possession and his love.

The cheer from the guests brought them to. Gavin released her, and she turned to smile without embarrassment at Don Esteban, the Ramirez family, and her relatives.

She accepted the congratulations graciously and acknowledged the compliments because from her earliest years she had been trained to be courteous to visitors to the rancho. But her only true awareness was of Gavin, of his kiss and the strange warmth that had flowed through her veins. So much yet to learn.

They rode together, looking at each other often, finding little need to speak until a small cry burst from Tessa as she spied the lone horseman ahead of them and traveling much faster than their leisurely pace. "It's Father! He must have watched the wedding from the trees on the hill."

Gavin watched her carefully, seeing the sudden tears in her eyes, saying nothing.

She took a deep breath, and then she said quietly, "It is sad. He is sad. But we will no doubt have ghosts of our own someday; we do not need those carried by others at our wedding feast. You are my love, Gavin."

They waited for Don Esteban to proceed them into the house to give them his blessing in place of her father's as they entered, and from that moment on, Gavin wondered ruefully if he would ever be allowed close to his wife again. Every time he tried to get to her or she to him, someone was in the way, demanding attention. There was music provided by *vaqueros* who made up for their lack of precision with their enthusiasm, and there was food enough to feed everyone many times over. Even though María had had the help of her husband and sons besides the servants, the amount of food offered was amazing. Tortillas appeared in endless stacks, and the grinding of the corn alone must have taken many hands and many hours. Beans steamed in large pots. Sides of beef turned and browned on spits. And wine flowed for everyone, most of it from casks supplied by Don Esteban. Not even that had he trusted to Michael Macleod. There was also fresh fruit from the earlier-ripening south, lying in jeweled profusion on wooden platters.

The day wore on to dusk while people danced, talked, and sang. Tessa lost track of what she had said to whom, and when she caught Gavin's eye across the patio, his comic grimace told her he was suffering from the same complaint. They hadn't even gotten to dance with each other since the first tune, during which Gavin had confessed himself lacking in the art while belying his own words with the strong grace of his body. Tessa sighed and lost her chance to capture him again because María had planted herself in front of him, and he was giving her his full attention. Tessa responded politely to the distant cousin who was gulping nervously with the weight of his dawning maturity, years which could not number more than her own. "You are José, aren't you?" Tessa asked and hid a smile at the blush which reddened his skin.

Gavin looked on María with real affection, loving her for her care of Tessa, but he was puzzled by her agitation. She wouldn't meet his eyes, and her hands twisted nervously around each other.

"Don Gavin, you will be kind to her?" she pleaded desperately.

He smiled and raised an eyebrow, not offended because her concern was genuine. "María, how else could I be? I will be kind to her, as kind as I can be, because I love her." He leaned down and kissed her on the cheek, adding, "You have raised a daughter beautiful in every way. I am grateful."

His affection completely disarmed María, who simpered like a young girl and hurried away with excuses of yet more food and drink to serve. Gavin looked after her, still not understanding her words, deciding they must be another product of a day that had been insane ever since they had arrived back at the house.

He turned to find Don Esteban standing beside him.

"This is madness, is it not?" he said in precise English, and Gavin laughed to hear the old man voicing his own judgment. They looked at each other with perfect understanding.

"I have heard that a Californio wedding feast is apt to go on for days," Gavin growled, not bothering to hide his feelings about it.

"Yankees seem to have no trouble changing traditions," Don Esteban commented sardonically, and added on a much softer note, "May you care well for each other, may your years together be long and happy ones."

He turned and walked away to answer the summons of one of the guests, his bearing as proudly erect as if he were no more than Gavin's age. His words meant more to Gavin than all the formal blessings of the day.

Torches and lanterns warded off the dark as the night wore on, and the musicians seemed to play faster and better with each jug of wine they drank.

Tessa no longer knew how she felt, hungry or tired,

99

happy or sad. She had eaten little and drunk less, but the noise and confusion had blunted her senses until she was numb. She didn't want to, but she agreed to nervous José's request for a dance, realizing he had been gathering his courage to ask ever since he had spoken to her hours before. And she started out decorously enough, arms at her sides, the toes of her slippers barely peeking from beneath her skirt. But even as the tempo of the music increased, she caught sight of Gavin leaning against the wall, watching her.

She danced for him and only for him. The pulse of the music and her heart were the same. She held the heavy skirt of her wedding gown in one hand, exposing her slim calves and ankles, and her other arm curved over her head, fingers snapping with the beat. Her eyes glowed violet under half-closed lids, and when the heavy mass of raven hair began to come unpinned, tumbling down her back, she ignored it, glad that María had long since taken the precious mantilla away to safety.

She danced everything she knew and much she had yet to learn of loving a man, of loving Gavin. She paid no attention when the other dancers ceased and drew back to watch. She did not see the shocked faces of some of her relatives nor the approval that lit Don Esteban's normally grim features. She saw midnight blue eyes and a thin white scar across a cheek; she saw the strong bones of the face which could be so harsh, the face young and gentle as he looked at her; she saw the lean, hard strength of him, and she danced to the glory of belonging to Gavin and not Luis.

Gavin watch Tessa and was amazed. His first feeling had been swift jealousy that older men should see her so, and jealousy was so new to him, he had some trouble recognizing it and was shocked when he did. But it was gone as quickly as it had come. She was dancing only for him, and he knew it. He saw the strange mixture that had made her so compelling from his first sight of her. The child was still there but quickly disappearing, and in her place was a woman who with love and care would give love every day of her life. Fear was as alien to him as jealousy, but he was terrified by his new responsibility.

The dance was finished, and she stood before him, and
100

still he saw things he would never have seen before. She was woman and she was triumphant, but beyond that she was Tessa, and she was on the point of collapse from weeks of strain. Her eyes were unnaturally bright and shining in her pale face; her body trembled slightly as though she were standing in the wind. He had done his best to follow the traditions of her country this day, to observe the conventions; he was beyond that now, as Don Esteban had known he would be. He picked her up easily and carried her inside to her room. He was not even aware of Don Esteban's sharp warning to the guests that the couple were to be left alone.

He held Tessa up long enough for his practiced hands to undo the complicated hooks and ties of her gown and lacy underclothes, and then he tucked her into bed quickly before she could take a chill. Her eyes were closed, but when he undressed and got into bed beside her, she nestled against him as trustingly as a child, murmuring, "Gavin, *yo te quiero*," before she was fully asleep.

He wondered at her trust as much as at his own reaction. He was aware of every line of her body pressed against his own, and this was their wedding night, yet he felt no urge to take her. Time enough now; they would have a lifetime together. His arms tightened around her, and he followed her into sleep.

CHAPTER X

Tessa wakened as she always did, in an instant with all of her senses alert, and for a split second her heart pounded so hard she could barely breathe. But it was Gavin, not Luis, who slept so peacefully beside her.

Slowly, patiently, she pulled her hair from under his shoulders which had trapped a few strands, and she raised her head cautiously so she could see him more clearly. The strange tide washed over her again as she looked at him. He was as spare and disciplined in sleep as he was in everything else. He slept without noise or bother, the firm line of his mouth only slightly softened, his breathing deep and even. Yet still he looked defenseless, younger, beautiful. The word came unbidden as it had with her great-grandfather, and she nearly laughed aloud at it in connection with the two.

Very cautiously she drew the covers off, and she regarded his body with curiosity and wonder. She had seen the hard, flat lines of muscle and bone on the terrible night when she and María had worked ceaselessly to stop the bleeding, but her will to save his life had blurred everything except the ominous red seepage. Though fully healed now, he would carry the scar of her blade always. *Esposo,* husband, her man until she or he died.

She had been in shock like any hunted thing, and only now did she fully comprehend what had happened. Against all odds she had been given in God's sight to this man. She had been raised in a world where the breeding of the male and the female in every herd was the sole support of life as she knew it. She knew she had yet to learn of a man's way with a woman, but it would be Gavin who would teach her, and she had no fear of it. Her fear was completely different.

From sleep to full awareness took Gavin no more time than it took Tessa. Even as his breathing altered, his blue eyes opened wide to regard her warily. He did not know quite what to make of her set expression. "Well, madam, you have succeeded in freezing me out of sleep. Having seen what you've got, are you sorry for the bargain?" he teased, even as he drew the bedclohes up to cover his reaction to her. Perhaps her fear was only surfacing now, he thought dismally.

She met his eyes, and he saw the depth of sadness in hers. "No, I am not sorry for that," she said slowly. "I am sorry because there will never be enough time, not even a hundred years from this day would be enough time for us to love."

She burrowed against him suddenly, kissing the scar on his shoulder and the thin one on his cheek, kissing his brow, his mouth, her hands touching him frantically as though to reassure herself he existed. He had never thought much beyond the next day, but now her urgent knowledge that day would not follow day forever became his own, and he held her fiercely, moaning against her hair, "Christ, Tessa, I want . . . no, not here, not now, away from Luis, your father, Don Esteban, all of them."

She went quiet in his arms, and then she pulled away to look down at him again. "Let us hurry and be gone from here. All of this is finished."

It was the ultimate gift, her childhood, all that was familiar and secure in spite of its hardships. He could not find the words, but his eyes and the strength of his arms as he drew her close once more said everything she needed to hear.

They accomplished their leavetaking as swiftly as possible, and Tessa held herself in rigid control as María sobbed in her arms.

Julio and Pedro had arrived home in the early dawn hours, and Tessa hugged them both despite Pedro's shyness. "But for the two of you, I would not have the joy of this day. God keep you both."

As Gavin wished, she was unaware of the exchange between her husband and Julio. He shook the young man's hand firmly. "My thanks, Julio," he said, as if the young man had equal claim to Tessa, and Julio managed to smile. "God's will, Don Gavin. I know you will care well for her."

Tessa gave Juan a swift kiss which left him blushing, and then she turned to Ramón. "My teacher, my father, so much I have learned from you," she whispered.

"My little one, my daughter," he answered, and all was said between them.

Tessa stood before Don Esteban, and their strange love for each other was cloaked in challenge as always. "For Amordoro, for the necklace, and for the Yankee I am grateful, Great-grandfather," Tessa said, mischief dancing in her eyes even with the sorrow of good-by.

The black eyes blurred for an instant, but his voice lost none of its dryness. "If I ever send such a gift again, I will also send my orders for its use. Had you let this one go, he would have been difficult to replace."

Swiftly she leaned forward and kissed him. "There will never be need for such a gift again. Eagles, you, and Gavin, I love them all." She felt him tremble before he was once more cold and withdrawn in his dignity.

Gavin was waiting patiently, but as she turned to join him, she caught sight of her father. He had opened the heavy wooden door soundlessly, and he stood half in the shadow of the entryway. She had not seen him since he had outdistanced them on the ride home. She looked to Gavin, whose quick-sighted eyes missed so little, and she saw his slight nod.

"It is all right now, Father. I love him very much," she said, kissing him briefly and hurrying back to Gavin before her father could lay any claim by his response.

Everything was arranged. They would keep in touch with Ramón and María who would in turn make sure Tessa's possessions would be delivered to Monterey. They were taking only one pack mule with them. None of that mattered to her. She was leaving with Gavin, that was all. She heard the old chorus, "*Vaya con Dios,*" but she did not look back. Gavin's straight figure on Diablo was all she needed to see.

Within the first hour of their journey, Gavin abandoned his original plan of returning to Monterey as swiftly as possible. Indian and business could wait. There was too much to learn about this woman he had married, too little time when they would have none but each other's company. And she needed all the rest he could allow her. He studied her pale face anxiously when he thought she was unaware of his scrutiny, watching for signs that they should stop, no matter how early it was. When they stopped for a midday meal he laughed aloud for the sheer joy of hearing her surprised, "Oh, I am so hungry! I'd almost forgotten what it felt like."

She ate heartily of the food María had sent with them, and then she looked at Gavin through eyes half veiled by her thick lashes. "You needn't worry, truly. I won't vanish. Not now," she added softly. He kissed her and decided privately that he would call the evening's halt long before darkness fell.

It was as though the place he chose had been created especially for them. A stream of cold, pure water tumbled through the clearing ringed and canopied by great spreading oaks. And not far away was a small meadow with good grazing for the animals. The dappled light cast a golden net as they accomplished the tasks of making

104

camp. He took care of the horses, started the fire and gathered extra wood for it, and he made his final trip for a great armload of soft, green branches for bedding, returning to hear Tessa singing before he saw her. He stopped and drank his fill of her before she was aware of him.

She was bathed in the shining gold of sundown filtering through the branches overhead. Every line seemed edged in flame. She was preparing their supper, each movement as quick and competent as if she had camped on the trail every night of her life. And he knew that the Spanish words she sang in her clear, surprisingly full voice were not those of a set song. The gay lilting tune told of finding a place in the forest where love would grow like the trees, where no one had been before, where the sun and the water and the night soon to come were wedding gifts of the earth.

She caught sight of him and finished the song without embarrassment, smiling up at him. "You see, Ramón and María taught me well. Wherever we are together will be home, even here in the forest."

He spent longer than he needed to prepare their bed for the night, fighting to sort out and control the unfamiliar tangle of emotions, giving up the struggle.

They washed the dust from their hands and faces in the icy water of the stream, but for all her care with the meal, Tessa was not hungry, nor was Gavin.

The sun was suddenly gone behind distant hills, and the dark invaded the glade until all light was focused in the crackling logs of their fire.

Tessa found herself in Gavin's arms, and then he was laying her down gently on the blankets of the bed he had made for them and his touch was the fire.

She saw his face grow taut, and she knew the cause— so had Luis looked at times when he had held and pawed her, but his face had had none of the tenderness of Gavin's. She was weightless, boneless, floating in a circle of light.

Gavin moved his hands over her, learning the delicate perfection of her body, so much more fragile than it should be now, the young hollow of her throat, the soft plane from shoulder to small upthrusting breasts, the long curve from waist to hip, the flat belly, the long slender legs. The firelight warmed her flesh, and her eyes were great shining pools. The smell of flowers filled his nostrils. She accepted his love-making without reservation, without cringing or trying to cover herself, giving her trust with her love, and he knew nothing that had gone before had anything to do with this. His experience did not include the teaching of virgins, and the terror rose again that he might do something that would ruin this for her forever.

"Tessa, I . . ." the words died in his throat, but she reached up to touch his face as though to reassure him that she knew what he wanted to say. He saw what he had not seen the night before, what he had thought was shadow until now—bruises on her ribcage, one on each side, faint but easily discernible now that he knew what they were.

He didn't need to ask; he had seen Luis grab her. He wished he had killed the man after all. His rage and his passion became the same and his fear was gone; he had a world to offer Tessa. Luis had offered hell.

She cried out at the sudden sharp pain, but when he stopped, she arched her body up to meet his, her fingers digging into his hard muscles as she held him fiercely.

She was the sky and fire, a storm wind, an elemental force she had never been before. And the only name she knew or would ever need to know was his.

Gavin woke in the pre-dawn chill to find the warmth of Tessa on one side, the freezing cold on the other. The fire had burned down to a few embers. It took him a moment to realize Tessa was awake already. He kissed her and murmured, "Are you all right?"

"No, I am not," she said, grinning at him. "I am starving. We missed supper, you know. I've been staring at you for quite some time to awaken you."

He laughed and held her close before he wrapped himself in a blanket and got to tend the fire. "I can arrange it so you never miss a meal. What would your choice be?" he asked with mock seriousness.

She appeared to give the matter due consideration. "It would be very sad. I would starve to death in a week."

She loved the sound of his laughter; she loved so many things about him, the joy of it poured through her, and Gavin's breath caught when the quick leaping flames illuminated the beauty of her face as she looked at him.

They shared the long delayed meal in quiet contentment, and they made love again in the pale gray half-light and slept until the sun was warm in the glade.

Gavin decided they would spend one more night here. He tried to make excuses to himself about Tessa needing more rest after all that had happened to her in such a short time, but it wasn't true. He was enchanted and loath to break the spell. Her innocent enjoyment of everything was contagious; he had never felt more alive than he did now. Her youth showed in her willingness to play, and his own matched hers though it was alien to his previous life.

She followed the water upstream and found a pool which, though much smaller than her old favorite, was large enough to bathe in, and she plunged into the icy water with delight, turning to find Gavin had followed her. She laughed and splashed him, but his hands were so much larger, he soon had a wall of water washing over her, and she surrendered, gasping and throwing her arms around him. "I wonder what it would be like here?" she asked, and Gavin answered, "Wet, difficult, and very cold. We're already turning blue," as he scooped her up and carried her out of the water to a warm patch of sun.

"You, Tessa Ramsay, have all the makings of a wanton," he teased, nuzzling her throat, moving his mouth lower until she fended him off with both hands on his chest. She wrinkled her nose at him. "I know that word. I have read it." She took her hands away, and he pretended to collapse against her. "I think it is a rather nice word, almost as nice as Ramsay," she whispered in his ear.

Though Tessa slept peacefully in his arms, Gavin lay awake for quite a while. Introspective moods, particularly ones concerning women, were not a normal part of his nature, though he realized with wry humor that they had gotten to be more familiar ever since the first day he had seen Tessa.

Only now, seeing the reasons for it, could he admit to himself that even while enjoying the benefits of it, he had been taken aback by Tessa's uninhibited sexuality. The promise he had seen by the pool had proved incredibly true. And he had believed since the dawn of his manhood that a high-born virgin was sure to be far more trouble than she was worth, needing months if not years to be coaxed out of corseted modesty and deep reluctance. Instead, Tessa had come to him with no reservations he had been able to discover so far. And he knew enough about a woman's body to be almost certain he had caused her pain even since that first time which now seemed a lifetime ago, yet by no sign had she betrayed anything but pleasure. He discarded the idea that she was dissembling before it was fully formed because he knew suddenly that had nothing to do with it. It was simply that she was opening her mind and her body to the delight of the experience with him, and her pleasure was greater than any hurt.

He did not blame himself for not finding the key earlier; she was unique in his experience, an innocent. Not a simpering parody of the word nor the wrong use for simple. She was innocent because no one had taught her to be otherwise. Her mother had died, and her father had been less than half alive for years. She had spent only a brief time with her restrictive relatives and had rejected the falseness of their lives. Ramón and María, who had had the most to do with raising her, lived lives tied to the harmony of earth cycles and to acceptance without definitions. Now he understood María's worried plea that he be kind to Tessa. It was her way of telling him she had neglected that part of Tessa's education.

He gave hearty thanks for all the neglect, accidental and otherwise, that had left Tessa free to use her mind and her senses fully and freely, without guilt. And he gave thanks that she was his, traveling north with him, not left to the cruelty of Luis, who would have destroyed her.

He thought of how close he had come to losing her, how close she had come to being lost to everyone. His world without her was unimaginable now.

He smoothed her hair back with infinite care so he

could see her face in the fire glow. She murmured his name and a small smile curved her mouth, though she did not awaken.

CHAPTER XI

Gavin figured they were still the good part of a day's ride from Monterey when he began looking for shelter for their last night on the trail. It was only early afternoon, and normally they could have had a few more hours in the saddle, but the sky was growing steadily darker, filling with great thunderheads that threatened a downpour any minute. A chill breeze brought the rain scent from somewhere else, and the first close crack of lightning and the long roll of thunder sent Amordoro skittering sideways with small bucks of panic.

Tessa had him under control in no time with her gentle voice and firm hands on the reins, and she brought him back up beside Diablo. "If you look like that every time my horse misbehaves, you're going to be an old man before your time," she teased Gavin, but though he smiled briefly, the worry did not leave his face. He had never felt this protective responsibility for anyone before—when the palomino shied he had had an instant's vision of Tessa lying broken on the hard ground, and the imminence of the storm showed him Tessa soaked to the skin and shivering with the chill.

But when the sky opened and the rain began, she laughed and turned her face up to catch the first drops. "I love the rain almost as much as I love you, my husband," she said gaily.

"My wife is a madwoman," he grumbled, but it was hard to resist her mood, even though the rain was coming down harder by the minute, drenching them.

It was Tessa who caught sight of the cabin when the shroud of rain lifted for an instant. "Gavin, look! Surely whoever lives there will not deny us shelter."

The rain poured down again, blotting out the landscape,

but they rode toward the spot where they had seen the building, Tessa confident of a welcome, Gavin hoping his rifle was not as wet as he was.

But the cabin was deserted and did not look as if it had been used for a long time. Gavin went in cautiously, and when he was sure there was nothing harmful living there, he ordered Tessa to stay inside while he took care of the animals. She protested vigorously that it was foolish not to let her help, but a sudden shiver betrayed the cold she was beginning to feel, and she obeyed him. She prowled around the single room trying to distinguish things in the gloom, and when Gavin had dumped the last of their provisions on the floor, she grabbed his hand like an excited child, tugging him from one thing to the next.

A battered tin plate held a short candle, and Tessa found two more stubs on the rickety table. The cabin was made of wood, and the roof leaked, letting water trickle in steadily here and there, but the place boasted a carefully built fireplace of stone, and there was enough wood stacked beside it to last the night. Now dry and dusty, brush had been piled before it for a bed. There was one small window, which could only be closed by latching the heavy wooden shutter in place.

It may have been built for *vaqueros*, for hide and tallow agents, for any weary travelers, or it might have been a stopping place for one of the solitary trappers who wandered the coast less often now. It was small and shabby, and Tessa could not have been more delighted had it been a palace.

Gavin was amused, but when he gathered her in his arms, he could feel her shivering even as he had feared, and her teeth were beginning to chatter. He moved swiftly to light a fire, and he made Tessa stand as close to it as she could bear while he stripped her of her sodden garments and wrapped her in the driest blanket he could find in the bundles of their gear.

"You are al . . . also wet," she said, reaching out to touch him, and his eyes glittered in the firelight as he undressed swiftly.

They lay in front of the fire, and Tessa, no longer cold, murmured against his mouth, "This is a wonderful way to grow warm, and the rain will be our music."

110

The rain excited her, adding another dimension to their love-making. He chided her softly for using only Spanish love words.

"They sing with the rain. That too I will learn," she laughed, "to make love with the sharp sounds of English."

When he would have taken her in his arms, she pushed him back until he was lying flat. "No, please, let me look, let me touch." Her eyes were wide, dark, and shining as she leaned over him.

Other women had touched him with practiced ease, well trained to arouse a man, but nothing had prepared him for this. The drying tendrils of her long hair brushed across his skin. Her hands and mouth touched, kissed, delicately mapping the planes of his body even as he had explored hers. Her hands slid down his lean belly to hold him, to begin moving again, and he groaned in pleasure.

So could a man be tamed, and so, Tessa thought, and her cry was wild and exultant when his control broke and he pulled her down on top of him.

She slept in his arms though he lay awake again. So much of his hope and all of his joy in life was now in the keeping of his quicksilver woman. But Indian was also part of his life, friend and brother. He dreaded their meeting. Indian had been furious at the debt he had incurred and disgusted at his mad haste to get back to Tessa. And Gavin had no way of knowing how Tessa would react to his friend. Many considered Indians and Negroes to be much less than *gente de razón*, people of reason. He tried to draw comfort from the gentle compassion she had shown for the poor Indians they had seen on their journey, shy woods creatures, thin and ragged, who lived mostly on seeds and grasshoppers and who slipped away in quick terror at the sight of the riders. But it wasn't the same.

He tried to explain his friend to her as they rode toward Monterey. "He's part Indian and part African. His mother was a slave in the South. She ran away when she was very young, but instead of going north to Canada as many do, she was taken in by a tribe of Indians. It's a strange story, because she was not only sheltered by them but was much loved by a high-ranking brave, and the result of their union was Indian. He would have remained with them

111

except there was nothing to stay for once the white men had decimated the tribe. His mother remembered white ways only too well. She ordered him into the swamp woods as soon as the attack began. She remained with her husband and the others. She wasn't killed there; she was probably taken back into slavery.

"Indian was eight or nine then, by his reckoning. He was lucky to survive at all, most didn't. He was even more fortunate to have been cared for by a white couple who were not slaveowners. They were God-fearing folk who abhorred slavery. They taught Indian what they could, and in return he worked with them on the land. They were childless. I don't think they were as harsh as my uncle and aunt—they certainly had no personal grievance against Indian—but they acted out of duty only, not out of love.

"He left when he was seventeen. His first years were still very much a part of him. He had the spirit of adventure, and more than that, he wanted to help his mother if he could, if she was still alive. He did the rest of his growing up very fast. He never found a trace of his mother, and he came close to losing his own life many times over. But he learned more about survival than any other man I've known, and I owe my life to him more times than I can count."

"As I'm sure he owes you his," Tessa interjected, unable to imagine any man more knowledgeable or stronger than Gavin.

"Luckily we don't keep score," Gavin said with a smile, but then his expression grew more serious. He still felt his description of Indian had been inadequate. "I've told you just about all I know about him. He seldom speaks of his past. You'll hear the South in his voice, more when he's happy or upset. He doesn't speak English the same way you do, but he always says exactly what he means."

Tessa raised an eyebrow in parody of Gavin's typical gesture. "Do you think so little of me that you believe I would judge a man less for not speaking as the daughter of a schoolmaster does?"

He flushed. "No, I think a great deal more of you than that. It's just that . . ."

He didn't blame her for eyeing him curiously and com-

112

menting, "I think perhaps you should leave it to me and to your friend to decide how we will share you."

He grinned weakly; put that way, his worry sounded ridiculous and vain.

They rode into town in the afternoon, and Gavin forgot everything except Tessa's delirious joy. Only on the visit to Santa Barbara years before had she seen any place other than the rancho, and then she had been miserable and afraid. Now she took in the beauty of Monterey with little cries of delight, twisting this way and that to get a better view of things, Amordoro prancing in nervous sympathy.

"Oh, Gavin, so many people and houses! And so many houses so tall! The flowers, aren't they beautiful? The walls, so white they are! And the sea close enough to touch!"

Gavin saw the curious stares they were getting—by now everyone surely knew of the Yankee's wild flight—and he saw the appreciation in the eyes of the richly dressed *rancheros* and *caballeros* who swept off their hats in extravagant tribute to Tessa. But he didn't care; he had enough to do answering her questions, seeing everything afresh through her eyes. Two-story houses with touches of New England from the ship's carpenters' art, so typical of Monterey, were a wonder Tessa could scarcely credit.

Indian's horse was tied outside the Vargas adobe, and as they rode up to the house a new thought struck Gavin, and he nearly swore aloud at his own stupidity. Not only would they have to face Indian, there was also Carmelita to be considered. True, she had been civilized enough about the end of their affair, but faced with Tessa, she might not be so obliging. He didn't even want to think about Tessa's reaction.

He dismounted and reached up to lift her down, explaining very quickly about how he and Indian had found lodging here. "Of course, we'll find our own house as soon as we can," he assured her.

She had no time to puzzle over Gavin's obvious nervousness. The man who emerged suddenly, glowering at them from the doorway, was the most enormous human being she had ever seen. She stared at him in wonder, and then she flinched at the soft, mocking words. "You paid all that

113

money for this piece of skirt? You had better here, little brother, cheaper too."

Gavin let go of her so quickly, she nearly fell. She saw the white fury blaze in his face, saw his hands clench into fists, and heard the sound, more threatening snarl than words. His whole body was tensed to spring at his friend.

The fight between Gavin and Luis flashed through her mind, and she knew this would be worse, far worse, because this time love for each other would be part of the battle.

"No!" she screamed, the sound harsh and piercing, and Gavin froze in astonishment as she turned her back on him and faced Indian.

The sheer size of him was enough to terrify her; she didn't need his murderous expression to make it worse. Her knees were shaking, and though she tried to make her voice firm, her face betrayed her fear. "Please, friend of Gavin, *valedor* of my husband, once already he has fought for me, it is enough, it is too much. Perhaps there are other women better for him, but there can be no other who loves him more than I do. Please!" she ended in a whisper.

Indian saw her clearly then. He saw the beauty of her, the strength, and most of all, the honesty and the pleading in her strangely colored eyes. When he had been blind, she had seen the pain it would bring Gavin if they could not be friends. When his jealousy had made him strike out, her love had made her offer peace despite the insult he had dealt her. He had not even granted her his normal care and caution in judging human beings. He was deeply ashamed.

His sudden vulnerability and his misery showed in his face even as Tessa's face had mirrored her own. Relief flooded her heart. The man was infinitely strong yet equally gentle, and she was glad he and Gavin were bound by deep friendship. She did not flinch when he took her slender hand in his huge paw. As carefully as if it were made of the finest porcelain, he cradled her hand and bent to kiss it. "I beg pardon for my words, Miz Ramsay. May your life with Gavin be joyful an' long."

She smiled up at him, color staining her cheeks because

up to this moment she had heard no one except Gavin call her "Mrs. Ramsay." "Thank you, er . . . Don Indian."

He laughed at the formalization of his name. "Jus' plain ol' Indian," he assured her.

"And I am just Tessa," she told him, and she rejoiced to see the bear hug Gavin and Indian exchanged, Indian accusing Gavin of being in league with Satan for luck, both of them laughing to ease their emotions.

Only when things had calmed down did Carmelita appear at the doorway, and Gavin spent a few anxious seconds wondering what she would do.

Carmelita was neither vicious nor stupid. One look was enough to tell her that the Yankee truly loved this girl, and that his love was returned in full measure. Nor did she misjudge Tessa—steel, no matter how finely formed and etched, is still a strong metal. Ruthlessly, she suppressed her painful knowledge of youth fading and chances missed.

She behaved graciously, in the warmest Californio manner, congratulating them both on their marriage, welcoming them both into her house, leading Tessa away so that she might wash and refresh herself while the men talked business.

"You are indeed kind to welcome me so warmly," Tessa said firmly, and Carmelita did not mistake her sincerity or her knowledge. She was glad she had not made a fool of herself by underestimating the Yankee's wife.

Word of the new arrivals had traveled fast, and that night Carmelita gave a *bailecito casero*, a little home party whose name was belied by the number of people who seemed to flow in in an endless stream. Though still shy of so many strangers, Tessa found it less difficult than she would have supposed because she had Gavin's comforting presence at her side. "I have no intention of being separated as we were at our wedding feast," he told her with a grin.

Abrego, Serrano, Pacheco, Estrada, Guiterrez, Stokes—she concentrated hard on remembering the names, but she needed no prompting when she was introduced to the Larkins. "I'm so grateful to you both for helping us so much, even to this," she added with a smile for Rachel,

115

holding out her hand so that the gold wedding ring caught the light.

"There are some things better trusted to a woman," Rachel answered, her eyes twinkling.

The only dancing Tessa did was with Gavin. Instinctively she wanted to reassure him that the extravagant compliments she had received from so many of the men meant nothing, that he alone mattered.

Her skirt swirled around them as they waltzed, and Gavin whispered against her hair, "I'll think I'll lock you up, hide you away after this evening. You've got even the oldest and most married men ready to slay dragons for you."

Her eyes were very wide as she answered, "If Señora Vargas was less wise, less kind, it would be I who would have to lock you up. The blue-eyed ones are much sought after in California, even when they do not have golden hair."

Gavin grimaced and made no attempt to deny it. However the knowledge had come to her, it was deep and sure. "I was miserable. You were driving me mad even from so far away," he said quietly.

Hours later he awakened to the silence of the house, to the moonlight streaming into the bedroom. He was panicked and disoriented, suddenly certain none of it had happened, but it was Tessa's face bathed in silver light, Tessa's voice which spoke to him, not Carmelita's. "My darling, what troubles you? I felt you waken."

He drew her roughly against him. "God, I thought I'd dreamt it all!"

His look of glad recognition and his words told her more than he knew, and she suppressed the image of him lying with Carmelita. That time was past. "No dream, this is very real, *mi vida*," she murmured, pressing even closer against him.

CHAPTER XII

The next month was the most exciting of Tessa's life. She had so much to learn. She and Gavin had set off to look for a place to live the day after their arrival in the capital, hopeful that they would find something suitable rather than having to build their own. Gavin took her to see a house the Larkins told him about, and to him it seemed adequate. He was disappointed and apprehensive at Tessa's reaction. She shook her head decidedly. "It won't do, it's much too small."

His words were gruff. "You can't expect to live as you did at rancho, not yet at least."

She looked at him in bewilderment. "But of course not. That would be foolish. But we must find a place where Indian can live too, and this house doesn't have enough room."

He hugged her, and his words were queerly muffled. "I never thought, and I know Indian didn't either. You have a right to your own home, to privacy."

She pushed away from him laughing. "I'm not expecting Indian to spy on us."

"Some people will think it very odd," he warned.

"I don't care about some people, I care about us. Indian is part of our family, and we're all the family he has."

They waited until they had found the house before they told Indian. It took Tessa a moment to understand the meaning of his curt refusal and rigid face. Gavin had taught her without knowing, and he, like Indian, had a basic generosity but almost no ability to receive. She was still learning how deeply a part of Gavin this was, still seeing the hesitation before the wondering acceptance every time she offered him another gift of herself when for her part, she wished each time the gift was finer.

Indian's harsh words still hung in the air, and his eyes looked as if they were carved from jet.

Tessa touched the lavender silk of her dress. Indian had

117

given her the exquisite cloth the day after the party. It had been a peace offering and a welcome, and she had accepted it as such. "If this is really how you feel, then I was wrong to take this," she said, deliberately holding his eyes with her own. "Such gifts in a family are acceptable. But even I know it is not proper to receive such personal things from a stranger."

He blinked at her in hurt surprise, and then his features softened into a rueful grin. "My yes, you do fight low when you've a mind to. Here I been feelin' sorry for you married to this clumsy friend of mine, now I ain't so sure where my pity lies."

Indian moved with them. Though there were much larger houses in Monterey, theirs suited them perfectly. The *ranchero* who normally took the house for the summer had broken his leg, and he and his family were unable to come into town. It meant the Ramsays would be able to rent the house for nearly a year at least. Though Tessa refrained from saying so out of politeness, Doña Josefa Abrego, who with her husband had helped them obtain the house, voiced her thoughts for her. "God's justice; one's misfortune benefits another."

Tessa and Gavin took the upstairs rooms. Tessa was enchanted with the idea of having two stories, and there was still room downstairs for Indian to have his own quarters. The house was built in the old Monterey style with an outside stairway leading to the second-story balcony, and Tessa loved the view from it. They were not far from the principal square, and they could see the ocean close by. Tessa was delighted to be able to hear the pomp and powder of the military in their daily ceremonies and to catch occasional glimpses of them, even though she agreed with Gavin that they were quite foolish when considered seriously.

Though Tessa insisted she did not need or want the swarm of servants common to most households, after catching sight of her hauling a heavy pot of water from one place to another as she scrubbed the tiles of the ground floor, Gavin insisted she have at least one. "Indian and I won't always be here to do the heavy work," he warned her.

She sat back on her heels. "So it would be better to

have some poor little woman doing this instead of Señora Ramsay?"

"Not little, I was thinking of someone rather larger than you," he said, and scooped her up in his arms, soapsuds and all.

The Indian woman Doña Josefa sent was at least three times as broad as Tessa. Her name was Rosa, and she was quiet, dependable, and strong. But she kept her distance carefully, reminding Tessa of her social position when Tessa herself would have forgotten it. Tessa learned quickly that Rosa and María were completely different episodes in her life.

But she did not lack for companionship. Rachel Larkin and Doña Josefa had given their approval of her, and the Ramsays were invited to nearly every social function from *bailecitos caseros* to more formal balls. They even saw a good deal of Carmelita, whose friendship with Tessa was growing despite its doubtful beginning. They went often to the Casa Abrego where Doña Josefa held court as if she were a queen, offering her guests chocolate or a glass of fine wine, presiding over discussions of the day's events, providing music for dancing, frequently closing the entertainment with a Spanish quadrille.

In spite of her rather imperious manner, both of the Ramsays liked Doña Josefa and her family. Her husband, Don José, had made a sizable fortune dealing in soap and hats, and he was also active in California's political life. Their children were not only well mannered but seemed happy as well. Even Indian felt comfortable in the Abrego household.

Gavin had been highly amused by Tessa's first reaction to the Casa Abrego. It was the first time she had ever seen a full-length mirror or a piano, and though she had done no more than quietly admire them while in the house, she chattered about them all the way home. Yet she had no desire to own such things; she simply thought them beautiful and unusual. Gavin wondered if the day would ever dawn when there would be nothing more to learn about his wife. She was greedy for new experiences but not for possessions. So unused to money, nevertheless she learned its value quickly and bargained furiously until she thought the price fair. At first this made Gavin uncomfortable, but when she explained to him, patiently, as if to a child, that it was a game between buyer and seller and would be a disappointment to both and a waste of money besides if it were not played, adding slyly that she was sure he and Indian would be ever more involved in the same game, he gave up and let her do it her way.

Sometimes he or Indian went out in the country and came back with wild fowl, fish, or small animals, and what they did not use at the house was good for barter. Tessa went with them whenever she could, loving the freedom of riding the open land again. And whatever meat the men supplied, she dressed and cooked to perfection for them. But Gavin accused himself of being very slow-witted when he discovered how she really felt about it. He had brought in a brace of ducks and two fat rabbits, and he was on his way out again to find Indian when he caught sight of Tessa's face.

Rosa had already gone home to her own family, and Tessa had all the dressing to do by herself. Her face was chalk white, her mouth clamped in a tight line even though her hands plied the knife with easy skill. Gavin realized then that she was usually out of his sight when she did this chore. And he judged himself even more dense when he recalled that, though she was an expert shot as far as inanimate targets went, he had never seen her shoot a living thing. She rode with them; she did not hunt with them.

"Tessa," he said her name softly, but still she was startled because she hadn't known he was watching her. "Why didn't you tell me you hate doing this so much?"

"I don't. It's all right," she protested, but his voice sharpened and cut her off. "Don't lie, I can see your face." To his dismay her eyes were suddenly filled with tears, her voice uneven with little sobs. "It is so stupid. María taught me well, and I've tried. Even with servants the mistress of the house must know how to do all. Here it is part of my work, and I eat from the same table. But when, when I do this, I see them alive as they were so little a time ago."

"My God, it isn't enough to cry over!"

"It's not that . . . not as much as wanting, wanting to be a perfect wife for you and not being able. There is so
120

much to learn and . . . there are so many women who seem to know it all already."

He studied the face upturned to his, shining with the marks of tears. He had not known until now the full extent of the change in her life nor how hard she must have been working to temper her wildness, to learn, to shoulder responsibilities even greater than those she had had before, all to please him.

"Let me know the day you become the perfect wife," he said quietly," because then I'll have to start looking for a suitable husband for you."

He washed the blood off her hands as if she were an infant, and though he picked her up with little more effort than were she a small child, he carried her up the stairs to their bedroom as his woman, not a child at all.

Indian arrived a short time later, saw the pile of half-dressed game, cast a speculative glance toward the balcony, and settled down, whistling as he finished the task.

After that day when Gavin or Indian presented Tessa with game, it was already prepared for cooking. They spoiled her in other ways too. Though she shopped for the kitchen and the house, she never purchased anything for herself. When Gavin asked her about it she insisted that though her wardrobe was limited now, it would not be as soon as her clothing arrived from the rancho. It made no difference to the two men; they could not be dissuaded from bringing her gifts from their cargo— beads, a fan, lengths of cloth. Secretly she was wryly amused, thinking they both had too much experience with women who demanded certain payment for their favors. Young as she was, she was old enough to suspect this. It never occurred to her that she was giving them gifts in return, gifts they had not received before—a place of contentment and joy to come home to, a woman's care, gentleness, and fire all mixed, though given in different ways, to Indian in friendship, to Gavin in love.

When Ramón arrived at the end of that first month, he recognized the happiness in Tessa and her husband instantly, and along with his relief was just enough jealousy to shame him. It seemed that even his own place had been filled, by the great dark friend of Don Gavin. This man named Indian looked at Tessa with the same protective kindness he knew showed in his own eyes. But Tessa's whoop of joy and her headlong rush into his arms had given him no doubt of her gladness in seeing him. Her questions poured over him at such a rate, he protested his ears were too old to hear that quickly, his tongue too old to answer so.

Juan had come with him along with Pedro and another *vaquero*. They had left María and Julio behind, María because she had to keep the domestic affairs of the rancho running smoothly, Julio because he was needed on the land and had already seen Monterey, no matter how briefly. Ramón was still scolding María even though she was so far away, and Juan told Tessa that his father had been doing so ever since they left the rancho. The amount of baggage María had sent to Tessa continued to confound him. Ramón insisted they could have arrived two weeks earlier had it not been for María's additions to the packs, which began in the morning and did not end until night had fallen.

Tessa controlled her mirth for a few minutes, and then she dissolved into giggles that had her leaning against Gavin for support. The unloading of the pack animals went on and on, and it was soon apparent that María had decided her child was going off to the wilderness rather than to the capital of California. Tessa's clothing and personal possessions were only a small part of the load. There were kettles and pots and knives for the kitchen in addition to four place settings of her mother's fine French porcelain which had come to California via Spain and Mexico, grudging or not, a gift from Don Esteban to his granddaughter on her marriage to Michael Macleod. There was a work basket with precious needles, thread, and an odd assortment of buttons ranging from bone, shell, and horn to some of silver and four of gold. Tessa's eyes went wider and wider, and her laughter infected Gavin; she could feel him shaking, but she didn't dare look at him for fear of losing control completely. María had sent some of her best tallow candles and more of the fine beeswax tapers than she could afford to spare; she had sent salted meat, dried fruit, and some of the hardiest cheeses, a rare gift given the great effort it took to milk the half-wild cows, all foodstuffs that would keep on the journey north.

122

But the most incredible thing she had sent was a crate of disgruntled chickens, flustered, pecked, and miserable from their long bumpy trip.

"She trusted me to feed you on love but nothing else," Gavin gasped, and then they looked at each other, both remembering their first night of love-making. "And I thought we were alone," Tessa said, setting them both off again.

Ramón was not offended; young lovers who did not laugh together often over their own private world did not love often either. He believed that firmly; he and María still shared both. A small smile lightened his face. It was good to see this place, better to know Tessa was all right, but it would be best of all to be home again with his woman.

Tessa was gaining quite a reputation for her easy and entertaining *bailecitos caseros,* and she would have liked Ramón and Juan to meet her new friends, but she knew it would only make them acutely uncomfortable.

As it turned out, the two *vaqueros* left to wander the town, taking with them stern admonitions from Ramón to sample its pleasures sparingly, and Ramón, Juan, and the three of the household spent a lovely evening talking and drinking wine. Tessa sat on the floor going through her baggage, jumping up every now and then to hold a dress before her, striking a pose and asking Señor Ramsay how he liked it.

Gavin raised his eyebrow and pretended to give her last question a deal of thought. "I like the dress well enough, but I like what goes inside it better, even if it is a little drunk," he said, causing Ramón to chuckle and Tessa to blush.

They stayed for only another day to rest the animals and could not be persuaded to tarry any longer, though Juan and the *vaqueros* were clearly eager to do so. It was Ramón's decision.

Tessa's last question was about her father, and she felt easier with Ramón's assurance that he was more or less the same and all right. "You need not worry, little one. María and I will take care of him and of the land."

"I am grateful, always. Remember now there is a place for you here whenever you, María, or your sons would

123

like to visit." Though she made the offer sincerely, she knew it would be seldom or never accepted. Monterey was a faraway foreign place to them.

Sensing she would be lonesome, Gavin took Tessa on a long ride after they had left. They stopped in a wooded glade that was much like the place of their honeymoon, and it was nearly dark when they arrived home.

CHAPTER XIII

It had been a week since Ramón and his companions had left when Gavin told her. She had dreaded it for so long she didn't even flinch. He and Indian had their boat for the coastal trade. The man who owned it was growing old, and he was tired of the endless short cruises up and down the coast. He was willing to lease the vessel for what Gavin and Indian judged a fair price. The boat had been native built in Santa Cruz and was in good shape even if a bit ancient. With luck they would be able to leave in a week.

There wasn't any use in asking to go with them. The ship at best would be cramped and reeking of hides and tallow, with negligible space given to the crew, let alone passengers. They would need every inch for their cargo.

When Tessa said, "You must let me know what I can send with you and Indian to make you more comfortable," Gavin knew she accepted the fact that they would both be going.

He watched her curiously. Nothing showed in her face; even the violet depths of her eyes, usually so quick to reflect what she was feeling, were calm. He felt foolish and angry with himself when he realized he had wanted her to show him how much she dreaded having him gone. The trips would only be for a couple of weeks at a time, three weeks or a month at the most. Her attitude was sensible.

She knew she had failed him, and she suspected the reason, but any other than her chosen course seemed

124

ridiculous. There was no choice. He was going. To rail against it would be futile and an extra burden on him besides. And she was never free of the knowledge of the debt he had incurred when he rescued her from Luis. It would have to be repaid before Gavin would be truly free to build his fortune and the foundation of their lives.

Their communication in the days before the first sailing was confined to such a mundane level that Indian could hardly bear to be around them. All laughter, teasing, and loving seemed to have vanished. They spoke almost entirely of household matters. Gavin had arranged for Rosa to stay at the house with Tessa while he was gone, or if that failed, she was to board with the Larkins. Tessa knew even as she agreed that she wasn't going to follow either plan. She didn't need a keeper, she needed Gavin.

Only in their richly covered bed, the traditional showpiece of a Californio wife, only in their love-making did her control desert her, thus destroying Gavin's. She was fiercely demanding, fiercely generous. Gavin felt as if he were living with one woman by day, another by night, and never more than the last night before he left. He was tired and his muscles ached from the heavy cargo lifting he'd done for days. He was in the middle of telling Tessa he loved her when he fell asleep.

He awakened with a grunt of protest, grabbing her and pinning her tightly against him to stop the sharp, jabbing blows of her fists on his rib cage. Her head sank forward, making him think she was giving up until her teeth nipped him sharply on his shoulder. "You little savage!" he roared, shaking her roughly. "What'd you do that for?"

"To mark you, both sides now, and to keep you awake. You can sleep on your damned boat." Her voice was low and husky, half threat, half promise, Tessa's voice, yet years older. He was intrigued and at the same time strangely disquieted; he had accepted the fragile childlike being so vulnerable to the pressures being exerted upon her. The sure, even aggressive woman he saw emerging was another matter entirely, and he wasn't sure how he felt about her.

"I ought to throw you out of this warm bed, or at the very least warm your backside," he growled, but the threats were empty. Already he was responding to the warm insistence of her body, her mouth, her hands. The next sounds he made had nothing to do with anger.

Only when she bade the last good-by the next morning was he able to see her clearly again. She was sixteen years old, and marriage and Monterey were only just beginning to be less foreign to her. He saw her eyes fill suddenly, her face paling, but even as he searched for words to comfort her, she regained control. Indian had withdrawn to a discreet distance, but she included him in her farewell. "Take care of each other. *Vaya con Dios.*"

Gavin kissed her hard and then let her go. She went into the house without a backward glance. She had told them she would not go down to the water's edge with them. But she broke her own promise to herself and went up to the balcony in time to watch the boat put out to sea. She watched until it had disappeared.

She told Rosa to go home early, explaining she would not require her to stay at night after all. The woman did not object; she was accustomed to obeying, and besides, she preferred to be with her own family.

Tessa waited until the house was empty before she let go, weeping and screaming, hating the sounds even though she made them, not realizing until she was exhausted that she was as angry as she was lonesome. It was intolerable that the center of her universe should be able to come and go as he pleased, for business or any other reason, leaving her to the desolation of waiting. And there was hate and fear mixed with her love at the realization of how completely lost was her independence, how completely dependent on Gavin she had become in such a short time.

She huddled in the gathering darkness. Her head ached, her eyes were swollen, her throat raw. Darkness was invading the house, but she made no move to light the candles. She felt as if she couldn't move at all, but her whole body jumped at the sound of a voice.

"Bastards, all of them, to give such hurt with the love." It was Carmelita, and Tessa found herself obeying her orders as if she were a child. Dazed, she washed her hands and face and sat down at the table, watching Carmelita's efficient movements as she unpacked the basket she had brought.

126

"We will have supper and some of the best tequila from Mexico, and you will feel much better. You are over the worst part now. It is always so the first time of parting in a marriage of love. And always worse for the woman who must watch the leaving." She smiled at Tessa's startled expression. "Yes, I know these things. I was not much older than you when I married my first husband. Pablo and I had so little time, two years only, and much of that he spent away from me because we had little, and he had to work hard for both of us. He died stupidly, not as he would have wished, of the fever and the flux. I could not save him." Her face was suddenly rigid with the memory, but then the lines changed again, and she was Carmelita, somewhat calculating and cynical, but most of all gay in survival.

"My second husband I married for practical reasons, and he was many years older than I. It was not a matter of love." She flashed a sudden wicked grin. "It was not difficult to be parted from him now and then, and he died as he wished, happily, in bed with me."

She had accomplished what she had set out to do. Tessa was in much better spirits, and they shared the meal and the easy mirth which came from the fiery tequila. But before she left, she warned Tessa quite soberly, "You have only two choices. You can die a little every time he leaves and not live again until he is back. Or you can belong enough to yourself so that no one, not even your husband, can take so much with him when he goes from you."

Tessa thanked her gravely, and her liking for this woman who had been Gavin's mistress was even greater than it had been before.

Though she was exhausted, she lay awake for a long time thinking of Carmelita's words. She saw the truth in them, and she knew what her choice would be. Though she was still horribly aware of the cold spaciousness of the bed without Gavin, and though she hated it, the loneliness was bearable.

The men were gone for two weeks, and in that time Tessa's life altered. She lost much of her shyness, even around people she didn't know well. She had no wish to cause a scandal, and so she tried to stay at least within the minimal bounds of propriety. But she had a good time too. She accepted invitations to ride during the day and to dance at private parties in the evenings. She simply made sure she was never alone with any of the gallants who seemed apt to push their attentions too far, despite the fact that she was married. The one social function she could not bring herself to make part of every day was attendance at Mass. She went once and felt false and uneasy in the dim, damp Royal Presidio Chapel of San Carlos, which smelled of wet earth, wax, and incense and was not improved in her eyes by the garishly painted wood of the ceiling, dirty reds and blues that made her feel as if the roof were going to fall in on her. Even the statue of Our Mother of Sorrows, believed to have been carried north by Father Serra himself, dismayed her. It looked like a crude, vacant-eyed doll lavishly dressed in stiff cloth. None of this had been part of her upbringing, and she could find no solace in it now. The God she believed in would feel as cramped by the ritual as she did herself, she decided. She knew many of the older generation condemned her lack of devotion, but she also knew they marked it down to her marriage to a Yankee, and she did not correct them.

Parodoxically, though she longed for Gavin and was seldom free of thinking about him, she sometimes felt as if she weren't married to him at all. Except for couple of brief visits with the Larkins, during which she assured them she was managing very well, she heard and spoke no English. Her days were filled with the sound of Spanish as much as they had been at the rancho after her father's withdrawal into his stuporous world.

She found a new interest. Because of the strangeness and isolation of her life on the rancho, she had had no knowledge of politics beyond brief glimpses in history books. Now she was fascinated, and frustrated too, because most of her Californio friends seemed to know and care so little. But by careful gleaning and by encouraging those who were concerned to talk, she began to get her first picture of the forces that might change this land and her own life. She could hear her great-grandfather's words and Gavin's about the changes the Yankees would make if they ever came in great enough numbers, and her conviction grew that that time was not far off.

Though they were not pouring into California yet, *los extranjeros* were trickling in in a steady stream. And a man named Sutter, though he was a Swiss rather than a Yankee, had begun a settlement to the northeast as far back as 1839, a settlement that seemed to be well on its way as the rallying point of most of the foreigners who were settling in the northern part of the country. But strangely, the biggest threat lay miles away, to the southeast. There were rumors that the Republic of Texas would be annexed by the United States, rumors that the Mexican government would not tolerate this, would go to war to prevent it. At first, Tessa could not understand how this could affect California, and then she cursed her own stupidity.

Don Francisco Barillo y Silveti was one of Tessa's more importunate admirers, only too willing to forget she was married, always ready with sly comments or stories about the Yankees, when others tended to be careful about what they said around her because of her husband. It was Don Francisco who told her of the silly antics of the American naval officer, Commodore Thomas ap Catesby Jones four years before. He had been in command of the United States Pacific Squadron stationed at Callao, Peru. He had received erroneous information that war had broken out between the United States and Mexico, and he had acted on it immediately, sailing for Monterey where he had sent his marines ashore to claim California for his country. There wasn't any resistance, and according to Don Francisco there had even been some amusement, especially when the commodore discovered his mistake and hauled down his own flag, replacing it with the Mexican ensign and apologies. The commodore had been fearful of an English takeover of California during the confusion of a war, and he had been willing to go even so far to prevent it, however ridiculous the outcome.

Tessa did not find it amusing. It seemed obvious to her that such an excuse or mistake or whatever the Yankees chose to call it could be made again and again until the conquest was a reality. The Californios numbered in their ranks too many like Don Francisco who, in his early thirties, was wealthy, indolent, and apathetic about his government, which was inefficient in any case.

129

She could not imagine their form of resistance would be anything against the brisk Yankee ways of men like Gavin, Indian, and Thomas Larkin, men whose numbers were ever increasing, men who would not tolerate forever the slow ways and endless bureaucracy of the Californio system, a system further weakened by deep sectional rivalries.

The thought chilled Tessa to the bone. By marriage and heritage she belonged to both sides, and by the same, she belonged to neither. Suddenly she longed desperately for Gavin, but even in the longing she realized her motive—when Gavin was with her, he filled her world, he was her world, making divided loyalty less possible. That too had to change if she were to belong as much to herself as to him.

She scanned the horizon the next day as she had every day for two weeks, but she saw no sign of the ship, and so she joined a riding party which, if it included the danger of Don Francisco's advances, also numbered enough people to ensure his good behavior.

They found a shady grove of oaks and spread a large white cloth that was soon nearly covered with food, and in the clearing beyond, the men showed off their excellent horsemanship, unchallenged by the women, though many were superb riders, until Tessa talked one of the younger men into loaning her his saddle so she could ride astride. She matched the riders trick for trick, ending with a race against Don Francisco for a handkerchief at the far end of the clearing. He was riding a big bay with good speed, and his attitude was that of a man sure to win. He was also treating Tessa's riding in a condescending manner which infuriated her. She held Amordoro for the first few seconds, and then she let him go. She streamed ahead of the bay, shifted her weight and hung off the saddle, her head terrifyingly close to the ground as she picked up the small white square, righted herself and went into the turn, arriving back at the starting line triumphantly far in advance of an astonished Don Francisco. She won applause and slightly stunned approval, and only then did she give thanks that the group was a fairly young one—by any measure of the old way, her conduct had been outrageous. She was further discomfited to discover that his defeat at her hands had only increased Don Francisco's pursuit in other areas.

She was wondering what she would do if he insisted on staying when the cavalcade halted at her house. She was weary from the hard riding, but it had been a good day. She was thanking her companions for it and receiving their teasing compliments of never risking a ride against her when she realized the house was glowing with light against the gathering dusk. The door opened, and she could not mistake Gavin's tall silhouette against the light.

Neither could anyone mistake the gladness of her cry, and no one was swift enough to help her down from her horse.

Gavin had spent the first days of sailing telling Indian how good it was to be free again. Finally Indian snapped, "When you got yourself told, tell me. Meantime, shut up!"

Gavin glowered at him and then grinned sheepishly. "You're right, of course. I miss her like hell already. How anyone can get to feel so married in such a short time is beyond me."

"Anyone with a gal like Tessa ought t' feel married an' a whole lot of other things," Indian said, not smiling, watching Gavin closely.

"She's not as helpless as she looks." Gavin spoke carefully, trying to explain the change in Tessa, finding it difficult because he was not used to talking about such things, more difficult because he did not want to betray the intimacies of their life together.

Indian listened patiently and thought a long while before he replied. "You married a scairt chil' but she growin' up real fast, gettin' to be a fine woman. Jus' depends what you want. 'Course I see how hard it mus' be for you to understand anybody who fights to keep what's theirs, you peaceable yourself."

Gavin knew the truth of what Indian said. Traits he considered solely his were part of Tessa too and growing stronger, but instead of admitting it, he asked, "You know so much about women, why aren't you married?"

" 'Cause I know so much 'bout women," Indian answered promptly. "But I find one like yours, I marry fast."

131

Their voyage was profitable. They put in where they could, sent in the longboat to bring back customers or show goods when they had to anchor off shore, and they were careful in their trading. They received some gold and silver for their goods, but barter was the general rule, with hides and tallow at the top of the list. They checked the hides carefully to be sure they were cured properly so that a bad one would not spoil the rest, and the tallow, whether in wood or in skin bags, had to have a fair degree of purity before they would accept it. They took on some fine fur pelts, and toward the end of the trip, they picked up some fresh produce, perishables they would have no trouble getting rid of in Monterey.

Gavin worked far harder than he had to, and his exhaustion helped him to sleep, though thoughts of his wife were the last to slip from his mind. They slept on the ship almost every night, and even when it was possible to sleep ashore, one had to remain with the vessel. Though the plan was that they would take turns with shore privileges, Gavin relinquished his after the first time.

They had anchored in a small bay and had been welcomed warmly by the lonely people of the rancho nearby. Gavin had been even more warmly welcomed by a young woman who seemed to know a great deal more than her position as seamstress in the household warranted. She was clean, well built, and possessed of the best features of both the Spanish and Indian blood of her parentage. Hers was not the kind of offer Gavin would have refused before. But now there was Tessa, and he was unmanned by the sharp image of her that he carried. He was no less amazed than the girl when he turned her down. He felt more bewitched than ever, and his rage against Tessa was the near equal of his love. His temper was so foul, Indian threatened more than once to find a new partner after throwing his present one overboard. The crew treated Gavin gingerly, comforted by the widely held belief that Yankees were more often than not a little crazy anyway.

They sailed back into Monterey Bay late on the fourteenth day, and when Gavin would have stayed to do his share in securing the ship, Indian shook his head. "You got a wife, go on home now."

132

Gavin went, and he found the house empty, Tessa gone, Amordoro gone.

Indian found him there in time to prevent him from charging out to search every house in town. "What you want, start good gossip 'bout how much you trust your wife? She probably jus' out ridin'."

He listened in wonder to Gavin's guesses that she might have been kidnapped, might have left him, should have been waiting no matter what.

"We been gone two weeks. She didn't know when we goin' to be back any more'n we did. You expect her to sit in this house day by day, waitin'?" Indian asked quietly, his voice lost in the sudden noise of the riders outside.

Gavin stood watching from the doorway, and even in the fading light he could see Don Francisco looking adoringly at Tessa as he added his own flourishes to the compliments being given her for her riding. He saw Tessa turn, heard her cry his name even as she sprang lightly to the ground and ran to him. The company moved on with good-natured complaints of having lost their champion to the Yankee, all save Don Francisco, who tarried a dangerous moment longer to call to Tessa, "The sea has been unkind to this unfortunate," before he too joined the others.

Gavin's body went even more rigid, and Tessa could see the clenched muscles of his jaw, the hard planes of his face. Though she reached out to touch him, he made no response. Her confusion made her slow to understand, but now she recognized his anger, and she was stunned. "Pay no attention to Don Francisco, he is a foolish man," she assured him, thinking that the cause.

"You have little idea of being a wife, but you play the whore to perfection," he said softly, viciously. "Not Don Francisco, but I am the foolish one to have hurried home. How is it done? Do I wait in line with the others?"

Her fury was the icy image of his. The change in her face was frightening. Her eyes glittered under narrowed lids, her cheeks glowed with sudden feverish color, her full mouth was taut and distorted as she spat the words at him. "You may wait in hell! Just leave my sight! Go find someone else to spread her legs for you. There are

133

many places in this pueblo where you will not have to wait." She called him an obscene name in Spanish, overheard long ago from the *vaqueros*, and pushed past him into the house, not looking back when she heard the heavy tread of his leaving.

She blinked in surprise at the sight of Indian, clearly having forgotten his existence, having forgotten everything except Gavin's words. Indian ached with the misery of it. He knew if he went after Gavin there would be a fight; he wanted to stay anyway, to comfort Tessa. But she wasn't going to accept that. She didn't throw herself into his arms to weep. She asked him with elaborate politeness if the voyage had been successful and would he like something to eat, and not heeding the answers, she set about getting a meal for him, cutting him off sharply when he attempted to explain Gavin's behavior. "Please, you may speak of anything else, not of him."

When she saw he had an ample meal before him, she excused herself as formally as if they had never met before. He heard her light step going up the outside stairs, and he sat hitting his balled fist into his open hand with hypnotic rhythm, making the sound louder when much later he heard the storm of weeping break in the chamber above.

Gavin did his best to get drunk, trying most of the places he knew that were reliable for serving *aguardiente* with mind destroying properties. He remained horribly sober except that each drink made his own words louder in his head. And he knew it wasn't true. He would have killed her if it had been. He ended up at Carmelita's, not knowing how he'd gotten there, pounding on the door, calling her name.

She was still dressed, having returned only a short while before from a party, and her annoyance changed to a welcoming smile when she saw who it was.

"So you are home." She peered behind him. "Where's Tessa?" Then she took a closer look at his face, and her own paled. "Holy Mother, what is it? Has something happened to her?"

He told her everything, the words wrenching his throat. "What should I do now?" he finished, and as angry as

Carmelita was, she felt sorry for him. But it did not stop her from scolding him. Grimly she told him of the lost Tessa she had found on the day of his departure and of the advice she had given her. "You are selfish and an idiot. And you should not be here. Go home."

She saw his doubt. "You are right, many women would not forgive such an insult. I would not. She will."

When Indian heard Gavin's step on the stairs, he fled. Carmelita, now clad in her nightrobe, was not surprised to see him. "Amigo, you are wise. Three in that house tonight is too many."

Tessa had never felt like this in her life, not even during the whole terrible time with Luis. When she had left Indian, she had felt hot and light-headed, so weightless that it was as if she were floating instead of walking. She hadn't even known when the tears began, the sound of her weeping came from a long way off. And when she was empty of tears, the chill had come so deep and penetrating that even her bones seemed to be shivering with it. She felt as if she were dying, and she didn't care. To belong to herself without belonging also to Gavin was the same as death.

Gavin had called softly before he entered their room so he would not frighten her, but even now standing by the bed, he knew she was not conscious of his presence. He had never seen anything like it. The whole bed was shivering, and when he touched her, he gasped at the ice of her skin. He lay down, taking her in his arms, holding her hard against his own warmth, rubbing his hands roughly up and down her back, saying her name over and over.

She had died. She was sure of it. Her idea of Paradise had never been very clear, but this was close enough, this sudden warmth flooding through her, the absolute knowledge of Gavin's body against her own, the terrifying cold gone as if it had never been. She opened her eyes cautiously, but Gavin was instantly aware of the change, and he let her go, trying to explain.

His halting words about jealousy, about choosing words

135

that would hurt her, words he did not believe—words. She understood everything he said, and nothing he said mattered as much as the fear she saw in his eyes.

Her hand found the soft dark hair at the nape of his neck and the cords beneath, and she kneaded the tense muscles gently. "My love, it is so hard for both of us, this belonging we have never known before."

No words of retaliation. He traced the strong slender lines of her body, and she moved to welcome him home.

CHAPTER XIV

Gavin made the decision as soon as he awakened. He leaned over Tessa and kissed her. "Lazy bones, wake up. We're going on a long ride."

She opened her eyes, asking mischievously, "Can't we just ride here?"

"For shame, madam. Hasn't anyone ever told you that overindulgence in anything causes terrible ills? I'm tempted to see if it's true, but if we're to be gone for a few days, we ought to get started."

"Oh, darling!" she cried, throwing her arms around his neck. "Do you really mean it? Just us? Where are we going? Can we?"

Yes, I mean it, just us, don't know exactly, we can because Indian will take care of things here," he laughed, answering her questions as quickly as she'd asked them.

Tessa didn't need any more urging. She could hardly believe her good fortune, and she had no intention of losing it by hesitating.

Gavin went downstairs in search of Indian and found him approaching the house cautiously. "You two friends again?" he asked.

"Friends and then some," affirmed Gavin wickedly, dodging a playful cuff from the other man. He explained what he planned to do and added, "I know it isn't just to leave you with all the work, but I'll make it up."

"You already made it up by gettin' rid of that bad

temper you been in. I handle things easy. Them that's friendly to me ain't no problem, them that ain't, I jus' scare th' hell out of them. Works easy both ways. 'Bout time you learnt th' courtin' don't end with th' marryin'."

Gavin was still thinking of Indian's words when they rode out of Monterey. He couldn't be angry; they paralleled his own thoughts. He looked at the happy, eager face of his wife as she rode beside him. She was at once easy and difficult to please. She demanded nothing beyond himself, but he was only beginning to learn how to give that essential gift. And he had been guilty of allowing himself the complacent belief that marriage settled everything, an idea as unreasonable as his rage had been at finding Tessa out when he arrived home. Marriage was only the beginning. He could see the leering face of Don Francisco all too clearly. He knew Tessa to be blameless as he knew the man was not. Don Francisco was the sort of man who, far from being deterred by the married status of a woman he wanted, would likely be even more intrigued by it. Gavin knew that reaction well; it had been his own on more than one occasion.

But for the present neither he nor Tessa was threatened; their focus on each other was too intense. Yet he wondered how long it would last, how long it could last. Sexual fidelity had never been part of his life, and Tessa was only beginning to experience that part of her nature. The thought of her giving herself to someone else as generously as she gave herself to him made him so furious he jerked on Diablo's reins, causing the horse to snort and sidle in protest.

He came to his senses to find Tessa watching him, obviously knowing his anger of the night before was somehow rekindled. He smiled at her, "Sorry, sweetheart, I was thinking of business."

"It must not be going well to make you look so," she said.

"But it is!" he protested, and the enthusiasm in his voice was genuine. "Figuring it all out on paper is difficult, but the selling itself went well indeed. California is so hungry for goods, we hardly had to bargain to get what we asked."

He would have left it at that, but Tessa wanted to know

more, and he was amazed by her agile understanding. He explained that while custom duties were very high, this was balanced by the fact that he and Indian had made and would continue to make an even higher percentage in profits on many of the articles. And they were only small traders compared to the big Boston firms.

"Their agents, I know they have them, do they not object to your taking a share of their business?" Tessa asked shrewdly.

"They're not overjoyed," he admitted, "but we simply didn't offer a big enough threat for them to do anything. We did stop at one of the hide depots, but they are so totally controlled by the big companies and their agents, trade for us was nearly impossible there. We did better with the small places, saved the ranchos the bother of contacting an agent, and we traded a little higher. The going rate for a hide is still two dollars, just as it's been for years. We allowed a bit more overall. Of course, the depots cure the hides better. They have crews of droghers washing them in salt water and scraping them clean. We had to be careful about the hides we took on."

Tessa began to understand the delicate balance that had to be found and kept. Gavin and Indian had invested everything they had in their cargo, money they had earned during several years of doing varied and often dangerous work such as their stint as a gunpowder blasting team for an eastern railroad. The mere fact of having gotten the cargo to the coast of California was the first victory. They would lose a little because of the overpayment for hides, but they would make up more than that from the rate of exchange for their higher-priced goods. The coin they had taken in direct sales was part of the profit, and it made no difference that the silver and gold was Mexican, French, English, and American; it was all acceptable. The other and greater profit would come from the barter they had collected and would in turn sell in small part in Monterey, the large part having to be sold to the ships taking raw materials back to New England for manufacture into finished goods. They had enough stores to keep them busy plying the coast until the autumn, but meanwhile they must be thinking constantly of how to replenish their stock. Though goods from Mexico—finely stamped leather,

138

vicuña hats, silver and gold ornaments, and certain articles of clothing—could be gotten in a relatively reasonable amount of time, goods from New England might take a year or more to obtain. And all the while how much of the profit was reinvested and how would have to be carefully decided.

Tessa was heartened by the idea of seeing more of Gavin once the trading season was over for a while, but she was not overly optimistic. He and Indian would never be able to bear too long a period of inactivity—they would have some other scheme going, she was sure of it. And she wanted to be part of it. She searched her mind desperately for something she could do to help, discarding one impossible idea after another, until she found one she knew would work.

Gavin had seen the rapid play of expression across her face, and he was less curious about the cause than enchanted with the effect. Her words took him completely by surprise.

"Soon, no, even now, you need someone to do that figuring on paper, to keep the accounts of what is sold and what is not, of the profits and the losses of your trading. I would like to do that. Perhaps also I could help you plan for the things women will buy for themselves and their households, things men do not think of. I know I could do it!"

His first impulse was to laugh at the idea of someone who had just learned the use and value of money offering to keep accounts, but he thought better of it in time to swallow his mirth. He didn't want to hurt her feelings, but beyond that, he began to see she really might be of use. She had learned quickly, and her bargaining powers, used in running their household, were as good as those of experienced women twice her age. And he knew he and Indian could use some help with the selection of goods for women. They had some bolts of calico whose patterns and colors he had only recently discovered were atrocities and would demand adroit bargaining to sell at all.

He answered carefully. "I'd be willing to give it a try, and Indian would let you sail the ship if you asked him. But I warn you, it won't make any difference that you're my wife. If you can't do the job properly, I'll dismiss you."

Tessa gave a whoop and took off on Amordoro, and Gavin didn't have to urge Diablo to join the fun. They kept the horses shoulder to shoulder at an easy, ground-covering lope, letting them stretch their muscles without allowing them to break into racing speed that would tire them too soon.

Tessa was so full of the joy of the day she wanted to laugh and cry and sing at the same time, feeling as if she must explode. And she could see the same delight in Gavin's face, making him look young and carefree, all trace of the earlier darkness gone.

They left the hills of Monterey well behind, traveling northeast toward San Juan Bautista. There were a few dwellings around the Mission, but the Mission itself had fallen into disrepair with the dispersal of its lands and its Indian laborers. There was more activity than usual because Governor Micheltorena had withdrawn to inland safety with his much disliked *cholos* due to yet another rumor of war between the United States and Mexico.

They felt no need for anyone else's company and certainly had no wish to tarry with soldiers, but they did ask for and receive directions to a pass to the north through the last of the coastal range. They rode swiftly, unhampered by pack animals, and it was as if they were on their wedding journey again.

They found the land on the second day. They were in the Great Valley. Tessa had never seen land so flat. Far in the east the great peaks of the Sierra Nevada, jagged and snow-capped, rose as if painted against the horizon.

They knew they were mad. The place was at best a long, punishing day's ride from Monterey into the interior in an area scarcely populated at all except by roaming bands of renegade Indians, beyond any possible protection by government troops which weren't dependable anyway, but worse, beyond any mutual protection by neighbors. It would take days to haul supplies in by *carreta*, and *vaqueros*, even the wildest of them, would be hard to persuade to work here. The summer heat was extraordinary, a heavy, gummy weight that made Tessa feel as if she were being squashed inch by inch into the ground. She longed for the cool relief of the sight and smell of the sea

140

slopes. But she no more than Gavin could deny the offerings of the land.

Mustard, tall grass, and here and there even heavy stands of trees grew in abundance. The soil was rich. A river, which Gavin was sure was the San Joaquin, was close by. Their approach had sent herds of deer and elk leaping for cover. It was land perfect for the raising of fine horses and cattle, orchards and gardens. And because it was still so isolated and beyond the heavy band of land grants along the coast, there was every chance it belonged to no one yet.

"No matter how carefully we manage, it will cost a great deal to build here," Gavin said.

"Yes, I know. I wonder if Indian will approve?"

"We couldn't possibly spend much time here until next year at the earliest."

"But we could begin." Tessa's voice was very firm.

"We will have new cargo to sell by then. We are too few to do both well."

"We are young. We are strong and willing. And I have heard tales and believe them true. More and more people will come to California, more and more from your country. This land will not always be without a master."

"It is far from the sea and would be lonely for you."

"Gavin, I am never lonely with you. We are speaking of small things. You are giving me every chance to refuse. I don't think we have any choice. The land has chosen us."

They stood arm in arm looking out over the land. It made no difference to either of them that the Rancho Valle del Mar would someday be theirs. It belonged to Tessa's father. They had need to make their own mark.

They spent the rest of the day exploring and determining the best details for describing the land and laying claim to it, wanting to be more specific than the old way of dragging a rope as far around as you could in a day's ride. They made camp near the river.

Their loving was fiercer than it had ever been, as if their separate visions of conquering the land were forged into one by the joining of their bodies. Gavin teased Tessa with his mouth and hands, touching every silken curve and hollow, spinning out the minutes until she was moaning

141

and raking his back with her nails, and when he entered her, she arched her body violently to meet him, taking him deep, making the act of possession mutual.

Later and very near sleep with her cradled against him, he felt the sudden warm wetness of her tears.

"Love, what is it, did I hurt you?" he asked anxiously, and he felt her head move in negation on his shoulder. "No," she murmured, "I . . ." she quickly abandoned English as inadequate. *"La tristeza que más duele es la que tràs placer viene."*

"The sadness that hurts the most is the one which follows pleasure," he translated aloud. "I do understand. Our loving, this journey, this land, so much joy does hurt. Oh, Tessa, I can see the herds. The rancho will be magnificent!"

"Rancho Magnífico, it has a good sound," she laughed, and relaxed against him in sudden sleep.

They left in the morning, but with great reluctance, trying to reassure themselves that no one would claim the land before they did. They were back in Monterey by the afternoon of the fourth day, and Tessa busied herself needlessly at the house while Gavin went in search of Indian. When she saw them, she knew Gavin had waited until she was present to tell him.

"All right, I'm waitin'," Indian said, glancing suspiciously from one to the other. "One of you better tell 'fore you both die of fits."

Tessa poured out her description of the land they had found, and Gavin watched Indian's expression change from skepticism to enthusiasm as he was charmed by Tessa's words. But when she had finished, the shutters came down again, and he said quietly, "I don' see what this has to do with me."

Gavin nearly laughed aloud at the unequal contest. Indian didn't have a chance. Tessa's eyes went wide and her voice was full of hurt. "I thought we were together, all three of us. Nothing will work unless we are, even now there is too much to do. Do you not trust us, then, that you would rather not do business with us?"

Indian spent the next half-hour assuring Tessa of his trust and his willingness to be part of the new venture.

"You are a witch, you know," Gavin told her later, and
142

she protested, "It isn't that. Men are not accustomed to doing business with a woman. It has its advantages."

"Which you fully intend to use. I'm glad you're my partner and not my opponent."

The rest of the summer passed in a frantic haze. The men continued to sell their goods, and Tessa set up neat columns of figures and tried with limited success to make the men think in orderly terms instead of the haphazard bartering they were used to. And all their time ashore was spent in planning for the rancho and in trips to the place when they had the time. Though Gavin's conversion to Mexican citizenship and Catholicism were doubtful, having been accomplished by Don Esteban's sleight of hand more than official means and the fee, Don Esteban's standing and Tessa's relationship to him helped with the grant. And in any case, the Californio government had long been generous with land for foreigners since there was so much to be had, and Rancho Magnífico was far enough away from heavy settlement to cause the government little interest.

The land-grant system was rather obscure, with strange limits here and there and casual definitions of boundaries, but the three were well pleased with the eleven leagues, nearly *49,000* acres, they obtained. "That's quite enough for a start," Gavin said with satisfaction. "Magnificent," and they laughed because their original name for the place had stuck. The grant would supposedly need approval by the general government, though this was often ignored, and the slow bureaucracy of the country would undoubtedly delay full title until at least the next year, but they all accepted this and were not fearful of the outcome, particularly since they had paid the grant fees already.

Indian and Gavin were away trading toward the end of August when Tessa received the wedding gift from Don Esteban. A *vaquero* found her at the house and handed her the letter from her great-grandfather, and then she followed him to the outskirts of Monterey to view the gift.

Every horse in the *manada* was perfect, the mares' rich chestnut, the stallion's palomino gleaming gold and silver in the sun. Many of the mares had foals at their sides, and

143

more than half of the young were also golden. The stallion sounded his commands and reassurances constantly. Even after the long journey, the horses looked sleek and well fed. The *vaqueros* had followed Don Esteban's orders religiously, bringing the horses up from his rancho by easy stages.

Tessa was half laughing, half crying as she looked at the animals. How like him to send such an incredible gift, not only a gift, but a charge. He fully expected she and Gavin would find a place to keep them; he wanted their investment in the land to begin as soon as possible. She knew he was aware of Gavin's plans for coastal trading, and she could almost believe he knew how hard Gavin's absences were on their marriage.

By the time the men returned, Tessa had found a place for the herd with the help of the Abregos. They had known of a *ranchero* not far from Monterey who had plenty of grazing. Tessa had to insist on payment, otherwise the *ranchero* would have given the herd the privilege of his land without cost. She preferred a business footing rather than having to give up any of the horses out of gratitude at the end of their stay.

Gavin knew instantly she had something to tell him. Her eyes were gleaming, and she could barely hold still for his kiss. She whirled away and got the letter from Don Esteban, giving it to Gavin only to snatch it back again when he took too long translating the Spanish script. "He wishes us joy in our marriage and sends a gift which he hopes will make up for my lack of dowry. The rest tells their lineage. The stallion is brother to Amordoro."

They waited only long enough for Indian to join them before they rode out to see the herd.

Indian whistled and swore, "Hell, if they ain't worth marryin' even my friend here. Now I see why you did it, Tessa."

"He could not have given you anything finer," Gavin said, and when Tessa protested, he was firm. "These are yours. You know more about horse breeding than Indian and I put together. We ride them, but one thing we've never done is to raise them. The market for good horses is going to get bigger and bigger with more people coming to this country." He shook his head ruefully. "I have a feeling Don Esteban knows all about the rancho, maybe he even knew before we found it."

"I do too," Tessa agreed, but only later when they were alone did she tell him of her plan. "It would be foolish for me to deny I think the golden horses are beautiful and that someday I would like to have them to raise on the rancho. But to keep this herd would also be foolish. I know I can sell them for a good price, and your debt to Señor Larkin will be diminished by that much."

"You know it is being paid off at a steady rate. You keep accounts," Gavin pointed out carefully. He was overwhelmed by her offer and not quite sure why she was making it.

"Yes, I know," she said, and the bitterness in her voice shocked him. "I know every time I look at the numbers how much it cost you to buy me."

"Have I made you feel that way?"

"No . . . I . . . ," she stammered, wincing at the hurt in his voice.

"But I must have. I thought I'd convinced you that I love you, that any price asked, since you think of it that way, would have been too little. I've failed, and I don't know how. I don't know any more ways of telling you I love you."

He had gone to the window, and he stood looking out, his back to her, his voice muffled. She wailed his name as she caught hold of him, turning him around, burying her head against him. "I'm so sorry! I was thinking selfishly of myself, not of you. I do know you love me. I could not live if I didn't know."

He tasted her tears as he kissed her and picked her up in his arms.

She almost told him that night, but she was not yet sure, not even of how she felt about it. She had never been so prone to tears and sudden shifts in emotion as she was now, and in the morning she felt slightly sick on waking, as if she were off balance, though the feeling passed and left her hungry by midday. She had missed three fluxes. Soon she must talk to some woman who could confirm her judgment.

She wanted to give Gavin a child, many children if it were possible. But at the same time, she was loath to relinquish the exclusive bond of their love, to have to share

145

it with a third person. She hated admitting that even to herself; it seemed so unnatural. And she feared the ordeal —her own mother and Gavin's had died of complications from childbirth—but she was more fearful of becoming less attractive to her husband, and of being treated differently and forbidden to be as active as she was. She decided to ignore it for a while longer, realizing wryly that nature would have its way in any case. One couldn't be partly pregnant.

Despite her best intentions, Tessa changed. Knowing she might be able to do far less before too long, she did twice as much and was exhausted by every nightfall. She was alternately irritable and clinging, but with a pattern so random, Gavin could make no sense of it. When he asked her what was wrong, she inevitably blamed the heat and the fleas. It was a reasonable enough complaint. Though the sea breeze kept things cooler in Monterey, still there had been a hot spell and it was far worse inland, and the fleas which seemed to spring up in California wherever two or more people gathered had fought a long seasonal battle to invade the house in spite of Tessa's murderous standard of cleanliness, which included the prohibition, enforced by most Californio women, against rugs or any other floor coverings which might harbor the pests. Now Tessa was apt to turn the house upside down in a fury of cleaning if so much as one flea hopped into her sight.

She changed in other ways too. Gavin caught her countless times in a reverie so deep it would take her a full minute to focus on him again. It made him feel strangely lonesome and jealous. It was as if she were listening to something a long way off. Or someone. He wondered if she were really as indifferent to Don Francisco's advances as he had thought. It hardly seemed possible, yet the man was becoming more and more openly a nuisance, performing a dangerous, flirtatious dance for her, often in sight of her husband, but so far cleverly enough to avoid provoking an open challenge. Gavin hated him without being able to blame him. Tessa was growing more beautiful every day. Even when she was tired and waspish, there was a luminous quality about her, a softening of the fragile lines of youth into gentle curves, a shining in the violet eyes which made it difficult to look away.

146

She was as contrary at night as she was during the day, sometimes exciting and demanding, other times refusing him, sometimes asking him just to hold her, then again holding herself apart so that no part of her body touched his while she slept. It made him nervous and bad tempered, and he felt like giving her a good spanking for behaving like a child.

Finally one night his endurance broke, and he swung out of bed, his feet hitting the floor with a thunderous sound. He found his clothes in the dark and dressed, letting his anger spill out all the while. "You, madam, are about as responsive as a corpse. I've had underpaid whores who were warmer than you are. I remember now why I never wanted to marry."

"Make sure you pay well tonight, else you might not get one warm enough," she snapped from the bed as he stamped out. She made no move to call him back. She sat hunched on the bed with her arms around her knees, rocking her body slightly for childish comfort. She was appalled at what she'd done, and yet unfairly angry with Gavin for not understanding, even though she herself did not understand. She was so confused. She put her head in her hands, trying to block out the image of Gavin making love to another woman.

He thought of it, but it wasn't what he wanted. He wanted the old Tessa back. Beneath his anger was a stronger misery. Their bodies together had been finely tuned, making an exquisite instrument capable of the most subtle melody. Now there was nothing except jangling discord.

He went to Carmelita's. She answered his knock, took one look at his face, and got out the tequila. "I should be a priest," she said drily. "It is getting to be a habit, this hearing of confessions. What is it this time, my friend?"

She understood more from his hopeless attempt to explain than she did from the actual words. She was angry at Tessa for making him so unhappy, but she was fond of both of them now, and she suspected her first intuition about Tessa's problem was correct. It was not something she could suggest to Gavin, that was for his wife to do, but her voice was very gentle as she struggled to enlighten him. "It is difficult being so young and loving so much. She

147

does love you, you know, she loves you more perhaps than is good for her, or for you. Many changes happen to a woman when she is learning of love." It was as close as she could get to the heart of the problem as she saw it without betraying Tessa, but she saw with despair that nothing flickered in the cold, deep blue of his eyes. *Mother of God*, she thought, *he is as young and unprepared for this as she is.* "If you will just have patience, it will be all right," she finished lamely, knowing she had failed to comfort or explain.

He looked at her speculatively, and she was not offended, only sad. "No, you don't really want me. Before it was different. Now you have a wife, and whether you still admit it or not, you love her, and she is my friend."

They talked of things that concerned neither of them for a while longer, and then Carmelita said, "Indian comes to see me quite often, you know. He told me you're leaving again tomorrow. I think you ought to go home now. Whether or not she can tell you, she needs you."

He left docilely after thanking her politely for putting up with him, and she knew he remained unconvinced. She would wait only until the ship had sailed before she went to see Tessa.

Gavin took no care to be quiet when he returned, and by the time he had undressed and gotten into bed, he was sure Tessa must be awake and still ignoring him. His sorrow and his anger were indivisible, and he wanted nothing more than the dawn to light the ship's passage from the bay.

Tessa's deep, even breathing was no sham. The huddled rocking had given way to exhausted sleep. She had no consciousness of Gavin's return. The warm weight in the bed was too familiar now, and she was too tired; without voice or touch, it did not penetrate her misery.

CHAPTER XV

Before she was fully awake, Tessa knew the house was empty. She turned her head, and her heart lurched as she saw the rumpled bedclothes on his side of the bed. Had he come back at all in the night? She didn't know. She got out of bed and moved to the window as if she were in a trance. The ship would soon be out of sight.

She was too numb to cry, too numb to do more than offer the barest welcome when Carmelita appeared. Carmelita took charge immediately, making sure they were out of earshot of Rosa who was already busy scrubbing.

She had thought of several ways to lead up to the point, but they fled as she looked at Tessa. *God help me*, she thought, *I'm nearly, not quite, but nearly old enough to be her mother, and that's just how I feel.* "How far along are you?" she asked bluntly.

"Nearly four months," Tessa answered dully. "How did you know?"

"Your husband."

Tessa's eyes widened, but Carmelita forestalled her questions. "He doesn't know. He doesn't even seem to suspect. But he came to me last night, not to anyone else, and all we did was talk."

She was relieved when Tessa's eyes met hers squarely, relieved when she heard her say with complete trust, "Thank you. You are a good friend to me."

"Why haven't you told him?"

Tessa tried to explain, feeling ever more hopelessly entangled in words that made no sense, sure she would earn Carmelita's contempt in any case. But Carmelita said, "My poor little one, so much has happened to you in so short a time, and now this brings its own confusion. You are not wrong to think these things. I have not borne a child. I tried very hard to conceive with my first husband, and I was very careful not to with my second." She got the response she wanted from Tessa, a wan smile for her wicked admission. "But I do know that everything changes for a woman while the child grows within her. She looks inward, and her needs are new. Gavin will understand why you have been behaving so if you give him a chance. Besides, you will not be able to keep it a secret for very much longer. You are too finely built."

"Poor Gavin. He has enough to worry about without this. I will tell him when he returns, and I will ask his pardon."

"After you give him the news, I don't think you'll have to say you're sorry for anything." Carmelita was well pleased with herself and with her friends. Marriage was bound to have its problems, but she was confident they could make theirs work. So was Tessa, and she waited peacefully for Gavin to come home again.

Aside from a couple of visits out to check the horses, she stayed at home, scanning the horizon frequently for the ship, and she was beside herself with excitement the afternoon it arrived. And to add to the splendid sight, another ship put in at the same time so that they swung into the bay with the wind and tide within hailing distance of each other. Indeed, there was quite a lot of good-natured shouting back and forth.

It was not until the ships were closer to shore that she was able to distinguish the figures and the voices. There was a woman on the strange ship, and somehow Tessa knew who she was even before the wind brought her the name. Soledad. She was deaf to the actual words of banter being exchanged in the mock race to land. *Soledad*. It did not matter that there must be hundreds of this name. This was the one Gavin had called to when he had lain unconscious by the pool.

Tessa kept hoping she would awaken from the nightmare, but it got worse. Don Francisco appeared at her side, taking her arm possessively. "I thought I might find you here. Such a beautiful sight, is it not?"

Tessa pulled her arm away and ignored him. Nothing mattered except Gavin. She did not even consider how it would look to her husband to see her standing with Don Francisco.

Gavin had thought constantly of Tessa, but now mixed with his desire to see her again was the fear that he would have to suffer more of her erratic behavior. He had always been able to leave the others at the first sign of a petulant, demanding nature; it was not the same with his wife. He had known so little love in his life, he had yet to learn the full power of it. And the deepest of all his childhood scars was his innermost conviction that he was unworthy to be loved. His father had left him while he was yet unborn. His mother had not cared enough to live for him after his birth. His aunt and uncle had never made any

150

pretense of loving him. He had always done his utmost to keep these thoughts hidden even from himself, and so they festered with poison grown stronger with the years. And he had never been so vulnerable to hurt as he was with Tessa.

He caught sight of her. She was wearing the lavender silk dress. Her hair was uncovered, neatly plaited, gleaming blue black in the sun. Not close enough yet to see them, still he traced her features in his mind—the fine, high cheekbones, the delicate brows over amethyst eyes so heavily lashed, the straight nose, the full mouth and firm chin. He could almost smell her flowery scent over the sea salt and reeking boat.

It hit him like a sharp, physical blow. Don Francisco stood beside her, garbed in rich blue with snowy linen and a wealth of silver trim. They made a handsome couple, both so obviously from the same high-bred world. If not he, some other don, some other minor prince of California carrying at least two family names to indicate legitimate birth.

Soledad. Much more his kind and without the complications of love. She seemed suddenly a timely gift of fate. The transition from the ships to smaller craft for landing on the beach was swift, and it seemed perfectly natural that Gavin should be beside Soledad when it was accomplished, and they stood on firm ground.

"You see what trouble I have taken to come to you, my tall, blue-eyed one," Soledad laughed, and she threw her arms around him and stood on tiptoe, tugging his head down to kiss him. Gavin returned the favor, conscious of Tessa watching them, conscious of Indian muttering beside him.

He stepped back, putting Soledad away from him. "Welcome to Monterey," he said, "and now you must meet my wife."

Soledad's eyes narrowed and her face was rigid for an instant, but Gavin missed it because he had started toward Tessa.

She stood frozen, waiting for him. The whole town seemed to have poured down to the waterfront to enjoy the excitement of not one, but two ships coming in at

151

the same time. Many would be rowed out to see the goods on the new ship.

She had waited so anxously for this, so sure that she would tell him and all would be well between them, and now there was nothing but a shattered world at her feet, nothing left but her pride. The woman he had left behind had followed him, and he had welcomed her in the sight of all. Tessa saw in her all the things she herself could never be. Soledad was a head shorter than she, and richly curved. Her eyes were big, bold, and black under sweeping brows; her nose and cheekbones had the slight exotic slant and flair of her Indian blood; her skin was golden, her mouth a perfect red rosebud. She had to be closer to Gavin's age than to Tessa's.

By comparison, Tessa felt too tall, too young, awkward in every way. Her stomach heaved unpleasantly, and she wanted to scream and claw at the woman's face, to drive her away. But she betrayed nothing. Even her eyes did not give her away as she greeted Soledad and welcomed her. She knew then exactly how Carmelita had felt, and she knew this woman bore no resemblance at all to her friend. It would make no difference to Soledad that Gavin was married.

When Don Francico was introduced to Soledad, she smiled up at him and said, "Oh, but it must be so comforting to Señora Ramsay to have such a handsome friend to care for her while her husband is away. She is so young."

"I look forward to attaining the wisdom of your added years someday," Tessa said sweetly, allowing herself one barb, and she had the satisfaction of seeing the woman's quick flush of rage for so stupidly trapping herself. The men ignored the byplay.

Poor Soledad and the hunched maid who trailed behind her, they had no friends except Gavin in Monterey and no place to stay. It worked with murderous ease. Indian escorted Tessa home; Gavin stayed behind to collect Soledad's luggage and to help her find lodging. Don Francisco was abandoned to his own calculating company. Searching for the smallest grain of comfort, Tessa found only one—at least Gavin had not insisted on finding room in their house for his whore.

Indian's misery was so acute, he was clumsy with it. He

152

kept silent until they reached the house, and then the words tumbled out. "I don' know, don' know what he doin', actin' like a crazy man when he got you. She—"

"No more!" Tessa snapped, and then her voice gentled. "Don't look like that. You are my most precious friend. Even your sorrow for my trouble is a gift. But I will not talk about her nor about any of it. Now, I ask of you a favor. There is to be dancing tonight. Will you take me?"

"But Gavin be back by then," Indian protested.

"I do not think he will be back. You will escort me?"

Indian agreed, wishing he could do something more useful such as finding Gavin, knocking him down, and throwing Soledad into the sea. But the situation was beyond any such simple solution now, and its subtleties were beyond him.

Tessa dressed that night in yellow satin, and she wore the emeralds and the embroidered shawl from María. The bright sunlight fabric of the low-cut, simply made dress enhanced the violet of her eyes and the darkness of her hair, which gleamed through a fragile mantilla. Defiance had put color in her cheeks. There were audible gasps of admiration when she and Indian arrived.

She had only attended one of these celebrations before, with Gavin, drawing the line of propriety here when he was absent, but all that was changed now.

These fairly public outdoor dances would be held as long as the weather permitted. The dance floor consisted of wooden planks laid down for the evening. Flaring balls of pitch topped tall poles and provided light and the sweet, sharp scent of burning resin. The wooden benches around the dance floor provided seats for the ladies, the unmarried with a *dueña* or a maid kneeling at their feet or standing behind them. The band was composed of soldiers from the Presidio and some Indians, and the music they made was lively and competent. Greetings, laughter, and the hum of conversation vied with the music and the tap of wooden heels on the floor.

Tessa plunged feverishly into the gaiety. By now many of the people who had not witnessed the scene on the beach would have heard of it. But they were wrong if they thought she was going to stay in hiding, suffering the role of the neglected and broken-hearted wife. Her task

153

was made easier by the absence of Carmelita. She doubted she would be able to fool her friend. Aside from Don Francisco, who was on the scene to make unwise comments in a soft voice she ignored, people were too polite to ask probing questions, and to their vague inquiries, she gave vague replies—her husband still had some work to do, and the visit of an old friend had further complicated things. Perhaps he would come later, perhaps he would not have time, perhaps he would come to the next dance. Her smile never faltered, and once the men found she would accept their invitations, she hardly had time to catch her breath.

They danced the waltz, the polka, the mazurka, but most fun of all were the old folk dances, many of which required the singing or reciting of verses, often improvised.

Tessa danced, sang, and took her turn at making up verses with convincing fire and grace. The rage and despair in her heart translated easily into the pure emotion of music and dance, giving everything she did a sharp edge. When a grave young man led her out for the *fandango*, the other dancers cleared the floor quickly to watch. This dance was for one man and one woman only.

Every tense line and arch of Tessa's body bespoke feline power, and her partner was wise and skillful enough to dance a complement to her, to make her the center of attention. The click of their heels made a furious sound, and when the music stopped now and then and the cry of "*Bomba!*" rang out, neither of the dancers ever missed a turn at singing a verse. Tessa heard herself compared to a lily, an angel, every lovely thing, and for once the extravagant words did not seem foolish but were balm to her bruised spirit. She wove and sang her answers cleverly, calling her partner a hunter, a valiant, but warning him she was bespoken, keeping her responses on the borderline of virtue.

The dance finished in a crescendo of heels beating on the hard wooden planks, followed by deafening applause and yells of appreciation. Her partner stepped back, and when the music began again, Tessa danced alone as one man after another placed his hat upon her head until she could balance no more and retired from the floor carrying the hats in her hands. The men came one by one, paying the tribute in coin to redeem their hats, and Tessa's wide smile was genuine—there was no higher praise a dancer could receive.

Gavin watched from beyond the circle of light. He had gone home, fully expecting to find Tessa waiting for him in a jealous rage. He hated himself as much as he hated her when he realized that. It had been a mean ploy, and it had failed utterly. He had never seen her look more beautiful nor dance better than she just had, not even when she had danced for him on their wedding night. The impulse to stride in and carry her off died quickly. He slipped away, back to Soledad.

Tessa had danced until she could hardly stand, and she had fallen into an exhausted sleep when she got home, but this time, not even that was a strong enough opiate to prevent her from knowing Gavin's return in the predawn. It was the alien scent which awakened her. Heavy, cloyingly sweet, nothing like the delicate fragrance she herself made from flowers and herbs. The musk clung to Gavin and filled her own nostrils, making her want to retch. But she lay very still with closed eyes, and when Gavin got into bed, he was instantly asleep.

She told herself she had no certain proof. She told herself several other lies even while she knew the truth. She was simply paralyzed, unable to decide what to do, waiting for the final blow.

It came after a week of the cruelest truce and worst tension either Tessa or Gavin had ever known. Tessa hardly saw Gavin. Sometimes he came home near dawn, sometimes he did not return at all. He did not touch her. The silence between them was only broken for absolutely necessary discussion of business and household matters. They avoided looking at each other. And when Gavin did spend a few hours in their bed, Tessa lay with body held rigidly apart from his, wondering all the while why he bothered to come home at all, and still unwilling to confirm where he had been.

Gavin could no more understand his behavior than he could understand Tessa's. He came back to her when he could bear being away no longer. She was as compelling as a drug to his system, and yet, he could no longer deal with her. Things had gone so sour so quickly. He knew he had been hideously wrong in trying to provoke her, as wrong as he had been in thinking Soledad could provide easy surcease for his pain when all she had to offer was her body and a great emptiness of spirit afterward. Yet he had lost the way to his wife. She seemed to go further from him each day.

She did not condemn him by look or word, even her silence was without heat. She seemed peaceful and uncaring about his infidelity. In the boiling heat of anger, Gavin felt they might have found a place to come together again, but not in this cold acceptance.

Indian's attitude added further agony. Here too Gavin would have welcomed a howling brawl, but his friend simply avoided him, making contact only when business matters demanded it, face stone-graven, eyes devoid of light.

Born of a harlot, fit only for a whore's love, Gavin judged himself each time he went to Soledad.

The night was oppressive with the burden of a late summer storm rolling in from the Pacific. The moon flickered, glaring brightly and then disappearing behind racing clouds.

Neither of the men was home, and Tessa was miserable. She could not doubt where Gavin was. The past week had been an eternity.

When Don Francisco arrived at the house, she told him curtly to go away. He was not deterred. His manner was silkier than ever, and she could feel his excitement and see it glittering in his dark eyes. She knew this was leading her to hurt. She had no physical fear of him; he would not try to gain his ends by force. He was a far more subtle man than that.

"I will leave, and you will go with me," he said, "just for an evening stroll."

"I am not going anywhere with you. I'll repeat, 'Go away!' "

"Ah, but there are many interesting sights and sounds to see and hear even in so quiet a place as this. It is to your advantage to come with me."

"And to yours, I'm sure."

"Perhaps. I am ever a hopeful man."

There could be only one thing his malice and covetousness could want to show her. Drearily she admitted to herself that she had been waiting for an excuse to finish it.

She got her cloak and went with him. They hadn't far to go. Soledad had taken the little adobe the Ramsays had first considered and rejected. Tessa had known that. Undoubtedly Gavin had helped the woman obtain the house.

She ignored Don Francisco's continuous stream of soft, mocking words. She knew she was going to her own execution, and she made no outcry when she saw it.

The house was brightly lighted from within and had no wall to shield it. No attempt had been made to guard the occupants from the eyes of passersby. The shutters were open to allow the least breeze of the oppressive night to cool the house.

Soledad was sitting in Gavin's lap, her hands playing with his hair, her mouth nuzzling his throat, kissing his mouth. Tessa didn't need to hear the words to know the kind of thing they were saying to each other.

"If you will be good enough to escort me home, Don Francisco, I will be most grateful," she said formally, and Don Francisco did as she bid without question and without conversation on the way. He was suddenly dreadfully aware that his plan had gone awry. Yet still he felt bound to pursue his course, and when they were back at the house he proposed staying to comfort her.

"You are a fool, Don Francisco, and worse, you are a vicious fool. That you should think so little of me to judge that I would take you because he has taken her is the worst insult you could offer. It was time I learned the truth. I must thank you for that. But no friend would present it so cruelly for his own gain. I hope I never see you again. Leave me."

He did as she ordered because he had no choice, and he felt as miserable as it was possible for a man with his limited moral sense to feel. She hadn't even raised her voice. She seemed totally in control. He would have understood hysterics far more easily.

Now that she had seen the reality of it, Tessa felt very little at all. She knew the calm would not last, and even that did not trouble her. The emotional shock was deep

157

and protective. Unconsciously she spread her hands over the small mound of her belly.

She had even slept a little by the time Gavin came in, though she awakened instantly when he entered the room. "Go back to your whore," she said quietly when he came close to the bed. "You stink of her."

She heard him gasp, but he waited until he had lighted a taper and could see her before he spoke. "Are you ordering me from my own house, my own bed. Is that what I heard you say?"

His face looked as cold and dangerous as when he had fought with Luis, but she paid no heed. "That's what you heard, you bastard!" Her control was breaking now under the heat of her rising anger and revulsion. She chose the word "bastard" at random, not thinking of its connection with him at all, but he didn't know that.

The word cut deep as he looked at the aristocratic features of his wife. The past days had taken enormous toll of his self-respect, and the anger he had wanted her to show had come too late. At this moment he hated her for being so able to confound him, so capable of making his life worthless. He hated her for driving him to Soledad. He hated Soledad whose soft words and softer body had been used as skillful weapons in her campaign to recapture him. He hated Tessa for being so right about the other woman. Most of all, he hated himself.

He lashed out to share the hate, using the words which would wound her the most. "I bought you, remember? It's strange to hear you call another woman whore. I own you, as I intend to remind you now."

He watched her through narrowed eyes as he undressed, and when she sprang at the heap of clothes, going for his knife, he was ready for her. He grabbed her, and she kicked and clawed at him in spitting fury. Her thin chemise ripped easily, and he threw her on the bed, pinning her arms back and thrusting his knee between her legs.

She fought valiantly, not ceasing to struggle until she was exhausted, but her strength was nothing against his. She would not ask for quarter, not for herself or for the unborn, and Gavin gave none. He took her swiftly, brutally, and she set her mouth against crying out from pain far greater than the loss of her virginity had caused. Then
158

she had been willing, now every tense muscle screamed her rejection.

He rolled off her and sank into a stuporous sleep. She waited only long enough to be certain he would not wake, then very carefully she rose and dressed by the light of the candle which was beginning to gutter down. She did everything very deliberately. She went downstairs and into the bottom floor of the house, finding that Indian's door still gaped wide open with his absence. She took Gavin's compass, and she took her own small rifle.

She had never felt this cold, bleak urge to destroy before. It was worse than anything she had felt against Luis; she had not loved him. She saw it clearly for an instant— Gavin and the woman dead, and she recoiled from it. Gavin dead? No, never by her hand, not even for this.

She made a hasty bundle of food and took a blanket from the linen stores and went out to Amordoro. That it would be a long journey foolhardy for her to attempt alone did not occur to her. The worst had happened. There was nothing more to fear. She had no other place to go.

Amordoro was strung high on the storm's energy, but he gentled at her automatic reassurances. She ignored the discomfort from Gavin's hard usage of her body. They had to go slowly and carefully when the clouds obscured the moon, increasing the pace when the white light poured down again. There were still several hours before dawn, time enough to travel a good distance.

CHAPTER XVI

Indian awakened with a start at the deafening crack of thunder. The woman beside him stirred restlessly but did not wake. Indian grinned wryly. Besides being very accommodating at a fair price, she offered the added benefit of a completely placid nature. Dull, but at least not dangerous. He had avoided his own bed for most of the week. The tension between Gavin and Tessa was unbearable, and her did not want to take sides again. He had even avoided going to Carmelita, which was hard because he had grown very fond of her. But she was too sharp, and he had begun to think going to her was disloyal to his friends.

He figured it was a little after daybreak as he rode toward the house, but there was little in the murky light and sudden sheets of rain to confirm it.

Many in Monterey still followed the old custom of letting their horses wander freely except for a trailing lasso around the neck, catching one or another when they needed a mount again. But in their household, they were not so casual, and when Indian led his horse to join the others in the back of the house, he was surprised to find Amordoro gone. He looked in the shelter, thinking the palomino might have taken refuge from the rain. His surprise changed slowly toward the first flicker of fear. Tessa's saddle was gone too. He moved slowly toward the house, thinking of all the things this might mean, not really wanting to believe any of them save the least plausible—that Tessa had gone for a ride despite the early hour and threatening weather.

Once in the house, it took his observant eyes no more than a split second to record the evidence: her heavy mantle was gone from the peg where it normally hung; there was an uncharacteristic mess on the table, bits of bread, meat, and cheese as though someone had prepared a hasty meal; and her rifle was missing from the gun rack.

He was outside, up the stairs, praying Gavin was there, in the room shouting Gavin's name as he shook him awake.

Even the storm breaking had become part of Gavin's nightmare, all of it loss. He could see Tessa so near, but he couldn't touch her, couldn't speak to her, couldn't make her understand. She wasn't aware of him at all.

Even while he focused on Indian, his hand searched the bed beside him, and asked her name.

"That what I been tryin' to tell you, she gone."

"Gone?" Gavin echoed stupidly.

"Yeah, gone, horse, saddle, rifle, an' her, they all gone," Indian roared.

Gavin saw it, heard it, felt it all vividly, every second of what had passed between them last night. He covered his face with his hands and groaned.

"You wearin' guilt like a bran' new coat," Indian snarled.

160

"You try it on again later. Right now get up off your ass 'fore I throw you off th' balcony." He was being purposely hard. His first thought that Gavin was not only responsible but didn't care had been fast replaced by the truth. He had never seen his friend look so miserable.

They went to Carmelita's house first, Gavin echoing himself constantly. Carmelita would know; why, Tessa might even be there. He didn't believe it any more than Indian did. He was fighting unsuccessfully against fear so palpable, it was making him feel cold and sick.

It took Carmelita several minutes to answer their summons, and when she opened the door, she stood blinking at them like a round, sleepy owl. She became fully awake far too quickly for her own liking at their questions.

"Tessa, here? No, she's not. I haven't seen much of her at all lately." Her voice cracked, and her mouth was dry. "You're sure she's gone?" She asked it only in a bid for time. The two huge frantic men were quite overpowering, threatening to make her concern for Tessa as paralyzing as their own. Even as Gavin explained, she maneuvered them into the house and lighted candles and lamps against the gloom, and she gave thanks when her first servant appeared. She whispered her instructions low and carefully to the girl, warning her of dire consequences if she failed to do exactly as she was told.

"I have sent for someone who might know where she is," she told them calmly when the girl had gone. She knew she was forcing the hand, and she didn't care. It was time and past. She met Gavin's eyes and nodded, "Yes, I've sent for Don Francisco. I am sure he will be at home, not with your wife. It should not even need proof, you and Tessa have so much to look forward to together now."

She saw his eyes narrow until even the pupils had contracted to tiny black points. "Mother of God, she hasn't told you!" She sat down abruptly, her calm command deserting her. "She was going to, we talked about it. I thought I had not seen either of you because . . . because you were so happy. I should have known, not seeing Indian either, I should have known."

"She did tell me," Gavin said so low the other two had to strain close to hear. "She told me in every way but words. I just didn't want to hear. I think I've known, some-

161

where inside. But her mother, my mother, they both died that way. I just didn't want to hear it."

"Enough of that!" Carmelita snapped; to see him in such torment hurt her. "When you find her, you can share the blame and the rejoicing."

The flustered girl burst into the room, Don Francisco on her heels. He checked at the sight of Gavin and Indian. The servant had followed her instructions, and he had not known the two men were here. His face paled, and his eyes were weary.

"Do you know where my wife is?" Gavin asked, and the look on his face made Carmelita shudder.

It did not have the same effect on Don Francisco. For the moment Gavin's obvious panic gave him the upper hand, and he could not resist it. "I have no knowledge of where your wife is, Señor Ramsay, but I have seen good reason for her to be gone. She saw it also. She graciously consented to take a stroll with me last night. There was much to amuse one."

He realized his woeful mistake even as he landed on the floor. He was no fighter, but he could not miss the blood light blazing in the blue eyes of the man who stood over him with knotted fists.

"Stop it! Stop it!" Carmelita screamed, even as Indian moved to put a restraining hand on Gavin. "This won't help Tessa. We must think now where she has gone."

Don Francisco picked himself up gingerly and edged out of Gavin's reach. Though his dignity was severely injured, he was grateful to be alive, and he was beginning to see this was more than the game of a runaway wife. The fear in the room was very strong.

"I was wrong, Señor Ramsay, to lead your wife to your sin," he said quietly, his Spanish very formal. "But you were also wrong to commit it. The woman you have married is worth many of the one you are keeping. I do not know where your wife is. I escorted her back to the house, and there she dismissed me. She did not come to me later. Perhaps she only needed a small time apart and will soon return. She is strong, young, and capable." He offered the flimsy comfort.

"She is also over four months with child," Carmelita

snapped, and had the satisfaction of seeing the fear in his eyes too.

The men, even Don Francisco, were all for setting out immediately, to search. It was Carmelita who made them tarry long enough to plan, she who packed and tied three identical bundles. And despite the gloom and the frequent heavy rain lashing the earth, she insisted on going with Don Francisco. They would search the peninsula and every other place in the surrounding countryside where Tessa had gone on outings. Indian would ride east toward Rancho Magnifico. Gavin would head south. He was almost positive Tessa was going home to the Rancho Valle del Mar. When he could not find his compass, he knew she had taken it, proof she had a definite destination.

He began to backtrack the way of their wedding journey. The rain made travel miserable and uncertain, causing the sodden ground to given way in small mud slides here and there. But Diablo was strong, and he floundered on gallantly even when the earth slipped treacherously beneath his hooves. Gavin scanned the landscape continually until his eyes began to ache from the strain. Once he met some *vaqueros* and another time a gnarled Indian shepherd. No one had seen Tessa. He did not stop at any rancho because he knew that in her solitary flight she would not.

Despair beat against him more strongly than the rain. He tried them all, all the reasonable ways out. Californio women were not like the frail eastern ladies who retired immediately into semi-invalidism as soon as they knew they were pregnant. Many of them carried on quite normally until just before the birth. Tessa was tough and fit. Nothing would happen to her. He didn't believe that. He was filled with a terrible foreboding, as if some disaster had already overtaken her and part of him knew it.

It was late afternoon, and the world was dissolving into distorted shapes as the storm intensified the failure of the sun. But Gavin saw it clearly, and Diablo traversed it nervously, a fall and tear of mud where the small hillside had given way. Anything could have caused it, and the rain had obliterated any clear tracks. It didn't matter. Gavin read the signs as if it were happening before his eyes. The earth had given way beneath Amordoro; he had

163

struggled to regain his footing; he had fallen. Gavin saw again the frightening vision he had had on their wedding journey when he had seen Tessa lying broken on the ground. She had teased him for his worry then, and now it was being fulfilled.

It was nearly an hour before he found her in the cabin they shared. He had had to remind himself constantly not to push Diablo too hard. It would not help Tessa if he were injured and unable to reach her.

No light or fire betrayed her presence, but Amordoro nickered a soft, nervous welcome from close beside the building. His saddle had been removed. Gavin smiled grimly to himself; it was typical of her to provide care for the horse while ignoring her own needs. Surely she was all right, Tessa who could be a bitch straight out of hell when she wanted to. She was probably waiting in the darkness of the shack, rifle loaded in case he had followed her. He wouldn't put it past her to wound him again; this time she might even hit his heart.

He called to her as he kicked the door open, stepping aside in the same instant. He had so wanted to find her unhurt, wanted even to hear the crack of the rifle aimed at him, it took him a moment to adjust to the lesser sounds, harsh breathing, a low moan.

He called her name as he stumbled toward the sound. He found her where she had collapsed on the floor. Her skin was cold, clammy, but the edges of fever were already beginning to touch her. He felt another warmth as he cradled her in his arms; it flowed over him, and he did not need the metallic scent of it to tell him she bled. Her body arched suddenly, and he felt every rigid sinew as she cried out. When the pain released her, she was limp in his arms again.

She stirred and his name was a question in the darkness. "Yes, sweetheart, I'm here. Rest now. I have blankets outside. I'll be right back.

She did not protest his leaving.

Without pack animals to share the burden, Carmelita had had to take great care in choosing what went into the bundles she had prepared. She had done the task well. When Gavin untied it, he found a little food, a flask of brandy, candles, but more important, two blankets, linen and lint, clear indications that Carmelita had feared Tessa would miscarry.

When he had the fire going and candles lighted, he wished for the shelter of the darkness. Tessa's mantle was covered with mud from the fall, and her clothes were soaked with rain and blood. He had never seen so much blood. He stripped her clothes off and watched helplessly as the pad of linen was stained, then saturated by the bright, terrible river. Her left side was badly bruised, but at least he found no bones broken. Sometimes she knew he was there, but her mind was working without pattern, wandering away only to be dragged back savagely by the pain.

Her eyes opened suddenly. "Not Amordoro's fault. I was careless, trail gave away. I'm losing our baby. You didn't know. Never told you. Meant to, should have told you." Her voice sounded pinched and far away, and when she whimpered against the next spasm, Gavin welcomed the frantic digging of her nails into his hands.

He lost track of time, of everything but Tessa. He willed her ordeal and his hopelessness to end; he willed her to live. And when the fetus was finally expelled, he stared at it in horrified fascination before he looked away, jamming his knuckles against his teeth, swallowing convulsively.

In all the terrors of his search and his finding of his wife he had not considered this; he had not even had enough knowledge to suspect it. In the carnage and torn membrane of the violent, untimely birth, the thing not as big as his hand was a tiny human being, even to hands and feet smaller than the tip of one of his fingernails, still with toes and fingers perfectly formed. It was a girl child. His hands trembled as he made a shroud of the bloody linen and put it in the furthest corner of the little room.

Tessa lay in a stupor muttering disjointed phrases, but Gavin understood enough to wince at the words. They were all concerned with him, his own nightmare of loss without hope.

The storm roared over and beyond them, leaving strange quiet in the hour before dawn. Gavin had done everything he knew to do. He had kept her warm. He had made her drink drop by agonizing drop of the sweet rain water, adding salt to some of it as she had once done for him. The

165

hemorrhaging had finally stopped. And she was still going to die.

Her pulse was growing weaker; there were longer pauses between each gasping breath. Her slight body was a leaden weight in his arms, as if the spirit that had made it strong and dancing was already fled far beyond his reach. He held her tightly, sobbing his grief as he had never done, seeing the endless years when he would remember her fierce, beautiful presence and would know her absence in the pale mockery of other women.

"God damn you, Tessa, if you die, I'll marry that whore and put her in your place! I swear I will. I will, my love." It was a howl of rage, fear, grief, and love so intermixed no one else could have made sense of it, but Tessa did, Tessa heard.

The ghost of her smile curved her mouth, and Gavin bent close to hear the faint words. "I'd . . . kill her first . . . and you. You are . . . *my* love." Even in the weak thread of sound, "my" was distinct.

He lay down carefully beside her and put his arms around her, molding the warmth of his body against hers. Her pulse was stronger, her breathing closer to normal, the heat of the fever diminishing.

He saw the pattern of their life together with great clarity. Challenge and love, there would never be one without the other.

He listened to a mockingbird singing stolen praises to the first light, and he breathed deeply as the scent of the rain-washed earth invaded the cabin, growing stronger than the smell of blood and death.

He left Tessa briefly at midmorning to check on the horses, finding her saddle on the ground near Amordoro, still with the rolled blanket tied to it. Even the rain that had soaked the leather had not obliterated the darker stain. It was a miracle she had even made it into the shack. He found himself giving thanks continually for anything that had helped to keep death from her.

Though he had no tools besides his knife, the earth was soft when he dug the grave and buried the pathetic bundle. He had no words. He wished he had no image.

It was Tessa who became his child. The severe blood loss and the stiffening muscles of her injured side rendered

166

her as helpless as a newborn. She lay very still, eyes closed, saying nothing even when he sponged her down with cool cloths and roused her at frequent intervals to drink small sips of water. He checked constantly for signs that the hemorrhaging had started again; each time it had not was another victory. Her fever, which he had feared might become the major enemy, broke and was gone by evening.

He prepared a meal for her, cutting the food into small pieces, wishing he had something better to offer than the bare provisions. He was aware of a sudden stillness, and he turned in panic, thinking something was wrong.

She was watching him. "Eyes like flowers." He remembered what he'd said the first time he'd seen them. Huge, vivid, bruised violets, the only color now in the transparent pallor of her face. He had a thousand things he wanted to say, a thousand more that needed saying, but his heart was pounding so hard he could scarcely breathe.

He went to her, kneeling down to put his arms around her, to bury his head in the familiar hollow of her throat. "I love you Tessa, no one else." The only words he could manage.

"*Mi vida*, my life," she whispered her love in both languages.

He coaxed her to eat a little and to drink watered-down brandy to help her rest more comfortably. And even when he fell into an exhausted sleep, his first in two days, he was conscious of her beside him and was ready to respond instantly should she need him.

When Tessa awakened the next day, her first thought was of how much she needed Gavin. She had never been this helpless nor felt so ill in her life. Lifting her head, every slight movement took enormous effort that left her sweating and caused the muscles of her bruised side to scream in protest. She could do nothing for herself. She remembered things clearly now. Amordoro had rolled in his fall, but the soft earth had saved her from being crushed, and the palomino had seemed all right too. She had mounted again and had thought they had both escaped serious injury. The first searing pain had taken her by surprise, nearly throwing her from the saddle. From then

167

on, even though she had struggled toward shelter with some last will to survive, she had known she was going to die. Gavin alone had kept her with the living.

She watched him as he tended the fire, and the sorrow washed over her. Here she had lost part of herself, part of him, joined. "I wanted a daughter before I gave you sons. Selfish. I know it was a girl. I didn't mean to kill her."

He heard every low word, and he kept his face rigidly expressionless while he saw again the eerie perfection of the fetus. He would never tell her it had been a girl.

He went to her and cupped her face in both hands while he kissed her tear-wet skin. "Perhaps we will have children, perhaps not. I did not marry you for a brood mare. And the blame in this is mine. Somewhere I knew, and I was afraid, and I gave you pain to ease my own. I drove you away. When you are strong enough, I will take you home. Then you will decide what you want to do." His voice broke on the last words, and she did not mistake his meaning.

"I will not lie. I do not understand how you could take another woman because I could not take another man in your place. Perhaps it is different for men, or perhaps I will learn someday that it is possible to love two men at the same time. But I have been a bad wife, pulling and clinging as a child fearful of the dark. I did not make it easy for you to stay with me." She closed her eyes and drew a deep breath, obviously exhausted. "Not Rancho Valle de Mar. My home is with you." She tried to open her eyes again, but her lids were too heavy.

Gavin watched her as she slept. They had said so many things, had left unsaid so many more. He had a sudden sense of the futility of expecting to know another person completely. He knew her fear of childbirth had not been based entirely on physical dread, but he would probably never understand the other factors, even while guessing they had much to do with himself. And though he had told her the partial truth about Soledad, he would never be able to explain the rest—the dangerous temptation of being able to seek the pleasure of another woman's body without the continuous thought and care involved in the loving of his wife, without the awe of her he could not

168

overcome, and the sheer relief in finding his body capable of physical response to someone other than Tessa, no matter how degraded he felt by the affair. Until he had gone back to Soledad's bed, he had not known how much he resented the power Tessa seemed to have over him. He had taught her a lesson, and he had taught it all too well, giving her a pattern of infidelity to follow, even as he had taught her to equate sex with love so that she could not help but assume he loved Soledad even as he loved her. He left the cabin and worked furiously to ease the tumult in his mind.

The sun was still high when she awakened again, and he wrapped her in blankets and lifted her with infinite care. She hid her face against his shoulder and made no sound as he carried her out into the light and laid her on the thick springy pile of evergreens he had cut. The tight planes of her face relaxed as the pangs of being moved passed, and her mouth softened in a smile as she tipped her head up to the sun. "Thank you. It feels wonderful," she murmured.

He scrubbed and aired the shack as well as he could with so little at hand, checking on Tessa often to see if she wanted anything. Once when he came out, he found she had pulled off the covering blanket. The bruises showed purple black against her fair skin, much clearer than in the dimness of the cabin. He feared she might take a chill, but when he felt the penetrating warmth on his own flesh and saw the pleasure in her face, he went back to his chores without comment, his whistling suddenly loud and cheerful on the still air.

CHAPTER XVII

It was nearly three weeks before Gavin judged Tessa fit to travel. She insisted she was fine days before that, but she knew he was right. Though she felt stronger every day, the slightest task took far too long and left her inordinately weak. She was content to rest most of the time. And with physical activity so radically limited, she had a great deal of time to think. The loss of the child was a deep, constant ache. The infant possessed greater reality in death than it had in life, but her maternal impulse, which had been as small and fragile as the seed within her, turned from the dead and grew stronger, forcing her to see Gavin with greater clarity than ever before.

He was not totally the invincible swashbuckler overburdened by love and adoration in every port. He was also the boy she had glimpsed so briefly when he had told her of his background, the boy with the white scar across his cheekbone testifying to the harsh, loveless years of his childhood.

At first she did not want to accept the truth of what she saw. It was terrifying to realize this man who was the center of her universe, her source of strength, was so vulnerable. But when the panic was controlled, she saw the beauty of it. She had after all something to give him— the assurance that he was loved and worthy to be loved.

He was both hero and child, and she had the ability to make the hero stronger and to comfort the child.

Gavin felt the change without needing to understand it. He felt the healing even though he had not consciously known he was wounded. He could hardly bear to leave her for an instant. When she was well enough to protect herself and to get about without his help, there was no excuse not to go after fresh game to make her stronger, yet he hated every minute of the hunt and used every vestige of his skill to shorten it. And when he returned it was always the same. She welcomed him with radiant joy and love. It shone in her eyes; it sang in her voice; it flowed from the slightest touch. It was as if they were making love constantly without making love physically at all.

They talked more easily. She told him of his crying out for Soledad while he was hurt, and he assured her it was only because he had so recently left the woman, making no attempt to give the affair false decency. He told her of watching her dance until he could bear it no longer and went to Soledad. Even in their sorrow for the hurt they had inflicted on each other, they were made stronger by the knowledge of the mutual power they had over each other.

170

"When first I saw you and next I married you, you were child as much as woman. Now you have grown quite beyond my knowledge," Gavin murmured, cradling her against him as they lay by the fire.

"Are you disappointed?" Tessa asked softly.

"I am rewarded beyond all justice," he said, and she smiled secretly to herself, knowing he had grown younger while she had grown older, in perfect balance.

Drowsily she nestled closer, but she grew more alert when she felt his muscles stiffen and heard the harsh breath he drew before he spoke again. "That night . . . the night you left, I . . . Christ! Sorry isn't a big enough word for rape." He stopped unable to go on, and for an agonizing instant, he thought Tessa was crying. Incredulously, he realized she was trying not to laugh.

"Oh, Gavin, I don't think it is possible. I have never heard of rape by a man on his own woman, his wife." She sobered, thinking about it. "Of course, it must be true, for some women it must never be anything but that terrible way. I am fortunate. We both are. That night, we were both angry. We fought, and each of us lost."

She had indeed been furiously angry, and she would fight him again if the situation were ever the same. But through it all and stronger than the abuse of it, love had been and would be the ruling impulse of their lives. She moved against him in invitation, knowing it would be all right now, but he refused firmly. "Time enough when we are safely home." His alone was the picture of the river of blood draining her life away, and he alone would have to overcome his terror of her fragility.

She fell asleep still smiling, encircled by his protective strength.

Within minutes after their return to Monterey, they had to endure the frantic greetings and questions from Carmelita and Indian. It had cost them a great deal of self-restraint not to ride blindly south after Gavin when their own trails proved cold. It was Tessa who told them quietly that the baby had been lost. And it was Carmelita who understood first that this terrible event had given her friends more than it had stolen from them, and she lost no time in convincing Indian when she saw that Tessa was in danger of being coddled to death by the big man,

171

who was reluctant to let her lift anything heavier than a fan or move more than a few feet without an escort.

The delayed last voyage had to be made, but when Indian volunteered to go without Gavin, and Gavin seemed about to agree with him, Tessa ordered them both out to sea. "It's important to all three of us, and you need each other. If only one of you goes there will be too much work and too little sleep for him." Her new maturity gave her words authority, and there was no more argument.

The one subject none of them had mentioned was Soledad, but Carmelita finally told them what had happened because she could keep it to herself no longer. "Don Francisco is not the best of men, even he himself would not so claim. But neither is he so bad as he sometimes appears. He too felt very helpless when we could not find you." Her eyes flickered briefly over Tessa, and then she avoided looking at either of the Ramsays. "I do not think Don Francisco has ever cared very deeply for anyone, but he did come to realize that you care deeply for each other. He wanted to do something to help and to ease his own bad conscience. He went to that woman, and he told her if she did not leave quietly, he would make her life a hell in Monterey by using all of his connections to make her a social outcast in this most social of all the pueblos. She believed him. She has gone."

"She no longer matters anyway. She never really did," Gavin said without hesitation.

Carmelita saved the rest of her words for Tessa alone. "There is one thing Gavin overlooks. Perhaps he does not know. That woman with her *puta*'s body and *puta*'s heart truly cares for him. And any feeling in such a creature is dangerous. You are well rid of her." Tessa did not dispute her.

That night, when Gavin would have done no more than hold her until they slept, she protested vigorously. "I am your wife, your woman, not your mother or your sister. There is nothing to fear now. I rode all the way home to Monterey without mishap. You sail tomorrow, but there are hours yet which belong only to us." Her mouth claimed his, and her hands began to rove over his body, now soft and playful, now using nails sharp enough to remind without hurting, stroking, nipping.

172

Even in his rising passion, Gavin fought the last vestiges of his fear, using Tessa with such slow delicacy, tracing all the nerves anew, she was crying aloud for him to possess her by the time he entered her. For an instant of separate wonder, he felt the hot, pulsing tide engulfing her before he was himself consumed by it.

Indian was well pleased with his friends as they said good-by the next morning. There was a quality to their leave-taking that had not been there before. Every time Gavin looked at Tessa, a rosy blush stained her cheeks, and Gavin himself looked so young and carefree that Indian, watching them, had to hide a smile.

Tessa slipped serenely back into the social life of Monterey, as though nothing had happened, and gradually most people came to believe it. Even Don Francisco now treated her with restraint and grave respect. And no one mentioned Soledad, at least not in Tessa's presence. There were more political rumors than usual to listen to, and almost all of them concerned the depredations of Governor Micheltorena's *cholos*. Tessa agreed with Gavin's judgment that an army of ragged chicken thieves was an embarrassment rather than a danger, and neither of them had shared the panic of some in Monterey during their August demonstration in favor of Micheltorena. But now there was a new element which made Tessa very uneasy.

Two foreigners, John Bidwell, an American, and John Augustus Sutter, the Swiss-born immigrant whose New Helvetia settlement was the rallying point for foreigners, had ridden to the capital with urgent news for Micheltorena. The supposedly secret nature of the news did not stop the leaks. A revolt was being planned against the governor by some prominent Californios.

Though she knew it was a callous attitude, Tessa didn't particularly care about the possibility of a revolt. There had been many in California's history, and the overwhelming majority of them had spilt more ink in proclamations than blood. There had always been sectional rivalry between the southern and northern parts of the country, and even stronger than that was the feeling against Mexicans, *de la otra banda*, of the other country, as Micheltorena was. The desire of native-born Californios to rule California was not new.

What did alarm Tessa was the idea of the foreigners such as Bidwell, Sutter, and their ilk becoming involved in any way in California's internal affairs. Everyone called each other cousin in California, and more often than not it was true to some degree. Bloodshed was therefore to be avoided at any cost. But the foreigners, even those married to *hijas del pais,* daughters of the country, were unlikely to feel this as deeply as the natives. And if the reports of the numerous new immigrants in the north were true, they were people with no ties to the Californios at all.

Tessa knew the plague of her thoughts came from uncertainty about Gavin and Indian. She dreaded their becoming embroiled in any conflict. Their lives in California were going so well now.

But nothing could dampen her joy in Gavin's return, and this time their reunion on the shore was warm and without interference. Even though November was beginning, the day was fair, a circumstance which Gavin claimed was only proper to provide a setting for his fair wife.

"You are being too gallant," Tessa teased. "Have you something awful to tell me? Did you throw all our profits overboard?"

"Suspicious wench." He kissed her soundly again. "You are more beautiful every time I see you. Perhaps I've married Lilith and should fear for my soul."

"It is I who should fear to have married a man so marvelously blind." She couldn't bring herself to talk of political matters yet, no matter how urgent, and put it off until Carmelita joined them for the evening meal.

She tried to introduce the subject casually, but the instant alertness on both of the men's faces told her that was futile. She told them what she'd heard, and she kept her voice calm until she described the two men who had brought the message to the governor. "It is not that they are harmful men by intent. They were entertained well here, and I met both of them. Señor Bidwell seems even a resourceful and rational man. There is no meanness in Señor Sutter either, but there is something perhaps more dangerous. His blue eyes are not like yours, Gavin. They are too full of dreams, a little mad. They glitter, and his cheeks look as if he always has a fever. I fear he is a
174

fanatic in his dreams of empire." Her voice trailed away. She didn't know quite what she was trying to say.

Gavin understood very well, and spoke kindly. "Indian and I are fairly reasonable men. We're not likely to borrow trouble we don't need. Micheltorena has been generous to foreigners. Sutter, Bidwell, and many others, including some of the local merchants, owe him a good deal." He gave a rueful laugh. "And from what I gather, the governor owes some tidy sums here and there. I suppose quite a few see it as mutual interest to keep him in power. He's really not disliked personally. It's that damn ragtail army of his. If he could just send them home, things would go a lot easier for him."

He kissed the worried line of Tessa's mouth and gave her a quick hug. "What the hell, maybe nothing will happen, as I've heard it so often does in California's politics."

Though Gavin held good-naturedly to his view, Tessa found it hard to believe in face of events. On the eighteenth of the month, Micheltorena issued a proclamation accusing the rebels of being horse thieves who should be tried as such, and warning that anyone foolish enough to join them would be treated likewise. Garbled reports did give the rebels credit for driving off government horses near Monterey and beyond to the Salinas Valley, and it seemed they had also seized what they wished of the guns and ammunition left at San Juan Bautista from the governor's summer sortie. It was difficult to discover exactly what was happening as one wild rumor chased another. But there was no doubting the governor's march from Monterey on November 23.

Tessa watched the man leave with nearly his whole force of one hundred and fifty men, and her heart pounded for fear that Gavin and Indian would find the procession irresistible. But Gavin eyed it cynically, and there was no admiration in his words. "They look like poorly made toy soldiers, and Micheltorena's pace will be no match for men on horseback."

Due to physical disabilities, the governor could not ride, and went everywhere in a strange vehicle not much lighter than a *carreta* and pulled by two men on horseback. Tessa

175

felt a sudden pity for the unavoidably amusing, even if pathetic, image the pompous official presented.

By the middle of December, the threat of civil war seemed to have been averted. There were no reports of fatalities; the governor had signed a treaty promising to send the battalion away; and the rebels were reportedly waiting peacefully at the mission of San José for the promise to be fulfilled. The governor's newest proclamation claimed that his good offices were in the main responsible for this pleasing turn of events. He chose to ignore the obvious fact that he had been outmaneuvered and defeated.

Tessa was not offended by Gavin's continued amusement regarding the whole situation. He and Indian stayed out of the whole thing, and that was all she wanted. They had even been careful to glean the best information available on the positions of the two forces so that they might avoid them both on the journeys they had made to Rancho Magnífico.

It seemed that Christmas would be peaceful after all, and Tessa turned her attention to the last feverish preparations. The one gift she wanted to give Gavin was beyond her control, and she had to swallow her disappointment every time she found time away from his eyes to work on what he would receive instead. She was still wondering how to send gifts to the Ramirez family when the problem was solved for her. Pedro arrived with a loaded pack mule and agreed willingly to take Tessa's offerings back with him. She hid her amusement when she discovered that the hatchet-faced *vaquero* could hardly wait to return to Rancho Valle del Mar. Monterey no longer held much fascination for him, at least nowhere near as much as a certain serving woman at the rancho did. Tessa could barely persuade him to rest one day before beginning the journey back.

She was astonished when she told Gavin and he did not laugh with her. Instead he held her by the shoulders and searched her face as he asked, "Do you want to go home? We can. We can leave right away and be in plenty of time to celebrate Christmas there."

She looked into the deep blue eyes darkened with anxiety, and her love for him and for the hurt child he was
176

at moments like this filled her until she was trembling with it. "My darling, my husband, home is a word without meaning except for you. I have told you this before. It seems I must say it forever to a deaf man."

The slow smile spread until it lightened the shadows in his eyes. "I hear you, woman. I hear you now."

Christmas had never meant much to him, but he was enchanted with Tessa's excitement over *la Noche Buena*. Her spirit could hardly have found a better place than Monterey to celebrate, he thought wryly, since the town which seemed to enjoy a constant fiesta was even more seriously bent on the pleasures of this feast day. The party she gave seemed to him as effortless and a lot more enjoyable than the ones they attended elsewhere. He realized he was having a difficult time avoiding the pitfalls of the doting husband.

They went to midnight Mass together, and in spite of his rejection of his harsh Puritan background, it made him uneasy. He felt dangerously stifled, and he concentrated on Tessa, finding that delight replaced every other emotion until he was hard put not to laugh aloud during the solemn ceremony. She had confided in whispers that she could almost bear to do this every day if the faithful were always so happy and the ceremony so beautiful. He watched her trying to emulate the practiced piety on other women's faces. She could hold the alien expression for only moments at a time before her excitement triumphed again in wide eyes vividly purple, in the delicate color in her cheeks, her whole body vibrating with joy.

Gavin leaned down to whisper wickedly in her ear, "I'm sure God is relieved that at least one person is enjoying His birthday party," and Tessa clapped her hand over her mouth to stifle her giggles.

After Mass they watched *Los Pastores*, the sacred drama of the shepherds, performed by a lively group of young people in bright costumes. The songs and comic incidents included in the performance added greatly to the fun even if they would have been impossible to find in the Bible.

Tessa had worked hard on her gifts to Gavin, Indian, and Carmelita, making everything with perfect stitches. Needlework had never been her favorite pastime, but

177

María had insisted she be as adept in it as in all other skills, and Tessa had finally found reason to be thankful for the long, weary hours of learning. For Carmelita she made a shawl much like the one María had given her, bright with flowers and birds worked in silk thread. For Indian, she had made a shirt, cut and stitched evenly to fit his broad form far better than any garment he possessed. To the Ramirez family, she had sent manufactured goods so scarce on the rancho—finely tempered hunting knives for the men, a new pair of scissors and some gay dress goods for María. To her father she had sent a ream of the finest paper she had been able to procure, knowing it was futile but still harboring a faint hope it would encourage him to return to his old scholarly pursuits.

But the best of her skill and love had gone into the poncho for Gavin. It was of the finest cloth, a deep, rich blue to accentuate his eyes, and she had worked the edges and the neck in gold thread in a pattern that appeared random until one looked closely and discovered the birds, beasts, and flowers curling into each other in a wholly original design.

They had insisted Carmelita join them, and the four made enough noise for double their number as the treasures were revealed. Ramón and the boys had sent a new set of reins to each of the men, and María had sent the daintiest set of undergarments for Tessa that she had ever seen. She held up the petticoat, exclaiming at the handworked lace that trimmed it, then caught sight of Indian's face and laughed at his discomfiture. "Don't tell me you've never seen one before!"

"Well, not one belongin' to a good woman," he explained solemnly, causing general hysterics and a sly, mocking look from Carmelita.

Carmelita gave Tessa a mantilla which Tessa modeled for the company, striking first an attitude of the utmost hauteur, quickly changing it to the coquette peeking over the edge drawn across her face. The women hugged each other, not only for the beauty of the gifts exchanged, but for the friendship they enjoyed.

But when Tessa saw what the men had given her, her joy deserted her as it had not done when she realized her father had not sent so much as a letter of greeting, prob-
178

ably being too unconscious to even realize what season it was. That she could bear; the men's gifts were far harder.

From Indian there was the most beautiful comb she had ever seen, of tortoise shell inlaid with silver, curved with strong teeth to hold it high on her head. And from Gavin there were three precious books, one in each of the modern languages she knew, English, Spanish, and French. As if the books were not rare treasure enough, the soft pouch of doeskin contained a necklace and matching earrings intricately wrought in gold and set with amethysts the color of her eyes.

"The books will begin our library. The jewelry is already part of history. It once belonged to a Russian woman to the north at Fort Ross, worn before that at the Tsar's court, or so I was told," Gavin explained happily, pleased with having found gifts so perfect for his wife.

He was stunned when she lifted her head to reveal her twisted mouth and eyes shimmering with unshed tears. She included Indian in her look, and her voice was small and tight with her effort to control its shaking. "The gifts are too fine, all of them. I gave you so little. You have given me the ransom for a queen."

Gavin stroked the rich embroidery of the poncho and said to Indian in a light, conversational tone, "I never had anyone spend hours making something beautiful just for me before. Never. Have you?"

Indian traced a seam of the shirt with careful fingers. "Naw, not even once before. Don't reckon I worth so much time an' love. Don't reckon you are either."

Tessa searched their faces, and she realized they meant it, that she could not have pleased them more nor shown her love better than she had. And her tears spilled over as she hugged first one and then the other, tears for these two whose lives had been so hard and lonely.

Only later when they went to bed with short hours left before the dawn did Tessa tell Gavin with soft, hesitant words of the gift she had wanted to give him.

By a sheer act of will he kept his body relaxed, his voice even. "The poncho will do for this year, thank you."

She giggled suddenly. "It is a funny comparison."

Not for the world would he tell her how glad he was she was not pregnant. His mind wandered back over the evening to recapture the quiet contentment, and a new thought struck him. "Tessa, how did you manage to buy what you needed for the gifts? I see the accounts regularly, and nothing indicated your purchases."

"Of course I didn't take the money from you and Indian to buy your gifts. That would have been stealing. I made a very good sum on the sale of two colts."

He heard the pride in her voice, and he was nonplussed. He wanted to shake her for the squandering of some of the promise of the herd and for her continuing refusal to regard the business as belonging equally to her. And yet, knowing how much she cared for the horses, he was infinitely touched by her gesture. Will and pride as strong as his own. His voice was a little strangled as he managed to say, "I'm sure I will be the only man in California wearing a poncho worth a palomino."

"Not quite a whole one." Her laugh was warm and husky as her fingers tangled in the soft hair at the nape of his neck.

They saw 1845 in with Indian and Carmelita, preferring that to the parties they might have attended. "I wonder what this year will bring," Tessa murmured softly, watching Gavin's face.

Gavin raised an eyebrow. "Are you still worried I'll support the governor?"

"Or fight against him, yes, I'm worried. I do not think the Californios will let him get away with the broken treaty."

"Then I'll make you a New Year's promise. I'll stay out of it. Not a hard promise to make, as I've no intention of getting involved anyway."

Even believing Gavin, Tessa was glad she had his word a few days later. On January 4, Micheltorena issued a new proclamation putting Monterey under martial law and entrusting *commandante de battalón* Don Juan J. Abella with its defense. Two days later the governor marched out of the town with most of his troops, hoping to effect a junction with Sutter before finding and crushing the rebel force.

Tessa shared the outrage of many Californios, even
180

while she doubted the wild rumor that credited Sutter with having two thousand Indians under arms marching with him. The fact that he would arm any Indians at all against a portion of the population when Indian attacks in the interior were one of the worst problems of the country's existence was infuriating. And in addition, he had a company of American riflemen with him. The deadly accuracy of the long rifle was legendary, and it was wholly an American weapon. It seemed impossible that the Californio tradition of bloodless warfare could survive in face of it.

Alvarado, Castro, Pico, and others—the rebel leaders— were among the most prominent men in California. It was the southern part of the country against the northern; it was the native-born against the outsider; it was California against the bungling, careless rule of stepmother Mexico. It was many things, but only one in Tessa's view—a foolish scrambling after danger and death that could have been avoided had rational thought prevailed.

Though he did not feel it as personally as she, Gavin sympathized with Tessa's distress and made every effort to make it easier for her, taking her for long rides away from the uneasy atmosphere that hung over Monterey. They made a couple of trips to Rancho Magnífico, keeping a sharp eye out for Indians and avoiding the two bands Gavin spotted, and Tessa was happy as she chose the spot for the house and visualized the gardens that would one day surround it.

She found contentment too in the progress of the herd Don Esteban had given them, and they went often to the rancho where the horses were boarding. Many of the mares were heavy with foals which would be born in the spring and were fast weaning their previous offspring.

"If we are fortunate, we will have half or more palominos again as there were last year among the foals," she told Gavin. His disappointed, "Only half?" confirmed his assertion that he knew little of horse breeding.

It pleased her that there was at least one useful thing she knew more about than Gavin. "Yes, half. You see, even breeding a palomino to a palomino is not sure for the color. Usually from such a match over the years a quarter of the colts born are chestnut, another quarter

181

albino, and half of them palomino. It is better to breed a palomino stallion to chestnut mares or a chestnut stallion to palomino mares because then you will have half chestnuts, half palominos, and no albinos, which see badly with their strange eyes and are not good tempered. But sometimes when there is a great stallion, he will sire more palominos than others do. Already that has happened here." Pride was strong in her voice.

"Don Esteban has been even more generous than I knew," Gavin said, thinking of the care and breeding that had gone into every animal of the herd.

"Do you think he will be all right?" Tessa asked hesitantly.

"Your great-grandfather is a wise and influential man who has no time for petty political quarrels," Gavin assured her firmly.

January faded into February, and the tension grew as one confused report after the other arrived. But Monterey had no intention of giving up her reputation as the most festive place in California, and Cascarone balls were planned for the eve of Lent as though civil strife did not exist. Ash Wednesday fell on February 12, and the balls the night before.

Tessa welcomed the opportunity to be gay. Following Carmelita's instructions, she filled goose eggshells with small bits of gold and silver tinsel and cologne, dividing them fairly with Indian and Gavin so that they too could go properly armed to the Larkins' Cascarone Ball. None of them had ever attended one such as this before, but Carmelita's vivid description had given them such a clear idea that Gavin wished privately he didn't have to attend anything so ridiculous, though he could not bring himself to disappoint Tessa.

Golden light poured from the windows of the Consulate, and music and chatter engulfed them as they walked in. There were lighted tapers everywhere, heavily laden tables of food, and generous glasses of wine, all typical of the Larkins' well deserved reputation for fine entertaining.

The Ramsays lost Indian and Carmelita in the crush, but they managed to hold onto each other while they greeted friends. People were enjoying themselves with
182

a will; this would be the last truly festive occasion until the forty days of Lent were over.

"It's awful," Tessa whispered, "but I can hardly wait to throw my eggs. I feel about five years old.' "

"So does everyone else, I think," Gavin commented drily, eyeing the weapons in possession of the guests and knowing there must be many more he couldn't see. He could see people watching each other surreptitiously, waiting for the right moment.

Shortly before midnight a young woman tiptoed up behind a striking-looking gentleman in military dress and cracked an egg over his head, showering him with tinsel and scent. He swung around laughing and returned the favor with his own weapon, and within seconds merry hell had broken loose. Tessa got Gavin and whirled away before he could retaliate, only to run into Indian who did the honors in the gentlest possible way.

There were shrieks of laughter, and the group broke apart into two armies, men and women, the men getting the worst of it as they ran out of missiles until some discovered that the ample supply of grapes on a food table would do as substitutes.

The air reeked of lavender, and Tessa was laughing so hard, she couldn't see to throw straight, but when the midnight church bells tolled, no one disobeyed the signal. The time for frivolity was ended. Lent had begun.

They thanked the Larkins and departed on foot, as was their custom though nearly everyone else had traveled on horseback even if they lived only a few streets away. They escorted Carmelita home first, and on the way, Tessa wrinkled her nose, sniffed audibly, and said innocently, "I never knew two tall Yankees could smell so sweet."

"I don't know, Indian, I just don't know. Some women are never satisfied. Here I've gone to all this bother to get rid of the horse, leather, and plain old sweat smell she's always complaining about, and she's still not pleased."

"Why, Gavin Ramsay, you liar! I love the scent of you. I've told you so a thousand——" she exclaimed, falling neatly into his trap before she could stop herself. She blushed furiously and was glad of the darkness as her three companions roared. "I deserved that," she admitted.

183

Later, in spite of all their efforts to wash it off, the sweet spice still clung to them. "Do you mind sleeping with a stranger for one night?" Gavin asked, and Tessa's eyes gleamed. "I'll trace the landmarks until I find something familiar," she murmured, beginning the journey.

Lent's bleak restrictions did not help to ease the taut atmosphere of the political situation. There were hostile demonstrations in Monterey, and toward the end of the month, on the strength of a rumor that Micheltorena had been defeated, a group of Californios outside the town demanded that Abella surrender the garrison and his authority. It was fortunate that the leader of the group, Gabriel de la Torre, was a reasonable man. Gavin went with the group of Yankee and native Monterenos to solicit his aid in avoiding an armed confrontation in Monterey, and Torre agreed to wait for more reliable news.

When Gavin returned to the house, he found Tessa waiting for him, eyes enormous, her body trembling as she hugged and patted him as though unable to believe he was unhurt.

"Honestly, you were foolish to worry," he assured her. "It was a very civilized conversation."

"I don't care!" she snorted. "If ever you go to battle, I will become a camp follower so that I can keep my eye on you."

Much to everyone's relief, news was not long in coming. In the first week of March, Andres Pico with a small group of men arrived in Monterey after forced marches. Torre put his men at Pico's disposal, and Abella now made no objection and turned his command over to Pico. Tessa was touched by Abella's behavior. He hadn't wanted a battle in Monterey and had simply tried to do his duty as a soldier.

Gavin pieced together what happened, and Tessa watched him struggling with laughter. "Micheltorena's progress was so slow, he lost quite a few men from sheer boredom on the way, and it seemed the two armies were never going to meet. But the Battle of Cahuenga was finally fought less than two weeks ago. Cahuenga is near Los Angeles, and there the two great armies faced each other. Then the Americans on one side realized there were Americans on the other side and vice versa.

184

Hell, most of them knew each other, and they had no intention of using their rifles on fellow countrymen. Guess right then they came as close to the Californio way as they'll ever get. They withdrew to visit. Of course, you can't have a war without casualties. It's been confirmed that the rebels lost a horse, and some believe the *cholos* lost a mule.

His restraint failed him, and the house echoed with the booming laughter of both men. "Oh, hell, Tessa, I'm sorry," Gavin choked, wiping streaming eyes, "but I'd have given just about anything to have witnessed the show. One horse and maybe a mule."

"Well, I hope it wasn't a good horse, and maybe it is untrue about the mule," she said with mock gravity, and then she was laughing with them. It was the purest joy to know that cousins had not killed cousins, to know that the deadly Yankees had not triumphed over the tradition of bloodless warfare.

When they had calmed down enough, he told them the rest. Micheltorena had surrendered and signed a treaty. Pío Pico, a Californio, was now governor. Micheltorena and his *cholos* would leave for Mexico before the month was out.

This time Micheltorena kept his word; he had no choice. The ship arrived in Monterey on March 19, and though the *cholos* were not allowed to come ashore, Micheltorena was, and he was treated with full honor and respect. He spoke with many of the town's leading citizens and even obtained statements in his defense. Tessa was most impressed by the behavior of his wife, Doña Josefa Fuentes. Bright, generous, and lovely, she had always been highly respected by the Californios, and she conducted herself with quiet dignity during what must have been a trying time for her. There was still enough strut left in Micheltorena to indicate that he continued to hold himself in high regard.

The exiles sailed on the *Don Quixote* in the last days of March, and as the ship left the bay, the guns of the *presidio* roared a full salute.

"I wonder what they do for you when you win?" Gavin inquired sardonically, and received a sharp elbow in the ribs from his wife.

Tessa could understand how silly it all was in his eyes, but at the same time, she felt a great swell of pride. No human lives had been lost, and no revenge had been taken. The few *cholos* who had wished it had been allowed to stay in California under terms of the treaty. Even Sutter had been detained and entertained in Los Angeles for only a few days before being allowed to return to his New Helvetia in possession not only of his previous rights but by all reports also entitled to the land granted to him by Micheltorena in exchange for the men who had marched with him in the abortive campaign.

Gavin watched the play of expression on Tessa's face as the *Don Quixote* sailed out of sight. "California has a generous heart," he said.

CHAPTER XVIII

Once Lent was over, the social season resumed with even more fervor than usual, owing to the presence of Louis Gasquet, who had arrived in March aboard the ship *Primavera* to serve as temporary French consul. Once she got over her initial shyness in the language she had not spoken for so long, and only with her father before that, Tessa found it great fun to converse in French with Gasquet. He was charming, sophisticated, and delighted by Tessa's interest in the places he'd seen.

The Ramsays were invited everywhere, and one of the invitations they could not refuse was for a day's festivities on the rancho where their horses were kept. The party was to go on for hours, and they were to stay overnight. Gavin thought it would be an enjoyable change, and he was hard pressed to understand Tessa's lack of enthusiasm, for which she offered no explanation.

They got an early start and arrived at a decent hour in the morning, but already there were scores of people, horses, and *carretas*, which had disgorged flocks of excited children with their attendants. Their hosts were a fine couple with some twelve children of their own, kind and hospitable. And still, Tessa's face didn't lose its white, tight-lipped expression. Her smile was only genuine when she discussed the palominos.

Once it began, Gavin understood. In the midst of the atmosphere of an hilarious picnic was more carnage than he had ever witnessed. The *ranchero* had ordered a *matanza*, a slaughtering, and it was as ritualized and graceful as a dance. Many of the wild cattle had been brought into the field by being lassoed and tied to a trained domesticated bullock which dragged them home more or less peacefully, solving the problem of transporting meat and hides too far in the warming weather.

The scene in the field was far from peaceful. Six *nuqueadores*, neckers, rode full speed on horseback through the field, their knives ready for the blow to the nerve at the nape of the neck each time they neared an animal, the cattle falling dead as if struck by lightning. They were followed by a swarm of *pleadores*, skinners, who stripped the hides from the carcasses with the easy skill of long practice. The *tasajeros*, the butchers, followed, cutting the meat into strips for drying, and in their wake came the women who gathered the lard and tallow into hide bags. And last of all came the sea of dogs, yapping and snarling over the rich feast of offal.

The noise was deafening. The cattle bellowed until the last one was dead. The Indian workers yipped and crowed. The dogs only shut up when their jaws were full. The spring air was tainted by the smell of blood.

Gavin had seen Tessa flinch the minute it began, and he had drawn her close to his side, whispering, "You needn't watch."

"I am the daughter of a *ranchero*, the wife of one soon to be. My cowardice is stupid. This is an efficient way of accomplishing a necessary task," she had answered stiffly, and she had watched it all.

The day wore on with singing, dancing, and daring feats of horsemanship. The color came back to Tessa's cheeks with the dancing she so loved, but Gavin grinned to himself with the knowledge that she would far prefer to have been with the competitors on horseback.

Makeshift tents had been erected for the overflow of guests who were to stay the night—if they ever wanted

187

sleep. Even after the long day, few except the children seemed tired. The dancing became livelier, and a new sound was added to the general din every time the musicians stopped playing for a short rest. Snorts and distant rumblings sounded from the moon-flooded field as if an army of giants were on the move.

Tessa was relieved when the chase began; it was better than waiting. And she was prepared for Gavin's response to the excitement. "You will be all right if I leave you for a while?" he asked hurriedly.

"Of course. Take care. It can be a dangerous sport." She knew if she asked him not to go he would not, but she wouldn't do that to him in face of the warm invitations he was receiving from the other huntsmen, who genuinely wanted the Yankee to join them. She trusted the more experienced among them to keep Gavin safe.

The night air was cut by the rawhide *reatas* being twirled and tested, and the horsemen rode off, leaving the older or more cautious men to tell inflated tales of their own exploits on the bear hunt.

Gavin felt wildly alive and exhilarated by the swift moonlight ride, and his concern that he and Diablo should acquit themselves well left no room for fear. It was the most severe test of a horse's courage and obedience to ask him to face one of his worst enemies. And Gavin knew it would be a test of his own skill also, for while he was capable with a lasso, he was nowhere as good as these Californios who had learned from the cradle.

Most of the men split off in pairs, Gavin with a *ranchero* a few years older than himself. Don Martín was the oldest in the group, steady, experienced, and perfectly willing to take the Yankee under his wing so that the lovely young wife should have no cause for mourning.

The field was not far from the house, and they were soon upon it. There were enough grizzlies feeding on the carcasses to offer sport to a far larger group than the riders who swept in among them.

Diablo snorted and shied in terror at the stench of dead meat and rank bear, but Gavin's heels, even without the spurs the others wore, and his hands steadied him, and he was obedient to the familiar voice.

"That one," Don Martín shouted, and together they rode

after the magnificent creature. It loped at good speed until it was near the fringe of trees on the border of the field, and then, as they closed the distance, it reared on its hind legs to face them.

"Damn! He's got to be over nine feet tall!" Gavin swore in admiration.

The massive head swung in rapid snakelike motions as the bear tried to gauge the strength and movements of his enemies, but he was already beaten. Don Martín's lasso flew out to snare the head and Gavin's was sure on a hind foot a split second later. Even Diablo behaved impeccably, keeping the rope taut as Don Martín's mount was doing.

They dragged the raging bear until they could tie him to a tree, and Don Martín gestured for Gavin to make the first kill. He recognized the honor and accepted it, moving in swiftly to finish the beast with his knife. Held by the strong rawhide and half strangled, the bear could offer no real defense, and in the moment of killing, Gavin was sickened. The head slumped limply in death, the long curved claws had lost their power to rend and crush. A constant hazard to livestock, a danger to men—it made no difference. The contest had been unequal, and there was no triumph in killing this way. Indian would never have done it at all; his respect for brother beast was too strong.

Gavin was thankful for the harsh light and shadow cast by the moon. Surely Don Martín could not see how he felt. He owed the man that much, the next kill.

Don Martín's words surprised him. "It is enough for one night's hunt. I have done this often before. My bones grow weary, but not so weary that I would not enjoy a dance with your most beautiful wife."

"Thank you," Gavin said quietly, and they left the wild sounds of the chase behind them.

Tessa saw him instantly when he returned to the dance, and she read all the signs. His hair still gleamed, his shirt showed damp marks, and the bleak lines of his face and the winter light in his eyes told the rest. He had been granted the privilege of the kill; he had taken it, but not all his scrubbing had relieved him of his distaste in the act. She was suddenly deliriously happy, and Gavin could not help but respond to the radiant smile she gave him.

She danced with Don Martín, who had only complimentary things to say about her husband, and when Gavin wanted to retire to their tent a short time later, she went without protest.

Not until they were lying close did Gavin try to tell her what had happened. Even the first few words were harsh, and Tessa stopped him with gentle fingers against his mouth. "You don't have to explain. I saw it in your face. Only a very strong man has the strength to despise cruelty in all its forms. Few are so strong. Many need to prove they are men even through it may hurt another creature." She thought of Luis and would not say his name. "And for some perhaps it rids them of the violence they might have used on their own kind instead."

"Tomorrow there will be worse, the same as in the Plaza de Toros in Monterey where I will not go. You hear still the sound of the bears, not dead and not far away." She paused and he did hear it—growls and shrieks of impotent rage. In the general noise of the festivities he had not sorted out these sounds as being anything more than the end of the hunt.

"They have brought in some of the bears and tied them fast until tomorrow. Then there will be fights between them and wild bulls. They will tie the hind foot of the bear to the foreleg of the bull to make the contest more even." Her voice was contemptuous. "Free to fight his own way, the grizzly bear is fierce enough to kill the wildest bull. Even the smallest children will watch and cheer; everyone will cheer. And there will be many wagers on the outcome. The long horns of the bull will rip and cut deep wounds in the bear; the strong muscles of the bull will shine in the sun and tear apart where the bear's claws have raked deep. There will be much blood."

"We won't be here to see it," Gavin said. "We are sorry we can't stay, but we have urgent business in Monterey."

His words were very nearly the same when they bade farewell to their host and hostess early the next morning, and Tessa could not have been more grateful.

The day after they returned was her birthday, and she had never been more excited about it than now. She had been appalled when she had learned that neither Gavin nor Indian had any idea of his birth date beyond a fair reckoning of the year. Neither one had ever celebrated one or had anyone celebrate for them. To Tessa, it was one of the cruelest deprivations of their lives, a confirmation of their lack of value to the people who had raised them, and she decided the twenty-fourth of April would serve for all three of them.

Pedro arrived with the usual bounty from the Ramirezes, and Gavin spent longer than usual talking with him, a fact that held no importance for Tessa until later. The day was simply too full for her to think of anything except the festivities. The gifts from Don Esteban arrived too—a bolt of purple velvet and more practical, four magnificent bullocks worth at least twenty-five dollars a head because they were trained to domestic tasks and the pulling of the *carreta*.

Tessa danced around the beasts, inspecting their strong promise, coming to a stop before Gavin, smiling up at him. "Now we need a . . . a *ganan* skilled with the *garrocha*," giggling because she didn't know the English words.

Gavin's eyebrow went up and he said to Indian, "I think she means a drover with an ox-goad."

Indian's own smile was broad, and he met his friend's eyes in perfect understanding. Though they loved her in different ways, this shared pleasure in Tessa was something they would never be able to explain to her. She would never understand how foreign and delightful was the image she presented—this lovely, slender woman who looked so delicately feminine yet rejoiced in the gift of these great, rough-coated work animals.

The letter from Don Esteban was simple. "*Feliz cumpleaños*, Tessa Ramsay," he had written. "The sea is no more beautiful than treacherous, trust in the land." His name was followed by the intricate flourish of his rubric, individual like all the others used by prominent men to prevent forgeries.

She showed the note to Gavin. "Don Eesteban is determined our rancho will claim us over the sea." She pointed to the rubric. "It is very amusing, is it not? As if someone else would send such a gift and pretend to be my great-grandfather." She paused thoughtfully. "You too

191

should have your own distinguishing mark. It is a thing of dignity. Even some Yankees have their own. I have seen Señor Larkin's."

Gavin's eyes twinkled. "My dear, even if I spent half the day as I've heard some men do penning my own fantastic design, my dignity would not be improved. I would still be nothing more than the Yankee rover you married."

"Thank God for that," she said without thinking, and laughed at the idea of Gavin's quick impatient body wasting half the day hunched over paper and pen for the sake of old custom.

He was glad of her laughter; it allowed him time to mask his emotions. Her frequent and spontaneous ways of expressing her love for him still had the power to shake him to the bone. And he found it no easier that evening when Carmelita joined them as Tessa's fellow conspirator, having known of the plan that took the men by surprise. She presented each of them with a bottle of the finest tequila from Mexico, and before either of them could say a word, Tessa followed with her packages for them.

"*Feliz cumpleaños* to both of you. I have decided this day will be for all of us from now on. Today I am seventeen. You, Gavin, today you are twenty-seven, so easy to remember, always ten years more than I have. And you, Indian, I don't know. I have not learned your age, but today you must confess."

He grinned sheepishly and shrugged. "I'm not so sure myself. Split th' difference an' call it thirty-two."

She kissed them soundly and urged them to open their parcels, but they were not content until they had brought out their own offerings to her. Indian had spoiled her again with the finest silk, more than enough for a dress in deep rose. Gavin gave her a pair of soft calfskin boots from Mexico stamped with gold and silver designs, dainty but strong enough to stand hard wear and protect against brush and snakes. And in one boot, she found a compass with a note: "May you travel safely in the direction you wish; and may we be fortunate enough to share the journey, always. I love you. Gavin."

To replace the ragged ones they carried on the backs of their saddles, she had given each of the men one of the justly prized black-and-white blankets woven by Indians
192

to the south. And in addition, to Gavin she gave one of the long, hard-to-obtain, double-edged knives, as deadly on the upstroke as on the down.

Their eyes met in perfect memory of their first encounter a year before, and Indian and Carmelita both looked away instinctively, not wishing to intrude on the intimate moment even though they did not know its cause.

Later Tessa played her guitar and sang, the others joining in when they knew the words, everyone having to take a turn when she played a catchy tune and offered the first impromptu lyric herself:

> My love and my friend,
> My tall Yankee men,
> Now home they are and home they'll be,
> Until they go once more to sea.

Carmelita had long experience with this form of entertainment, and her verse was gracefully turned into a thank-you for the evening. Indian, though he was shy about it, did very well, proving himself the possessor of a lovely bass voice and a sly wit which poked fun at Gavin's incredible luck in California. But Gavin capped them all, singing his words with mock seriousness:

> My own love, my wife,
> Gave me a sharp knife,
> She knows I can't bear the delight,
> Of nudes who bathe in my sight.

"Gavin Ramsay, I believe you've done this before!" Tessa laughed, and her cheeks matched the silk Indian had given her even though she knew the double meanings only made sense to her.

"You've done this before too," she whispered later, shivering at the lean beauty of the gold and dark image looming over her, illumined by the candles they'd left burning.

"I have, I have indeed," he murmured against her skin, tracing the sleek line from shoulder to breast. "But never this until you. My darling, if I live to be a hundred, I will still see you as I saw you a year ago today."

193

The flame was in his eyes, striking blue sparks in the flickering light, and she wanted to tell him how strange the idea was of his being an old man, so old, and she would be ninety, but the wanting of her body was stronger, and she lost the thought and the words in a shiver of pleasure as she guided him home and arched her body to take him deep.

Gavin awakened knowing several things at once: it had been one hell of a night; dawn was just filtering into the room; he'd hardly slept; he felt marvelous anyway; and the incredibly beautiful eyes in the incredibly beautiful face belonged to his wife who had obviously given some thought and a long stare to wake him up.

"If you want more of me, love, I fear you'll be sadly disappointed. I am now ten years older, as well you know," he teased, his hands already moving to belie his complaint.

Tessa slipped away, out of his reach. "I can't think when you do that."

His grin broadened. "I'll have to remember that. It's awfully early. Couldn't you have let me sleep while you thought?"

"Gavin, this is important, for both of us. It really is, for Indian too. We must think of the rancho, and more, we must begin to build there, or it will never be anything but the wild land it is now. It's no good this way, seeing it only now and then, and having our animals kept by others."

"You're right," Gavin agreed quietly. "I've been thinking about it too. I even spoke to Pedro about becoming our *mayordomo*, only with Ramón's permission to leave, of course. I think it will work out. It's a beginning at lease. Don Esteban will be pleased. Hundreds of miles away though he is, sometimes I get the feeling he's right here with us," he added wryly.

"That would be most embarrassing," Tessa laughed as she snuggled close again. "Enough thinking."

CHAPTER XIX

Never had the difference between the Californio and the Yankee way been clearer to Tessa than in the preparations the men made to make the rancho habitable. What would have taken weeks in the normal manner of the country they accomplished in days, patient but inexorable in their pursuit of what they wanted.

Indian was as dedicated to the project as the Ramsays, though he admitted to Tessa that he had strange feelings about it. "Th' Indian half of me don' believe land can be owned anyhow, an' th' other half remembers slaves work other people's land, don' own it neither. Not sure I believe any this happenin'." He seldom mentioned anything about his background, and Tessa was touched with the realization that the rancho was beginning to mean a great deal to him also, even if he was not yet sure of it.

They designed and registered their brands in the *libra de registro*—*el fierro para herrar los ganados* for signifying their ownership, and *el fierro para ventear* for selling the beasts. They figured carefully and procured *carretas* to move what they needed to the rancho. And they coped as well as they could with their main difficulty, which was in staffing. Even with the ample promise of food, clothing, and payment in goods, it was difficult to find Indians willing to live in the dangerous territory of their renegade kin.

Denial of the parallel between the status of the Indians in California and the black slaves in the southern part of the United States would have been useless, and Tessa did not attempt it. Nor did she claim ignorance to which she was not entitled. In his clear-sighted days, her father had been too good a teacher to allow such a comparison of human follies to pass unnoticed. It was not only morally wrong for a small, elite group to claim ownership of another people, it was tactically dangerous. Overlords had ever to fear being overthrown.

If the labor system in California was less obviously

structured in the buying and selling of human beings than the South, still the result was the same. The *padres* had in many ways, sometimes literally, captured thousands of Indians, ostensibly to civilize them and save their souls. Indeed, the first soldiers of the Church had been most dedicated and pious, willing to endure the worst hardships and even death for the sake of winning souls for their Savior. But despite the intent, the result had been the creation of a large, captive labor force whose lives were dictated even to the point of who could marry whom, if at all. And when the missions had been stripped of their lands and possessions, many of the neophytes had been absorbed by the rising rancho system and its labor needs and had been provided with fairly stable and comfortable lives, ill treatment being almost nonexistent. But there had remained a great number who had no work and few ways to survive. Many had simply died of neglect and white man's diseases. And many had fled to the interior to take on the characteristics of the fiercer Indians inland and to form bands of raiders who swept down on the ranchos to murder and pillage.

With his New England and morally rigorous Scots background, it had made Tessa's father uncomfortable to know that most of the people who worked on his rancho were little more than slaves. Tessa had shared his discomfort, but both of them had lived with it, and now Gavin, and Indian, who must have the most bitter feelings about slavery, would also have to accept it. The hard fact remained that there was no other work force available in the country.

Tessa took little part when the men discussed the situation, letting them come to their own conclusions, agreeing with their decisions. They would do their best to see that their workers received above-average food, shelter, clothing, and goods in payment for their labor.

As for the wild Indians, the bands of neophytes and those who had never been captives at all but who had learned to prey on the white man's plenty as the invasion of old hunting grounds continued, there was no way to know the exact situation they would face. The rancho might be left alone or it might be raided occasionally for the horsemeat the Indians favored above all other flesh.

197

Tessa tried her best not to consider that—the thought of one of the palomino's slaughtered for a feast horrified her.

If problems did arise, they would do their best to use the approach that had worked so well for Sutter in the north. He had greeted the hostiles with a smile and generously open arms, and they had responded well, working and hunting for him, receiving more of the goods they coveted than they would have gained by slaughtering the foreigner and his company.

The arrival of Pedro from Rancho Valle del Mar proved a great help. Ramón and María had sent him and two others with their blessings, and Pedro quickly proved himself capable of recruiting others, a fact that startled Tessa since he was the most silent, unobtrusive man she'd ever known. But then, she had known little of him on the rancho except that he was judged dependable by Ramón, and even now she learned there would always be a great barrier between the man and herself. He would serve her as well as he would serve Indian and Gavin, but they would never be friends as she had been with Ramón. To Pedro that would be like stealing something from the man who had been his superior. But she guessed that if she had children—she rephrased it firmly to herself—when she had children, Pedro would be there for them as Ramón had for her.

Thinking it over, she knew why he was willing to assume the risk of working at Rancho Magnífico, why he was putting such effort into collecting other *vaqueros*. At Rancho Valle del Mar, Ramón and his sons would continue the chain of command both by tradition and by capability; on the new land, Pedro would be the *mayordomo*. From that point of view, it was not difficult to see why he regarded his jump in position as a miracle worth working for, even worth leaving the woman who was now his wife. This he had explained with some diffidence and a great deal of pride. Don Esteban's priest had returned out of good conscience to perform several marriages and baptisms. Tessa had to hide a smile, thinking of how lost the priest must have considered the souls at the rancho to make the long journey again.

The other two *vaqueros* were also married, as was one

of the three additional men recruited by Pedro, but all had decided to wait until there were suitable quarters before bringing their families to the rancho. It was a gesture of protection, of not wanting their families exposed to danger they were as yet unable to judge. Whenever Tessa detected the same speculative gleam in Gavin's eyes, she was swift to point out they had discovered the land together. However, she could not accompany the men every time, as it was her charge to pack their household goods and to make sure the house was in clean and perfect shape for the return of its owners.

Carmelita offered space in her own home for anything Tessa wanted to leave behind should there be a lack of space or use for it in the wilderness. Even having ridden out and admired the beauty of the land, nothing could shake Carmelita's conviction that her friends were mad to be giving up the gaiety of Monterey for the dangers inland.

"I say all these words, but it is my selfishness which speaks," she admitted. "I will miss you all terribly."

"Maybe not so much. We will probably come visiting so often you will wish the rancho was farther away," Tessa teased to cover her own sorrow at the thought of losing the comfort of her friend's proximity.

By June, Gavin, Indian, and their workers had accomplished great things. The adobe bricks they were making on the site would take longer to cure and would be used for additions and expansion, but in the meantime, there was a little house of hewn wood with a hard-earth floor, a tiled roof, barred windows, and closely chinked walls. The wrought iron that was ornamental remembrance of more dangerous days along the coast was here a functional device that would make it harder for marauders to enter, as the tile of the roof was good protection should someone try to fire the house. This one had not one, but three rooms—a main one for cooking and daily living, a bedroom, and a small study where the accounts and books could be kept. Having expected to live in one room for some time, Tessa was delighted with her home. And not far away, a smaller version of it was taking shape for Indian's bachelor needs, it being well understood that he would eat and spend much time at the Ramsay's house anyway.

Even the long, low structure of the *Indiada* that would shelter the *vaqueros* and their families some distance in back of the houses was growing day by day, Indian and Gavin making sure it would offer as much protection against the elements and enemies as their own quarters.

They were conscious of being observed now and then, but Gavin's instructions were clear. No one was to offer any hostile action to any visiting band of Indians unless there was absolutely no choice. It was an edict that displeased some of the *vaqueros*, but they bowed to the *patrón*'s will, especially since he was supported by Pedro, their direct overseer.

They had discussed it, including Pedro in their council, doing their best to predict the natives' reaction to their presence. Their every action betrayed the fact that they were settling in and would be bringing in stock; no raiders would mistake that. And it followed that they had not been attacked so far because of this—to wait would mean greater spoils.

The day they drove the palominos, many of the mares with their new foals at their sides, and the small herd of cattle into the valley and onto the rancho, they knew their own waiting was near an end. The cattle were on loan from the rancho where the horses had been kept. It was a tradition started by the missions when their herds were vast and now carried on by some of the *rancheros* with their own numerous cattle. The loan of cattle helped friends build their own herds, and it was understood that the same number and perhaps a few more would be returned after a period of several years.

Gavin knew the advantage they had in the valley—there were many wild cattle long strayed from herds and unbranded that could be enticed to join the more domesticated beasts, thus building a large herd far faster than usual. He only hoped his plan for the Indians would work. The alternative was all too easy to visualize—the rancho stripped of every beast and a death toll horrible to contemplate.

Most of all, he wished he had stood firm about making Tessa remain in Monterey until this was resolved one way or the other. Then he admitted to himself that making Tessa do anything she didn't want to do was impossible, and she had been a good deal of help in driving the stock in, her skill and Amordoro's making easy work of bringing back strays.

He watched her now, and his face softened. She was pacing off land with one of the *vaqueros*, clearly seeing a large and productive garden.

His smile was gone abruptly, and his face was etched in hard, sharp lines as Indian rode in at top speed. "We got it, daylight visit, right behind me, 'bout thirty!"

Gavin barked his orders, warning everyone within hearing to have their weapons ready but to hold fire until he or Indian gave an order to the contrary. "Tessa!" he shouted, "Run for the house!"

She wheeled around, staring at him with wide eyes, not taking in what was happening for a moment because she had been so deeply absorbed in the future, but when she started to run, Gavin shouted again, "Here, by me," realizing it was too late. The Indians were riding into view, and it could only make them angry and uneasy to see someone disappearing into the house, perhaps to shoot at them from its shelter.

Tessa stood frozen at his side. She wanted to touch him to reassure herself they were both still alive, but she didn't want to interfere with his use of the rifle cradled with deceptive casualness in his arms.

As long as she lived, she would not forget the peculiar clarity of her perceptions when the fear of immediate death had passed. The Indians were alert and wary, but they were making no overtly threatening gestures. They had obviously scouted the rancho well and knew they far outnumbered its forces; they would never have come in daylight otherwise. She realized it was just as obvious that they had come in hope of gifts, more appropriately named bribes, preferring that to a confrontation with the long rifles, even in darkness. That they knew the dangers and accuracy of the rifles was clear—they eyed Indian's and Gavin's weapons constantly.

Curiosity had played an equal part in the visit, and Tessa had to stifle nervous giggles as she read the reaction showing in so many dark eyes. She had not until this

201

moment seen herself and the two Yankees as others did. Now she saw what an odd trio they made; the two tall men, the one so dark as to make the other, tanned as he was, pale by comparison, and herself, taller than most women. And added to that were her strangely colored eyes, the foreignness of Gavin's deep blue ones, and Indian's, which were reflections of the warriors' staring at him now. She saw the subtle gestures and understood them. They were being regarded as not quite human, perhaps the haunt of evil spirits, perhaps of good, but not quite human in any case. Tessa widened her eyes deliberately and met every sliding glance with a bold stare.

The easing of her terror and the dawning sense of her power finally allowed her to see the Indians clearly. They were a mixture of several groups, formed into one band for the sole purpose of survival by horse and cattle thievery. Some of them were of the short, squat build, flat-nosed, roundheaded, with broad-faced countenances familiar from many of the coastal and mission Indians and from most of the *vaqueros* and other servants she had known. But many were proof that the legend of the tall, graceful people first seen inland by missionaries was true.

They were magnificent. Broad-shouldered and muscular, they were given added height by being mounted on horseback, but even on foot, several would be six feet and taller. The oiled copper of their skin gleamed like metal in the sun, and scantily clad as they were, there was a lot of skin to see. Some wore strings of glass beads, and a few had feathered ornaments. All were armed with a knife or a lance, but only two had guns.

No wonder the Indians of the inland valleys and the eastern mountains were respected and feared; even the neophytes riding with them gained stature by the association.

Tessa's senses seemed to be working separately, and it took her a moment to realize that Gavin and the man who appeared to be the leader were conversing in stiff but intelligible Spanish. She felt a great surge of relief; it was an unlooked-for blessing. As far as she knew, there were so many, no one had ever counted all the dialects of the Indians in California. The man could have pretended

202

ignorance of Spanish; it was heartening that he chose the common ground.

She was achingly proud of Gavin. He was greeting the man with all the courtesy he would have accorded an admired acquaintance, as calm and grave as if nothing more than that were occurring.

The whole meeting could not have lasted longer than two hours, but Tessa lost all sense of time in the tension that made minutes stretch beyond counting. They fed their visitors, Pedro and another *vaquero* going to the house to bring out the food. Gavin's subtle orders made it clear that Tessa had special standing. He had not missed the uneasy signs of awe either, and he did not intend to let the Indians feel things were more natural by having Tessa take the traditional woman's role of waiting on the men. He had also seen the looks directed at her which had nothing to do with spiritual impulses, and he knew if she went inside and one of the braves followed her, all hell was going to break loose. He'd make sure of it.

Much to his surprise, he found himself liking his adversary more and more. He had an unexpected degree of shrewdness, seeing the promise of future gifts the instant it was offered. That he was willing to judge any white man as separate from others was a measure of his caliber, though Gavin knew his friend had much to do with this. Indian and Tessa were letting him do the talking, but he deferred to them constantly, letting the brave understand their status. The man was clearly fascinated by Indian, looking at him often with unconcealed wonder. Indian returned the compliment with his own grave stare.

Tessa was not neglected either. Gavin turned down the generous offer of pelts and horses stolen from other places, informing the man that he had paid far more than that and had no intention of giving up the comforts of his woman anyway. He blessed Tessa for her good sense. She made no indignant outcry, and only the heightened color in her cheeks gave any indication of her feelings about the matter. She knew as well as he did that the offer was a compliment to her husband's taste in women and to her own beauty.

The beads they had brought along for expressly this purpose were accepted, as were the hunting knives, adequate and shiny, if not the best. And the talk moved inexorably to the true object of the visit—the horses.

Gavin's smile was genial, but his eyes were not. He pointed out the special color and the fineness of breeding. He explained that the powerful elder of his wife's family had given them as a gift to be treasured and protected. "For these, we will fight. And though you are more than we are, we will take a fair number with us in death." He looked straight at the leader. "You will be one of the first. I will see to it. If it happens now or if you come at night, it makes no difference. I will see to it."

He let the small silence stretch for a moment before he added, "But we will be honored if you will accept one of the mares with a golden foal at her side." It was his final offer, and the man knew it.

Tessa had known that some sacrifice of the herd had to be made, and she had been steeling herself against protest, but now the words burst from her, clear and piercing. "They will serve you well and long. They will carry you swiftly. There are no finer beasts anywhere. You must care well for them. Shoot the deer for food. Let the horses live!"

It was not a plea; it was a command. The glinting black eyes bored into her, and she did not flinch but met his stare.

Gavin had gone rigid at her outburst, thinking furiously that if they lived through this he'd wring her neck, but as he watched the staring match, he realized Tessa was winning.

The pattern of sunlight on the copper skin shifted suddenly as the brave smiled, and Tessa felt the impact of him as a man, undoubtedly respected and well liked among his own people. She smiled back.

"You have my word," he said, and she thanked him.

She went with them for the choosing, and her admiration for the man increased, albeit grudgingly since she was losing something precious. He had an excellent eye for horseflesh. The mare he chose had fine, strong lines and a healthy palomino colt at her side. And the ache in Tessa's heart eased a little when she saw the way he handled the horses. Though many of the foals would be taken and trained for riding, the breeding stock was fairly wild, yet the man had a rope on the mare and had calmed the nervous threats of the stallion very quickly, using soft strange words and no violence, even as he had stilled the protests of his followers, who would have liked to have left with the entire herd.

Before the band wheeled away, the leader gave Tessa one more long look and smiled briefly again as he said to Gavin, "If you grow weary of trying to tame your wild mare, remember there is one who would pay well for her."

They were swiftly out of sight, guiding their mounts without bits or spurs, the newly acquired mare and foal moving off with them.

Tessa slumped weakly against Gavin, and she wasn't sure which of them was trembling the hardest with reaction to the long tension.

"God, what a day!" Gavin breathed, tightening his arm around her, tipping her head up to kiss her soundly. "If he'd upped that bid by a few head of horses and a few more furs, I might have taken it," he said reflectively.

"If I had had a little longer to get to know him, I might have been pleased to go with him," she replied.

Gavin's face was suddenly solemn. "He's quite a man. I know it was hard to see those horses go, but I think we've gained quite a bit. This is his territory, and we'll be a lot safer with his protection than without it."

"Strange, we don't even know his name," Tessa mused. "It was said a few times, I think, but it was such an alien sound, I could not learn it. I christen him 'No-Name'."

"Why, you little minx! You *did* fall for him!"

"How could I not? He is so much like you," she told him, her laughter easing the final knots of tension for everyone, and the air was filled with whoops of joy as they all grinned foolishly and congratulated each other on the calm handling of the situation. Even Pedro's normally solemn countenance was shining.

"Wish I could claim that No-Name for a relation," Indian chuckled.

They heard wolves howling at night sometimes, though more often there was the far less majestic yipping of the

205

coyotes. They had to be on guard against the depredations of the grizzly bears, and Tessa was sickened by the loss of a colt to a puma one night. They heard the wild screaming of the herd, but were not able to get there in time. The puma hadn't dragged the carcass far, and Gavin waited for it to return to feed the next night and shot it, noting with grim satisfaction that the cat had already received some good kicks from the stallion or the mare whose foal had been killed. There were undeniable hazards to living in the wilderness, but they all seemed slight now the worst danger, the threat of attack from their own kind, was past. No-Name was keeping his spoken and his implied word. Only Indian had seen him and his band since, having found himself suddenly in their midst while he had been out riding in search of likely looking wild cattle. He returned slightly bemused to the rancho, relating that he had even shared a meal and had found horsemeat rather tasty, if a little sweet, not thinking about what he was saying until he saw Tessa's stricken face. "Tasted like bay, not palomino," he assured her, essaying a weak grin. "An' besides, he tol' me th' mare an' th' colt are doin' fine, an' I take his word."

"I do too," Tessa said, succumbing to his woebegone expression.

She was enormously content with life on the rancho; it was much more the life she was accustomed to than the festival atmosphere of Monterey. She missed Carmelita and other friends, but nothing could lessen her enchantment with the progress made on the land. The horses were flourishing; the cattle were constantly increasing in number; and even with late planting, the corn and a few other staple crops were showing strong stalks under the bright sun. Not even the heat, which was so much greater than any she had known before, had the power to dampen her spirits. She wore her hat and gloves when she was outside; she kept herself and her clothing immaculate no matter how tired she was; she used the concotions of flowers and herbs to keep her skin soft and sweet-scented; and she gave thanks daily for the lessons María had given her. And never suspecting the effort it took, Gavin marveled that he never found Tessa anything but cool, neat, and soft with the scent of flowers, a willing delight for his body and his soul.

The women would be coming to the rancho toward the end of July or the beginning of August, and though it would make her work load lighter and would relieve the *vaqueros* of chores they considered women's duties and were embarrassed to do, Tessa was secretly glad she would have time to settle in before they came. She hated to admit it even to herself, but she was apprehensive about training a staff to run Rancho Magnífico as smoothly as María had managed Rancho Valle del Mar. She supposed she'd muddle through.

Her greatest concern was for Gavin and Indian. They were working so hard, they scarcely had time to draw breath and were totally exhausted by sundown. One night Gavin grinned wearily at her and asked, "How long has it been since I made love to you?" and was asleep before she could answer.

Toward the end of June, just when things seemed to be settling down, they received word that the new cargo was in. Tessa was all for having both of them go, insisting she could now handle things at the rancho until they straightened out their business in Monterey, could even manage if they were both still needed for the coastal trips. But the men had already agreed between themselves that Indian would go to Monterey and take the ship on its first run and probably continue the trade after that, sending for Gavin if he needed him. Both had learned a great deal the year before about getting through the bureaucracy that hampered business at every turn, even as they had discovered the best stops for trade and the shrewdest ways to buy and sell without ever breaking the rules of courtesy. And their connection with Don Esteban was an undeniable asset.

Indian admitted frankly that he was getting the best of the deal, since he would spend days doing little more than watching the shoreline while Gavin would be working all day long.

Tessa hugged him fiercely before he left. "*Vaya con Dios*, my friend. We'll miss you. And do not hesitate to send for Gavin if you need him."

CHAPTER XX

He watched them from the trees. He had been watching since dawn, and the day before he had watched. It was unfortunate they had built in the old way, in a clearing that offered no shelter for approaching enemies. He couldn't hear what they were saying, but it didn't matter, he could see them well enough. The man he had sent in had been accepted. He would know very soon now if his plan would work. He had known Teresa María for a long time, long enough, he was sure, to judge what she would do. If he was wrong, he would have to change his strategy, nothing more.

He hissed at one of the men behind him to be quiet. In case their moral outrage was insufficient, they were being well rewarded to help revenge the supposed injustice he had so carefully elaborated. He rubbed the muscles of his twisted arm. It was always more painful when he was tense. Over a year now, and it would never be right. It would grow worse, more twisted, more useless, because the bones had been shattered and inadequately reset, and the muscles were warping with the bones. Over a year now, and time past to punish them, not swiftly but with exquisite attention to drawing out the pain and humiliation. It gave him pleasure, deep and sexual, just thinking about it.

He waited until he saw the Yankee taking leave of his wife before he withdrew with his men to a safer distance where there would not be so much chance of discovery. Teresa María was staying at the rancho; it was exactly what he wanted. He knew enough now—where the horses were kept, how many *vaqueros* these were. All that remained was the waiting.

The word from Indian was a shock. The Ramsays hadn't heard from him since he'd left and had assumed all was going well. And now this short verbal message—trouble with the authorities, would Gavin please come to Monterey. The messenger was no help. The large, dark man had given him the directions, that was all, but perhaps it was important since he had been paid extra to ride during the night.

Gavin wanted Tessa to accompany him, but he had to bow to her logic. At least one of them should be at the rancho, and more important the mare she had been worrying about for weeks still had not foaled. The *vaqueros* should have no trouble protecting her since the threat of Indian attack was past.

He kissed her thoroughly before he mounted Diablo. "What am I supposed to do at night in Monterey?" he asked, deviltry in his eyes.

"You're supposed to miss me dreadfully and sleep alone," she shot back. "Besides, last night should have left you in need of a few nights' rest."

He ignored the watching messenger as he kissed her again. "It should work that way, but it doesn't. The more I have of you, the more I want. You are a witch, just as I suspected from the first," he said softly, and she held onto him for a moment before she pushed him away playfully. "If you don't get started, you're going to have a difficult time getting there. Give Indian and Carmelita my love. *Vaya con Dios.*"

She watched him out of sight, and he turned to wave to her at the last moment. The messenger left a few hours later when his horse had been fed and watered and he himself had been politely served a hearty meal by Tessa. She was glad to see him go. She had taken an instant dislike to him. His words had been brief and courteous enough, but she had caught him staring at her several times as if he could see her stripped bare, something entirely different from the appreciative looks she was accustomed to from most men. And for a hireling, his speech and hands were strangely smooth, his whole aspect high bred despite his dishevelment from the long ride. She was thankful Gavin had been too preoccupied with Indian's need to notice anything amiss, otherwise, he would undoubtedly have delayed his journey until he could make sure the man rode out with him.

Gavin pushed Diablo hard. Indian would not have sent for him unless there was real cause. He must just be back from the first trip, which could only mean some new bureaucratic ruling had been handed him. It was odd, since it seemed the outward voyage had been allowed. Gavin fretted about it the whole way and hoped it was something that could easily be cleared up. He already missed Tessa and wished she were riding beside him. If he had to stay in Monterey for more than a few days, he'd send for her, and to hell with the horses and the rancho and everything else.

He covered the whole distance in one day, arriving in the town in the glow of the long summer light. He saw the boat swaying peacefully at anchor in the bay and went to Carmelita's house, sure that if Indian wasn't there, there would at least be word of him.

Carmelita answered his knock, and his nightmare began. Indian was there with her, and both of them were astonished to see him.

"What you doin' here? Don' trust me with that little ol' boat? Everythin' went fine. I goin' ride out tomorrow to—" Indian stopped abruptly. He saw the grayness in Gavin's face and the pupils of his eyes shrink to tiny black points; he saw the way he moved to sit down, shaking like an old man. "Sweet lord, where's Tessa?" he breathed.

"At the rancho, waiting for a late foal," Gavin croaked, and he told them the rest, the words grating against his dry throat.

"Didn't sent no one for you, no reason. Mebbe it's jus' a mistake," Indian offered uncertainly.

"The horse was wet, just wet, there wasn't any foam," Gavin mumbled, ignoring him. "I didn't know until now what bothered me about the messenger. And his hands, too smooth and clean." He came to enough to see their blank stares. "Don't you see? Not from Monterey. The horse, doused with water and dirt for good measure to look like he'd come a long way. He hadn't. Whoever sent him was right there. *Is* right there." He shuddered as he stood up. "Got to get back."

Carmelita grabbed him, sinking her nails into his arms. "You'll eat and drink first. It won't help her if you drop dead on the way back." She turned to Indian. "Saddle your horse for him. Diablo must be all in. He's got to go back. We'll follow on the best horses we can find."

Indian didn't protest her orders. As much as he was beginning to understand, he knew she understood more for some reason.

She realized Gavin was in shock from the long ride coupled with his overwhelming fear for Tessa, and she took full advantage of it, making him eat and drink before she dealt the final blow. He was finished and rising to go before she spoke.

"It is partly my fault. I never suspected. The day after Indian left on the ship, a man came looking for Tessa. I see now he must have asked in many places to know to come to me. He called her Teresa María and mentioned her great-grandfather. He claimed to be an old friend who wished news of her. I told him, as I am sure everyone else did, that she was happily married to a Yankee and living on a new rancho in the Great Valley. He was well mannered and high born. I saw him in the town a few times after that, so he must have spent much time asking many people about you. It does not matter, the name he gave me. I think you will know his true name. He looks much like any other son of a wealthy don except that he is a cripple. His right arm is useless."

She shrank from the blazing fury on his face and the snarl of a name—"Luis!"—and then he was gone.

The day was unbearably hot, hours too long, and uneasy in its stillness. Tessa knew her miserable judgment of it stemmed from Gavin's absence. She had been without him for days and nights the summer before, and she would have to bear it again if Indian needed him. But it was harder now. She was more used to having him with her; and she loved and needed him even more than she had then. She wished she had gone with him, but then she admonished herself. It was right that she had stayed on the rancho. The mare she had been watching with such anxious eyes seemed in worse condition than ever. All the others had foaled long since, and even if this one had bred late with the stallion, her burden was weeks overdue by the look of her—belly so distended, milk dripping

211

from her swollen bag, head drooping. Tessa left her with the herd, but checked on her constantly. As soon as the mare showed signs that labor had begun, they would move in to help her. Tessa saw her own guess that the foal was dead reflected in Pedro's tense face. Even though it was an act of nature beyond his control, he would consider any loss of stock a blot on his record of stewardship, a sin made worse by the absence of the *patrón*.

The day wore on, and the only relief in sundown was a slight easing of the heat as the shadows stretched over the land and a small breeze began to blow down the valley. At least they would have a good moon tonight.

They planned carefully. Pedro would not tolerate having Tessa take a shift to ride out and check on the mare, but he promised he would send for her immediately if the birth had begun. They would not keep a constant vigil. The mare was not a pet; she was a half-wild and private creature like the rest of the animals in the *manada*, and she would be better off beginning her labor alone, without having to keep a nervous eye on the humans.

Tessa stood outside for a while, letting the air cool her skin. The wind was blowing harder now, summer gusting without a hint of moisture. She saw Pedro and another *vaquero* go out and come back. Nothing yet. She went inside and paced restlessly, wondering what Gavin was doing. She was sure he would have arrived in Monterey by now, and though he would be very weary, it would be pleasant for him to see Indian and Carmelita. She hoped they missed her as much as she missed them. She brushed out her hair but remained dressed. Surely whether it was dead or alive, the mare must relieve herself of her burden soon.

She left the door slightly ajar, and even when she picked up her guitar to ease her tension, she stilled the strings often to listen for the summons that would come over the wind.

The rumble of thunder, it made no sense, and she froze in total confusion for an instant before she was outside screaming for Pedro. The horses swept by on the outer fringes of the clearing, turned to bronze and silver by the moon. She saw darker shapes driving them, and she heard the high-pitched yipping of the raiders.

Pedro and the other *vaqueros* were out, grabbing for their own nervous mounts, Pedro yelling at her to go back inside and bar the door. She didn't argue, not wanting to delay his pursuit. There was no danger here; the raiders would stay with the horses they were stealing. She would get her rifle and Amordoro and follow. To lose the herd was unthinkable. And she would not believe No-Name had broken his word until she had proof of it.

She ran for the house. "Rifle, then Amordoro," the words were an eerie chant in her brain.

He grabbed her as she entered the house, his arm an iron band around her, lifting her off her feet. She screamed in terror and clawed at the arm, wrenching her body so desperately that he lost his hold. She saw the cruel white planes of his face in the moonlight. "Luis, bastard, horse thief!" She continued the spitting list in Spanish, using every terrible word she knew, her hands curved into talons ready to tear at his face. He only had one good arm, she could see that now; it would give her some advantage. Then she saw the others, three of them, and she knew it was hopeless.

She quickly learned why he had her gagged so quickly; it had nothing to do with his excuse that there might yet be one of her *vaqueros* prowling around. He feared his men might believe her if she had a chance to speak. His lies washed over her in a sickening flood. Here was the woman who was a traitor to her own people who had once been his intended bride. Here was the woman who had instead gone off with two Yankees, one of them no better than a beast, a Negro. Here was the woman who had encouraged the savage attack on himself that had left him crippled. Here was the whore who with her two men was growing rich and strong by stealing from the true Californios. Tonight she would get what she deserved.

It went on and on, and her eyes searched wildly for a familiar face other than Luis's. Two of the men were strangers to her, as hard-eyed as Luis, the sweat of lust already oiling their faces. The other was the messenger.

She went on fighting even after they had stripped her and tied her to the bed, pulling against her bonds, arching and twisting her body helplessly.

213

Luis took her first, and she moaned and choked against the gag at the tearing pain of his entry.

Her mind refused to stay with her body after that. It swayed and drifted, taking note of the obscenities being done to her flesh, noting even the separate pains of the tight bonds and the pulled joints, but refusing to believe fully that any of it was happening. One of the men went to a lot of trouble to indulge his preference when he raped her, turning her on her back again and retying her when he was finished in courtesy to the next, who did not share his taste. Was he the second or the third after Luis? Her mind worried the question as if it were terribly important to know the answer. There was a space of blessed darkness, but she couldn't even hang onto that. First and last, Luis, privilege of the leader.

They were finished. One wanted to kill her. She was, after all, a witness. They all laughed at that. Another wanted at least to cut the pretty face to remind her should she forget. No, she might bleed to death before the Yankee —he corrected himself quickly—the Yankees found her. She must be alive for them. The rest of the plan would never work otherwise. It was Luis speaking, Luis who wanted to get to Gavin through her, not just to kill him, but to draw the process out with as much pain as he could cause. She knew that with a clarity nothing else had. She drifted in the dark again, drifted in and out, praying that no matter how horrible it would be to have him see her thus, that Pedro would return and find her before Gavin did. If only the knowledge could be kept from Gavin.

The horse Gavin had borrowed was like all the other mounts Indian had had—big, raw-boned, and strong to carry the huge man. He didn't have the fine carriage or fiery speed of Diablo or Amordoro, but he carried his rider at a steady, unfaltering pace all through the night.

"Just let her be alive." Even when Gavin had forced himself to quit repeating the words aloud, they went on echoing around him.

He rode into the rancho shortly after dawn, and the ominous stillness pounded against him. His last hope had been that Pedro and the *vaqueros* would have offered a
214

strong enough defense to keep Tessa from harm, but there was no sign of them.

He was sobbing her name by the time he was inside the house and his voice rose to a scream when he saw her, bruised and spread-eagled on the bloodstained lace of their bed. He believed she was dead as he cut the leather thongs that bound her and removed the gag, believed it until she moaned a feeble protest and opened her eyes thinking to see Luis, thinking it was all beginning again.

He cradled her in his arms, his grief and rage making wrenching animal sounds deep in his throat. She shuddered and tried to pull away. "I . . . am filthy. Must get clean. Don't touch me." Every word was a deliberate effort, but she could not begin to tell him how she felt, beyond the pain, being filled with the slime of Luis and his men.

Gavin paid no heed to her command. He gave her water for her parched throat. He massaged her arms and legs until she could move them again. He bathed her and salved and bandaged the livid cuts on her swollen wrists and ankles. He brushed the tangles from her long hair. The soiled bedclothes and the dark streaks he had washed from her flesh gave evidence she had bled from the attacks, but the amount was less than it might have been, and she was no longer bleeding, giving Gavin at least some small comfort that she did not have serious internal injuries. She kept her head turned from him and her eyes closed while he ministered to her, and he knew it was from the shame she felt at his discovery of all that had been done to her.

He dressed her in a fine white nightgown and put a robe on over it, receiving no more help than if she were a child's doll. He carried her into the main room and sat down with her on his lap. He stroked her hair and traced the soft curve of her cheek for long moments before he gently but firmly tipped her head up. "Open your eyes, Tessa, look at me."

He looked into the shadowed, desperate eyes, seeing even the splendid color changed to cloudy gray, and he had to swallow hard before he could find his voice again. "I know it was Luis and his men." She shivered, and he held her tighter. "They raped you. You will never forget it. I would not expect you to. But they did it. Luis did it.

215

It is not your shame, it's theirs. And at the very least, Luis will pay with his life. It makes a difference to me only because you have been so grievously used. It makes no other difference. Do you understand? You are my woman, my love."

She understood more than he. She believed his love unchanged by what had happened to her, and that was balm to her spirit, which was even more bruised than her body. But nothing mattered as much as the fact that somehow he knew it had been Luis, and unknowingly he was going to do exactly as Luis wished. She didn't have the words to dissuade him, but she burrowed close, holding onto him. If only she could do that until he no longer wanted to go after Luis, until it was too late. She held onto him drowning, knowing it would never be too late until Luis or Gavin was dead, not knowing what else to do.

Pedro found them first, and Tessa saved him. She had forgotten he existed until she heard his hail as he rode in. She heard Gavin's growl of anger too. "He ought to be dead. It's the only excuse. I'll have him off this place in two seconds."

"No, Gavin, please. I couldn't bear for him to know. It wasn't his fault." She pleaded quickly, desperately. "We had no idea the horses weren't the only reason, but even so he warned me to get back inside. It was just too late." Her voice shook as she finished.

Gavin sighed wearily as he put her from him and went to greet his steward. Her words were just, but what he really wanted was to vent his fury on someone before he exploded with it.

Pedro was obviously confused at having found Indian's horse before the house, the lathered coat drying stiffly without a rubdown, and his confusion did not lessen when Gavin stepped out to greet him.

His swarthy face paled visibly. "Doña Tessa, she is all right?"

"She is all right," Gavin lied. "I had a sudden hunch that messenger was not from Indian, so I came back. The horses?"

It was no wonder Pedro had come back so late. The others were still on the way with the herd. Pedro had ridden ahead with the news. They had driven off the raiders, white men as far as they could see, not Indians. Pedro was sorry they had not killed or at least captured the men. But it had been a task to gather the herd. The stallion would be all right, but he was lame. Perhaps he had fallen. The mares must have panicked then, and it had taken much looking to find them all.

Pedro crumpled the brim of his sombrero nervously, and Gavin felt the first stirring of sympathy for him. "Don Gavin, there has been sadness tonight. One of the colts, the race was too swift for him. He broke both of his forelegs, and I killed him quickly for his suffering. And the mare who was heavy with life, she too is dead. But I took the foal from her body with my knife. It is a palomino and lives, a large, fine stud colt grown beyond birthing time. I think the mare who has lost her own will take this one to raise at her side."

"You've done a good night's work," Gavin said, and he meant it. "Tessa had a worrisome night waiting for news of the horses. She is very weary. But when she is able, I know she will want to see the new colt. In the meantime, Indian and Carmelita will be riding in shortly. Please make sure there is enough food ready for them, and please take care of Indian's horse now."

"And food for you, Don Gavin," Pedro ventured hesitantly. "You have had a long journey." He knew something was terribly wrong. Gavin's words made no difference. He could see it in the *patrón*'s eyes and in the lines of his face, a man still young who suddenly no longer looked young. And he had orders to feed the other *patrón* and the friend, a task always performed by Doña Tessa. His dread was greater than his curiosity; he hoped he never would find out what had caused this change.

Gavin dragged himself back into the house, his body protesting ever more vigorously the long hours of hard riding without rest. He told Tessa about the horses, and she nodded in acceptance. He wished she'd scream or cry, anything to let the poison out, but he realized the curious blankness settling over her was protective and must not be tampered with until it had run its course.

Her eyes narrowed in an attempt to focus on him. Her

217

voice was slow and slurred as if she'd been drugged. "You look so weary. Must rest. There is food."

For answer, he settled down again with her in his lap, and when Indian and Carmelita found them, they were both asleep. The two friends had been greeted by Pedro, who had told them his part of the night's work and had added that Don Gavin was with Doña Tessa. They had been wise enough not to betray their knowledge of Luis by asking foolish questions.

For a moment they thought their prayers had been answered and no harm had come to her, but when Gavin awakened and raised his head to stare at them, the illusion was shattered. And the tight fetal curl of Tessa's body against his was plainly no relaxed sleep but a drawing inward from a consciousness too painful to be borne.

It was Carmelita who took charge while Indian struggled to regain control of himself. Gavin could not bear to look at him. He had never in all the long years of knowing him seen him weep, but now the dark face glistened with tears, and the broad chest heaved as he struggled to breathe without sobbing. He fled outside.

"She will be more comfortable in bed," Carmelita whispered, and Gavin shook his head. "No, not yet. Take the linen and burn it, all of it," he ordered. He didn't bother to whisper; he had felt Tessa stir.

Carmelita asked no questions and had them all answered when she gathered up the lace and fine linen Tessa had been so proud of. She took them out to Indian, asking that he burn them at his house, away from the prying eyes of the *vaqueros*, who could think him crazy for a summer fire.

Indian had mastered his grief in the only way he could. It pulsed in him now, changed, a clean, raw hunger for vengeance. When he knew enough, the man would die.

He took Carmelita's arm. "I have a bottle, an' I think we both needin' a drink. Come with me."

"She's awake, I think."

"So much better reason. Give her time to face us."

Carmelita went with him obediently, waiting only until she was inside to scream against what had been done to her friend before she let her grief overwhelm her.

"They're gone, but they'll be back, and you can't avoid
218

them," Gavin said gently. "They're here because they love you almost as much as I do."

His victory was a futile one. She insisted on getting dressed, hesitating only a moment before she went into the bedroom. She put fresh linen on the bed, fussing with it until there were no wrinkles and everything was perfectly straight. All her movements were stiff, laborious, and obviously painful. And when Indian and Carmelita entered the house cautiously, she greeted them with bright, blank politeness as if they'd just called for tea and nothing at all had happened. Gavin suffered it all without knowing what to do.

Pedro brought food from their stores and hurried away from the tense atmosphere in the house. Tessa insisted on preparing the meal, though she allowed Carmelita to help, and though she pressed food on everyone she herself ate none.

The day faded into the long evening and another meal, and the three were paralyzed by Tessa's behavior and their own weariness. And then Indian finished it. Normally reticent and unwilling to trespass, he could bear no more. He stopped her in one of her vacant courses of the room. He held her by the shoulders, his huge body towering over her, his eyes demanding she meet them with her own. "Chil', don' do this to us, don' do to Gavin. You half his heart now. What he do, you leave him this way? Th' pain is his also, you not comfort him?"

Her tears were scalding as she hugged Indian convulsively, and then she was in Gavin's arms, and the others had left them, and she went on weeping and choking for breath, mouth twisted with the ugliness she was telling.

He heard her out without a word of his own, simply holding onto her until the storm had quieted. And when he took her to bed, she made no protest against being there. Even in his sleep, he cradled her as if she were an injured child, and if she chose never to be a woman again, he would not blame her.

Only Carmelita had seen the panic in Tessa's eyes when Indian had broken her control. Control it had been far more than shock, a deliberate, planned act. Carmelita slept badly, worrying the problem even in her dreams until

Indian drew her close, whispering, "There now, it been a long, bad time, but she alive. Sleep peaceful now, Lita." She smiled and relaxed at his use of the nickname none but the two of them had ever heard.

CHAPTER XXI

Tessa was stiff, sore, and bruised, but that was all. She wasn't ill as she had been when she lost the baby. Mentally she was all right too as long as she blocked the hideous images of that night from her mind. She didn't need Gavin's constant care, and he knew it. Kind and attentive though he was, she could feel him getting ready to leave, and she was terrified.

She told Carmelita first because the woman asked her point blank. "My dear, you're up to something. You are afraid, and I don't believe it's all from what happened to you. What is it?"

"Luis," Tessa admitted dully. "He wants Gavin to come after him. What he did to me was only to make sure of it."

Carmelita regarded her gravely, knowing little more than that Luis was the man who had lost Tessa to Gavin and had punished Tessa so cruelly for his loss. "Then he is a madman. Gavin will kill him."

"He is mad, but he is equally clever. He would never fight Gavin man to man. He will lay some trap, perhaps with the same men he brought here."

"Then you will warn him."

"I will, but do you believe it will make any difference?"

"No," Carmelita admitted. "Nothing will make any difference. Gavin is a man of honor, a fierce man. Such men have few choices. They must always do as honor bids them. Gavin will not rest until he has his revenge."

"This I know, but he is little use to honor or to me if he is dead," Tessa said bitterly.

Not even Indian could dissuade him or convince him to allow his friend to go with him. They nearly came to blows over who should have the privilege of tracking and killing Luis. But Indian had to bow to Gavin's stronger right. And Tessa's warning was received not better than she had expected. The blue eyes were remote, glittering coldly with anticipation of the kill. "Thank you, my love, I go forewarned," he said, and she raged at him desperately. "You still don't know him! You still have no idea of how evil he is, and how powerful. You are doing just as he wishes."

"Then he is a fool who wants his throat cut," Gavin said, his smile thin and unpleasant. He could not blame her for believing overmuch in Luis's ability to harm.

Everyone fell in with his plan. They had no choice. He took command and held it. He would take Carmelita back to Monterey, pick up Diablo, and begin his search. Indian would stay with Tessa on the rancho.

Tessa argued no more with him. She was cold and sick with despair. She would never see him alive again. Luis would make sure of it. She clung to Gavin fiercely for a minute and then stepped back.

"No 'Vaya con Dios'?" Gavin asked softly, and she shook her head. "I doubt God goes with those who ride for revenge."

Carmelita put her arms around Tessa and whispered as she hugged her in farewell, "I will do my best to slow him down."

It took Tessa twenty-four hours to convince Indian that she would accept nothing less than following Gavin, with or without an escort. Nothing short of holding her prisoner would stop her, and he wanted to follow as much as she did. But he made her tarry long enough to pack carefully selected supplies.

"We need nothing for a dead man," she protested grimly, and Indian snapped at her, because he was thinking the same thing. "Your bones, my bones, say different things, dead, alive, so different things." He prayed the lie was true.

Carmelita had been listening for them, and she was outside before they dismounted. "He's twelve hours ahead of you in spite of my reluctance to ride too fast and the time he spent picking up the trail. You have one of two choices. If you plan to go on tonight, I won't give you one bit of information; you can waste time discovering it on your own. If you promise to rest here for the night, I'll tell you everything I know and what I suspect. What will it be, Tessa? You look ready to fall out of the saddle."

Tessa straightened her back deliberately, but it was true. She ached all over; she had given up trying to think or see clearly hours before, and Indian's obvious worry about her, now strengthened by Carmelita's, was an added burden. "All right, we'll stay," she agreed wearily, and she let Indian lift her down from the saddle and carry her inside.

Carmelita made them eat first, and then she told them. "The man left no doubt about where he was going. He meant to be followed, just as you said, Tessa. He went to Montejo's rancho, two days' ride northeast from here. I do not know whether the other men were still with him or not, but it matters not. There will be others there."

She looked into Tessa's shadowed eyes. "I may be very wrong, but I think I know what this Luis is planning. I am with the many who know the English or the Yankees will take California. It will not be long. And like many others, I am only a little saddened by it. We have long been ill served and ill protected by our government. Perhaps a change will be for the better. But there are some who fear and hate the Yankees more than anyone else. Montejo is one of them, and he has friends. I think Luis is using them against Gavin. From what you have said, it is a way he would choose so that the danger and the wrong will not be his alone. He must fear not only Gavin but your great-grandfather."

"But how could he do this?" Tessa asked breathlessly.

"It is simple. He is high born, and few know him for what he is." Carmelita restrained herself from using the description which came to mind. "He need only convince them that Gavin is guilty of some crime. Who knows, perhaps it will be the killing of another's *vaquero,* the stealing of cattle or horses. Montejo and his kind will believe anything said against a Yankee. For that, I am ashamed."

"I am a Californio also," Tessa reminded her quietly, and she stared blankly, knowing Carmelita's guess was correct, seeing only too clearly the penalties for the crimes accused—flogging, branding with a hot iron, even death. Such a death would be all Luis desired.

"It would make no difference if you found your husband tonight," Carmelita said. "You cannot take him from his purpose." She felt a thousand years old, and she was glad of Indian's reassuring strength as he put his arm around her. They both knew Tessa was beyond their help, and they shared the silent agony of wondering what she would do without Gavin, what they would do without him. Savagely Carmelita forbid herself the threatening tears. There had been enough useless weeping. Tessa was dry-eyed now, so could she be. "You've been through worse than this," she told herself, and knew it for a lie.

She saw them off at dawn. Tessa was rigidly upright on Amordoro, and her face was as cold and hard as polished marble. It was to Indian that Carmelita whispered, "I will wait to know. *Vaya con Dios.*"

Tessa was mindless on the journey. She dismounted to rest Amordoro at Indian's command. She ate when he told her to. She even slept for short stretches when he ordered it. She trusted him to find the way, and the difference between what she wished and what must be the truth was so great, she denied thought of it lest she go mad.

The numbness broke and left her painfully alive on the second night when Indian reckoned they were within the boundaries of Montejo's *rancho*. "May be guards. You wait here," he ordered harshly. He did not even suggest the possibility that he might not return.

He slipped away, and she shivered, bones colder than the night. A coyote yipped and others answered. Even the small whine and scrape of insects seemed unbearably loud. A chill night breeze blew fitfully. She thought she could hear the faraway hum of human voices. Picking up her tension, Amordoro snorted nervously.

A soft warning whistle and Indian was back. "Th' man must have little fear of bein' stopped. Only found one sentry. He sleep th' night an' then some. He don' see a thing."

"Luis judged Gavin well," Tessa moaned, her misery rising to choke her.

"We have this to finish," Indian spoke softly, but it was another command.

She would know hell if she saw it again. They rode in without being detected, the *rancho* dogs so excited by the strangers already there that they gave no added alarms. There were no women in the scattered group of fifteen or so men. Pitch torches lit the scene with flaring yellow light. A few of the men stood near the red embers of a fire. There were enough jugs in evidence and the talk and laughter were shrill and erratic enough to give proof that some had needed false courage for their work. Their work sagged in limp unconsciousness against the tree they had bound him to. His back was a bloody ruin.

She saw it all in a split second and heard the words of Luis and another man before they were aware of the invaders. Luis wanted to finish the Yankee horse thief; the other man thought he was nearly dead already and couldn't see how he would serve as an example if none but they knew. Luis's voice rose peevishly. "He hasn't admitted it. I want him to confess."

He shrieked in fear then as the torchlight caught the metal of the rifle muzzle and showed him Tessa's face as her mantle fell back and she took aim.

Indian whispered desperately. "Don' fire! It start, we dead! Got to git Gavin out of here!"

He switched to his oddly accented Spanish and his voice boomed out. "No one moves, no one gets hurt. There are more of you, but we'll take some to hell with us." No one had difficulty understanding him.

The mist of rage was clearing, and Tessa saw that Indian was right. One shot, and the frozen figures before them would dive for weapons and cover, while for the moment, they were as stunned by her presence as they were by Indian's commanding roar. She pressed the advantage.

"I am Teresa María Julieta Margarita Macleod y Amarista de Ramsay." Her voice was steady, and every syllable gave arrogance to the aristocratic name. She followed it by spinning out the full weight of her great-grandfather's name, and she was sure she felt the fearful jolt of recognition from some of the men. "Your prisoner is my husband. We were married in accordance with the law of the Church and the law of the government with
224

the blessings of Don Esteban. My husband is a citizen of California and Mexico. He has stolen nothing. Our horses were a gift from my great-grandfather." As she talked, she watched Indian's slow, steady movements. He dismounted, led Diablo from where he stood with the other saddled horses nearby, cut down and lifted Gavin's body effortlessly and tied him face down over the saddle.

Even with only one gun trained on them, none of the men moved. They listened as if hypnotized to Tessa's voice telling them the same things the Yankee had claimed earlier, before they had silenced him. She took heart from their stillness, though she recognized none except Luis. "You have listened to the lies of a madman, a coward, a violator of women. He has disgraced his name and the honor of all Californios." The rifle moved slightly, but Indian was beside her leading Diablo. "Don'," he whispered. "Leave him. Gavin alive."

Luis's courage broke then, and he scuttled into the darkness behind two other men, going for a gun or just running, they didn't know. "Ride!" Indian shouted and they wheeled away, hearing a rising, angry hum behind them, but no shots.

They rode as fast as they dared at first, both straining to hear pursuit over the pound of their own mounts, not stopping until Indian judged it safe.

"Cain't do much, but I try make him more comfortable," he muttered.

He more than half expected to find him dead, but as he lifted him from Diablo, Gavin came to, struggling and screaming in agony until he recognized Tessa's sobbing voice and his jaw clenched as he opened his eyes and looked at her.

Tessa crumpled to the ground, and Indian laid Gavin face down in her lap and worked swiftly to pad the saddle as well as he could with their blankets. Tessa poured small, broken words over Gavin, but she knew he no longer heard. He did not even come to when Indian lifted him and placed him across the saddle again.

The nightmare seemed endless. Gavin's blood was everywhere, on Indian, on Tessa, fresh red and dried black on his own body, showing ever more gruesomely as the

225

sky lightened into dawn. Twice Indian left them to double back and both times he returned, sure they were not being pursued.

"Where are we going?" she asked finally, not caring beyond the need to free Gavin from the added torment of the ride.

"He cain't make it all th' way to Monterey, an' that's th' only place we truly sure of friends. No matter his marryin' you or what's right on paper, he a foreigner, jus' like me. We still don't know what those men goin' do. Reckon some are powerful. They believe you while you talkin' an mebbe they go on believin'. But mebbe too, even believin', they jus' as soon not have no one know. We goin' where we don' be bothered for a while." His words were uncompromising, but she accepted his reasoning, she felt as alien as he in the country of her birth.

They rode into the foothills, and Indian chose their stopping place, a grassy clearing by an outcrop of rock, surrounded by dense foliage and watered by a clear stream.

"Won' move him more than we mus'," he said briefly, dismounting and working with furious speed to make camp, snapping orders at Tessa, who followed them without question, as she had on the ride. The only thing she was prepared to argue about was a fire, but even that was in Indian's plan. "They not find us here," he said with absolute certainty, and she believed him.

Indian carried Gavin's large frame as if he weighed no more than a child and laid him tenderly on the brush bed by the rock. "There now, little brother, there," he whispered softly. Tessa touched his cheek gently, and together they stripped off the bloodstained leggings and breeches.

He lay breathing in short, shallow gasps as though trying to keep movement from his wounds even while unconscious. Tessa covered him to the waist and forced herself to look at his back, at the swollen flesh and bloody gashes, some so deep that his muscles gleamed whitely through the red. Her stomach knotted convulsively when she recognized the curving furrow, blacker than the rest, for what it was—the letter C, for *cautrero*, horse thief, crudely executed by a hot iron and surely Luis's own work.

She sorted through her supplies while Indian heated

water. Her hands trembled as she fumbled in her saddle-bag and found needle and thread, but it had to be done. One of the gashes was as deep and long as if it had been sliced with a knife and would never heal properly unless stitched.

Indian held Gavin still while she cleaned, stitched, and salved. She worked with deep, forced concentration, trying to ignore the reality of it being Gavin's twitching flesh beneath her hands, Gavin making the inhuman sounds that beat against her ears.

Without Indian, she was sure she could not have borne it. For days, Gavin was never free of excruciating pain. Even though he was unconscious most of the time, he moaned with every breath he drew, and his body writhed in protest until exhaustion overtook him for a while before the whole cycle began again. It was worse in the brief periods when he was conscious. Then he lay in rigid control, making no sound, his tightly clenched jaw and knotted muscles screaming in the silence.

Rationally Tessa knew she was taking the best possible care of him, using every herb Indian could find for her, every ointment she could make to keep his wounds clean and to prevent the ragged, overly thick scar tissue, which would stiffen his back, from forming. She knew because María had taught her well, and María's healing powers were long since proven.

It was Indian who built the thatched shelter against the rock to keep the sun and heat of day from them, the chill away at night; Indian who often lifted her bodily from Gavin's side, taking her outside and holding her upright until her cramped muscles could support her, ordering her to wash and walk and remember she too had to live. And it was Indian who followed her when she staggered from the shelter on the third day.

He had seen it too, a deep weal near the waist, the only one which wasn't healing properly. His hands were hard on her shoulders. "I been tellin' you get out for a while, now I tell you go back in there."

"I can't!" Her voice was strangled. "I just can't! Every time I touch him, I hurt him."

"He already hurt. You make th' difference whether he

live or die. Somewhere you know that. You don' help him, I have to. I don' know what you know, don' know how to do it gentle. But I know cain't be left that way, poison spread, kill him. You choose. My way, your way."

It was Tessa who lanced, cleaned, and cauterized the wound. Indian held her hands tightly afterward, letting her draw comfort, listening to the shaking rustle of her voice. "Seeing him suffer like this, it's horrible. Every time I touch him I want to scream and go on screaming. But that's not all, the rest is selfish. I've accepted that part of him inside is a child, but that's different. Even when I nearly killed him with the knife—" She saw Indian blink. "He never told you?"

"No, but I figure somethin' like that."

"It was a serious wound, with much bleeding, but it was clean, and even though he was weakened, he could . . ." she struggled to explain. "He was somehow in control, not like this. Now he is helpless, it terrifies me. I depend on his strength, use it for my own. Selfish."

Indian's voice was low and warm. "Why, if that don' beat all, callin' it selfish. If th' husband an' th' wife don' take th' good an' the bad of each other, th' strong an' th' weak, what for they marry? I don' lie, it bad this, I never seen him so bad. But he heal. You watch, soon he be strong an' want to fight everybody again."

"Then I will leave him just long enough to find Luis. A woman can get closer. I will kill him." The words were so softly spoken that Indian knew she did not realize she had said them aloud, and he did not betray his hearing of them.

Tessa noted with satisfaction on the sixth day that all of the lacerations were healing well. No telltale red streaks traced the path of blood poisoning, and even the burn had stopped weeping. Indian was in his customary position, holding Gavin's shoulders against movement as Tessa worked. Gavin's head turned and his eyes opened. His voice was no more than a whisper, but it was firm. "It's all right, Indian, I can do that now." Indian released him instantly.

With great precision, Tessa finished her task before she met his eyes. The deep blue showed vividly again. She sat back on her heels, covering her face with her hands, taking deep breaths that turned into sobs in spite of her efforts not to cry. The tears overflowed and spilled through her fingers.

"Women, I never understand," Indian snorted in mock disgust. "Never she cry all th' time mebbe you dyin'. Now you gettin' better, tears come." He left them without a backward glance.

"Your hand, Tessa," Gavin said reaching out with his own, wanting to see her face. She took his hand in both of hers, and still the tears rained down. She looked years older, her hair and skin lifeless, her face thin and drawn, her eyes ringed by dark shadows that made her look as if she'd been in a terrible fight. She had, he knew. He wondered if he would ever be able to explain. He had never experienced anything like it before, a red sea of agony that had engulfed him relentlessly, beyond his power to escape or control unless he surrendered and slipped away from it into death. He wanted to die, and he would have except she had not allowed it. Even when all else had vanished, he had know she was there.

Her tears stopped, leaving her completely drained. "Lie down beside me. You are so weary, my little one, and so am I," he said, and she did as he wished, taking care not to jar him. Exhaustion was fast overtaking him again, making it difficult to think or keep his eyes open, but he managed to kiss her and to murmur, "I knew you were here, always." He fell asleep knowing he did not have to explain further after all. She understood. The memory had come suddenly to him. When she had lain bleeding to death from the loss of the baby and the loss of her own will to live, he had called her, and she had followed him back to the living, back to himself.

When Indian checked on them, they were sleeping, and he roused them only briefly hours later to make sure they both ate something.

"You'll spoil us," Tessa accused him, smiling sleepily. Now that she knew for certain that the crisis was over, she was giddy with relief, not even conscious of the number of times she reached out to touch Gavin's face or to hold his hand.

"Spoil you all I can," Indian replied promptly, and he tidied up the camp quietly, seeing they were asleep again.

He schooled himself to patience; he could not leave them until Gavin was able to move around.

Gavin regained his strength much more slowly than he would have liked, though Tessa considered the speed of it miraculous. He hated being helpless and dependent, and she clamped her lips tightly over words of warning and let him find his own limits. The day he insisted on getting up, it took Indian's strong arms to help him stand, and Tessa had to look away from his set face. He only managed a few steps and short minutes outside the shelter before he swore viciously at his own weakness and lay down again with obvious relief, his whole body trembling. But it was a beginning, and each time he got up, it was for longer periods. Tessa made him flex his arms and stretch his back muscles endlessly, and her panic began to cease when she saw that none of the muscles had been irreparably damaged and the scar tissue wasn't thick or puckered enough to have pulled the skin too tightly across his back. It was her private grief that she could see what he could not— the splendid smooth satin strength of his back which her eyes and hands had so loved was forever marred, and falsely proclaimed him a thief. She was thankful at least that his own vanity was less than hers for him.

Neither she nor Indian questioned him about what had happened; it was he who told the story briefly and without excuses for himself. "It happened just as you warned me, Tessa. He set a trap, and I blundered right into it. I underestimated him and the support he could muster. He left a trail. I followed it, and his friends were convinced they had caught a vindictive Yankee horse thief who was bent on killing Don Luis in addition to stealing his horses and his woman. His elaborate lies suffered no lack of detail. He even pointed out the knife scar as his own work, the token he had given me in the valiant fight he had waged and lost at the cost of a crippled arm." Despite everything, there was a gleam of wry humor in Gavin's eyes as he looked at Tessa. "I didn't even try to explain how I'd really gotten it. I gave up explaining much of anything once I understood how it was."

Tessa dug her nails into the palms of her hands, transferring the pain, keeping her expression bland in comparison to what she was feeling. Nothing had been broken,
230

and his other injuries were so much more serious, but the bruises on his face had given ample evidence of why explanations or any speech at all might have been beyond him. The bruises were fading now, paling purple, yellow. She focused on his voice again.

"There was a mock trial, a delay for which I will be eternally grateful. It gave me time to be rescued. Alive is much better than the alternative." The eyebrow went up, lessening the tension, but neither of them doubted the depth of his gratitude. "The sentence was a celebration, a fiesta of joy." His voice was devoid of expression, flat and cool.

Indian made sure they were well supplied with game, though he knew that in spite of her aversion to hunting, Tessa was a good shot and wouldn't allow Gavin to go hungry should their supplies run low before he was strong enough to go after meat.

It was time for him to be on his way. His lies were as smooth as glass—Carmelita must be half out of her mind with worry. He'd not only visit her, but he'd find out which way the wind was blowing, whether anything was known in Monterey about what had happened, whether feelings against Yankees were running particularly high. Intent on each other, Tessa and Gavin didn't even think to question him.

It was two weeks before they saw him again, and during that time they did little more than rest and survive. They slept close and touched often but without sexual overtones. To be alive was enough for a while, and to go further than that was impossible to handle right now. And they drew strength from their separate plans for revenge on Luis, each planning excuses to leave the other long enough to accomplish it once Indian returned.

He rode in and only afterward did they realize how little he had said, how hard he had studied them both before he told them.

They had dined well on succulent rabbit, which much to Tessa's relief, Gavin had snared and skinned. They were replete with the meal and at peace to have Indian back with them. Insects sang around them and a yipping coyote chorus echoed in the hills.

Indian's voice was sudden, sharp, and final, and all the

231

golden firelight seemed caught on the dark planes of his face. "I see now my hope. You strong enough to go on for lovin' without th' killin' need. Th' man, he dead. I kill him. Again, he leave a wide trail, this time not hard to follow either 'cause he think no one will. Die like he live, coward's way, not clean. I cut from him his manhood so he know. Let him know for some long time, then cut his throat. I come with th' shadows, leave th' same. Some mebbe know. None will say. Th' others, some place they live, yes, but he th' one, an' he finish."

Tessa felt the shock of anger running through Gavin's body, and she felt it as her own for an instant before the realization of the enormity of what Indian had done for them erased everything else. She rushed to fill the silence before Gavin would say the words to end his friendship with Indian forever. "There will never be any way to thank you enough. You succeeded where both of us failed. We are three, friends and together in everything. I have never known that more truly than tonight. I am only sorry the ugliness is equal to the beauty."

"Never be, never," Indian said firmly, and finally Gavin spoke. "My thanks, my brother. I know the cost. You are not a man for executions."

It was not a realm she understood easily, but Gavin had made it painfully clear. She saw graphically what Indian's brief description had meant. She saw him stalking Luis, saw the torture he had inflicted for retribution, saw the final death stroke of his knife. A foul, fitting end for Luis, but one which had exacted great price from the gentle, fair-fighting man who had dealt it.

She left Gavin's side, going to Indian, putting her arms around the broad expanse of his chest, hugging him hard and kissing him on both cheeks, telling him by touch that nothing had been changed or harmed between them by what he had done. His shoulders heaved, and she felt the tension drain out of him before he whispered, "Now I thank you. Could not lose my family an' live like a man."

CHAPTER XXII

They left the next day, traveling first to Monterey, Tessa claiming fatigue whenever she thought Gavin ought to rest. Indian had in fact seen Carmelita on his hunt for Luis, and though he had not confided in her, she had had little trouble divining his purpose. She deserved to know it was over.

The visit was quiet and brief. They had no wish to see other friends, though they were glad to find the attack on Gavin had been an isolated case of evil and had not led to violence against anyone else. Gavin had no wish to bring charges before the authorities against the men, especially as it might mean making what had happened to Tessa public, and even Carmelita agreed grimly. "It is good, is it not? Now they will walk in fear that someone will come in the night to kill them as Luis was killed."

No one could have been more relieved to see them than Pedro when they returned to the *rancho*. He had been told so little, and he had begun to wonder if his superiors would ever return, but he had continued doggedly with his work and had seen that the other *vaqueros* did the same. When he was told that the vicious horse thieves had inflicted the wounds on the *patrón*, he accepted the explanation, still not wanting to know any more.

They tried to settle back into the life of the *rancho* as though nothing had happened, but both Tessa and Gavin were restless, uneasy, and growing strangely out of touch with each other, each not wanting to burden the other with dark thoughts, thus hampering the sharing they had had.

"I wish we were there," Tessa said softly one morning. She was standing in the garden, but her eyes were gazing far away to the east, to the great peaks of the mountains. She was unaware that Indian had heard.

He could hardly wait to find Gavin, and when he did,

233

he plunged right in. "Tessa wants to go th' mountains, an' you goin' take her."

Gavin gazed at him in astonishment. "She tell you that?"

"Naw, tol' herself. I hear."

"Well, you know it's impossible. There's too much work here, besides the rest of the cargo to sell."

Indian rejoiced; Gavin wanted to go as much as Tessa. "Now, listen, little brother," he growled. "Mebbe not be so much money when th' year over, but Pedro an' I, we do fine. You take your woman, an' you go, jus' th' two of you to learn each other agin. Way now sad, too damn polite."

Gratitude closed Gavin's throat. His body had healed rapidly, but his spirit had not. He worked grimly, without joy, and he slept in constant dread of the nightmares— Tessa beyond his help in the hands of Luis; the fire of the lash burning across his back again. And even when she reached out to wake him when he moaned and thrashed in the grip of the dreams, they held to each other not like lovers but like numbed survivors of a catastrophe, strangers to each other. He wanted desperately to go away with her, away from other people, to a place where they might have some chance of rediscovering what they had lost.

He gripped Indian's hand and managed to say, "We'll repay you somehow, someday for this."

"Don' know what ails your memory, but you sure do forget sometime. I be dead now or else somebody's field nigger, weren't for you. You want talk 'bout owin', that heavy debt."

They regarded each other with full understanding, full awareness of the fathomless bond between them. Indian could see Gavin clearly as he had seen him eleven years before, a young man of sixteen cloaked in a calm maturity far beyond his years, the young man who had taken the sudden appearance of a bleeding, half mad, dark-skinned giant as a matter of course, who had reacted without alarm or threat. "Do they have dogs?" were Gavin's first words, complete understanding even then. "Naw," Indian had answered, and though the boy was younger than himself, he had given himself into his keeping. He would never forget lying in the tree-root hollow covered with leaves and brush while Gavin spoke with cold disdain to the slavers, his false accent holding more deep South than Indian had ever heard before or since. Later they had even been able to laugh about it.

"Better find Tessa an' tell her there some travelin' to do," Indian suggested gruffly, and Gavin obeyed him.

They left at first light, and despite the stifling heat pressing them against the floor of the Great Valley, by midday Tessa was singing without even knowing she was, a gay lilting song that made Gavin smile and softened the stern lines of his face.

They had a pack animal with them, and the easy pace suited them exactly. They knew they were traveling toward each other again, and with the destination sure, it was better not to hurry. Even when they made camp at night and slept touching, they made no demands on each other, wordless in agreement that they would somehow know when it was time to be one again.

It seemed they had ridden forever toward an unreachable goal, endless flat miles across a valley burned to brown and golden stubble by the relentless sun, and then suddenly the mountains took them, lifting them up through the foothills to cooler, thinner air sharp-scented from the pines and deep green thickets, alive with game and birds, singing with clear icy water from the snow runoff of the high white peaks.

They were in a kingdom ruled by the fiercest Indians and the wildest beasts—bear, lion, and wolf—and they were careful, but not afraid. Their own kind and color had dealt so savagely with them, the wilderness of the Sierra Nevada seemed almost kind. And they were not dismayed when one way presented them with impassable cliffs or impenetrable brush; they simply chose another. They had no mission to chart this world, no destination beyond themselves.

The pines would whisper all night until the breeze was stilled by dawn. Water tumbled forever over the pebbles and worn runnels of stone. The horses swished their tails, cropped grass, and made comfortable settling-down sounds close by where they could be protected from marauders. The mournful power of a wolf's howl drifted over them from far away, answered by a fainter echo from another quarter.

Tessa heard all the sounds, and she shivered, not in fear,

but with the deep throb of joy beginning. She felt washed clean, reborn, part of the earth. She would have to tell him eventually, but not even that held any terror now. She felt him watching her, and she met his eyes over the glow of their fire.

"Now, my love?" he asked huskily, and she came into his arms and he held her against his heart. "Tessa, it is up to you, you must decide. . . ."

She stilled him with gentle fingers tracing the firm sculpture of his mouth. "What Luis and his men did has nothing to do with us, with our loving." She could say the words and mean them now. "The victory is not his, only death is his."

He denied his own urgent need and took her as slowly and carefully as if it were the first time for her, reclaiming her body with exquisite delicacy, seeking to obliterate all traces of the other men who had used her. And when he finally entered her, they shared only a stop second of painful memory—her fear, his hesitation—then he was smooth gliding deep into her welcoming body, her own fierce rhythm of love meeting his, two voices in one wild, triumphant cry.

Tessa awakened first at the dawn and drew far enough away that she could see Gavin's face, and the blankets slipped from both of them. Her breath caught at the youth and vulnerability of him, his body curved protectively toward her. Even the livid stripes on his back had become beautiful to her, reminding her every time she touched them that he bore the scars for her.

He opened his eyes and considered her silently for a moment before he observed, "In Boston you would be arrested for looking at a man like that."

"Isn't it fortunate we're not in Boston," she answered, and he grinned at her pronunciation, which made the first "o" a "u."

"Can't think why, but I'm hungry," he teased.

"So am I. Breakfast can wait." She was laughing as she pounced on him, pushing him flat on his back, straddling him in mock victory.

Her body was rosy in the first light, her eyes deep, gleaming violet, the black silk of her hair touched him softly. She looked young again, young and shining and more beautiful, stronger than she had ever been.

"Tessa, my life," he whispered low, reaching up to stroke her face, feeling the cold dawn on her skin. "You'll take a chill, sweetheart."

"No, I will take Gavin, my husband, *mi vida,* and he will not be cold," she murmured, and savoring the warmth and strength of him, she lowered her body slowly against his.

The healing grace of the mountains affected them tangibly. Their bodies were stronger and more supple than they had ever been, radiating health and joy. Physically they came together often, and with gay abandon whenever and wherever they pleased, feeling as if they were alone in the world. Mentally, they made love constantly, more closely attuned to each other than either would have believed possible before. Sometimes they spent an entire day without needing words, communicating by a touch, a sudden stillness that said plainly there was some new vision to share. And everything was made more poignant by the knowledge that like the first couple in Eden, they too would have to leave the Garden. Their life was in another place, and the first snow would be no less deadly here than the first sin. They prayed it would be late in driving them from the mountains.

One day they discovered a beaver pond and spent hours watching the peculiar-looking creatures waddling on land and gliding swiftly through the water bent on the endless tasks of eating and building. Not once did they betray their observation post, and no warning slap was given.

So many of the fur-bearing creatures had been decimated by hunters and trappers in more accessible areas, it was the purest pleasure to see them alive and free. Gavin found a family of otters and took Tessa to watch them playing on their mud slide, and it took all her control not to laugh aloud and scare them off. With their plump, silky bodies and inquisitive little faces, she thought them the most enchanting animals she had ever seen. They slid down the smooth run, chasing each other and their own tails, barking and squeaking hysterically as if nothing were more important than having a good time.

Even the sky was alive with the sharp silhouettes of

falcons and the grand sweep of hawks and eagles. Sometimes Tessa felt so much a part of it, she could feel her own body soaring, bones gone hollow, wind all around her effortless flight.

They saw herds of elk and deer, and rabbits and game birds abounded. Gavin hunted carefully, taking only what they needed. Even with her aversion to killing, Tessa could understand Gavin's quiet enjoyment in providing food for her and for himself, in being part of the same pattern of all the animals, predator and prey, without rancor or waste.

Wherever they went Gavin scouted the area thoroughly, and only once were they taken unawares by the approach of a band of Indians who rode suddenly into the meadow before them. Even then, Gavin's skill kept them from harm. Within seconds, he had the pack mule muzzled and his arm around Diablo's nose, leaving Tessa with nothing to do except keep Amordoro quiet also. They waited, frozen in the dark of the forest that rimmed the meadow. The Indians here were noted for their efficient massacre of soldiers and surveyors who had tried periodically to map their land. Even thinking of that, with her heart pounding in her throat, Tessa could feel a strange kinship with them, and she thought of No-Name. As strong and beautiful in their way as the wild, free beasts of the mountains, having little resemblance to the cowed peoples of the coast, they were justified in believing that with the white man came their destruction. But even this knowledge did not prevent her trembling relief when the Indians had disappeared without sensing their presence.

Indians were not the only predators to be avoided. The bear population was large and busily intent on foraging, needing enough fat on their bodies to survive winter hibernation without starving in their sleep. But as long as they were not threatened or approached too closely they gave no trouble, and the Ramsays kept a sharp lookout for them, especially where there were thickets of late berries or anything else that looked as if a bear might like it for a meal.

Their closest call came from another quarter. They had made camp for the night, but instead of settling down, the horses stamped and whinnied nervously. Finally Gavin moved back out of the fire's glow, ordering Tessa to do the same. They waited, both of them armed with rifles. Gavin was relieved when he heard the spitting scream—he preferred a cougar to a surprise attack by Indians.

The horses grew more agitated, pulling at their ropes and staggering in their hobbles as the lion's scent grew stronger in their nostrils.

Tessa was curiously unafraid; there was a sad inevitability about it. The lion could be dangerous if cornered, but he would be no match for two rifles. It took him a long time to come in. He could probably smell the humans and surely the fire. But finally the rich scent of horseflesh was stronger than the warnings.

The eyes flashed irridescent golden green as the lion sprang. Gavin felled it with one shot, and for an instant, Tessa felt her own death in the great cat as if she had become the long, sleek, tawny body with the small neat head so finely marked. It was not the same to kill him here in his own territory as it had been to hunt the one who had trespassed on the *rancho*.

Gavin echoed her thoughts. "There is no joy in this kill. It is such a splendid beast. I only hope there is no mate close by."

They did not see another lion in all their days in the mountains.

Every new place they had explored had seemed more beautiful than the last, but Tessa insisted that they would never find a spot more lovely than their present campsite.

There was a meadow with good grazing for the horses; tall timber for shelter and shade, and a pooling waterfall that delighted her in spite of the icy water so barely translated from snow. The colors of autumn were seeping into the landscape, touching the foliage with gold, orange, and soft browns. The air smelled different, softly scented with the change, and every night brought a deeper frost. Large flocks of birds flew purposefully southward, and often the geese passed so low at evening, the singing of the wind in their heavy pinions was clearly audible. The mountain sheep were coming down in greater numbers every day, the rams magnificent with their heavy, curved-back horns. Their passage to the lower meadows was a sure sign that winter was coming to grip the high country until the spring. The new snows had already begun to fall on the high peaks. They had watched them disappear several times in the thick cloud banks.

Very soon it would be time to leave the mountains, and Tessa and Gavin were both aware of how precious was each minute left to them.

It was a perfect, still morning which Tessa announced she was going to spend in complete laziness by the waterfall.

"In order to allow you that, I'll just have to take myself off and find something else to do," he said, eyeing her wickedly as he stood over her.

"I'm never that lazy!" she protested, grabbing for his legs, but he was too quick. "Ah, no, you've lost your chance. I'll see you later." She watched him walk away, never tiring of the long, easy stride that gave such grace to his tall, lean body.

He had no intention of wandering too far from her, and the richly flowered patch was no great distance. He had seen the late blooms the day before, and even though he felt a bit ridiculous, he wanted to pick a bouquet for her. He already had a good fistful of yellow flowers when he heard the sound. He put the stalks down and took up his rifle. The mournful whimperings grew louder as he traced its source. "Well, I'll be damned!" he swore softly.

It was a wolf cub held fast by a front paw in a fall of timber. It must have been after some small rodent when the logs had shifted slightly, enough to trap him neatly. It made a half-hearted attempt to snap at Gavin, but it was too shocked and miserable to manage more than that. Gavin covered the cub with his shirt and levered the log until he could lift the animal free. The paw was badly mangled, and had been made worse by the wolf's own sharp teeth trying to gnaw away the pain.

Gavin wondered what he was doing. The sensible course and the kindest would be to put the creature out of its misery, but there was something pathetically appealing about it, with the look of a large, though underfed puppy, feet too big and ears triangular. It should have been with its parents until the early spring mating season of next year, but there was no sign of the adults or other young, no sign that any but this little one had been here. Perhaps

Indians or a solitary trapper had taken the pelts of the others, leaving this one to wander alone.

Tessa saw Gavin coming and eyed his bare chest and the shirt bundle he carried.

"I meant to bring you flowers," he said, looking as guilty as a little boy who had been caught with a frog in his pocket.

Her love for the wolf was instantaneous, and with awe, Gavin accepted the idea that it appeared to be mutual. "He won't hurt me. You needn't hold him," she said as she went to work to bathe and bandage the injured paw.

He watched the animal carefully, not wanting the sharp teeth to slash Tessa's hands, but the wolf bore the ministrations with closed eyes and still patience.

"It's as if he knows," Gavin breathed.

Tessa glanced up. "Of course he knows. Wolves are intelligent beasts."

She gave a little sigh when she had finished. "Now we must let him be peaceful, and he will decide whether or not he will live. I am only sorry that even my best will leave him lame."

She put a piece of meat near his muzzle, and they stood looking down at the cub for a moment.

"I don't know quite how we're going to take him home with us. We will have to be on our way long before his leg will support him again. But I guess we'll find a way," Gavin said gently, and Tessa hugged him and felt the comfort of his arm going around her. She did not protest. He had made the necessary decision. To tarry too long was to court a grim death.

"When?" she asked.

"The day after tomorrow. The weather is already changing. I can feel it; I've been in high mountain ranges before."

It was time now, and a place near heaven for the telling. She felt a surge of joy mixed with apprehension. "Come," she said, slipping out of his hold and tugging him by the hand. "The afternoon is yet warm enough for a swim."

"How you can stay so long in that icy water and call it warm is beyond me," Gavin marveled, willing to go along with her, wanting them to be happy for the time left, but puzzled by the strange excitement he could see in her eyes, feel in her touch.

They splashed each other and played until Gavin gave up, getting out of the water to watch her freeze by herself, as he put it. He lay propped on his elbows on the warm stone bank, savoring the sight of her.

She made faces at him and called him disrespectful names in English and Spanish for being so lily-livered. Then, her heart pounding, she climbed up to stand on the rocky shelf in the shallows by the side of the waterfall. She turned her body in profile to him and pushed her small round belly out deliberately.

Her sudden stillness drew his attention even more sharply. A fine spray from the fall surrounded her with silver light. Hair so black, skin so honey golden now. So slender and yet round in the right places. Why, she'd even gained weight in spite of their lean wilderness fare. He'd tease her about that stomach she'd acquired. He'd . . .

For an instant, he was paralyzed; even his heart felt as if it had stopped. He didn't know he had moved, didn't know anything until he scooped Tessa off the ledge and had her on dry ground again. "When? How long have you known? Why haven't you told me before?"

The questions poured over her in a quick frenzy, his eyes were narrowed, dark glittering blue, but with anxiety for her, not with anger or suspicion. She felt a sweet, engulfing calm. Her first realization and terror had been changed by the strong, beautiful days here. Against great odds, the seed had remained planted in her womb and was even at this moment growing to fruition. She did not know whether it was Gavin's child she carried, conceived before the rape, or a child of that violent night. She would not know until she saw her child. But she believed now and would go on believing unless proved wrong that it was Gavin's. Even if it were not, a respect for the life she was carrying had been growing steadily as the fetus—the tiny, barely formed beginning she carried gave every indication of being fiercely bent on living. The only thing that mattered now was that Gavin should know no doubt, nothing except joy in his approaching fatherhood. "It is over three months. The baby should be born in April." She saw his eyes darken momentarily as he counted backward, and she gave him no time to let the thought take hold. "I had missed one flux right before that night, which proves now that I was pregnant then. But I don't think any woman dares to believe it true until two or even three months have passed without bleeding. And after being raped"—she forced herself to say the word—"I feared to lose the babe." A swift, mischievous smile eased the tenseness. "And when that fear proved needless, still I did not tell you, because I wanted to be here with you, with no others near, and I know you too well. You worry overmuch." She stilled his protest. "I know I gave you cause for worry, but that was different. I have not even been sick of a morning with this one. And any child who chooses me for mother must live as I do. I could not bear to be shut in and cosseted. I would go mad, and the child would be less than he must be for the life we lead."

"He?" Gavin asked, one eyebrow quirked.

"Yes, I'm quite sure."

As sure as she was with the last one and as true, he thought in a spasm of memory, but looking down at her, he saw the absolute serenity of her face, the eyes without shadow, and his heart lifted. "Yo must think me a clumsy fool of a man to have been with you all these days and to have noticed so little," he mumbled apologetically.

She giggled at that. "Your body runs no monthly course to remind you, and now I need not mark the days either for months to come, so we are more alike."

He looked scandalized at the idea before the humor of it dawned on him, and a rueful smile curved his mouth. "That is a terrible falsehood, my love," he murmured, and he leaned down to touch the gentle curve of her belly with the most delicate of kisses.

The beauty of the gesture caught her throat and filled her eyes with tears. She drew him close. "You do know, my ignorant husband, that nothing is changed between us, not for a long while yet." She knew that much instinctively and hoped Carmelita could supply her with a more specific timetable; the older woman hadn't had a child herself, but she seemed to know a great deal. Tessa nearly laughed aloud again from sheer joy, amusement, and tenderness all mixed. Here she was already worrying about the time when she and Gavin could not make love, and there he was, having known so many women without knowing a woman at all, and yet possessed of such a deep ac-

243

ceptance of a woman's body and his own that her monthly courses did not dismay or repulse him, did not to such an extent that he hardly noticed, and certainly had no memory that her body had not failed its schedule until after the rape. That he believed her was the greatest joy of all.

She was glad to let the complexities drift away, her body claiming her mind under Gavin's caresses.

CHAPTER XXIII

Tessa accused her husband of speaking with God; how else could he know so exactly when to ride west? A light snow fell on them their last night at the waterfall camp. Tessa was enchanted with it and with the way the world looked on the last morning; living so near the coast, she had seen little snow. Gavin, more practical, was relieved it wasn't enough to isolate them.

The wolf cub went with them, sometimes draped over Tessa's saddle, sometimes curled asleep in the hastily made bag on the pack mule. He had accepted food, and sure he was going to live, Tessa had named him *Sombra*, shadow, for his black coat. When she was very young, she had dogs that were special pets among the multitude on the *rancho*, but none of them had appealed to her as the wolf did. Despite the lameness he was sure to suffer, he gave promise of being a magnificent and intelligent creature. Even his acceptance without protest of her ministrations, though his amber eyes were wary, showed his clever adaptability.

"Sombra makes it easier, as if something of the mountains goes with us," she murmured.

Gavin grinned wryly, "I know what you mean, but for my taste, too much is coming with us." She laughed in agreement. The light snow of the night was revenging itself on the sun of morning, falling heavily now. Even when they rode below the snow line, it was into drizzling rain, and there was no use in looking back. The world they had

244

shared was shrouded, as forbidding and inaccessible now as it had been welcoming so short a time before. When Gavin saw Tessa eyeing the lowland meadows with a peculiar expression, he said, "No, love, you can't have it. We have land enough now to worry us aplenty. And it wouldn't be the same as where we have been."

"You're right," she agreed, and she kept her eyes resolutely to the west.

The rain stayed with them halfway across the Great Valley until they emerged into a world of clear skies and much higher temperatures, and suddenly they were ready and anxious to be home, longing to see Indian and Pedro, wondering how things had gone in their absence.

The changes were loud and obvious. A swarm of dogs boiled around their arrival, the challenging roar changing to uncertainty and in some to outright fear as the wolf scent reached them, coupled with the swift, well-aimed kicks Amordoro and Diablo administered to those who came too close. Added to the din were the nervous shrieks and giggles of the women who emerged from the now completed *Indiada* at the news that the Ramsays had returned.

They looked at each other, laughing helplessly. The noise was unbelievable after the long quiet. Nothing could have been more welcome than the sight of Pedro and Indian riding in furiously from near by in response to the din.

Indian was beside himself. He had seen the storm race to the east to close the mountains, and he had been trying to resign himself to wait until spring before he accepted the death of his friends. Yet now he saw them younger and more in love than ever, and he could feel himself smiling and hear himself saying foolish words and swearing grandly, without being able to do anything about it except hold out his arms to both of them.

Tessa left Indian's embrace to thank Pedro gravely for the good care she saw, restraining her impulse to hug him too; he was already ruddy cheeked, obviously fearing the possibility. He introduced her to the now timid women, and she fixed their names—Rosita, his wife, and Conchita, Flora, and Dolores.

The dogs had slunk off to watch sullenly, their attention riveted on the mule, and Gavin broke off his conversation with Pedro and Indian abruptly when he saw Tessa lift Sombra out of the sack. He started to edge toward her fearing the dogs would attack, but his fear turned to amazement when he saw Sombra take command, with a low-throated growl and the barest curling of his lips to show fangs. The dogs backed off, succumbing to their in-bred terror of wolves, no matter what size. Pedro and Indian smiled as though it was perfectly natural that Tessa would have a pet wolf rather than a dog.

The horses were fine; the cattle were increasing; the garden plot had yielded generously. Some of the cargo had yet to be sold, but no worry. Best of all, the land grant was now officially confirmed. Indian and Pedro had done so well in their absence, Gavin suggested that perhaps he and Tessa ought to leave again to insure success. Indian protested the plan, claiming he wanted someone to blame his mistakes on.

It was good to be home and marvelous to be with Indian again, and a few days later with Carmelita, fetched as promised by Pedro as soon as the Ramsays showed up.

She gave them all the gossip of Monterey, and they shared their own news of the coming child. Not by the slightest word or gesture did she betray her suspicions about the date, and Tessa loved her for it.

Only when they tried to describe what it had been like in the mountains did they fail, as if it had been a religious experience for which there were no adequate words. But Indian and Carmelita could gather all they needed to know from their shining contentment.

The fact that the *vaqueros* and their wives were all young helped Tessa take over management of the house-hold. Even Dolores, the oldest of the women, was only a few years older than Tessa, and all were willing to please the *patróna*. Within a few days, "Don Gavin" and "Doña Tessa" were names used with easy respect and affection, as "Don Indian" already was, despite Indian's embarrass-ment about the title. As the *mayordomo*'s wife Rosita held the top position among the women, and helped Tessa with the cooking and the household tasks. She was a small round girl of nineteen with great dark eyes, a ready smile, and endless adoration for her husband who had risen so swiftly in the world. Dolores helped in the house also.

Conchita was the laundress and a fine seamstress. Flora's only task was to grind meal for tortillas and bread. They were left with ample time to be with their husbands and care for their children and their own quarters. Dolores had two sons, one still nursing and the other a year and a half old. Conchita had a baby daughter. Flora would be delivered of her first child before Tessa, and Rosita couldn't wait to get pregnant.

"If there's a younger, more fertile *rancho* in California, I've yet to see it," Gavin commented drily, but he shared Tessa's relief that there was surely enough midwifery skill among the women to assist her when her own time came.

She was gentle but firm with her involvement in the *rancho*. She had no intention of becoming totally useless and lazy, as so many women did with servants to perform every task for them.

She also resumed her keeping of the neglected accounts. They had far more obligations now and many supplies had to be purchased: salt, sugar, chocolate, coffee, wine, cloth, particularly for the servants as part of the keep, and a myriad of other things which could not be grown or made on the *rancho*. But the land would continue to produce more and more with care; they had a small reserve of coin from trade; and the debt to Thomas Larkin was being paid off at a steady rate. With prudence they would do well.

They spent the Christmas holidays quietly and Tessa's greatest excitement had nothing to do with the gifts exchanged. She had felt strange flutters before but nothing like this, a hard, sure kick as if the baby was suddenly in a hurry to grow and be born.

"Oh, my!" she gasped involuntarily the first time it happened, and her hands gripped her belly. Gavin paled, asking anxiously what was wrong. Her face was suddenly soft and radiant, and she guided his hand to the expanding curve. "Nothing is wrong, it's gloriously right! Your son is kicking to be free." She giggled at the look of incredulous wonder on Gavin's face when he felt it.

The child took on a greater reality for both of them after that, and Gavin fussed about Tessa doing too much, but he need not have worried; she remained active, but she took no foolish risks.

Flora was delivered of a girl without complications one

February night, and Tessa didn't even know about it until the next morning. She was confident that if Flora could do it so easily, so could she.

She had shown so little in the first months, it was a shock to feel and see the growing bulk of the last weeks. The rest of her body remained slender, but her stomach seemed to know no limits, bulging out until she confided to Gavin that she felt quite grotesque and couldn't wait to see her feet again. "I think your son wants to be born as large as you are now."

Though Gavin had made one trip to Monterey for supplies and business affairs in January, he had not wanted to leave Tessa since, and so Indian had been their contact with the pueblo. And when he arrived at Carmelita's toward the end of March, he was bombarded by her questions about Tessa. "She doin' fine, baby gettin' big an' strong." His smile faded. "That don' please you?"

"You silly man, of course it pleases me, to a point. But Tessa is very small here." She patted her own wide, strong hips. "I just hope the baby does not grow too large while she still carries it."

She saw the look on his face. "Pay no attention. I worry as if I were her mother. And don't tell Gavin. She has women to help her now, and I don't want to frighten her with my love, but promise you will send for me in good time."

Indian promised, and tried not to watch Tessa too intently once he was back on the *rancho*. He rather wished Carmelita had not shared her fear. It did seem to him that Tessa's burden had grown alarmingly out of proportion to her slight body.

It seemed that way to Tessa too. The first days of April brought increasing discomfort. She could find no easy way to sit or lie down, and she was disgusted with her walk, which was a most undignified shuffle. The first protective glow of knowing she carried a child inside had long since given way to a heartfelt wish that he would quit her womb as soon as possible. Sometimes she even chided him aloud, telling him that surely after such a kick he was ready to be born.

She could scarcely forget that women died in childbirth, as her own mother had, and sometimes the ripple of fear
248

was tangible. But stronger than anything else was her eagerness to see the child. She prayed he would look exactly like Gavin.

Even with her limited knowledge, she knew when the baby dropped, settling so low and heavy that her back ached continually. She grew more and more sharp-tongued, quite unlike her normal self; everything made her furious, including Gavin's unending kindness in the face of her temper. Everyone at the *rancho* treated her with patient, soft words and smiles that made her grit her teeth.

April was more than half gone when the first pain hit early one morning while Gavin still slept beside her, and her elation that at last the waiting was over was boundless. Gavin awakened at her sudden movement, but the deep, low spasm had passed, and she was able to lie smoothly. "He just kicked harder than usual."

He studied her face and then accepted her words. He was doing his best, but he knew he was out of his depth, and the terror he had been determined to deny had risen full force in the last weeks, so that he had all he could do to keep from giving it to Tessa to carry with the child.

The sun was hardly up before he had ridden out on the land—early out, early back, somehow it was important, weren't babies always born at night? He laughed at his own idiocy and wondered if all fathers were so foolish the first time.

Tessa was relieved to see him ride off. The anxiety he was trying to conceal was obvious to her. If she needed him in a hurry, one of the *vaqueros* could go for him. She didn't think she'd need him for hours. The first pain was only now being followed by another. She bent over, clutching her belly and breathing hard, sighing in relief when it had passed. It wasn't pleasant, but was bearable, and she took comfort from that. Gavin and everyone else would know soon enough. For now she wanted to be alone to adjust to this new experience. She sent the women away as soon as she could. Dolores asked if all was well, and had to accept Tessa's firm assurance that it was. It was understood that Doña Tessa's temper was uncertain these days. She even banished Sombra, who was large and annoyingly underfoot, whining a constant question as if knowing something was wrong.

She got linens ready, laid a nightgown out, and smoothed the bedding in the cradle Gavin had made with such loving skill. She paced the house and lay down to rest now and then. The pains crept in, spreading from her back across her abdomen, but they were still random and far apart. It was nerve-racking; she wished her labor would start in earnest and be done with. Gavin's son. No one else's.

She might have kept it from him a while longer, but he came in in late afternoon just as she had another contraction, and before it was over, his face was as white as hers. He wanted to go get every woman on the place immediately, and it was difficult to convince him there was no need yet, difficult to convince him that once the spasm had passed, she felt perfectly all right.

When Gavin told him, Indian groaned, "Lordy, I should be in Monterey days back. Carmelita want to be here. Jus' 'bout think Tessa her chil'. Well, I get her here time to see th' baby 'fore it grows up."

Gavin didn't protest the night ride or anything else; he wished he had something as active and purposeful to do.

It was long after sundown before Tessa allowed Gavin to send for Dolores. The intervals between pains were becoming perceptibly shorter, the contractions stronger. She tried to be glad to see the woman; after all, she must know something about childbirth, having two children of her own. But the only person she really wanted with her now was Gavin, no matter whether he knew what to do or not. She clamped her jaw against the words to call him back and endured the next contraction.

He thought it would be easier away from her where he would not have to see her suffering, but his imagination worked vividly to make it worse. He heard Sombra howl disconsolately outside, and he shivered in response to the desolate cry. He was on his way back when Dolores met him outside the door. Her voice was low and hesitant. "Don Gavin, you must understand, I am no midwife." It took Gavin a moment to identify the unfamiliar word in Spanish. "My own little ones were born as Flora's daughter was, at their appointed time without more pain or trouble than is expected for giving birth. Doña Tessa
250

is small here"—she used the same gesture Carmelita had used in explaining her fear to Indian. "It is not going well. Her labor is already hard, but the waters of birth have not even come."

He tried to whisper. "One of the other women, surely someone knows."

She shook her head. "We are all young. There is not a wise older one among us. I know more than they, and much too little." She dabbed at her tears with her apron. Gavin wanted to rage at her for showing his own fear and lack of knowledge, but he controlled himself, knowing her distress for Tessa was genuine and arose out of affection. He knew Tessa would see it too if Dolores went back to her. "Stay out here. Sleep if you can," he ordered. "I'll call you when she needs you." The woman did not protest.

Tessa was gripping the bed linen convulsively. Gavin put his hands over hers and felt her fingers twist to hold onto his, the incredible strength of them telling the agony even while her mouth was closed against sound. She writhed violently, and sweat gleamed on her skin.

The spasm released her, and she lay with eyes closed, breathing hard, her body looking small and limp save for the grotesque mound of the child. Gavin wiped her face with a cool cloth and raised her head, urging her to take a small sip of water.

Her eyes opened, enormous dark pools. "It is better with you here," she whispered. She tried to smile. "I don't think I'm very good at this."

"You're doing fine," he lied. If he lost control as Dolores had, he would never forgive himself.

Her fingernails bit into his flesh again, and to her shame, she knew the wild screaming was her own. She had fought the pain for so long, she couldn't fight it any more. Each time it was worse. She was being crushed and torn asunder at once. Those first warnings an eternity before had been but shadows of this. She swam in and out of knowing Gavin was with her, feeling the strength of his hands, seeing the reflection of her agony in his face. And in one short period of calm, she gasped, "Hard with the first, I know, but something's wrong, isn't coming, no nearer now. I know."

He knew too, with utter finality, the truth of her words. He had had a moment of relief and hope when the fetal waters had drenched the bed after a particularly violent time, but that had faded with Dolores's grim expression, and he had sent her from the room again. That had been hours ago. He had scarcely noticed when the dawn had broken, and now the morning was late. He went out to Dolores again. He told her what she must do, and she refused. "I cannot. I do not know how. I would kill her."

"It must be done. It's her only chance, and your hands are smaller than mine," he blazed at her, and she stepped back from his fury, still shaking her head in refusal. She was trembling violently, and he saw in despair that her fear and her acceptance of death in the house made her useless.

It could not end like this, not after all they had survived together, not after the love they had found. He knew he might kill her, but she was surely going to die anyway unless he helped her. The violent contractions still ripped through her body, but her strength was so depleted, even her screaming was reduced to low whimpering.

He anointed his hand with the sweet oil that was ready to be used on the tender skin of the newborn. He waited until the next contraction had passed, and then he reached into her.

He cursed himself for his lack of knowledge; he cursed the God he did not believe in; he cursed his unborn child and his own seed; he cursed aloud without knowing. All of his senses were concentrated on the blind passage toward the child. New contractions pressed the birth canal around his hand, and each time he waited until they eased, but finally he found the mouth of the womb.

At first he could not comprehend. He felt the tight pressed lump of flesh and thought wildly that he had fathered some brutish thing without arms or legs. Then he understood. The baby was not breech, as he had vaguely suspected; it was lying crosswise, an impossible position for delivery. The sweat poured into his eyes and every muscle trembled as he tried to find the child's head in the tight space, and he heard Tessa's renewed screaming with every nerve in his body. The child was probably dead already, but even if it weren't, he had no doubt about his

252

priorities. He would save Tessa even if he had to tear the child to pieces.

His hand found the shoulder, the head. He could hardly believe it, but he felt the body rotating as he brought the head toward the birth canal. Tessa screamed again as her whole body bore down to expel the child.

He saw the head as it emerged, and he held it, knowing instinctively he must let the baby come in natural stages now.

It was quickly done, and he bellowed for Dolores, whose shaking terror vanished at the miraculous sight of the child. With all of the efficiency that had deserted her earlier, she cut the cord, bound it, helped Gavin clean the signs of birth from the baby, and delivered the afterbirth.

A large baby, mottled from the hard birth, but very much alive, squalling angrily now. Perfectly formed, flaunting a crown of black hair. A son.

He saw the violet eyes open in her drawn, white face as Tessa heard the cry. "We have a son," he said shakily, and he placed the baby beside her and watched as her arm went around him and held him close. Dolores bundled the signs of battle away and slipped out to tell the joyous news.

"Oh, my God, Tessa, at such cost," he gasped, and he wept. With great effort she reached out and drew his head down to lie in the hollow of her neck near the baby before exhaustion overcame her and she slept. The last thing she heard was his voice whispering love words, Spanish and English mixed.

He watched over her anxiously, but none of the things he dreaded happened. She was simply bruised and exhausted by her ordeal, content to sleep most of the time as he was content to watch over her. The focus of his world narrowed until he saw nothing but his wife and child. He hardly noticed when Rosita, her superior position reinstated, came to insist he eat the meal she had prepared while she fed rich broth to Tessa. He ate as she bade him, without tasting anything, wanting only to be back with his wife.

He laughed aloud at her exclamation when the baby first suckled, rooting around in the fullness of Tessa's breasts until he found a teat and clamped his small mouth around it. She started, her eyes widening. "He's so strong, your son!"

Gavin did not hear the emphasis on the last two words, for he was watching another expression dawn on Tessa's face, the same faraway look she had when he was pleasing her. He wondered if fathers always became jealous of their sons. He would not, he vowed; Tessa had enough love for both of them.

Having had so much to do with the birth, he had no fear of handling the baby, and it was he who carried the child out at Dolores's timid request so that the people of the *rancho* could cheer the heir. When he returned, Tessa asked if Indian had seen their son yet.

"Not yet, but he will soon. He rode off last night to bring Carmelita back."

"I am glad she was not here," she murmured sleepily. "She might have sent you away." She looked fixedly at the baby, a deep slow smile beginning until it illuminated her whole face. "Gavin, I had feared . . . Oh, my beloved, it is so hard to tell with the newborn, but I see it now. He is your son. His eyes, his chin, his ears, his nose, his hands, they will all be images of yours. Nothing of Luis or——"

She swallowed hard and stared at her husband.

It was the first he knew of the burden she had carried along with the child for nine months. The lie he had accepted had given him ease and pride in his fatherhood, despite his fear for her, for all these days while she had waited to discover whether she bore a child of love or rape.

"I have no doubt," he said, gathering them both gently into his arms.

"Gavin," Tessa whispered, "I know what you did. We truly belong to you. We would be dead except for you."

His answer was to hold them closer, and Tessa could feel the heavy beat of his heart and the small, warm presence of her son.

Indian and Carmelita checked at the open doorway. Carmelita murmured, "*Madre de Dios,*" and it was closer to a prayer than it had ever been in her speaking. Indian's eyes were suspiciously bright as he took in the scene before him.

Gavin greeted them and invited them to meet his son. Indian chuckled. "Wonder if all new papas smile wide as a river."

They exclaimed over the baby and congratulated Tessa and left her to fall asleep again.

Carmelita asked anxiously, "Is she really all right to leave alone? She's so pale."

"She's all right, but she had one hell of a time," Gavin said slowly, the light fading from his face, and he told them what a close thing it had been.

"These things happen once in a while, an accident of nature. But it is seldom, and you must not fear it will be so again."

"It won't be so again," Gavin answered firmly, and Carmelita sighed inwardly, thinking Tessa was going to have her work cut out for her to make Gavin forget. Strange that a woman could so quickly forget the birth pain in the wonder of her child.

CHAPTER XXIV

Tessa regained her strength rapidly. Each day the shadows around her eyes lessened and the color in her cheeks was better.

Carmelita stayed through the twenty-fourth for the triple birthday, and Tessa was well enough even by then for Gavin to carry her out to the main room for the celebration. They shared a good deal of laughter over Carmelita's refusal to become the fourth to age that day. "I do know when my birthday is, and I've been doing my best to ignore it ever since I became twenty some years ago," she insisted.

In keeping with his desire that they build a fine *rancho*, Don Esteban had sent a *carreta* that creaked under the weight of rose cuttings and young fruit trees. Tessa could not have been more pleased when Gavin told her about it; she knew immediately where she wanted each plant to go. "We will send him news of Brand in return," she said.

Gavin had been startled by her choice of a name. She had wanted no long tangle of Spanish names, just Brand Gavin Ramsay. "Brand," an odd, but strong, masculine name. For a few blank moments he had wondered why she wanted to call the baby that. And then he understood. She meant it in its most literal sense. As Luis had marked him, so he himself had branded his son—every day his own image was clearer in his child. The name was all Yankee crispness, Tessa's final repudiation of Luis.

Tessa's delight in Brand was limitless. She was enchanted that he looked so much like Gavin, enchanted with the perfection of him, the growing awareness in the eyes she knew would remain deep blue. And she admitted to Gavin that she was indecently proud of being able to nurse their son herself, obviously to his good, for he was round and rosy and seemed to grow perceptibly by the day.

It was wonderful to be alive, and she found amusement and joy in a thousand things. One day she overheard Pedro and Indian discussing quite seriously their plans for teaching Brand to ride and hunt, as if the baby were capable of throwing a saddle over a horse already. Sombra too gave her cause for many smiles. He was a beautiful animal, big and powerful, his black coat tipped with silver. His slight limp in no way hindered his speed and strength. He tolerated everyone on the *rancho,* and had even made peace with the dogs, albeit by firm dominance. But his devotion was to her, and Tessa knew what fine protection he offered; just the look of him was enough to frighten off most creatures, man or beast. He was always the first to hear riders coming in, and his response was to find Tessa immediately, warning her with low growls and standing as close to her as he could to defend her. But he was well mannered, and settled down as soon as he knew there was no threat. She knew there was every probability he would leave, perhaps in the next winter, returning to the wilds to find a mate, and so her joy in him was made more intense. Her only fear had been that he might prove dangerously jealous of the baby, but he had not. Brand was part of her, young and defenseless, and Sombra regarded him as an extension of his charge. To Gavin he gave polite attention and what affection he could spare from Tessa and the baby, which Gavin agreed wryly was better than a wolf's animosity.

With so much happiness, feeling the life pulse so strongly, she was slow to realize that something was dreadfully wrong. Gavin had taken to sleeping on a pallet in the study since the birth of Brand. At first it had been reasonable; she had needed a quiet bed and all the sleep she could manage to recover. And then she had unconsciously excused his absence on the grounds that he worked hard, long days, and the baby might disturb him. But it wasn't true; Brand was a happy, contented child who seldom cried and slept through most nights at least until dawn.

More than six weeks had passed since the birth. The early June weather was warm, soft, and lovely. She was fully recovered, and she wanted Gavin. She knew there was no physical reason why they could not be together again. Yet he did not seek his place in their bed. He spent longer and longer hours away from the house, leaving early, returning late.

She knew her body should please him, yet the more physically attractive she felt, the more he retreated. He seemed now to be in full flight from her at the merest suggestion of anything sexual between them, and still she could see the want in his eyes when he thought she was not looking. It took her longer to see the fear, and finally she thought she understood.

She brushed her hair until the heavy dark tresses gleamed to her waist. She perfumed herself with the scent Gavin loved. She fed Brand and put him down, trusting he would sleep the night. She dressed in her finest nightgown, and then she blew out the candle and sat on the edge of the bed, waiting in the darkness. She heard each step as he came into the house; she heard the silence as he paused outside the door, and the renewed sound as he turned and went to the study.

She waited a few minutes longer, then followed him, opening the door quietly.

He lay on the pallet, but a candle still burned on the desk, and he was not asleep. His eyes looked nearly black as he gazed blankly at the ceiling, and it took him a moment to realize Tessa was in the room with him.

257

Startled, he sat up quickly, pulling the bedclothes around him, asking anxiously, "Brand? Is he all right?"

"He is fine and sound asleep. This has nothing to do with him. It has to do with me, with you, with us." She moved into the circle of light and Gavin could see every line of her body through the thin gown. She had never looked more beautiful. He felt as if he were drowning in the enormous amethyst pools of her eyes shadowed by the heavy fringe of black lashes. He wanted to look away and could not. He watched as she deliberately untied the robe and let it fall to the floor. His eyes took in the full upthrusting breasts, the narrow waist and small belly, the dark ruffle of hair, the softly molded thighs. All the slender, supple strength was still there, but all the angles of youth were now rounded into a woman's body. He turned his head away with a groan and closed his eyes, but he saw her as clearly as if he were still gazing at her. "Get out, get out, Tessa!" he snarled.

She moved swiftly, pulling the bedclothes away, touching him, seeing his flesh respond to her with the same fierce quickness as it had always done.

"Gavin, my love," she moaned, "why? I cannot bear to be without you any more. You want me as much as I want you. It is all right now. I am well. It is you who are ill."

He stood suddenly, grabbing her arms and holding her away from him. "You little fool, can't you understand? I might make you pregnant again. Surely women cannot forget so much of childbirth! Twice you nearly died!" His voice was vicious with agony even greater than what she had suffered giving birth to Brand, and she finally knew the full cost to him of the long labor.

"The first was my fault, the second was no one's fault, not yours, not mine. These things happen rarely." She echoed Carmelita's words. "There is no cause to think it will be so again. And a woman while she nurses her child seldom conceives another. But even so, even if, I want you. I am not dead, but I am only half alive without you. Did you think to go on the rest of our lives this way?" she finished, half pleading, half accusing.

His resistance broke, and he pulled her against him, feeling her velvet skin rubbing against him, feeling her

258

mouth nuzzling and kissing as though she could not taste enough of his flesh, hearing the whimpered words of love and need. He pulled her down on the pallet, and when he would have waited, Tessa found him and urged his entry, moaning with pleasure. With all of the times of their lovemaking, none had been like this, not even in the mountains, coming home to fire and storm and infinite peace all one and the same. Tessa heard Gavin's wild murmuring, and she gloried in the love words. And when she felt him try to withdraw, she held him fast within her body and met his joy with her own. They fell asleep without separation, and when they awakened again, it was to a slower rhythm, drawing their love-making out, rediscovering everything of each other.

Brand did not cry until early morning, and Tessa laughed softly as she slipped from Gavin's arms, thinking how comfortable they had been on the impossible bed. She brought the baby back into the room and lay down again, nursing Brand while Gavin watched from a propped elbow.

"I hope my son doesn't find his breakfast in short supply this morning," he said solemnly, his eyes gleaming wickedly, and he watched in delight as a delicate blush stained Tessa's skin.

When Tessa got up to take Brand back to his cradle, Gavin stretched elaborately. "I think I'll stay in bed late this morning. You wouldn't think of hurrying back, would you, Mrs. Ramsay?"

"I would, I would indeed."

They were blissfully happy with each other, with Brand, with their rich yielding land, but the peaceful interlude lasted for far too few days.

Indian rode in from Monterey in the third week of June, and they had never seen him so distraught. He didn't even bother to wash, but dirty and travel-stained as he was, he plunged into his story.

"Th' damndest thing happenin' up north. Some Americans steal some horses, an' now looks like they goin' steal th' country along with th' herd."

Tessa listened in stunned silence while Gavin asked questions and patiently sorted out the story. Even sorted out it was nothing short of fantastic. More and more immigrants had been coming to settle in the valley of the Sacramento River, where the man Sutter's fort remained a gathering point. Some had taken Mexican citizenship to acquire land, others hadn't even bothered to do that, but even so, the government had been tolerant of them, partly because it had always been to immigrants and partly because it didn't have the forces to drive them out anyway. But now a most incredible thing had happened. A herd of nearly two hundred horses had been dispatched from Sonoma to Monterey in the charge of a Mexican officer and several *vaqueros,* and a wild rumor had sprung up that this foretold the coming of a fully equipped army to drive the foreigners out. A group of settlers had taken it upon themselves to steal the horses, and this accomplished, they had ridden to Sonoma where, on June 14, they had demanded the surrender of General Mariano Guadalupe Vallejo, the ranking Mexican military officer of the region. Having no other choice, he had surrendered like a gentleman.

"Vallejo!" Tessa exploded. "But surely he has always favored that the United States should have California someday. So it was said in Monterey. To subject him to such indignity!"

"It's true, he is known as a friend. Those idiots! I can see the shabby reasoning behind this. They stole some horses, and stealing horses is against the law here and everywhere else, so they decided to move right along to something they no doubt believe ranks with Independence Day for sheer patriotism." Gavin's face was grim, and the rest of the information didn't ease his expression, not even when Indian described the Californios' reaction to the flag the rebels had hoisted—a rag sporting the Lone Star from Texas, plus a grizzly bear and the words, "California Republic." It was badly executed, in berry juice, and the natives insisted the bear looked like nothing so much as a pig. "Th' Americans pretty drunk, so I 'spect th' drawin' suffered."

"What's happening now? Does Larkin have something to do with this?" Gavin asked.

"Didn't talk to him, but hear he ragin'. Seems he know nothin' 'til it all done. Nobody knows much, but there sure be lots of loose talk. War with Mexico seem close, an' if that true, California don' be neglected. 'Nother thing, there be a man, a Captain Frémont, engineer in th' United States Army. He be all over California now, an' if he's leadin' them horse thieves, then our government at home ought'd be shamed." Indian was looking at Tessa when he finished, and Gavin's words were for her too.

"I won't deny the United States has wanted California for a long time, nor will I deny that Thomas Larkin as the country's representative here has worked diligently to that end, urged on by his fear England might beat us to it. You know as well as I do, the Mexican government has never given enough care or attention to this land to hold it or defend it, and the Californios in charge now aren't doing any better. But I swear to you, it was to be by gentle persuasion or outright purchase, not this way. Our government doesn't work through horse thieves and renegade army officers."

"Doesn't it?" she asked coldly. She thought of Micheltorena's finish, which had also begun with the theft of horses, but a Yankee war would not be so bloodless. And then her face crumpled. "Oh, God! I don't even know how I feel about it anymore. After what happened to you, after my father, after everything, I just don't know. I'm part of both sides without belonging to either. What will happen? There will be a war?"

"To have a war, you normally need two opposing armies at the very least," Gavin said slowly. "And that's hardly the case in California. But there might be marauding and skirmishes here and there, which is why I'm going to take you and Brand to Monterey."

"I won't go!" she protested.

"Yes, you will, without choice this time."

"Gavin, be reasonable. If there is trouble, it's much more likely to be in the capital than out here." Like many others, Tessa still called Monterey the capital, though Governor Pico had changed it to Los Angeles, a move which had done nothing more than to increase the rivalry between the northern and southern sections of the country.

"Anything that happens in Monterey will be accomplished with a drumbeat, fancy uniforms, and a minimum of bloodshed. Out here it might not be so civilized. I don't want to argue about it."

261

She made one last attempt. "What about the other women and children?"

"It's up to them and their husbands. They can all come to Monterey if they wish."

It did nothing to improve her temper to find that the *vaqueros* and their wives were serenely decisive about staying at the *rancho*. These troubles had happened before in California, no need to worry. Indian raids were dangerous; political upheavals were ridiculous. She felt as if she'd been defeated before the first battle, but she could not blame Gavin—remaining on the *rancho* without him had once proved disastrous. Indian too would stay for a few days at least.

Traveling with a small baby was extremely fatiguing, even though Gavin fashioned a carrying sling and had Brand with him for more than his share of the time. They had left Sombra tied and howling dismally, to be released when they were well away, but before the day was half gone he had joined them, looking very pleased with himself and trailing a chewed-through length of rawhide.

"Christ, that's all we need, to ride into Monterey with a wolf!" Gavin swore, but Tessa insisted she'd feel much safer with him along, and she was kept very busy when they finally reached the outskirts of the town until she had Sombra safely stowed at Carmelita's. Sombra obviously knew this place was not his territory and he did not go out of his way to be aggressive, but he had no reluctance in putting dogs who got too close in their places.

Carmelita greeted them laughing and shaking her head. "The Ramsays don't even travel as other families do. No servants, an infant, and one very large wolf."

They asked her immediately for news, and she threw up her hands in mock despair. "Anyone who believes even half of what is said in Monterey is a gullible fool. There are tales of armies marching, but I ask you, where would such armies come from? There are stories of Yankees stealing from Californios and the other way around. There are proclamations from both sides claiming God for an ally. The strongest rumor is that war is now a fact between the United States and Mexico. That, I fear, I believe."

262

There was confirmation that there had been bloodshed in the northern affair. Joaquin de la Torre had collected a small force south of Sonoma after the capture of the town and had marched to liberate it. The Bears, *los Osos,* as the insurgents were called by the Californios, had marched out to meet him. The Californios had no weapons to match the Yankee rifles and had lost two men and had had several wounded in the first fire. Only by the ruse of a supposedly secret message telling of a march in one direction had Torre managed to escape in another. But compared to what the toll might have been, the battle had been fairly bloodless. If there was to be more trouble, it would be in the south where General Castro and Pío Pico were endeavoring to overcome their sectional difficulties in order to mount some resistance against the invaders. Gavin had been in California long enough now to know the hopelessness of such an attempt, and he only hoped as few as possible would die.

They hadn't long to wait for the truth of Carmelita's belief. War with Mexico was a reality, having begun somewhere outside of California along the lower Rio Grande weeks before in a clash between Mexican and American cavalry patrols. It seemed to make no difference that there was good reason to believe the Americans had been defeated in the first encounter on Mexican territory, where they should not have trespassed in the first place.

Word had traveled across Mexico to Mazatlán, and the United States Pacific Squadron under Commodore John D. Sloat had set sail. Carmelita and the Ramsays watched the arrival of the flagship *Savannah* to join two others in port at Monterey on July 1. An officer came ashore from the flagship to offer the usual civilities—a salute to the Mexican flag, but the honor was declined because there was not enough powder to return the gesture, and the flag hadn't been flying for several months anyway.

"So much for the dangerous Californios," Tessa commented bitterly. "Surely this man has come to join the conquest, so why does he offer to salute the country?"

The answer became apparent in the next few days. Though indeed Sloat's orders had been to come to California and to hold her, mainly against British intervention, until the war with Mexico should be concluded and a decision made, the news of the insurgents in the north and the presence of an army officer with them had shocked him and made him even more hesitant than was his normal habit. And perhaps his indecisiveness was deepened by Larkin's attitude, which was becoming clearer by the day. The consul hated the *Osos* nearly as much as the natives did, and he was appalled at their actions. He still hoped desperately for a voluntary, peaceful conquest by means of the Californios simply choosing his government over their old system, and he was enraged by the actions of the Bears, which made his plan more sure to fail each day. Larkin was the highest-ranking American in California, so it would not be surprising if Commodore Sloat listened to him. Larkin visited him for a long while on the second, and received a nine-gun salute when he departed the ship.

Sloat's men had been given leave to come ashore a hundred at a time for twenty-four-hour periods, and Monterey had a strange flavor, not quite under siege but certainly aware of the military presence. The ship was dressed and her guns fired on the fourth in honor of Independence Day. Tessa observed waspishly that even if it weren't a war, it surely sounded like one, particularly on a day of such mockery.

Finally on the seventh, the Stars and Stripes were raised above the old capital. It began early in the morning when Sloat sent several officers ashore with a formal demand for surrender of the post. The message was delivered to Mariano Silva, an old artillery captain, who answered politely that he had no authority to submit, no arms, troops, or public property to relinquish anyway, and suggested the demand be made to General Castro, to whom the summons had been addressed in the first place.

Since Castro was not in Monterey, Sloat proceeded with his plans. At ten o'clock, two-hundred-fifty men, seamen, and marines, were landed from the squadron with strict orders against pillage or violence of any sort. They marched to the Customs House, a proclamation written by Sloat was read, and the flag of the United States was raised. The troops and the spectators gave three cheers, and Tessa thought sourly that the latter joined in because
264

anything was better than what they'd heard of *los Osos*. Each of the three men-of-war fired a salute of twenty-one guns, and it was done.

Indian was with them, having ridden in to report that all seemed calm and safe at the *rancho,* and they all stared at the flag fluttering in the light sea breeze.

"It's forever, isn't it?" Tessa whispered, and she longed for the secure weight of Brand in her arms, but he had been left behind in the care of one of Carmelita's servants who could serve as wet nurse.

Indian nudged Carmelita, and they drifted away to share their own feelings about the change.

Gavin put his arm around Tessa, dreading to find her resistant, but she pressed close without hesitation. "You will find this hard to believe, my love, but I am not even sure of what I feel right now. The flag was not my father's, but it was my mother's and mine. But I was a rover until I met you, and rovers depend on countries more or less respecting each other and allowing free trade. War and conquest are only profitable if you are an army supplier." He paused before he added quietly, "None of that answers your question, does it? I expect it is forever. The United States has a habit of holding on to what it takes."

A few days after the flag had been raised in Monterey, Admiral Seymour of the British fleet arrived aboard the *Collingwood.* He accepted what the Americans had done with dry humor, having neither the means nor the inclination to undo it.

"It's a good thing the British recognize the difficulties of supplying an army this far from home," Gavin commented, "for if ever there was a time when their intervention to help the Californios could be justified, it's now. It seems their intentions were severely misjudged."

He pursued every piece of information relentlessly, doing his utmost to assess the situation. It was clear that the Stars and Stripes now flew over all the major northern towns. It had occurred to him from the very first that any change in the easy-going California way was going to raise questions of land ownership sooner or later. Would the old grants be recognized? And even if they were in principle, how would that work in fact with so many of the boundaries so vaguely defined? His future, Tessa's, Brand's, Indian's—all tied to the land now.

Sloat's proclamation, posted in Spanish and in English after the reading, was very conciliatory, containing such phrases as "its peaceful inhabitants will enjoy the same rights and privileges as the citizens of any other portion of that territory," going on to predict the bright future of California, especially in her land and products, and assuring that "all persons holding titles to real estate or in quiet possession of lands under a color of right shall have those titles and rights guaranteed to them." But the fact remained that it was an odd business for the United States to be claiming to be fighting the invasion of Texas on one hand while invading California on the other. And one would have had to be blind and deaf to assume that Sloat's kindly view was the only one in California. The part the *Osos* would play in the new government was unknown and potentially explosive. If the proclamation that had been issued by one of their leaders, William B. Ide, was any indication of their attitude, the outlook was grim.

Ide's proclamation lost none of its onus in view of the fact that it had been written for and read to the people imprisoned in Sonoma for the express purpose of explaining to them in the loftiest terms that their arbitrary loss of liberty was for their own good and would lead to even greater benefits for them.

For once, Gavin had wished he had a wife less intelligent and aware. Laboriously hand-written copies of Ide's words had reached Monterey, and when Gavin had read it, his first thought had been that he hoped to God Tessa never saw it, a foolish hope.

She had been furious, eyes flashing dangerously, the color bright on her high cheekbones. "You have read it! This imbecile of a man writes as if to serfs who have lived under a wicked king and have now been freed by Heaven's own angels. He even deigns to tell us how we may now become true human beings under this new rabble of a government. It is the worst of insults!"

"It is indeed," Gavin agreed wearily. He considered trying to explain to her how exotic, sinful, and backward California would appear to a narrow-minded and strictly

266

Protestant New Englander, but he had decided against it. He thought of his uncle, and for an instant all the old hurt and anger raged in him again. It was impossible to explain the rigid intolerance and unending self-righteousness of such men to someone like his wife.

And because Ide's proclamation had preceded Sloat's, Gavin could not blame Tessa's skeptical opinion of the latter—voices of moderation were so often drowned by those more strident.

The arrival on Sunday, July 19, of a battalion of Bears with Frémont leading them was not a reassuring sight. They had been preceded by another troop of Americans, sailors so clumsy on horseback that Tessa, bred to grace and ease in the saddle, marveled that they remained on their horses at all.

Frémont and his men were not so easily dismissed. A vast cloud of dust was first sighted and from it emerged a long file of the wildest looking men Tessa and Carmelita had ever seen. Even Gavin and Indian, who were familiar with the type, were amazed by the stream of so many.

Frémont rode ahead, lean and active looking, dressed in a blouse and leggings and wearing a felt hat. Behind him came his bodyguard, five Delaware Indians, in charge of two baggage horses. They were followed by the others, two by two, rifles held by one hand across the pommels of their saddles. Many were so dirty and weathered, they were darker than the Indians.

Gavin explained the differences, making a quick count and estimating that about forty of them were Frémont's regular men, mostly backwoodsmen from Tennessee wearing what passed as their uniforms—long, loose coats of deerskin tied in front with thongs, homemade trousers of the same, and hats and caps of various designs—and riding on several types of saddles, according to their own preferences. The rest were an even more disreputable-looking lot Frémont had picked up recently. Many had hair and beards that suffered from infrequent trimmings and even more seldom washings. They all bristled with weapons, revolving pistols, and long knives in addition to their deadly rifles.

There had to be at least two hundred, and they drove with them even more horses plus a brass field gun, the horses and the gun recently acquired in California.

"And they think us uncivilized," Tessa sneered. "I have never seen such savages, nor have I ever smelled such a stench. No animals would ever be so filthy!"

The battalion set up quarters in the open air on the hills near the town under the shelter of some large firs. Though they were supposed to be well disciplined, forbidden the use of liquor, many spent the next two days in drunken debauchery in the town, and a few were simply missing by the time the rest of the offenders were marched away to be confined to camp. Tessa and Carmelita kept close to the house during those days.

For Tessa, having to meet Captain Frémont socially was the final straw. At first she refused to go at all. "Monterey is such a place that if the devil himself came calling, there would be a party given for him, but that does not mean I would have to be one of the guests," she protested.

"Not unless you had to deal with him," Gavin pointed out. "We will have to deal with Frémont and his kind. We are landowners, and we will be affected by the new government in California. I can't force you to go, but I must, and I would prefer to have you at my side, always."

She would never be able to refuse when he put it like that, and he knew it, but he had to grant the victory was partially hers. He liked Frémont no better than she did, and he watched her reaction to the man with amused wonder. She had never looked so much the aristocrat, so haughty, elegant, and unyielding. Her English was far more precise than usual, and everything she said was sweetly, subtly barbed. Even the conquering hero seemed daunted by her icy courtesy that bordered on contempt.

However, Gavin was not sure who had won the final round after he heard Frémont's last words to Tessa. "You remind me of my wife, Jessie. She too is a most formidable woman. My compliments, Mrs. Ramsay." The captain gave her a formal bow and moved off.

Jessie Benton Frémont, a well-known name now though the lady herself was at home in the States, well known because her father was one of the most powerful men in

Washington, Senator Thomas Hart Benton of Missouri. For the first time, it occurred to Gavin that Frémont's activities in California might well have arisen from the machinations of the ambitious senator, having nothing at all to do with the normal decision-making process of the United States government. It was a chilling thought, all too probable in light of what had happened, and he didn't hear what Tessa was saying until she tugged at his sleeve and repeated the words more strongly.

"I want to go home. And if you won't go with me, I'll take Brand and Sombra and go without you. Brand howls every time those cursed guns salute something and so does Sombra, who is as miserable as I am at being a prisoner here. Another day or another Frémont, and I'll be howling with them."

He looked down at her, seeing her more clearly than he had for days, seeing the faint shadows under her eyes, the pale, too delicate cast of her face, the loss of the rich bloom of health and happiness she had had so short a time ago on the *rancho*. He knew these were the physical signs of the deeper mental and spiritual strain of the past weeks, and he didn't think the immediate future was going to be any easier. Commodore Sloat had announced his intention to retire from his position in California at an early date the week before, and Commodore Stockton, who had arrived from Honolulu, had been appointed by Sloat commander-in-chief of all forces and operations on land. Stockton gave every indication of being Frémont's willing listener.

Gavin restrained his impulse to take Tessa in his arms until he had guided her through their ritual good-bys and thanks and had signaled their departure to Indian and Carmelita, who appeared bent on watching the fascinating spectacle for a while longer, but once they were outside in the sheltering dark, he took full advantage, holding Tessa so tightly she squealed in protest against the pressure on her full breasts.

"We'll go home, love. It's time, and I am as ready as you are to quit this place," he acknowledged, holding her more gently.

He waited until she had fed the baby and had joined him in bed, settling against him with a tired little sigh.

269

He stroked her hair and traced the planes of her face, and his voice was as soft as his touch. "Sweetheart, we've come this far. We've lived through a great deal together, and we haven't only survived, we've got a fine son and our love for each other. It's time we paid a visit to Rancho Valle del Mar." Deliberately he did not call it her home, knowing she did not regard it thus, glad that she did not in spite of the untruth. "It is only just. Ramón and María have a right to see and love Brand. Even your father has that right."

When she stiffened and would have pulled away, he held her. "They can't bind you or hurt you by love or by hate any more. You are part of me as I am part of you now. Nothing, no one has a stronger claim than that."

He was filled with joy at the sudden softness of her body relaxing against his. He didn't need her murmur of compliance to know it was accomplished. He hardly understood his own motivation. He suspected that his own lack of roots accounted for his belief in hers. With all the confusion of the past days and the painful changes, some yet to be, he wanted her to be able to draw strength from the familiar land of her childhood. And his mention of the people who must see Brand was more of the truth than he would tell her. He had never thought to feel any kindness toward her father, but when Tessa had so nearly died in childbirth, he had suffered an agonizing moment of kinship with the man, knowing how mad and meaningless life would be without Tessa, knowing how Michael had felt at the loss of Tessa's mother.

CHAPTER XXV

The trip to Rancho Valle del Mar was filled with memories for both of them, some separate, some shared. But Gavin saw with great pleasure that the color was returning to Tessa's face, the tenseness draining away, her eyes gleaming with anticipation, and he was glad to know the decision he had forced on her was a good one.

The first twenty-four hours of their visit were chaotic. The Ramirez family seemed little changed. María made vain attempts to control her tears, but she appeared to have an endless supply for the joy of seeing her darling again and of holding Brand, whom she considered her grandchild, an idea wholeheartedly accepted by Brand, who beamed and laughed every time María took him onto the broad comfort of her lap or ample bosom. Ramón wore a wide continuous grin, and Juan and Julio regarded Tessa with awe for having produced this fine son and for being so obviously the mature and loving wife of the Yankee.

Tessa did not feel mature. She felt young and carefree again, wanting to behave like Amordoro, who seemed to recognize his old pastures and was as frisky as a colt. Even Sombra behaved himself, settling down contentedly once he was assured that all were friendly and no one was going to threaten his mistress or the baby. The people of the *rancho* regarded the wolf as yet another proof that Tessa had never lived quite like other girls, and they were proud of the difference and careful of the wolf.

The only dread was the inevitable meeting with Michael Macleod, which the sooner faced and gotten over, the better. But they saw no trace of him until the second day, and even Gavin was shaken by the change in him. María had tried to warn them, but it was still a shock. He looked old, tired, and feeble, though he had obviously made a pathetic effort to appear washed and brushed. And the worst of it was, at his first sight of Tessa, he blinked and called her softly by her mother's name.

Easily she did what she could not have done before. She went to him, putting her arms around him, and eyes bright with tears, said gently, "No, Father, I'm Tessa. We've come to show you your grandson."

They found some comfort in the fact that even in his vague and weak condition, there was no doubt of Michael's instant love for Brand. And Brand was happy and contented in his grandfather's arms as if he recognized a kindred childish spirit.

Only once did a spark of Michael's old malice show when he asked without preamble, "Did you know Luis is dead?"

Tessa felt a small shock run through her, but she answered evenly, "No, how should I know that? I can't say the news saddens me. What happened, did he finally fall off his horse and break his neck?"

For a moment her father's eyes were sharp and alert. "He was murdered, emasculated and then killed with a knife. No one knows who did it."

"Bless him, whoever it was," she said flatly. Gavin said nothing at all.

Gavin took care that no one saw his back during the visit. Even when the servants brought in water for warm bathing, he was always covered until they had departed. But when he and Tessa visited the pool they did not need to fear discovery. They stripped, swam, and played as they had in the mountains. And when they made love in the place where Gavin had lain bleeding from Tessa's knife, their spirits experienced as much as their bodies. "But for that day, there would never have been this," Tessa whispered, and Gavin heard it as his own voice.

Having been in the thick of things in Monterey, they found it hard to accept the political indifference at the *rancho*. Since couriers had been riding up and down the coast and had occasionally begged hospitality here, there was some idea that the government was changing, but there was little concern about it. Gavin spoke at length to Ramón to make sure the man understood the gravity of the situation and would seek him out if ownership of the land was challenged. He believed Michael's original United States citizenship would be of great advantage should problems arise, but he wanted to see the papers of the grant, and with María's help, he and Tessa slipped into Michael's study while he was in the garden with Brand and María.

They found the documents blotched and stained with age and sealing wax. Tessa translated, because her knowledge of written Spanish was so much better than his. She recognized all of the landmarks used to define the boundaries of the *rancho*, but she had to agree that they would be difficult to defend to someone who had not been born and raised on the land.

"We will just have to wait and see what happens," Gavin said. "There's no sense in making an issue of it now."

272

They stayed less than a week, traveling back to Monterey to spend one more night at Carmelita's to glean the latest news, something Tessa felt she could do without even while she recognized Gavin's need to know. They found that Commodore Stockton had wasted no time in his desire to subdue the south and had already sailed off, as had Gillespie, a government agent turned captain, a shadowy man who had been with Frémont for most of the time since his brief visit in Monterey with Thomas Larkin before the rebellion. It was difficult to ascertain what his role had been, and it hardly seemed important now anyway. Frémont himself, now a major of the volunteer battalion, the California Battalion, once the Bear Flag soldiers, had migrated south with the others. Even Larkin had followed in their wake, still desperately hoping for a peaceful takeover.

They thanked Carmelita for the care and shelter she had given them and bade her come to visit Brand, of whom she was very fond, even if she didn't miss the rest of them. And with great relief, they turned homeward to where Indian and their household awaited them.

But though Gavin was as glad as Tessa to be back on their own land and to find all undisturbed, he had no intention of losing track of what was happening in California. He and Indian took turns making regular trips to Monterey for news, and when they felt they must both be attending to business on the *rancho,* they sent a *vaquero,* though they could ill afford his labor loss, not to mention their own. They both knew that periods of transition in any country are dangerous, and neither one had ever trusted to ignorance to get himself through. Staying alive as they had had always demanded every bit of available knowledge.

They were helped somewhat by the publication of *The Californian* in Monterey. A dingy, badly done job, the first newspaper in California was still better than nothing. If for no other reason, Tessa delighted in it because it was something new to read, and she swallowed her bitter reactions to some of the columns for that reason.

With the newspaper and the ever numerous rumors, they did their best to piece together what was happening. One of the most startling events, confirmed as true, was that

273

a shipload of more than two hundred people had landed in Yerba Buena on San Francisco Bay at the end of July. They included among their number some one hundred children and a roughly equal number of men and women. The women and children were strange enough, but the fact that they were almost all members of the Mormon sect was a far greater oddity. Almost every citizen in the town had turned out to stare, and many had been disappointed by the absence of cloven hooves, horns, and tails. The Mormons were not popular in the States, their practice of polygamy being thoroughly condemned, at least outwardly, by almost everyone outside their brotherhood. They had sailed with no idea of the United States takeover, intending to meet their leader, Brigham Young, with other followers who seemed to have tarried elsewhere, all of this in the firm belief that California was outside of the United States' territory, a land of milk and honey free for the taking. They seemed to be adjusting well to the somewhat different reality.

The south seemed fairly quiet, General Castro and Pío Pico were both reported to have fled to Mexico. And they heard that Larkin had been appointed Naval Agent for the Coast of California by Commodore Stockton. They were glad for their friend, whose life was so bound up with the country's, and they hoped the official confirmation from Washington would be forthcoming by the next year.

And then quite suddenly all of Gavin's attention was refocused on his wife. He was watching her brush her hair with long, steady strokes, watching the grace of her slender arms, the soft curves of her body showing through the thin gown. He didn't even know all the subtle signs his subconscious was picking up, but he recognized the total.

He sat up in bed, and his voice was so sharp, Tessa dropped the brush. "Are you pregnant again?"

She took her time retrieving the brush and putting it down again before she faced him. "I'm not sure. My body has been a bit confused, but I think so. I think I'm about three months along."

"Nursing Brand, it wasn't supposed to happen," he said desperately, and she went to him swiftly, cupping his face in her hands, seeing the fear reawakening in his eyes.

274

"Don't, Gavin, don't feel this way! It will be easier this time, and I'm happy about it, truly I am. It is my joy to be able to give you children, and I don't want Brand growing up all by himself. It must be so much better and so much more fun to have brothers and sisters to share your childhood with, not just other children, but children who are close by blood and the same in many ways. Besides, there is nothing to be done now anyway—except this." She kissed him deeply.

"Perhaps this time we'll have a daughter," Gavin murmured against her throat, and the words were the best acceptance she could have wished.

What she had told Gavin was true; she looked forward to the new baby with far more anticipation than fear. Her fear stemmed from an entirely different source. They had heard the news that on September 22, hostilities had been renewed. Gillespie had been put in command of Los Angeles and had so insulted and mismanaged the people that trouble between the citizenry and the soldiers was inevitable. The Californios had laid siege to the small American garrison in Los Angeles and had won, taking some twenty Americans prisoner. At the end of the month, Gillespie and the Los Angeles force had been permitted to depart for San Pedro with the promise they would sail from California, something they had no intention of doing. They had joined with a relief party at the port and had marched inland again to try to recapture Los Angeles. The Californios had won again, forcing the Americans to retreat back to San Pedro.

Things seemed to quiet down for a while after that, but even Tessa, who would so have liked to believe there would be no more trouble, knew it wasn't over. The Yankees would never leave the south in Californio hands, and Tessa could not blame them. Such a situation would mean endless years of petty wars. She had come slowly but steadily to the knowledge that since this American takeover had begun and was now in earnest, it would be best for all when it was fully finished. Even Thomas Larkin, who had hated the mode of conquest, was now proceeding to do his utmost to help the new government run smoothly. And the undeniable fact was that the Americans would come in ever greater numbers with their superior weapons and fighting knowledge, and though the Californios must be proud of their recent victories, if not amazaged by them, surely the best of them must know they could not continue to win. Tessa's terror was that Gavin or Indian would be moved to take an active part in the fighting. She fought the possibility by never mentioning the idea.

But in late November, they received such terrible news, silence was no longer viable. Thomas Larkin had been captured and was a prisoner of the Californios. Rachel had gone to Yerba Buena, a predominantly Yankee town —a move Tessa insisted must have been on the advice of others and much against her will, since Rachel was terribly fond of Monterey and her home there—and their little girl, Adeline, had fallen seriously ill. Larkin had been in a hurry to cover the distance from Monterey to her bedside and had been less cautious than usual in his anxiety and had fallen into enemy hands. Enemy hands— terrible to think of them that way when many were his own longtime friends.

"Do you go to fight now?" Tessa asked bluntly, unable to keep up the pretense that there was no reason. To prevent Gavin's action either by silence or tears was a risk too great to take any more, a chance of earning his resentment forever.

Gavin looked at her for a long moment before he spoke. "I won't deny that Indian and I have talked about it, and this makes it more difficult. God knows. Thomas Larkin has been kind to us. And for both of us, doing something is easier than standing aside. But I'm not going and neither is Indian." His eyes held hers. "In spite of what Luis and his men did, we have been well treated by the Californios. My wife is one of them, and so is her great-grandfather, a man I greatly admire. I approve no more than he does of the way this conquest had been accomplished. I have something to show you."

He was back shortly, handing her heavy sheets of parchment. She did not need the signature and rubric to recognize the handwriting of Don Esteban's.

"He sent this to me with the gifts for Brand," Gavin explained. He had sent news of their son's birth southward by courier, and Tessa had been delighted with the ex-

276

quisitely carved yet sturdy toys from Mexico her great-grandfather had sent to Brand along with a small saddle with richly embossed leather to be used when the boy first learned to ride. She had had no knowledge of the letter to Gavin until this moment, and her hands trembled. Don Esteban had written in English so there would be no misunderstanding on the part of the Yankee.

"Don Gavin, husband of my beloved great-granddaughter." She blinked away tears at his use of the word "beloved," beautiful even in English, so that she could see to read the rest:

> This is a time of grave trouble in California. But the weakness has been in our own government for so long, this was sure to happen. You Yankees are a young, strong people. Until you become as old as we are, nothing will stand before your strength. But I am saddened that it has come to pass in this way, in this uncivilized and savage manner. We Californios have always welcomed you and bid you live in peace on land we have freely granted to you. The repayment of our generosity is bitter and unjust. The end is sure. It matters not how long or how hard we fight, the victory will be yours. I am almost able to see the light of hope in change. Perhaps life will be better here for many. But I am too old to welcome change so great as this for myself.

> I write to you these words as one man telling another the things of his heart. But there are more important things to say to you. You, and Tessa, as she has always been more than Teresa María, are well matched for life together. She is of both worlds, though I judge the greater part of her heart is Californio. She must change to go on with you in this new world, and I would not desire that it be otherwise. You must not allow her to take you from your purpose. If it is necessary in your spirit that you join your countrymen in their fight at this moment, then so you must do and she must accept. It will not change my rejoicing that my great-granddaughter belongs to no other but you. I will always believe that I chose most wisely for her.

> If Death neglects my aged bones until there is peace again in this country and it is possible once more to move

277

from place to place without an army, I will do my utmost
to gain sight of your son and your land.

Go with God.

She let the tears blind her then. "Oh, Gavin, I was so
sure of his power, I haven't worried about him at all! Yet
he is sorely troubled and still takes time to bid you follow
your own conscience even if it leads you another way
from his. And I have done nothing except pray that you
stay by me no matter how the war fares. I am ashamed
at the selfishness of my love, selfish in so many ways since
the day I met you."

Gavin drew her close. "You are the mother of one
child born, another unborn. If you did not do your utmost
to preserve the lives of those you love, you would be a
strange woman. I doubt that many women have sent their
husbands and sons to wars willingly. And I suspect Don
Esteban of being no less lovingly devious than you are.
He gave me a clear choice, trusting I would not choose to
march away from you with Frémont troops. And as for
your great-grandfather himself, his power is still great.
He is a longtime and honored citizen of California, besides being a wily old fox, not an easy man to threaten
or ignore."

She relaxed against him, letting herself draw strength
and comfort from him, knees weak with relief that he
was not going.

Indian made a trip to Monterey and brought back the
news that the Californios had won yet another victory in
the south, this time against the Great Army of the West
led by General Stephen Watts Kearny marching in from
a bloodless conquest of New Mexico. However, the Americans had not been at full force, Kearny had thought the
conquest of California well nigh complete, and had sent
most of his troops to aid General Zachary Taylor in
Mexico. The Americans had used poor judgment. Weary
and lacking a clear sight of the unfamiliar terrain due to
fog and a cold, heavy mist, they had attacked a force
under Andrés Pico near the Indian village of San Pasqual
not far from San Diego on December 6. Their gunpowder
was wet; their guns silent. Their mounts were mostly tired

mules and undisciplined horses recently seized from the Mexicans. They were no match for the lances and superb horses of the Californios. Reports gave each side eighteen wounded, but Pico had lost only one man, Kearny more than twenty.

Tessa took no joy in the news; she went on praying the war would be finished. But another piece of news interested her even more than the battle. Rachel Larkin had returned to Monterey. Her daughter had died in Yerba Buena, and Thomas was still a prisoner. Tessa was determined to go and see her, and nothing Gavin could do or say was going to prevent the visit, so he gave in and took her, cursing most of the way, fearful she would sicken in the damp winter weather, fearful she would lose the child she carried.

Though neither of his fears were realized, it was a miserable trip, especially for Tessa who had left Brand behind to be wet-nursed by Flora and missed him horribly, having never been so long away from him since his birth. She missed Sombra too, and secretly wished he'd find a way to get free again and follow, but she knew once he found that Brand was still at the *rancho*, he would settle down to his guard duties.

But they both admitted they were glad they'd gone. Not even Rachel's self-reliant New England character prevented her from showing her pathetic pleasure in the effort they had made to visit her. She too was carrying a child, due in April, and she was terrified that her baby would never see its father at all and she never again. Tessa kept every trace of doubt from her voice when she reminded Rachel that Thomas had many California friends who would keep him from harm. It did not help Rachel that her two eldest sons, Oliver and Frederic, only twelve and ten years old, had left in the spring and were away in the States for schooling, though Oliver had been away before to Oahu for the same purpose. Tessa hoped there would be fine schools in California before Brand and the baby yet to be were ready to attend. She shivered inwardly, thinking of Rachel's lot—a pregnancy nearly every year since marriage in 1833, a child within her, two young ones at her side, two so many miles away, and the dead. Her own did not seem far different—a child

279

within, Brand, and the dead, the hardest to accept, the abrupt finality she prayed would never be so again.

Rachel's gracious nature made the hardest factor of the visit unimportant. They had dreaded her reaction to their noninvolvement in the war, but Rachel judged them wise, pointing out that even her husband, who wanted California for the United States, had been dismayed by the means used to take the country and had been careful about his own involvement in the conflict.

They were back at the *rancho* for Christmas, and had convinced Carmelita to come with them. It might have been a sad, tense time had it not been for Brand, whose presence made gaiety not only mandatory but surprisingly easy. He was so bright and responsive, it was difficult not to spoil him, and everyone did. Tessa knew she was no better than the rest. Brand looked more like his father every day, his eyes ever a deeper blue with mischievous light in them, his hair glossy black. Even his hands looked like Gavin's; small though they were, they gave promise of the same long strong lines. She thought it would be none too soon when he would share the attention with another child.

Carmelita watched and fussed over her until Tessa took her in hand. "You've got to stop it, my friend. You'll have me an invalid. The ride to Monterey did no harm. The babe stirs, and I feel very well." It was perfectly true, and in addition, the thought was never far from her mind that she had Gavin beside her while Rachel waited to know what would happen to her husband.

They saw 1847 in with one shared wish, that the war would be over soon, and the wish was granted in short days. Frémont, in command of the California Battalion, was marching south. There were reports of an indecisive battle at Navidad in the Salinas Valley. Mud and rain were slowing him down far more than the opposing army. Stockton and Kearny led a force of some six hundred Americans from San Diego overland, north to Los Angeles. They too engaged in a skirmish, this early in January, on the banks of the Río de San Gabriel.

And then it was finished. The Californio forces were unorganized, split by endless internal squabbles, and badly armed. They made their last stand on the banks of the

Río de Los Angeles, but retreated quickly under light artillery fire. Hostilities were formally ended on January 13, when what remained of Andrés Pico's command surrendered to Frémont near Los Angeles at Cahuenga, the same place where Micheltorena who been defeated. As Gavin had observed when it all began, two armies were needed to make a war, and despite their valiant efforts, the Californios had never quite managed to field anything that could properly be called an army.

Frémont was appointed civil governor at the end of January, but his rule hardly extended beyond his headquarters in Los Angeles and his time in office was short, as General Kearny had the position by March. There was a bitter quarrel beginning involving Stockton, Kearny, and Frémont, which seemed based in jealousy over who had the most authority. Sly tongues had dubbed Kearny "the rising sun" and his lack of popularity worked to opposite effect for Frémont, who seemed to many much more palatable.

It was a strange time of transition. Though the war was over in California, it continued in Mexico, and until that was concluded, there was little that could be done with California either, though there was also little doubt that the United States would hold onto her, whatever the outcome in Mexico. The government was mainly military though local *alcaldes* were chosen or remained in office. The law was a mishmash of Spanish tradition and Yankee on-the-spot rulings. Land-grant confusion was already beginning, with more Americans coming in and holding to their belief in squatting. It had worked everywhere else in the West, why not in California? Gavin sincerely hoped the situation would ease when a uniform code of laws and courts was adopted, though when that would be was anyone's guess. He and Indian were doing all in their power to file papers with every official they thought might be of use to reconfirm their right to Rancho Magnífico.

The best news they received was that Thomas Larkin was back with Rachel. He had been released after Cahuenga, though he had been delayed because he had had some trouble finding a ship to travel north, a necessity at the time since land travel was still dangerous with the restless aftermaths of war. Though his confinement had been a severe mental strain, he had been well treated and protected from the few who had wanted to kill him.

The worst of the winter's stories had nothing to do with the war, but rather with a group of immigrants from the States. They had delayed so long before they reached the Sierras that an early and heavy snowfall had caught them in the mountains. Some of the people had stayed in the mountains while others had gone for help. Both groups had suffered starvation and the deaths of some of their fellows; both groups had eaten of the dead. The Donner Party would be long remembered.

When Indian told them the story, Tessa huddled close to Gavin. "We were in those mountains, and it was so lovely."

His arms were warm and comforting as he held her. "We knew what we were doing and when we had to leave. To ask the mountains for kindness in winter is foolish, no matter how tragic the outcome."

They were cushioned. Nothing seemed as real as the approaching birth. And in that they were both together and separated, both wanting another healthy, bright child like Brand, but Gavin again had all he could do to control his fear for Tessa while her joy and anticipation were boundless. She was simply convinced it would not be a repeat of Brand's difficult birth. And she was now sure it was going to be another boy. She even had a name ready for him. He would be called Jefferson Ray Ramsay, after Indian and Ramón.

It had taken a lot of subtlety to worm it out of Indian without arousing his suspicions. She had gone to great lengths before she had asked with elaborate casualness, "Indian is your perfect name; I can imagine calling you no other. But it does seem odd that you have been called so all of your life. Or did you have another?"

His skin grew even darker than normal as he blushed. "Th' name my folks gave me was in my father's tongue, an' as near as I can tell you, it'd be 'Shadow of the Forest' in English. Th' people who took me in cain't match their plain speakin' with that. They call me 'Jefferson,' after th' president. He die 'fore you born, I think, but I near full grown then. Keep slaves an' all, but he known to be a good man an' a fine president." He grinned when he saw
282

the mischief in Tessa's face. "I do forget your father come from th' States, 'spect he tol' you enough 'bout th' man."

"He did indeed," Tessa laughed. "And I can't name all the kings of Spain. But tell me, why didn't you keep the name? Didn't you like it?"

"Like it fine, but jus' too late. Didn't feel up to livin' it. Already on my way an' not to be president. 'Indian' enough to cover it."

Thinking of naming the new baby after Ramón and Indian, even though in this indirect way, made up in some part for Tessa's conviction she was not going to have the daughter she so longed for. Gavin was touched that she wanted to name the baby after his friend, though he still wanted the girl for her. And he was amazed that she had gleaned this bit of information he himself had not known.

The baby was born at the end of March, and though giving birth would never be easy for Tessa, Jefferson's delivery was so much easier than Brand's had been that she considered herself lucky. Carmelita was with her this time, and so was Gavin. She wanted him there, and his wish was twin to hers. They had been through so much together, including Brand's birth, this was no time to be apart.

Her labor started in the afternoon, and all the way through it she was aware of Gavin, of his hands giving her strength to hold onto, of his face bending over her tense with love and concern, of his voice encouraging her. Carmelita was further amazed at the depth of their love, and she claimed to have had no midwifery duties at all.

The baby arrived with the dawn, and Tessa laughed softly at her first sight of him. "He looks like a little owl!"

"You spite yourself, my love," Gavin said. "I think he will look quite a bit like you before long."

Indian was overwhelmed at having the baby named for him. He tried several times to express in words what he felt, giving up finally to stoop from his great height to give Tessa a gentle kiss before he grabbed Gavin in a bear hug that would have broken weaker ribs.

Brand was the only one who did not immediately rejoice. He eyed the newcomer suspiciously and behaved

283

badly for several days before quite suddenly he seemed to realize he too was still much loved.

CHAPTER XXVI

Rachel Larkin had been delivered of a boy on April 10; the child was well, though Rachel was not fully recovered. In his new position Thomas Larkin had lifted the blockade on Mexican ports so that imports could come from San Blas or Acapulco, though not from Mazatlán or Guymas. It was well that he had done so; manufactured goods were still in great demand in California and were not forthcoming from the States. A famine in Ireland and assorted other troubles in Europe had turned the ships to that trade. Gavin and Indian waited in vain for word that their goods from Boston had arrived, filling their time with work on the *rancho*. They were all too aware of the possible complications in such a situation. When the delay was over, there could well be a glut on the market from back orders arriving at the same time. They could only hope that their selection of merchandise, should they ever receive it, had been shrewd enough to carry them through. Gavin was glad Tessa had helped them, writing very precise descriptions of certain items; he was certain her taste would stand them in good stead. There were rumors that the prices for hides and tallow in the States were falling, and the men expected that was true, but since there was nothing they could do about it, they ignored it. And they were heartened by the fact duties under United States rule would vanish unless the shipment came from ports outside U.S. jurisdiction.

Politically things remained an unsettled combination of civil and military rule, judged by no one to be anything more than an interim, not very workable solution. The war in Mexico went on. Frémont and Kearny had left by the end of spring, and there were yet more rumors on this score, all of them suggesting that Kearny would do his best to make sure Frémont reaped his share of trouble from military officialdom in Washington. Since Kearny was so little liked, sympathy seemed slightly in favor of Frémont, though out of sight was out of mind, and no one cared very much in any case.

Most of the new emigrants from the States were soldiers of the Third New York Regiment of Volunteers, notable hellraisers, and the "Mormon Battalion," most decidedly not. All of them had arrived too late to do any fighting, but they were to be used as garrison and occupation troops until their enlistments expired. Given these roles, they were hardly likely to be popular with the natives, but they were treated in most cases with typical Californio courtesy. Not even war and defeat had been strong enough to kill the old habit.

Every time she heard a new tale of nonpayment Tessa gave thanks that Rancho Magnífico had been on the outskirts of the war. The Bear Flaggers and then the California Battalion had given paper promises up and down the coast for goods, horses, and cattle, and these slips were proving worthless in far too many cases. One *rancho* was reported to have lost five hundred saddle horses, receiving nothing in return. She turned pale at the thought, seeing their own horses now under training being driven away by uncaring troops. Gavin had sent messages to both Ramón and Don Esteban to find out how their herds had fared, being very careful not to let his words sound patronizing but still wanting them to know that he was willing to use whatever power his original United States citizenship might offer had injustice been done.

Since the Ramsays had visited Rancho Valle del Mar after the end of hostilities, they were fairly sure nothing would have been taken since their visit, and word came from Ramón confirming this. But they heard nothing from Don Esteban, a fact that troubled Gavin no less than it did Tessa. Gavin knew he had the old man's respect and as much fondness as the man would ever feel for anyone not of his blood, and both meant a great deal to him.

Toward the end of August without any warning, Don Esteban appeared in person.

The land was seared to gold and brown except for the land near the river and the plants and plots they kept watered by the irrigation system Gavin, Indian, and Pedro had devised. The heat was so intense, the *rancho* had long since redesigned its days to fit it. Morning began very early, before the sun was fully risen, and when the heat was most intense all work ceased until the temperature began to fall in late afternoon. Last chores were done right up until the dark came down, but the middle of the day was given to sleep, or at least complete inactivity.

Gavin rode in totally exhausted and overheated, and Tessa, brooking no nonsense because she was worried about him, poured buckets of cold well water over him until she claimed she could touch his skin without burning her fingers. He thanked her meekly, filling the bucket again with slow, deliberate movements, and before she knew what was happening, she was sopping wet.

Giggling and sputtering, she admitted it felt marvelous, and hugged him. "This is the only way one can make love in this weather."

"Would you be willing to settle for just thinking about it while we sit on the porch?" he asked with a smile, and she traced the upward curve of his eyebrow as she answered, "More than willing. It's still too hot."

He called it a porch; she declared it grander than that, and called it a verandah. She was infinitely pleased that he and Indian had built it for her, a lovely shaded appendage to the house, a place to catch the breeze and overlook the land.

She went to check on the boys and found a harried Rosita, who agreed that the babies were not going to sleep any more this afternoon.

She fed Jefferson and carried him outside, preceded by Brand, who walked easily now and enjoyed the independence it gave him. He squealed in delight and said, "Papa!" as he hugged Gavin. His vocabulary was growing rapidly, some words in Spanish, some in English. Rather than confusing him, his parents trusted he would learn the difference between the two languages eventually. Gavin wanted Tessa to teach the child French also before he was too old. The first recognizable word Brand had said had been "Papa," even before "Mama," and Tessa took great joy in that, as she did in seeing them together. The softness in Gavin's face when he played with his son never failed to touch her, and she knew Jefferson would receive his share of attention as he developed too. Gavin had no intention of letting his children suffer from the neglect that had warped the planes of his own childhood.

Tessa settled down on the porch again with Gavin and Jefferson while Brand wandered here and there, bringing back sticks and pebbles to show them.

Sombra had been dozing a little way off, opening a watchful eye now and then to check on his charges, but suddenly he stood up, head cocked and ears twitching, and came to Tessa, giving his low warning growl. It took the *rancho* dogs several minutes longer to hear the approaching riders.

Automatically Gavin checked to make sure his rifle was in easy reach, though there was little cause for alarm at this time of day. Indian had gone to Monterey and was due back any time, but when he appeared, he was not alone.

"Well, I'll be damned, it's Don Esteban!" Gavin breathed.

Tessa started up in shock, clutching Jefferson so tightly that he gave a whimper of protest. Then she gasped, "Oh, Gavin, look at us, look at me!" and she dissolved in nervous giggles.

Gavin had to admit they were a sight. His clothes and hers still clung damply to their bodies, hers made semi-transparent by the water. Her hair hung in a long braid down her back, she was barefoot, and even with the baby in her arms, she looked no more than twelve years old. Because of the heat she had allowed Brand to go without clothing, and he stood beside his father, a sturdy little nude, regarding the approaching riders with interest.

"Inyun!" he called with glee when he spied one of his favorite people, and then he turned his attention to the stranger, giving him a long, unblinking stare before he looked up at his mother. "Eagle," he said in a pleased voice, obviously proud to have made the connection with the only other white-headed creature he had seen.

"Mother and son have much in common, I see," Don Esteban observed drily, and he smiled.

Tessa's laughter spilled over again as she kissed him. "Great-grandfather, I swear I did not do more than tell him the name of the bird we see often here. I was not even sure he had learned the word," she managed to explain.

She was suddenly deliriously happy to see the old man, and it didn't matter any more that they were not properly clad to receive him. It did not matter to Don Esteban either; he had found Tessa and her family glowing with happiness; he could ask for no more. Looking at Brand, he said wistfully, "I envy the privilege of extreme youth. He is the only one suitably attired for so hot a day."

He stayed with them for a week, sharing Indian's bachelor quarters as if he had never known more comfort. He had made the trip to Monterey aboard a ship and inquiries had led him to Indian, but he undoubtedly would have found his way to the *rancho* in any case. It was difficult to imagine any obstacle that could prevent Don Esteban from doing what he wanted. His only regret was that he had been obliged to use a horse other than his own; as far as he was concerned, only horses bred from his herds were fit to ride.

He approved of what they had built on the *rancho* and of what they were doing with the horses, keeping the *manada* intact except for the few losses they had suffered and training some of the offspring, even fillies, to the saddle, while planning the next *manada*, which would be all palomino mares and a likely chestnut stallion they would find at Valle del Mar or buy from another *ranchero* when the time came. The outside stallion was needed to keep the breeding from being too close. Don Esteban agreed that the market for good horses could only increase with the influx of immigrants.

The conquest was accomplished, had to be accepted, and he spoke little of it except to assure Gavin and Tessa that he had lost no stock to the invaders. "I made sure the herds were difficult to find," he remarked.

He and Brand got on very well. Tessa often had to hide a smile when she saw Brand imitating some of his great-great-grandfather's characteristics, especially when he attempted to hold his small, round body rigidly erect to walk as the old man did.

The only bad moment of his visit came when he saw Gavin's back. Gavin had stripped off his shirt to wash, not even thinking about it because he was used to everyone at the *rancho* knowing.

Don Esteban's face went ashen. "My son, how did this come to be?" he asked hoarsely.

Gavin turned to face him. "I am sorry, sir," he said quietly. "Had I been thinking, I would have spared you the sight. It does not matter now how it happened. It has been revenged."

"Luis." The old man made it a statement, not a question. "I heard of his death. Now I rejoice in it again."

He did not bring up the subject again, but his pride in them was even greater than it had been. Without being told the full of it, he knew his great-granddaughter and her Yankee had come through hell together and emerged even more finely tempered than before.

One thing he did ask about was their seeming indifference to the threat of Indian attack. "The raiding has been very bad in many places since spring, yet you seem to inhabit magic leagues."

Tessa told him the story of No-Name, adding, "He has kept his promise. The men have seen him twice this summer, and once they took grain and goods and left them where they knew he would find them, but no more horses. Both times they saw him, he was riding the chestnut mare."

"I share your relief," Don Esteban admitted. "I too am distressed by the idea of anyone dining on one of my beautiful horses."

The men had many lively discussions of California's future, and how fortunes would best be made in the years to come. Tessa often joined them, impressing her great-grandfather with her astute questions and judgments. But now and then she caught a feeling of suppressed excitement from Indian and Gavin, and she wondered what they were up to and when they would tell her.

She kept sadness at bay until she and Gavin had watched Don Esteban's departure, again with Indian as an escort. Wordlessly she had embraced her great-grandfather, only at the last minute managing a strangled, "*Vaya con Dios.*" The sad acceptance in the dark eyes had acknowledged what she knew—they would not see each other again.

Don Esteban was a very old man; not even his valiant spirit could continue to deny that. He had made the trip to Rancho Magnífico because he knew he would be unable to do so before much longer. The ride that would have meant nothing in his younger days had greatly taxed his strength. The first two days of his visit, he had been content to remain quiet, aside from a short walk with Brand. Out of respect for his pride, Tessa had pretended not to notice his weariness and the pinched blueness around his mouth, and had resisted the impulse to fuss over him, something that would not even have occurred to her previously. She wished he did not have the long journey back now.

He had mentioned his own home and the welcome the Ramsays would receive there only once, and very briefly. Tessa knew as well as he that the visit would never be made. It was not the great distance as much as it was the involvement with despised relatives and a life that had nothing to do with hers and Gavin's. Don Esteban wanted her eyes to be on the future, not the past.

She leaned against Gavin, and he held her, saying gently, "Cry if you wish, my love, but for yourself, not for him. He has lived a long, rich life, long enough to see his great-great-grandchildren. He came to bid you farewell with dignity, and that he has accomplished."

He held her while she cried, and he suspected he would weep with her before this was over.

That night, wanting to take her mind off Don Esteban and knowing it was time to tell her anyway, he and Indian told her their plan.

At first she just stared at them, and when she found her voice it was high with incredulity. "Two lots in Yerba Buena, or San Francisco, or whatever they call it now! But why! I have never seen the place but have heard it is a windswept, desolate place of sand and scrub, full of fleas and Yankees and little else."

Neither of them tried to tell her that her description was wrong. It was in fact, quite accurate. They had visited the town a couple of times on trading trips. Even the part about Yankees was true. The population of San Francisco was fully four-fifths American. The name had been officially changed from Yerba Buena this year before any of the new upstart settlements could claim it. It seemed only fitting that the oldest town on the bay should bear the name.

Gavin told her of the beauty of San Francisco Bay and his absolute certainty that it was destined to become a trading center of the West. Even Indian couldn't contain his enthusiasm, echoing Gavin's thoughts. "I see big ships there, 'fore long, an' where they be there be big town, mebbe even be 'nother Boston."

"But our debts are almost paid, and now this!" she stammered. Gavin heard the real panic behind her words.

"Thomas Larkin is turning ever more to investing in the land. He told us about these lots; he already has land in the town and his eyes are on Bernica City, a new settlement on the bay. The prices are rising rapidly now, but we can buy both of them for two thousand dollars." He ignored her gasp of dismay. "Larkin has been hard used by the war; he is having difficulty calling in debts, but he has given us an introduction to another merchant who has guaranteed the loan for fair interest."

She had no right to gainsay it; Gavin had, after all, gone into debt to buy her. Her misery threatened to engulf her and then was miraculously gone with Gavin's next words. "Tessa, this makes no difference as far as the *rancho* is concerned. I have no intention of uprooting you and the children to go live on a sandpit. The land in San Francisco is a gamble, that's all, but both Indian and I think we can win with it someday. Even Don Esteban saw the possibilities. Are you willing to agree to the risk?"

Suddenly she realized he was really asking her. He and Indian had planned and plotted and wanted this very much, but if she refused, they would not do it. And her fear that it would mean leaving the *rancho* had been seen and dispelled.

Very deliberately, she raised her glass of wine. "To the risks. May we never be too old to take them."

She thought of her words later. Chirstmas was only bearable this year because of the children and because Indian and Carmelita were such kind and understanding friends. Don Esteban had taken his last great risk in coming to visit them. He had died toward the last of November, but the word did not reach them until the week before

Christmas. The *vaquero* who served as courier was still shaken by the death of the man he had honored and served next to God, but he ignored the tears staining his weathered cheeks as he told the Ramsays that Don Esteban had died as he would have wished. He had been very quiet and contented after his visit to the north, but this day he had ridden out once more to see the herds. He had gone alone. When it grew late, and he had not come home, his most trusted men had gone in search of him. First they had seen the horse Don Esteban always rode. "The stallion stood as if he were carved of golden stone, and there we found *el patrón*. There was no sign of struggle. Perhaps he had wearied and had dismounted to rest a little. Now he rests with God." The last things Don Esteban had seen were his finest horses on the best grazing land of his *rancho*.

Even with all of the other dependents he had, Don Esteban had left Tessa two more *manadas* of his prize horses and gold and silver in the amount of two thousand United States dollars. In the documents the *vaquero* had brought to her was a brief missive from her great-grandfather, written a week before he died, telling her by the date that he had foreseen his death, and telling her much more. "I believe your Yankees are correct about Yerba Buena, now San Francisco. Let this be your part of it, and a legacy for your sons. I am well pleased in you, Tessa. Go with God."

She had waited to read it until she was alone with Gavin, and she had read it haltingly, translating into English as she went, managing to get through it before she wept. And in wonder, she saw that not all the tears were her own.

CHAPTER XXVII

Despite the fact that the drive had to be made in wet winter weather, the horses arrived at Rancho Magnífico in January. One stallion of those *manadas* was gold, his mares chestnut, while the other stallion was a chestnut with golden mares. And there was more than one young chestnut colt that looked as if a couple of years would give him the growth and power to make him master of the palomino mares, offspring of the first *manada,* that were yet to be formed into a family. Tessa knew these were among Don Esteban's most magnificent horses, and she was certain he had left instructions for them to be driven north immediately for the express purpose of keeping them out of the hands of greedy relatives.

The money arrived too, but at first Gavin refused to take it for the San Francisco investment. Tessa was adamant. "It is what my great-grandfather wanted. It is what I want. I could not help before with the grant fees, with anything. Do you not see? Finally my guilt for the debt you took with me will be eased."

She knew she wasn't fighting fairly, because he hated mention of the debt, but that made her no less happy when he capitulated.

The practical side of her nature accepted Don Esteban's death, but there was another part which saw the horses, thought of the San Francisco land, and believed that somewhere the old man still lived. She had seen so little of him, and yet his influence had been so powerful, it did not seem possible that she would not see his lean, fierce visage again. And gradually she came to accept that she would see him again, did see him, simply changed into the only kind of immortality that made sense to her. His influence was still in their lives; her memories of him were sharp and clear; and every time the eagle soared over the *rancho,* she thought of Don Esteban and was glad.

The year 1848 started out so peacefully, Tessa and

Gavin would remember it later as the calm before the great storm. They were enjoying each other and their children more and more. Brand was increasingly active, and his vocabulary was expanding at such a rate in both languages that the men learned quickly that they had to be careful of what they said in his presence. He spent an entire week prefacing everything he said with a very recognizable version of "God damn it!" Tessa tried to explain to him that it wasn't the sort of thing he ought to be saying, but her authority was undermined by the laughter that threatened every time she tried to discuss it with him. Finally, he just seemed to tire of it, leaving Gavin to wonder what his next choice would be.

They were both amazed to see the differing personalities of their sons emerging so early. Brand, nearly two, was bold and quick, capable of thinking out the consequences of what he did but not bothering to most of the time, preferring rather to plunge right in. He already had a keen sense of balance and seemed to have no physical fear, which in turn made Tessa fearful for him, but she was determined not to coddle him or make him timid on her account.

Jefferson, even though he was less than a year old, showed traits very different from his brother's. He seemed to consider everything deeply and thoroughly before he committed himself. Where Brand would reach out quickly for a new object, Jefferson would regard it solemnly for a long time before touching it. He wasn't fearful, just thoughtful. Tessa still sometimes called him *poco buho*, little owl, though in truth Gavin's prediction was proving true. Jefferson looked very much like her, his bones finely sculpted, his eyes a deep gray violet. But he was the one who had his father's tilting eyebrow. Tessa suspected the boys were going to be lady-killers when they grew up; she was relieved there were still years to go before that began.

The news came to them gradually. Sutter had been building a sawmill on the American River for some time. On January 24, James Marshall, one of Sutter's cohorts, had found gold in the tailrace. At first the news was received calmly. After all, gold had been found in California before; there were still placers being worked in the south-

295

ern part of the country. It seemed more important that the war with Mexico was finally won, a United States victory, the Treaty of Guadalupe Hidalgo having been signed on February 2, including the provisions that the United States would pay Mexico $15 million plus assuming Mexican obligations to Americans up to $3.25 million, small enough concession in return for the vast tracts of land now in American hands. At last the position of California as a United States possession was assured, and the business of setting up uniform systems of law and commerce could begin.

The spring wore on, and the rumors of gold increased and then exploded. Sam Brannan was a rowdy, very unMormon-like Mormon, a blustering fellow who had managed to enrage most of his fellow churchmembers and seemed not to mind that he had. He had just opened a store at Sutter's Fort, which probably had a good deal to do with the effort he made to create a scene in San Francisco. He was successful. He rode up and down the quiet streets roaring, "Gold, gold, gold from the American River!" and brandishing a bottle filled with flakes.

By the time the Ramsays heard the story, the whole country had gone mad. These were not the small-yield placer strikes of the south, there were large nuggets to prove the vastness of the treasure, washed down from the mountains for centuries into the riverbeds, giving rise to the legend that the Mother Lode to end them all, a solid gold mass, existed somewhere, just waiting to be found, the mythical country of El Dorado.

The male population joined in a mass exodus from the towns and *ranchos*. Buildings were left half-finished, crops went unharvested. The pueblos of the coast were well-nigh deserted. Though the Yankees in the eastern states seemed skeptical and slow to act on the news, men from Oregon showed no such reluctance, nor did those from Hawaii and Australia or from Chile and Peru and most of all from Mexico, many Mexicans being already highly skilled in mining techniques in their own country.

Trading ships were left to rot in the bays for want of crews who deserted for the gold fields. The only way a captain could be sure of sailing away was to forbid his crew to go ashore at all.

296

Indian came back from Monterey looking positively dazed. "I tell you, it like times in th' Bible when God smack down his hand an' everybody gone. Carmelita say th' silence 'nough to make her crazy. More goin' on out here than there."

Tessa saw the sudden gleam in her husband's eyes, a sure sign of a scheme beginning to take shape. "Gavin, you're not thinking of going to dig for gold?" she asked, nearly shouting.

"No, and at this stage I believe it's panning, not digging. But I'm not going to do either one," he said slowly, and then the faraway look left his eyes, and he took her by the shoulders. "Tessa, with that many people, there's a ready-made market for almost anything we can offer. I'd be willing to bet anything that most of them are completely unequipped and ill prepared for this venture, and they'll pay in gold!"

She caught fire from his idea then, seeing it as clearly as her husband. She had come to enjoy the trading game as much as he did, even though she saw most of it only on paper in the accounts, and she made no protest against him and Indian going to see for themselves. She missed Gavin dreadfully, and the nearly three weeks of his absence seemed more like three years, but there was an inevitability about what was happening, and it would be foolish to deny it.

She didn't need the words; she could tell immediately by their faces that Gavin's judgment had been sound. But the images he conjured with his quick, excited words sounded like the tales of a madman.

"It is unbelievable. The hills are crawling with men now. You hear shoveling, shouting, hammering, and God knows what else all day long, and it isn't much quieter at night. At a place called Coloma there are already hundreds of frame buildings and a big hotel is being built. Most other camps have tents, but Coloma is growing up right by Sutter's Mill so they have plenty of cut lumber, at five hundred dollars a thousand feet, no less. The prices for everything are beyond crediting. Eggs are going for a dollar and a half a dozen and up, if you can find them, pork and bacon are near that a pound, flour, beans, and rice for more than any but starving men would pay.

297

Picks, pans, and shovels are worth nearly their weight in gold. A shovel can go as high as twenty dollars. Horses cost one hundred dollars and a blanket the same. There is a shortage of everything because few are willing to pull themselves away from panning for gold in order to procure supplies. And it's going to spread further. They're finding more gold in every creek bed every day. But it's still a game of chance; one man finds a fortune, another can't even pay his daily expenses, and it means standing knee deep in freezing water for hours whether you hit pay dirt or not. And they mean pay *dirt*, back-breaking tons of black sand to go through looking for the gold."

"And when do you and Indian plan to go trading there?" she asked quietly.

"As soon as we can get enough merchandise together to make the trip worthwhile. We're only going to be able to make one big run this year; the winter weather and the wet are going to drive people out of the hills for sure in a few months," he answered promptly and then paused, skeptical of her calm acceptance of what would be a repetition of his recent absence and his coastal trading days away from her.

She managed a small smile. "I am being civilized because there is no choice now. But next year the boys will be old enough to leave in Rosita's and Dolores's care for a time, and I will go with you." She was not asking his permission; she was telling him what she would do. He didn't argue; he was too relieved to have no opposition now. Next year seemed a long time off.

Not even their beginning days at the *rancho* had been as hectic as this time was. Most of the time now, even the hottest part of the day, involved some kind of labor, and sleep came late as lists and bundles were rechecked.

Indian had made the trip to Monterey and had come back with the news that their cargo was in, though there was no one to unload it. Gavin kept one *vaquero* to help him on the *rancho* while the rest went with Indian to Monterey to unload and bring back the cargo on pack animals.

Tessa set the women to making soap, which they cut into large cakes—this lowly commodity was in great demand in the camps. And the chickens, which despite losses to weasels and skunks had increased greatly in number from the original flock sent by María, were deprived of every egg anyone could find. Brand thought this treasure-hunting great fun and didn't even fuss over the scratches and pecks he received for his efforts. The eggs were carefully packed in barrels, in layers of straw. Dried fruit, salted meat, beans, corn, and wheat were also to go as proof of the *rancho*'s productivity, along with a small herd of beef on the hoof to be driven with the caravan.

Indian stored the dress goods and other items designed to catch a woman's eye in Monterey—women were a rarity in the camps. But there was a great deal that would sell immediately to the miners: blankets, pails, tools, nails, a dozen pairs of men's boots in various sizes, sugar, coffee, flour, rice, salted pork, sea bread, ale and beer; the list went on.

He secured extra pack animals and returned with the *vaqueros* to the *rancho* to find Gavin champing at the bit to be off trading. But they still had a good two days' work to do making sure everything was as compactly and securely packed as possible.

Tessa worked as hard as everyone else, deliberately keeping overly busy to avoid thinking of Gavin's departure, but on their last night together, she could deny it no longer. In spite of her struggle for control, tears overwhelmed her, and she sobbed against him. And when she found her voice, the weeping was in the words. "*Arriesgía mi vida por amor a ti.* I would risk my life for love of you. But I cannot care for you where you are going. I was not afraid before, but now hearing of how many are there and how much gold there is, I know it must be dangerous. Take care, *mi amado*, take care!"

Gavin held her gently against him, rubbing her back and soothing her with calm words. "It is not like that. I can't tell you exactly why, but I swear it is uncommonly safe in the camps. Indian and I both wondered at it. There is little stealing, little death aside from natural causes. Perhaps it is because all are so intent on finding gold, but I think it is more probable that the simple necessity of survival makes its own laws and most men obey them for their own protection so that their fellows will not turn against them. Even leaving Pedro here with you, I worry far more for your safety than you should worry for mine."

"Next year, next year I will see for myself," she murmured, and when she laughed softly a moment later he knew she had accepted his comfort. "You are not thinking of going to sleep, are you?"

His hands began to rove her body with skillful abandon. Before he kissed her, he whispered against her mouth, "Oddly, I have no desire for sleep, my desire is all in another place."

Tessa let everything go, everything except loving Gavin until she was only love for him. Her mind and spirit and heart were as open to him as her body, and his possession of her was no less an act of worship than her gift to him. He cried out her name as the fire consumed him.

She saw them off in the morning with the old blessing and no tears, proud in spite of her sadness that her Yankees had managed to assemble such an impressive venture in a fraction of the time it would have taken other men.

Gavin swung Brand up for a last hug and a kiss, and the boy knowing that something big and new was happening, said, "You and Inyun, come back." It was half a question, half a command.

"You can be sure of it, my son," Gavin told him, and then the long procession was off.

While they were gone, Tessa worked harder than she ever had in her life. Pedro had no men to help him, and sheer need forced him to accept the unsettling situation of having the *patróna* ride out to help him with the herds. Tessa grew even more fond of Pedro than she had been, seeing with ever more clarity what a competent *mayordomo* he was. Though it must have been hard for him to see the other men go off on an adventure, he did not betray disappointment in any way.

The only real benefit she could find in the men's absence was that it gave her more time than she usually had with the children. Even they seemed to sense that this was something different from their father's and Indian's recent absence, something more risky and uncertain. The study had long since been made into sleeping quarters for them, and a new room would be added when there was time. At seventeen months Jefferson was a capable if careful toddler, and he and Brand would often tiptoe in early to stare at their mother until she woke up, kissed them both, and allowed them to climb into the big bed with her for a tussle and a discussion of plans for the day before she had to ride out with Pedro. Brand always had a thousand things he thought he might do, and the words would tumble out faster and faster until Tessa had all she could do to keep a straight face. Jefferson would chime in here and there with a solemn word indicating he would join Brand for this or that. She loved the relationship between them. Brand was protective of his small brother and very patient with him, and though Jefferson looked up to him, he had a mind of his own. Sometimes he would simply plant himself and refuse to play the part Brand gave him. He seemed to enjoy playing by himself as much as with other children, which was a relief to Tessa because when Brand joined the *vaqueros'* children, Dolores's two older boys plus Conchita's and Flora's daughters, the games were often rough and tumble. And the numbers were increasing, Conchita having produced a son the year before, while Flora had had another girl. Dolores was pregnant again, and Rosita was still hopeful. An army of infants, Gavin called the collective offspring of the *rancho*. Strangely, despite the older children, Brand was always the leader, not by virtue of being the son of the *patrón* and *patróna,* but because he had that quality, recognized by the others, young as they all were, in their games. He was always the one who seemed to lead them on to new circle, stick, and ball games. But Tessa was most proud of the fact that both of her boys were generous with their playthings, sharing them with each other and the other children without having to be told to do so.

Brand and Jefferson both had already been held securely in front of riders in the saddle by their parents, by Indian, and by Pedro, and neither had any fear of the height and excitement of being on horseback. Given the joy they found in it now, they both promised to be fine horsemen someday. It wouldn't be long before Brand would be using the small saddle Don Esteban had given him. But when there was much and hard riding to do, it wasn't convenient to take them, and even with the servants watching them, Tessa felt even more secure having Sombra to guard them, and he was obedient to her command to stay with the children.

She still regarded the wolf as a kind of miracle. On occasion when wolf packs had crossed the *rancho* in winter Sombra had answered with his own voice and once he had even vanished for a week, but she had ceased to dread his final desertion, especially now that he seemed to have claimed one of the dog bitches as his own. She was as light as Sombra was dark, and she looked more than a little like a wolf herself, showing much in long, tawny eyes and her general shape to suggest that her bloodlines had been wolf-crossed in the not too distant past. Gavin had teased Tessa about the match, pointing out that if the tales of wolves' fidelity to their mates was true, Sombra and his bit of muslin were going to have endless domestic squabbles, given the immoral character of dogs. Tessa had responded by naming the bitch Pureza, purity, and indeed, Pureza seemed to be living up to her name. Sombra tolerated no other males around her, and in any case, Pureza was haughty and proud in her possession of the dominant male.

Tessa was thinking of various things, including the wolf and his mate, wondering what their pups would look like if they ever had any, as she rode in from the pastures one afternoon. The men had been gone for nearly a month, and the one thing she didn't want to think about was how much she missed Gavin. It was stiflingly hot, and she wished she'd quit hours ago. The world was shimmering unpleasantly, and she couldn't tell if it was from heat waves or from her own dizziness. And then she wondered for a split second if the heat had affected her brain. The calm scene she had seen before her—Brand playing in a shady, flowered spot, Sombra, aside from the brief glance he'd given her, watching the child, and Pureza dozing nearby—erupted in sudden madness as Sombra grabbed Brand's outstretched arm and hurled the child backward with a twist of his massive head.

Tessa heard Rosita's scream from the porch in chorus with Pureza's startled yip, and later she knew she'd screamed too, but now all her consciousness was focused

302

on aiming her rifle at Sombra before he could savage Brand further. Never, never had she thought the wolf would revert to the wild, harm the children. She was in the act of squeezing the trigger when she heard Sombra's cry of pain and saw the long, dark shape that had caused it. Her shot sent the snake flying in two pieces.

The cold sickness hit her like a physical blow as though she had never known what it was like to be too warm in her life, and she staggered as she slid down from Amordoro, but she went on with murderous intent, finding the rattler and cutting its head from the still writhing half length of body. Rosita, holding Brand, assured her that he was all right, although he had begun to cry in a dazed fashion. Tessa went to Sombra.

Even through the close, heavy fur of his sound front leg, she found the puncture marks and the swelling flesh. His half-closed eyes already had a slightly glazed look, but he managed to lick her hand, and he bore her ministrations even as he had the first time she had seen him. She cut and sucked the wound just as she would have done for a human, but she knew the poison was already spreading. It took all her strength and Rosita's combined to carry the animal onto the porch.

Brand was coming out of his shock, and though Sombra's teeth had broken the skin and he was bruised, he was not seriously hurt. Every time Tessa looked at him, she thought of how easily he could now be dying of the venom so dangerous to the young. Brand knew what Sombra had done, and he stationed himself by the great head, stroking it gently and saying, "Thank you, Sombra, thank you, was a bad snake," over and over as Tessa poulticed the wounded leg, hoping to draw the poison. "My lovely, brave one," she crooned, and her voice sounded very like her son's.

Despite her revulsion, Rosita buried the bits of the snake, knowing the head could still bite for hours after death, and when she could slip away, she took the tale of the wondrous deliverance to the other women and was the first to greet Pedro with the story when he rode in. Everyone agreed it was permissible to pray to the Virgin to intercede for the life of a wolf in such a case.

Pureza and Tessa kept the vigil on the porch through

the night, and Brand would have remained with them had not sleep overcome him deeply enough to allow his mother to carry him in and put him to bed.

Gavin and Indian rode in ahead of the others to head confronted by the sight of Tessa cradling Sombra's head on her lap while Pureza kept watch beside them. Tessa's face was pale with fatigue, but her smile was wide. "He'll be all right now. He told me you were coming long before the others barked."

Gavin lifted her from her cramped position, and then she was weeping in his arms. Between sobs she choked out the story of how Brand, who knew the difference between harmless and poisonous snakes, had startled the rattler, so rare near the house, sleeping in the cool under a bush into striking without warning, and of how Sombra had saved the child.

"My God," Gavin breathed on a long sigh. "It hardly seems important now to tell you we sold everything—our saddlebags are full of gold, and though everyone tried their hand at fortune hunting, we haven't lost a single man; they're all right behind us."

She drew away to look up at him, and then they were both laughing, much to Indian's relief. "Our trip peaceful-like hearin' this," he said, and he joined Gavin in making much over Sombra. And when the children came out to greet them, with glad cries at the familiar voices, both men managed to listen gravely to Brand's version of Sombra's bravery accompanied by a "baddie snik" chorus from Jefferson. Tessa took one look at the contortions Indian's face was going through to preserve a serious expression and didn't dare look again until the boys' recital was over.

And finally Tessa did see the gold, from dust to good-sized nuggets, just enough temptingly poured out in revelation by Gavin from deerskin pouches. She reached out to touch it, and drew her hands back.

"It doesn't have fangs like the rattler you and Sombra just dealt with," Gavin said. He meant to be funny, but he felt a horrible squeamishness in the pit of his stomach at the image of Brand lying mortally ill. It took him a moment to register the strange look in Tessa's eyes.

"Doesn't it?" she asked, and deliberately she put her
304

hands out again, fingers spread to touch the treasure piled on the table. "Everything is changing, changing even more than my great-grandfather foretold." Her hands came down on the gold. "I accept it, and next year I will be part of it."

Her eyes, wide and violet, challenged both men. Indian looked at the floor, and Gavin answered slowly, "I expect you will. I think things happen where you are, and I'd rather have them happen where I can watch."

Only later, when night had fallen, Sombra had been judged well on the way to recovery, and the boys were asleep, did Gavin make his confession. Tessa was brushing out her hair, and she kept on, but she heard the same note in his voice as his eldest son's had when he wanted to tell her about something he'd done before Rosita or someone else did.

"We did sell everything, and at very good prices. And to make it better, the gold which is worth anywhere from twelve to fourteen dollars at the camps is worth from seventeen to eighteen dollars an ounce once shipped to the States. But that's not the way we made all of it. There's a small fortune there, enough to pay off all debts and a good deal more." His voice trailed away.

She put down the brush carefully and turned to face him. He looked so much like Brand anticipating trouble, it was all she could do not to go to him and tell him whatever it was, it couldn't be that bad. And his eyebrow, seemingly frozen in its upward quirk, as Jefferson's sometimes was, didn't help. "Just what have you and Indian been up to?" she asked as gently as she would have asked one of her sons.

"Ah . . . well, I've thought of how you might feel about it, with your father and all. But there's not . . . there really isn't much to entertain the men in the camps at night, no women to speak of." He was actually blushing, something she could not recall seeing him do before. "Oh, hell, Tessa, we gambled, offered Lady Luck. We didn't cheat. You don't have to when you're the house and know how to play. The house almost always has more money than any one player—we had the stakes from selling our goods —and almost always wins eventually if the dealer isn't a complete idiot. Indian and I have made our living more

305

than once with cards, and we've done it again, this time for pure gold."

She thought of her father only briefly. He had gambled stupidly, using her for the stakes, but most Californios made wagers on everything with an element of chance involved, and never lost more than they could afford. She thought of her own fascination for the account books, for figures that progressed in an orderly manner. She thought of how, for a small yet endless space of time, she had thought Gavin was talking about procuring women for the gold miners.

Purposefully, she widened her eyes and asked with mock innocence, "I am quick with figures—do you think you could teach me the games with cards?"

He blinked in sheer surprise, and then he opened his arms. "Come here, Tessa, come here, my love. I'm certain I can teach you very quickly."

"This I already know," she giggled.

They had both been exhausted to begin with, and had added much to their exhaustion by the time dawn broke.

"Tell me, wife," Gavin whispered in Tessa's ear, "is this a habit in my absence?"

Tessa raised herself on one elbow and sleepily regarded her children, who were standing by the bed. "Good morning," she said to the boys, and in a soft aside to Gavin, "Yes. We were lonesome for you. Don't yell at them."

"I do have some vague ideas of being a father," he protested and he reached for first one and then the other, hugging and kissing them soundly before he said, "Brand, why don't you take Jefferson with you, find Rosita, and see if Sombra is better. Your mother and I are very old, you know, and we're still tired."

Brand considered his words, blue eyes meeting blue eyes, and then he nodded, took his brother by the hand, and even made sure the door was securely closed behind them.

"He believes it, but we are not very old," Tessa managed before laughter overcame her.

"Just think, when they're grown, we can be young again," Gavin said, sharing her mirth as he pulled her close. "Here's to Forty-nine, Tessa."

"To Forty-nine and Lady Luck and me with you wherever you go," she replied, and the way she was touching him made Gavin acutely aware of how lonely the gold fields had been without her.

CHAPTER XXVIII

"Are you cheating?" Gavin asked, his eyebrows slanting.

"Of course not. I don't know how yet. Do you want to teach me that now?" Tessa asked with mock seriousness.

Indian's deep laughter boomed out, despite his effort to keep it down so as not to wake the children, and Gavin laughed with him. Teaching Tessa to gamble had proved to be quite an experience for both men. She grasped the rules of the dice and card games so quickly, they rarely had to be repeated. She figured swiftly and played without hesitation, her normally expressive face wearing a look of bland innocence throughout. And beyond this, she had natural card sense and a sure feeling for when luck was running with her and when it was cool, things that could not be taught. Gavin gave thanks that her father had lacked these talents; otherwise Michael Macleod would surely never have forfeited his daughter.

"What are you thinking about?" she asked softly, and he smiled at her. "You, what else?" She followed his thought then, and her eyes were huge and shining. "Yes, it is good he played so badly."

" 'Nuff gamblin' tonight, think I be goin' now," Indian said as he made for the door to their vague chorus of good-nights. He was accustomed to his bachelor existence and seldom minded, but sometimes when he saw the Ramsays looking at each other like that, he felt damn lonesome. He wished Carmelita were waiting for him in his little house.

She had come to spend Christmas with them, and she was highly amused and just a little shocked by Tessa's new skills. Gavin, Indian, and Tessa had been enjoying their nightly gambling practice for long enough so that Tessa could explain with great authority monte, faro, *vingt-et-un*, *lansquenet*, and a host of other games including roulette, which she knew well in theory though she had not yet seen a wheel.

"I did not know that respectable ladies with children committed such sins," Carmelita teased, forbearing with great effort to comment on her friend's determination to go to the gold fields.

"These are among the least of my sins," Tessa replied, mischief lighting her face, and Gavin added a heartfelt, "Amen!"

"She keep all th' money she win from us, we be walkin' 'round nekid," Indian claimed, beaming proudly because he had helped teach her.

"I would like that," Tessa giggled, "but it wouldn't be fair since I started with your gold."

The holiday proved to be a joyful time shared among friends, with Brand and Jefferson in such a continual state of excitement that they were exhausted by nightfall and usually sound asleep on any convenient lap long before their bedtime. But Carmelita quickly discovered that the one subject she wasn't going to be able to discuss, no matter how carefully she approached it, was her friend's plan to accompany the men in the spring.

Tessa's voice was even, but her eyes flashed dangerously. "There is nothing to discuss. I will go with them," she said, and Carmelita knew better than to pursue a hopeless cause.

Tessa meant what she said, but that didn't ease her guilt. It did not matter that the children would be well cared for on the *rancho*. She was their mother, and she had every intention of leaving them because she couldn't bear to be left behind by her love. No one could have called her more terrible names than the ones she called herself. And still she went on relentlessly with her preparations, dosing the boys with herbal brews at the first sign of any winter complaints lest they fall ill and keep her home, feeling nothing but relief when the threat of another pregnancy passed with nothing more than a day of feeling ill after two months of worry. She wondered if Gavin had suspected, but he said nothing, and she certainly was not going to enlighten him. She pitched in with wild fervor to help with the chores that would provide them with ample goods from the *rancho* for trading. And here too,

Gavin said nothing beyond thanking her for her help and warning her not to overtire herself, but she caught him looking at her with a speculative gleam now and then, and finally one night curiosity overcame his restraint.

"What have you been stitching so busily these last days?" he asked, propped on an elbow, looking down at her, his free hand savoring the satin of her skin. "You're not letting any of the women help you, and you're spending every spare minute at it."

The question took her by surprise, especially because all her senses had begun to spiral inward to be conscious of nothing except his touch. "Not fair," she murmured, "not fair to make me feel like this and then pounce with questions."

"I know," he agreed, leering wickedly. She pushed him away suddenly and slipped out of bed with one lithe movement. "Close your eyes for a minute, and I'll show you," she commanded.

"I like what I'm seeing right now," he said, but he closed his eyes obediently, pointing out that it was a solemn act of trust given her present mood.

She got the finished article out of the wardrobe and donned it. She was proud of the workmanship. She had tanned the doeskin herself from hides Indian had given her, though surely he had not had this purpose in mind, and she had done all the painstaking sewing herself.

"You can open your eyes now."

"Jesus!" Gavin gasped, staring at her. "Breeches!"

"We'll be riding through rough country, and skirts simply won't suit," she pointed out defiantly. "And with my hair tucked into a hat, I can pass for a boy, and that ought to make things easier."

That was too much for Gavin. The doeskin fit her like a second skin, molded to the tiny waist and the feminine curves of hip and thigh. The image of a boy was rendered even funnier by the firm upthrusting breasts with the nipples still standing in excited peaks and the long shining tresses of black hair framing her face and falling down her back.

"Tessa, a boy in your condition would be past saving!" he gasped before he succumbed to a paroxysm of laughter that shook him and the bed.

She jumped on him, pummeling him with her fists in mock anger for making sport of her efforts. Still laughing he grabbed her, holding her down while he stripped off the breeches. "These are covering something I want, madam. They fit so well here, and here, and here."

Her own laughter turned to a gasp of pleasure as he thrust into her, but a last rational thought remained—he had laughed, but he hadn't said No.

The next day when Gavin rode out, Tessa went with him. With spring well on its way, the hungry predators were too often taking livestock to fill their winter-starved bellies, especially the grizzlies, which seemed to be leaving their drowsy months with a vengeance to invade the valley. So far Rancho Magnífico had lost no horses, but the toll in cattle was heavy. There were rumors that in some places, the bears were being poisoned with some success, but the Ramsays and Indian were agreed that they would not use that way unless driven to it.

"Die bad an' ugly that way jus' for bein' hungry. All die, th' bears, th' wolves, even th' birds who peck a little for their younguns. Till we don' got enough, don' seem right poison 'em." Indian's way of stating things had a pointed clarity. There was little left for them to do except to patrol the land looking for kills, tracking and shooting the most persistent raiders.

Tessa hoped continually they would find nothing amiss. Though neither of them admitted it aloud, she and Gavin both knew the reason they took this duty on themselves whenever possible. Any of the *vaqueros* or Indian or Gavin by himself could do it, but when Tessa and Gavin went out together, it meant they could be alone without even Sombra, who was now wholly concerned with guarding the spring pups Pureza had presented to him. Tessa was highly amused by his harassed expression and nervous fidgets—his long-muzzled, apologetic grin saying as plainly as words that his charges, human and otherwise, had grown too numerous.

She pointed him out to Gavin as they rode away. In deference to Sombra's feelings, they refrained from laughing aloud when he dashed after them only to be halted abruptly and drawn back by Pureza's troubled yip.

310

The joy of being together on a fine spring day in a greening world lasted until they found the cow. She was so newly dead, the feasting had not begun, though the vultures were beginning to float down when they were disturbed by the riders' approach. The cow had not been killed by a predator; she had died trying to give birth to twin calves.

Tessa settled herself on the grass a little way off while Gavin went to work. This was the penalty for the freedom of this duty—to salvage at least the hide and the best cuts of meat whenever possible. They even had a pack mule with them for just this eventuality. At least Gavin was skilled and quick enough to need no help from Tessa, for which she was deeply grateful.

She concentrated on looking everywhere, anywhere except where Gavin was butchering out the cow. Even though she had not seen it, she could envisage it clearly—the birth struggle, the hard, long fight, the total loss.

She saw the movement out of the corner of her eye, and at first she didn't take it in at all. Her gaze kept wandering, savoring the new green fertility of the place. Her eyes shifted back, focused, and knew an instant before her mind understood.

Now standing on its hind legs, it was the biggest grizzly she had ever seen. And suddenly she could see it all too clearly. Its head at least four times the size of her own, its enormous paws armed with lethal claws, it stood caught in dappled light before it dropped to all fours and went for Gavin, while the horses screamed in terror.

She knew it was happening very fast, but her mind had slowed it down to a slow, eerie dance of death. She yelled at Gavin even as she grabbed her rifle. He had no time to get to his own weapon. His head and then his body jerked up, the knife in his hand, silver in the sun.

Oh, God, what had Ramón taught her about shooting a bear? Why hadn't she done this before? Gavin's knife would be pitiful against the monster; Gavin would be torn to pieces. The bear reared up snarling on its hind legs, towering over him.

She fired, aiming mid shoulder in the broad expanse of fur, hearing the deafening report, not knowing for an

311

agonizing moment whether she'd hit the beast at all. Then Gavin ducked and rolled sideways as the mammoth form swayed and crashed to the ground.

He approached it cautiously and then exclaimed, "Damn! Tessa, what a shot! You killed him."

"Yes, long ago Ramón told me where to aim," she said, her voice oddly flat and prim. He saw the sudden chalky whiteness of her face and the blindness of her eyes before they closed, and he leapt the distance and caught her as she crumpled.

She came to to the soft sound of Gavin's laughter, but his eyes were dark and anxious. "You are an astonishing woman, Mrs. Ramsay. You managed to shoot him in the only vital spot, a shot any marksman would envy, and when you were sure he was dead, you fainted."

"It didn't seem a very good plan the other way around," she managed, but her smile wavered, and she reached up with urgent hands to stroke his face. "I could see him tearing you to pieces. He didn't touch you, not at all?" Her hands followed the frantic course of her voice, touching, patting as though she could not believe there was no wound.

He gathered her close, and she could feel the heavy beating of his heart. "I'm perfectly sound, thanks to you. Indian and I will breathe easier with you along to protect us in the gold fields."

She burrowed closer, holding him, beyond words. It was the final capitulation and a tribute to her strength, a recognition of her right to make her own choice even when it would lead her from the children into a man's world. Her guilt about leaving the children was no less, but it was easier to carry without the added burden of Gavin's silent uneasiness.

"Are you ready to ride?" he asked finally, and she nodded.

"Come along then, let's quit this place."

They counted themselves lucky that though their mounts were still snorting and sidling in fear, they were too well trained to have gone far. And even shaken and sickened by what had happened, Tessa worried about whether or not the bear had been a female with cubs near by that would now die.

312

Gavin had a momentary picture of her being followed around by a couple of young bears in addition to the wolf. "Consider it a mean old male whose greed got the better of him," he said firmly.

It was so much easier now, and the words tumbled out. "Gavin, it's harder with spring all around and everything reminding me of what good mothers the wild things are, so much better than I am. I know it's wrong and even unnatural for me to leave the children. I love them, I love them dearly, but I love you more, and I can't seem to change that."

He kept his voice steady with an effort, remembering how he'd feared being jealous of his own children. "Please don't try. I haven't made it easier for you, and I'm sorry. I'm ashamed to admit that my mind is as cluttered up with old ideas as anyone's. But it isn't as though we're leaving the children to starve alone; our people take fine care of them and their own children. And it is *we* who are leaving our sons, not just you, so we'll share the blame if they are spoiled rotten in our absence. You're going along to work, and there isn't any reason why you shouldn't have the same right to do that as the rest of us."

"Thank you, darling," she murmured, and Gavin brought Diablo close and leaned precariously from the saddle to kiss her.

She giggled suddenly. "We won't be able to do this when I'm dressed as a boy; people would think it very odd."

Brand and Jefferson demanded endless retellings of the bear story and took turns with the other children of the *rancho* in playing the part of the creature against a single-shot hunter, and Tessa blushed when she heard the flowery song the *vaqueros* had made up and sang in tribute to the brave *patróna*. But the best of the episode for her was the strength Gavin's words had given her. She needed every bit of it when the day came to tell the children that when the men left the following morning, she would be going with them.

"Me too?" Jefferson asked, his lower lip beginning to tremble, while Brand's expression was suddenly rigid, watchful and unchildlike.

She drew them both close, ignoring the stiff resistance of Brand's body. "No, my little ones, you're going to stay here where your friends are and your toys, books, and everything. Your father, Indian, and I will be riding all day long into very rough country to sell all the things we've been raising here. It's too far for you now, but when you're bigger and older, you'll be able to go along and help. For now, I would very much like you to be good while we're gone."

She sighed inwardly, thinking how unjust was the complete tyranny of adults over children. Brand and Jefferson were already showing signs of acceptance because they had no choice. As indulged as they were, they had learned early that temper tantrums would not avail them, and they recognized the tone of voice in both parents that brooked no argument. And Tessa knew that though Jefferson was the younger, his thoughtful nature made it easier for him to adjust than Brand's own quicksilver temperament. She tried to make it easier for Brand by getting him alone later to tell him that she was counting on him particularly to keep an eye on his little brother, and she was pleased by his response, the sudden smile and easing of tension, his confident, "Oh, yes, I take very good care of him, Mama, an' he won't even know I am."

Brand's change of attitude helped, but the dawn leave-taking was still a painful wrench. Tessa kissed away Jefferson's tears and ignored the condemnation in the women's eyes, which said so eloquently what their mouths would not dare. Her last sight of the children showed them waving, Brand's arm protectively around the shoulders of his little brother. And it was Brand who called, *"Vaya con Dios,"* to the departing calvalcade, his voice high, clear, and brave on the sweet spring morning.

CHAPTER XXIX

To avoid brooding about the children, Tessa concentrated on the trail, glad she was riding near the front, since they had enough men, beasts, and carts to stir up a thick dust cloud from all but the dampest ground. It gave

314

her great pleasure to see Indian on the palomino she had given him on the shared birthday the week before. She had waited and hoped that the colt would prove large enough to carry the huge man. Now in his fourth year, the stallion had more than fulfilled his early promise. He would still muscle out more with added years, but he was already taller and more sturdily built than Amordoro, and having been handled and schooled from the beginning as were all the foals destined to be working stock, Tesoro was already much better behaved than one would expect of so young a horse.

Tesoro, treasure. Indian had named the animal himself. She smiled tenderly thinking of it. She had had Pedro lead the stallion in at dusk, after the men were back from their day's labors, and she had led Indian out of the house, Gavin grinning widely behind him because he knew.

"Happy birthday, my friend. May he carry you long and safely and may you never ride one of those ugly beasts again." She stood on tiptoe and tugged his head down so she could kiss him on the cheek.

His chest heaved with his struggle for control, and he started the old lament, "Cain't take it, jus' cain't," but then he stopped abruptly, drew a deep breath, and the new words were a soft whisper. " 'Course I goin' 'cept it, 'cause jus' lookin' I know he raised jus' for me, growed up big to carry this too big man." He put one arm around Tessa, one around Gavin, and drew them close in warm tribute to their bond of friendship, and they had spent the rest of the evening celebrating and teasing Indian as he rejected one name after another before deciding on Tesoro, beaming at his choice, turning the tables on them since the word began with the sound of Tessa's name. The only thing lacking in their gaiety had been Carmelita, who for a vague jumble of reasons hadn't been able to join them.

Gavin brought Diablo up beside her and followed her glance. "Before too long that horse is going to be the biggest baby and the best-trained animal in the country. I told Indian that if he doesn't have a care and cut down the time he spends talking to Tesoro, he's going to forget how to talk to us. Mrs. Ramsay, how do you like your first day with the Yankee traders?"

"Very well indeed!" she replied pertly. Not for the

world would she have admitted how weary she was that night or any other. And to her relief, day by day she could feel her body growing stronger and reaccustomed to long hours in the saddle. Because of the beef on the hoof and the cartage, their pace was slow, and though there were now more people in California than ever before, the way was still marked by nothing more than meandering cattle trails over rough country. Most hopeful miners arrived in San Francisco and took any kind of crossing they could procure until they could get space on a launch or even a leaking rowboat going up the Sacramento River, proceeding from there to the gold fields. But the Rancho Magnífico entourage had to go overland, up the great Valley.

Tessa donned her breeches the second day out to a collective stare of astonishment from Indian and the *vaqueros* before their politeness reasserted itself, but her bizarre attire was soon accepted for the practical answer it was. In some places the brush was so thick, it would have torn skirts to shreds in minutes. And more, the breeches offered some added protection against insects. The plague of them was the hardest thing for Tessa to bear. Clouds of flies followed the animals. Voracious mosquitos made any stop near water a torment, and fleas were the undisputed rulers of the earth.

When they made camp at night, they burned pitch to ward off the attackers, and though it helped a little, one would have had to sit in a dense cloud of smoke to be fully immune.

Tessa felt that her insistence on coming had negated her right to complain, and she was determined not to, even though the insects seemed to find her flesh particularly delectable. She patiently applied salve to each new bite and made sure everyone else who needed the medicine had it, but she would have loved to have vented her discomfort in the same spontaneous curses she heard from the men.

Gavin, watching her slapping ineffectually against a particularly persistent horsefly, said, "Go ahead and let it out before you choke. I promise not to say I told you so." He was trying not to laugh.

Tessa glared at him. "It's a good thing I have only pure thoughts about you. It's unkind to read people's minds."

"Pure thoughts!" Gavin snorted, and won a smile from

her, followed by a succinct, satisfied curse as she killed the horsefly.

She had at least a partial shelter in the half tent, half lean-to Gavin erected each night and shared with her when it was not his turn for watch duty, and she considered herself lucky, but this was another aspect of the journey that she had simply not thought about. Privacy was nearly impossible. It was all she could manage to dress and attend to her personal needs without an audience of *vaqueros*.

Snuggling against Gavin one night, she sighed. "To think how chaste we have become. But perhaps if we were very careful and quiet . . . "

Gavin muffled his mirth against her hair. "I can just see it! This contraption would come right down on us." She was suddenly asleep in his arms, and his smile was gentle in the darkness. "My gallant Tessa," he whispered.

They rode into Coloma on a Sunday, and Tessa's view of the world was forever changed. They had seen people on the way, mostly hopeful would-be miners heading for the foothills and some new settlers on the land, but they had aimed for Coloma as their first large settlement.

The very un-Sunday-like noise reached them before they breasted the hill, and then they were looking down on the multitude of shacks along the south fork of the American River. Tessa blinked and stared and caught herself just in time before she made the childish admission that she hadn't known there were so many people anywhere. Reading about it was not the same. Only now could she begin to comprehend how vast and peopled a power was the United States. The closer they rode, the more detail they could pick out, and Tessa could see that while there were other nationalities represented, the overwhelming majority were Yankees. And if so many could be in this place, and so many more scattered through other mining camps, leaving yet legions who had not come to California at all, the total number was unimaginable. Not since she had seen the Stars and Stripes raised above Monterey had she felt the eclipse of the Californio way so deeply.

But it was impossible to hold a somber thought amid the gaiety. Sunday was the only day the miners took off to wash their meager wardrobes of work pants and red

317

flannel shirts and to attend to other domestic chores, accomplishing it all in a spit-and-fly fashion to leave most of the day free for drinking, gambling, and general carousing, activities restricted by mining to nightfall during the week.

The main thoroughfare was crowded with great knots of men on foot, not to mention the many whooping around on mule and horseback. Gavin and Indian flanked Tessa protectively, Indian dropping back only when the way became too crowded or narrow. As far as Tessa was concerned, she might have been on the other side of the moon. The babble of tongues and the range of facial types was incredible. French, German, and Italian blended with the various forms of Spanish from Peru, Chile, and Mexico. There were Kanakas from Hawaii, mulattoes from Jamaica, and Negroes darker than Indian from the South. Even hearing English, Tessa felt disoriented, because each Yankee seemed to speak it a different way.

"Heys boots fer yer road-smashers," yelled one man, and Gavin chuckled at Tessa's baffled expression. "He's from the state of Maine, can't mistake that accent. You'll find great differences in speech from one state to another."

"I'm hearing it already, complicated by the rest of the world," she murmured.

"Vhat vill you have? Only de best from me, only de best," a little peddler with a handcart called out.

"Six ounces, gentlemen, no one can tell where the little joker is!"

"Bet on the jack, the jack's the winning card! Three ounces no man can turn up the jack!"

"Here's th' place to git yer money back."

Games of chance were being touted on every corner by a profusion of thimble riggers, French monte dealers, and string-game tricksters. Tessa had never been so thankful as she was now for Gavin and Indian's wide experience; without them to interpret the scene, her confusion would have been complete, and her danger equally so. It was not that the men were trying to be threatening, it was just that women were the rarest treasure of all here. Gavin had suggested Tessa don her skirts again before they rode into Coloma, and she had complied, agreeing that it would save

318

confusion when they started trading, but now she wasn't sure it had been a good idea.

The word spread like fire that there was a woman riding through town, and the sea of men shifted until the waves were all around the Ramsays. "Keep Amordoro moving," Gavin whispered to Tessa, but his grin was affable as he called out to the men, "Don't crowd my wife, boys, we'll be in town for a while. Let the lady through, now."

Tessa's face was flushed with embarrassment. "Beautiful lady, throw us a kiss." "Just a smile, just a little smile." The pleas for attention engulfed her. It was a little better once they established their camp on the edge of town because there she could occupy the center of a protective circle of *vaqueros,* and her erstwhile followers moved off to other pursuits, taking with them the assurance that she would be more accessible when the selling and gambling began.

But Gavin offered her a way out, assuring her it would be perfectly all right if she chose not to take an active part in their dealings.

"I see," she said thoughtfully. "You'll keep me in a magic circle just like some captive princess in a romantic tale. Fie on you! I'll admit I wouldn't take a Sunday stroll by myself, but I'm certainly not going to be useless baggage on this trip. And they mean well, I'm sure they do— they're just lonesome."

" 'Just lonesome' is enough to drive some men mad," Gavin snapped.

"Why, Gavin Ramsay, you're jealous!"

He grinned wryly. "Now that you mention it, I can't think of a better word. I had an intense desire to smash a few lecherous bodies on our way in."

Her laughter was low and throaty, and she hugged him, ignoring the watching eyes. "I'm glad you feel that way; it's good for my vanity. But there's not a man out there, nor all of them together, to match you in my heart."

His voice was muffled as he held her in a suddenly fierce embrace. "You unman me, my dear."

She giggled irrepressibly. "I hope not! Even if this is to continue a celibate summer."

When they began to sell their goods, she was in the
319

thick of things. The first items they offered were produce that wouldn't keep indefinitely and things delicate to haul, better unloaded as soon as possible. Tessa's eyes widened at the confirmation of the men's claim of high prices and the miners' willingness to pay them. She calculated rapidly. They were getting nearly a dollar's worth of gold for each egg they sold and an equally exorbitant amount for other lowly items such as flour, beans, salt, corn, coffee, and smoked and salted meat. The fruit they had brought with them, most of it dried, and even the last autumn's rather sad-looking apples were gone in no time, and the bidding for the beef on the hoof was brisk. Coloma was surely the best settled and supplied of the gold-mining towns, but its hunger for foodstuffs and other goods was ravenous because so few wanted to abandon the chance of a lucky strike to engage in commerce.

And even with the sky-high prices, when the miners were paying Tessa, they tended to do it with foolish grins and a liberal hand, so that she was continually telling them they had given her too much.

Indian chuckled and said to Gavin, "We got her along, we sell rocks an' these men buy 'em an' eat 'em without knowin', 'cept you keep watchin' her like that, people goin' think she married to a turkey buzzard waitin' swoop down on 'em."

Gavin was amused by the image, but he had no intention of letting Tessa out of his sight.

They did a fine business in the picks, pans, shovels, blankets, shirts, pants, and boots they offered, their only regret being that they had not had more to offer despite Indian's winter efforts in Monterey and elsewhere to increase their stores.

They kept to their plan of retaining some of their merchandise for other settlements and all of their whiskey and wine to sell by the glass in their gaming tent. They had no intention of dumping their goods on one market and scurrying home. They had a lot of territory to explore and a great deal of gold to glean on the turn of the cards.

They had the tent up by Monday night, not Tessa and Gavin's little shelter, but stout sprawling affair of stitched canvas capable of holding a good many people in its lantern-lit interior. It was filled to overflowing, and there was no doubt why—Tessa's table was mobbed. The miners were even more generous here than they had been in the trading; many of them seemed willing to hand over their full pokes just to keep their places. And once word got around that she had been heard singing at the Ramsay campsite, nothing would do but that she play the guitar and sing at intervals during the evening. Leather pouches of gold and even gold coins rained about her then, and she gave up trying to dissuade them because it was no use. Her first embarrassment at performing before so many people quickly gave way to quite another feeling. She did not attempt to explain to Gavin and Indian because she sensed it was purely feminine. After the first frightening press of sheer numbers, she began to understand the deep loneliness of these men. They had left their loved ones far behind them for a desperate venture. There were big strikes to be sure, but for most it meant standing bent-backed and knee-deep in icy water for all the daylight hours six days a week, hoping to see a generous amount of "color" in their pans, more often collecting rheumatic joints and scarcely enough gold to cover the day-to-day expenses of survival. And the life was so strange and hard, that even when the men did accumulate a good hoard, they could hardly wait to gamble or drink it away, anything to soften the hard edges of existence.

Tessa felt motherly toward them; she couldn't help it. She was young, but many of them were even younger. And most were ill equipped to hazard the rough life. The cheap resale value of used frock coats, dress shoes, and other formal articles of clothing testified to the myths they had followed of easy treasure. Now the clothes were most often bought and used briefly by those setting off for a fling in San Francisco. There was surely no use for them here, even if Coloma did boast a rickety hotel. And Tessa was appalled by their lack of knowledge about even the most basic of survival skills. Scurvy was a constant plague, especially among those who had wintered in the mountains, and few of them knew enough to eat green shoots and drink tea brewed of spruce bark. She found herself giving more than one lecture on the necessity of keeping body and soul together, and she found it easier to do as the mob separated into individuals, each with his own story. Jeb,

Bob, Dick, Kani, Miguel, Fritz, Jean, and endless others—she didn't believe all their names, but she believed in their essential goodness under the weathered exteriors, and they responded in kind, mooning after her like anxious puppies whenever they were not hard at work.

But it was not all one-sided. These first comers of forty-eight and forty-nine were, for all their lack of previous experience of the sort of life the gold camps dictated, the best of their civilizations, bright, adventuresome, and strong enough to have survived the rigors of overland or sea journeys to California. And to her delight, Tessa found that an astounding percentage of them were well educated and some had managed to keep in their possession precious books, even when they had been forced to abandon other personal belongings. Once word got around that Mrs. Ramsay liked to read, she suffered an embarrassment of riches—everything from novels to poetry to religious tracts were generously offered her. She spent every spare minute absorbing them greedily, and Gavin teased her with the fact that he knew even better than before how to keep her out of trouble. "If I could just keep you supplied with books, I could lock you in a tower, and you would never notice."

"I would unless you supplied me with a thousand candles as soon as the sun went down," she replied pertly.

"Oh, I would supply you with other amusements for the dark," he said, his eyebrow at an exaggerated angle.

"To read all day and make love all night, I can't think of a nicer life," she sighed.

He shook his head in mock despair. "You're hopeless."

But he was proud of her. The few other women in the place were the wives of Mexicans and South Americans and much more restricted in their movements than Tessa, spending most of their time in the area of their husbands' mining efforts, closely guarded, though they did sometimes hold small soirées after sundown for singing and talking. Tessa, on the other hand, was in the middle of things, and yet had quickly managed to establish her own dignity so that no man ever addressed her with anything less respectful than "Mrs. Ramsay." Gavin knew this resulted from deliberate effort on her part, far more effective than his glaring. Despite the fact that she dealt cards, poured drinks, and sang for the players, Tessa had presented herself as a married woman with no intention of behaving otherwise.

They moved on after two weeks, able now to send some of the *vaqueros* back to the *rancho* since their load was so much lighter. The men were glad to go, anxious to be with their wives and children again.

Tessa found herself having to swallow hard as she bade farewell to some of her special friends in Coloma and wished them luck, but she shared Gavin and Indian's desire to see more of what was happening in the foothills.

She had them both whooping with laughter while they rode along over her playful lecture on the new language she had learned. "It is called the language of the mines and has little to do with English. I heard one man say he was weary of the 'quicks and slows.' I thought he was suffering an ailing stomach and offered him herbs, but no, he was speaking of fleas and lice, horrible creatures! If one has drunk too much, one has a 'brick in one's hat.' Who would have thought such a thing? If one is nervous, one has the 'peedoodles,' or should one raise a fuss, it is a 'conbobberation.' And if one dresses smartly, it is to be 'ripsniptious.' But 'to see the elephant' is the phrase I least understand. It is not likely one would find that fabled beast here."

"Stop it, please, Tessa, before I fall of Diablo!" Gavin gasped, wiping his streaming eyes while Indian chuckled through several ways of saying 'ripsniptious.'

When he had his breath back, Gavin explained. "The elephant story is an old one in the States. Supposedly there was a farmer who had wanted to see an elephant ever since he was a small child, and one day he heard that a circus, a traveling show with animals and performers of all sorts of tricks, was coming to a nearby town complete with an elephant. So the farmer decided to mix business with pleasure, and he loaded his wagon with eggs and vegetables and set off. Lo and behold, he met the circus procession being led by the elephant. But though the farmer liked what he saw, his horse didn't. It took off, kicking the wagon to pieces on the way and spreading eggs and vegetables over several counties. But when people commiserated with the farmer, he replied, 'I don't give a hang. I seen the elephant.' So you see, it means the excitement of searching for and finding something exotic along with the disappointments and hardships that almost always come with it."

"Yes, I understand," she said earnestly, "but what is a 'hang' and would anyone have wanted it if the farmer had been willing to give it?" That set them off again.

Late spring in the foothills of the great Sierras was profuse and exquisitely beautiful, creating riots of rainbow color everywhere, slopes flaming red, gold, and pink, sudden forest clearings of lavender and yellow, and delicate hollows of blue and purple beneath the trees. Bees hummed loudly in the new warmth, butterflies drifted gossamer bits of brightness, and dragonflies added their own iridescence to the singing of birds amid new foliage.

One day Gavin called a halt, dismounted, and disappeared into the shadows of the forest, to return to Tessa with a generous bouquet of violets. "For you, my love. They are the color of your eyes," he said softly.

The fragrance enveloped her, and she looked at the deep purple blossoms through sudden tears, overwhelmed by the sweetness her rough-hewn man was capable of. She leaned from her saddle to kiss him, murmuring, "Could we make camp early tonight, before we chance upon another Babel?"

Indian and the remaining *vaqueros* treated the situation with the utmost delicacy so that somehow Tessa and Gavin's shelter ended up a good distance from everyone else, and when the couple set off hand in hand on foot toward the afternoon shadowed trees, no one followed. "Sometime bein' safe ain't everythin'," Indian observed to no one in particular.

Gavin knew what Tessa was looking for long before he heard the sound of the little waterfall. "You're going to freeze to death one of these days," he said before they'd found the small pool.

"I would if I didn't take the precaution of having you to warm me when I get out." She sniffed audibly. "Then again, I think you could stand a bath too; and we could warm each other."

They played in the water, laughing at each other for the
324

tanned signs of the sun, golden on Tessa's skin, deep bronze on Gavin's, against the modest white of the rest of their flesh induced by the crowded places where they had been.

Gavin retreated from the icy water first, warning Tessa that if he did not, there would be no way for him to warm her at all. And rubbing himself briskly with a rough blanket, he complained, "Being married to you is like having a pet otter; there's no peace unless I can find a swimming hole for you to play in."

She slipped from the water in a flash to rub her cold body against his renewed warmth. "An otter indeed!"

"My, yes," he murmured, the image perfectly fitting for the damp, sleek body twisting sinuously against his and for the sounds of pleasure humming in her throat under his mouth.

He drew her down with him on the blanket. "This is to be warm," she whispered, and though no longer cold, she shivered with the fire.

After their first urgency, their love-making was tempered. That night as they lay together outside the shelter, hearing the soft soughing through the trees, seeing the separate brilliance of the stars against the dark vault of the sky, Tessa felt an exquisite tenderness for her husband, something part of and beyond her body's hunger for him, and she knew he felt the same for her, knew in the low caressing note when he spoke, knew in the gentle play of his hands on her flesh.

"This is the first time the mountains have seemed as they were when we visited them on the edge of winter," she said.

"Sombra found and Brand yet unborn—how long ago that seems." Hearing the echo of her own sadness in his voice, she realized suddenly that that was what had made these last hours so special for them. For a brief time, they had recaptured the mountains' fastness which had healed them and lifted up their bodies and their souls when their need had been greatest. But they knew it was an illusion. Gold had broken the solitude, men were coming to delve in the streams and pick at the hillsides in ever greater numbers. New strikes were being made daily, the trail of the miners taking in ever more territory. Even with the excitement and the profit it meant for them, Tessa and Gavin knew better than most what had been lost.

"We were fortunate to have known it together," she whispered, and she gladly lost sight of the stars in Gavin's lean, dark silhouette.

CHAPTER XXX

Even in the foothills, the swelling heat of summer pressed against them. The insects were worse, and there were sounds Tessa didn't ever need to hear again: the all-day clatter of picks, pans, gravel and water; the grinding of stone against stone of the *arrasta,* quickly shortened to "raster" by the Yankees, its use learned from South Americans but confined to those who had a patient mule to plod around and around, turning the top stone to crush the gravel against the bottom stone with endless noise; and the overwhelming all-day sounds of human voices shouting, swearing, groaning, and singing in raucous chorus. She never needed to hear some of the night sounds again either; the scrape of a fiddle or the wheeze of a concertina, even the high clear notes of a flute well played could pierce the nerves after too long. She hoped grimly that she would not grow to hate the sound of her own guitar. And there were songs worn out with constant repetition, but she had learned them dutifully and went on singing them for the miners. "The Old Oaken Bucket," "Dearest Mae," "I'm Sad and Lonely Here," were always popular, and there were special favorites that had become the anthems of the times—"Coming Around the Horn," "Sweet Betsy from Pike," and "Oh, Susanna!" Tessa had grown to loath both Betsy and Susanna.

She was sustained by her first realization of the loneliness of these men and by the fact that even though she was tired and homesick for the children and the *rancho,* she was with Gavin. That alone kept her smiling, kept her from asking to go home.

She lost track of the number of camps named Ophir for the lost Biblical city, of the ones named Poverty Bar, Long Bar, Murderer's Bar, Dead Man's Bar and every other kind of descriptive name for an obstruction in a river. There seemed to be endless Coyote Diggings and Old Dry Diggings. Places were named for the men who had staked the first claims, for nationalities or remembered home states and cities, for animals, for good and bad luck, for recent local happenings, for favorite curses, and sometimes for pure whimsy. After pushing their way through thick brush up and down steep hills, they had chanced on the town of Volcano. It was immediately apparent there were no volcanoes in the region. Tessa thought that one of the most nonsensical names of all, and she wondered who had been drinking what when the name was chosen.

But still, the towns differed in flavor, even if their names were sometimes the same. It was usually determined by who had arrived first or in the greatest number and how strikes were running. Tessa liked Sonora best of all. Though many Americans and other non-Mexicans were beginning to fill the town, it still had a distinctive Mexican air.

Great trees gave ample shade, and the shelters built by the inhabitants were the most charming Tessa had seen. Rigged of canvas or cotton cloth or even of stocks with branches, leaves, and strong vines interwoven, they were decorated with hangings of silk, cotton, or any other bright material available. Mexican dress was favored, adding yet more color to the spectacle, the brilliant dyes on scarves, shawls, ponchos, and serapes shining in the setting sun.

The Saturday night they spent there so enchanted Tessa that Gavin teased her that he had not thought to travel with such a child. She didn't care; she skipped at his side, pointing out this and that, while Indian obligingly directed the setting up of their equipment.

Lights shone from the houses with their fronts open to the streets, and even the streets themselves glittered with lighted tapers. And on both sides of the streets were gambling tables covered in scarlet cloth with counters holding a multitude of liquor bottles behind them. In fascination, Tessa watched one man buy a bottle of brandy

327

priced at an ounce of gold and pour the whole contents into a wine glass, letting all the overflow puddle at his feet while he pridefully drank what was left.

"Easy come, easy go," Gavin commented drily.

Circles of men sat on the ground and conducted private games using a serape or a blanket for a table, losing their week's earnings as easily there as to one of the professionals.

There were refreshment tables offering every kind of sweetmeat, cakes, dried fruits, hot meats, and pies to be washed down with beverages cooled by snow from the high slopes of the mountains. Tessa tried not to gorge like a greedy child, but finally she gave up. After the lean trail fare, all of this was too much to resist.

"Well, if you follow my example, you'll be sick," Gavin remarked, licking his sticky fingers.

The air was filled with the noise of drums, fiddles, guitars, and Mexican lutes, and here it all sounded fine, so fine that Tessa had to restrain an impulse to dance and sing in the street. It was with reluctance that she accompanied Gavin back to their spot to begin the business of the evening.

They had decided to follow local custom, and the bright lighting made it simple while the soft summer evening made it possible, so they had not set up their tent, but had a table like everyone else.

They did well, but even in this the difference of the town showed. There were many more women in Sonora than in most other camps, wives of the Mexican and South American miners, and mistresses of some of the Yankees, women who would live happily with a heretic but wouldn't marry him. When Tessa realized this was the case for more than one couple, she sighed dolefully. "You didn't really enter the Church's fold. I expect I shall go to hell for marrying you."

"It'll be all right," Gavin retorted with a wicked grin. "I'll be there too."

The relative abundance of women in Sonora made it much easier for Tessa because she didn't have to fend off the first sight crush of lovelorn men as she did in most of the camps. The liquid Spanish compliments she received here were echoes of the days before Yankee rule.

328

A week later, Sonora seemed like a pleasant dream long past. The weekend found them in another of the endless "Diggings," aptly named "Devil's Diggings." They stopped and set up the tent because to miss a Saturday night and Sunday when the heaviest gambling was done seemed foolish, but the place was not promising. Already it had the air of desperation of the camps where gold was petering out, or at least the easy gold. Gavin predicted that it would be a ghost town by the end of the season. But here as in every other camp, they found men willing to buy a drink and risk their fortunes on the cards.

Indian was selling the liquor while Tessa and Gavin dealt for the house. What followed happened so fast, it took Tessa a moment to realize what was going on.

She had been trying to persuade one of the players that he'd had enough to drink and enough bad luck. "Señor, what you really need is some sleep now," she finished gently.

"Need kiss from you." The words slurred drunkenly.

His eyes were beginning to glitter feverishly, but Tessa was not alarmed, having seen her share of men in this state by now. "No, you don't need that at all and certainly not from a married woman with her husband right beside her." Her voice was still calm, but the warning was plain. A man would have to be mad to challenge the combined muscle of Gavin and Indian. She glanced aside nervously, relieved to see Gavin intent on his dealing, hoping the drunk would just go away quietly.

But the man was beyond reason. Tessa could almost hear something snap inside of him in the instant before he raised his voice and bellowed, "Wahl, jus' listen to th' nigger's whore, this little greaser sayin' she too good for Pete! Bet she ain't worth a Chinaman's diggin's in bed."

The tent was suddenly as quiet as the eye of a storm, the players frozen in various attitudes of shock. Tessa stared at the man, unable to believe she'd heard correctly. Indian stood as if graven of dark stone. But Gavin did not share the general paralysis. His face contorted with fury, he flew at the man and his fist slammed into the jawbone with such force, the man was laid flat out on the packed dirt.

"Kill him, dirty bastard ain't no good anyhow," someone yelled and found assent in other voices.

Gavin was ready to do just that as he loomed over the fallen man, his clenched fists still aching to batter bone and flesh, but Indian was beside him now, whispering low, "Don' do it, brother, don'. Ain't worth killin' that kind. He ain't gon' get up. What he drank an' what you gave him put him to sleep but good."

Gavin backed off, his rage lifting, his mind clearing. "Play is over for the night, gentlemen," he announced in a clear, hard voice. "And I would be obliged if you'd take this carcass with you."

The miners, rough lot though they were here, were genuinely sorry for what had happened. They had quickly discovered that the Ramsays and Indian ran fair games, and beyond that, they had recognized Tessa for the rarity she was in the gold camps—a virtuous woman. One of them, though as scruffily bearded and dressed as the rest, was obviously recognized as a leading citizen, for there were nods of approval when he said, "We apologize for Pete's words. He's been a troublemaker ever since he staked his claim here. We'll send him off in the morning with a good flogging."

"Thank you, but there's no need. The man got ugly because he can't hold his liquor. We're moving on anyway, so there shouldn't be any more trouble," Gavin said smoothly. Only Tessa, standing beside him, felt the ripple of remembered pain running through him. Not even for this miscreant who had so insulted them, and who undoubtedly deserved punishment for other reasons, would Gavin condemn a man to suffer the same agony he had known under the lash. There was no organized law in the camps, but the miners' "Ten Commandments" had already become a standard text wherever more than one miner stopped to pan for gold. Though whimsy entered the rules in some camps, the basic tenets were the same from place to place, designed to protect person and property. They were respected to the extent that a shovel and a pan were enough to notify all comers that the land was claimed. Even the size of the claims were well governed, the allowable space being smaller where gold was plentiful, growing larger in direct proportion to poor promise. And with

330

every miner, except the accused, serving as judge and jury, retribution was swift—hanging for the most serious offenses such as murder or bold theft, flogging and banishment for lesser crimes.

Once in their summer wanderings the Ramsay entourage had witnessed, quite inadvertently, the flogging of a man who might or might not have stolen another's poke of gold. Had the proof been clear, he would have been hung. Tessa had heard Gavin's muttered words as the lash fell: "They would be kinder to kill him." His face was ashen, the skin stretched tight across his cheekbones. She had pressed against him, gripping his hand, flinching with him, able only to whisper, "My poor love." Since then they had avoided the dealings of justice in the places they visited.

Tessa's love for him washed over her now as it so often did, offering no warning of its force, so that she had to struggle against tears. Only when the tent was empty of all save the Ramsays and Indian, did she speak. *Mi corazón*, I'm so proud of you," she said softly, and she put her arms around him. "A small man hurts another and goes on wanting the hurt to be forever."

The old ghost of Luis rose between them, and Gavin's voice was raw. "Don't give me too much credit. If he'd gotten up, I would have killed him."

"But he did not, and you did not. And you did not wish him to suffer tomorrow, that is the difference." She burrowed closer against him, feeling his tense muscles relax as he put his arms around her, returning the pressure.

After a moment he raised his head and met Indian's eyes. "I think we've won enough this time around. San Francisco and then home, how does that strike you?"

"Strike me jus' fine." Indian was smiling, as much because his own urge to kill the foul-mouthed man had cooled as for the proposed plan.

The next morning before they left, Tessa had received a bouquet of wildflowers and renewed apologies from the bearded spokesman, who assured her that Mr. Ramsay had been right—Pete was suffering sufficiently from overindulgence and the well-placed fist.

They did not discuss the broader implications of the incident, but they were all aware that already the idyllic time of good fellowship was beginning to tarnish, greed begetting bigotry, especially in places where gold was scarce. "Greaser"—Tessa had heard the term before, it was an old one from the hide and tallow trade when the handlers, both Yankee and Californio, had gotten greasy hands—but never had she heard it applied to herself as it had been last night. And "nigger," no less ugly, both words somehow worse than "whore." The Chinese, arriving in ever greater numbers, kept to themselves, and were kept away from the richest land so successfully that the poorest diggings were described as places even a Chinaman wouldn't touch. The arrogance of the Yankees, so newly arrived themselves, in terming everyone else a foreigner was something Tessa found no easier to comprehend now than she had during the Bear Flag days.

They sent the last of the *vaqueros* home. Tessa was almost tempted to go with them, but she wanted to see the journey through, and she had a growing desire to visit this fabled city of San Francisco and to survey the land they had there.

When they arrived, the men quickly abandoned their pose of knowing all about the city and showing the country lass; they were as stunned as Tessa.

The bay was a forest of masts, grown up now of hundreds of deserted vessels. Gone forever was the sandy waste boasting a few huts and one brick building huddled at the base of the hills. There was a sea of tents and shacks. The din was even louder than the most populous gold camp. Many who had tried the gold fields had returned to San Francisco to glean treasure an easier way, selling goods and services. Several thousand people were now permanent residents of the city, in addition to the many thousands of the floating population which drifted back and forth from the diggings. How unknowingly apt Frémont had been to name the entrance to San Francisco Bay the Golden Gate, two years before Marshall's discovery at Sutter's mill. But not even Frémont claimed to have had second sight. He had chosen the name as a classic conceit, comparing the entrance to the bay to the Golden Horn of Byzantium, foreseeing trade from the Orient, not gold from the hills.

They rode slowly through the dusty, potholed streets,

finding some places paved with flattened sardine tins and rough planks even more treacherous than the bare earth. Merchandise spilled out from rickety stores, bales and bundles making an obstacle course. Hawkers with baskets and carts and small stands called for them to buy everything from tinware to ribbons to boots and fruit and a cup of whiskey.

Tessa could feel Amordoro trembling with each step he took in his effort to behave in this terrifying place, and she sympathized with him. She had never felt so crowded by noise and confusion in her life, not even in Coloma. The men too had all they could do to control their mounts.

At Portsmouth Square, more popularly known as the Plaza, they found gambling tents in full operation, charging a dollar a shot for bad liquor and jammed with men as they would be for twenty-four hours a day, the abundance of red-painted sail cloth, light, ornate bars, and gambling tables making them warm gathering places.

Gavin glanced at Tessa's face and grinned. "No, you aren't going to deal or play here. We haven't time."

"I wouldn't think of it," she protested with assumed innocence. Her eyes were wide, glowing deep violet. Gavin was glad she was used to the stares of the woman-starved populace of the mining camps—she was making every bit as much of a stir here, causing men to stop in their tracks and gaze longingly at her or to join the group which took the time to walk along beside her, embroidering the air with compliments. One group had appointed themselves her official escort and handily cleared the way ahead, their orders being good-humoredly obeyed. Her admirers' fascination became her own when four women rode by at a speed reckless for the congestion. Two of the women were clad in bright riding habits, and the other two were dressed in men's clothing, tailored prettily to their generous curves. All had vividly painted faces, rouged cheeks and lips, darkly outlined eyes, which Tessa found quite exotic.

"Oh, my heavens, they're——" she gasped, and both of her companions roared with laughter.

"I'll say they are!" Gavin agreed, and Indian asked, "What that we come for?"

"To check on the lots and nothing else!" Tessa giggled.

333

They stayed for three days, setting up their own tented sleeping quarters on the sandy outskirts of town rather than trusting themselves to the overcrowded and flea-infested partitions of the outrageously priced boarding houses and hotels. They avoided the section euphemistically called "Happy Valley" where most newcomers camped until they could find their way to the gold fields. It was a perfect place for the plague, Tessa remarked in disgust. The drinking water was foul, sanitation nonexistent, and wharf rats moved about in broad daylight with little interference. Due to the lack of warehouse space, enormous piles of boxes and bundles, goods of all sorts were left on the beach where they had been unloaded until they could be auctioned off on the spot. Many of the new immigrants sought shelter in the mess or slept on any handy box. There wasn't a section of the city, including this one that didn't look as if it would make a perfect bonfire.

Fire was an even greater hazard to health here than disease.

When they checked on their lots, they found both occupied, but what could have been ugly situations were avoided in both cases by the amazing wealth pouring in from the gold fields. The prime piece of land was on the Plaza, and Mr. Peniston, the gambler who had pitched his tent there, was a hard-headed businessman who considered himself fortunate to have enjoyed free rent for several months and who could well afford to pay the $30,000 a year rent Gavin and Indian asked. He knew there were other lots, not so well placed, that were going for more, and the profits of his gaming tables were enormous. He had had no illusions, sure from the first that someone owned the land and would show up in time, and more, he had no taste for violence, especially not with two huge men who looked so fit. His own style favored a Derringer and only then in extremity.

The other piece of land, further from the center of things, sported a ramshackle general store run by a whiner named Smythe whose protestations of poverty were made ludicrous by the constant traffic of customers and gold dust. Gavin and Indian remained impervious to Smythe's alternate threats to vacate and pleas of ruin, and in the end, all were satisfied with the agreed rent of $15,000,
334

the men because that was what they had decided on for the property, Smythe because he felt he had cheated them.

Night and day the city raised its raucous voice like a monstrous infant struggling to grow in a confined space. Already the back hills were being eaten away and leveled, and the edges of the bay were being filled in to provide more usable land. Abandoned ships were transformed into restaurants and boarding houses and storage space. As the land encroached further on the sea, it wasn't unusual to find a land-locked vessel sandwiched between two buildings on inland streets.

Even their short stay allowed them an ample view of the new alien shape of California, far more noticeable here than in the gold camps. President Polk's announcement in his December State of the Union address had not been the only one. The news had been carried by ship, rider, and word of mouth and was still spreading to every corner of the earth, setting mankind on the march in unprecedented numbers. "God and gold, the two things worth a crusade," Gavin remarked cynically.

Logically, the nearer a country was to California, the sooner its citizens arrived. The few foreigners Gavin and Indian had noted the year before had been for the most part simply fortunate enough to have been in California at the time the gold discovery was being taken seriously, and they had been very few in number compared to the purposeful immigrants of this year. Though Yankees were beginning to arrive by ship and the fever-ridden crossing of the Isthmus of Panama and by land after weeks of perilous wagon travel, the bulk of the new arrivals were from Mexico and Central and South America, and were of Spanish or French descent. There seemed to be far more of them in San Francisco than in the camps, where Yankees often matched or outnumbered others.

It was the women Tessa noticed most of all. Accustomed as she was to only Californio women and a very few Yankee wives, she found the foreign females of San Francisco, the vast majority of them prostitutes, fascinating. And though the ratio was better in the city than in the gold camps, women were still greatly outnumbered by men. The Mexicans dressed very much like Californio women though their clothes were brighter in keeping with their profession, but those from other countries wore very different garments when they retained their national dress. The Peruvian women had a common costume, the *saya y manto,* a hooded dress that left only the eyes and feet to be viewed. Indian claimed the way to a Peruvian woman's heart was to flatter her feet; he had the grace to look discomfited when Tessa asked him how he knew. The matter of social class was delicate even within their ranks and depended on their skin color, which varied from the *cholos,* who were part Indian and part white, to the mulattoes, to the Creoles. But they all shared the astonishing habit of smoking cigars.

Peru was also responsible for the export of some of the French women because of the French colony in Lima. Valparaiso, the French Marquesas, and even the populous Hawaiian Islands had also lost quite a number of their French females. Although they appeared overdressed and overpainted to Tessa, these women still showed a Gallic, quintessentially feminine flair and style, their ruffles, flounces, lace, and feathers worn with a sure sense of the portrait.

The largest number had come from Chile. They tended to dress like the Mexicans, and even those with the emptiest purses managed somehow to acquire a vividly colored dress and silk stockings. Their hair hung in single long black braids down their backs. Their complexions were dusky, their cheeks rosy, and their eyes gleaming black. And they already numbered enough to have given the name "Little Chile" to the southern slopes of Alta Loma, where most had their tents. But in spite of their healthy country look, there were facets to their lives that Tessa found nearly impossible to think about. In some of the tents, five or six girls might be serving their customers at the same time, and some of the girls were no older than twelve or thirteen. The Frenchwomen seemed for the most part to control their own lives, while the South Americans were almost all in bondage to the ships' captains who had brought them or to the men who had paid their bonds on arrival. For six months or a year their preferences would be ignored and their earnings confiscated.

By far the most intriguing woman in San Francisco was Ah Toy. Though Chinese men were beginning to filter into California in fair numbers, fleeing famine and war, there were only two Chinese women in all San Francisco. One was a servant and the other was Ah Toy, who had lines of men waiting in the alley by her house and who charged an ounce of gold for the privilege of "gazing on her countenance."

When they saw her near the Plaza on her second day, even the men were wide-eyed. Ah Toy wore apricot silk trousers and a lime-green tunic with a little standup collar. Her face was rice-powder white, her brows slim black curves, her lips ruby red, her ebony hair oiled and dressed neatly on top of her head. She was fine boned and graceful, appearing taller than she was because she wore clogs four or five inches high.

Despite all the strange sights and sounds, the overwhelmingly fast pace and foreign pulse of the city were finally so pervasive that Tessa was glad to leave. She sensed personal danger in the place. It was a world of bachelors. Even the men who were married had for the most part left their families far behind, and though they might have virtuous thoughts of making a fortune to sustain their wives and children, their present lives were not family centered. The elite of the city were already emerging—almost all gamblers and prostitutes. It was no place for marriage and children. Tessa had not seen more than a handful of women who were not prostitutes. It was a chilling thought, raising the ugly, painful memory of Soledad. And she was incapable of imagining what it would be like to sell herself to any man with the gold to pay. She thought of the intimacies her body and Gavin's shared and of how endlessly specific and intertwined were her lust and love—it was always and only Gavin she wanted, with her body and her spirit. She felt as if the whores had a weapon she would never possess, an ability to separate sex from love and to use it for gain, while she was forever enslaved by her need for one man. She drew a grain of comfort from the thought that surely, in giving nothing beyond their bodies, the women received less in return, while her own days and nights were filled with Gavin's gifts.

He was watching her now as they rode along. "I trust

337

I'm not the cause of that dark frown," he observed, his eyebrow up.

There was no way she could explain, but the sweetness of the smile she gave him made up for inadequate words. "I've seen so many different things in such a short time, I'm having difficulty putting them all together."

"Don't try," he advised. "San Francisco is the closest thing to total bedlam I've ever seen." Indian agreed, and the two slipped into reminiscences of the cities they had seen and how unlike San Francisco they all were. Tessa could not mistake the excitement in both of them. San Francisco. A place to be reckoned with before too long.

A lumbermill, now that was something which would turn a profit for years to come, and yes, a warehouse too would be needed that also meant more land even at the extravagant prices asked. The fortune they had amassed during the summer would probably barely cover it.

Tessa was glad their enthusiasm was masking her silence. She wondered whether she would ever reconcile the two halves she recognized in herself—the one wanting adventure as much as the men did, the other wanting peace and roots, her husband and her children safe and together.

She swallowed her panic, praying she would be able to cope with the city when the time came. And then surprising even herself with the firmness of her voice, she said, "I don't think I could run a lumbermill very efficiently. I will have a store with the most tempting goods to offer. I'll have it where the weasel Smythe is now. By then I think he will have gone away."

The men stared at her in astonishment, and then Gavin grinned. "If it will keep you out of the way at the mill, a store you will have, and I expect your profits will match ours."

"They will indeed," she agreed. *I'll think of the silks and satins and lace I'll sell those ladies—well, women—I saw*, she decided inwardly. *I will not think of leaving Rancho Magnífico for such a long time, perhaps forever. I will not.* She kept her eyes very wide so the tears would not spill over and turned her head away as if admiring the landscape so the men would not see.

CHAPTER XXXI

There was pandemonium when they rode into Rancho Magnífico; even their weary mounts seemed to recognize the home pastures and quickened their paces. *Vaqueros* greeted them with joyous yips, and they heard Sombra's full-throated howl before they saw him, hurtling toward Amordoro and Tessa. He escorted her in, bouncing around and making happy squeaking noises as if he were a cub instead of a full-grown wolf.

Then for Tessa there was nothing except Brand and Jefferson, both of them looking as golden brown as the summer-seared valley. Jefferson greeted her with a glad cry and open arms, but Brand held back for a moment, very much on his dignity, not sure he could so easily forgive the long absence. Tessa met his eyes and smiled at him through her tears. "You've taken very good care of your brother. Thank you," she said softly, and he was undone, throwing his sturdy little body against her, nuzzling hard as though he couldn't get enough contact.

She clung to them, overwhelmed with tenderness. Even in so short a time they had visibly grown and changed. The round warmth of them, the clean sun and earth on skin smell of their outdoor days, the fine soft silk of their dark heads—the sensations were so intense that she was almost relieved when it was Gavin and Indian's turn to swing them up in strong arms.

She thanked Rosita, Dolores, and all the other women for their generous care of her sons, and she ignored their disapproval for the next few days when she, with Gavin's full agreement and Indian's gleeful cooperation, ignored the boys' bedtime and indulged them with stories of the gold camps and San Francisco. It made little difference; they were so exhausted by nightfall, they fell asleep at their usual hour anyway.

It was so good to be home. Tessa found herself touching once familiar things, even pots and furniture, and seeing them all with new eyes. Everything was so beautiful. Not even the oppressive heat of the valley summer could defeat her. The cattle were too many to count; the horses were fat, lazy, and perfect. Hawks and eagles drifted over in all the daylight hours, and she soared with them. She thought often of Don Esteban and felt as if he knew and blessed them all.

The children and the people of Rancho Magnífico had their own tales to tell—tales of good harvests, peaceful days, and not too much trouble yet with the seasonally shortened supply of water from the river and the wells. But they had had their own adventures too—adventures like the grizzly who had managed to kill three bullocks before the *vaqueros* had dispatched him. Had Doña Tessa been there, they acknowledged with the utmost courtesy, it would have taken much less time with fewer losses. Tessa counted herself lucky not to have been at home. But she mourned the fact of her absence when she finally sorted out what the children were saying about No-Name.

"The man who has your horse came here," Brand said, and Jefferson added, "Pretty horse, pretty man."

"My horse?" Tessa said, thinking of Amordoro, but the sense of it hit her at the same time Gavin and Indian understood. "No-Name!" the three of them said at once, leaving the children puzzled in their turn.

They got the details from the *vaqueros*. No-Name had paid the rancho a visit shortly after they had left for the gold fields. He had been as princely as the first time he had visited. He had come to breed the chestnut mare to the golden stallion. Tessa laughed when she heard this: No-Name was no fool; he had obviously grasped the intricacies of breeding palominos. He had come for another reason too and had been disappointed to find the Ramsays gone. He wanted the woman who had defied him to know that the horses were well cared for and had become no one's feast.

Tessa was touched, but she was also uneasy. There was no systematic campaign being waged against the Indians of California. There was something that was almost worse —an assumption that it was perfectly all right to shoot an Indian if he got in your way. The Californio policy hadn't been much different, but there had been far fewer
340

people to kill Indians. Now the countryside was swarming with greedy men. Tessa shivered, and Gavin took her hand, pressing it gently, reading her mind as he so often did.

"There's nothing we can do but hope his cleverness will continue to serve him well."

They spent a great deal of time with the children, going over their letters and numbers, singing songs and playing games, taking them on rides whenever possible. Perhaps separations between parents and children weren't so terrible after all, Tessa thought; not if they ended this way, with a fuller appreciation on both sides. Even Sombra and Pureza seemed to parade their offspring by for a share of the attention. She laughed inwardly at herself, wondering what other sop for her conscience she would imagine.

Their bedroom was a new and luxurious place after the struggle for privacy on the trail, and Tessa and Gavin took full pleasure in each other. They were often forced to laugh at themselves when one touch or gesture would lead to another so that they were ready to go to bed before the children were.

But there was one worrisome note. Indian had now made two trips to Monterey since their return to the *rancho,* and each time he had brought bits of news from the town and assurances that Carmelita was fine and sent her love. But there was an uncharacteristic reserve in his manner, a sadness in his eyes that haunted Tessa.

One night as she lay with Gavin, feeling safe and languorous in the after-passion peace, she propped herself on his chest so she could look down into his eyes. "Do you know something I don't know—what is troubling Indian, for instance?"

Gavin had been drifting toward sleep, and her question took him by surprise. "I know a lot of things you don't know and several I hope you never find out," he said, smiling at her.

But she wasn't deterred. She had felt his guilty start, had seen his eyes flicker away from hers in the candlelight. "You haven't answered my question."

He studied her thoughtfully for a moment, then sighed. "I can't. I know Indian is your friend now as much as he is mine, but I can't tell you. That's up to him."

341

He expected further protest, but she asked instead, "He's not in any danger?"

"No." He reached up to stroke her hair back from her face. He knew what she was thinking, that perhaps the murder of Luis had finally been traced to their friend. "No, it's nothing like that."

She settled down against him and murmured, "I'm sorry, darling, I should not have asked. The loyalty you and Indian have for each other is a thing of great beauty. I would never wish to make it less so. He will tell me if and when he wishes to do so."

Gavin loved her dearly at that moment, but he still dreaded her reaction when inevitably she found out.

And suddenly the peaceful interlude was over. It was as if they had all known it would last for all too short a time, and that had made it more precious. After the United States Congress had adjourned for the third time without making any provision for a true government in California, the current de facto governor, General Bennett Riley, had issued a call for a constitutional convention to be held in Monterey. Gavin was to be one of the delegates, his name undoubtedly put forward by Thomas Larkin and some other old friends. Tessa was enormously proud of him, and even Gavin's normal composure was shaken by the honor.

Indian brought word that Carmelita was offering them the hospitality of her house and fully expected them to accept it and of course to bring her favorite children. When he had delivered this message, he had more to tell, and Tessa knew it.

"Indian, what is it?" she asked softly.

He did further damage to his already battered hat, twisting it in his hands before he spoke. He had dreaded this moment and wished he could avoid it forever. It hadn't been difficult to tell Gavin; Gavin was a realist like himself, but Tessa was different.

"Got to tell you, ain't no way 'round it no more. Carmelita gettin' married," he mumbled finally.

Tessa gave a whoop of joy and hugged him. "That's wonderful! You silly man, didn't you know I'd be happy for both of you? It's perfect!" But then the misery in his face and the unyielding tenseness of his body hit her, and she backed away.

342

"I say it wrong an' clumsy like, don' meant that. She ain't marryin' me, marryin' Sam Collins."

Tessa's eyes were wide with shock. "Who in the hell is Sam Collins?" she demanded.

"Don' take on like that!" Indian protested, and for him, his voice was sharp. "Sam Collins a good man. Come from th' States this spring an' he already got a nice little store doin' fine. An' he love Lita an' she love him back, so that's all."

His inadvertent revelation of his nickname for Carmelita made his pain all the more tangible. "I don't understand how she could do this to you!" Tessa wailed desperately. "You were lovers! You were good and kind and beautiful together. How can she marry anyone else?"

"Things change, don' always stay like you want 'em. An' I never asked her t' marry me, never. Jus' went along think' everythin' fine. That Sam, he smart. He see she need somethin' more an' he goin' give it to her—his name, his love, a regular kind of life. He win, I lose. An' I don' want talk no more 'bout it." He stalked off, unable to bear the pity in her eyes.

Tessa found Gavin and flew at him like a whirlwind. "We can't stay with Carmelita, not after what she's done to Indian!"

"What she's done to Indian? And what precisely is that? She gave him some good times and a great deal of love. And now she is going to give the same to this man Collins and marry him besides. She has a perfect right to make that choice. If you let that destroy your friendship with her, you will prove yourself a far less compassionate woman than I think you are. And we will stay with her. Her offer is most generous. Monterey is going to be crowded. You have a choice—either that or I'll go alone and you'll stay here with the children. I won't have Brand and Jefferson made uncomfortable because your plan for the universe has been altered."

She paled under the harsh, cold words, and Gavin drew her to him remorsefully. "Ah, Tessa, I'm sorry. I'm worried about my fitness as a delegate, and I just can't manage a war with an old friend at the same time. And I feel as badly for Indian as you do, even if it was his fault for not asking her first."

Tessa relaxed against him. "Do you think she would have said Yes?" she whispered.

"We'll never know, but one thing I'm sure of, if she had said No, it would only have been because Carmelita doesn't want the kind of life we all lead. She's a cat-on-the-hearth sort of woman, and she knows it. And don't ask me if I'd like a cat-on-the-hearth woman, because surely you know better."

Tessa was grateful for his reassurance, but one fearful fact remained—both he and Indian seemed so ready to accept the idea that even the deepest bonds of love between a man and a woman could change, shift focus and break apart. It was a concept that chilled her to the bone when she thought of herself and Gavin. If the bond between them were ever broken, she was sure he would be the destroyer. She could not imagine loving another man.

She attacked him fiercely that night, nipping, scratching, and writhing against him, demanding possession of every part of his body, giving hers in return until he pinned her to stillness beneath him. "If you're trying to kill me before I change my mind about you, you're doing a good job of it," he groaned. "Never, my love, never." A caress in the words as deep as his mouth claiming hers, his body invading.

They left for Monterey the next day. "Are you fit to ride?" Gavin whispered in mock concern, his eyes glittering devilishly.

"Surely as fit as you are," Tessa returned saucily, but she felt the blush on her cheeks that grew deeper when Brand crowed, "Oh, look, Mama's turning red!"

The trip was uneventful, the children well behaved despite their excitement. Indian rode ahead at the last to warn Carmelita of the imminent arrival, and then the moment was upon Tessa as Carmelita stood at the door to greet them with Sam Collins beside her.

She had the grace to be ashamed of herself even as she did it, but she simply couldn't believe Carmelita had chosen this little round man over Indian, and her response to the introduction was cold—Teresa María at her haughtiest. A tall, virile Yankee like her own she might have accepted, but not this man. Sam Collins was scarcely taller than Carmelita. The little hair he had left was a short, gray fringe skirting a bald dome. Tessa saw little in his face beyond the fact that his nose was crooked from some old fight or accident.

Indian and Gavin were almost overhearty with Mr. Collins, as if to make up for Tessa's behavior, and had Tessa been observing him, she would have seen a good deal of awareness in his expression. But she was too intent on Carmelita to notice anything else.

Carmelita had seen everything, and her anxious smile disappeared abruptly to be replaced by an expression no less coldly courteous than Tessa's had been to Sam.

"You are welcome in my house," she said, the emphasis on the pronoun, and she turned swiftly from Tessa to hug Brand and Jefferson.

Tessa would have felt better if Gavin had rebuked her for her rudeness, but he said nothing, obviously leaving that up to Carmelita now. She hadn't long to wait; Carmelita soon sought her out. Her face was hard and set as Tessa had seen it seldom before, and she made no pretense.

"In my life, I have not had many women I could call my friends. I hoped you were one who would never fail me, but even so, I feared telling you of my plan to marry Sam. I see now my fears were more than justified. I will not try to tell you why I love him. If you cannot see that he is a good man, my words will not help. But I will tell you, little cat, sink your claws into Sam even one more time, and you will leave my house!"

Carmelita was gone before Tessa could say anything. She felt absolutely miserable. No matter how good her motives, and some of them she knew weren't anything but selfish, she had behaved very badly, much more like a child having a tantrum than a grown woman. If Indian could bear it, certainly she could.

It was worse that evening when she found herself studying Sam and seeing all the things she should have noticed on their meeting. His eyes were blue—not as blue as Gavin's but very near—and they were the kindest, wisest eyes she had ever seen. Even when he looked at her, the serenity of his gaze did not falter. He was short and round, but now she saw that there was no sign of sloth in him. It was muscle, not fat, that gave his frame its stocky look. His movements were slow, steady, and sure, every one bespeaking a man competent and unruffled in all he did. His crooked nose was not the only sign of character; the rugged bones of brow, cheeks, and chin were all there to see beneath the weathered skin. And his voice was full of New England, much more than her father's or Gavin's. She almost laughed aloud when it occurred to her that Sam sounded a lot like the peddler who had been offering "road-crushers" in Coloma.

She saw another parallel just as suddenly, and she stood up abruptly. "Señor Collins, if you would be so kind, I would like a few words with you."

She saw the frozen expressions and then Carmelita's eyes narrowing and Gavin putting a restraining hand on her. Only Sam looked completely calm. "I would be honored, Mrs. Ramsay," he said, and he offered her his arm and led her outside into the soft September night.

"Señor Collins . . . er, Mr. Collins," she began, but he corrected her firmly with, "Just Sam, if you'd be so kind."

"All right, Sam it is. And I am Tessa." She took a deep breath and realized that he was not going to hurry her, that he carried with him a circle of timeless peace and acceptance. For the first time she knew how truly lucky Carmelita was.

"When I first met Indian, he was so afraid for Gavin, he couldn't see me at all. He saw only a scheming woman who had trapped his friend into marriage. It wasn't true. I loved Gavin then—I love him now and will forever. Indian paid dearly for his mistake; it took him months to believe he had made it up to me, even though we were by then fast friends. And he was far less guilty than I. He had no one to reassure him about me. I have had my husband, Indian, and Carmelita herself to assure me that she has made a good choice. I was too stubborn, too set on my own to heed them. I have only myself to blame. Can you find it in your heart to forgive my rudeness? Can we begin our acquaintance again?"

"Course we can. I think we could be fine friends with no trouble a 'tall. An' it just wouldn't do to have two people Carmelita loves spattin'." Sam's voice was as mel-

346

low as the night, and Tessa had a sense that he, even more than Gavin and as much as Indian, was a man of the earth as rooted in it as the great oaks, as steady and dependable as sunrise following sunrise.

His voice flowed over her as if he had heard what she was thinking. "Weren't a storekeeper to home. Had a farm, a pretty piece o' land even if th' ground were more stone than soil. Had a wife too, Amelia. Knew her from th' time we both began an' married her not long after. Small an' lovely as a summer rose she were, but th' winters were never kind to her, an' five years ago came her last one. No children livin' an' th' farm seemed to get bigger an' bigger. So finally I sold off the land an' came here, figurin' at least th' winters wouldn't be so hard." He paused, and the sound of music and laughter came to them from another adobe. Even the lap of the ocean seemed audible, and the stars were bright and separate without even the barest wisp of fog to obscure them. Tessa felt no need to fill Sam's silence with nervous words, and had no sense of how much time had passed before he spoke again.

"I haven't seen a California winter yet, but I've found all th' spring an' summer I'll ever need in Carmelita. I love her, an' I'll take th' best care of her I'm able."

"That's all and more than I need to know, Sam," Tessa said. Sure that he wouldn't take it amiss, she leaned forward and kissed him on the forehead, just as Carmelita opened the door and saw them in the flood of light.

Tessa saw the flashing smile, and then Carmelita was hugging them both, saying in Spanish, "I could not have borne it if the two of you had not made peace."

"My Spanish is gettin' better by th' day, an' I gather everything's settled, so I think I'll just take myself back inside with th' other menfolk."

Carmelita turned to watch him go, the light from the house illuminating the softness of her expression, and then the two women were hugging each other tearfully.

"He is wonderful, he really is!" Tessa gasped, and Carmelita agreed wholeheartedly. "I never thought to feel this way about a man again," she added, and everything was understood between them without the mention of Indian's name. It even eased Tessa's insecurity about the changeability of love. Carmelita had loved Indian, yes, but not the way she loved Sam. And that made all the difference.

In the next days she and Carmelita made up for lost time, finding endless things to tell each other. Tessa confided that her initial relief at not being pregnant at an inconvenient time was being supplanted by growing concern that perhaps she would not be able to give Gavin any more children at all, because she was now sure she had been pregnant at least two times and probably more since Jefferson's birth without being able to carry the child for more than two or three months. Carmelita had a sensible and comforting reply. "Perhaps your body knows this time in your life is not a good one to be burdened with a child. And childbirth has been difficult for you. Look at the two fine sons you have. I do not think Gavin feels cheated in any way. Though I confess, I do. Since the children decided Sam is their friend, I have hardly gotten to spoil them at all."

Tessa was doubly grateful to Sam and Carmelita for being so good to the children, for soon Gavin could think of nothing but the daily doings of the convention, and his involvement became her own.

The convention met in Colton Hall which had served as a jail, though most recently as a school, and had been built mostly by the fees from those fined for drunkenness and disorderly conduct. There were forty-eight delegates, seven native-born Californios while five had been born in such disparate places as France, Scotland, Switzerland, Ireland, and Spain. At thirty-one Gavin was one of the youngest delegates, as all of the men were over thirty, but still, they were a young body, the oldest being only fifty-three and more than thirty of them under forty. They were lawyers, farmers, and merchants. Gavin told Tessa that he was glad he had some standing in both of the latter categories, since the title of professional gambler would hardly suit in this case. There were familiar names among the delegates: Carrillo, De La Guerra, Larkin, Pico, and Vallejo. But it soon became evident that even though many of the men knew each other, their ideas were very different, shaped by diverse backgrounds, and that the chief work of the convention would be to formulate a plan on which all could agree.

348

The greatest difference had not even occurred to Tessa until Gavin explained it. Despite all the changes in California, she still found it difficult to credit that the United States government, representing a land and a people foreign to her in spite of her father and her husband, were now the rulers here and that their internal affairs affected California's. So it was a shock to learn that while twenty-three of the delegates were from northern states and most had been in California for some years, the fifteen men from southern states represented a power to be reckoned with, a power that wanted California to come into the Union as a slave state.

"It can't be possible!" Tessa gasped in horror, and Gavin drew her close. "It's a possibility in all new states admitted to the Union. There's a dangerous game being played, trying to balance slave and free states. It won't work forever. There's going to be hell to pay sooner or later, and California will trip the balance toward the free states because your people, the Californio delegates, are as violently opposed to slavery as we from the northern states are, and that gives us a pretty solid block."

She clung to him, seeing it in terribly personal terms because of Indian, who might have been a slave himself —Indian, whose mother had once escaped only to be taken back and forever lost.

She fretted so over it, it was a welcome diversion to find that even with the serious business at hand, the social life of Monterey went on.

It was grand to see the Larkins and many of their old Monterey friends again, but Tessa wasn't as pleased when the evening came to attend the Frémonts' reception. She had still not forgotten her feelings about the man during the Bear Flag days. But she realized Gavin was right— the man was a political force, and the better dealt with, the better for all.

Gavin smiled and commented, "The spirit of California leading her people, I presume," when he saw what she was going to wear—a dress of white lace and satin with the neckline off the shoulders and the bodice fitted to the full skirt of many tiers.

"Would you prefer I wear something else?" she asked sweetly, but her eyes flashed mutinously.

He laughed outright. "I'd prefer to strip you down to nothing and stay right here. You look enchanting." And he meant it. The white set off the summer gold of her skin; her shining black hair was piled high on her head and held in place with the comb Indian had given her; and the wide, glowing amethyst of her eyes was matched by the jewels encircling her slender throat.

He moved behind her, trapping her in his arms, planting a kiss on the temptingly soft nape of her neck. "A few more moments, and we will stay here after all," she murmured before she whirled away from him, even the sensuous rustle of her skirts making Gavin wish they had no social obligations.

Sam Collins shared that wish, fooling with his collar and adjusting his uncomfortably new frock coat until Carmelita scolded him. "Brand and Jefferson will be well cared for by Alma; the house will not burn down while we are gone; and Indian and the Ramsays await us. If you tarry a moment longer, we will be the last to arrive and all will notice us."

It didn't take Tessa long to understand the change in Captain Frémont, and she had to hide a smile at the irony of it.

The man had been tried by court-martial in Washington for his altercation with Kearny. He had been judged guilty on several charges and sentenced to be dismissed. But President Polk, while agreeing with the verdict except for the mutiny charge, had remitted the sentence. That had made no difference to Frémont; bitterly he had resigned. His latest explorations had been financed by his father-in-law, Senator Benton.

But the change in Frémont went far beyond his altered military status. He was now a landowner in California, a role far different from that of the roving conqueror. The purchase itself contained a puzzle hard for most to understand, particularly people like the Ramsays who knew Thomas Larkin fairly well. Frémont had left Larkin with a commission to buy acreage near mission San José, good coastal property. Inexplicably, Larkin had bought the selfsame land for himself while purchasing more than 40,000 acres at the foot of the Sierras for Frémont, land that had been part of an old grant named *Las Mariposas*

—"The Butterflies," surely the friendliest of the inhabitants, since the territory had been controlled by hostile Indians, and most of the soldiers and surveyors who had tried to map it had been massacred. Gavin reckoned it included the same land Tessa had eyed longingly on their return journey from the mountains.

Understandably, Frémont had been furious when he first learned of the switch, but no longer. The Indians had virtually disappeared with the onslaught of the gold seekers, for the land turned out to be very rich in the precious metal. It still did not explain Larkin's behavior, but it made everything except the wealth of the land insignificant. Far from wanting less of that location now, there were rumors that Frémont had every intention of proving his claim extended for a good long distance beyond what one would have supposed to be the boundary lines. He and his wife, Jessie, had plans for building a home and settling there.

And that was the other great difference in him. His wife and daughter had now joined him. Tessa could not help but respect the courage Mrs. Frémont had shown. She and her daughter, Lily, has been the first white women to cross the insect-and-snake-infested, disease-ridden Isthmus of Panama. They had arrived in San Francisco to be met not by Frémont but by the news that he had surely perished on his latest exploration. Jessie had steadfastly refused to believe that, and now she was basking in the rewards of her faith with her husband in the lovely adobe house they had rented in Monterey.

Tessa knew instantly when they were introduced that she and Jessie would never be friends. There was too much of another culture, another way of life and privileged power gleaming in the dark eyes, showing in the aggressively regal set of her head. But Jessie was gracious in the introduction nonetheless, and Tessa even detected a humorous gleam in Frémont's eye that said very plainly that he remembered their first meeting and his comparison of her to his wife. Tessa had to smile in return; even not wanting it to be true, she saw many of her own traits in Jessie Benton Frémont.

And then the social amenities were over, and she had nothing more strenuous to do than dance with Gavin. He didn't make any effort to hide his amusement. "You and Jessie Frémont, my, my," he teased, confirming the fact that he had made the same comparison Tessa had. But it made all the difference when he whispered, "Not really the same at all, because I wouldn't trade for the world. Let's go back to Carmelita's as soon as we can."

They left as early as possible without rudeness, with Sam in Carmelita's capable charge and Indian deep in conversation with three men who had also been on the Santa Fe trail. Tessa sighed inwardly, wondering if Indian would notice the attractive young woman who was eyeing him and tapping her foot impatiently to the music. She admired the easy camaraderie that Indian and Carmelita had so carefully established now their love affair was finished, but she wanted Indian to have something more from a woman, something he surely wasn't going to find unless he started looking again.

But she forgot everyone except Gavin when they got back to the house. They sent Alma home, and the children were fast asleep.

"I've been wanting to get back here for hours," Gavin murmured, his mouth caressing Tessa's neck as he unhooked her dress.

"I can think of some other places I would have you visit," Tessa said, stripping off the last of her undergarments, her hands impatient at the fastenings of Gavin's clothes even as she kissed him.

That night became a treasured memory in the weeks that followed as the convention consumed all Gavin's energy. Tessa was prouder of him every day. It became increasingly clear that the men like him, those who had been part of California in the peaceful days before the gold discovery, were providing the voices of reason and justice in the drafting of the constitution. It was evident they were needed, and from Tessa's point of view and that of many others, tragic that they were not heeded in all things.

Should the property of a woman remain hers after she married? Should dueling be forbidden? What of education, how much support should the government give it? Who should be given the right to vote and who should not?

There was no precedent for it; the convention was deliberating as if California was a state already, not a territory with years to wait for full process, because few doubted she would be quickly admitted to the Union. The gold pouring from her mountain veins was sure to hasten the birth of statehood. But free state or slave, that was yet to be determined.

Gavin was obsessed. He talked of little else, and often awakened Tessa with his restless nightmares. Gwin—the name of the man she came to hate, a Southerner bent on any strategy to establish California as a slave state.

"Christ almighty!" Gavin roared without preamble when he came back to the house late one evening long after his sons were abed. "God damn Gwin and his cohorts to hell! We thought we had them licked, thought we had the makings of a free state. Now Gwin's proposing extending the boundaries of California so far, they would take in most of the Far West. There would be at least enough territory to make two big states, vague now but no doubt clear in his mind for the future—a free state up here and a slave state in the southern regions. And the worst of it is that some of the Californios who have been with us up to now are listening to him. I can't blame them; they see only too clearly that it's Yankee rule all the way up here, and they're hoping that the quieter pueblos of the south might be left to them for the old way of life. They haven't a chance. Gwin and his people are simply using them."

"My poor husband," Tessa said softly, her heart aching. He looked unutterably weary, even his tanned skin had an unhealthy gray tinge. No amount of physical labor could have so depleted his strength. He sank into a chair, and she dropped a kiss on the thick darkness of his hair, then began to knead the steel-tight muscles of his neck.

Carmelita and Sam were out, but Indian had heard every word and made no pretense about it. "You doin' all you can, little brother, ain't no use beatin' yourself to death. Ain't so many of us black men here. Sure, I seen some those freedmen workin' on the wharves in San Francisco an' some in them southern gentlemen's camps what say no slaves here, nigras jus' love that workin', but still, not many. An' mebbe I th' only one of all who got a white man for part my soul. Cain't 'spect them others to know what you know or change for what you know."

Gavin swore so viciously, Tessa jumped, and when he continued, his voice grated with barely suppressed violence. "I *do* expect them to know! It's wrong, it's the worst evil for one man to think he can own another. And beyond the moral hideousness, it's impractical. It never works. The hindsight of history shows us it leads to battle every time. You and I, Indian, or at the very latest, our sons are going to pay the price of that morally blind, greedy southern system. So don't you go patient and forbearing on me!"

"Jus' nuff to keep from bustin' heads an' gettin' hung." Indian's voice held a deadly note, and then he was gone.

Gavin rubbed his face wearily. "That's arrogance for you—me lecturing Indian on the evils of slavery!" His voice took on a strange, faraway sound. "You can almost be lulled into believing it's all right in the border states. Most of the places look like well-run farms where the Negroes have a good life. Almost you can forget they're slaves, no matter how well they're treated. Almost you can convince yourself that since they're in this country and have been for generations, it's just as well there's work for them to do and a place for them to be. It's such a comforting way out, especially when you know the color of your own skin. Almost. But you can't do that in the deep South." His voice quickened. "My God, you can't imagine! Nothing here could possibly prepare you for it, not even the shabby treatment of the Indians. It's a vision of hell. Hours and hours, dawn till dusk in forced labor in the hot sun under the lash." His body quivered involuntarily in memory. "Sold away, so often they are sold away because so many of the plantation owners are living on credit, have been for years, and when ready money is needed, the slaves are easiest to sell. There's a shortage, don't you see, with it being illegal to bring in and sell new souls, so you have to depend on your neighbor's breeding stock if you're short. Would you like a good buck, good for work, good for stud? Or do you need a house slave, a biddable little woman trained in all the arts— laundry, cooking, even a lady's maid, maybe some other services for the master? And these pickaninnies, good promise here, and cheap. No matter that all together they're a family, no matter. What do niggers know about
354

family? Buy what you need, no matter if you don't want them all."

He took a deep breath. "That's the big plantation in the deep South, and not all the so-called good masters make up for one bad. They never will. And we're all part of it because we buy the cotton, the rice, the indigo." Only then did Gavin recognize that the strange warmth turning cold on his skin was not strange at all. "Sweetheart, to make my bad dreams yours, to make you cry, I never meant——"

Her fingers against his mouth stopping his words; her own words filling the silence. "Never try to keep me from that. Your dreams, good and bad, are mine, as mine are yours. If that ceases, we cease. And I promise, the Californios will not fail you; they will not let slavery happen here! I know these men; I know their kind. Nothing for their own gain will blind them to that injustice." She could not tell him that for her not even the terrible image of slavery matched the horror of his acceptance that either he and Indian or their sons would fight a bloody battle over it. Their sons meant only hers and Gavin's now. Gavin and Indian, Brand and Jefferson; the choice was intolerable. She shivered violently, and Gavin drew her close.

They were both asleep when Carmelita and Sam came in, Tessa curled in Gavin's lap, her head tucked in the hollow of his neck, his arms holding her even in sleep.

"Let us not disturb them," Carmelita whispered. "They need the sleep wherever they find it. Our plans won't change if we wait until morning to tell them."

Indian did not come back that night at all.

CHAPTER XXXII

Carmelita became Mrs. Collins in a quiet civil ceremony with the Ramsays and Indian in attendance. Sam had expressed his willingness to join the Church, but as Carmelita confided to Tessa, she didn't feel strongly enough about it to put him through that, his taste in worship being far

355

more simple and direct. "I fear if God is not as understanding as Sam thinks, I'm lost in any case."

Tessa agreed with her. "At least, in that, things are now better. A more unlikely Catholic than Gavin I cannot imagine, and yet he had to pretend conversion to marry me."

When Sam and Carmelita had been pronounced man and wife and the groom had given his bride a hearty kiss, Indian claimed the privilege next, kissing her on both cheeks and whispering for only her to hear, "Be happy always, Lita. Sam, he one good man."

Through her tears, she saw Indian and Sam shaking hands, genuine liking in their eyes and perfect understanding.

When Tessa gave Carmelita a hug, she said, "You look absolutely beautiful," and she meant it; she had never seen her friend more radiant, nor as soft and young as she did now.

It was a good thing to have something to celebrate as the debates at the convention continued, but finally it was over, and the constitution was ratified by an almost unanimous vote on November 13. A system of government was provided as well as a system of education. Duels were unlawful; a woman's property remained her own after marriage; religious freedom was guaranteed; and many more rights and privileges were delineated. Suffrage was limited to male whites of twenty-one years and over, though some exceptions were to be made for some native Indians in special cases.

"My sex and your race, Indian, seem to be similar barriers," Tessa remarked wryly, but she was proud of Gavin and the other delegates. California was to be a free state. These men of various backgrounds had come together and drafted a document in English and Spanish simultaneously. And through their labors, they had minimized their differences enough to come to agreement on a system of government as fair as any in the world.

Tessa cried when she read the delegates' advice to their constituents. Not only did it address a free people and warn them that only their own vigilance would preserve their freedom, but it stated very clearly that while it was understood that the people of California were of differing origins, it was profoundly hoped that the Constitution would provide a uniform and just code of government for all.

Tessa was not so naïve as to believe that such a document could change the hearts of men, any more than she believed the document itself was perfect and without omission. But she knew it was a fine, brave start for what only the citizens themselves could prove the country to be.

"Did we write something badly?" Gavin asked teasingly.

"It is just so very beautiful," Tessa answered, for which her husband kissed her soundly, tasting tears and love.

By the time the Ramsays and Indian left Monterey, a man named Peter Burnett had been elected governor and Frémont seemed a sure bet as one of California's first United States senators, as soon as admission to the Union was ratified. It was no secret Jessie wanted it as much and very likely more than her husband did, particularly as an agent to remove the stigma of court-martial. But even Tessa, despite her initial antipathy to the man, felt he would be a good choice. She felt much more kindly disposed to him now she knew he was antislavery, even though he had been born in the South. Already he had strong enemies in the proslavery people. That alone was enough to soften Tessa's attitude.

She would have liked nothing better than to return to Rancho Magnífico, as Indian did, but Gavin was quietly adamant about their visiting Valle del Mar. She knew he was right, and she was ashamed of her reluctance. Jefferson hadn't even been introduced to his grandfather and the others. But Gavin's insistence on the visit went beyond that. Eventually, he hoped, Tessa would be able to draw strength from her roots as she once had. He was no longer jealous of that source of power, but rather fearful that Tessa would harm herself with its denial.

Even though the children were more patient than one had any right to expect, the journey was miserable. The winter rains had already begun and were unusually heavy. The horses slipped and skidded and were trembling with exhaustion by nightfall. Though they did not speak of it, Tessa and Gavin carried vivid memories of the disastrous journey made in this kind of weather years before.

But the weather produced its own reward, wearing away at her defenses so that by the time they reached Valle del Mar, she was yearning for warmth and light, and it seemed nothing had ever felt so welcoming as María's arms.

María was a little broader, Ramón a little leaner, and both a little older, but that was all. The changes were greater in Juan and Julio, who were very much the contended married men now and whose wives had produced a grandchild apiece for Ramón and María.

The greatest change was in Tessa's father. He was old, dry and fragile as a withered leaf. There was a feeling of impermanence about him, not a threatening vision of death but a peaceful acceptance of the last season of life coming to a close. It was this peacefulness that made it bearable for Tessa. The devils that had haunted Michael Macleod for so much of his life had departed, and if there was little of the old fierceness left, there was less pain.

Most of the time he thought Tessa was her mother, and she did not disabuse him. He seemed to require no explanation for Gavin's presence, nor that of the two little boys who were so fascinated by him.

"Three children," Gavin said gently, watching his sons playing with him some game only they and their grandfather understood.

The Ramirez stewardship showed in the careful tending of everything at the *rancho,* and as long as Michael with his Yankee background remained alive, there should be no trouble with the deed. Ramón and his sons had had some trouble with some summer squatters, but they had managed to drive them off with relentless politeness, the use of Michael's name, and no bloodshed.

When the time for leave-taking came, Tessa went last to her father, knowing there was no certainty that she would see him again.

"Good-by, Father," she murmured, not caring that she was crying and not expecting him to know who she was.

But his eyes were suddenly very clear and focused. "You are happy, Tessa?" he asked.

"Yes, oh, a thousand times yes, Father! I love Gavin even more now than when I first married him."

"And you have two fine sons. Don't weep, my child, there is no sorrow in this. The sorrow was all before."

She clung to him as though she were a small child again, and then she let him go.

Never had she been so glad to see her own home as she was on their return to Rancho Magnífico. Rain had lashed them all the way. Every valley was rapidly becoming a sea of mud, every stream and river swelling to dangerous limits. She was glad they had built on high ground, and could only hope it was high enough.

It was a miserable winter. It seemed the rain would never stop. It was hard on everyone, but hardest for the children, who couldn't be outside for more than a few minutes without getting cold, wet, and mud-covered. Tessa spent hours with them, devising games to amuse and some to instruct them as painlessly as possible in the arts of reading and counting. Brand was already capable in both, and even Jefferson was intrigued, especially by the idea that several letters together could make a word. Gavin and Indian had made marvelous wooden blocks, includings a set on which Tessa had carefully painted the alphabet, and she blessed the men every time the boys settled down to build something or to play with the letters. But even the best amusements wore thin, and sometimes Tessa had to clench her jaw to keep from wailing along with the children.

And there were still tasks to be done on the land, much of it now consisting of moving the livestock from one place to another to keep them out of the spreading lakes and in areas that still had enough grazing to sustain them.

Indian came down with a bad cough that threatened pneumonia, and he gave into Tessa's orders that he go to bed and stay there because, as he finally admitted, "My knees won' stay put."

Some of the *vaqueros* succumbed to the same malady, and Gavin's burden grew that much heavier. He came in in a foul mood one evening.

"Goddamn horses are the dumbest beasts in the world!" he swore, causing his sons to regard him warily while Tessa flew to him in concern.

His heavy poncho was wringing wet, his skin icy cold. The scar stood out whitely on his cheek, and he couldn't control his shivering.

Tessa started giving him orders, and when he protested, she snapped, "Shut up! A frozen husband is of no use to me!"

"I don't think this one is going to be much use even if he does thaw out," Gavin conceded, submitting meekly to her ministrations, suddenly glad of the help in ridding himself of his wet clothes and donning warm dry garments. His own hands were so numb it would have taken him forever to do it by himself.

Gratefully he drank the hot spiced wine she gave him, and he managed to eat most of the rich beef stew on his plate before his eyes began to close. Vaguely he knew he was leaning on Tessa as he walked, and then he knew nothing beyond the softness of the bed that seemed to rise up to meet him.

When he awakened he knew he had slept a very long time even though the gloomy light didn't give him much clue, and he was appalled to discover it was late in the morning.

"Before you bellow," Tessa said sweetly, "I would like to point out that we simply can't afford to have you fall ill along with the others. The dumbest beasts in the world, as you called them, are not worth that. You needed sleep more than they need you. When you're ready, I'll ride out with you. And please, don't refuse me, for, as surely as I love our adorable offspring, I shall go mad if I'm locked in with them for one more day. Dolores will watch them, and I think they'll enjoy the change as much as I will."

Even their celebration of Christmas was dampened. Sam and Carmelita had made tentative plans to join them if the weather permitted, which it obviously did not. As the days moved into 1850, Tessa felt more and more as if Rancho Magnífico were an island floating on an alien inland sea. Even Sombra was given to dismal howling bouts for which Tessa hadn't the heart to discipline him. At least there was some cause to smile when Sombra's offspring tried to reproduce their father's voice.

One visitor did ride in, Sombra giving a warning that

quickly changed to another note and then expectant silence signifying the wolf recognized the person. Tessa went out to the porch, peering through the gray drizzle, completely puzzled. There were few people who received such a greeting.

He took shape suddenly, emerging from the rainy distance, and the first thing she noticed was that he was not riding a chestnut or a young palomino. And then the other images crowded in. The splendid copper of his skin was muddied as if the harsh winter had seeped into his bones. He looked so much thinner, so much older, her eyes widened in concern.

Just for a moment, the No-Name she had first seen appeared again as he smiled and assured her he rode neither the mare nor her first golden colt today because to risk such precious animals on the treacherous ground would be unwise.

"They are well. To dine on gold is a foolish man's wish," he told her in Spanish, and then the smile faded and his eyes were as old as the mountains.

No, he would not stop for a meal or to get warm; no, he had only one purpose. He refused all her offers with the utmost politeness and thanked her when she told him where she thought Gavin might be found.

She was so attuned to his trouble, she did not even know that Jefferson and Brand had come to stand in the doorway behind her until No-Name's gaze shifted. "Your fine sons. May the land have room for them to grow into fine men."

"He's not riding the horse you gave him now," Brand observed.

Beyond words, Tessa held her sons close as they watched the rain swallow horse and rider again. She wanted to follow him to make sure he found Gavin, to hear what he had to say, but she would not commit such a grievous discourtesy. She was certain No-Name had known where Gavin was. He had come to her first in rare tribute. She winced away from the reality and still could not deny it— the vibrant sureness of command that had made him so compelling was gone. His hope was gone.

"Cwyin', Mama?" Jefferson asked nervously, and she buried her face in the soft darkness of his hair. "Yes, I

361

am a little, because sometimes things are sad, and someday I'll explain why. But you and Brand make me very
happy."

She knew it made some kind of sense to him because
he looked less upset. Brand's too-thoughtful expression also
eased. She struggled desperately not to worry them further
as she waited for Gavin to come home, and she was thankful that both the children were asleep when he did.

He put his arms around her and held her hard against
him. His voice was ragged. "I have never felt so inadequate
to any task. He is wiser than I will ever be, and a leader
of men. Yet he humbled himself to come to me. He paid
me the tribute of trusting me despite my white skin. And
I could not help him. He and his people are being hounded
from one place to another, some have already been shot
in cold blood just for the hell of it. He knew I was a
traveler. He wanted to know if there was a place to which
he could take his people in safety. To the south, to desert
country ruled by other tribes and completely unlike the
land No-Name and his people are accustomed to? To the
north, through the heavy band of murderous whites and
beyond to land that is also controlled by fierce and alien
people? To the west, to the sea? To the east beyond where
No-Name has roamed, to the peaks of the Sierras where
nothing can live? There is no place I know of. I wanted to
weep. I asked him to forgive me. He said there was no
blame, that not all white men are the same, any more
than all Indians are. He wished me a good life with you
and the children, and then he was gone."

The first months of the year were haunted by sadness
and loss. In February Indian made the trek to Monterey
as much because he was getting claustrophobic as for the
business necessity. The only good news he brought back
was that the Collinses were well; the rest was dreadful.
The havoc of the floods was widespread. Sacramento had
been under water for most of January, causing people to
take shelter in their attics over streets that had become
waterways navigable only by boats. The reports of damage
to every town and camp in the north were endless, and
the southern part of California seemed to have fared little
better.

And then, a scant time later, Ramón rode in, flanked

by his sons, their presence and their grave faces telling Tessa what they had come for before a word was spoken. Her father was dead. He hadn't had the strength to withstand the damp winter. He had been buried beside her mother and infant brother.

The distress on Ramón's face hurt her more than anything else. "Do not mourn for him or for me," she said gently. "I knew when I saw him that it was the last time. He has been old and tired for a very long time. He had no reason to live any longer."

Gavin spoke at length with Ramón about the stewardship of Rancho Valle del Mar. At least Michael Macleod had used one of the saner periods of his life years before to write a will leaving everything to Tessa except for special and generous bequests to the Ramirez family. Gavin trusted Ramón and his family to continue their excellent running of the *rancho,* but he reiterated his plea that they send for him should any challenge be made. Though unspoken, it was understood between them that in the new order of things, Yankees did not always respect the word of Californios.

Even with the devastation of the rains, Ramón and his sons found much to admire at Rancho Magnífico before they returned to their own home, and Ramón was pleased that he would be able to carry such a description back to María. But he worried about Tessa's lack of visible emotion over the death of her father. He knew his little one too well—he knew she was feeling far more than she was showing, and he dreaded the final price.

Gavin shared Ramón's uneasiness, but he too knew Tessa well, and his knowledge made him helpless. No-Name's sad visit, the devastating storms, her father's death —together they had brought her to a point beyond tears, a terrible place of waiting for the next disaster. She seemed to need to touch him for reassurance and to hold the children more often even while she struggled not to be overprotective. He wondered if she would ever learn to bend rather than chancing the breaking point.

Tessa's questions about herself scarcely differed from Gavin's. She felt as if she were poised and waiting for the next blow, unable to deal fully with what had already happened lest it make her less capable to face new threats.
363

She felt something strangely akin to relief on the day one of No-Name's band rode in. She had only seen this man that first time, but recognition was not difficult, since behind him trailed the mare No-Name had chosen that day four years before. The mare was heavy with foal, and with her were her offspring, not only the original colt, now a bright golden cream color with a high, arching neck and proud carriage, but two more, one light, one dark, the youngest nudging its mother nervously when they stopped. For one wild moment, Tessa tried to believe that that was all it meant—No-Name simply wanted her to see how splendidly his promise had been kept.

She knew it was not true even before she saw the man's face clearly and heard the harsh spitting sound he made of the Spanish he hurled at her. "His, now yours, woman."

This was a ritual. It must all be said, even though she knew the words to come. She motioned away the *vaquero* who was approaching. She regarded the man calmly, and her voice was steady. "They are indeed his. He has given us much for them. I have not asked that any of them be given again to me."

"He has no need of the horses now. He is dead. Before, he asked that I bring them to you. I have obeyed him."

She understood the frozen mask with the black, hating eyes. It was true; nothing could undo it. She had known it would be, and this young follower was suffering the ravaging pain of grief for a much beloved leader.

"How?" Her voice was a small whisper the Indian answered with the dry rustle of his own voice. She heard again the alien name, the melting purr of syllables she had never learned.

They had not even been raiding; to have died so would have been honorable. No. They had been riding, just riding when the white men with the long guns saw them. The white men had laughed and given chase as if they were driving a herd of animals. They had shot many, killed many. No-Name had ridden swiftly away with the others who had survived, but he was grievously wounded. Death had come to him before the sun had fallen. He had been riding the tall colt. He had ordered the colt, the mare, and the others to be taken back to the woman with the eyes of the far mountains. This was now done.

364

Please God, she screamed inwardly, *let this fearful still-ness in myself end now. The worst fear has become the truth. Let me weep.* But the unwanted calm would not break. "I have no words for my grief for him, for you. What will you do?" It was all she could offer.

"We will flee to the higher country in the mountains. We are too few to fight. We have many women and children and old ones in need of safety."

He knew as well as she did that there was no chance for them, no place, as Gavin had told No-Name months before.

"The horses, if they will help in your journey, take them with you."

"No. He would not rest."

"Then wait, just for a moment, please." She turned and went swiftly into the house, not looking back, trusting the man would wait, glad no one was inside except her napping sons.

He was still there when she struggled outside again with the bulging sacks. He looked down at her for a long moment before he reached for the food, and she learned what she should have known before he said, "Yes, for my father. From your hands he would take it now. There is hunger among our people." It was said softly, and she knew he had finally accepted her grief as genuine, seeing her frozen emotion as counterpart to his own disciplined acceptance.

The ghost of his father's smile touched the young man's face and was gone. "Live long and without sorrow," he said.

"Vaya con Dios," Tessa called after him, knowing the words were futile—God seemed to have no room for Indians.

The few people of the *rancho* who had witnessed the meeting and kept their distance because of her silent order now moved closer, but Tessa ordered them to see to the horses and to go back to their other tasks in an imperious manner totally foreign to her normal way with them.

The day was filled with sunlight as though the rain had never been and the early spring would last forever, but to Tessa it might have been the rain-shrouded day of No-Name's farewell. No-Name robbed of all splendor by his senseless death, part of a grim pattern she could not yet summon the strength to understand or deal with. The grass was going to be plentiful for grazing this season, but all she could think of was the livestock that had not made it through the winter. She could see a barren land more clearly than the thrusting green shoots. She could feel her own barrenness. Another child beginning this winter and gone now. She hugged herself, wishing desperately that another heart beat beneath her own.

Gavin and Indian had been told about the visitor and the return of the horses, and even suspecting the cause did not prepare Gavin for Tessa's reaction. She was sitting on the porch with Sombra lying close beside her. One of her hands played idly with the wolf's ears and stroked his massive head, a gentle gesture. But her face was not gentle when she looked up at the men. Her eyes were narrow, hard, and glittering in the pallor of her face. But her voice reflected nothing. She told them the story of No-Name's death as if it had no meaning for her at all.

Indian's face twisted with grief before he could turn away. He had felt a deep respect and kinship for No-Name.

Normally Tessa would have seen Indian's reaction and immediately sought to comfort him, but not now. Indian left them abruptly, and Gavin pulled Tessa roughly to her feet.

"God damn it! What's the matter with you? Don't you feel anything any more?"

She pulled away from him and regarded him coolly. "Yes—I feel the truth of Don Esteban's words. Remember? Years ago he said I would have to change or perish in the new order of things. I didn't understand then. I do now. I have every intention of surviving."

"If you survive this way, it makes no difference. You'll be dead already!" he snapped.

"How unfortunate for you to learn so late that people change."

Gavin's hands clenched with the effort not to slap her, and he cringed inwardly from the vast loneliness that filled him.

CHAPTER XXXIII

Tessa's distance from everything widened in the days that followed. The only close contact she seemed able to make was with her sons, and even that now had a quality of fierce protectiveness that often caused them to squirm uneasily in her hold.

Gavin's sense of helplessness deepened. He couldn't reach her. Even when they lay together at night, they were apart. Only once since the news of No-Name's death had Gavin tried to make love to her, but her body had remained cold and unresponsive, and he shuddered at the idea of taking a "dutiful" wife.

The preparations for the trading and gaming journey were beginning in earnest again. He had no idea whether Tessa meant to go with them or not, nor did he wish to ask her. He didn't know how he felt about it. Part of him thought it might be a healing process for her to get away from the *rancho* and perhaps get closer to herself and to him again; but another part thought it would be a relief to go without her.

And then to add to his burden, Pedro found him one day to announce that there were squatters in the northern pastures. The *mayordomo* was still trembling with rage. He had politely informed the people that they were on the *patrón's* land and asked them to leave. They had laughed, called him and the other *vaqueros* "no-account greasers," and driven them off at rifle point. Pedro was perfectly willing to go back with more of the men and do battle, but he awaited orders.

Gavin sympathized with him and shared his anger, but the last thing he wanted was a massacre on Rancho Magnífico. He and Indian gathered the men, gave strict instructions about holding fire, and headed north.

Gavin's temper was not improved by the realization that the smell of roasting beef coming from the squatters' campfires undoubtedly had its source in the *rancho's* herds.

367

And as they rode in, the discarded hides gave proof of it.

The squatters were full of food and drink and had mistaken Pedro's prudence for cowardice. The men from Rancho Magnífico swooped in before any alarm could be given, and when Gavin saw men reaching for their rifles, his voice rang out, clear and cutting. "Don't touch those! You are already tempting targets."

There was a sudden, deadly stillness as the two groups surveyed each other. The squatters were a sorry lot. Even with water easily available, none of them seemed to believe in bathing. The men wore greasy buckskins and faded flannel. The women were clad in limp and tattered calico. Even their equipment, the wagons, harnesses, and tack for the scrawny horses, showed a lack of care. Unless there were more hiding in the wagons, they numbered about thirty men, women, and children. A child whimpered and his mother cuffed him automatically.

Gavin wrinkled his nose in distaste at the stench that not even the odor of roasting meat could disguise. "Do you have a leader?"

A big man with a greasy beard and little pig's eyes shuffled a few steps forward, and Gavin judged him quickly—the kind of man to watch out for in dark alleys, the most dangerous kind of coward. "Ephraim Thomas," the man mumbled.

"I'm Gavin Ramsay, and this is my partner, Indian," Gavin said with icy courtesy, and when he heard the man start to frame the incredulous words, "that nig——," he snapped, "Don't say it! You're in enough trouble already. You are trespassing on our land and you've stolen cattle."

Thomas started to protest about not knowing they belonged to anyone, but Gavin cut him off. "Even an illiterate can recognize a brand when he sees it." He gestured toward one of the hides. "Are you blind, Mr. Thomas?" His smile was so unpleasant, the man took a few steps backward.

"Don't bother with the next lie. You know by now this is not open land. We have the documents to prove it though I doubt any of you can read. We'll give you twenty-four hours to move on peacefully. If we find you here after that, it won't be peaceful. Understand?"

The man nodded, but whined, "Th' young'uns is plum wore out from all this travelin'."

Gavin was disgusted with himself, but the man had hit on his one vulnerability. The children did look exhausted, but more from a life of neglect than anything else. They were uniformly pinch-faced, tangled-haired, and scantily clothed, peering at the strangers with eyes which were far too old and patient.

He sighed. "All right. You have three days, but no more. That ought to give you time to finish off the beef you've slaughtered. You might even find a minute to clean yourselves up. There's plenty of water." His sarcasm wasn't lost on Ephraim Thomas, whose beady eyes flashed angrily before he managed to resume his expression of servility.

Pedro felt that his honor had been vindicated, but he agreed with both of the *patróns* that the squatters would bear watching during the next three days. His wife had done much to soften his nature, but she would not be happy if she knew what he was thinking now. He still ached to open fire on Thomas and the others.

When the men had ridden out, Tessa had made no attempt to go with them, seeming as indifferent to this problem as she was to everything else these days. But by the time they returned, she was not so calm. It had occurred to her with jolting suddenness that these squatters might be very dangerous—that the men might have ridden into a trap to be wounded or killed.

She had sent the boys with Dolores to play with the other *rancho* children, and she was waiting for the men when they rode in, her eyes scanning their ranks anxiously for signs of anyone missing or wounded. And when Gavin dismounted, she leaned against him, her knees giving way.

"You're all right, all of you? Were they still there? Did they leave? What happened?"

Despite the gravity of the situation, he almost smiled. This was the Tessa he loved, so urgent and alive, not that cold withdrawn stranger. "We're all fine. They were there, but they'll be gone in three days. And if you'll give me a chance, I'll give you the details."

He tipped her chin up and kissed her while the men pretended not to notice, and then he led her into the

369

house with his arm around her, his heart lightened because she pressed against him rather than pulling away.

She was outraged by the squatters' behavior, but she couldn't blame Gavin for his decision. "Such children would have swayed me also," she admitted. "But I do not understand. How can these people just come and think to take land that belongs to others? Would they do the same in the states they have come from?"

"Not in the settled states in the east, they wouldn't, though even there that was the practice in the beginning and a good many Indians died as a result. In most parts of the Far West it's been like those beginnings all over. California should be different because even though there's still a vast amount of land available, there's also a settled population that goes back a long way. The squatters seem unwilling to accept that." He stopped, finding it difficult to explain without being offensive.

"Unwilling to accept it because how can a Yankee be expected to honor the word of a greaser or any other foreigner, and of course, all of us who were born here can be called one or the other. One might as well take the word of an Indian or a nigger." Tessa's voice was silky with mocking hate, but she relented instantly when she saw Gavin's expression. "*Mi corazón*, not you, never you. I'm sorry, but it's hard for me to be sensible about this."

She was suddenly very, very tired. It was as if this was the final threat she had been waiting for, the land itself in danger. All the old ways, the old promises, the old honor, all being swept away. But she saw the one hope. Gavin would never be like the brutal, unthinking parts of his people any more than she shared those characteristics of her own background, but he was enough a part of his own culture to be able to deal with it where she could not.

She nestled against him, sighing like a weary child. He held her gently, stroking her hair, feeling the nervous tension drain from her until she was nearly asleep. He carried her into the bedroom and set her down on the bed, covering her warmly. She stirred and mumbled, "The children . . . "

"Are with Dolores and will be here soon, and surely I

can manage them for one night," Gavin finished for her. A smile curved her mouth before she was sound asleep.

Gavin found his sons were willing to join in the game of letting Mama sleep, and Dolores tarried long enough to make sure the house didn't look as if the stormy season had hit again after one meal. Gavin enjoyed the time with his sons, and let them stay up a bit longer than usual. He was amused when Brand observed wisely, "It's good for Mama to sleep. She been actin' funny for a long time." But later, when the children were finally asleep, he reflected that Brand's comment was far more sobering than amusing. How easy it was to forget as an adult how acute one's vision had been as a child! He felt there was even less excuse for him to lose sight of this. For him, it had been a matter of survival to watch and listen and get out of the way whenever he could. He realized he was tracing the scar on his cheek involuntarily. He had never struck either of his sons, and he hoped he never would.

Suddenly he was desperately hungry for Tessa's warmth, and though she did not awaken when he got into bed beside her, the instinctive curling of her body against his was enough to ease the old nightmares.

Tessa awakened feeling more rested than she had in months. She reached for Gavin, still drowsy with the waking knowledge that he had held her all night long, and he was so much in her mind, it took her a few seconds to realize he was gone. But there was the crackle of paper under her hand and the words he had left:

> I love you. If you must ride out today, go south. I don't trust the squatters. Take Sombra with you, if he can be persuaded to leave his expectant wife. In any case, take your rifle. Best of all, stay home.   Gavin

She laughed aloud. How well he knew her! Though he would prefer she stay close to the houses, he knew that the healing that had begun could only continue with the land.

Brand and Jefferson made little fuss, accepting her promise to take them out the next day. Dolores and Rosita were not so understanding, but when Tessa pulled rank they

371

had no choice, though that did not stop them from muttering about the evil men of the northern camp.

"I'm not going north, I'm going south," Tessa told them sweetly as she calmed a prancing Amordoro who was as anxious as she to get out. Only her care for his dignity kept her from laughing aloud when she asked Sombra to go with her. He looked back and forth from Pureza to Tessa, snapping a warning at the largest cub from last year's litter when he ventured too close, and made worried sounds in his throat as he tried to decide where his duty lay. Finally he got up, shook himself, nuzzled Pureza, and trotted to Amordoro's side.

The sun, which had been so rare in the winter months, felt heavenly. Soon even Sombra ceased to look hag-ridden and was gamboling like a puppy.

Tessa rode for a while and then chose a favorite resting place, a grassy slope shaded by oak trees above a swift bend of water. It was a marvelously peaceful place and despite the good sleep she had had the night before, she felt her eyelids growing heavy as she watched Sombra ranging further and further away until he was out of sight as he chased mice and anything else that jumped in the foliage. She heard Amordoro cropping the new grass, then she heard nothing more.

Pedro searched frantically for Gavin or Indian, cursing despairingly when place after place proved fruitless. When he finally found Don Gavin, he was nearly incoherent with relief. "Perhaps it means nothing, perhaps it is foolish to worry," he sputtered, "but the man among those squatters, the one who spoke for them, he is not at their camp. The others are there, but not that one."

Gavin's face paled. "Tessa!" he breathed, and he shook his head to clear it of the old, dead images and managed to steady his voice, giving his orders calmly. "You were wise to come to me, Pedro. I too hope it means nothing, but Tessa might be out on the *rancho* and I would not like her to meet Mr. Thomas. You go home and see if she is there after all, and whether she is or not, bring back any of the men who are available. I think I know where

Tessa might be." He gave Pedro a brief description, and they parted, each riding hard.

Tessa awakened to a confusion of impressions, not sure at first where she was. The breeze was chill on her skin; Amordoro nickered nervously from near by; there was a terrible stench—her eyes flew open, and she tried to scream but no sound came.

The man looming over her laughed as if her terror were the most amusing thing he had ever witnessed. "Been wonderin' when you was goin' wake up, been starin' at you fer some time now. Saw a pretty hoss an' found a pretty woman, cain't ask fer more than that."

Tessa found her voice, screaming for Sombra even though he was nowhere in sight and she had no idea how far he had ranged in his hunting, and she reached desperately for her rifle.

He kicked it out of reach easily and grabbed for her as she pressed herself against the trunk of the oak. "Now, now, you be good an' quiet an' ol' Ephraim'll take care o' you an' hisself too."

He jerked her to her feet, running a heavy hand down her body, then holding her head in a viselike grip while he tried to kiss her.

"My husband will kill you for this!" Tessa hissed before his slathering mouth found hers. She bit his lower lip hard, and he gave a yelp of pain and cuffed the side of her face, but still did not release her. "Damn hellcat, ain't you! This might be more fun'n I thought. Which one your husband, th' white man, th' nigger, or one o' them greasers? Or mebbe all o' 'em take their turn. Let's see what we got here." He laughed again, and his hand clawed at her skirts and under them, tearing at her underclothes and her flesh.

He was a big man and strong, holding her easily with one hand, anticipating her attempts to kick and scratch, laughing as he tormented her. It was all happening again, Luis—the worse nightmare of her life. The final threat, not just an invasion of the land, but of herself, her body, and her soul.

The world began to recede in whirling blackness and she went limp. Thinking she was giving in, Ephraim re-

373

laxed his hold a little, grunting with pleasure and expectation as his other hand found the warm softness between her legs.

The pain of the vicious probing seared away the faintness that had engulfed her, and she went mad, writhing and screaming and kicking with incredible strength. She fell to the ground as the man staggered back. She crouched there, teeth bared, hands curved into claws. It wouldn't happen again, never. She would die before she would let it happen again.

"You little bitch!" the man swore as he advanced on her. "I'll learn you!"

The wolf came out of nowhere, leaping and hitting the man from the side with such force they both crashed to earth. Tessa saw the man's knife flash and her own screaming blended with his and was still not as loud as Sombra's frenzied snarling. The two forms were already crimson stained and blood flew around them in an ugly vapor. She dove for her rifle.

She knew the instant Sombra died, even before his voice was silenced and his body slumped heavy on the man. She knew in the fierce wild part of herself that had recognized Sombra as kindred even from the time when Gavin had brought him to her as a wounded cub.

She saw knowledge of the death in the man's eyes, saw his hands and body move to shift the dead animal. The man was weak from his struggle and growing weaker from the deep, bleeding gashes inflicted by the wolf's fangs. He was no longer any threat to her; she was in complete control.

What he had tried to do, what he had done—rage boiled in her and faded abruptly, to be replaced by chill purpose. Even her hands felt cold, cold enough to sense the sun warmth of the rifle. The man's eyes met hers and widened in terror. "No, lady, no, you cain't!" he gasped.

"I can," she said, the words as soft as velvet. She took aim and fired, blowing part of his head away.

She put the rifle down very carefully. Some part of her knew that soon she would have to acknowledge that she had killed a human being in cold blood, but she silenced the voice with the same icy savagery that had enabled her to pull the trigger.

Sombra was over a hundred pounds of dead weight, but Tessa managed to drag him off the man, and she kept on, sweating and whimpering in frustration until she had gotten him well away. Then she sank down and buried her face in his bloody fur. "My lovely, lovely Sombra, poor beautiful beast, better to die in the high mountains with your own kind than here with mine." She moaned it in English, in Spanish, in a thousand variations, huddling in misery against the lifeless form.

Gavin found her there. He had died a thousand times since he had heard the shot, but even so, the sight that met his eyes so shocked him, he flinched and roared Tessa's name as he threw himself out of the saddle.

Her clothes were torn; she was covered with blood, even her face was smeared with it, and it took him several frantic moments to discover that very little of it was hers, because she didn't respond to his anxious queries and was still under his hands as he searched for injuries. But she reacted violently when he tried to pull Sombra's body away.

"No!" she shrieked wildly. "Maybe it isn't true, maybe he lives!"

"Tessa, he's dead, there's nothing you can do for him now." He picked her up and for a moment, she resisted fiercely, kicking and trying to claw at his face, her eyes glazed and wild as a trapped beast's.

"Tessa, it's Gavin, my love, it's over, you're safe!" The sharp pain in his voice reached her, and she went limp in his hold.

He held her tightly, rocking her in his arms, crooning to her until the speeding beat of her heart slowed, and she was breathing more evenly. Then he put her down gently and got the flask from his saddlebag.

"Drink it slowly," he cautioned, and she sipped the fiery liquor obediently when he held the flask to her mouth. He soaked his neckerchief in water and washed the blood from her. She bore his ministrations in silence, not even wincing when he discovered the swelling bruise on her cheekbone, until he began to work on a particularly ugly scratch on her thigh.

She stared at it in fascinated horror as if noticing it for the first time, and he was glad when the words began to pour out. He needed to know what had happened to her as much as she needed to tell him.

She described everything, her voice rising as she finished. "Luis all over again. I couldn't bear it! I would have died first, but Sombra came. He wounded the man badly before the man killed him. I knew that, but I killed the man anyway. I shot him on purpose." She paused for an instant, taking deep gulping breaths. "I don't know how I could do that. I killed a human being. But I would do it again. I would like to kill him again right now!" She spat out the last words, and Gavin pulled her roughly into his arms again. "You'd have to wait your turn," he said savagely. "The man deserved to die, but I should have been the one to kill him." He stroked her hair and kissed her face over and over. "Jesus, I couldn't bear it without you!" She heard the break in his voice and felt the tears on his lean cheeks, and his fear and need and love gave her the comfort nothing else could.

She drew a long shuddering breath. "I do not care what happens to the carcass of the man, but I will not leave Sombra for the vultures."

She was speaking Spanish as she so often did under stress, and it took Gavin a moment to remember what "*buitres*" meant. The image of the great, black, naked-headed death birds pleased him; he'd like to leave the man's body to be stripped and shredded of all dignity by those hard talons and beaks, but he had another use for it.

But his voice was gentle and did not reflect his grisly thoughts, "Of course, we will take him home. Pedro and some others should be here soon."

When Pedro rode up not only were several of the *vaqueros* with him, but Indian was there too, arriving first at a breakneck pace that had Tesoro skidding on his haunches.

It was Tessa who spoke first to ease the pain on Indian's face. "It is finished. And little harm was done me."

Indian buried his face in his hands, and his broad shoulders heaved before he regained control of himself. He took Tessa's hand very carefully in his own huge ones and raised it to his lips to touch it with the lightest of kisses. "You mus' keep safe, so many hearts in your hands."

She was quiet while Gavin told the others what had happened. She ignored the gasps of shock and the expressions of murderous rage. And she looked away when one of the *vaqueros* threw the dead man's body over the back of his saddle, tying it on like a sack of meal while his horse snorted in protest. But when she saw the same was to be done with Sombra, she protested, "No, he goes with me."

"All right," Gavin agreed gently, and he waved the others off. Diablo liked his bloody burden no better than the *vaquero*'s horse had, but he carried it obediently, his nostrils distended and blowing hotly at the death scent.

Gavin took Tessa up in front of him on Amordoro, who was trembling with distress for his mistress, but they rode without mishap until Tessa mumbled, "Stop, I must get down, going to be sick."

Gavin held her head and gave her a drink afterward, and assured her calmly that it was natural after the first kill.

She thought about what he'd said all the rest of the way home. The very casualness of his observation sobered her own reeling world and gave her a new focus when she felt the nausea overtake her again. She had known he had killed before; she had wanted him to kill Luis and had feared only for his own safety. But then she had not killed; now she had. Now she understood what it meant to make another human being into nothing.

She had done it, but she could not accept it. She wanted to commit the act over again even while she refused to believe she had done it at all. Gavin accepted it totally and was willing to do it again if he thought there was cause. That was the difference—the vast difference.

Gavin had no intention of going back to the squatters' camp until the next morning. He had coldly logical reasons for his decision. He wanted the squatters to wonder what had happened to Ephraim Thomas for just that much longer. And though he had a tight rein on his fury, he wouldn't test it yet at that close range. It would be too easy to open fire and shoot every one of the bastards, and he knew Indian, Pedro, and the *vaqueros* wouldn't hesitate to join him. But most of all, he didn't want to leave Tessa until the first shock had worn off.

377

Tessa was kept busy by the children's need to be comforted. They had loved Sombra, and their cries were no less pitiful than Pureza's whose high keening wail was a clear recognition of the death of her mate, the voice of her wolf's heart with nothing of her domestic breeding in it. When they had buried Sombra, Pureza lay whimpering near the stone-weighted mound.

Tessa held the children, drawing comfort from their warmth, explaining that the way she looked came from a fight she'd had with the very bad man who had killed Sombra.

"Did you win?" Brand asked, momentarily diverted from his grief by his curiosity.

"Yes. I did." She shivered inwardly and hoped they would never learn what form the winning had taken.

"That's good. Maybe now Sombra be all well again," Jefferson suggested hopefully.

"No, my darling, Sombra is gone from us now. But we still have his beautiful puppies." Not the same at all, she cried inwardly. What a terrible thing this is to try to explain death to a child who is all life.

At least their grief exhausted the children and allowed them to sleep while Tessa remained as tightly strung as a bow, prowling the house restlessly, heating water to bathe again and again, as if to wash away not only the touch of Ephraim Thomas but her own killing of the man, and Sombra's death as well.

Finally Gavin could bear it no more. He caught her to him, holding her as if he feared she would shatter in his hands. "It's finished, my love. You've got to accept it, and you need to rest."

She let him lead her into the bedroom, let him help her undress. He felt the first tremors rippling through her like the warning breeze before the rain, and he was ready when the storm broke and she wept. "All the wild things are dead or dying. No-Name and by now surely his son. Don Esteban. Sombra. Even my pitiful father. All of the wild things, one by one." Her voice was choked with tears, but Gavin understood.

"If I really knew why, I would be God," Gavin said slowly. "So much seems to make only the cruelest kind of sense. But life does go on, in us, in our children—even
378

Sombra's blood continues, and we can always hope that somewhere another child of No-Name will grow to his wisdom. Even the land is green again after this harsh winter, greener than it would have been without the long rains. None of this is any answer, I know, but it makes it more bearable."

Tessa tried to steady her voice. "You and Indian, you both have the gift of acceptance. I wish I could share it, but just when I think I've learned, something happens to show me I have not changed at all."

"Don't change, don't ever change, Tessa! Between the two of us, we ought to be able to handle just about anything."

He felt the pulse in her even before she murmured, "Love me, love me so that not even death matters." Her mouth sought his, opening, eager and demanding.

The long distance that had separated them was bridged in that night, bridged so fiercely that both were shaken, unsure of their separate boundaries for longer than ever before.

As Gavin took her he felt himself in turn taken, held a loving prisoner in the depths of her. And Tessa, opening her body to lure him in and possess him, was herself possessed until she felt herself flowing out to become part of him. She knew the scars on his back and her own on his chest, the lean strong lines from neck to hip, the firm beauty of his flat stomach and the hard eager flesh of his manhood, the perfect musculature of his long legs; she knew his body better than her own until she was part of him thrusting into her, and the separate entity of herself was unimaginable.

She blushed when she opened her eyes to his in the morning.

"Considering the woman I slept with last night, that's an intriguing reaction," Gavin chuckled.

Neither of them mentioned Ephraim Thomas, and Tessa did not ask to go with the men when they rode out with their shrouded burden. But her voice was steady when she bade them go carefully and with God.

Gavin felt as if he were two entirely different people. Part of him was still languorous and satisfied from the night of loving Tessa, while the other was intent on deal-

379

ing with the unpleasant matter at hand. But at least he knew his judgment had been good; his rage was still there, but it was controlled now.

This time when they rode into the squatters' camp, there was a change. The men were no more capable of defending the camp than they had been before, but there was an air of guilty waiting, of eyes and bodies shifting uneasily, an acknowledgment that they had known Ephraim had wandered off to no good purpose, probably to steal horses or anything else that caught his fancy. Tessa.

Gavin's face was devoid of expression as he cut the ropes and gave the body a shove. It fell out of the canvas and landed with an audible thud, and there were gasps and horrified cries at the mangled remains, but Gavin's were the first words. "He tried to rape my wife. You are fortunate that he will be the only one to pay the price if you leave immediately. My men will see you on your way."

One of the women screamed then, a high shriek of hysteria. "He was my husband, you kilt my Ephraim! I'll have th' law on you!"

Gavin's cold stare silenced her. He saw the bruise on her jaw, the mark on her arm, and the gaunt, worn look of years. Ephraim Thomas had been no kinder to his wife than he had been to his random victim.

"I'm surprised you didn't kill him long before this, Mrs. Thomas. You would have saved yourself, my wife, and undoubtedly many other women a great deal of trouble. You're looking at all the law there is here, and the verdict is that carcass at your feet. Take it with you. We don't want it poisoning our land."

The woman's eyes shifted, but not before Gavin saw the truth—she was indeed relieved her husband was dead.

"Looks like the devil hisself kilt Ephraim," one old crone quavered. Gavin did not enlighten her about the origin of the fang and claw marks.

"You go back to Tessa," Indian said softly. "I see they leave this time."

Gavin wondered as he rode back to her if she would ever know how lucky she had been in her first kill. The taking of a life was grim any way you looked at it, but she had slain a man who was clearly evil. His own first kill had been far different. He'd been eighteen, the man he'd shot not much older. The man had been very drunk and in the bad light and murky atmosphere of the saloon, he'd mistaken Gavin for someone else, going for his side-arm, leaving no time for anything but self-defense. It had been justifiable and unavoidable for survival, but that had not eased the pain of looking at the young face so relaxed and defenseless in death, nor had it helped to learn that the kid had been steady and well liked except for his inability to handle liquor. No one blamed Gavin, no one had had to—he would remember that face and the name Willie Curtis for as long as he lived. He only hoped that with time, the image of Ephraim Thomas would fade from Tessa's mind.

For now, he awakened her and held her when she had nightmares about the man; he shared her pain and the instinctive searching of her eyes when one of Sombra's older cubs gave voice suddenly in his father's primal tongue. When Pureza's new litter was born, he shared the bittersweet sight of one puppy that looked almost exactly like its sire, and most of all, he understood Tessa's new, urgent need for him in a world that threatened chaos at every turn. He knew she was going to go with them when they left the *rancho* before she told him.

"I had thought to stay home this time, but I can't. I must go with you. It's selfish, I know, but I need you more than the children need me. Surely the time will come when I will be better able to bear being without you." Her face was as troubled as her voice, and he reached out to smooth away the tension.

"I hope that time never comes," he said gently. "I'm glad you will be with me. I would not care to be without you either."

Nothing would make it easy, but Gavin's words helped to sustain Tessa when she told her sons she would be leaving them again for a while.

CHAPTER XXXIV

They traveled much further north than they had the year before. Though there were some practical reasons for it with more men coming to the region in the wake of ever more gold strikes and therefore more customers to buy goods and to gamble, curiosity was their major spur. This was an area they hadn't seen, so they would go there. It even made sense to Tessa, despite the added days on the trail.

They found a well-established town with grandly false-fronted buildings lining the main street in the place now called Hangtown, the name having been changed from "Dry Diggin's" the year before, for good reason. The hanging tree had already been well used.

It was an unfortunate symbol of the changes they found everywhere. Far sadder than the marks of flood damage left by the winter rains were the signs of erosion of the human contract. The idyllic time in the mining camps was fast fading. There were more shootings, stabbings, floggings, and lynchings. In many places, it was no longer enough to leave a pick and pan as proof of a claim. The easy gold was gone in places where many had searched, and it was growing more and more necessary for several men to band together to survive. A simple pan no longer did the job, and miners had turned to "rocking the cradle," a rectangular wooden box on rockers set on a slope, the top having a sieve, the bottom a series of cleats. Dirt was poured in the top, a bucket of water was added, and the cradle was rocked to swirl the mixture and make it flow through the box, with the result that the larger rocks were caught in the sieve, the waste flowed out the lower end. If one was lucky, there was a noticeable amount of heavy gold particles trapped on the bottom, more if the men were able to afford a mercury coating that could be vaporized from the gold, condensed, and used again.

Some men were working in even larger teams, using Long Toms, greatly enlarged, elongated, and modified versions of the rocker. But in addition to needing more men to operate them, the Long Toms also needed a steady stream of fast-moving water. Tessa watched in amazement as men bent their backs to divert streams to rich but dry dirt when the sites on the banks of the rivers were exhausted.

But even with these combined efforts among small groups, the overall feeling was shifting away from the early sense of community. The situation was not helped by the constant filtering in of Sydney "Ducks," criminals from Australia, or the "Hounds," who had for the most part arrived with the New York Regiment after all the fighting was finished in California and who had been recruited from the ranks of criminals in the first place. They were men who remembered the corruption in New York City's politics with longing. It was every man for himself and his immediate friends and devil take everyone else, particularly anyone who was different, any "furriner."

It was ironic that while Gavin could understand the causes of the situation, this was one case where Tessa could accept it better than he. While he fretted because the worst of other societies were being introduced into this new one, which needed only the most able and conscientious, Tessa accepted it as simply one more calamity of a chaotic time. But she was more thankful than ever for Gavin and Indian's protection. The crowds at night in the gambling tent tended to be rowdier than they had been the year before, but Gavin and Indian compensated by being much more obviously watchful of Tessa, and it would have taken the most foolhardy of men to challenge them.

They journeyed northwest from Hangtown for no other reason than they heard there was fairly well-established gaming in Marysville. They found the rumor to be true at the New World gambling house, spacious, plush, and well lit.

It was crowded, and Gavin and Indian stayed close to Tessa to protect her from the appreciative press of men. Gavin bought drinks at exorbitant prices so they would have an excuse to take up space. The barman eyed Indian

385

and muttered, "He gets his first drink free and that's all he drinks here, just like in San Francisco."

"We pay for what we drink, and we drink what we want unless you know how to use those fists for something better than opening bottles," Gavin shot back, and the man subsided with bad grace.

If Indian had heard, he gave no sign, and Tessa pretended complete ignorance, fixing her smile in place and thanking Gavin when he handed her the first glass of French champagne she had ever tasted. "Oh, my!" she exclaimed, blinking at the first sip. "The bubbles are treacherous! I expect this could make one quite foolish in a very pleasant way."

Gavin's face relaxed, and he laughed. "Why do you think I chose it for you?"

"Well, look there, I bet Natchez or New Orleans," Indian whispered, and they followed his glance to one of the dealers. He was a sturdily built man, but where many professional gamblers were pale-skinned from their indoor lives, this one had a naturally swarthy complexion, coal-black hair, and a luxuriant, drooping mustache. He was richly dressed with a large jeweled stickpin underlining his proficiency in his profession.

"Natchez, New Orleans? Why? I'd guess another country," Tessa said.

Indian smiled. "Ain't talkin' 'bout where be born, but how he dealin'. That man's good as they come, an' th' best is from New Orleans or Natchez way. Lot of gamblin' there, lot of money in th' houses an' on th' riverboats. Gavin an' I live to be a hundred, we still ain't goin' be that good."

Tessa's protest to that died unspoken as they edged closer to watch and she could see what Indian meant. The man's well groomed hands controlled the cards with absolute grace, while his large dark eyes watched the players. His expression was one of bored indifference except for the alertness in those eyes.

And then Tessa saw an amazing change as the man glanced up briefly, his rather craggy face suddenly much softer and intensely alive, his mouth curving in a small smile before he concentrated on the play again.

Tessa followed his gaze. The crowd had swirled open to

allow sight of the most beautiful woman she had ever seen. Her skin was very fair, her hair was thick and gleaming, brunette with just enough hint of auburn to be spectacular. Her heavily lashed eyes were hazel, but even at this distance, Tessa could see the deep, predominant green. Her features were delicately perfect, and the voluptuous curves of her body were so daringly displayed Tessa couldn't help wishing she herself had not dressed so demurely.

She knew she'd been caught staring when the woman cast a speculative eye at her. Tessa smiled tentatively, and the woman smiled back before a group of miners reclaimed her attention.

Gavin had seen the woman too, but had turned his attention back to the cards until he felt Tessa tugging on his sleeve.

"Isn't she lovely! And the way the dealer looked at her! Perhaps they are married."

Gavin snorted. "I think the champagne is giving you a rosy view of the world. Of course, she's lovely, that's one of the first requirements in her profession, and I doubt very much she's married to anyone."

"You're not a very romantic person, and that's an awful thing to say about her," Tessa protested.

Gavin looked down into the slightly flushed face of his wife and marveled anew that she was so beautiful and so unaware of the extent of it. "My dear, have you ever known a so-called decent woman to dress as that one is dressed?"

"I was just wishing I was dressed more like that than this," Tessa confessed, touching the high neckline of her dress.

"If I ever catch you displaying that much in public, I'll give you a sound thrashing and exile you to the *rancho* forever."

"I'm in no danger," she giggled. "I don't have that much to display."

"If you're fishing for a compliment, consider it caught. And now, if you'll cease distracting me, I'd like to watch the play for a while longer."

Tessa didn't mind. The champagne was making her feel pleasurably warm and weightless, and she was enjoying the spectacle, especially the glimpses she caught of the fascinating woman, and the snatches of her conversations with admiring miners. Gradually she realized that the information the stranger offered differed from minute to minute. She had been born in several cities in the eastern United States; she had had several sets of parents of various means; several tragedies had befallen her (these related with downcast eyes and the hint of tears, especially the one about the dead baby); and she had coped and come to California in several ways.

Tessa heard about yet another set of parents, this one complete with a blind father, being presented to a gullible-looking young man, and she couldn't prevent a laugh from escaping. The woman heard, and her hazel eyes narrowed as she looked at Tessa with complete comprehension. Then she grinned and shrugged her elegant shoulders, and a few minutes later she was standing beside the Ramsays and Indian. She offered her hand to Tessa first. "I'm Belle Ryan, and that's fairly true, though Belle is short for Arabella, a little high falutin' for me."

"I am Tessa Ramsay, and this is my husband, Gavin, and my friend, Indian."

Tessa wanted to laugh again because both of the men looked so discomfited; they had not been paying attention to Belle's remarks and had no idea why she had introduced herself. And despite the fact that neither of them could be classed as inexperienced, they were not accustomed to meeting prostitutes socially, and especially not while in the company of a woman like Tessa.

Tessa was not only amused and interested, she was also charmed. There was something very likable about Belle. There was a force and confidence to her sexuality which Tessa envied without feeling threatened. She was nothing at all like Soledad. Her eyes sent no special messages to Gavin or Indian, acknowledging Tessa's existence as fully as the men's. Men came to Belle, not the other way around.

Tessa liked her even more when she said frankly, "I'm sorry about Croper's rudeness earlier." She gestured at the barman. "He came whining to me, and I gave him some clever suggestions about what he could do with his complaints. He's a fool, but he knows how to pour and collect, and it's difficult to find anyone to work with gold glittering

388

in their eyes. This place isn't mine—I just help the hospitality along now and then—but it belongs to Charley"—a nod of her head toward the dealer and the same softness in her face that had been in his—"and his two partners. They don't give a damn what color a man is as long as he can cover his drinks and bets."

"That good to hear these days," Indian said, and Tessa saw he meant it and that his eyes were warming toward Belle. Even Gavin seemed less ill at ease.

Another man came to spell the dark dealer, and Belle was instantly at his side, drawing him with her, introducing him simply as, "Charles Cora, my friend." His dark eyes took a quick, wary inventory, and then he relaxed and smiled. "I noticed you watching. You don't play?" His voice like Belle's was cosmopolitan, perhaps holding a faint trace of the South but nothing that bespoke a particular region.

Gavin explained their travels briefly and added ruefully, "I'd think a long time before I'd bet against a house with a dealer like you. No offense—I could see the game was honest, but anyone who can handle cards like that has to have more than a passing acquaintance with Lady Luck. Indian guessed Natchez or New Orleans."

Charley's smile widened at the tribute. "Natchez it was."

They walked outside for a breath of air, finding it delightfully easy to converse despite having been complete strangers so short a time before. Tessa decided it was because there was a forthrightness and basic honesty in both Charles and Belle, and she was flattered that they seemed to find the same qualities in the Ramsays and Indian.

They listened with a great deal of interest to Belle's description of their trip to California. "My God!" she swore, "I'll stay in California forever before I'll do that again. We crossed the Isthmus by dugout canoe surrounded by insects large enough to carry us off, and when we got to Las Cruces it was still twenty miles or more to Panama City—that trip was on horseback with mud up to the horses' bellies most of the way. We kicked our heels a while in that hell hole before we managed to book passage on the side-wheeler *California*. It might not have been so bad on the boat if she'd only been carrying the two hundred and fifty people she was built for, but there

389

were nearly double that number of us stuffed on board. Some days I thought there must be five thousand, all of them seasick. I would have been sick too, only I worried it would spoil my looks." She gave a gurgle of laughter. "We weren't very well liked by the respectables aboard, so we raised a ruckus now and then just to keep things lively. We got to San Francisco in late December and decided to head out to the provinces, but one of the first places we tried was Sacramento, which happened to be under water. Neither Charley nor I find it comfortable to do business that way, so we moved on. Charley's doing pretty well at the New World, and I can't complain either, but I expect we'll be in San Francisco before the year's out."

They talked for a while longer. Tessa described Rancho Magnífico and the children, trying not to brag too much about either subject, and then it was time for Charles to return to the tables and for Belle to return to her house.

"I'd invite you to visit me there, but I think it might be better if I came to your camp instead. Would that be all right?" It was asked with diffidence, and Tessa replied without hesitation, describing the place where they had camped, glad to hear Gavin and Indian adding their own words of welcome.

They walked back to the camp, Tessa feeling warm and protected with Gavin on one side and Indian on the other against the occasional lurching drunk. The last effects of the champagne were making her feel sleepy too, but not too sleepy to ask the question that was troubling her once she and Gavin were alone.

"Charles and Belle are surely lovers. In fact, they seem as married as we do. So how can she be . . . er, how can she do what she does, and how can Charles bear it?"

Gavin groaned. "Of all the questions to ask a man when he's too tired to think! I expect she separates her life very neatly, loving Charles on the one hand and conducting her business on the other. And I expect Charles understands that very well. Anything beyond that, you'll have to ask her."

She let the subject drop because she knew he was suddenly thinking of Soledad as she was. He had gone to Soledad as something separate and without love. She understood it no better now than she had then. But she did not want it to interfere with her first liking for Belle, and so resolved simply not to think about it.

Charles and Belle appeared at midmorning, and the Rancho Magnífico crew promptly shut down their trading, suggesting the miners come back in a few hours' time.

"I hope you're suitable honored. This is early for Charley an' me," Belle announced irrepressibly.

Tessa had to hide a smile at the men's eagerness to talk to Charles about odds and dealing techniques and a thousand and one variations of the games. Normally they were so competent and in command, but they knew a master when they saw one, and were not about to let false pride keep them from some of his secrets.

"I don't really envy you," Belle said softly, "because I'm happy with my lot. But if I were going to live a different life, yours would do nicely. And another thing, I have this strange urge to tell you the truth after all the lies you overheard last night. I'm lucky the men don't pay such close attention to what I say—their minds are on other things."

"You don't have to tell me anything," Tessa interjected, and Belle laughed. "Honey, I know that. I don't do anything unless I want to, not any more. I used to; when I was small I was a very good girl. I grew up in Baltimore. My parents were Irish and Catholic, good, kind people who saw a life of toil as just punishment for being born. I have a sister, Anna, she's two years older. We both quit school when we were pretty young to work in Betsy Osbourne's dressmaking establishment. Among all the other customers we sewed for were twenty girls from the Lutz. It was a house favored by English sea captains. Anna and I might not have finished school, but we weren't stupid. We figured it would be a lot better to wear the dresses than to make them. So, to put it as politely as I can, we left Osbourne's for jobs at the Lutz. But after a while, I got bored and I drifted on south to Charleston. Met a fellow who kept me very well until he was killed in a needless accident." She did not elaborate. "I did a few more things you'd never do, and then, two years ago, I met Charley. I'll never know if it's true, but it's the best compliment he could give me. He swears he and his best

391

friend saw me in the café at the same time and to avoid drawing blood, they flipped a coin to see who would make my acquaintance. Charley won. Thank God, Charley won! We've been together ever since. I hope we always are. I love him dearly." Her mouth twisted in a wry smile. "Your face is very calm, but your eyes betray you. I don't ask you to understand how it is; you would be lost if you did. But I do ask you to believe I love him."

Tessa studied the flawless face and the depths of the hazel eyes, doing so without embarrassment, taking her time, knowing it was important to be sure. "You're right, I don't understand it, but I do believe in your love for him," she said finally.

"Your husband is a lucky man. In my business, you could make a fortune," Belle said, and their eyes met for an instant before they broke into peals of laughter. Belle's tribute, so honestly given, was a peculiar one for a respectable married woman.

Belle pressed Tessa for details of her own upbringing, and Tessa was disconcerted to find that Belle regarded her background as virtually that of an exotic foreign princess. But that was preferable to talking about her father's dissipation or Luis or Soledad, so she did not say the words to change the image.

"Tell me more about your sons," Belle urged. "That's another lie I think you heard. I never did have a child. In my profession, that would be a foolish thing to do. It's the one thing I think I shall miss later, but there's a price for everything." Complete acceptance and no bitterness in her words.

They talked on and on. Gradually it dawned on Tessa that her hunger for the friendship and understanding of another woman near her own age (Belle would be twenty-three this year and even that thrilled Tessa because a scarce year was all that separated them) had been intense for a very long time. Her mother had died so long ago, and María had taken her place as well as she could, but she, like the women on Rancho Magnífico who cared for Tessa's welfare, was ever conscious that Tessa was the *patróna*. Even Carmelita, who had been the only one to partially fill the need, was older, and embarked now on a new life with Sam that left her little time to bridge the distance between her life and Tessa's.

But Tessa's attention wandered when she realized that the men were talking about San Francisco.

Belle studied her set face. "Don't let it frighten you," she said gently. "It's a big town, growing bigger. It's noisy and a little mad, but you'll have him with you." She gestured toward Gavin.

"You're right, of course," Tessa agreed slowly. "And it's something I've known I was going to have to face since my first sight of the city. I just keep balking like a stubborn horse because it's all so strange and new."

When they had to move on, Tessa's parting with Belle was not as sad as it might have been because Belle whispered, "See you in San Francisco." Tessa was quite sure they would indeed meet again.

East from Marysville, in Grass Valley, there were reported to be rich finds of gold-bearing quartz. It was the first time Tessa had seen the men show interest in an actual strike rather the business opportunities surrounding it.

"Don't tell me you have finally caught gold fever," she said, eyeing them suspiciously. "What makes this any different?"

"A good vein of gold in the quartz will yield a lot more gold at a steady rate than a stream with random nuggets," Gavin explained patiently. "But it also takes more work and more equipment to extract the gold, and that means capital to back it. Don't look so worried, darling, it's an idea for the future when the first hordes have gone on in search of easier pickings."

Tessa didn't bother to point out that lately the future seemed to be arriving in the present with alarming speed. And the key to it all was San Francisco. It throbbed in her brain, a painful, unkeepable secret that would surely out sooner or later. She was determined she would not be the one to raise the subject, but in the end that was exactly what she did, and it was precipitated by something that had nothing to do with the city.

The men held more conversations out of her hearing than they ever had before. She knew that most of them were about San Francisco, and she felt shut out and resentful, even though her attitude had undoubtedly gotten her into this fix. But when she found that was not all they were keeping from her, she was furious.

They had set up camp in one of the new settlements in Grass Valley, and she was dealing a monte game in their tent when she heard two miners talking about the Foreign Miners' Tax which had been levied since April. "Damn righteous, I call it," one man said, and the other agreed. "You give them furriners jus' th' littliest inch an' they take a mile from ya. Greasers an' Chinaboys, cain't abide 'em."

Tessa went on dealing, smiling and acting her part as the charming hostess while anger seethed beneath the polished surface. This was beyond acceptance. Only when they closed down the gambling in the early morning hours did she let her temper out.

"This Foreign Miners' Tax, you both knew about it, didn't you? Did you think I would never hear of it?" she snapped, taking the men totally by surprise, seeing them start in guilty unison.

"We hoped you'd never hear of it, a foolish hope to say the least," Gavin ventured sheepishly. "It's so unjust, surely it won't last for too long. Twenty dollars a month to mine when you've already been forced off the best claims is a criminal amount—any amount would be." He studied the cold hauteur of his wife's face for a moment before he finished. "I know, the prejudice is damnable, but there's an even simpler reason. The Chinese will work patiently for all the daylight hours, hardly taking time out to breathe, and the South Americans and many of the Californios know a whole lot more about mining than most Yankees do. Sheer greed and envy of other people's skill had a lot to do with getting that tax started."

The still, withdrawn expression softened and vanished as Tessa considered his words. "I know you were trying to protect me from something you knew I would hate, but please, don't do it again. And the two of you can cease whispering about San Francisco also. Let us speak of it together. It is time to go there again, most probably it is time to stay there for a while." Only on the last few words did her voice tremble, but there were no tears when Gavin kissed her and Indian gave her a hug, admitting they'd both been fearful of broaching the subject to her.

It was midsummer when they arrived in the city, and the mudholes of the winter rains had long since dried up and baked to fine dust. There was more of everything: more gambling houses and brothels, more hotels, stores, and warehouses, more landfill in the bay, more abandoned ships, the masts now indicating more than six hundred vessels, more cuts in the surrounding hills, many more people despite the absence of those at the mines for the season, more fleas, rats, dirt, confusion, noise, and lawlessness.

Tessa liked it no better than she had the first time, but now she had had a voice in the decision to come here, and even if she never grew fond of the city, there was surely challenge enough.

They spent two hectic weeks preparing the way for a more permanent commitment to the place. Mr. Smythe, true to Tessa's prediction, was not averse to leaving when he found he could not whine his way to a lower rent. He had already made more money than he had ever hoped to see, and he wasn't the sort to want to work longer than necessary. When the men discussed various uses for the lot, Tessa reminded them sweetly, "That's the place for my store." They did not gainsay her, because their lives had been made so much easier by her cooperation lately. And as Gavin confided to Indian, "She just might make a success out of it." Indian had fewer doubts that Gavin.

Mr. Peniston, having fully expected to be evicted when the landlords returned, was delighted with their offer. They had plans to build a much more elaborate gaming house than the ramshackle affair he had put up, but for a good share of the take, he was welcome to stay and oversee things for them with the full understanding that the slightest hint of chicanery would see him on the street faster than his legs could carry him. It was fine with him. He was a good gambler, but he had no desire to take the risks of building an empire. And it was fine with them too because while Mr. Peniston was not of the caliber of Charles Cora, he was easily recognizable as a competent professional, always preferable in this business to even the most talented amateur.

Their hardest and most time-consuming task was to acquire more land, a process they had started the year before. Even with the astronomical prices being asked, good lots were seldom long without buyers. But with the quickly turning tides of fortune and the speculators, it was possible to find parcels coming up for sale and possible to buy them if one were quick and had the gold to pay.

Gavin and Indian had had their eyes on a piece of land that they judged perfect for a warehouse and brokering concern. After days of feverish bargaining, they had it, because the previous proprietor had a bad habit of neglecting everything to play cards for stakes over his head. They were also helped more than a little by Jordan Ames, now their lawyer.

They had not sought him out. He had simply appeared, openly admitting he had heard about them and their desire to purchase more land and that he was in a position to help. Among other things, he knew the owner of the potential warehouse property, and it was he who told the Ramsays and Indian of the man's gambling addiction. In addition, he had some suggestions for a lot that might serve to hold living quarters.

They were not such country bumpkins that they had not heard of the overabundance of crooked lawyers in San Francisco. Some people even contended that it was this population which was causing all California's lawlessness by their manipulations. But there was something very engaging about Jordan, and the fees he suggested were reasonable considering the vast amounts of money involved in the purchases.

He was nearly as tall as Gavin, but his coloring was completely opposite. His hair was thick, wavy, and so fair that it was as much silver as gold. His features were so straight and symmetrical, he might have been in danger of being called beautiful had it not been for his eyes. It was not that they were not also beautiful, for indeed they were, a deep gray with gold flecking, the color enhanced by lashes and brows many shades darker than his hair. It was what the eyes held that changed the face, gave it character and caution.

Jordan offered his credentials cheerfully. He had been raised in the South, in Georgia, but had attended schools in the North, including Harvard where he had studied law. He had then been a law clerk in a Boston firm. He had come to California slightly over a year before, and he intended to stay because he felt a man's opportunities were far better here than back East. He had found San Francisco a wide-open place where one could learn a great deal by simply listening. He was twenty-eight years old.

It was credible as far as it went, but Tessa read so many other things in his eyes, she was unnerved, especially when she realized that Gavin and Indian weren't conscious of the discrepancies at all. It wasn't all that unusual for sons of wealthy Southerners to go North to the great universities, even she knew that. But why had Jordan gone, and for so long? Had he gone willingly or been sent? Had his life really been as smooth and uneventful as he described it? She doubted it. His eyes. There was nothing evasive or dishonest about them, but they were deep, sad, and knowing far beyond his years, belying the confident and easy-going façade. And they were telling her more than they were telling her men. She realized it with a shock which made the muggy day of their first meeting with Jordan even more uncomfortable. The man was looking at her in a gentle, intimate way, the way lovers look at each other for reassurance, the way she and Gavin often did. There was no offense intended, she knew. It went beyond that, as if Jordan had known her for a very long time. And her greatest terror was that she was seeing him sexually, seeing the trim strength of his body, his strange fair coloring, hearing the patterns of his speech, cultured and cosmopolitan and even less touched by the South than Belle and Charles's voices. She was perceiving him as she had never done any other man except Gavin.

She did not know what to do as the days passed, and they saw more and more of Jordan Ames. She could not accuse him of any kind of discourtesy. In word and gesture, he was as courtly as the long-vanished knight of old in all his dealings with her. How could she explain to Gavin that that was part of her disquiet, part of Jordan's intimacy? She could not explain to him any more than she could to herself the sensations on her skin, the quickened pulse of her body, the feeling of Jordan touching her and of her own response every time she saw him, though their only physical contact had been the touch of their hands when they first met. And worst of all was her feeling that they had known each other before. Of all the madness she had steeled herself to face in the city, this she had never considered at all. Even her prayer that Jordan would prove incompetent in his legal work went unanswered; he was efficient in every phase of the business transactions.

Finally Gavin noticed how subdued she was and asked anxiously if something was wrong. It was her chance to try to explain, but something stopped her. She shook her head and managed to smile. "Nothing is amiss except that I'm concentrating on learning so many new things, I haven't time for anything else."

The place Jordan had in mind for them to live was a surprise. It was in Happy Valley, a location they would not even have considered in the previous year. But the great fires that had swept the city beginning with Christmas Eve of the year before had done some constructive work in Happy Valley. It was much less crowded and pestilential now and even boasted a good number of brick and frame buildings as opposed to its old shambles of tents and packing crates. It wasn't far from the warehouse site on Montgomery Street nor from Tessa's lot on Kearny, and even the Plaza and the gambling houses would be possible on foot and an easy horseback ride. Though the original shoreline was fast creeping away with landfill, they would not be far from the bay, and that was somehow comforting to Tessa, a way to keep in touch with nature even in the midst of so many people.

With bricks going for a dollar apiece and scarce even at that price, and with the labor shortage still so chronic, they decided they must begin with a prefabricated house. Many were coming to California from New England, from Europe and Asia. Some were of wood, others of galvanized sheet metal and corrugated iron. Though the metal might provide a little more protection from fire, they decided on wood because at least it did not get so hot or cold as metal with changes in the weather. They would not be alone in the nature of their shelter; everything from churches and hospitals to bowling alleys and hotels were being shipped in from various corners of the earth to be erected in San Francisco.

It was while they were surveying the Happy Valley land that Tessa finally summoned the courage to face Jordan

Ames. Indian and Gavin were a short distance away, engrossed in discussing various aspects of the work to be done, and Tessa felt protected yet uncrowded by their presence.

"Have I met you before, Mr. Ames, in one of the mining camps perhaps?" she asked politely.

His face was lighted by a swift smile. "Ah, at least you feel something! No, we never met before. But I saw you when you rode into San Francisco last summer. I followed you for several blocks, and I, for one, did not look away when the *hetaerae* rode by. I feared then that the blue-eyed man was your husband, and now I find my lot even worse because I like him. It won't change my loving you, but it will guarantee my good behavior."

Tessa's eyes widened, and she stared at the man, unable to credit she'd heard right. "*Hetaerae,* that's Greek, is it not?" she stammered and blushed deeply for the foolishness of the remark. "I'm sorry, I'm not accustomed to casual flirtation." Almost she could remember his face in that crowd of men.

The smile was gone and his gray eyes were grave. "I am—but that has nothing to do with this. The women I have known would have slapped my face for my effrontery. You, on the other hand, stand before me with color in your cheeks and confusion in your eyes, as if it is all somehow your fault. It is not, but that you would have considered it so is just one more reason to love you. I mean what I say. The fact that you are married and quite obviously in love with your husband does not, unfortunately for me, change my feelings."

His face was suddenly flooded with remorse, and he barely checked himself from taking her hands. "Don't look so frightened. I am used to a world where things are never quite as one would wish them. I will never press you; you have my word on it. But surely it cannot be so tragic to know someone else loves you and would do anything to make you happy."

She could not conjure up any of the reactions she thought she ought to have. She wanted to tell him it was impossible to love someone just like that, but she could not; she remembered her first day of knowing Gavin. She wanted to dismiss the whole episode as this man's calculated approach to married women he desired, but she could not—the depths of his golden-gray eyes forbade it. She felt a welling sadness for him, for the waste of this man's heart, but she also felt her uneasiness ebbing away. Now she knew, and she knew he would be true to his word. And since she loved Gavin, there was nothing else to be known.

"Thank you, Jordan Ames," she whispered finally. "May you be happy also and find someone else to love as much as I love Gavin."

He bowed his head in a brief but eloquent gesture of acceptance.

Indian and Gavin returned to them, and they rode back to their camp to wind up details of this additional venture. It was difficult for Tessa to believe the passage between herself and Jordan had happened at all. He betrayed nothing.

When she and Gavin were alone, Gavin said, "You look happier than you have in days. Maybe it's because now you have an idea of where we're going to live?" His raised eyebrow underlined the question.

"Indeed, it's a great help. I can see Brand and Jefferson quite happily settled there."

Not until he was fast asleep beside her that night did she realize this was the most unnerving thing of all. She had lied to him so easily and convincingly. It was as if their lives had already begun to run separate courses. She moved to rest her head against his shoulder, to encircle him with her arms. He did not awaken, but he murmured her name and his body shifted instinctively to settle her more comfortably against him.

CHAPTER XXXV

The time had sped so quickly since their return from San Francisco, more like a flying visit than coming home —days filled with deciding what to take and what to leave behind, days of comforting the distraught people of the

400

rancho who recognized the seriousness of this change; days of trying to reason with Brand and Jefferson, who were sometimes excited, sometimes terrified, and always confused by this inexplicable reorganization of their lives; and some long days without Gavin and Indian, who had to visit the city frequently to make sure things were progressing as well as could be expected. Even Sam and Carmelita added confusion, her friend suddenly losing control and weeping against Tessa's shoulder, calling herself every sort of fool because after all, the trip from Monterey to San Francisco was easily made by ship, wasn't it?

The Collinses were gone now, and so were the days. Tomorrow they would leave for the city, and there was still much to do, but in the midst of the bustle, Tessa suddenly stopped what she was doing. "Gavin, please, ride out with me," she pleaded, and he responded to her need without question while Indian let the children "help" him so they wouldn't mind not going with their parents.

They rode and rode until they stopped by mutual and unspoken consent at a place where the world was theirs for a vast reach and some of the best of the golden horses grazed nearby.

Tessa remembered how they had found the land; she could feel the love and excitement of that day, see it as if it were happening again. The cycles of creation sped through her mind: the crop land, wider greenswards every year; the gardens and the orchard, roses blooming all summer now, many of the fruit trees mature enough to bear sweet, heavy burdens at their appointed times; the herds producing fine strong offspring; the *vaqueros* and their families now numbering enough to populate a small town. The terrible night of Luis and his men. The return from the mountains. The births of Brand and Jefferson. The bear. The squatters and Ephraim Thomas. Sombra. The days and nights of love and toil and danger she and Gavin had shared. The images flashed faster and faster. Grief rose in her throat until it was agony to breathe. They would come back, of course they would. But the beginning here was ended. Their birth cords to the ranch were being cut as surely as the children's had been cut from the nourishment of her own body.

And she still feared the city. Gavin had known great

401

cities before, had been raised in one of them. But nothing in her experience, not Monterey or the gold camps, had prepared her for the noise and confusion of the sprawling growth on San Francisco Bay. She was afraid of being swallowed and dissolved in the spawning creature.

Gavin's arm came around her, strong, warm, and comforting as he held her against his side, tipping her head up with his free hand so he could see her face. Her eyes were swimming with unshed tears, the violet as deep as the shadows on the distant mountains. "It is still ours," he said gently.

"But not the same," she answered, her voice shaking.

"I know. But we can always come back if life in the city proves too much for us. As competent as Pedro is, we will have to keep close ties in any case."

Her voice steadied. "Nothing is too much for us, and we are not backward-going people. Pedro can manage very well here. Wherever you are, wherever we are together is home. I am foolish to forget that even for a moment."

He kissed her then, gently at first, growing more insistent until all the golden images of that day were fused in her mind with his dark beauty forever.

The first month in the city was the most hectic time Tessa had ever known. The frame house, sparkling white with slate gray trim (a color Tessa had chosen over the green most of these houses sported) provided more than adequate space with an upper story, even if it did leak when the wind blew. But though she had been well trained by María in domestic work, the only time she had had to do everything by herself had been for that brief time in Monterey and there had been no children then. Gavin had suggested they ask one of the *vaqueros* and his family to accompany them, but Tessa had refused. Their own uprooting was bad enough; she could not imagine any of the *rancho* couples being happy in the city. Now it was difficult for her not to regret her kind impulse. Women to do domestic chores were well-nigh unattainable. The few there were were making fortunes by simply running their own laundry businesses, charging fees so high some men sent their shirts to Hawaii or even China to be washed and ironed.

Tessa found herself gritting her teeth through most of the daylight hours as she tried to keep everyone decently fed and clothed, the house and the children as free of dirt and fleas as possible, and her own temper from exploding. Brand and Jefferson had been at a high pitch of excitement since they arrived, wide-eyed and voluble about every new thing they saw. And not wanting herself or them to be prisoners of the house, she often took them out walking or shopping with her while the men were busy at one lot or the other, supervising the raising of the buildings. Though the wooden structure for her store was going up rapidly, she thought in despair that she would surely never be able to run it if her life didn't change drastically.

It affected their marriage too, both of them so exhausted at nightfall that the best they could manage was to crawl into bed and immediate sleep. But one night, Tessa was so tired she couldn't sleep. Her body ached and twitched with fatigue, and the gulls that mewed over the house all day seemed unwilling to stop for the night, a final insult.

She sat up in bed. "God damn them!" she swore. "If they don't shut up, I'm going to get my rifle and blow them out of the sky!" And then she burst into tears.

Gavin who had been startled out of sleep, put his arms around her, patting her back as if she were a child. "It will get easier, things will settle down," he assured her anxiously. Suddenly her mood changed, and she started to giggle at the mental picture of herself standing outside shooting at the night. Even in a place as mad as this one, that would surely be noticed.

Gavin joined in her laughter. "I'd just tell everyone you're part cat and hunt better at night for the makings of gull stew," he choked.

They rolled around wrestling and giggling like children until they fell asleep in each other's arms.

October 18 proved to be the most hysterical day they had yet witnessed in San Francisco. The Pacific Mail steamship *Oregon* steamed into the bay with the news that on September 9, California had been admitted as the thirty-first state in the Union.

Bands assembled as if by magic and blared forth on every corner; flags and bunting engulfed the city; volunteer fire companies raced around in uniforms ranging from heavily trimmed pseudomilitary outfits to full evening dress, and they dragged their pumps with them, clanging the polished bells. Regular business was forgotten, and the streets seemed crowded with more people than could possibly be living in the city.

Tessa thought of it always not only as the day the final link in the chain that bound California to the United States had been forged, but also the day her own chains had been broken and her involvement in the city had truly begun.

They were all together, Indian and Gavin each with a child on his shoulders, but the press of people was so great that at one point, Tessa was separated from the others. With both the men so tall and given the added height of the children, she could see them easily, but getting to them was more difficult.

It all happened so quickly, she hadn't time to think. A burly veiny-faced man who had obviously overindulged was also trying to get through the crowd, and when he saw his progress impeded by the small form of a Chinese, he picked him up and threw him against some other people.

Tessa saw red. She didn't like being so hemmed in anyway, and this was the final straw. The Chinese had been doing no more than patiently following the flow of the crowd. The big man was right beside her, and she turned to improve her chances and kicked him as hard as she could in the shin with her hard, pointed boot. He gave a roar of pain, and she yelled at him, "I hope I've broken it, you bully! He wasn't doing anything to you, and he couldn't get out the way!"

A small circle cleared around them, but it took the man's befuddled brain a moment to understand what had happened. "Why you little——" he snarled, but a sharp voice cut him off. "Little what? Be very careful. She's my wife."

Gavin had come back for her, and she had never been so glad to see him in her life. She noted with grim satisfaction that the man took Gavin's measure quickly and subsided into apologies, mumbling inarticulately about be-
404

'ing kicked in the shin. She turned her attention to the little man and saw with relief that he had picked himself up and appeared to be all right.

"Tank you, missee. You do velly kind," he said solemnly. There was an immense dignity about his diminutive person, and Tessa smiled at him. "I would have liked to do more damage to him than I did. I hope the rest of your day proves more peaceful."

She had no way of knowing how good his knowledge was of English, but the brief smile and little bow seemed to indicate he understood, and then her attention was fully taken by Gavin. She told him what had happened and he shook his head. "Jesus Christ, Tessa, what would you have done if I hadn't happened along?"

"Kicked him again. What would you have done?"

He grinned at her. "Broken his nose or his jaw. But then, my fists are bigger than yours. I wish you didn't always have such good reasons for getting into trouble. Come on, let's go rescue Indian. I left him saddled with our offspring."

When Tessa looked around, the Chinese seemed to have disappeared, but she kept thinking she caught glimpses of him during the day. She couldn't be sure. He wore the same loose-fitting coat and trousers so many of them wore, and they all seemed to avoid direct eye contact, so it was difficult to get a good look at their faces.

The crowds thinned a little toward sundown as people headed for meals or for more liquid refreshment. The children were asleep on their feet, and Tessa wanted to take them home. But when the men proposed accompanying her, she refused. "No, it's not that far, and I can see you both are dying to check on things."

They agreed because it was true; they didn't know whether the rowdy crowds had damaged any of their half-finished buildings or not, and it would be just as well to know now as later. The streets looked quiet enough, and there was light enough left to make Tessa's homeward journey tame.

She wasn't far from the house when she became convinced she was being followed. Wisps of fog had begun to roll in from the sea, and with the leftovers of the crowds still on the streets, she hadn't been sure when the

405

first feeling of pursuit had made the back of her neck prickle. She turned, seeing no more than a myriad of scurrying figures, each seeming intent on his or her own business.

"What's wrong, Mama?" Brand asked plaintively, and Jefferson stumbled.

She hoisted Jefferson up into her arms, and he burrowed his face sleepily against her neck. "Nothing's wrong, Brand, and we're almost home," she assured him.

The footsteps came closer, short rapid footsteps. She couldn't turn around. She felt as if her heart was going to burst, and then the voice came to her. "You go velly fast, velly hald catch up."

It was all she could do to control her nervous laughter as he came up to them.

"I cally dis one, den much betta fo' both," he said matter of factly. She was quickly adjusting to his lack of Rs and the other irregularities of his English that was otherwise very direct. But what he wanted and why he had followed her, she had no idea. She wasn't the least afraid of him, but she was embarrassed, and she made some mumbled excuse about Brand not needing to be carried because she was sure he would scream in protest if the strange man touched him.

Brand and the man ignored her. The man said something she couldn't hear, and Brand considered him for a moment, opened his arms and allowed himself to be picked up. "I'll teach you how to say Rs," he offered.

"I teach you Chinese," the man replied equably, and the odd procession went on to the house, the man showing his wiry strength in the effortless way he carried his burden.

Jefferson awakened briefly once they were inside. Before Tessa could caution him to be polite, he observed, "You're funny lookin'."

Tessa could have sunk through the floor with shame, but the man didn't seem in the least upset. "You funny lookin' to me too, but no matta," he said, and while Jefferson was considering this, Brand piped up. "He says Chinese too, whatever that is."

Tessa was speechless, nearly strangled with the laughter rising in her again. The children had had so many treats from vendors during the day, they were not hungry, and she bustled them off to bed to give herself a chance to recover.

"Is he goin' to stay?" Brand asked, settling down on his bed with a blissful sigh.

"I don't have the slightest idea, darling, but I expect you'll know in the morning."

"I hope he does. I like him," Brand said and followed Jefferson into sleep before Tessa stooped to kiss them good night.

What she had told Brand was only the truth, and she was at a loss. She didn't know whether the man simply wanted to thank her for what she had done to his attacker or whether he wanted something more. Thinking hunger was a common ground, she offered him food.

"Latta maybe, talk now, please."

Tessa nodded, sat down, and waited.

"I watch, I see you got two big mens, two little, an' nobody wok fo' you. I, Chong Sai Sing, wok fo' you. Hunded dolla a month. Do laundee, take cale childen, cook too. You can call me jus' Chong Sing."

Tessa was glad she was sitting down. She thought of what he had just offered. The hundred dollars he was asking was too good to be true. Men could make eight to ten dollars a day for almost any work they did in the city and even a prejudice against Chinese could be overcome when someone needed something built or cleared away. Some of the prefabricated houses from Canton even came with their own Chinese crews to assemble them. But her wonder went beyond that. It had never occurred to her that a man might be hired to do the household chores she had so rapidly grown to hate.

"Can you really do all those things?" she asked finally. He nodded vigorously.

"Why do you want a job like this and for such pay?" She had to ask it.

His dark eyes met hers directly for the first time. "Much fighting, much hungly in China, no good now, so come fo' de Golden Mountain, maybe betta. But no, many, many don' like man flom China, many, many bad mens, maybe kill me. So I come San Flancisco, find jus' same kind. Den you hit bad man, tell him no do dat. You husband come

407

say same. Dis famly maybe good fo' Chong Sing. Maybe I good fo' famly."

"I think maybe you're right," she said slowly, making the greatest effort not to say "light." She couldn't stop her smile. It should have made sense from the beginning of this day, she thought. Her life had been so peculiar in so many ways since her marriage, she should have seen Chong Sing's advent in it as perfectly reasonable. What a pity she had wasted so much energy hoping for a strong woman who wanted domestic work when this capable little man had been the answer all along.

The first thing Gavin and Indian noticed when they walked in was that there was a Chinese working busily at Tessa's stove, and the next was that Tessa looked happier and more relaxed than she had since they'd come to live in the city.

They froze. Gavin found his voice first but only managed, "What the hell——" before Tessa said, "I would like you to meet Chong Sing. I have hired him to help run this household. I expect he's a better cook than I am, though I'm quite capable. We'll know shortly. Would you care to wash before dinner?" Her voice was as sweet as honey.

"Nothing's been torn down," Gavin offered, his voice sounding peculiar, and then he and Indian turned and went outside to the washing basin as obediently as if they were children. Once there, it took them longer to stifle their mirth than to wash.

"She sure do keep us hoppin' an' now she got that little bitty man to keep hoppin' too."

"I don't know," Gavin said, still laughing. "I have a feeling this Chong Sing chooses his own pace."

Dinner was a success even if Gavin did grumble under his breath about the difficulty of adding up all the small pieces of meat to make one good beefsteak. "You would have to cut it up to eat it anyway," Tessa whispered back.

Chong Sing had taken common ingredients and made them into an uncommon dish, everything cut into delicate strips and shapes as appealing to the eye as to the palate, everything so quickly and perfectly cooked that each substance retained its individual texture and taste. But Chong Sing could not be persuaded to sit down with
408

them. He had a sense of propriety even if they did not; he made that clear in the politest way.

He moved into the little ground floor room that they had been using for storage, near to Indian's quarters. Tessa thought it much too bare and austere once they had cleared away the boxes; Chong Sing did not. He could not abide clutter, and his quiet intolerance of it soon had everyone, even the children, being neater than before. The children adored and obeyed him. Tessa was fascinated by the spell he seemed to have cast over them. He did not expect them to behave as anything other than small boys with a good deal of growing and maturing to do, but they quickly learned the limits he placed on their mischief. It was impossible to discover how he did this. His voice was never raised, and he never scolded. But he did away forever with the legend of the inscrutable Oriental in the Ramsay household. Though the signs were subtle, they were clear. Disapproval came with a deeper blackness in his long eyes, a prim stillness to his face. The eyes widened and sparkled, the face eased, his body moved with fluid grace when something made him happy or won his approval. Anger they had not yet seen, and no one wanted to.

They learned very little about him. The only time he ever spoke of China after his brief words to Tessa on the first night was to the children, and then only in the form of fabulous tales of dragons and spirits, good and evil. Tessa ceased to worry about the effect of the stories once she realized that good always won out, and even the most horrific monster had its power somehow blunted in Chong Sing's telling. It was impossible even to tell his age, and no one asked. There was something about him that said very clearly that if he wanted you to know something, he would tell you, and otherwise it was not a good idea to ask. Sometimes he looked very young and sometimes ancient. Tessa guessed he must be somewhere approaching thirty. She dismissed the idea that it was difficult for them to tell simply because he was Chinese and not a part of their experience until now. It went beyond that. There was something ageless about Chong Sing, something wise beyond any normal span of years. He knew how to do so many things and learned things without effort. It occurred to Tessa he was very probably much more than he had seemed at first.

She listened more now to the talk of China. Though Chinese women were still very scarce, there were more and more men coming to California. One section was already almost wholly Chinese. And for many, internal strife had been every bit as much a reason for immigrating as famine and poor chances. Tessa knew there must be many side issues, but the two major sides seemed to have been drawn from those loyal to the imperial rule and those who were discontented and fighting against it. The two groups had fought each other constantly, and members of both were coming to California because the fortunes of war shifted so continually in China. There was talk of *tongs* growing stronger here, the strange term applicable to family groups in China but taking on a broader, more sinister meaning here, different factions crossing family lines to band together against other factions. A way of belonging, of achieving identity in a foreign land, but also possibly a way to transplant the very violence they had sought to leave behind.

Tessa wondered which side Chong Sing had chosen. She was sure he had been involved. He was too alert, too deep to have been apart from it all. But she had to agree with Gavin's viewpoint when she spoke to him about it.

"I expect you're right. I've thought about it myself. But you've sung the song often enough for the miners. Didn't you listen to the words?"

She joined his soft, mocking voice as soon as he began:

> Oh, what was your name in the States?
> Was it Thompson, or Johnson or Bates?
> Did you murder your wife
> And fly for your life?
> Say, what was your name in the States?

"It goes as well for the name Chong Sing and a Chinese origin. As long as he takes good care of you and my sons, I won't ask any more from your Chinese dragon."

"You're right as usual," she complained, giving him a swift kiss. "But I'll bet even you don't know that his name in the English way would be Sing Sai Chong. Chong is his surname. It's all backward."

"Does it make any difference?"

She puzzled out his mischievous look and laughed. "I see. No, it does not. The saying is the same if one prefers it that way, Ramsay Gavin. But it isn't kind to call him my Chinese dragon."

"Isn't it?" The eyebrow went up, and she had to laugh. Chong Sing was kind to everyone in the household, but she was, she knew, his special charge. It had been so from the first evening. If she started to leave the house on a chill day, he would suddenly be there, the heavy cloak he held out a kind rebuke for her failure to dress warmly enough. If she were feeling tired, Chong Sing would appear out of nowhere with a hot cup of tea. At first she had barely been able to swallow it, preferring coffee or chocolate to the strange brew that had never been favored at the *rancho,* but now she suspected she was becoming addicted to the taste, which was like flowers, spice, and not unpleasant wood bark. Sometimes she wondered what he put in it besides tea, but she didn't stop drinking it.

Sharing their lives with Chong Sing was not without its problems. It took Tessa quite a while to convince her oldest son that his name was still Brand, not "Bland."

"Chong Sing doesn't say it that way, so why should I?" he demanded.

She had had enough of the argument. "When you can speak Chinese as well as Chong Sing does, then you may decide whether or not to dispense with Rs in your English." He caved in under the weight of adult logic, as she had known he would. Even with his quick ear and his ability to speak Spanish and English interchangeably plus a good smattering of French, the subtle intonations of the Chinese Chong Sing spoke eluded him, despite Chong Sing's patient repetitions. The totally alien shape and tone of the Chinese words made it easy for Tessa to see why Chong Sing's English had its own sound.

She was grateful that he had immediately shortened "Jeffelson" to "Jeff."

And then there was the matter of food preferences. The first time Chong Sing shopped for and cooked "good China food," there was a near revolution. Gavin walked into the house, and instead of returning his wife's kiss, wrinkled his nose. "Whew! If I didn't know how much he loved them, I'd swear Chong Sing has roasted one of our sons for dinner. Or is that just singed gull I smell?"

Indian who had come in on his heels, took one whiff and wheeled around, saying over his shoulder, "I jus' 'membered other things I got to do, like eatin' somewhere else."

"I think that's how dragon smells when it's cooked," Brand told Jefferson, but neither of them looked as if they were going to be able to eat it, both turning slightly green.

And when they sat down and Chong Sing served them, Gavin whispered, "I've never considered myself a coward, but Tessa, I can't eat this. I swear there are eyes in it, and they're staring at me."

The children were immobile, waiting for the parents to taste the dish first.

Tessa was torn between her desire to laugh hysterically or to cry. Gavin was right; there were most surely eyes in this dish, probably squid or octopus eyes, but eyes nonetheless. She wasn't going to be able to eat it any more than the others were. But she couldn't bear to hurt Chong Sing's feelings.

She thought of the platter of meat and cheese the men had fixed for themselves when they had come home unexpectedly for a midday meal. They had not eaten it all. It would do.

"I think we should make this an international meal," she said brightly. "We will begin with some cheese and meat and then we'll go on to Chinese fare." How they were going to avoid the second course was beyond her at the moment.

Chong Sing himself saved her. He was right beside her, making little noises of protest as she picked up the platter. "Dat cheese velly bad food, velly smelly, bad. Bland an' Jeff too little eat dat."

She blessed whoever had first discovered cheese. "Chong Sing, the way you feel about cheese is the way we feel about 'good China food.' We have been raised in different ways, and one of the things we find difficult to eat is eyes."

"Jus' little fishy eyes, fish gotta lookee too," he ventured.

"I suppose they do," she agreed, pursuing the subject grimly. "But we don't like cow eyes either, despite all the beef we eat."

"Dem potato tings got eyes, dem okay?" he asked, and she thought he was serious until she saw the gleam in his eyes, the smile pulling at his mouth.

"I undastand, food too China tonight, jus' like I newa eat cheese no matta how long I be heah."

He was not in the least offended, though he did look a trifle condescending as he removed his masterpiece from the table.

Tessa restrained herself until she and Gavin were alone before she told him about the potato eyes. They laughed until they wept, trying to stifle the sound so as not to wake the sleeping household. And then Gavin's mood changed, and Tessa's with it. "God bless your dragon," he said and kissed her. Her mouth opened to his and their bodies shifted, moving without thought in perfect harmony for the ancient dance.

Chong Sing was in fact very much her dragon, as if by magic making her life so much easier than it had been before his coming. The children were safe and well cared for now, as was the house, and she was free.

CHAPTER XXXVI

It was possible now, when they had the energy, to sample the pleasures of the city. There were cooks from every country and restaurants of every description from French *cabarets* to Spanish *fondas* to German *wirtschafts* to Chinese *chow-chows* and American dining rooms. But the Ramsays soon settled on a favorite, a little French restaurant, La Belle Maison on Jackson Street. It was relaxing for them both to know the children were at home and secure with Chong Sing while they themselves shared an intimate meal and discussed business and events of the day.

There were more and more entertainments being offered,

413

new theaters and music halls opening constantly in addition to the gambling houses. Gavin was remorseful when Tessa asked him if they might attend a theater just to see what it was like. Sometimes he simply forgot how isolated her upbringing had been. He himself had seen so many second-rate shows in his life, along with a few good ones in the East, he didn't care about going one way or the other. But he dutifully took Tessa to a performance one evening. It was an unfortunate choice, a minstrel show. Tessa squirmed restlessly in the seat beside him and finally asked in a small voice if they had to stay until the end.

"Of course not," he replied, and he got a good look at her face. She looked as woebegone as a small child who has just been told there is no Christmas.

"What is it?" he asked when they were outside.

"It was horrible! I hated it!"

"Well, I admit they weren't the best I've ever seen, but they weren't all that bad."

"It was everything about it, white men with lampblack on their faces, pretending to be black men, making Negroes seem like overgrown children who sing and dance and smile big, white smiles. I'm glad Indian isn't with us tonight."

"There are a lot of other kinds of theater to see," Gavin informed her gently. The next night he took her to a Shakespearean reading, which she enjoyed immensely while he enjoyed watching her rapt face. He realized ruefully that he was never going to enjoy a minstrel show again, good or bad. He had seen so many of them and yet had never once seen them as having any connection with Indian. It was frightening to realize how blind and insensitive custom could make you. Now that he thought about it, he could not remember that Indian had ever gone with him to any of the shows.

But even though they sampled the city's pleasures, most of their waking hours were taken up by business. Many people had suffered such losses in the year's fires, there had been a small financial panic in September. It was hard on those who had lost, but it made the Ramsays and Indian's position that much stronger. Still, it terrified Tessa sometimes when she thought of the fact that the wealth

414

they had amassed from their trading and gambling was nearly all tied up in the city now except for the amounts set aside for buying new merchandise. And the first night she saw the sky alight with the ominous red-orange of fire, she huddled in the house with Chong Sing and the children and died a thousand deaths before the men returned at daybreak to report that all was well with their buildings. She vowed then that the next time she would go with them rather than waiting helplessly for news.

Her store was finally becoming a reality. She had great plans for its future, but she had decided to begin with women's fancy goods, or as she called them privately, fancy women's goods. She had quickly seen the pattern— what the parlor house madams and the better paid prostitutes, especially the French women, adopted in dress, other women soon copied, pretending ignorance of where the mode had begun. And in any case, the greatest number of her customers would be prostitutes.

The Ramsays and Indian had a good deal of enjoyment out of considering various blends of their names to make one for the enterprises. When the shop opened the sign outside read "RAMIAN'S FINE CLOTHING FOR WOMEN" in dark blue letters with the finest line of gilt around them. Tessa kept the jumble inside to a minimum; she detested it in the city's shops she had visited. Counters were clearly marked for thread, needles, buttons, fabric and trim, for gloves, reticules, and wraps, for shoes, imported scent, and even lingerie, which Tessa insisted those garments be called despite the fact that "white work," "white sewing," and other terms she considered equally unattractive were considered more decent. And one section held lavish models of some of the gowns that could be made to order on the premises.

Molly was responsible for the quality and availability of this display. Her real name was Mary Barker, Mrs. George Barker, and Tessa considered her as much of a godsend as Chong Sing. She had found her wholly by accident. Having decided a good seamstress was absolutely necessary and then having despaired of finding one, she had read the small advertisement in the *Alta California* several times before she realized the brief lines offering "plain and fancy sewing at reasonable rates" might mean the answer to her prayers. She found Molly and George living in a rickety shack, the two giving ample proof that not everyone found easy wealth in California. She was touched by the courage they had shown in leaving the civilized farmlands of the eastern shore to come west. They were not nearly as young as most newcomers, both appearing to be closer to forty than to thirty. All George had gotten from his experience in the camps was a severe attack of arthritis in his knees and back. They had come to the city, and though George did earn a bit here and there with light labor, Molly was the one who was really supporting them, though she charged far too little for her sewing. They were childless, so at least there were only two mouths to feed.

Tessa had had her doubts with her first sight of the woman. Molly was such an unfittingly gay nickname for her. She was small with timid brown eyes and graying brown hair, and she was dressed in a severely plain brown gown. Her husband was a fitting match for her, albeit he was a bit bigger and his eyes were faded blue instead of brown. It seemed highly improbable that Molly would be able to do the kind of sewing the shop would need, but Tessa tried not to betray her doubts when she asked to see some samples.

She quickly found how woefully wrong it was to judge Molly's work by her sober demeanor. One dress she was working on was bright red satin trimmed with jet beads with a matching many-tiered petticoat. She had almost finished a set of sheer undergarments edged in the finest tatting. Even the brown dress she wore, when considered more carefully, showed her skill. Her stitches were perfect, and her voice took on a more positive note when she explained to Tessa that she had been trained as a dressmaker before she met and married George Barker.

"Your work is beautiful," Tessa assured her enthusiastically. "And I am relieved to see the red dress. It leads me to believe you are not overly harsh in your judgments of customers. I could not tolerate that in my store. Most of the women who have the money to buy the kind of clothes I'm going to sell are less than respectable, to put it politely."

416

Molly smiled, revealing a fleeting glimpse of the girl she must have been before years and toil had stolen her youth away. "I should surely be ashamed of myself, Mrs. Ramsay, but I like working on fancy goods, and it's fancy women that wear such."

Tessa offered them both good salaries plus a percentage, and the bargain was happily struck. She needed a clerk and thought George would do very well. He could read, write, and keep simple accounts, and there was nothing about him to make any woman feel threatened by his presence.

Her greatest problem had been and would continue to be stocking the store. Goods sailed into the bay in an unbelievably erratic pattern. The various storekeepers kept their orders secret, each hoping to make a greater profit than the next, with the result that often several shiploads of the same item would arrive at the same time causing a glut on the market. One street was already paved with iron stoves, so many having been shipped in at one point that there had been more than one for every man, woman, and child in San Francisco. And speculation was rife, fortunes made and lost in a day by men who cornered the market on one item or another in the hope that they would then be able to name their own extravagant price. The stoves had accounted for several lost fortunes, but sometimes it did work. One man had done exceedingly well with carpet tacks, his common sense telling him that in a city of board and canvas structures, the tacks would be useful indeed. And a Frenchman was rumored to have gotten himself quite a stake though he had arrived with little more than a large box of toothpicks. He had sold them at various prices, finally settling on two for a dollar's worth of gold.

In a city that was slightly mad in all its aspects, Tessa could think of nothing more insane than the way trade was carried on. Her problems were compounded by the fact that in many instances in order to purchase the specific goods one wanted, the whole cargo had to be bought. And this often meant bidding at the raucous assembly on the beach where boxes and bales had been dumped because of the continuing shortage of warehouse space.

Sometimes it was difficult to judge the quality of the merchandise from these brief glimpses, but there was no help for it, speed in acquisition being so vital.

Tessa didn't know what she would have done had they not had several businesses to absorb the variety of goods typical of most cargoes. The gambling house, to Tessa's delight, the men had named "The Golden Horse," could use any amount of liquor and glassware, the breakage rate being high, and the warehouse could use almost anything for future selling, all of which was a great help to Tessa in her pursuit of goods she wanted.

But nothing could make the task truly easy, and the amounts of money involved and the speed of the transactions made her heart pound. Nor was it convenient here to be a woman. While there was no problem when Gavin and Indian were with her and she simply gleaned goods from a cargo they bought, it was a different matter when she was bidding on her own.

The first time it happened, Gavin and Indian were bidding on a cargo that included a good supply of brandy and champagne besides several cases of tinned oysters, a favorite delicacy in the city and at the gold camps. Tessa had been following the transaction with interest until she noticed with dismay that another cargo was going on the block a short distance away. It was one that contained some fine China silk and French damask. She slipped away from the men and joined the crowd at the other auction.

The first thing she discovered was that she had to pitch her voice to a near scream to be heard above the rough male voices, and the next was that she just wasn't being taken seriously. No one was threatening her, but it was almost worse to hear the jests at her expense, the comments about how the little lady was going to carry all this home. And the auctioneer was paying no attention at all to her bids. When hers was the last before the silence and yet the auctioneer was counting down the sale to the bid before hers, her temper flared. "I am not aware that gold has any sex!" She heard the discomfited gasps because she had said the word at all. "You're a fool to judge that it is male. I'm sure the owners of this cargo would prefer the highest profit to your stupidity."

418

The mood of the crowd veered, and they gave her a ragged cheer. The auctioneer, flushing beet red, mumbled that her bid was accepted, the cargo hers.

She paid him and turned to find Gavin watching her. His face was closed, giving nothing away. He waited until they were alone before he said, "That was quite a performance, the screeching fishwife. And do you know you've purchased 80,000 gallons of vinegar along with your fripperies?"

She turned on him furiously. "How dare you! I got the cargo and at a good price. You can shut up about the vinegar. The fripperies, as you call them, will more than pay for it even if we can't sell it! You and Indian might know a lot about many things, but you're near idiots about what women will buy. I can still remember that ugly cloth you brought to California. Did you think to let me have the store as a plaything only, is that it? Something to keep me out of your way? A place where I could play with ribbons and be a perfect little lady and let all the life of the city pass me by?"

Her eyes were bright and narrow with anger, her cheeks were flushed, her breast rose and fell with her rapid breathing, and Gavin was ashamed. His attack had been totally unfair, and the worst of it was that there was a part of him that wished she was just like the deplorable description she had spat at him, even as he knew such a woman would bore him to distraction. But she would be so much more predictable, and more, so much easier to protect. Part of his anger had come from the fear he had felt when he noticed she was missing from his side and discovered her in the midst of the jostling crowd of men.

He rubbed his face wearily. "I'm sorry. And you're quite right, Indian and I seem to have no talent as modistes."

Her anger dissolved in the face of his sheepish, endearing grin, and she put her arms around him, burying her face against his shoulder. "So many changes for both of us, but it will be all right, it will!"

The next day he gave her a gift, a small pearl-handled lady's derringer, and he stilled her protests with his plea, "Please, for me. It hasn't any range, but it's deadly up close. I hope you'll never have to use it, but I'll sleep better

419

knowing you have something more than a boot in the shins to defend yourself with when I'm not there."

It was strange, how much more ominous this weapon seemed than her rifle even though she had killed a man with it. But the rifle had the excuse of being a weapon for survival and defense in the wild country. The neat little citified derringer had been made for only one purpose—to kill another human being at close range. Even at first, when she handled it as if it were a rattlesnake taken mistakenly for a pet, she knew Gavin had been right to give it to her. The lawless elements of the city seemed to gain more power by the day, and just as the men never left the house unarmed, it would be foolhardy for her to do so.

Gavin had the added grace to store the vinegar in the warehouse without further complaint.

She soon gained a reputation for being a shrewd buyer at the auctions and one who paid promptly for goods received. And it only took a couple of incidents with the unwise before word also went out that Mrs. Ramsay not only had a husband and a large black friend to defend her, but that she was also capable of making a deadly little gun appear in her hand as if by magic. She still went with the men whenever possible, but she no longer had any reluctance to go alone when necessary. Only Chong Sing remained steadfast in open disapproval, shaking his head and making clucking noises whenever he suspected she was going on one of her buying missions.

Not only were the goods available at the shop growing more numerous, but so were the people who patronized it, many of them, to Tessa's initial surprise, men who came to buy lavish gifts in the hope of bribing their lady friends for lavish favors in return, and many accounts were billed directly to men who were generous to their mistresses. But it was the women themselves who were responsible for the success of the business, even to letting their gentlemen friends know that their favorite shop was Ramian's and a gift from there would be well received. The word was spread quickly that Mrs. Ramsay carried the finest and that though she was apt to talk a person out of the quantity of furbelows one had in mind, a finished gown was sure to be perfectly made and flattering to the wearer. And more important, Mrs. Ramsay wasn't like some who looked down their noses at you just because your business was different from theirs. If you could pay your bills, that was all Mrs. Ramsay asked, and she would be as polite to you as she was to one of the respectables.

Business was so good, Tessa hired two more clerks and another seamstress to help Molly. The girl they decided on wasn't as proficient with a needle, but Molly was sure she would be in time. Molly herself had recommended Anne Long and her husband, Walter. The Barkers had known them for a while as neighbors and had found them kind and engaging despite the fact that Anne and Walter were much younger, Anne having just reached eighteen and Walter only a year older. They looked more like brother and sister than husband and wife, being an even closer matched pair than the Barkers. They both were tall, with freckled skin, russet hair, and prominent, rather knobby features. But they were good, cheerful workers and inveterate city dwellers. They had taken one look at the lonely spaces—to them lonely, to Tessa fast becoming overcrowded—and headed for the biggest city they could find. They had scrimped, saved, and sold everything they could to make the journey from New York City, and they hadn't been doing so well so far in San Francisco, but they were born survivors. It was the old song again, "Tell me what was your name in the States?" Given their youth and the fact that neither of them ever referred to his or her parents, Tessa suspected theirs had been a runaway marriage, but seeing them happy together made her like them more for the idea.

The other clerk Tessa hired was Pierre Lamont, a young Frenchman who was slightly too fastidious in his dress and manner for her taste, but who quickly proved himself an able salesman. She, Anne, and even Molly sometimes had to stifle their giggles and avoid each other's eyes when Pierre went into his full Frenchman's act to charm a woman into buying something.

Tessa found Pierre through Jordan Ames. Jordan had visited them frequently since they had moved to the city, sometimes calling on business, just as often on pleasure. And gradually Tessa relaxed in his presence. The children adored him and the men enjoyed his company and had no guilt about picking his brains for useful information. He knew more about what was happening in San Francisco than the newspapers. He dismissed it carelessly as a necessary talent for a lawyer, but Tessa knew it went beyond that. Jordan had one of the most acute minds she had ever encountered, and the education he had received had not been wasted. He was a voracious reader not only in English, but in French, Italian, and German as well. The Latin required for his profession was no problem to him, and he had been adding Spanish to his vocabulary since the day he had arrived in California. And his concern for people was as vast as his education. Tessa could not fail to be charmed by it. Even when Brand or Jefferson was taking far too long to tell a simple story, Jordan's face remained alight with interest. And though he probably knew enough to blackmail a good number of San Franciscans, he was no gossip. If he did have a good story to tell at someone's expense, the names were missing and the story became an amusing fable of the human condition.

Only once did Tessa know of his telling a salacious story with all the characters boldly drawn and named, but in this case there was no sense in disguising them, as the tale was fast becoming a city favorite. Irene McCready, a madam, and her lover, James McCabe, a gambler and part owner of the El Dorado gambling house on the Plaza, had arrived together the previous year. Irene's jealousy and their lovers' quarrels had quickly become the stuff of legend, with people as anxious for the next installment as if it were a specialized novel in one of the papers. Jordan provided the final chapter. Irene had finally made so many jealous accusations, some of them loudly proclaimed to all in the El Dorado, James had thrashed her. But Irene had had the final word. She had sent messages that she was pining away for her love. He with a foolishly good heart had gone to call on her and had drunk the drugged wine she gave him. While he slept, Irene had played Delilah to his Samson, but she had not stopped at the hair on his head. He awakened bald all over. His friends had seen little of him lately, though it was rumored that the tall figure in the slouch hat who haunted the region of the Plaza was none other than he.

It was typical of Jordan that while he told the story to Indian and Gavin, he would never have done so in Tessa's
422

presence. She heard the men laughing uproariously and demanded the reason from Gavin that night. He told her without hesitation, his voice still choking with laughter. And when they settled down to sleep, he made a great show of looming over her with his eyes open. "What are you doing?" she asked.

"Making sure you're asleep before I am."

"Oh, I would never do that," she giggled. "What if it never grew back? I would be an object of pity. 'There goes poor Mrs. Ramsay,' they'd say. 'Her husband's as bald as an egg, has been since the fall of fifty. No one knows why she stays with him.' " She tugged at his thick hair, pulling his head down so she could kiss him, both of them deciding they weren't ready to sleep after all as her hands explored other places where poor James McCabe was bald and Gavin was not.

She couldn't resist it. The next time she saw Jordan, she smiled sweetly and remarked, "I'm so glad to see you haven't lost your hair. I've heard a man must be careful of the company he keeps in San Francisco."

She expected him to laugh, but instead he flushed scarlet and his face was suddenly taut. "I apologize, Mrs. Ramsay, I did not mean for you to hear that tale."

She regarded him in amazement. "No, Mr. Ames, I think it is I who must apologize for teasing you. But surely you must know that with the clientele of my shop, I was bound to hear it sooner or later, and an amusing one it is."

She won a rueful smile from him. "It's background, Mrs. Ramsay. Somehow one can never totally escape it. The women I grew up with would have fainted dead away with shock and never forgiven the teller. I am apt to forget that western women are quite different."

"I suspect those women who fainted away would also laugh themselves silly later on in private," she observed, and Jordan had to laugh with her at the probable truth of it.

The incident taught her something about Jordan. She had managed since her return to the city to put him into what she thought was proper perspective—a charming man who had an easy and appreciative way with the ladies. Now she knew again, as she had on their first meeting, that Jordan was not to be so easily dismissed. They never even addressed each other by their first names, but their formal-

423

ity had the mocking edge of a delightful game, and his eyes still gave him away. And when he allowed himself to pay her a compliment, the artful ease did not cloak the fact that he meant every word. She knew that now, as she knew that he was deeply protective of her. And even though she sensed that the change in herself might be dangerous, she no longer felt any unease in Jordan's presence. As Jordan had promised, their relationship would only move beyond friendship by her choice, a choice she would never make because of loving Gavin.

Jordan made himself useful in many ways, and Tessa ceased to feel any guilt when she realized that he was, despite his self-assurance, often lonely in his bachelor's existence and glad to share the family life of the Ramsays. Sometimes he came by the house on steamer days, the first and fifteenth of the month when the mail steamer came in and the city used it as an excuse for festivities. Even Chong Sing trusted him to take the boys out for a few hours to enjoy the sights. And if the flags on Alta Loma, now renamed Signal Hill, indicated that one of the more beautiful clipper ships was gliding into the bay, Jordan was sure to have the children out in time to see it. From him they learned how to read the multitude of flags, each one meaning a different ship. When Tessa scolded him for neglecting his business, he assured her that was one of the advantages of being a lawyer—the privilege of choosing one's own hours except when one waited on the pleasure of the court.

He seemed to sense when Tessa was feeling particularly rushed and harassed by business at the shop. He would appear and coax her out to lunch, and she found herself giving in more and more often because she always felt so much more relaxed and able to cope after the time with him, a time when Gavin was scarcely ever free. Jordan stimulated her mind and gave her rest at the same time, even though they often discussed serious subjects. It was he who gave her a broader view of what California's admission to the Union really meant, the shaky compromise between northern and southern interests that had allowed it. California had come in as a free state, but the territorial governments that existed in the remainder of the land of the Mexican cession would decide for themselves on the question of slavery.

His voice was harsher than she had ever heard it when he enumerated the other provisions. "The slave trade has been prohibited in the District of Columbia, but slavery itself as it now exists there will not be abolished without the consent of the residents of the District and of Maryland, nor will it be abolished without compensation to the slave owners in the District. All that is bad enough," he said slowly, "but there is much worse. There's now a new fugitive slave law in effect. It's inhumane in every sense. Even should a slave win his way to a free state, and many are hunted, maimed, and die in the attempt, the law now requires that the slave be returned to the 'rightful' owner. There is no safe haven left anywhere in the United States for slaves. They must win their way clear to Canada to be free of their shackles. And all power has been taken from the Congress to promote or interfere with the slave trade in slave-holding states."

"What a dreadful price to pay for California's statehood," Tessa said in a small, cold voice.

"I'm every kind of fool," he said contritely, "to lure you away from the shop only to distress you so."

"No, that isn't true. You never distress me even though not all subjects are pleasant. I should hate to be treated as a frivolous woman fit only to discuss the newest Paris fashions. I expect Gavin and Indian have known all about this from the beginning, but they are sometimes too careful of me. I can't really blame them. I find it difficult to be calm about the subject of slavery. In my love for Indian, I have lost the ability to be impersonal about it." She paused, searching the depths of the golden-gray eyes. "You are not impersonal about it either, are you?"

His eyes darkened with pain, eclipsing all the gold. "Ames Pride, as straightforward a name for a plantation as you could hope to find. And primogeniture as sure as in the Bible. I was the eldest son. Ames Pride was to be mine as it had been the eldest son's for generations. Martin was mine, born the same year as I, just a few months earlier, given to me as my personal slave when we were both infants. We grew up together, and until I went north to school, I thought him only the luckiest creature not to have to share my lessons. And then in that foreign place and with more and more joy coming from my studies, I began to

425

see it in an entirely different light. I was sure my family would see it the same way. How naïve I was. I had great plans to take Martin back north with me after one of my school holidays. It was not that unusual; many young gentlemen had their servants with them." His mouth twisted over the words "young gentlemen." "At least I did intend he would have the chance to learn everything I was learning. When I first told Martin of my plan, he looked as if I'd offered him heaven, and then he looked quite different. I'll never forget it—so very old, so resigned. He told me my father would never allow it. He was right. My father told me that educating Negroes above themselves was as dangerous as striking a match near a keg of gunpowder. We had a terrible row, but in the end, I backed off because he threatened to prevent me from returning to school, said I ought to be taking more of a hand in running Ames Pride anyway. I compromised, just as our government's done now. And it brought nothing but death just as this will."

She formed the word in the silence which seemed to envelop them even though the restaurant was a busy place. "Martin?"

The grief and pain in his eyes was unbearable, and she looked away, but she could not avoid his words.

"Yes, Martin. I had a plan, you see, and perhaps I should have told him about it, but I feared disappointing him again. On my eighteenth birthday I was to come into money left me by my grandfather, as my brothers would also when they came of age. It was laughingly called the 'Rakehell Fund,' which is precisely what Grandfather had meant it for. He believed that parents were too often too restrictive as his had been, and he did not think any man could be a gentleman until he had been less than one. He cloaked it in fancy words, but basically his theory was that the way to virtue was through vice. He even went so far as to insist that the best husbands were those who had been trained by the best whores in their youth." Tessa knew he was so far back in his past, he was not even conscious of saying "whores."

"It was all so simple. I was going to turn the tables on them all. The papers proving my ownership of Martin were also to be mine on my eighteenth birthday. On that day

426

I was going to turn vice to virtue, free Martin and take him north with me where the money would be enough for both of us to live and learn. I came home a week before my birthday. I wanted that much time to say farewell to the land. Ames Pride was beautiful, despite the ugliness of the system that kept it so. It was already much too late. Martin had been dead for nearly a month. He had given up waiting for his life to change. He had run away. My father hired slave catchers. They tracked him down. There were three of them, and they had dogs besides, but Martin fought them anyway. It made them angry to get so much sass from a nigger. They maimed him. He bled to death before they ever got his body back to Ames Pride. It was just as well. Because of what they did, he was no longer a man. He could not have borne to live that way."

Fitting justice for Luis, the most horrible injustice for Martin, the thought spun in a crazy spiral in her head, and Tessa dug her fingernails into her palms, making no sound, waiting for him to finish.

"I did go north. I haven't been home since then. My parents, three brothers and two sisters, not one of them or all of them together could make up for Martin. He was more than a friend; he was more my brother than my real brothers were. They killed him, and I killed him. I compromised. I should have run away with him the day my father refused permission to take him north with me. We would have made it somehow. And that is not the end. It goes on and on. The North, the South, the leaders bicker and compromise and bicker again. They are all afraid and equally guilty, and they all know the end will be vast and bloody, all this country will ever need to know of hell."

His voice trailed away, and Tessa was frozen for an instant, wailing inwardly, *Gavin, Indian, Jordan, they all see it coming, this terrible war. They all share a vision of destruction that is against everything life should be, everything I want it to be.*

But then Jordan's pain touched her again, and she reached across the table for his hand, cradling it in both of hers. "My dear," she said as gently as if he were one of her sons, though she had never before called him anything but Mr. Ames, "it is so difficult to learn that we can never go back, never live anything over again, never. We think

427

of all the right things to do, but it's useless because the chance will not come again. You were young and yet you had the courage to reject your background and the comfort it offered because you found it unjust. That's a tremendous accomplishment for a man or a woman at any age, and you did it before you came to full manhood. I do not suggest that you forget the pain of Martin's death; pain like that is never forgotten, it becomes part of one even as it happens. But the blame you must forget, and yourself you must forgive. If you cannot be just and kind to yourself, how can you be to another?"

"Thank you," he said finally, his voice soft and unsteady. "Because you believe it, perhaps I can learn to believe it also."

Outwardly, it was compromising in every sense, their hands clasping, each searching the other's eyes so deeply, it took them disoriented seconds to waken again to the reality around them. But inwardly, neither felt any shock or guilt. Jordan had been suddenly overwhelmed by pain he had never admitted to anyone else, and Tessa had responded to it and offered comfort. It was that simple. And it was that complicated. Their game of formal address ended that day, and new games began, but only much later did Tessa realize that coming so close as human beings, without the disguising roles of man and woman between them, had been the most dangerous and intimate step of all, to be understood only when all else was gone.

Gavin was as lulled by Tessa's unknowing innocence and the city as she herself was. None of the rules for other places applied here. It was a city of bachelors who were willing to pay an ounce of gold simply to talk to a woman for an evening in a gambling house or saloon, a city where men gave women expensive gifts, often for nothing more than friendship. Women were so in the minority, the least attractive were courted and the beautiful were worshipped. And it was a city where the women, by the very virtue of the courage and perseverance it took to get here and to survive, were unwilling to accept old rules, determined to establish their own. There was much to be gained and much to be lost, but few places in the world offered them so much freedom.

Gavin expected every man to love Tessa. He could not

see how they could fail to do so, but he never even considered the possibility that Jordan Ames was in love with her. He would never be as close to any man as he was to Indian, but he had come to regard Jordan as a friend of nearly the same caliber. He trusted him and was thankful for the protection and company Jordan offered the children and Tessa when he himself didn't have the time.

He didn't puzzle it out consciously, but the deepest part of him believed that, in fact, he no longer had to consider, as he had once, whether or not men were in love with Tessa. Tessa loved him even as he loved her, a continuous stream that knew the magic of flowing both ways at once. And as long as both continued, no other single current could match or break their strength.

CHAPTER XXXVII

They had optimistically made tentative plans to spend Christmas at the *rancho,* but it proved impossible; all the businesses were demanding more rather than less time. Indian did make one trip right after Christmas, to take late gifts and greetings and to check on things but also because he, even more than the others, missed the freedom of the land. Though Gavin and Tessa went out of their way to protect him, and though he knew their care arose from love, even his great patience was galled by having his status so dependent on his friends. San Francisco's first great fire had begun at Denison's Exchange because a black man had refused his one free drink that included the agreement to leave after its consumption, and had requested the privilege of paying for his first and second should he want it. He had been stabbed and killed for his attempt at equality, and as he had fallen, a lantern had set the canvas afire.

The only times Indian was assured there would be no trouble if he ordered a drink or food was at the Golden Horse or when he was with the Ramsays. He had long since learned to control the deep, hard knot of rage. His very size and strength had made that necessary, or he would have been executed long before for leaving dead bodies in his wake. But the grief he felt was not so easily controlled. The continual assaults on his dignity as a man, the continual assumption that the color of his skin meant he had no right to dignity nor any desire for it, were enough to bring him near the breaking point sometimes, enough to make him want to weep without ceasing. Not even his friends could ease his heart when this was upon him, but the land could, the land that did not ask the color of a man's skin but only the quality of his labor and understanding. In this, Indian sensed that he and Tessa were closer than he and Gavin, Tessa also needing the renewal of her earth roots. Though he did not speak of it, he worried about her in the city. There was a brittleness about her that had not been there before. And he knew exactly what she meant when she asked him as he set out for the *rancho*, "Please, look carefully at everything so you can tell me when you come back."

He did as she asked, returning with the essentials engraved in his mind: the horses—where they were pasturing for the winter, the gains and losses, the most promising colts; the cattle—how fat they still looked despite the dryness of this winter; the people of the *rancho*; the very color of the earth. He had also been to Monterey to see the Collinses, who were prospering.

Because Indian was still away at the time, Tessa and Gavin had New Year's Eve to themselves. Chong Sing had no objection to staying at home with the children as he knew the celebration of this day to be white idiocy, the proper date of course being the Chinese one. It was most convenient that he celebrated only Chinese festivals.

They walked to La Belle Maison for a late dinner, for though the night was chill, it was clear and free of fog, and they wanted to savor the sights and sounds of the festivities. Never lacking an excuse for a party, the city was even noisier and more brightly lit this night than usual. And at one corner where a fiddler was sawing away and an impromptu street dance had begun, Gavin asked Tessa with mock formality if she would care for a dance. She went into his arms and they danced by the light of flaring torches, both of them felling more carefree than they had for too long.

The owner of the restaurant presented them with a bottle of champagne, not only, he explained in his rapid tongue, because they were such faithful customers, but because they were always as if they had just met and were still courting each other with love.

Tessa blushed at the compliment, translating it for Gavin, and he smiled as he raised his glass. "To us, my darling, may we never disappoint Jacques. To 1851, may it be a good year."

"And a thousand following after, all with you," she returned softly.

Bells clanged, horns and whistles blew, and people yelled as midnight turned to the first instant of the new year, but Gavin and Tessa scarcely heard them as they walked home arm in arm, murmuring nonsense to each other, stopping frequently to savor long kisses, hurrying the last blocks and laughing aloud because they couldn't get to bed fast enough.

Their hands were still cold as they helped each other undress, and even that became a sensual delight.

Don't ever let us lose this, Tessa pleaded inwardly, not knowing whom she was asking or why but feeling as she had as a child when something was too beautiful and too brief to bring joy without equal pain.

His hands began to trace the silken curves of her breasts, belly, thighs, circling, teasing, asking, and promising until there was only the beauty of Gavin in the universe, only the pulse of him deep and full inside her, no grief and no future.

"Not yet, not yet, stay with me!" she cried urgently, and Gavin spun the moments out until they were both mindless with the need for release and could wait no more.

"Happy New Year," Tessa whispered as she fell asleep, and Gavin drew her close in answer.

But the year did not seem as intent on peace and prosperity as they were. The violent and lawless elements of the city grew bolder by the day. And on the evening of February 19, a particularly brutal attack was made on Mr. Jansen of Jansen and Company, Merchants. Mr. Jansen, having surprised robbers, was assaulted and left for dead. Though badly injured and unconscious for a good length of time, he lived to tell the tale.

Though murders were so frequent as to be nearly commonplace, the attack on Mr. Jansen proved to be the trigger on the tempers of the law-abiding citizenry. In the following days, arrests were made, and the person supposed to be responsible, one Burdue, was imprisoned, even though the case against him was compounded more of his general bad character than any real proof.

Large crowds gathered around the building, threatening to tear it down and hang Burdue. They were deterred from their immediate purpose only by urgent promises of a speedy trial and just punishment. But it was rumored they had little faith in the promises and planned to gather in even greater force.

And when Sunday morning came, Tessa knew Gavin was somehow involved. In the past few days she had quickly come to dread being anywhere in the city except in the house or the shop. There were knots of men everywhere, the sound of their voices the same, an angry murmur that would become an ugly, deafening roar when all the parts of the beast came together. It was the first time she had ever experienced the frighteningly singular character of a mob. There was just cause for grievance and for the demand for public safety, but this response terrified her.

"Where are you going?" she asked sharply when Gavin started to leave the house. "And don't tell me to the warehouse, because I won't believe you."

"I won't tell you that," Gavin replied quietly. "I'm going to the jail to see what I can do to help. A group of us, mostly merchants, have been discussing this since Jansen was attacked. We cannot allow mob rule. We will all be lost. There's got to be a legal, workable alternative. And perhaps if there are enough of us asking for that, the others will listen."

"Or perhaps they will hang you along with Burdue!" Tessa snapped. "I'm going with you."

Gavin's even tone deserted him. "For God's sake, don't make this any harder! That's all I need, to try to speak with the voice of reason while I'm wondering if you're being crushed to death by an angry crowd!"

There was tense silence between them for a moment, and then she stood on tiptoe to kiss him. "*Vaya con Dios*,

432

querida," she murmured. He hugged her hard and was gone.

She jumped at Indian's soft voice. She hadn't even known he had come into the room. "I watch out for him. No hurt come to him."

"Nor to you, Indian. God be with you too," she blessed him gravely.

She passed the time with the children and drank the hot tea Chong Sing provided. She tried not to think at all of what might be happening at the jail.

It seemed inconceivable that the children were going to be five and four shortly. Despite the great changes that had marked her years since she had given birth to the boys, it still seemed they were growing up far too quickly, especially since she was becoming ever more convinced she could not have any more children. In spite of the upheavals it would cause in her life, she had again the sudden, deep longing to bear another child. Perhaps this year.

"Are we ever going home?" Brand asked without preamble, startling Tessa so much she nearly dropped her teacup.

"This does not feel like home?" she asked in return.

"Well, it sort of does, and then it doesn't," Brand said, struggling to explain, and Jefferson chimed in with his own succinct appraisal. "Not enough trees or horses, and too many people."

Tessa deliberately assumed her most thoughtful expression while her mind raced. Had the children's uprooting been even more drastic than her own? She didn't think so. They had seemed fascinated and happy enough ever since they had come. They were well cared for by Chong Sing, and they had even found some children in the neighborhood who were good for a game or two when they tired of each other's company.

"Home is most of all a place where you have someone who loves you," she said finally. "And you have lots of people who love you here and many who love you at the *rancho*. Truly, I think we are all very fortunate because we have two homes. But it took us a few years to make the *rancho* a safe, good home, and it will take us some time to do the same here. Perhaps we can visit the *rancho*

433

soon just to remind ourselves what it looks like. But would you not miss San Francisco if we left for good? You wouldn't see your friends or Jordan Ames any more or the ships coming into the bay."

"Oh, I would miss the ships!" Brand agreed.

"Me too, and Jordan!" Jefferson added fervently.

She could hardly wait to repeat Jeff's description of the city to Gavin. She knew exactly what he meant. Good-sized trees were indeed a rarity here, though more and more saplings were being planted; there were plenty of horses but not in the free-running herds Jeff was used to; and too many people was surely the problem of the moment. That Gavin and Indian would be home soon, safe, was the only acceptable thought.

The hours seemed endless, but she knew the instant the men returned that they had been successful. Though tired and drained by tension, they were all right, and their satisfaction showed even through the fatigue.

"We weren't needed after all. Some good men spoke and the crowd listened. There was a trial, a hasty affair, yes, but still a jury trial. The jury couldn't agree. Burdue is being remanded to the authorities. There'll be another trial and maybe he'll be lynched someday, but it won't be here. The mob ceased to be; men returned to their senses and listened to reason." Gavin's face sobered. "They are for the most part good, honest men. But they've had enough. We all have. Between those bastards from the New York gang and the criminals from Australia, there isn't much room for a peace-keeping man in this city. They haven't had real opposition since some of them were thrown out after they destroyed the Chilean settlement for Sunday sport."

Tessa shivered, remembering the blackened ruins she had seen on her first trip to San Francisco nearly two years ago.

"What happened today proves that most citizens want to be law abiding, and they recognize the danger of mob rule. But it can't go on this way. What authority there is, isn't enough, and is too damn corrupt to be much use anyway. The next time something like this happens, there's going to be hell to pay." His words carried deadly conviction, but Tessa's answer was no less sure.

434

"Then we'll just have to face it when it comes." It was one thing to decide to leave, quite another to be driven away. Only then did she realize she had answered a question that had not even been asked.

But it was difficult to sustain the defiant courage of a moment through all the days that followed. The whole city was nervously on edge—the criminal elements openly boasting of what they had done and what they would do; the law-abiding citizenry, which in this strange place included many gamblers and prostitutes who had no more desire than any one else to lose life and property, steeling themselves to withstand further depredations and assuring themselves the criminals would pay, one way or another.

Mr. Peniston ran The Golden Horse anyway; Indian could handle the warehouse; and Tessa had to trust her clerks to manage the shop adequately for a while, because she and Gavin had finally decided to return to Rancho Magnífico, if only for a few days. Part of it was for the very practical reason that this winter had been drought-stricken, in complete opposition to the flooding of the year before, and now with spring beginning it would be possible to make some judgment about the year's grazing. If the grass was going to be insufficient, animals must be culled and sold so the prime breeding stock would not be weakened by lack of food. And even this far removed from them, the horses remained Tessa's when decisions were to be made. But she and Gavin admitted the reason beyond the practical—the peaceful land would be so welcome after the tensions of the city.

The children would go with them, of course, but they weren't quite sure how to approach the problem of Chong Sing. He would be much more useful staying in San Francisco to keep the house tidy and to cook for Indian, but they didn't want to offend him. Tessa solved their dilemma by putting the question to Chong Sing himself.

"Someday I go see dat place, but not now. Dis time I stay heah, take cale of house an' Indian. Childen be fine wid you." His answer, as grateful as she was for it, made Tessa want to smile; he obviously felt he was conferring
435

a great privilege in trusting them with the children without himself in attendance.

The trip was wonderful. Despite the lack of rain, the land was doing its best to bloom, sending out ripples of green and sudden gifts of flowers. And the people of the *rancho* were overjoyed to have the Ramsays there again. Even Pedro lost all semblance of his normal control and grinned, hugged the children, and muttered hoarse words of welcome.

There was a fiesta the first night, the music, dancing, eating, and talking going on almost to dawn. When Tessa wasn't dancing with Gavin, she was answering the women's shy but endless questions about San Francisco, and she soon realized that they wanted to know every detail of the place even while they had no wish to go there. The city might well have been the moon. She was glad for the *rancho's* sake that they felt that way, and she wasn't at all sure their satisfaction with their lives as they were wasn't just as good for themselves as it was for the land. Time, if it did not stand still here, at least moved slowly enough to be understood. Even violence lost its final power against the healing of the land. She knew that better than most.

The children were asleep, blissfully exhausted from the renewal of friendships and familiar places. And they in their way knew the same things she knew. Jefferson had sought her out after they had been at the *rancho* for only a few hours.

"I looked around an' I thought about it, Mama," he began, and she knew by his solemn tone and his expression which so fitted his "Little Owl" nickname that this was something of great importance to him. "He's really not here any more. I kept thinkin' he would be. His puppies are here, lots of 'em, an' some of 'em look like him, but they're not. They're not Sombra. An' I don't know why, but it's all right now."

Only at the end did his voice betray his panic at finding the once unacceptable acceptable without understanding how it could be so.

She drew him close, trying not to burden him with the full weight of love she felt for him in this moment of perfection. "How right you are, Jefferson. Sombra is gone, and we'll always miss him. But the land goes on

436

and on, from spring to summer to autumn to winter and back to spring again. As long as you can remember to look for that, and to believe in it, you'll never lose too much because, even though it isn't the same spring any more than Sombra's puppies are the same as he was, it will always be a new season with just enough of the old to make you happy."

He regarded her gravely for a moment, understanding far more than she hoped or knew. "The house was waiting for us too," he said, and then he smiled and gave her a quick kiss before he was off to rejoin the other children.

She thought of it now in a brief respite between dances and chatter, and her vision was a little blurred. Jefferson had been right about the house too. In spite of their parting instructions that it should be used for living quarters or storage or whatever was necessary, they had ridden in without warning to find it well aired and gleaming, a trifle bare because of what they'd taken with them to the city, but still warm and welcoming. She knew Indian's little house was kept in the same readiness. Now she understood the significance of his remark that he had walked into his house and felt he'd only been gone for a few minutes.

Gavin caught sight of her face and excused himself politely from a conversation with Pedro and some of the *vaqueros*. And for a moment he just watched her, savoring the sight. Gone were her complicated city clothes. She was, in fact, dressed much less elaborately than some of the *vaqueros'* wives. She wore a low-necked peasant blouse and a long skirt bound at the waist by a sash. And her hair was dressed as simply as the rest of her, hanging in a thick gleaming braid down her back.

"You look very much the way you did when I first met you," he said softly as he came up to her.

"Except that I am wearing a bit more," she pointed out, smiling up at him.

He took her arm, and they went for a walk in the moonlight, not caring that their intention was marked by indulgent smiles.

The stars were brighter, closer, and more numerous than they ever appeared to be over the city, where the white mist from the sea so often obscured them. And

437

the air smelled different without the salt tang, smelled of green growing shoots and the earth itself.

"For a moment back there, you looked very sad," Gavin said finally.

"No, not sad, just a case of the doting mother," she hastened to assure him, repeating what Jefferson had said. "It's strange, isn't it, that no matter how hard we try to explain to the children, there are certain things they must come to know by themselves."

"Perhaps it protects them from growing up too quickly and too harshly," he mused. "After all, it isn't really possible, try as we might, to remember what the world was like and how time moved when we were children."

It touched her deeply that he could know that, he who had been given so little time to be a child. She was thinking about that, and so the question he could not forbear to ask took her by surprise. "Do you want to come back here? We could sell out in the city now and make a good profit."

She answered without hesitation. "I want to come back, as often as we can, to visit. But to leave the city now would be to leave so much unfinished. I have never liked to leave a task uncompleted. But I doubt we will ever finish all that we have begun in San Francisco, so we shall just have to accept that we share our hearts with more than one place." She was offering him the same comfort she had offered the children, and he was taking it as gratefully, but only now did she realize she truly meant the words—in her struggle not to be beaten by the city and to find a place of her own in it, she was coming, albeit grudgingly, to love it.

The moonlight was silver on her face, dramatically lighting the hollows and planes, casting a web of light on her black hair. Gavin saw the utter tranquility, felt the strength and peace-giving spirit of her more clearly than he ever had before. He trembled with his need for her, his body suddenly quickening, desire throbbing painfully in his loins. He drew her close and held her body against his own.

She gave a soft gurgle of laughter. "They will know and forgive us, and they will go on dancing. Come, my love." She pulled him toward their house.

It was like the magic of New Year's Eve in the fullness of their joining, but this night Tessa was the aggressor, hovering over Gavin, taking his body with her hands and her mouth, ministering to him like a priestess performing a rite of worship. He could taste himself as she kissed him, as her body settled down against him, taking him into her warmth.

They fell asleep comfortably intertwined, neither wanting to curl away into a separate entity, and Tessa awakened to Gavin's blue eyes watching her in the first pure rose of dawn, Gavin's flesh the sun rising inside of her, filling her with light, taking her into morning.

They spent the day riding far, checking on the herds, finding every reason to praise Pedro and his men for their excellent care of everything. The grass was indeed going to be less this year, but with care it appeared possible to get all but the weakest animals through what would undoubtedly be a dry summer. And best of all to Tessa's mind, there had been no more trouble with squatters.

They planned to sell all excess produce from the *rancho* in San Francisco this year where there was always an avid need for fresh food, and they discussed the probable dates of the various harvests with Pedro who, while he preferred to work with livestock, was an uncannily good judge of nature. And when they headed back to the city, Tessa insisted on taking a crate of chickens with them, much to Gavin's amusement. "I had almost forgotten how delicious fresh eggs are," she said, defending her cargo firmly. "And the children have promised to help take care of them."

The love they had shared on the *rancho* with each other and the land, the peace they had felt there, quickly took on the quality of old and precious amber as they were caught up in the race of the city's pulse again. Even their shared birthday celebration was less than a total success, all of them feeling older than their years and anxious to go to sleep long before the champagne Gavin had provided for the occasion was finished.

Tessa's clerks had done their best in her absence, but there were decisions they simply hadn't been able to make without her. And the men had a backlog of orders to ship

439

from the warehouse, goods they had resold that were not only going to various addresses in the city but to other towns and mining camps. Their hours were even longer than Tessa's. It seemed as if they might never sit down to a meal together again, and the only time Tessa saw Gavin was when he fell into bed and exhausted sleep beside her late at night.

May was only three days old when everything got worse.

CHAPTER XXXVIII

Tessa had come home late as usual in the past weeks. The children had already been fed and were on their way to bed, but she let them keep her company while she ate the supper Chong Sing had kept warm for her, then told them a story and settled them down for the night. The men still weren't home when she crawled wearily into bed. She wanted to stay awake until Gavin came in, but sleep overcame her.

She awakened abruptly with a cold start of fear, reaching out automatically for Gavin even as she tried to understand what had broken her sleep. Gavin wasn't there, and it was not her own nightmare; the pandemonium outside was real—the racing thud of feet, yells, bells clanging the horrible signals, the lurid orange glow when she looked out the window.

She threw her clothes on, instinctively deciding on the buckskin breeches, knowing trailing skirts and a woman's appearance would hinder her progress, willing her hands not to shake as she pinned up her hair and clamped the battered felt hat she had worn on the trail over it. She tucked the derringer in her waistband.

She found Chong Sing already with the children, who were whimpering as they woke up. "Darlings, it's all right, Chong Sing is here with you, and he won't let anything happen to you. There's some trouble in the city, a fire has started, and I'm going to go help your father and Indian.
440

Do whatever Chong Sing tells you to do and be my two brave boys."

They stared at her, their eyes wide and frightened, but they nodded obediently. Brand spoke for them both, making his "We will, Mama," as brave as he could.

She drew Chong Sing aside and shook her head at his mutinous expression. "It's no use looking like that. I'm going, and I haven't time to argue. If the fire threatens anywhere near here, take the children and go to the beach, you'll be safe there. And to hell with saving anything but your lives. Agreed?"

"Agleed," he said reluctantly. "But Mista Lamsey not goin' like dis any mo' dan me." His expression softened the tiniest bit. "I know you, you go no matta what. I ask China gods take cale of you."

To his surprise and her own she hugged him, and then she was running out of the house.

She was glad she was on foot. Not even Amordoro's willingness would have overcome his terror at the chaos on the streets. Fire companies raced and clanged in the wake of the torch boys. People clogged the streets, dragging what they could of their possessions. No voice was lower than a scream, and the sound of the spreading flames and exploding buildings was the loudest of all. Ashes and sparks were falling everywhere, and the murky orange glow of devastation lighted the way through hell.

The warehouse. She knew they would be there. She saw the tinder-dry sidewalks, put in the year before at great cost, and the piles of surplus goods acting as long, running fuses to the buildings on Montgomery Street. And then she saw Gavin wrenching a burning plank from a section near the entrance to the warehouse, tearing it away with his bare hands.

She screamed his name as she ran to him, and he turned on her, looking like the devil himself with his face soot blackened and his blue eyes blazing in sudden fury. "What in the hell are you doing here? Where are the children?"

"I'm here because you're here!" she screeched back at him. "The children are safe with Chong Sing. If the fire goes that way, he'll take them to the beach. What can I do to help?"

441

He slumped against the wall in sudden overwhelming exhaustion and defeat. "You can help me get Indian home," he mumbled. "He's inside where I left him and pretty groggy. A falling board hit him. There's not enough water even if one of the pumps got here. Just have to let it go, I guess."

She stood paralyzed. She had never seen him so beaten, knowing what the loss would mean to them, seeing no solution until she remembered. She went to him, reaching up to shake him fiercely by the shoulders, hearing the fire roar ever closer. "Gavin, the vinegar! We have 80,000 gallons of it—it will do as well as water!"

Her urgency pierced the layers of fatigue and pain, and he grinned. "It will serve Indian and me right, won't it, if it works?" He wanted more desperately than anything else to send her home to safety, but he knew she would refuse to go, and more, he needed her here.

She found Indian propped up against a bale of goods. Shaken, he admitted that the board had "shuffled" his brains some, but he managed to get to his feet. Even diminished, his strength was more than enough to splash vinegar wherever fire threatened.

They worked for hours. People, pump gangs, and the fire roared around them. A pack of men, obviously bent on looting, paused only briefly when they saw the quickly drawn sidearms of the warehouse defenders. Tessa felt a terrible urge to shoot one of them even as they retreated, and she saw the same desire on the men's faces, but to pause even for a vengeful instant in the fight was to lose.

She would never have guessed that the tart clean smell of vinegar could be so nauseating. She swallowed and kept on wetting the building down with the stuff. It seemed to take a long time for her to realize the sound she was hearing was Gavin's voice. "It's over, Tessa, you can stop now. The danger's past. We've saved the warehouse."

She stared at him stupidly for a minute, handing him a crock of vinegar automatically. But when some of it splashed on his hands and he winced, the world was in sharp focus for her again. His hands were a mass of blisters and raw flesh, and her stomach heaved at the idea of what it must have felt like to have the acid vinegar splashing on them for hours. She could not get him and Indian home fast enough, her voice harsh and insistent when she thought they were lagging.

The smell of smoke and charred wood was all around them, but there was no damage to their house. Chong Sing met them at the door, his face a paler ivory, but his manner as composed as ever. "Jeff an' Bland sleepin'. I tell dem dlagon all gone now," he told them. He set calmly to work, brewing tea and fixing a meal for them all while Tessa attended to the men's injuries.

There wasn't much to do for the bump on Indian's head except to give him cold compresses to hold on the spot. There was only a small cut on the scalp, and Tessa didn't think the skull was fractured despite the heavy bruising. She kissed him gently on the forehead, saying, "I know this won't help your headache much, but I love you dearly, my friend, and I'm glad you're more or less in one piece."

"He hurtin' pretty bad," Indian whispered worriedly.

"I know, but he'll be all right," she murmured, determined it would be true.

She soaked his hands in the strong tea she had allowed to cool, and Chong Sing gave his approval. "Tea good fo' all sickness," he claimed.

Gavin looked down at her drawn face and smiled wearily. "It looks worse than it is."

"It doesn't," she returned flatly. "Your hands are badly burned. I'm not sure I know enough to cope with this. Should I find a real *médico?*"

His head fell back and his eyes closed, but his voice was very sure. "No, you've seen me through worse. I'd trust you any day to an old sawbones who got thrown out of Boston and came here."

She worked doggedly, trying to keep everything very clean, salving his hands after the tea and wrapping the fingers separately to prevent any of the damaged tissue from healing together. He was beyond hunger but she got him to drink a tisane of herbs to ease the pain and bring sleep in addition to the effects of the brandy Indian had already given him. And waving Chong Sing and Indian away, she supported Gavin's sagging frame to their bedroom.

443

He sighed deeply as he sank down on the bed, and she thought he would lose consciousness immediately, but he lasted long enough to put his arms around her, clumsy bandaged hands and all. "You and your damn vinegar," he managed before his eyes closed. She settled down beside him, knowing neither Indian nor Chong Sing would fret when she did not return to them.

The city still smouldered and in some places still flamed brightly against the light of morning, and the task of clearing away and building again, though already begun, was not made easier by the growing conviction that arson was surely responsible, as it well might have been for some of the earlier conflagrations. It was May 4, the anniversary of a great fire the year before. There had been rumors that another would be set to commemorate the day. It surely seemed proven true. This fire had begun in a paint shop, and millions of dollars' worth of property was now ashes; worse, reports were circulating of hundreds of lives lost. And the wind had been right to keep the fire away from the area most heavily populated by the Sydney Ducks and their cohorts. Looting had been widespread. Never had the small peace-keeping force of the city and indeed of the state been shown to be more ineffectual than they were now.

When Tessa had made her decision to join the men at the warehouse, she had resigned herself to the fact that her store would surely be lost. She was overjoyed to find that it still stood—her clerks, even Molly and George, had hastened to the scene when the first bells rang. Their determined bucket brigade had kept damage to a minimum. She thanked them all, her voice unsteady, and even Molly looked less restrained than usual, eyes still sparkling with accomplishment. Walter Long spoke for them all when he assured her that they had fought as much for their own jobs as for the business. "We kinda like workin' for you, Miz Ramsay," he finished with a shy smile, his arm around Anne.

The Golden Horse had burned to the ground, but as Mr. Peniston pointed out, the gold on hand had merely melted, and had already been recovered and taken away for safekeeping.

Tessa felt as if they had waged a war and come out

the victors. Not only were they alive, but their commercial lives were also intact. It was a shock to her to find that Gavin did not feel that way. The pain in his hands he ignored, as he had always ignored physical discomfort—even when the lash had laid open his back and would have killed most men, he had lived and surmounted the pain in a miraculously short time. But now he was intolerant of the helplessness forced upon him. He hated every minute of it; it made him ill-humored and worse, it sapped his belief in their victory.

"Perhaps we ought to get out while we can, sell everything off and go back to the *rancho*," he suggested.

"You can't mean it!" she cried, but she saw by the look in his eyes that he did. "Oh, Gavin, to let it defeat us when we have fought so hard and done so well!"

He studied her face, flushed with passionate will, and he was not at all sure he liked what he saw. There was a sharpness about her, a quick edge to her voice, to the way she moved, even to her features and the shape of her body, as if she were a thoroughbred in constant training for a demanding race, her race with the city. It was as if softness only came with effort now. The brief respite at the *rancho* seemed a thousand years past. He felt old and tired beyond his years, as if the strength he had had for their ventures here had passed from himself to her.

She knew something was terribly wrong, something deeper than the cause they were considering in the open. But she did not know what it was or how to cope with it. She took his bandaged hands in her own with infinite gentleness and kissed each wrist. "My love, they are healing. Soon the bandages will be off, and your hands will serve you as well as they ever did. You will feel so much better then."

He was undone by her sudden tenderness, and he forced spirit he did not feel into his voice. "As long as one of us goes on believing, it ought to be enough. To us and to the city, my dear." He raised an imaginary glass. Her head buried against him, Tessa did not see the winter in his eyes.

The city was more than ever like an armed camp. Groups of businessmen took turns prowling the streets at night, heavily armed and quick to fire at any shadow that

445

might conceal a vandal or arsonist. It was enough to keep the law-abiding off the streets. What effect it was having on the criminals was more in doubt.

It was June 3, a month since the fire, and Jordan Ames was with the Ramsays and Indian. They had seen a good deal of him during the past weeks. He had felt the increased tension in the household and had been doing his diffident best to ease it. And he had joined in their endless discussions of what could be done to insure the safety of life and property in the city. He was as much on the side of moderation as they were and as helpless to find a way to guarantee it.

But this night was in the nature of a celebration. The bandages had been off of Gavin's hands for a few days now, and though his skin was still streaked with angry red and pale white stripes that would take time to fade, he had full use of his fingers and of all the muscles of his hands. He flexed them constantly without Tessa's urging, working diligently to banish the last traces of stiffness.

He raised his wine glass, holding it by the delicate stem as clear proof of his dexterity: "To the best doctor in San Francisco." And then he froze, as they all did, one by one picking up the growing swell of sound outside, becoming aware of the false dawn beginning to light the sky.

"It can't be!" Tessa cried in futile protest, knowing it was. "Wait for me!" she called even as she ran upstairs, tearing at the fastenings of her dress as she went, struggling into the buckskins which still bore the stains of the last catastrophe, returning to the men who made no protest except for Jordan whose horrified "But surely it would be better——" was cut short by Gavin. "Save your breath for fighting the fire. It's no use wasting it on her."

Even Chong Sing was instantly intent on his own duty, assuring them briefly that the children would be well cared for before he hurried away to be with them when the noise awakened them.

It was worse than the month before. There was even less water to fight the fire this time. The warehouse was in no immediate danger, but the roof of Tessa's shop was already flaming brightly. Her clerks arrived even as she, Gavin, Indian, and Jordan did and together they managed

446

to get a few of the more precious items out—silks, Oriental and French fans of ebony, ivory, delicately painted silk and chickenskin, silver-threaded and beaded shawls and reticules, kid gloves, fur and feather trims, lace from the Continent. But what they saved was pitiful in comparison to what was lost. When Tessa felt the heat becoming more intense and heard the ominous creaking, she screamed at everyone to get out.

"It's not worth dying for! Leave, leave all of you! Molly, drop that, it's too heavy, it will slow you down!" Molly let the bolt of velvet fall with reluctance. "Pierre, never mind that. Gavin, your hands, enough! Make sure Indian and Jordan get out!" Together they herded everyone out of the building, and they all spent the last safe moments carting the goods they had saved as far from the flames as they could.

Tessa watched the building collapse on itself, and she felt Gavin's arms come around her, holding her tightly against his side. She turned her head and kissed the hand on her shoulder. "No new burns. It's all right. We're all safe." Her voice had ceased to shake by the time she finished.

By morning they had moved the shop's goods to the warehouse. It was the only one of their businesses that was still standing. The newly rebuilt gaming house had burnt to the ground again, and this time Mr. Peniston had nearly gone with it, suffering smoke inhalation and surface burns in an heroic attempt to save the place, an attempt he was the first to admit was uncharacteristic when they located him among the night's wounded. "I just got so damn mad, begging your pardon, Mrs. Ramsay, I guess I thought even spitting on the fire might help," he told them hoarsely.

He had been removed to the boarding house where he lived, which was luckily still intact. His landlady made every promise to look after him, and Tessa was sure the ample, kind-looking woman would keep her word.

"Mr. Peniston, when you're well again, you'll find a new Golden Horse for your talents," she assured him.

"Always did like someone who could beat the odds," he said. Gavin said nothing at all beyond expressing his hope that Mr. Peniston would be feeling better shortly.

Their house was still standing, Tessa saw with overwhelming relief as they neared it. Gavin stopped suddenly and grabbed her, swinging her around violently to face him. "Don't you know when to give up, don't you ever know? What in the hell do you think you were doing, promising Peniston another place?"

She stared up at him from eyes as smoke-reddened as his own, her face black-streaked. "I will not be beaten! We are no worse off than most people. We're surely better off than many. Some must have lost everything this night. We have not. We can build again. I will build again even if you will not, even if I have to sell every palomino. And if you want to hold me, you can do it without hurting!"

His hands fell away as if he had been burned again, and she caught at them with an inarticulate moan. "Oh, Gavin, what's wrong? It's not like you to surrender!"

"It was different when I had no wife or children and the risks were all my own. But now I must think always that you or my sons might be burnt to death or killed in some other savage way. Christ, you've been through this night and the one a month ago! Are you blind? There's a civil war going on here! And it will get worse before it gets better." What he said was true, but was only part of what he was feeling. He could not find the way to say the rest, but Tessa heard the unspoken words all too clearly.

She let go of his hands and drew back from him, standing proudly alone in the raw, smoke-tainted morning. "I have survived a civil war here before. I don't know why you find me unworthy now. Or our sons. We have changed as we have had to change, and we still look on life with joy. It is unjust of you to judge us unequal to the task."

He wanted her back, the girl he had known by the pool, the girl hard enough to defend herself so effectively he had nearly died, but soft enough to have long depended on him to understand the swift new life. The cold, still beauty before him seemed to need nothing from him at all, seemed capable of going ahead whether he was with her or not.

He bowed his head, searching desperately for the words to explain without offending, but when he looked up again, she was disappearing into the house. Wearily, he followed in her wake. When Indian, who had preceded them, cast him a troubled glance, Gavin frowned his refusal to answer.

448

Chong Sing produced an enormous amount of food in a short time. They ate mindlessly, too tired and hungry to notice much about the food except that it was hot and filling. But after they had assured the children that everything really was all right and had stripped and fallen into bed, Gavin noticed the bruises appearing on Tessa's skin where his hands had gripped her. "I'm sorry," he murmured, kissing first one shoulder and then the other.

"It's all right," she whispered back. "We are both very tired." She was asleep before he could say anything more.

The situation in the city grew steadily worse, and the cries of outrage were as loud as the hammers of rebuilding. Arrests had been made and there was firm evidence of arson against some of the men. Crowds grew violent, and attempts were made to hang the prisoners. But the mayor and other officials made fervent promises that the criminals would be severely dealt with. The grand jury was already in session and found a true bill against some of the prisoners. But then the incredible truth swept the city—the indictments had been subverted by technicalities and the prisoners had disappeared.

It was enough, more than enough, an end to patience. When Gavin said he wanted the children sent to the *rancho*, Tessa made no objection.

"I don't suppose I could persuade you to go with them?" he asked drily.

"No, you couldn't, but I think this time Chong Sing will probably want to accompany them." She was right. Though he muttered against families being separated and worried further about what would happen to the house without his care, he had no intention of letting the children go without him, since this time they would not have their parents' protection.

Tessa was glad he felt that way, because it made it easier to convince the children that not only were they lucky to be returning to the *rancho* for a summer holiday, but now they could show Chong Sing all their favorite places.

Indian was going to escort them, returning immediately to the city. Though none of them discussed it, the reason was understood. Gavin's ability to participate in events

449

and to be heard would always be greater than Indian's simply because Gavin was white.

Even though she knew it was for the best, Tessa had to struggle for control when the moment came for her to kiss her sons good-by, and she thought of how odd it was to see them riding away from her rather than the other way around as it had been. She had a sudden sense of what it would be like when they were men and really rode away from her.

She was saved by Chong Sing from breaking down and weeping openly. Though both of the children were competent riders now, the journey was too long and tiring for them to make on their mounts, so the men each had a child up with them on their saddles. Chong Sing had Jefferson, and Tessa heard him explaining to her son that China was so big and horses so many less than in California that to have one was a symbol of wealth and gave a warrior the power to control vast amounts of land.

Tessa was sure whatever he had been in China, Chong Sing had not been a warrior on horseback. He sat his mount with the same competent authority with which he did everything, but it would have been a great exaggeration to have called his seat either casual or graceful. Tessa was glad they had had the wisdom to procure this docile mount for him. His pride would have suffered badly from any overt struggle for control.

"That horse is going to speak fluent Chinese long before he gets to Rancho Magnífico," Gavin whispered, and Tessa was able to bid her sons good-by with a smile.

She saw very little of Gavin or of Jordan Ames in the next few days, but her heart was with them both, knowing that they were meeting with other cool-headed men in an effort to avert mob rule.

She focused her own energies on directing the rebuilding of the Golden Horse and her store. It was being done without further discussion between herself and Gavin, but at least he had made no inquiries or objections when she began ordering materials and seeking out work crews, offering them extravagant wages in return for speed.

One night Gavin did not come home. At first Tessa didn't worry. He had warned her he would probably be late, confirming her suspicion that something was to be decided this night, something momentous, but he had stopped her questions with a plea. "Please, Tessa, don't ask me now. I promise I will tell you when I can, if it works, if there's anything to tell."

She had to respect his request. It was not just his secret; it involved a great many others.

It was more difficult to abide by her promise not to worry or to seek him out as the tenth of June drew close to midnight and became the morning of the eleventh and still he had not come home. She thought she heard a fire bell, but no glow illuminated the sky and no other bells took up the notes.

As the day drew on toward dawn, it was more and more difficult to fight her terrible imaginings. *Surely,* she thought, *Jordan or someone will come and tell me if something has happened to Gavin.*

She was outside again, eyes straining toward the center of the city, the first soft light of morning touching the sky, when she heard the footsteps and saw Gavin looming through the faint mist. She hurled herself at him and his arms came around her and held her so hard her ribs ached.

"Oh, my God, I thought something terrible had happened to you," she sobbed. Then she realized that something had. He was holding her as much for his own comfort as hers; she could feel the high tension in his body, and as the light broadened, she could see the ghastly, pale set of his face. "Come in where it is warm, and you can tell me," she said gently, drawing away from him and then pulling him by the hand into the house as if he were one of the children. He sank gratefully into a chair and closed his eyes for a moment. Still he said nothing. She handed him a steaming cup of coffee heavily laced with brandy, and he took a deep, scalding gulp of it before he finally began to talk.

"Tonight we formed the Committee of Vigilance of San Francisco. There must have been about two hundred men there who enrolled at the meeting. We pledged our lives, our honor, our fortunes to the protection of our fellow members and to the cause of purging this city of those who threaten its welfare. In order to accomplish this we vowed to 'watch, pursue, and bring to justice the outlaws

451

infesting the city, through the regularly constituted courts, if possible, through more summary process if necessary.' Those are the exact words. They sounded very civilized then. We arranged for watchwords, patrols, and a signal to call us to the rendezvous, and then we adjourned for the evening.

"I lingered a little longer, discussing what we'd done with Jordan. He's a member too, of course. It is a dangerous thing when citizens take the law into their own hands, but we felt we had no choice because there is no law here, none that works, and the only other alternative is mob rule. The city has been moving very quickly in that direction. The committee's purpose is to prevent that as best we can.

"We all meant what we said, but we did not expect to have to act so quickly after we had made our pledges. I was on my way home when the fire bell rang three times. I turned back, as did the others, at the signal."

He stopped, covering his face for a moment, and Tessa's heart jumped against her ribs. The bell she had heard when there had been no fire. The most ominous sound in San Francisco—for what reason this time?

Gavin's hands dropped away, and his eyes bored into hers. "We hung a man; we executed a man named Jenkins in the darkness."

She felt very cold, but she did not cry out or look away from him. "Was justice done?" She could not prevent the harshness in her voice.

She knew she had chosen the right thing to say because she saw the slightest easing of the tautness in his face before he spoke again.

"That's really the only thing that matters, isn't it?" he said slowly. "Several of us, including Mr. Coleman, the merchant we chose as chairman, objected to the implied cowardice of hanging a man in the dark, but there were reasons for it. Jenkins was caught stealing a safe from a store. He was a well-known ex-convict from Sydney who has repeatedly broken the law and escaped punishment. He was insulting and cocksure all during his trial, bragging that even while we tried him, his friends knew of our activities and were gathering to attack us in force. And some of the newly elected officers of the committee con-
452

firmed this even while scores of citizens converged on the place to sign with us and offer any support we might need. So everything moved very fast from trial to hanging, though Jenkins' friends didn't appear to rescue him. Perhaps they would have if the word had not gone out and so many men had not pledged themselves to our cause. I just don't know. But I do know that Jenkins was an evil man with nothing to offer his fellowman but hurt. He even vilified the minister who came in good faith because Mr. Coleman insisted the condemned should have the chance to speak with a man of God." A wry smile lit Gavin's face briefly. "I've never had much to say to men of the cloth myself, but I would certainly never say what Jenkins did to a priest or anyone else."

His eyes were blind and inward looking for a moment, and then he nodded. "Justice was done. I believe it is fair to say that. I only hope we will be able to say that of all the committee's work."

CHAPTER XXXIX

When Indian arrived back from the *rancho,* he was, as Tessa had privately requested, not alone. With him were fifteen proud golden horses, all dark-skinned under the gold, dark-eyed and with flowing silver manes and tails. They were the oldest and best trained of the offspring of Don Esteban's stock, and they were no more wide-eyed and nervous than Pedro and the three other *vaqueros* who had helped to bring the animals to San Francisco.

She had planned everything very well. Space for the horses and already interest being expressed by the potential buyers Jordan had helped her to contact, men who were wealthy enough to pay the prices she would ask, men whom she judged would be acceptable owners. She had even arranged boarding space for Pedro and the *vaqueros* so that they might have some comfort while they stayed to help handle the horses at the sale, with time enough allowed for them to see some of the city sights.

She had planned everything except Gavin's reaction. He was furious, his anger made even worse by the fact that Indian and Jordan had both been in on her scheme while he had not.

"Don't you dare blame them!" she snapped. "I asked them to help me, and as gentlemen, they could hardly refuse. And you have always said the horses are mine, even when I would not have had it so. These are ready to be sold, and with this dry year, it will not be amiss to have fewer to feed at the *rancho*. I don't understand why you object."

"I think you do," he said coldly, "or you would not have arranged this so cleverly behind my back. What is it you want that makes you willing to part with the horses?"

"Bricks are what I want—what I *have*. The shop and the Golden Horse will be almost all of brick this time, not wood that burns so quickly or metal that does not burn but twists and melts and bakes everything inside." She shuddered, remembering graphic descriptions of bodies found after the fires, bodies of people who had made the tragic mistake of thinking the metal would protect them. "I want buildings that stand a better chance of surviving than those we have had. You have been busy with the work of the committee, otherwise you would have seen the brick walls going up."

Gavin realized he was losing track of where their argument was heading, and bafflement replaced much of the anger in his voice. "All right, I'll grant you that brick is a sensible idea, but why sell the horses to obtain it? We've lost something, it's true, but our general funds could still be stretched to cover that. We could even arrange a loan from any one of several sources."

Suddenly she wanted very much for him to understand. "It will still require a substantial amount from our monies. The horses will not pay for all the building. But they will help. And it is important to me that they make some difference so that if a good cargo is offered, we can buy it, so that we need not be in debt to a money lender, so that what I want will not make things impossible for you and Indian. I don't even know how Indian feels about it, but I do know how you feel. You told me very clearly. You did not want to rebuild. I do, and in brick. It is only just

454

that part of the means should come from what is precious to me."

"I can see your point," he conceded finally. What he could not admit even to himself was that her capable handling of the rebuilding, her dedication to it, even to being willing to sell the horses, was making him feel not only obscurely threatened but lonely besides. He tried to mark it down as simply one more complication of these complicated times. Though it was necessary, this work of driving human rats from their holes and occasionally killing one was not to his taste.

Despite the governor's nominal opposition to the Vigilance Committee, it operated for a month, banishing about thirty men against whom there was no clear proof of murder in the state, arresting some, hanging four, and scaring many other criminals away from the city. Then, judging the job well done, and not wanting to push the established authorities too hard for too long, the committee adjourned. But it did not disband; the organization was to remain in readiness for any emergency.

Tessa realized the full cost to Gavin when he came home and announced, "It's finished, and I hope to God I never hear that signal again." He didn't even want anything to eat, though Tessa doubted he had had a proper meal all day, not to mention his spartan eating habits for the last month. All he wanted to do was sleep, and sleep he did, not even stirring when Tessa worriedly touched his face for signs of fever. Indian thought it was the best thing in the world for him, and wouldn't hear of having him awakened for work the next morning.

"I been in it, doin' a little here, little there, but not like he been. He wore out, 'specially from all his frettin' 'bout whether th' committee doin' th' right or th' wrong thing day by day. I cain't manage a day without him, I ain't worth much."

His cheerful assurance eased her worry. She went to the shop only briefly. Her clerks were busy in the new brick building. There was still much to be done before the opening planned for the next week, not to mention a great deal of stock yet to be replenished from heaven only knew what sources. But she did not want Gavin to awaken alone. She knew it was a foolish thought, as if he were

455

one of the children, but it made no difference. She did only a few essential things at the store before she made her apologies and went home again.

She needn't have hurried. He did not wake up until late at night. He looked at her with a puzzled frown when he saw her reading beside the bed, the lamp flame low so as not to shine in his face. She heard him stir and saw the disorientation of his long sleep in his eyes.

She rose swiftly and bent over him, laughing softly as she kissed him. "You've slept for twenty-four hours, my love. And I would guess that now you must be very hungry."

He stretched luxuriously with a groan of pleasure, then grabbed her so swiftly she gave a startled yelp. He pulled her down on top of him, nuzzling against her neck and the soft lace of her wrapper. "I'm hungry for all sorts of things, but I think food first, to give me strength for the rest."

If Indian, who had retired hours before, heard them rummaging around in the kitchen, he gave no sign, and Tessa felt a great surge of warm satisfaction from the simple task of making a meal for Gavin and watching him eat everything ravenously.

"I'm strong enough now," he said with a grin when he had finished, and he picked Tessa up, ignoring her laughing protests, and carried her upstairs. It was the best sharing of each other they had experienced since their visit to the *rancho*, and they both knew the sadness of that realization along with the joy of their loving.

The city gave them no chance to rediscover the path to joy they had once known so easily. With San Francisco safer than it had ever been, it was time for the children to come home, and even with Chong Sing setting the house to rights again, they added their own confusion to every day. But nothing could dim Tessa and Gavin's gladness at seeing them again. Both boys seemed to have grown, even though their absence had been little more than a month, and they were both surely summer brown and sturdy-looking from the days on the *rancho*. Gavin told Tessa he even thought Chong Sing had acquired a deeper color, though he would never be so bold as to mention such a thing. Chong Sing himself admitted he had found it quite nice on the "*lancho*," but the way he said it indicated clearly that to him it had been like visiting another foreign country. And he wasted no time in reestablishing his contacts in Chinatown, bringing home foodstuffs that he politely kept separate from the household's supplies.

Giggling, Jefferson and Brand gave Tessa their own account of Chong Sing's stay at Rancho Magnífico. "Nobody there could understand what he was saying," Brand informed her, "but they all did what he wanted anyway."

"We had an awfully good time," Jeff said, "but we missed you and Papa and Indian and Mr. Ames and the boats." He gave her a hug to emphasize how much he meant it. She wondered if anything on earth smelled and felt as lovely as a small, warm, slightly grubby child.

But the children were not all. Her shop was open again, doing such a brisk business in its new and more luxurious quarters that Tessa was frantic in her search for goods to buy and had to spend even more time than usual inspecting available cargoes and warehouse supplies other than those from their own that was growing increasingly well known under the name the sign boasted—"Ramian Mercantile Sales and Storage."

The Golden Horse was ready to open again before Mr. Peniston was recovered enough to handle the long, demanding hours. He had competent people working for him, but he did not judge any of them fit to take responsibility for the whole operation. Tessa left this decision entirely up to the men, offering to do whatever she could to help, but not pushing them one way or the other. It was they who decided the Golden Horse had to stay open, and stay open for all hours as it had before; it was their most direct and easiest source of income, capable of building up their depleted capital. Tessa had never kept the shop open seven days a week as most merchants did, but a gambling house was another thing entirely.

It put the final touch on their hectic days and nights. As often as not, Tessa found herself spending a good many of the late hours at the gaming house with the men, dealing, acting as hostess, or entertaining the gamblers with songs.

As they rode home in the dark hours one early morning, hoping for at least a few hours of sleep before the day began in earnest, Tessa yawned audibly. "I've been practicing praying again for the first time in years. I'm asking for two things—Mr. Peniston's speedy recovery and Chong Sing's continued patience. He doesn't approve of this, you know, and if he leaves, I'm going to jump into the waters of the bay and swim through the Golden Gate to China to see if he left any willing brothers behind."

She was rewarded by the men's laughter, rare sound these days, and Gavin held her a little longer than necessary when he helped her down from Amordoro. They had long since given up walking to the Plaza, having neither the time nor the energy.

She wondered whether Chong Sing ever slept. No matter what hour they came in, he was waiting, looking alert and insisting they eat before they slept, even while he grumbled under his breath against the unsuitability of what they were doing.

Not only did Chong Sing show every sign of staying with them, but the other prayer she had joked about was answered in a completely unexpected way. She was glad she was singing, not dealing, when they walked in, or she would have abandoned the table no matter what stakes it held. As it was, her guitar and her voice went silent as she stared.

"Sorry, boys, but I'll sing for you later. Right now I have some friends to see," she managed, and then she was running swiftly through the obligingly parting crowd, hugging both of them, wanting to weep because she was so glad to see them. Belle was even more beautiful than memory, and Charles was at his city best in an immaculate suit complete with pleated shirt, richly embroidered vest, gleaming stickpin, and kid gloves.

"It wasn't just the name and that pretty horse's head on the sign that gave you away," Belle laughed. "I saw those big gold brutes and the chestnut outside, and I figured it had to be the Ramsay outfit. I think your horse even recognized me."

"He might have," Tessa giggled. "He hasn't made many new friends here."

Charles bore their nonsense with a tolerant smile while
458

his eyes watched the action at the tables with keen interest. His bushy eyebrows lifted in surprise when he saw Indian dealing, and there was no offense, just real interest when he asked how that could be. It was one thing in the outer regions where men were so hungry to gamble, quite a different thing here where there were enough places for them to indulge their whims and prejudices.

"Only by the best of luck," Tessa admitted frankly, and she told them of the fire and Mr. Peniston's injuries. "We simply couldn't keep everything going without Indian, and he'd never let us try since the responsibility is half his. We've learned something you must surely know very well, Charles. Gamblers are strange in their ideas of what makes good fortune and what does not, and for those same strange reasons, enough have decided Indian is lucky for them so that he never lacks for players. And now I want to know what good fortune brings you here. Is it for good or just for a visit?"

"We haven't really decided yet," Belle said. "We've been doing fine in Sonora. But I don't think we'll be able to resist San Francisco much longer. However, I can see it's not without its problems," she added, eyeing Tessa with kindly concern. "Looks to me like you could use some quiet time out in the country."

"We're all a little weary," Tessa admitted. "There just don't seem to be enough hours in the day or the night.'"

The men greeted Belle with extravagant politeness and Charles with so much warmth that Tessa knew what Gavin was going to say before he said it. "If I had any manners at all, I'd wait a while and work up to this subtly, but I'm afraid I'll miss my chance," he confessed with a smile. "If you haven't any other immediate plans, we could sure use you here until our head man is able to take over again. That shouldn't be more than ten days at the most."

"It would be my pleasure," Charles said without hesitation, a smile lighting his craggy features. His hands already moving as if they held invisible cards.

"God works in mysterious ways," Tessa said piously a few days later, and Gavin burst out laughing. "Your view of God is unique to say the least. Where I came from even considering the idea that God would send a gambler and

459

a prostitute in answer to a prayer would be enough to merit eternal hellfire. But then again, I expect even God has to make do with what's available out here."

Whatever providence had sent them, Charles and Belle couldn't have been more helpful. Charles quickly had everything running smoothly and profitably at the Golden Horse, and Belle was a great deal of help to Tessa at the shop, suggesting patterns, fabric, and color combinations enthusiastically once she knew that neither Tessa nor Molly Barker was offended by the advice.

By the time they left, Mr. Peniston was fully recovered, and life seemed generally more manageable than it had for a long while.

"We're forever in your debt," Tessa told them, giving them each a hug.

"That's not a word between friends,'" Belle said. "Charley and I have few enough friends to be damn thankful for those we've got. No need to look so sad, anyway; we'll be back, and shortly I think. We've been bitten by the same bug that makes everyone crazy to stay here."

As Charles stood talking to the men, Belle had only a brief moment to speak the words for Tessa alone, but she made the best of it. "Take care, my dear. You and Gavin have something very special. Don't lose it. It's one of the few things I know anything about, that magic that happens every once in a while between a man and a woman. Take time for each other, no matter what else you do." She did not have to say outright that she had seen the changes in them and feared for them.

"We'll try," Tessa promised softly. "Oh, Belle, it will be so good when you live here too!"

She was glad of Gavin's comforting warmth beside her as they watched Belle and Charles ride out of sight. Aside from Jordan Ames and a few business associates, their own close friendships were very limited in this city of strangers. They had even lost touch with their old friends the Larkins, who seemed to be dividing their time between trips to the East and the speculative community of Benicia in which Larkin had invested. Though Benicia was not too far from San Francisco, the Ramsays had only seen the Larkins once in the city. Sam and Carmelita were in Monterey, and close as she was to Anne and

Molly, Tessa knew there was always the barrier of her being their employer. To have Belle nearby to confide in and laugh with would be wonderful. It no longer seemed even the least bit odd to her to have chosen a prostitute for a good friend.

She knew Belle's warning was one to be heeded. She had known from the beginning that San Francisco was not a healthy place for any but the strongest of marriages, and though she hated to admit it, hers and Gavin's had been showing alarming signs of weakness lately. The pressure they had both been under was somehow causing fissures and separations rather than a stronger fusing. She wished she had not chosen that comparison; base metals always cracked under pressure.

She vowed that would not happen to them. Even with her determination to succeed in other things, the center of her life was Gavin, and to lose him would be to lose the purpose for everything else. She ceased to allow herself to be coaxed out to lunch by Jordan, and she ignored the disappointment in his eyes. She tailored all her activities to allow her more time at home, wanting to be there when Gavin came in, even though it often meant spending hours of waiting. But even that had its benefits, because it gave her more time than she'd had in a long while with the children.

And Gavin did notice, giving her a longer kiss than usual one evening when she greeted him at the door and saying, "Seems I've been seeing more of a particularly beautiful woman lately."

"Are you complaining?" she asked saucily.

"Indeed I'm not," he murmured against her hair. "I'll do my best too, sweetheart. We need more time together than we've had lately."

"Amen," Tessa said fervently. "And what about this Sunday, just for the two of us?"

"I think I can manage that, ma'am." He meant it, and his disappointment was just as great as hers when the day began to fall apart. The week as usual had not had enough hours to finish all that had to be done. Indian, always so sensitive to their moods, had elected himself to finish up tasks at the warehouse, but still Gavin wasn't free to spend the day with Tessa. They had paid little attention when

461

the Land Act had been passed this year, but now Jordan was warning them that it might have a profound effect on their ownership of Rancho Magnífico, and even more on Tessa's claim to Rancho Valle del Mar. The documents were at Jordan's office, and a Sunday meeting was simply too convenient for Gavin to refuse.

"I'll be back as soon as I can," he promised ruefully. He refused her offer to go with him, pointing out that since they would both undoubtedly be involved before everything was settled, she might as well enjoy her Sunday while she could.

She made a face at him as he went out the door and muttered, "This lonely splendor wasn't exactly what I had in mind." Even the children were gone off with Chong Sing to visit some of his friends in Chinatown.

She settled down to work on the myriad accounts that always seemed to outdistance her, and she tried not to think of the Sunday slipping away without Gavin.

He took much longer to return than she had thought he would, and when he walked in, he was not alone.

She stared at both of them. Gavin looked uncharacteristically nervous and unsure. The first thing that registered about the small figure at his side was that it was the thinnest, dirtiest little boy she had ever seen. She caught a glance of deep brown eyes before the child returned to his study of the floor.

"I bought him!" Gavin blurted out suddenly.

"You *what?*"

"Oh, Christ! I'll explain it later. First he needs a bath and food. His name is Paul." He sounded much more confident with something specific to be done.

"Yes, of course," Tessa agreed serenely, as if small boys purchased at the marketplace were a daily occurrence. She had seen the trembling the child was fighting so hard to control, and pity flooded her heart.

He began to wolf down the food she offered him so ravenously, she snatched the plate away from him. "You'll be sick. I promise you you can have all you want to eat, but only if you eat it slowly and carefully."

The boy hadn't made a sound, and she wondered if he were deaf and dumb, but when the tousled head came up and the brown eyes stared at her, she knew there was

462

nothing dim about this child; malevolent perhaps, but not stupid. He regarded her with a crafty, defiant look, and then he shrugged and took a slow, deliberate bite of the bread he still clasped in his grubby fist. She put the plate back within his reach.

The bath was not so easily accomplished. Gavin helped her prepare it, helping strip off the filthy clothes and dumping the shuddering child in the tub. But then he stepped back helplessly to let Tessa take over. The first thing she received for her care was a painful bite on the arm.

"Why, you little savage," Gavin growled, but Tessa warned him away with a swift look. Very deliberately, though not hard, she bit the child back, causing his eyes to go wide in shock. "That's how it feels. Don't ever do it again," she said severely. "In this house, we don't use teeth or fists or any other violence, and you won't either."

Though her hands remained slow and steady as they washed away the accumulated grime, her pulse jumped and pounded in outrage at the bruises and weals revealed on the clean skin, and she wanted to wrap her arms around the child and hold him. She didn't need Gavin's white-lipped expression to tell her this was why—he had seen himself in this waif. And she understood the dull flush on the child's skin; whatever else he was used to, it was not having a woman bathe him. He couldn't be more than seven or eight years old, and yet he was acutely embarrassed by her ministrations. She sighed inwardly, wondering if he would ever be able to tolerate anything but maltreatment. Unconsciously she had already accepted him as part of their lives from now on.

The rapid shocks and changes of the day coupled with the food and warm bath took their toll. He was so sleepy by the time Gavin lifted him from the tub, he made no protest as Tessa dried him swiftly before he could take a chill, and he was sound asleep by the time Gavin set him down on the bed they hurriedly made up for him in the boys' room.

They stood for a moment looking down at him. Even with the shadows under his eyes and the pathetic thinness of him, he was a handsome child with clean straight features, long dark lashes, deep brown hair with chestnut

463

highlights, and pale skin only faintly golden from the sun.

"He's a beautiful child," she said when they were downstairs again.

"Physically, yes, but I don't know, maybe it's too late."

She regarded him in surprise. "Are you already regretting bringing him home?"

"Yes, I guess I am. It was a mad thing to do, and I can hear it in your voice, you've already adopted him. But there's more than an even chance it won't work. I know, I was the same sort of child, though probably not so canny. I saw this huge drunken son of a bitch slapping the boy around, and I went sort of crazy, knowing what it was like, wanting to kill my uncle as much as I had ever wanted to. Before I knew what I was doing, I'd knocked the man down. The boy never made a sound, just stood there shivering, staring at his father. When the man came to, that's what he claimed to be, and I believed him. He's much coarser looking than his son, but the coloring's the same. I asked where the mother was. Dead back in England—the man made it sound like she'd done it on purpose to spite him. I offered him five hundred dollars for the boy. He made some obscene suggestions about what I wanted the child for, and I could have beaten his brains out. But in the end he agreed and came along with me to get the money and sign the papers. I left the man and the boy with Jordan while I got the money from the Golden Horse; I didn't want the man knowing where the gold came from. I got Jordan to draw up the papers and a judge friend of his to confirm them even if it is a Sunday. But it's still highly irregular and probably not legally binding. Even so, I don't think the man will be a problem. He's one of the Sydney Ducks the committee missed. He obviously hasn't any use for his son beyond abusing him. And God knows how many criminal arts the boy has already learned. You're right, I am regretting it."

"Don't please, not yet. Let's give him a chance. Humans don't seem to breed true, do they? Our own sons are very different from each other and even from us. And if blood does count so much, who knows, maybe Paul's father was the first bad one in the line. Maybe Paul's mother or other people in his family were truly beautiful and that's why he is such a beautiful child, and maybe somewhere in the
464

battered little body there's a beautiful spirit to match. Surely we have enough love in this house to change what has been!"

Her words were so quick and pleading, Gavin grinned wryly. "I think you missed your calling. You would surely make a better lawyer than Jordan. He called me every kind of fool and elaborated quite grandly on the theme while he drew up the papers. I must remember when I want something to pretend that I do not. I can scarcely believe I'm the one who started all this."

He drew her close. There was unspoken agreement between them to give it a try, and a mutual refusal to consider what they would do if it did not work.

For Tessa most of all, it was a hellish week. She neglected the store, concentrating all her energies on getting through to Paul and feeling increasingly frustrated that so small a person could prove so resistant. He spoke to no one, and if he looked at you, it was only to glare with silent fury. He did what he was told to do, no more, except for exchanging blows with Brand in one row. Brand gave as good as he got because though younger, he was stronger than the skinny interloper. There was no doubt that Brand regarded Paul with dislike and suspicion and had since he had first been taken to see the strange boy sleeping in his and Jefferson's room. He had tried to be friendly when the situation was explained to him, but he had received nothing but cold silence and a basilisk stare for his pains. He was not accustomed to being snubbed, and it rankled. Jefferson, sweeter and more thoughtful by nature than his brother and far less sure of his own charm, remained patiently kind toward Paul, though puzzled by him.

"That's a sad little boy," he observed to his mother, and she hugged him for echoing her own hope. Surely sadness and lack of love could be more easily overcome than wickedness. But she could not deny her growing conviction that Paul was simply biding his time before he ran back to the streets, eating well in the meantime and paying no heed to the other inhabitants of the house. Chong Sing added nothing to Tessa's comfort with his muttered comments about "bad blood" and the need for "honolable palents" that the child might also be "honolable." He

465

ministered to the child's needs efficiently, but with none of the warmth he gave Brand and Jefferson.

Indian's policy of staying out of the business while regarding her with sympathetic eyes helped no more than Chong Sing's attitude, and Gavin made it hardest of all, especially because he was the one who had brought Paul home in the first place. The altercation with Brand had sat ill with him, and he had become so watchful of Paul that though he said nothing, he made it clear he would allow no one, child or adult, to interfere with the lives of his own sons. If Paul could not get along well with them, he would have to go. Gavin was willing now to consider the unthinkable alternatives.

Tessa knew why she was so determined to keep the child. The years were different and the reasons, but still she felt a particular bond with him; his father had sold him to Gavin, and her father had tried to do the same to her.

And finally her waiting for something to happen was over. She had made no attempt to force Paul to go anywhere with the family, nor had she locked him in. The decision to stay or go had to be his own. She suspected he was more than a little fearful of meeting his father again and preferred some time to elapse, perhaps hopeful that the drunk who had sired and sold him would forget his existence entirely. Her greatest fear was that he would do something terribly destructive before he left, such as setting the house on fire. God knew, the Sydney Ducks had had enough to do with hell in the city. She had quietly made sure that Paul was never alone in the house for long.

Everyone was gone, all of them having found excuses to leave her to yet another Sunday, even the children gone off again with Chong Sing. She couldn't blame them; the household had been tense since Paul's arrival.

The house was very still as she worked over the accounts, finishing what she had started on the Sunday that seemed a year rather than a week before. When she heard the noise of the squeaking door hinge and the giving creak of a floorboard, she knew Paul thought himself alone in the house. She closed her eyes for a moment and the ache in her heart was close to physical pain. She stood up wearily and went soundlessly upstairs, avoiding all the stairs that might betray her until she stood outside of hers and Gavin's bedroom. The door was slightly ajar, and she did not need to look inside. She could hear the careful rooting sounds of Paul rifling their belongings.

She grabbed him as he came out the door. He was so frightened, he uttered only one sharp cry and froze, making no attempt to pull away. She took the handkerchief bundle from him and pulled him with her back into the bedroom. She let him go and locked the door.

Paul stood where he was, his head bowed, as she opened the handkerchief on the bed. The emerald collar from Don Esteban and the amethysts from Gavin glittered a fiery rainbow.

"You have very good taste," she said drily, "though I'm relieved to find you aren't very good at thievery yet. These pieces are quite unique. How did you plan to explain having them in your possession? They are hardly the sort of thing a small boy would own."'

She regarded him steadily, hoping the wild pounding of her heart was not audible. It was the only sound in the room to her ears; all else was the deadly silence between them, and a distance far greater than the few feet that separated them. Tessa had the unnerving sensation of facing a very old man in a child's body. She was filled with a wordless prayer that the hard and burdensome shell around him would shatter into a million pieces. If it did not happen now, it never would.

He raised his head the smallest fraction, just enough so he could peer at her through his shielding lashes. She had thrown him off balance, taken away all that had been predictable in his life. She had abused him neither physically nor verbally. The snare of quiet was trapping him as nothing else could.

She saw him clench his small fists, saw the bone-shining knuckles and knew his nails were biting into his palms in a frantic effort to transfer the pain to something he could handle. His whole body shuddered, his face twisted; and still she waited for the full surrender.

The brown eyes were suddenly as wide and young as a fawn's and drenched with tears. Tessa moved swiftly

467

then, gathering him into her arms, feeling him pressing close, desperate for comfort.

"That's right, my little one, let it all go. It's all over. You're safe now." Her own tears closed her throat, and she let her body go on speaking to Paul, hands rubbing his back gently, tousling his hair, the warmth of her flesh telling him he was a child to be loved and protected. When he began to talk, she had one wild instant of struggling against laughter born of sheer relief and real amusement. Of course, he would speak with an accent— she simply hadn't considered it.

"Oh, aye, mum, oye ban't ever be in sech a place afore."

She questioned him gently but firmly, leading him on, wanting him to be free of all of it. Sometimes she had difficulty understanding specific words, but it didn't matter, the pieces fit together, however jaggedly.

He was seven years old. He knew that for certain. There had been a gentle woman, his mother. He still remembered her, as an almost mystical figure of kindness and soft words. Tessa gathered that she had been a seamstress of some sort in London, but more important, she had been able to keep Paul's father more sober and steady than not. Then she had died, and the little boy's hell had begun along with his father's. Drunkenness and thievery, a sure road to the gallows transmuted to deportation probably only because some kind judge had thought of the child, who would surely go to the workhouse because he had no other living relatives. Paul's description of the ocean trip to Australia led Tessa to believe he was surely the only one who had found enjoyment and adventure aboard the stinking ship. The child, despite all, had the spirit to survive and even to be charmed in the midst of darkness.

Australia had not altered his father's habits one jot. In addition, the colony was growing weary of English castoffs and was seeking to establish a more respectable society. California seemed a perfect dumping ground for unwanted rubbish. The authorities in Australia were not too careful of "ticket of leave" men who moved on.

"My dear, I'm so glad you came! How else would Gavin and I have found our other son?"

He looked up at her in wonder, then burrowed closer like a small, nestling animal. Even tear-stained, the beauty of his face startled her. He was all child now, a beautiful, vulnerable child. She bound him closer to them by telling him of Gavin's lost childhood and the death of her own mother long ago. "You see, we're all orphans in one way or another."

He was drugged and drowsy with his release from tension, and his voice rambled, but nothing could dim his quick, observant mind. He was sorry about Brand; he knew Brand didn't like him. But it was almost worse about Jeff, who had gone on being so kind to him, no matter what. He hoped Jeff would still want to be friends. He was afraid of Chong Sing. He thought Gavin must be just like God. He had never had such nice things to eat; he had never slept in such a soft bed. And no one had ever been so kind to him as she and the mister. He hadn't known how to accept that. He had thought he must be dreaming. Maybe he was.

"No, love, no dream. You're home now," Tessa said softly. "Sleep now, you've had a weary day." She set him back on the bed, covered him, and watched as he fell asleep.

When Gavin came home, he saw the excitement and joy in Tessa's face before she said the words to confirm it. "We have a new son," she told him. She felt as if she had in a way given birth to the boy. How strange it was that she had so wanted to have another child this year, and suddenly there had been Paul.

CHAPTER XL

Paul was a changed child. He was eager to please and to learn, and his face wore a look of wonder as if he had just discovered that Christmas was forever. For him, his new life was very much like that. What he had told Tessa was true. He had never had so much food, nor had he ever lived in a place where it was so easy to be clean. And the constant affection offered to him was nourishment to his parched soul, so that Tessa could see him blossoming day by day.

Even Chong Sing warmed to him. As if to make up for his first bad opinion, he was even more insistent that Paul eat and rest properly than he was about the other boys. "Make you stlong like Mista Lamsey, eat, eat," he continually urged.

While Chong Sing politely listened to the boys' attempts to teach him to speak proper English and made absolutely no changes at all in his speech, Paul listened avidly and asked Jefferson for added help. More than once Tessa heard Paul carefully repeating words and phrases to himself, making every effort to rid himself of the accent that made him different and reminded him of the bad times in the past.

Everything would have been perfect had it not been for Brand. The first rebuff had been enough to start it. He could not abide Paul, and nothing Paul did to try to make it better made any difference. Forbidden to fight physically after the first encounter, Brand resorted to emotional violence, which was so effective, both of his parents began to wonder if fists might not be better. He never looked directly at Paul and only spoke to him when he had to, and worse, he teased Jefferson unmercifully for befriending the "duck." Tessa tried to talk to him with no success; he simply denied anything was wrong. Gavin did better, because his temper started to rise, and Brand could not remember his father being really angry with him before. It touched him on the raw, and he blurted out things he had never meant to say.

Gavin's voice was grave when he told Tessa. "I suspected part of it, but I didn't know how deep it went. He was used to being our oldest and Jefferson's older brother. Now he feels that Paul has taken both of those places. And it's more than that, it's jealousy over you."

"Over me!" Tessa looked at him in alarm. "Why?"

"Because he's gotten this strange idea that love is something like bricks or nails or money in the bank; there's only so much and no more. And he thinks a lot of his share is going to Paul now. He says he 'never ever,' to quote him, gets to talk to you or ask you things without Paul around."

470

Tessa wanted to deny it all, but she could see Brand's point. It wouldn't matter if he liked and accepted Paul, but as things were, it did matter a great deal. "I suppose that's true," she said slowly. "With only two it was somehow easy to have time for each of them, but with three it doesn't seem to work that way. I can see I'm going to have to make sure it does. It's strange, but I love Paul so much, I expect everyone else to love him as well, and it gives me a nasty feeling to find that Brand does not. What an unfair choice that is, between my natural-born and my adopted son."

"But it isn't a choice you're ever going to have to make," Gavin assured her gently. "Paul is our son now, and Brand will just have to accept that eventually."

"I love you," she said. For once, the words seemed inadequate, because what she really meant was that she loved his justice. When Paul had been causing trouble for Gavin's natural-born sons, Gavin's grim visage had made it clear that such behavior would not be tolerated for long, and yet now, he could see with equal clarity that Paul was doing his best and Brand his worst for the cause of peace in their home.

Whenever any of the men, including Chong Sing and Jordan, planned an outing for the boys, he took all three to keep things equal, but now Tessa took them carefully in rotation, making sure each child had his own time with her. It didn't solve the basic problem, but it seemed to ease some of the tension between Brand and Paul. It gave her a chance to observe Paul more closely, too, and she looked forward to the day when he would cease glancing around fearfully for his real father the minute he left the house.

Each in his turn, she took them on walks and small errands and made a game of reading shop signs to improve their skill. It took some of Paul's fearful watching away—he could hardly wait to be able to read a book, and studied hard. Brand read so easily, it was a pity he wouldn't help Paul. But Jefferson wasn't far behind him and had endless patience in sharing this knowledge as well as everything else with his new brother.

Tessa did not want to have a favorite child and fought against showing favoritism in any way. But deep inside

471

of her was something that responded with deep flowing joy to Jefferson's sweetness. He was so aware of how others felt and so careful of their feelings. And his thoughtful consideration of everything in his world delighted her. He was quick to observe something new but slow and deliberate in making his decision as to what it meant to him, even as he had been since birth. Whereas Brand and Paul saw things and accepted them more or less at face value, Jefferson wanted to explore the unseen facets. While they never tired of the ships in the bay, the older boys accepted them as simply being there. Not Jefferson; he wanted to know where they had come from, who had built them. How did they know how to find San Francisco, the ones that were left here, would the people who owned them ever come and get them? He never asked questions idly, and Tessa was amused by her own anxious desire to be able to answer him.

She enjoyed the times immensely when it was his turn to go with her, and she was savoring that knowledge and focusing her attention on him as they walked along on a late summer day, she carefully suiting her strides to his short ones. But she was startled when he stopped suddenly and tugged at her hand.

"Oh, my goodness, there's a lady Indian!" he said, his voice squeaking with excitement.

Tessa hadn't the slightest idea of what he was excited about. He had seen Indians before, though not many Indian women. She didn't know he had learned to single them out. When he pointed at the object of his interest, she ordered him to stop it.

"It's rude, Jefferson, it's . . . " her voice trailed away as despite her objection, her eyes followed the direction of his. She stifled a laugh. It was indeed a lady Indian, one who had nothing to do with California Indians. Jeff was being very specific indeed; he had seen the female equivalent of his friend Indian.

Though surely there must be others in California now, Tessa had never seen a Negress before, and there could hardly be many like this one anywhere. The woman was magnificent. Taller than Tessa and more amply endowed, she moved with a lovely flowing dignity. Her mouth was full and well defined; her cheekbones were strong and
472

slanted upward a bit like Indian's; her nostrils flared proudly; and her eyes were large, dark, and slightly elongated, giving the final touch to the exotic face framed by a wrap of bright cloth. She was one of the most beautiful women Tessa had ever seen.

Only when the woman returned Tessa's thoughtful stare, wary and inquiring, did Tessa realize that she herself was being even ruder than her son. She blushed and turned her head away in confusion, wondering what in the world she could do. Go up to the woman and say, "Good day, I'm Tessa Ramsay, and if you're not married, I would like you to meet my friend, Indian." She cringed at the thought, and when she looked back, the woman had disappeared in the crowd.

It didn't matter. She would find her again and discover more about her. Not until now did Tessa know how very much she minded Indian's solitary state, which had deepened with Carmelita's marriage to Sam. He was too beautiful a man to go forever alone. She wanted him to have a woman to love him and to love in return, and children he could spoil as he did her sons. And she knew him well enough to doubt that he would ever take a white woman.

She considered it an outrage that people should make it their business to dictate who should marry whom, but it was a social reality that they did. Things were difficult enough for Indian as they were; life would be intolerable if he took a white wife—if he could even find someone who would marry them. Perhaps after all, he and Carmelita had accepted that when Tessa had not.

But now she had found the perfect solution. She refused to think of it as matchmaking, preferring loftier terms because she knew what Gavin's and Indian's feelings were about the former. Surely there was finer weaving in the pattern than that. After all, Don Esteban had sent Gavin to her, and causing a holocaust came closer to describing the result than matchmaking did. She knew in her bones that this woman and Indian would generate the same force.

Jeff's impatient tug at her hand brought her back to the present, and she sighed. It served her right for her plotting —of all the people she had to have with her today, it

473

would be this child who was so observant and so open he found it nearly impossible to keep a secret. The minute he got home he'd chatter about everything he'd seen, and he'd surely ask Indian if he knew about the lady.

"Jefferson, do you think you can keep the lady Indian a secret for a while?" she asked.

"Why?" He was looking up at her with a puzzled frown.

She wished she could fall back on the parental tyranny of "because I'm asking you to," but she couldn't, not with Jefferson. She took a deep breath and plunged in. "You know how you feel when I ask you to eat something because it's good for you? You usually decide you don't like it even before you've tasted it."

He nodded, amazed that his mother knew that.

"Well, the lady and Indian don't know each other yet, and if we go home and tell Indian about her, he might decide he doesn't like her before he meets her, and I think that would be a pity because they might be good friends someday."

"But Indian eats everything," Jefferson protested, and Tessa nearly choked trying not to laugh.

"That's because he's grown up; he knows what's good for him, and he chooses for himself. He wouldn't like it if I told him to eat this or that." Jeff was much too polite to point out that he didn't like being told either, but she could see the expression on his face.

"You see," she continued desperately, "we're going to play a little trick on Indian, a nice one. We're going to let him think he chose the lady to be his friend all on his own, without any help from us. Please, Jeff? It will make him happy. You mustn't tell anyone else either."

Jefferson paused only for an instant before he nodded vigorously, and Tessa sighed in relief. Jeff would always spot faulty logic in an argument, but you could get around him by appealing to his heart. She bent down to give him a hug and a swift kiss just because she found him to be such a lovely human being, and while Brand would have squirmed in embarrassment and Paul would have blushed to his toes, Jeff kissed her back and said happily, "I love you, Mama."

Tessa had more trouble than her son in keeping the secret. Jeff, having promised, seemed to remove the sight of the woman from his mind, while his mother became more and more obsessed with her. She went back to the wharf area alone again and again, searching among the stalls of the vendors and the stacks of merchandise for another sight of her. She thought of various excuses for introducing herself to the woman, but when she was finally rewarded for her persistence, she was nonplussed. The black woman was with a blond woman and a blond little boy. Tessa studied the trio and came to the obvious conclusion. The black woman was carrying a large wicker basket into which various purchases disappeared; in addition, she was obviously minding the little boy, who was as sadly overdressed as the woman who had to be his mother. She chided herself for her stupidity. There was only the slimmest chance that a black woman could be in California as a free agent. She would most certainly be the wife of a freedman, or a prostitute, or a servant. This one was obviously a servant, though that told Tessa nothing about her marital status.

The woman turned her head suddenly, and there was more than annoyance in her expression as she gazed at Tessa. Tessa gritted her teeth in self-disgust. She was making such a bad job of this. She wasn't any closer to meeting the woman, yet the woman knew she was being stalked, and didn't like it one bit.

The little boy tugged at the woman's skirts, and they moved on, stopping inside a dry-goods shop, which renewed Tessa's hope. She knew the shopkeeper, a gossipy little twist of a man who minded more business than his own.

When the trio emerged and continued on their way, Tessa went into the shop. The proprietor greeted her effusively, not, she knew from any personal liking but because the Ramsay household patronized his store now and then, always paying on the spot, never asking for credit.

Tessa cut his syrup short with firm politeness and asked, "The two women and the little boy who just left, could you tell me who they are, please? I'm sure I've met the woman before, but I can't recall her name. It's most embarrassing. I didn't dare greet her."

"Why, that was Mrs. Carlton Fitz-Williams and her

nigger. They've only been in San Francisco a short while, and betwixt you an' me, that drawl of Mrs. Carlton Fitz-Williams gets thicker by the day. Don't think she's too happy tradin' Mississippi for California." He stopped abruptly, frozen by the look on Tessa's face, and he had the grace to look abashed. "No offense intended, ma'am. I forgot about your friend," he muttered.

"I'm sure you did," she agreed coldly. Thinking of Indian, she had also to think of his quiet tolerance of people's ignorance and bigotry, his insistence that tempers be held unless there was great provocation.

She managed to make her expression more pleasant as she lied about remembering the woman's name now that she'd heard it again, thanked the man for his help, and quit the place.

She should have known Gavin would sense her preoccupation, especially because they were now so conscious of each other in their continuing efforts not to neglect each other. Their quiet Sunday had finally come though it was late now and the rest of the household were home and asleep. They were lying in bed, and Tessa was feeling cat boneless with pleasure as Gavin played with her hair, draping the long tresses across her breasts in patterns that pleased him, changing them, running his fingers softly over her flesh. She was in a state for which she had no single name, enveloped by a warm tide that was more than sexual, a feeling infinitely peaceful of being cherished, another gift from Gavin, appreciated every time she drifted into this wondrous place, a place where in recent weeks she had been much too seldom.

"I can hear you purring," he said lazily. "Would you like to tell me what you're up to?"

She was so comfortably drugged by his touch, it took her a moment to hear the question, and then she started so guiltily, she knew her protestations of innocence were futile even as she made them. "Nothing, nothing at all, Gavin Ramsay, and you're no gentleman to make me feel like this and then pounce. Speaking of cats!"

"Feeling like what?" he asked with feigned puzzlement, his eyes glittering with blue mischief. He knew her so well, he wasn't alarmed, just curious and amused. He, as much as she, was lulled by their closeness. Her odd comings and

476

goings, her neglect of the shop lately, her overly intense response when he surprised her in some reverie, he was sure they pointed to nothing sinister, but rather to some plan she had for which she didn't want to risk ridicule. Had he been paying attention before, he was certain he would have found out about the shipment of palominos too.

"You and Jefferson aren't worth a damn when it comes to keeping secrets," he murmured, and her stricken look told him that Jeff was in some way in on it. "I promise, I won't ask him. I have better things to do," he managed, but his laughter vibrated against her.

"Oh, you!" She meant to scold, but it didn't sound like that at all as his mouth moved downward.

The next day, she sought out Jordan. Despite his northern education and cosmopolitan ways, he usually knew all the doings of the southern part of San Francisco's population.

She found him at his law office. He was in a playful mood, and she bore his flowery nonsense as long as she could before she pleaded, "Please do stop it! I need some information, and I'll never get it at this rate."

He grinned impishly, not in the least offended. "Actually, I'm glad you called a halt; I was running out of clever compliments. Now, how can I help you?"

She asked about the Carlton Fitz-Williamses, and Jordan nodded. "Yes. I've met them. They're from Mississippi. They've only been here for about a month or so, and the lady of the house swears she will never become accustomed to the savage West. She's a perfect example of that special product of the aristocratic South, a will of iron disguised by lace and vapors. Her husband is a retiring sort with generations of money behind him, beginning in the Carolinas before the Revolution. I think the woman is still stunned that her husband made the decision and brought her West. They have one child, a little boy who is in danger of being smothered to death by the doting attention of his parents."

Tessa knew it would never occur to Jordan to mention the servants, so she had to ask outright, "What about the black woman? Does she live with them? Is she married?"

"The slave they brought with them? Of course she lives
477

with them, and since I helped them hire men for the heavy unloading, I don't think she has a husband." He checked for a moment at her expression, and when he continued, his voice was grim. "Look, you know I'm no more fond of the peculiar institution than you are, but it still exists."

"Not here!" she protested.

"No, not officially. But I'd be willing to bet money that the Carlton Fitz-Williamses owned that woman and still do, one way or the other. Of course, they couldn't have brought her into the state as a slave, they would have had to free her, but undoubtedly she is indentured to them in some way, perhaps for the cost of the journey. Why are you so interested in her, anyway? Planning to steal Mrs. Fitz-Williams's help?"

"Something like that." Obviously it did not even occur to him that it might have something to do with Indian.

"Well, I think you'll find it difficult even with your brand of determination. Slave or not, the woman is very definitely an integral part of that family. After all, if I'm correct about her origins, she's probably been with them for all of her life, and even if it is involuntary, that can be habit forming. And now that I've told you everything I know about that subject, can I talk you into lunch?" His mood was light again, and his gray eyes gleamed.

"No, you can't," Tessa laughed as she rose to go. "I think a tête à tête might be dangerous with you today." She spoke only half in jest. Their friendship had grown steadily deeper since the day he had told her about his past, and she was thankful for it, but sometimes she felt a tremor of alarm at the realization of how close she and Jordan had become.

"Ah, well, I shall simply have to bide my time. I'll come by soon to take the boys on an outing. I'm growing as fond of Paul as I am of Brand and Jeff. My compliments on your maternal instinct for seeing what a charmer was hidden under that grime. Take care of yourself."

Tessa decided she had to act before all of San Francisco started buzzing with her interest in the Fitz-Williamses. Indian had been very busy at the warehouse in the past weeks, so she knew her request would be an imposition, but she trusted his kind patience to give her her way.

"Indian, would you be so kind as to accompany me this

478

morning? There's a lovely cabinet I'm interested in, but you know so much more about wood, I'd like your opinion on its quality." It had to be today. The only fairly consistent pattern she had discovered was that the woman, with or without her white family, often visited the shops on Tuesdays and Fridays. It was Friday now, and Tessa couldn't bear to wait until the following week. She saw Gavin opening his mouth to offer to go in Indian's stead, and she held her breath and then blessed him when he changed it to a smooth, "Sorry, Indian, I'd go myself, but I've got business at the Golden Horse." A bright knowing light shone in his eyes.

Indian consented gracefully, though he did point out that knowing about wood and whittling on it didn't make him any expert on furniture. He made no mention of the many other things he had to accomplish this day, and Tessa felt a twinge of guilt for taking advantage of this gentle man, even if it was for his own good.

She simply had to find her. She wanted it so badly, and searched so anxiously, she couldn't help bobbing with excitement.

"This cabinet you lookin' for, it have th' habit runnin' all round by its own self?" Indian asked softly. Tessa looked up at him guiltily, and his grin widened. "You goin' tell me what this 'bout?"

"Nothing, it's nothing except that I can't remember where I saw the cabinet. Maybe it's been sold. Oh, this is embarrassing, to drag you away and then not be able to . . ." her garbled explanation died away as she caught sight of the woman. The woman was alone.

"I think it was this way!" she said, pulling at his arm frantically.

A few more seconds and the woman was going to be swallowed by the crowd again. It wasn't going to be as casual as Tessa had hoped, but it was going to work anyway. She made Indian quicken his pace until they were in danger of knocking down innocent pedestrians, and he was laughing and protesting, "That cabinet run damn fast!"

She glanced sideways, seeing they were abreast of the woman though separated by others. She went a bit further and then cut left abruptly, dragging Indian with her. She

479

glanced out of the corner of her eye, took a deep breath, and pretended to trip on the hem of her dress.

Indian was quick, and he attempted to steady her, but she was strong with purpose. She crashed into the woman, sending the basket flying, hearing the outraged gasp and saw the dawning recognition.

Tessa forestalled her with elaborate apologies. "I'm so terribly sorry, that was so clumsy!" She stopped to gather the contents back into the basket.

Indian wasn't helping her. She glanced up at him. He and the woman were staring at each other, staring as if in a long passage of strangers, each had just recognized an old and dear friend.

Tessa tucked the last spool of thread she had retrieved into the basket along with the packets of chocolate and coffee and managed to stand upright despite her trembling knees. "I think everything's here," she said, offering the basket to the woman. "I'm Tessa Ramsay and this is my friend, Indian. He did his best to prevent such a silly thing, but——"

"But you, Miz Ramsay, was in full sail," the woman drawled, and Tessa felt the blood staining her skin under the knowing look from the dark, exotic eyes. With relief, she saw humor and understanding there too.

"I'se Armenthia." She offered it with pride, the long name probably given to her by her white owners.

It took Tessa a moment to understand what the woman was saying because the deep, slow drawl was alien to her despite that of the Southerners she had met, but Indian had no trouble with it at all. "Pleased t' make your acquaintance, Armenthia," he said, and he made the trite greeting sound completely new.

"I've changed my mind about the cabinet, but there's some silk I'd like to look at, and I don't need your opinion about that. Please, if you would see Armenthia home, it might make up a bit for my nearly oversetting her."

Tessa eased away even as she made the transparent excuse, and though Indian flashed her one distracted glance, obviously feeling he should continue as her escort, he remained where he was.

Tessa beamed all the way home. It had to work, and it would; Indian and Armenthia had gazed at each other
480

as if they had seen the beginning and the end of the world right there. Armenthia, however she had acquired it, it was a beautiful name for a beautiful woman. Tessa laughed aloud, ignored the inquiring looks she got. She was on the point of skipping, as if she were a young girl again instead of a married lady.

Gavin was lying in wait when she got home and took her completely by surprise, picking her up and whirling her around before she could catch her breath. "I've been patient, I have, but no more. Why'd you lure Indian out on that specious errand? I've wasted the whole morning doing nothing but dying of curiosity."

"What will you do if I refuse to tell you?" she teased coyly, nuzzling her head against his shoulder, overwhelmed by the beauty of that rare world where everyone was in love.

"I'll break your ribs," he answered with mocking matter-of-factness, and he gave her a warning squeeze completely belied by the kiss he added before he set her back on her feet. "Tessa, have mercy!"

"Where are the children?"

"Stowed away with Chong Sing as soon as I caught sight of you. If you invoke any other delays, your health will be in danger. You look ready to burst."

"I am! I've found a wife for Indian!" she pronounced triumphantly. Gavin was too stunned to do more than stare at her, so she pressed her advantage and raced through the story, relieved that he managed not to laugh at anything except Jefferson's first description of Armenthia and Tessa's vigorous collision with the basket.

"I presume you're going to let Indian take it from here?" Gavin said, eyebrow going up.

"Of course!" Tessa pretended outrage, but she could sense Gavin's approval, and his next words confirmed it.

"If I had any sense, I'd tell my friend to run, but having experienced wedded bliss for several years now, I fear the warning would lack conviction."

"You're very sweet sometimes," Tessa allowed, curling into his lap as he sat down.

"Just sometimes?" Gavin asked softly, his fingers tracing the hollow of her throat.

"Gavin, the children," she murmured.

"The children are prisoners of your Chinese dragon," he finished for her. "We've already wasted most of the day, or at least I have."

They did not see Indian until late in the afternoon, but one look at his face confirmed what Tessa had hoped. Even Gavin, who had known Indian for so long, was amazed at the change in his friend. The huge man looked ten years younger, his eyes alight, his smile quick and ready. He gave Tessa a gentle hug and said simply, "Thank you, thank you for all my days."

CHAPTER XLI

Indian in love was a new and charming companion. His laughter rang out frequently. He sang snatches of gay songs. Always clean and tidy, now he took special pains with his clothing and had new garments tailored, often asking Tessa for her opinion, wanting things to be just right. He chafed at the days Armenthia's duties kept her from seeing him but rejoiced in the time they did have together.

When Tessa judged that surely the couple knew each other well enough, she suggested a family picnic, asking Indian if he would care to bring Armenthia. He hesitated, and Tessa guessed the reason, but finally he agreed, obviously wanting Armenthia and the Ramsays to be friends.

Tessa suspected it had taken a fair amount of cajoling, but in any case, Armenthia agreed to come and the picnic was arranged, even to hiring extra and gentle horses. Tessa blessed the fall weather for holding so fair and golden, and her spirits rose in delight along with her guilt. The children were so excited about riding out of the city on this adventure, she realized that times when all of them, adults and children, were together at once were far too rare. Gavin looked young and carefree, and even Chong Sing showed his happiness in increased bustle over the food preparations and a haughty lord-of-the-world look once he was mounted on his horse.

It was not difficult to see how much Armenthia wanted to please Indian, for not only was she shy of the Ramsays, but she was also leery of riding. She had done very little of it in her girlhood on the plantation, and then only on a mule. Indian confided this quietly to Tessa. Tessa applauded him silently for being so tender of Armenthia's fear, not asking her to go too fast or risk too much despite his own great skill. There was no question of very hard riding anyway, as Paul was only beginning to feel confident on a horse.

They rode south into the rolling hills, determined to go far enough to be free of the noise and confusion, threading their way through scrubby growth and stands of taller trees.

After the first greetings Armenthia had spoken little, seeming to give all her concentration to managing her horse, gentle as it was, but Tessa caught the furtive, speculative glances she cast at her companions now and then. She wasn't being rude, just very wary and acutely uncomfortable in the presence of Indian's white friends. She was even more beautiful than Tessa had first thought; the sun on the rich brown skin made it look like smooth satin. And she was scarcely older Tessa was sure than she herself. The dignity and self-possession she had witnessed in her previous glimpses of Armenthia were still there, but slightly eclipsed by her vulnerability.

Tessa had an intense desire to know more about her, to know what her life had been like as a slave, to know if she could adjust to Indian's way of life, but her attitude did not invite the probing of such delicate ground.

It was Jefferson who helped ease the tension. Tessa had had the foresight to warn him that their little plan had worked and to congratulate him for being so good about the secret. And he was still being good, having greeted Armenthia with a wide smile and his best manners, but watching him during the ride, Tessa had the distinct impression that his restraint wasn't going to last too long.

She was proud of all three of her sons, Brand and Jefferson both so straight and easy in their saddles and Paul doing his best to copy them. But whereas Brand looked calm and dreamy with his private thoughts and

483

Paul's face was puckered with concentration, Jefferson was positively glowing and spending most of his time stealing glances at Armenthia when normally he would have been pointing out any object that caught his fancy on the trail.

They chose a small, tree-circled clearing for their stopping place and found it even boasted a trickle of a stream and a murky puddle that might once have qualified as a pond before the dry year and still boasted a private host of dragonflies zipping overhead in vivid blue and orange. Tessa felt the soft warmth of the day seeping into every hollow of her body, and she stretched luxuriously as soon as her feet touched the ground, causing Amordoro to look back curiously and nicker softly for his share of comfort. She loosened his girth and then let him rest the hard sculpture of his head against her shoulder while she stroked the velvet of his ears and the close hair of his forehead and watched the picnic preparations.

Chong Sing was in instant motion, determined to establish domestic order here as he did at the house. The boys took the time to secure their mounts and loosen their saddles before they raced off, and in her fond following of their progress, Tessa nearly missed the exchange between Indian and Armenthia, but when she noticed it, her dismayed attention was riveted. She couldn't hear the words, just the low murmur of their voices, but the pantomime of their bodies was too eloquent to need words. Indian's face was miserable with pleading, and he kept shaking his head; Armenthia clearly wanted to go help Chong Sing. Tessa knew Indian was protesting not only because Chong Sing would take an offer of help as an insult to his capabilities, but because Indian did not want Armenthia to take refuge in her familiar role of serving white people.

Tessa didn't know what to do to help, and she stayed where she was, feeling paralyzed. "Trouble?" Gavin asked softly as he came up beside her. She nodded slightly, about to explain when Jefferson came racing back to them. He was already grubby, and his face was flushed and beaming with his exertions. He carried a fistful of dusty yellow flowers.

He stopped in front of his mother first, dividing the
484

flowers carefully into two bunches, handing one to her. "I looked for purple ones to match your eyes, but I couldn't find any," he explained.

She leaned down to kiss him. "These are perfect, Jefferson. Thank you so much!"

"The rest are for Indian's friend," he said, wheeling away.

He held the flowers out to her and struggled to pronounce her name correctly, obviously having practiced it but still not getting it quite right. "Arimenth . . . ah, Airymenthe . . . Thia, these are for you."

The woman looked at him in solemn wonder for a moment, and then she smiled, a wide lovely smile of tenderness and amusement which illuminated her face and made her look happy for the first time this day. "I thanks you, Jefferson Ramsay. Been a long while since anybody brung me flowers. An' I likes de name Thia jus' fine, so you jus' call me dat."

Trust Jefferson to make it right, Tessa thought, her eyes misty as she watched him running off again to rejoin his brothers. When Gavin asked what exactly the trouble was, she replied, "Nothing at all now." And it was true. Armenthia made no further attempt to help Chong Sing, and more, she showed every evidence of enjoying the outing and Indian's company, her earlier reserve gone as if it had never been.

She even chatted with Tessa, though she said little about herself, confining herself to observations on the strangeness of San Francisco and admiration for the Ramsay children. "Deys all good childun, but dat little Jeff, he special fo' gettin' to de heart."

"He is that," Tessa agreed with a laugh, and she thought of how foolishly easy it was to touch a woman's heart by praising her children.

The afternoon was soft and warm, even Chong Sing let down his dignity enough to fall asleep after lunch. The children went off to play again, even the usual disharmony between Brand and Paul lulled by the day. Indian and Armenthia strolled off together arm in arm, and Gavin settled himself comfortably at the base of a tree, Tessa leaning back against him, her head against his shoulder.

"What a perfect day it's been," she sighed, and though she had meant to keep it a secret for a while longer, she found herself telling him.

She felt his body stiffen and then relax with a deliberate effort. "When is it due?" he asked.

She twisted around so that she could see his face. "She's due at the end of March, I think. With three boys, even though I can't really count Paul for my luck, surely this one will be a girl. Please be glad about it, my love."

"I will be glad because you are," he said firmly, kissing her and holding her tightly against him. He thought how foolish he was to have thought he could know her secrets so easily.

She should have remembered that the beauty of fall days was the last ghost of summer, not the beginning of a life season. She thought of that the next morning when she awakened to the heat and then sudden cold of her body, the dull low ache blossoming into a sharp cramp, and then the warmth again, warm and wet between her legs, so warm for death.

"Damn, damn, damn!" she swore, and Gavin was awake, knowing. He had his arms around her before the first sob wrenched through her.

"I'm so sorry, shouldn't have told you. Oh, Gavin, I was so sure it would be all right this time," she moaned.

"*Mi vida,*" he crooned, using the Spanish deliberately. "Only you are my life. You have given me two sons at great cost, and now we have Paul. They are enough. I love you more, fear losing you more than any want I could ever have for another child." He spoke no more than the truth. He knew she still wanted a daughter, and he wouldn't mind having a little girl to spoil, but his response was automatic—when Tessa was pregnant, he was terrified.

At least in this there was no panic; the routine of miscarriage was drearily familiar. He ministered to her tenderly, and when dawn broke weakly through a cold, drizzling rain, Tessa was sleeping exhaustedly while Gavin watched over her, fighting his old nightmare memory of the first baby she had lost.

He told the boys their mother had caught a chill and must rest for a couple of days, but he did not forbid them
486

to see her, hoping that their warm bright reality would help her as it had before. He was rewarded when he heard her laughing because Jefferson had announced plans to build a "tike." Brand hastened to correct him with, "You silly, it's kite, not tike," and Jefferson shot back, "It'll fly anyway, even if I am mixed up." Paul in his continuing role as diplomat suggested they should all build it together and let Chong Sing paint Chinese magic on it when it was finished.

Gavin had told Indian because they had few secrets from him, but when Tessa was up and about again and saw Indian, she knew the sadness in his eyes had been deepened by the Ramsays' loss but had other roots. When he put his arms around her gently, she asked the name in a whisper, "Armenthia?" and felt his whole body stiffen.

"Jus' cain't talk 'bout her right now," he mumbled, and Tessa didn't press him, but finally he did talk.

The children were in bed, and Tessa was downstairs in the main room curled up in her favorite position on Gavin's lap, listening to the comforting beat of his heart under her ear. A fire burned and crackled in the grate, warding off the damp winter chill, and Tessa felt truly content for the first time since the miscarriage. Acceptance was subtly easing out sorrow and turning the thwarted instinct to nurture the unborn toward Gavin and the children. She felt so close to Gavin again. She had so much to be thankful for.

They heard Indian come in, but they stayed where they were, unalarmed. The house was as much his as theirs and he came and went as he pleased. Tessa smiled to herself, imagining the late hour meant he had spent a good evening with Armenthia and had straightened things out. She knew the futility of that hope the minute he burst in on them, not apologizing, startling them both so much that Gavin nearly dumped her off his lap.

Indian's face looked carved of unyielding ebony, and his voice was as hard and sharp, totally unlike him. "Mean more work for you, but I got to go out to th' *rancho,* leavin' first light."

While Gavin stared at his friend, Tessa blurted out, "It's something to do with Armenthia!" She wished she hadn't.

"Yassir, yassir, Armenthia, dat woman's a nigger, an' I

487

don' need no niggers in my life," he snarled in parody of Armenthia's drawl.

They moved like badly managed puppets. Tessa pulled her skirt down and got up with a stiff primness totally alien to her. Gavin spilled the brandy before he managed to pour a glass and hand it to Indian. The ugly word echoed in the silence.

Their utter shock reached him. He put the glass down carefully, and he lowered himself into a chair as if he were a very old man. His hands came up to shield his face, and he wept, his body rocking in misery, his words choked. "I want her like I never want nothin' before, love her like I never know lovin' before. She say fine, ol' Indian, you come courtin' any ol' time for th' rest of your life, but ain't never goin' be more than that, ain't never goin' marry you, be your wife, never. She born slave to white folks an' that's all she goin' be, all she want t' be. That her place an' she like it better'n she like me. She goin' be good nigger mammy to that white chile, ain't never goin' take my seed for her own."

Tessa put her arms around the great shoulders, cradling him as if he were a small child. "I am so dreadfully sorry, so sorry I ever got you involved. It's foolish and dangerous to tamper with people's lives like that!" If only she had listened more carefully to Jordan!

Indian's voice was still muffled, but he was regaining control of himself, and he couldn't bear for Tessa to feel guilty on his account. "Ain't your fault, way I feel 'bout her, jus' know I find her anyway."

Tessa and Gavin knew what he meant. Later, as they clung together fiercely, Gavin said, "Jesus, the poor bastard, to know this exists and not to be able to have it!" His mouth claimed hers in hard demand.

They saw Indian off in a rainy dawn. Trips to Rancho Magnífico had heretofore been cause for excited anticipation and renewal, but this departure was like seeing some one off on a funeral procession. Tessa was thankful that Chong Sing had heard them moving about and insisted on joining them, muttering, "No good big man not eat, velly bad big body."

Not even Indian could resist the humorous comparison of his own great bulk towering over birdlike Chong Sing, and he managed a wry grin and meekly ate the meal prepared for him before he left.

"It can't make things any worse. Good luck." Gavin said as he left for the warehouse and various other points. He had seen her beginning to plot before Indian was even out of sight.

She had to force herself to wait until a decent hour to call on the Fitz-Williamses' household, not even daring to pass the time at the store for fear she would vent her nervous temper on the clerks. She spent far longer than usual over her toilette, choosing a soft blue wool dress with wide sleeves, a fitted waist, full skirt, narrow dark blue trim, and a bonnet to match. Over it all went a closely woven cloak to keep off the rain. She giggled a little at her reflection in the mirror, still so often finding it amusing to see herself dressed in what she considered Yankee style even if it was most often a translation of the French mode. She knew she possessed good taste and that it had become an even finer talent with her experience with her business, but she was always conscious of being a Californio woman masquerading as a Yankee.

But today was different; today she would go dressed to the teeth in the height of fashion, not because Armenthia would care what she wore, but because if Jordan's description of her fit, Mrs. Carlton Fitz-Williams would, and that might help make up for the fact that Tessa was calling without prior introduction or warning.

The woman fit Jordan's picture of her so well, she was like a caricature. She went through all the motions of being gracious though distressed at the advent of this unexpected pleasure—the house simply wasn't in the order it should be, still settling in, the languid drawl went on and on, and Tessa could see beneath it that the woman had taken her measure by her appearance and believed herself to be the recipient of a high society call which was only her due. And the house was in perfect order.

Her features were too small and petulant to be beautiful, but there was a delicate porcelain perfection about her that had its own appeal, a doll to be taken care of. The image was clear and frightening to Tessa. She could see what Jordan had described, the predator lurking beneath the butterfly flutters, but she also saw that his cynicism had

489

given him an easy judgment. Mrs. Carlton Fitz-Williams undoubtedly did have her strengths and her ways of getting what she wanted, but her weakness and her fears were every bit as real, and Tessa was sure they would prove the greater part. She felt treacherous sympathy. The woman had been raised to be the image of that doll, to be protected and coddled; even though she had been uprooted from Mississippi, it was far too late for her to learn self-reliance. And Armenthia must certainly be one of her major props against life.

The tedious welcome seemed to be over. Tessa took a deep breath and spoke quietly. "I am very pleased to meet you. However, I'm here under false colors—actually I would like to speak to Armenthia."

The woman blinked at her, her mouth gaping open unattractively before she closed it enough to sputter, "Armenthia? But whatever could you want with her?"

"Armenthia and I have a mutual friend. I would like to talk to her about him."

The fair skin was rapidly mottling with anger. The drawl was noticeably less. "You must be speaking about that buck she's been seeing. That's all over. Armenthia told me so herself."

Tessa controlled her own temper with difficulty. "Are you forbidding me to speak to her?"

She would never know what the woman would have answered because Armenthia herself was suddenly there. "Dis wone take long, missee," she said calmly. "Little Carlton would jus' love some time wiff his mama. Why don' you go to him an' I brings you tea in jus' a while."

Mrs. Fitz-Williams was obviously only too glad to have Armenthia deal with a situation that was getting out of her control. She produced a handkerchief from her lacy cuff and dabbed pathetically at her mouth as she got up. "I bid you goodday, Mrs. Ramsay," she said icily as she left the room, her skirts rustling with her angry progress.

Nothing could have given Tessa more ample proof of the woman's dependence on Armenthia than this little scene. Her heart sank, but she was more determined than ever on her mission.

"I'se sorry you took all dis time come callin' on my account, Miz Ramsay. Ain't nuffin' to say 'bout Indian an' me. Dat's all over. He gots plans I don't wants no part of."

They stared at each other for a long instant before Tessa spoke. "In the first place, my name is Tessa which you know and by which you called me on the day of our picnic. And in the second place, I cannot believe you can dismiss Indian so easily and so finally. I saw the way you looked at him as well as the way he looked at you. It's not one-sided. Perhaps he has planned too quickly for you, but surely you can forgive him for that; surely you can't bear him to be as unhappy as he is now, unhappy as only you can make him."

She watched with grim amusement as Armenthia struggled to maintain the protection of her subservient demeanor against the force of her rising temper. She nearly crowed aloud when she saw that Armenthia was losing.

"My place here, not wid dat man! I gots dis chile here to care fo' an' de missee, dey needs me an' I belongs to dem!"

"Who are you trying to convince?" Tessa asked coolly. "Yourself or me? You may have belonged to this household in Mississippi. You don't belong to them here. This is a free state. God knows that is true and at great cost! I watched my husband and other men nearly kill themselves to make it so." Her voice lost all semblance of calm. "You would give your life, all the years left, to this simpering woman and her sickly-looking son rather than to Indian? You must be mad! I haven't even seen the man of this house, but he can't be much better than they are. If any of my sons looked like that little boy, I'd fear for him. He needs to be out more; he needs to wear clothes that can bear the dirt; and he needs that very dirt of play, and other children to share it with him. He looks as much like porcelain as his mother does, not human at all. And you help keep them that way! You make them useless by doing everything for them. I grew up with servants too, but none of them would have tolerated such ignorance and helplessness in me. You all should have stayed in Mississippi. San Francisco is a place for people who want to make their own lives. You are a coward, and I am sorry for the day I saw you." Her heart was pounding, and she regretted her loss of control more than a little, but Armenthia's anger was more than a match for hers.

"You wan' t' meddle an' decide fo' me jus' like dey do, ain't no different. But you don' know everythin', you don'. Now I tell you. I jump de broom 'fore, when I 'bout fifteen. I chose de man eben knowin' he not allus de best. Massa not wantin' me wiff dis man, but he let it be 'cuz I wants it. An' de man a debil jus' like everbody 'ceptin' me knows. He damn near kill me, so near I lose de chile I carries. I don' know what I'se gwine do. An' den, de massa sell dat debil man. Nebber no sellin', nebber no breakin' up de famblies by de massa, but dis time fo' me, he sell dat man. An' I hears fo' long dat man died, kilt by 'nother slave whan he feelin' good an' mean. So I'se truly free den, an' I'se truly free now, as free as I wants t' be. Indian change all dat iffin I lets him."

Tessa listened very carefully because Armenthia's English was so difficult for her to understand. Even with her attentiveness, she had trouble with some words and phrases, but she understood more than enough, and she was deeply ashamed of herself. She bowed her head for a moment and swallowed hard before she was able to speak.

"I apologize with all my heart. I saw things in a very simple fashion because I love my friend Indian and I know how much he loves you. I didn't even consider such things as you have told me. I am very blind about Indian because of my love for him. I could not imagine there was any good reason why you could not accept him. Now I see that there are many reasons, and only you know what the right choice is for yourself. Indian is gone now, to Rancho Magnífico. The land is a healing place for all of us, so perhaps his heart will be lighter when he returns. I must tell you, he did not send me here. He would be angry if he knew I had come. But surely you know, he is no devil. He's one of the kindest men I've ever known." She settled her cloak around her shoulders and picked up her reticule. "Good-by, Armenthia. For selfish reasons, I am as sorry for myself as I am for Indian. I had looked forward to our friendship."

Armenthia's face was impassive. Tessa was halfway out the front door before the footsteps and the quick spate of words stopped her. "Miz Ramsay . . . Tessa, iffin dat ol' Indian ain't jus' right when he gets back, iffin mebbe he still lonesome an' not too angry wiff me, you tell him fo' me dat Armenthia'd like fine to see him agin."

There were tears in her dark eyes, and Tessa took her hand. "You won't regret it, I know you won't! Indian's the most forgiving man I know. He'll be here."

CHAPTER XLII

It all seemed to happen so fast, but when Tessa looked back, she could see everything in a long, slow progression which might have been stopped at any one point and had not been.

There were so many good things. Armenthia's invitation to Indian had been accepted by him without hesitation, and Indian was once more joyful. Tessa had no doubt he would persuade Armenthia to marry him within the year. Armenthia had even grown less shy and much more sure of herself in the company of his friends. And there was the house, the plans for which Gavin had given Tessa for Christmas, telling her with a smile that while she could make any changes in the rooms, the basic material would be brick. "It's time, you know. We could use the extra room and so could the children. They haven't much space to get away from each other when they need to."

She knew he was right, and that there was a gift beyond the house itself, the symbol of it, in brick, a sturdy commitment to the city. There was room to build it on this lot without tearing down the frame house. Indian would need his own house soon, and the frame house would do until the day came when he and Armenthia needed a larger one.

Not only did work on the house begin in the new year, but also Belle and Charles returned. "We'll be in business before 1852 is a very old year," Belle vowed happily, and no one doubted her.

There were so many good things, it took the bad longer than it might have to make themselves felt. The rainy season had come again this year, and even with recent

493

improvements, the legends of San Francisco's quagmires proved true. The favorite sign erected by some wag a couple of years before seemed more fact than humor: "This street isn't passable, it's not even jackassable." Tessa could well believe the rumors that some of the mud holes were deep enough to have claimed human and animal victims. The mud and the wet slowed down work on the house, but that was to be expected unless they wanted to wait until spring to build. Far worse was the effect the weather seemed to be having on the children.

Tessa hadn't known before how lucky they had been in the health of the boys. Of course, she had watched them carefully and dosed them faithfully with María's remedies when she saw some illness coming on, and she continued to do both, but nothing seemed to have any effect. She began to wonder if there was some jinx on the number 3. First one child would get sick, then another, and then the third, and scarcely would they all be well, when it would start all over again. They had chills and fever, rashes, deep coughs, and stomach upsets. They had them in various combinations and in various cycles. The only thing Tessa could find to be thankful for was that they had all been vaccinated against smallpox and showed no evidence of getting any of the other plague diseases—cholera, yellow fever, and diphtheria—which were always a danger, especially in a place like the city where so many people lived closely together and sanitation was still primitive at best.

But the complaints they did suffer from were not without their own dangers. Jefferson in particular had an alarming tendency to develop a high temperature when he was ill, and Tessa, knowing the damage that could do, spent frantic nights wrapping him in cold cloths while he babbled in delirium. It tore her heart to see any of them ill, their eyes too bright, their little faces flushed and miserable, and it frayed her temper when they were on the mend and had the energy to bicker among themselves. Chong Sing did his best to help, and she didn't know how she would have coped without him, but she was the one the children needed when they were sick, and in any case, she could concentrate on nothing else when they were.

They might be healthier on the *rancho*, but she would not consider it. To send them there when they were feeling fine and able to enjoy it was one thing; to send them when the land would be as rain shrouded there as here for days on end and they were not feeling well and needed her was quite another. And it was impossible, now more than ever, for her to leave with them.

All their businesses were proving enormously successful; enough so that they could afford not only to build the house, but to buy the site for the lumbermill the men had long wanted and to construct the wharf for receiving the wood to feed the mill from the northern coastal communities with tall timber. But a steady and considerable amount of their profits came from Rancho Magnífico and Rancho Valle del Mar, in addition to the fact that the land provided a living for the many souls who were dear to them beyond the honest and efficient work they gave. And now it was the land that was giving them the greatest problem.

Jordan's dire predictions about the Land Act were proving all too true. At first there had been little they could do except understand it and prepare to fight against it. Tessa even voiced the hope that it would be repealed, as the unjust Foreign Miners' Tax had been, but Jordan grimly denied that possibility.

"There's already another miners' tax in the works though it won't be as high as before. As for the Land Act, too many people stand to gain too much by it. That alone is enough to keep it in effect."

She hated the idea that his cynicism was justified even while she knew it was.

Basically what the Land Act required was that all save the very recent buyers prove their ownership of their lands. It seemed superficially a reasonable proposal; in fact, the proving was beginning to show itself to be an expensive process that could take years. The courts were already bogging down with the land cases, and all the costs for proving their claims were to be paid by the landowners. Gavin, Tessa, and Indian were all agreed that whatever resources it took from their San Francisco ventures would be committed to saving the land. They had a chance, though the fight would surely be bitter, but Tessa could see only too clearly that most *rancheros* who had nothing but the land would surely lose in the end because the land

495

could not be bled forever, the balance between profit and loss being so delicate and varying so year to year, and so much of the profit being the non-negotiable security provided for the people who lived on the *ranchos*.

Even Frémont was appearing as a litigant in court, and it didn't look as if past fame was going to do him any good. He had indeed been one of California's first senators, but only for the short term, the pro-slavery forces defeating him in his bid for reelection, so he and Jessie were developing their land in earnest now. The Ramsays didn't believe his claim to the extended boundaries of his Mariposan property was wholly legitimate; there were still strong suspicions that the lines had expanded and followed the discovery of gold. It was a chilling thought that despite the amount of gold being taken from the Mariposan land, it appeared that nearly all of it was going to be needed to pay the court costs.

"At least we have Jordan working for us," Gavin commented with relief. "His fees continue to be very reasonable. He does hours and hours of extra work without charging us." He paused before he asked diffidently, "I must go to court with him tomorrow. Do you want to go with us?"

She shook her head. "I know what you're thinking, and you're correct. I don't find it easy to hold my temper in all of this. And you are the Yankee, not I, so let it be you who appears to ask that we may keep what is already ours. If I'm needed, I'll go. Otherwise, it's well that one of us concentrates on business. I'm glad Don Esteban didn't live to see this," she added harshly.

Gavin had no easy comfort for her. He agreed with her. The law could not have been better tailored to punish the old Californio landowners.

He spent more and more of his time poring over documents concerning the Land Act. He even had to go with surveyors to both *ranchos*. With so many duties in the city, Tessa could not accompany him, nothing could have seemed odder than to be traveling to these places, to be seeing the people she loved without her. It took him quite a while to ease the look of fear from María's eyes; she was convinced something terrible had happened to Tessa because she was not with Don Gavin.

Tessa shut her mind to the image of these visits and pursued her own tasks. They moved into the new house in the first week of April, while Gavin was still gone. She told herself he would just have been in the way, but she cried herself to sleep from sheer weariness and the loneliness of being in this big, new luxurious house and their familiar bed without him.

Indian saw them drifting further and further apart, and his heart ached because he could do nothing to help them. And his own life was separating from theirs as he and Armenthia drew closer to each other. He had not asked her to marry him again, but he knew he would soon, and he knew this time she would say Yes. He was alone now in the frame house, but not for long.

Tessa even found it increasingly difficult to concentrate on business at the shop. The skirts on women's dresses were growing wider with more and more petticoats underneath and flounces outside, and Molly was worrying about getting the dress she was working on just right. "Mrs. Ramsay, do you think this will suit?" she asked, pinning a flounce in place.

"I don't give a single damn whether it suits or not! Nor do I care if skirts this year are three leagues wide or as narrow as your needle!"

She was instantly sorry and more so because Molly's eyes filled with tears. "Oh, Molly, please don't cry! I didn't mean that! It had nothing to do with you or the dress. It was just everything together."

Molly gulped, nodded in understanding, and her tears ceased, but now Tessa felt like weeping, and only Belle's voice saved her. "Well, I'm relieved to find it wasn't my dress that caused all this after all. Molly, I trust your judgment, otherwise I wouldn't keep impoverishing myself with orders. And Tessa, the least you can do is offer me a cup of tea in the back."

She shepherded Tessa away from the eyes of the clerks, and Tessa went gratefully, still feeling as if she might shatter into a thousand pieces. Never had she been so grateful for the privacy of her office, an alcove screened off from the rest of the storage and work space.

Belle poked at the embers in the little stove and took her time making the tea, giving Tessa a chance to recover before she asked, "Now, my dear, what's wrong since it isn't my dress?" Her voice was easy and kind, but her eyes were worried. The thin, sharp, almost feverish look of her friend formed a terrible contrast with the woman she had first met in Marysville.

Tessa covered her face, but the tears leaked through her fingers. "I'm as bad as Molly," she hiccoughed.

Belle put her arms around her, holding her without regard to the fact that her dress was green satin and tears would surely leave marks. "There, honey, there," she crooned. "Cry it out. Then tell me why if you can."

A glimmer of Tessa's sense of humor surfaced in her realization that Belle must have comforted many weeping women in her time and thus did it very well. It helped her to stop crying, but she couldn't find the words to tell Belle what was wrong. "Everything together," as she had told Molly, was as close as she could come, and the words made her feel ashamed. She had so much to be thankful for.

She pulled away from Belle and made an effort to get a grip on herself. "What a foolish display that was," she said shakily. "I haven't any sympathy for women who suffer attacks of the vapors.'"

Belle remained unappeased. "There's a limit to what any one person can do. And I think you've stretched yourself a mite thin. I know it must be nearly impossible to keep regular hours with three children and everything else you've got going, but couldn't you take just a bit more of each day for yourself? I have two hours a day I consider my own. My girls know better than to bother me, and even Charley respects that time because he knows the more of myself I have, the more I have to give him." She laughed, easing the seriousness: "Not to mention my customers."

But Tessa heard the unspoken comparison—Belle's troubled knowledge that Tessa and Gavin's relationship must surely be suffering with Tessa in this state.

She donned a bright, false smile. "Your advice is sound, and I'll try to follow it." No use in admitting that things seemed to have gotten so frantic and out of control, she could imagine nothing short of a miracle that would provide her with Belle's cherished two hours a day.

Belle sighed inwardly. She had grown very fond of the Ramsays and Indian, particularly of Tessa, who was surely as close a woman friend as she would ever have. She recognized in her her own sense of self and the will to meet life on one's own terms even though the ways they accomplished this were vastly different. To see her friend faltering was to feel herself falter. But she also felt the wall of politeness beginning to encircle Tessa, and she knew she dare not trespass any further.

She was even tempted to abandon the errand that had brought her to the shop today, but then she decided that would be cowardice, and her instinct that Tessa should be warned was still very strong.

"I didn't really come to check on the dress," she began, and her tone of voice caught Tessa's full attention instantly. "All the work you and Molly have done for me has been exquisite; my gowns are the talk of the town, or at least that part of the town which allows itself to notice such things." She knew she was taking too long to get to the point, but the huge lavender eyes watching her so intently made it harder. "I hate to upset you further today, but I think you ought to know that there's a woman who is much too curious about the Ramsays. She's been here for some time, but lately she's been asking an awful lot of questions about you and Gavin. She even came to me directly because she'd heard I knew you. I showed her the door. I disliked her on sight. She has opened a brothel; whatever her pretensions, she will never run a parlor house."

Even with the alarms beginning to scream in her head, Tessa wanted to smile. It was impossible to live in this city and not know the difference. The product was the same, but the price charged for it, the setting, and the social distinction were all quite different. A brothel offered only one thing, with no refinements and strict time keeping. Belle definitely ran a parlor house, a place where entertainment and companionship beyond the basic commodity of sex were offered her clients in a setting rich with lace, crimson velvet, shining wood, crystal, silver, and offerings of the finest food and drink. She had proudly invited Tessa, Gavin, and Indian to come see it the day before her official opening. Tessa had thought that even if it was luxurious

499

and overdone to the point of decadence, still it would surely be a happy place for a lonely man to be, and she had nearly laughed aloud at the uncomfortably aware expressions on the men's faces. She did not think she would laugh now. The full weight crashed down on her.

"Is Soledad still beautiful? I had hoped by now she would be old, fat, and ugly." Her words were flat and calm, and it was Belle who suddenly had trouble keeping her voice steady.

"I'm so sorry! Soledad, yes . . . that's her name. I . . . I didn't know, I wish . . . " Tessa's eyes continued to watch her. "Hell, yes, all right. I don't know how she looked before, but she's beautiful now." She was stopped by her own expertise and Tessa's lack of it. How to explain that the woman was ripe rather than beautiful, that she exuded sex like a constant perfume any man could sense, that every move she made with her round, sleek body was an invitation and so much a part of her she didn't even cease the pose when talking to a woman? Impossible to explain and impossible to admit that she had shown the woman the door not only because she resented the questions about the Ramsays, but because she recognized her as a real threat, the kind of woman she would never employ in her own house. Belle was supremely confident of her own beauty and her attractiveness to men; in her short months in San Francisco she had already become the most admired of her profession, and she knew men considered it an honor to be accepted as a client at her house and a great privilege granted few by the gods of pleasure when she deigned to serve them herself. But confidence did not make her complacent, and she was no fool. The girls who worked for her made good money and had a certain loyalty both to her and the other girls beyond their basic self-interest. Even in their short encounter, she had recognized the absence of all of these qualities in Soledad. Soledad was dangerous, most dangerous of all because she did not even possess loyalty to herself. What she desired, she would take, even at the risk of losing herself.

Belle had hoped against all reason that the woman's inquisitiveness about the Ramsays had no personal basis and stemmed only from the profession's policy of knowing the territory, rich men always being preferable to poor.

But Tessa's knowledge of Soledad had banished all hope of that. "I wish I'd never mentioned the wretched woman," she said fervently.

"No, you were right to warn me. Once, years ago, I nearly killed myself because of her. This time, perhaps I'll kill her instead." There was obviously going to be no further explanation.

Belle shivered inwardly at the icy words, but she made one more attempt to help Tessa. "Perhaps there is no need for any of this. Just because she's been asking questions doesn't mean that you or Gavin ever need see her or be troubled by her."

"Perhaps. And perhaps the moon will fall into the Bay and drown some night." The thin, knowing smile was the worst of all. Belle wanted to shake her and order her never, ever to show this face to Gavin—so exquisite, so perfect in every feature, and so cold, so haughty that the warmest man would lose his fire before it. But there was nothing she dared say.

She wondered where Charley was right at this minute. She had a sudden overwhelming desire to nestle into his arms, to feel his silky moustache tickling her cheek, her mouth before he kissed her. She could hardly wait to find him, and she hoped he wasn't involved in some high stake game. She was more glad than ever that she and Charley were not married and had no children; it seemed those encumbrances made it so difficult for love to survive.

Tessa roused herself enough to feel Belle's distress as she said her halting good-by.

"Give my best to Charles. And my friend, do not let my troubles become yours. I thank you for your care, but I don't want you to dread our visits together. May the next day we meet be more pleasant." She kept her smile in place even after Belle had left, and Molly and the other clerks were relieved to see it, none guessing that she was conscious of little else except the name screaming in her head.

She didn't know what to do. She felt like an animal at bay, back against stone and no place to run. It was terrifying that the image of Soledad still had so much power to hurt, and worse that Soledad was obviously still interested in Gavin. Tessa knew she would have been better able to handle it if relations between herself and Gavin were easier, but the demands and tensions of their separate tasks seemed to increase rather than lessen. Sometimes she felt that the distance between them was so thinly spanned, the weight of one untoward thought would break the bridge.

Her first impulse, to simply ask him if he knew Soledad was here, was quickly gone. If he knew and had not told her, she would feel that much worse. If he did not know, her question would tell him and perhaps tempt him.

She tried to convince herself that with so much living and three children between them, Soledad no longer had the power to threaten her. But she did not believe it.

It colored everything, and she was powerless against it. She found herself judging herself and Gavin with a merciless eye. The joint birthday this year, before she had known of Soledad's presence—Gavin just back from his travels and very weary, she as tired from nursing the children through their last lingering winter ailments, besides seeing to business. Only Indian and Armenthia had been happy and without shadows, doing their best to participate in the festivities but finding it difficult to concentrate on anything except each other. Tessa remembered only too clearly that she and Gavin had gone to bed and to sleep, and nothing more.

Had Gavin known about Soledad then? Had he seen her? Had he? Was he? She knew how madly destructive it was to be thinking such things, but she couldn't stop. And though part of her desired him as much as ever physically and sorrowed because they made love so seldom these days, there was another part of her, a new and frightening part, that was too drained to want to be touched at all. She was so terrified of that, she went out of her way to wear the sheerest nightgown, easy to untie and slip out of in seconds, made to entice even more than bare skin; she made sure her hair was always brushed to gleaming and her skin clean and sweet scented; she did everything a good whore would do to please a customer, and she felt very little more than a whore must feel for the stranger in her bed. She pretended pleasure when she felt none. She wanted so much to tell Gavin how she felt, but she could not. Her body's response to his had been the
502

surest thing in her life since she had met him, and to have lost it was devastating.

And finally she did what she had never considered possible; she refused him.

He had come in late when she had already been long abed. Normally he would not have disturbed her, but this night he reached for her, his body urgent, his voice a murmured plea. "Tessa, please, wake up. I need you, my love. Please."

"Leave me alone. I am very tired." Her words were unyielding, separate stones, and she moved so far away from him, she was balancing precariously on the edge of the wide bed. Gavin reached out to touch her in a gesture she didn't see, and then he drew back.

He got up, dressed again, and left the room without another word. Tessa jammed her knuckles against her teeth to keep from crying out. It was almost a relief that the blow had finally fallen. She knew she was not mistaken; though faint, the scent of Soledad had come to her clearly from Gavin. It was a perfume as unique to the woman as was her own delicate one to herself. She had never smelled it on any other woman, and she remembered only too clearly the first time it had choked her with its message. She heard Gavin come back to the house just at dawn, but he did not come into their bedroom, and he had left again by the time she came downstairs. She smiled at the children, chatted with them and Chong Sing, and pounced on Indian as he left his own house for work.

"Have you seen that woman Soledad too?" she asked, surprising him so much that the answer was written plainly on his face before he could prevent it.

He nodded miserably. "Yeah, I seen her couple times. She come 'round pesterin' Gavin, but he tell her plain he don' want nothin' she got."

"Well, that's a relief!" Tessa lied. "You needn't tell him I asked you about it. That would only trouble him more. He'll just have to handle this his own way."

Indian tried to accept her words because he so much wanted them to be true. He was so happy with Armenthia these days, he wanted everyone else to be happy also. He didn't even want to think of the time before when Soledad had caused so much havoc, and he assured himself that certainly Tessa and Gavin had both grown up and had shared so much since then, it couldn't happen again. He did not believe his own arguments. And he could think of nothing to do that wouldn't make things worse.

Tessa went along to the shop as if nothing had happened, and she mocked herself for so fast developing a talent for subterfuge. She performed her tasks by rote, her mind wholly concentrated on Gavin. She had sent him away last night without asking him a single question or giving him any chance at all to explain because she wanted neither the lie nor the truth from him. And now she had to live with that and the knowledge that he had seen Soledad several times and had said nothing to her about it. She tried to think of it fairly. He was, after all, a separate human being. He had no obligation to tell her if it did not involve her, particularly since he knew the news would upset her. But it did involve her now. She could not be detached and just about it. The remembered scent was ugly in her nostrils. She could not share her bed with another woman. She wished there was a way she could kill Soledad, just as she had told Belle, without being punished for it. But even as she thought of it, she knew that Soledad had only triumphed because there were already problems in the marriage, even as she had gained by their troubles before.

"You've certainly gotten what you deserve," she told herself grimly. "You were the one who wanted to stay in San Francisco when Gavin would have moved back to the safety of the land."

She didn't know what she would do. That was the part her brain seemed incapable of dealing with. The idea of seducing Gavin back, away from his whore, filled her with self-loathing. Nor had she any desire to run away this time, conceding defeat. She thought of Jordan, and even as she whispered, "Oh, no, I couldn't!" a stronger voice inside said Yes.

Gavin had been completely stunned by Tessa's behavior, and his anger was nothing to his hurt. He hurt in so many ways that even his body felt as if it had gotten the worst of a fight. He had known as well as she that things were strained between them, but not like this. He had needed the reassurance of loving her physically, and her rejection of him had been absolute, as if his body and the very idea of making love with him was disgusting.

He realized long afterward that if he had not had just enough guilt gnawing at him, he would have asked Tessa what the hell was wrong.

He had been stunned and immediately uneasy when Soledad had first appeared at the warehouse. He had certainly never wanted to see her again, and her pose of simply coming to say hello to old friends was transparent. But his rudeness had not deterred her, because she had seen his response to her, despite his attempt to conceal it.

That was the source of his guilt. He would have gladly killed the woman once, and he would never forgive her or himself for the damage they had caused. And yet, still his manhood responded to her. She was not beautiful in the way Tessa was. And her age showed in new tiny lines around her eyes and mouth. It made no difference. Soledad was pure sex, more so than any other woman Gavin had ever known. She was a bitch in perpetual heat—he used all the foul images he could find, but none of them cooled the fire that rose in his loins every time he saw her.

She had come to see him again today, late in the afternoon, eyes sparkling wickedly as she asked him specious questions about the city and pretended to be much in need of his advice. Her smile showed openly when Indian stomped away in disgust. She had no more use for him than he had for her.

And suddenly she had pressed close to Gavin, putting her arms around him, and laughing when he pushed her away. "You are not ready yet, but we have time. You will come to me when you have need of a real woman. That haughty stick you married, does she look more like a woman now?"

"Keep your foul tongue off my wife and get out!" he had snarled. Even his anger had pleased Soledad, though she had risked no more and left.

Gavin had worked late to calm down, and then he had gone home, his need for the reassurance of Tessa's love growing with each pace nearer until it had been a fierce ache. And she had rejected him. He had no idea that

Soledad's scent clung to him, no idea that Tessa knew she was in the city.

He had left the house blindly and walked the distance to the Plaza. He had spent an hour in the Golden Horse, Mr. Peniston and the others quickly leaving him alone when they saw his mood. And then he had decided the draught was bitter in any case and might as well have cause.

He went to Soledad's house, and if she had been entertaining another man, he had been quickly gotten rid of. Her words and her body said she had been waiting only for Gavin. Her girls were ordered not to disturb them for anything before morning.

Gavin took her roughly, without any pretense of love or tenderness, wanting to punish her and himself. Soledad was well pleased.

CHAPTER XLIII

Their marriage moved into a strange twilight state that made Tessa suspect they had both gone slightly mad. They made no pretense that everything was well between them. They hardly looked at each other, and confined their speech to necessities. And without any discussion at all, Gavin moved most of his belongings into the guest room down the hall from their bedroom. In the old frame house there would have been no space for this, but in the new brick house, there was plenty of room. Gavin spent little time at home in any case. The business of their lives provided perfect shelter for both of them without either making any special effort. The separateness that Tessa had once fought against was now a welcome retreat that fooled most people except Chong Sing and Indian, who each in his way tried to ignore the disastrous change as long as he could. And they both found they had to continue to ignore it because neither of the Ramsays were in any mood for sympathy or advice. Indian spent more and more time
506

with Armenthia, preferring even the risk of encounters with Mrs. Fitz-Williams (whose initial antagonism to him remained but was now cloaked by coy resignation and comments about "stealin' our little Armenthia away") to the atmosphere at the Ramsay house. He dropped by and shared meals as seldom as possible now. Chong Sing went to visit his Chinese friends more often, but his chief concern was not for himself, but for the children. He was uncharacteristically short with Tessa, who seemed just not to be there any more, even when she smiled and spoke. Finally he forsook his caution and confronted her.

"Summa almos heah. I take children out to land. Good for dem. Betta dan dis place now. Children velly wise, see too much an' be sad."

The naked honesty of her grief showed in her eyes for an instant and was gone. "I think that's a very good idea," she agreed quietly. "And I'm sure Gavin will consent."

Gavin did, having no more choice than she, knowing it was only fair to get the innocents away from the battle-field, though when they discussed it, they spoke only of the healthy benefits of summer on the *rancho*.

Tessa realized that Chong Sing's plan had come just in time. Jefferson was already beginning to look troubled whenever he saw his parents together though he had as yet not said anything openly about it. She diverted his attention by speaking at length with him about how much she trusted him to make Paul feel happy at the *rancho*. And with Jefferson's enthusiastic descriptions and Tessa's reassurances, Paul's pinched look of fear eased. Though he could not admit it to anyone, not even to Tessa whom he adored, he had thought at first that perhaps they were planning to take him somewhere and leave him there without the comfort of this family, which he still found miraculous, even while he sensed something was wrong between his adoptive parents.

Indian volunteered to escort the party again, this time having his own special reason—he was going to take Armenthia with him.

"How are you going to manage that with the Fitz-Williams woman?" Tessa asked.

"Oh, I got her tamed 'cuz she know I ain't too fond of

507

Armenthia workin' for her anyways, an' she afraid I take her away for good sooner than later. Ain't even makin' any more noise 'bout bonds t' pay now I got th' means."

"I'm glad someone is winning," Tessa said, but when Indian would have spoken further, she shook her head in a small gesture of denial. "*Vaya con Dios,* Indian. That is all there is to say. My sons are always safe in your care."

And this time when she kissed each of the children good-by and saw them off, she did not weep. She stood very still, a little apart from Gavin, but when the caravan had disappeared from sight and he turned to speak to her, he found she had already quietly gone inside. He felt that a vital chance between them had been refused by her, even as she had refused him that night. He went off wearily to check progress at the lumbermill and the wharf, wondering if he would ever again feel the joy of accomplishment that used to come to him from new ventures.

Tessa had not been aware of Gavin's feelings at all as she watched the children ride away, Brand proudly riding alone this time so that Paul could have the comfort of sharing the saddle with Indian. The thought had taken hold suddenly, and possessed her—she was free. It was not a state she would have chosen or wanted now, but it was true. She did not even question the idea that Gavin would be with his whore most nights. The house would be empty, as intolerably empty as her bed had been these many nights.

She left the house after dusk. There was little chance Gavin would know she was missing even if he did return to the house. He had not once tried the bedroom door. If he had, he would have found it unlocked, though Tessa herself could not explain why she left it so.

Her face was deeply shadowed by her hood, and she had the derringer ready, but no one impeded her progress.

She climbed the outside steps which gave access to clients who had business at the law office and not the storage space which occupied the ground floor. Her knock was timid, but Jordan heard it and opened the door, flooding her face with light from inside. "My dear, what's wrong?" he asked involuntarily, unable to credit that she was standing on his doorstep at this time of night.

She answered with a question of her own, asking if he were alone and then blushing deeply, her eyes wide and frightened. She had suddenly considered the embarrassment she might cause him, and she felt like fleeing down the stairs and away.

"I'm quite alone," he said as he put his arm around her and drew her inside. He could see her panic, could feel it in the tremors running through her body. His voice was warm and gentle, and he blessed the training of his profession that allowed him to maintain a calm façade no matter how he felt. Inside him there was no quiet at all. He forced himself to be ready to accept the fact that she had probably come because Gavin or Chong Sing or Indian was in some kind of trouble. But he did not really believe it. She didn't appear to be in a fighting mood; in fact, he had never seen her look so vulnerable.

He led her through the little anteroom into the room that served as both office and living space. It was cheerful with lamp light and the glow of fire in a potbellied stove that served to ward off the sea damp chill that still came with darkness even at summer's beginning. There were books everywhere and comfortable places to sit, but he led her to one of the chairs arranged in front of his ample desk.

It is like a very strange dance without music, she thought as he took her cloak, heavy with the weight of the derringer in one pocket, and held the chair for her. But there were sounds, the bell of struck crystal and the gurgle of liquid poured from a small necked decanter. She did not look around to watch him. *His bedchamber is right through that door,* she thought. *I have seen this room before, though I did not notice until now how comfortable and comforting he had made it for people in trouble, for his own moments of needing peace. But I have never seen the bedchamber.*

He broke the silence of words as he came back to her, offering her a glass of amber liquid. "Sherry, so much more soothing to the nerves than brandy." He raised his own glass to her. "To you, Tess. May the trouble that brings you here be less than the shadows in your eyes." He seated himself in his chair behind the desk, allowing her the added security of that barrier between them, but

509

finally she had recognized the depth behind his steady voice; she had heard his deliberate use of "Tess," so small a difference, but not the name anyone else ever called her.

She put her glass down carefully and laced her fingers together tightly. "Jordan, do you mean it, have you always meant it?" she asked desperately, her body still braced for his denial.

He did not hesitate nor question her. He went to her, drew her up into his arms, and held her tightly against him before he cupped her face in his hands and kissed her, his warm insistence taking her by surprise even though her own journey had brought her to this.

"Don't tell me why you have come to me," he commanded, his voice no longer calm. "It is enough that you are here at last."

She lost all sense of time: she lost all sense of everything but Jordan's love pouring over her, first in words, soft spinning the web of his desire, the tale of his own enchantment with no need to condemn or even mention the absent Gavin, then in the first delicate testing of her by touch, his hands still asking the question gently, still ready to let her go if she wished escape, until her own answer was so strong that escape was no longer possible for either of them.

Without knowing quite how she had gotten there, she was in the bedchamber, the room she had never seen and did not see now, and Jordan's hands began to rove her body feverishly. But there was expertise in his touch, and a small separate part of her mind was cynically amused by it. He was deft at removing her clothes and his own. This was most assuredly no virgin she had come to seduce. Her guilt eased. Jordan had wanted this from the first day and now she wanted it, needed it too.

"Oh, my God, you are even more beautiful than I imagined!" The words were wrung from him, the depth of his perception of her sounding in every syllable.

She felt her hair tumbling down her back as he removed the pins; she trembled as his hands ran down the line from rib cage to hips, circled back to etch her neck and shoulders, cupping her breasts as he kissed her again, stealing downward to find her warm female promise.

510

The bed was soft beneath her. She felt a moment's panic and revulsion. This wasn't Gavin looming over her; it wasn't Gavin's hard flesh probing for entry. Her body froze, closing, drying the easy way. But Jordan knew even as it happened and his hands were magic, his murmured words reassurance, his mouth a caress as deep as the wound of Gavin's return to Soledad.

She had not been so aware of what the act of love entailed for years. Gavin's body fitting against her own, into her own—it had become so familiar, she had ceased to know. Now it was new and strange again with all the nuances to be learned, the questions being asked and answered without words, to move this way or that, to shift a leg and turn a little, to meet the new rhythm, does this please, or this? Like Gavin in lean strength, yet not like him at all, Jordan's body so unscarred, the curve of waist to hip so different, the texture of his hair so alien she could feel the sunlit color, the opposite of the midnight black, his scent clean and urgent but not Gavin's. Not Gavin's coldness either, or the scent of Soledad on his skin. Jordan's body worshipping hers even in the act of taking, Jordan's love pounding in the heavy beat of his heart, sounding in the sweetness of his endearments, Jordan's love shining over her until she was floating in a sea of light after the long darkness. Her body blossomed suddenly, petals opening outward to welcome him in, nerves so attuned to his long sleek thrust that the ripples of sensation spread and consumed all else. She was no longer Tessa or Gavin's wife or the children's mother, nothing beyond this woman filled with power, filled with love, flesh of Jordan's flesh.

It was no longer fully dark outside when she opened her eyes to Jordan's gray ones, the gold flecks shining in the lamplight. "I must leave now," she said with soft regret.

He held her down for a moment. "I will only say this once. Whatever you want, I will abide by it. I will take you and the children away with me or I will stay here and endure the knowledge that you live in another man's house. Whatever. I love you, Tess. I will love you until I die."

"Jordan, what have I done to you?" she whispered,

suddenly fearful of the intensity of his love which had so pleased her earlier.

"You have made me happier than I have ever been," he answered smiling. "But this is dangerous for you. We must find ways to make it safer."

"It won't be dangerous for me at all, not for many days," she corrected him firmly. "The children have gone to Rancho Magnífico for the summer and Chong Sing with them. Only Indian will be returning in a fortnight and to his own house. I must be careful of him because I would not hurt him." She paused only for a brief moment before she went on and her voice was very strong. "You don't want to know, but you must. Gavin has gone back to a woman he loved before he ever saw me." Even though she had no compunction about calling Soledad a whore and thinking of her as such, she had no doubt that Gavin loved her, despite what he had told her long ago. "He won't know whether I'm in our house or not. We no longer share a bed or anything else. It's not very dangerous to me as long as I am careful."

Jordan knew then that he was lost. Some last dream in him had hoped she had come to him only because of himself. He knew the truth was not the truth she saw. He had seen the Ramsays together too many times. Whatever Gavin was doing with another woman, it was not for love of her. He damned the logic of his mind, which insisted on the correlation—whatever Tessa was doing here with him, it was not for the love of him. He doubted she herself knew that. But not once had she said, "I love you, Jordan." Not once, even though he knew he had brought her great pleasure. He heard the voice from the past, Tilly, Martin's mother. "Massa Jordan, ain't nuffin ever quite likes we wants it, jus' gotta make do wiff what we gets." She had told him that for some childish disappointment and held him close to her warmth to belie the harsh reality, but she had lived by the words, going on, he knew, just as before after Martin's death, only her eyes betraying her grief. She had been harder to leave than his blood kin.

He heard the worried asking of his name. "It's all right, Tess. For whatever reason you have come to me, I love you." He had no guilt about Gavin, even though the
512

man was his friend and client—any man who was so foolish as to let this happen deserved the loss.

She got up, and he helped her dress, even that a new erotic ritual for them. But when his lips touched the nape of her neck, she shivered and turned quickly to face him, her thoughts an ironic parallel to his. "My only regret is that surely I have made it impossible for you to deal with my husband any longer, and you have had not only business but friendship between you." She buried her face in her hands. "What a fool I've been in my selfishness! I've only thought of that now. And it affects Indian too!"

He captured her hands with one of his own and tilted her head up with the other so that she could not look away. "This affects no one except you and me. God help me, my darling, but I can be as two-faced as any man. Neither Gavin nor Indian will know anything from me."

She knew it was wrong that she should be the cause of such duplicity in a good man, but she rested her head against him for a moment in a gesture of submission, and for the first time in a great while she gave the burden of herself into another's keeping.

But when he would have escorted her home, she gainsaid him. "Even when there is magic, there must be a little sense." She showed him the derringer. "I know how to use it. I'll be perfectly safe." She reached up to kiss him. "Thank you, Jordan. Unless you tell me otherwise, I will come again as soon as I can."

"I will never tell you otherwise."

She drifted home in the blue gray chill of morning as safe as she had promised Jordan she would be. But she did go very carefully once she was near the house. She could imagine what a hideously ludicrous scene it would be if she and Gavin met at the front door after their night rambles. And her basic instinct warned her that while he might no longer be interested in their marriage, he probably still considered her his wife, his property. She had no doubt that he was capable of killing her if he were angry enough.

Now we are really enemies, she thought, *and I am planning everything I do as if it were a battle.* She knew this was a tragedy beyond any other in her life, but it did not still the warm joy coursing through her. Jordan had re-

513

stored her pride in herself as a woman, had eased the terrible hard coldness that had begun to possess her. Desire had filled her again, and she had pleased him even as he had pleased her. She refused to consider what the future would do to them. Each day in its turn was enough.

The night had been long, but she felt no fatigue. She felt young and quick again. And she barely restrained herself from singing aloud until she was sure the house was empty.

Gavin heard her singing as he came in the door, and he froze at the sound, the gay notes making him want to shout at her to stop. He hadn't spent the night with Soledad. He had spent hours at the Golden Horse and hours more simply walking the streets and thinking. He had steeled himself to have it out with Tessa, to ask if there was not some way for them to put the shattered pieces back together again, especially now that they had their world to themselves for a while. Soledad was as poisonous and unfulfilling a drug as she had ever been and no answer to his pain over Tessa. She filled his body with sensation and left his mind and spirit as empty and desolate as she had in the beginning.

He went wearily up to the guest room to change and make himself presentable for the day, pausing only briefly outside the bedroom door. Tessa was singing in Spanish now, a love ballad. He shivered.

She found she was ravenously hungry and remembered she had had nothing to eat since the previous morning. She was making herself an ample breakfast when she heard Gavin come down the stairs. *My God!* she thought, *that was close, he must have come in minutes after I did!* Her heart was still beating jaggedly but her face was carefully composed, her eyes blank when he appeared. She offered him breakfast and smiled as politely as if he were a boarder in her charge.

"Thank you, I would appreciate that," he managed, but then his control slipped, making his voice uneven. "I'm sorry, I'm so accustomed to the house being full of people, I didn't think of its being empty last night. You should not have been left alone."

"I didn't know I was. I assumed you had just come in late," she lied. "So you see, in my ignorance I was quite

514

safe and will continue to be. Here I have not only the derringer but my rifle also."

She could not bring herself to look at him while she spoke. A glance had been enough for her to see how haggard he looked, and she fought against the pull at her heart by thinking that Soledad must surely be a demanding lover. And she considered the frustrating knowledge that now she must wait at least until the following night to return to Jordan. It would be the worse irony if enough of Gavin's sense of duty toward her remained to hamper her freedom.

Gavin's hopelessness increased. Her voice betrayed not the slightest shade of anger or interest. And she looked so much younger, more beautiful and happier than she had in months. He could think of nothing except that she was obviously *relieved* to be free of him and the obligations of their marriage.

He did not know what to do about it. It had been an even longer and more difficult winter for her than for him, because of the children's illnesses. He realized that now. It was no wonder she was glad to be free of all responsibility except the shop for a while, no wonder she looked better than she had. Free for a while, though he did not even want to consider that it might be longer than that; he was afraid to press her now because he did not know what he would do if she told him she wanted it this way forever. He prayed he had enough strength and patience to wait this out. It did not even occur to him that she might have taken a lover.

Nor did it occur to Tessa that Gavin loved her as he would never love Soledad. She mistook his patience for indifference, and she put her will to continuing the affair with Jordan as fiercely as she had to anything in her life.

For two nights Gavin was home too early for Tessa to get away, but she grew bolder when she realized that he was spending a lot of the day at the lumbermill, making sure it would be in working order soon, and he was tired enough to sleep deeply. Poor Soledad, she thought with grim satisfaction. She listened carefully and not once did she hear him stir from his room, and she knew she could slip out of the house without him hearing her. She admitted to herself that the danger of discovery added much

515

to the spice of the game, so that often when she reached the sanctuary of Jordan's room, her body was already flushed and humming with excitement. It was easier when the hour grew late and Gavin was not yet home, for then she simply closed the bedroom door and left the house as she had the first time.

Jordan had not sought her out in the two days. He had waited, scarcely daring to hope, unable to think of anything but Tessa. But when she came to him again on the third night, he knew the first had only been the beginning, and he welcomed her with a full heart, his only regret being that there seemed no way to prevent the risks from being so much more hers than his.

Now the strange dance had its own music, his voice joining hers or deep and sure singing songs she had never heard before in the various languages he knew. Now that the first desperate need no longer possessed them, their love became many faceted. Jordan made love to her not only with his body but with his mind and heart, and Tessa felt infinitely cherished. His mind was princely in its riches, and he opened it to her as never before, presenting her with endless treasures, poems he particularly liked, bits of philosophy and humor from the ages, discussions of books they had both read over the years and tantalizing glimpses of many she had yet to read.

It was impossible for her to avoid the comparison of Jordan's mind with Gavin's. Gavin was well educated and well traveled, but he had so long been concentrated on survival and practical considerations of life, he had had little time to develop a sense of whimsy as deep as Jordan's, little time to spend pitting various ideas against each other for the sheer joy of it.

Despite the fact that he already had all she could give him, Jordan courted her. In the ugly pursuit by Luis and the close escape into Gavin's arms, there had been nothing like this. Having no kitchen or cook, Jordan lived like most San Francisco bachelors, eating his meals out except for scattered times of cheese, bread, and tinned food. But often Tessa arrived at Jordan's to find a lovely cold supper from a fine restaurant awaiting her with champagne to wash it down, and she felt a sad well of tenderness when she realized that he had undoubtedly gone to the same trouble when she had been unable to come to him. And there were almost always fresh flowers in the bedchamber with a love note, sometimes teasingly written in German so she would have to ask him to translate it, which he gladly did as he held her. She giggled as she opened one slip of paper and beheld the exquisite calligraphy. "I know that's Chinese, and I'm sure you don't speak or write it, as talented as you are!"

"You doubt me, ma'am?" he said with pretended hurt, and then he joined her laughter. "I got a scribe, or whatever the Chinese call them, to do this for me. For all I know, it says, 'Go away, crazy man, and may all the fleas of San Francisco follow you.' I think there are enough characters there for that. But what it is supposed to say is, 'Flower of my life, I would stay forever in the night garden with you.'" He quoted it without embarrassment, his voice suddenly low and as gentle as the touch of his fingers tracing the shape of her face he already knew so well.

The scent of roses will mean Jordan forever to me now, she thought, and she would not let herself admit the image of Chong Sing's doleful eyes conjured by the brush strokes.

But Jordan heard the fresh and fearful urgency in her words, "Hold me, my darling, hold me tightly! You alone are the garden," and he did as she asked, his love for her coursing through him. "Darling" now, "my dear," and still he knew the lack; never "my love" or "I love you"—those words given by her forever to another man.

With Indian due back to complicate things further any day now that nearly three weeks had elapsed, and with too many nights proving impossible for Tessa's escape from the house, she and Jordan grew even bolder, the danger of discovery paling before their need. But it was Jordan who took the first step in daylight, coming to the shop, greeting Tessa casually and proceeding to tell her he needed assistance in buying a special gift. His eyes gleamed more golden than gray with as much mischief as warning, and Tessa swallowed hard and found her voice.

"Have you anything particular in mind?"

"Yes, very particular indeed." His eyes left her face to roam the store and settled on one of the garments displayed as a sample. It was one of the most rare and expensive items in the store, a robe of the finest velvet trimmed in fur, the material, even the fur, imported from Europe. Though floor length and long-sleeved, it was anything but demure, the neckline being cut in a low deep V to expose the cleavage of the breasts between two borders of rich fur, and the total effect of fur and velvet designed to delight a man's touch before he claimed the satin of the skin beneath.

Jordan eyed it critically. "It's lovely, but it's the wrong color for my friend. Have you other choices?"

Tessa could control everything but the blush rising hot on her cheeks. The robe displayed was deep green with brown fur, not her colors at all; the only other was royal purple with the silk of sable borders, perfect for her but something she would admire and never consider for herself. "Yes, we have one other. But truly, there must be something else that would do as well for a gift. The robes are unique, and very expensive."

He shook his head decisively. "Nothing else will do. May I see the other one?"

Molly brought the other robe before Tessa could do anything about it.

Jordan smiled in satisfaction. "That is quite perfect. I will take it with me, if you please."

Tessa made one last attempt. "It might not fit her. Perhaps you should send her in so we can make sure." Hardly likely, since the robe had been fitted to her.

Sheer deviltry glinted in his eyes now. "If it doesn't fit, she can bring it back for alterations, but I think it will. And I want to surprise her."

He paid on the spot, charming Molly with his smile, so that by the time he left, she was quite pink-cheeked. "I know I shouldn't approve of such gifts from an unmarried man to his lady friend, but husbands so seldom buy such beautiful things for their wives. Such fabric and such fur! We might never see the like again. It looked wonderful on you. I wonder how it will look on Mr. Ames's friend. It's nice indeed to see him so happy and in love. He's a fine gentleman, but I've often thought he seemed lonely. The lady is fortunate." She paused thoughtfully. "But isn't it odd that you haven't met her, Mr. Ames being such a good friend of you and your husband?"

"Perhaps they prefer their privacy," Tessa said pointedly,
518

thankful to be able to make any comment at all, even if it were so dangerously close to the truth. "If Mr. Ames wishes us to meet her, I'm sure we shall."

"Well, at least she will be well dressed," Molly sighed.

"Or undressed," Tessa quipped with a smile she couldn't prevent. She had suddenly seen the direction of Jordan's game and the sly wisdom of it. To discontinue the outward trappings of their friendship would be odd, not the other way around. And under cover of those trappings, they could steal more time for each other. She started going out to lunch again with him though they seldom went further than his place, and when his afternoon was clear of appointments, she was often late back to the shop. She told Molly that Jordan was boring her silly asking for advice about his friend.

"Maybe he'll marry her," Molly offered hopefully.

There was no sham in Tessa's suddenly grave expression. "No, I don't think he will. I have not yet met her, but I fear she will bring him sorrow in the end."

"At least he will have you and your family to comfort him."

Tessa was glad Molly returned to her work, obviously expecting no answer to such an obvious statement. The fear she tried so hard to keep at bay flashed through her. *My sweet Jordan*, she thought, *I am destroying you.*

And then Indian rode in one evening so full of his own joy, it took him some time to sort out his impressions of the Ramsays. The boys were all fine, even Brand behaving with some kindness toward Paul as he and Jefferson introduced him to the various delights of Rancho Magnífico. Chong Sing had taken command from the first day, just as he had the summer before. "I think they jus' give him his way to keep from havin' to figure out extra English th' way he talks it."

He went on to tell of how grand the land looked with good crops coming in and the animals sleek from the grazing provided by the winter rains. He had brought back beef and produce which was even now at the warehouse, the last securing being done by Pedro and the other two *vaqueros* who had come with him. He even had careful lists to give Tessa as a special gift, showing the increase in the horses even down to detailed descriptions of the new foals

519

and the progress of the older animals. And then his joy spilled over and he couldn't keep the news back any more.

"Best of all, Armenthia jus' love it out there an' th' land got to her so deep she tol' me she loves me too, got right down to it an' asked me t' marry her!" His shoulders shook with his laughter. "Me, I jus' bein' patient as can be, not wantin' t' scare her off again. Well, I so patient, she get tired of waitin' an' she ask. I say Yes 'fore she change her mind."

"That's marvelous! When will you be married?" Tessa crowed, hugging him.

"Come th' fall when the' children back an' Armenthia have everythin' sorted out at th' Fitz-Williams place."

"Congratulations, my friend," Gavin said, and Indian knew he meant it, but he was rapidly becoming aware of other currents. He had instinctively searched Tessa's face first because so much of what she felt was always reflected there. And he knew that his first instinct had been valid— she was happy, feverishly happy for the first time in months. She was happy in the way a woman is when she is well loved. But now Indian knew it had nothing to do with Gavin. The Ramsays were together welcoming him, but they were not together in any other way. Gavin's face was drawn and grim despite the smile he offered his friend.

Indian's sorrow was vast. He had hoped desperately that the Ramsays would find a way back together in their time alone, and now he found them further apart than ever, and he felt real fear. The unthinkable had happened. Tessa had taken a lover. He had no doubt of it, and he knew Gavin did not even suspect. If he did there would surely be hell to pay. Inwardly, Indian cursed the man, wondering who he was and knowing in all honesty that he could not blame him; moral scruples could so easily prove a flimsy barrier against loving a woman like Tessa, especially in this city.

"You look very tired," Tessa said suddenly. "Let me fix something for you to eat and then you should sleep."

He refused politely, offering as an excuse the fact that the *vaqueros* would soon arrive at his house for food, drink, and sleep. "They don' wan' trouble you tonight. They come see you in th' mornin'."

Tessa felt duty bound to point out that they had plenty of room in their house too, but Indian remained adamant
520

about the arrangements he had already made. He did not want to linger any longer in this atmosphere or think any more about it.

And that night, Tessa did not go to Jordan, or the next. Despite the fact that Indian lived in the other house, from now on, she and Jordan would have to be more careful than ever. The freest time of their affair was over. And for the first time the end seemed closer and more real than the beginning.

CHAPTER XLIV

Tessa blessed her early and rigorous training in the courtesy owed by a California hostess to her guests. It enabled her to converse adequately with Pedro and the others, to ask them about their families and to listen patiently to their proud replies. And she gave Pedro cheerful, innocuous little notes, for each of her sons, bidding them to continue to enjoy themselves but to help with the work on the *rancho* whenever they could. The two days that Pedro and his men stayed seemed an eternity.

And now even with the lumbermill open and producing at last and demanding much time and energy from Gavin and Indian, the world seemed to be seeking Tessa out and closing in on her. A letter came from Carmelita protesting the long separation and suggesting a visit in the fall, one way or the other as long as they got together. Tessa's heart beat thickly in her throat when she thought of being under Carmelita's knowing eyes. And closer to home, she already had to deal with Armenthia and Belle. Thia's reserve would never allow her to ask personal questions, but sometimes Tessa thought she detected a puzzled look when Armenthia was with Indian and the Ramsays at occasional meals and gatherings Tessa could not avoid without being openly rude.

Belle was worse because she was so much more direct, finally seeking Tessa out at the shop, waiting patiently for her until she came in late in the afternoon.

"You've been avoiding me," she said quietly. "And I'd like to know why. Charley hasn't seen much of Gavin lately either."

Tessa made feeble excuses. Belle took a closer look at her, at the glowing eyes and still pink cheeks and full mouth, and she smiled warmly. "So the rumors are true! How glad I am! I can well see how you might have been busy lately!"

"What rumors?" Tessa asked through dry lips, her face suddenly deathly pale. She felt as if the tracks of Jordan's hands and mouth were glowing scarlet on her flesh.

"I don't understand. I thought . . . the way you look, happy and all, that . . . well, I heard that Gavin had been seeing that woman and I could understand why maybe you wouldn't want to see many friends but now, now people, er . . . rumor has it that there's been a terrible ruckus and that Soledad woman is in a fury because she knows she's lost him. So surely Gavin and you . . ." Belle's stammering voice ceased as she stared at Tessa in complete confusion.

Tessa had her breath back. Nothing could be so terrible as having her liaison with Jordan discovered, and that hadn't happened. She was thankful he had not escorted her back to the shop this afternoon. Briefly she considered an outright lie, to tell Belle she knew all this, that she and Gavin were doing fine, and to leave it at that without further explanation. But she knew it would never work because her reaction had been too strong and the lie would surely be obvious if Belle saw her and Gavin together. "I had not heard he had left her." It was the only honest thing she said. "Perhaps he needs some time to decide what he wants to do. But you mustn't worry. I'm really quite happy, and what will be will be." Words of María from the past and never meant for this. "It was a hard winter with the children so constantly sick and so much going on. And now with the children at Rancho Magnífico, I've had time to collect myself and enjoy a little quiet."

Peace and being alone do not make a woman look as you do, Belle thought, and for the first time she was sorry she knew as much about women as she did about men. The wall was firmly in place again around Tessa, and she knew how futile it would be to batter against it. "Take care, my

522

dear, and I hope Charley and I see more of you," she said, kissing her softly on both cheeks, feeling totally hopeless inside, and forbidding herself to speculate about Tessa's lover. But once settled in her carriage whose horse and driver had waited patiently as ordered, she could not banish the image of Gavin's lean face from her mind. "Holy Mary," she beseeched for the first time in years, "protect her when he finds out." She had no doubt that he would.

Tessa's knees supported her until Belle was out of sight and then she sank into the chair at her desk. Gavin had left Soledad. The full impact of it began to hit her, and she felt the whole structure of her sanctuary with Jordan begin to sway and crumble as if it had been hit by an earthquake.

"No!" she said aloud. "It makes no difference. Perhaps they've just quarreled. And he has not come back to me." And even as she said it, she knew she had made it nearly impossible for him to approach her even had he wanted to.

Even though she had just left him, she wanted Jordan desperately, wanted him to convince her everything was going to be all right. She was tempted not to go back to the house at all tonight, but she steeled herself against the impulse, knowing that now less than ever could she afford a stupid, willful mistake.

She went home and waited, her nerves screaming, until she judged the hour late enough, and then she slipped out of the house, nearly cursing aloud at the bleaching light pouring over the earth from the full white moon without even the grace of fog to obscure it.

Only the high pitch of her nervousness saved her. There were always a few people about on any street in the city no matter what hour, but her eyes caught and focused on the man coming toward her, far up the street, far enough for her to duck into a narrow alley between two buildings, pressing her face against a wall to make her cloaked form nothing more than another dark shadow cast by the bright moon. She bit her lip until it bled in her effort not to whimper aloud, and she held her body rigid against the trembling that threatened to betray her. If Gavin had seen her and found her now cowering in an alley, nothing on earth could save her, and there was no way out; she could see the stacks of boxes and goods blocking the passage.

She had no idea how long she waited, expecting any second to hear his voice, to feel his hands grabbing her, but finally she turned her head, searching the opening, finding it empty. She walked unsteadily forward until she could see the street and no trace of Gavin.

She wanted to run the rest of the way to Jordan, but she made herself slow down to avoid attracting any undue attention. It made little difference; by the time she was safely in Jordan's arms, she was breathing as if she'd run for miles.

He held her close for a moment, not asking anything, feeling her heart hammering against his chest, tasting blood when he kissed her. "It's all right," he crooned. "Whatever it is, my love, it will be all right."

He felt her head moving in frenzied negation against his chest before the broken words poured over him. "It's not all right, and it will never be. Too many people guessing, maybe knowing, too many people." Before, he could not possibly have made sense of the fragmented outpouring, but now he knew her so well, he understood. Indian home and Armenthia with him, Belle, and now nearly meeting Gavin.

He held her a little away from him so that he could see her face, compelling her to meet his eyes. "Tess, you are so innocent in so many ways." He gave her a little shake when he felt her flinch from the word. "It's true. You feel as if you wear a scarlet letter like the heroine of Mr. Hawthorne's book." He smiled openly at her. "Yes, I've read it too. Perhaps in that little inbred New England village people had time to care so much for what Hester had done, but not here, not here where everyone wants only two things—good fortune and freedom to live as he or she wishes. It's your own harsh judgment of yourself that makes you see eyes watching. People are much too selfish to care much what anyone else does as long as it takes nothing from them. And besides, Hester was the best of the lot, the only decent person in that story."

She had to laugh with him, and she wanted terribly to believe him, but the small clear voice left within could not be stilled. She had taken something from all of them—
524

trust from her friends, and the best of herself from Gavin, everything that had belonged only to him until now.

She knew the piece the minute he began Jonson's "Song To Celia" with only the name changed to her own. He had quoted it for her before, but now she really understood the words:

> Come, my Tess, let us prove
> While we may the sports of love;
> Time will not be ours forever,
> He at length our good will sever.
>
> Cannot we delude the eyes
> Of a few poor household spies?
> Or his easier ears beguile,
> So removed by our wile?
>
> 'Tis no sin love's fruit to steal;
> But the sweet theft to reveal,
> To be taken, to be seen,
> These have crimes accounted been.

She heard him to the finish, but the deep, gentle sound of his voice made no difference. "That fits too goddamned well!" she swore, then burst into tears.

Never before had Jordan regretted his knowledge of the appropriate word. He had never seen Tessa cry, and for a moment he was frozen with the hurt of it. But then for the first time anger rose in him against her, and he shook her roughly, his eyes blazing golden. "Don't do this to yourself, don't do it to me, to us! No one knows!"

Her eyes still glittered, but the overflowing tears had stopped. "Jordan, I'm so sorry," she whispered. "Why is it so difficult to remember that no one alone is strong enough for two people?" She was thinking not only of Jordan but of Gavin; she had asked him to be stronger than one so many times.

Jordan pulled her close again, and she did not resist, her body hungry for his, her mind desperate not to think any more. They made love fiercely as if they were combatants in a battle to forge one perfect being from two flawed creatures. And Tessa could not stop her frantic memorizing of Jordan's body: remember the smooth tautness of his skin, the sleek muscles, the eyes golden like a hawk's when he is angry or intent, kind gray to drown in when he is peaceful, remember the sunlight silk of his hair, the scent of him, and the sound of his voice, and remember the way he makes love with his heart and mind as well as his body. Remember, remember, the way one wants to after someone has died or gone away forever.

She was so exhausted, for once she did not awaken instinctively before the dawn, but Jordan, alert for her safety, did. He kissed her cheek and whispered to her until her eyes opened without alarm to the gentle waking.

"I wish you could stay forever and never have to leave at this ungodly hour again."

"So do I, but you must not malign this time of day. I have learned how beautiful the world is just before the sun." She touched the velvet and fur of the robe spread out at the foot of the bed regretfully, wishing she could just put the robe on and watch the sun come up with Jordan, but with a sigh she got up and began to dress. Jordan watched appreciatively and helped with the fastenings. He nuzzled the nape of her neck. "One of the countless things I like about you is that you don't creak," he said. "Women are beginning to make more terrible squeaking and creaking noises by the day in their corsets."

Tessa giggled. "Jordan Ames, have you been making a survey of San Francisco's corsets?"

"No, I just have very acute ears."

Their nonsense stopped abruptly as Tessa caught sight of the statue on the little table which usually held flowers. There was a note at the base of the figure.

"I should have given it to you last night, but I forgot it, and you didn't even notice it. I'm flattered your eyes sought me out and were not greedy for a gift." He was making light of it, but nothing could diminish the beauty of the jade glowing opalescent spring green. The statue was nine or ten inches high, the figure a sinuous curve in soft draperies, the face absolutely serene under its headdress, the whole carved from one piece of jade.

The note said nothing more than, "I love you, J.'"

"Who is she?" Tessa, still gazing at the statue in awe.

"She is actually a he or better yet, an it, or so I understand. Kuanyin is a giver of mercy, intelligence, tranquility, and magic. And the jade itself is supposed to be magic."

"All things we need," she said softly. She picked it up with infinite care, and she was amazed by the sensuous feel of it, cool smooth with a silken sleekness that made her want to run her hands over every line. It was almost as if the stone were alive, pulsing with its own light.

She put it down carefully. "Jordan, it's one of the most beautiful things I've ever seen. But you must cease. First the robe and now this, and I have given you nothing."

"You have given me everything. And you count me more unselfish than I am. When you are not here, the robe remains sweet with your scent, and now Kuanyin carries the image of your hands stroking the jade."

She looked up at him, a small smile on her lips. "Another word and I will not be able to leave. Thank you, my darling." She kissed him and was gone. Jordan picked up the jade and held it for a long moment.

Because she had so nearly run into Gavin the night before Tessa was even more careful when she approached the house this morning, and she breathed a sigh of relief as she always did when she found it shrouded in silence and darkness as it was now. She nearly had the door open when a soft voice stopped her. Just her name, but enough to spin her around with a barely stifled scream.

She looked at Indian for as long as she could, and then she closed her eyes and still could not banish the well of sorrow in his. "If it will make it easier for you, you can pretend that I have been out for an early walk," she offered in a small voice.

"Cain't pretend no more. Been tryin' hard ever since I got back an' find you happy an' Gavin not. But no more."

Tessa's head came up and her eyes opened wide in defiance. "All right then, you must do whatever you need to do, just as I have done. Gavin needs Soledad. I need someone too. It's as simple as that. What has been between my husband and myself is no longer. Everything changes; everything ends."

They stared at each other for an endless moment, and then Indian shook his head. "You wrong, firs' time I ever

527

know you so wrong. Many things change, pass by, but not what you an' Gavin got, not what yours an' his together. An' you both crazy if you think you goin' slip out like a snake out of old skin. An' both cowards if you let this bad time be th' last time. But ain't nothin' I can do to make it right, an' I ain't goin' do nothin' to make it worse."

Tessa drew back a step, resisting the burden of his hurt, and fearing suddenly that he knew Jordan was the man. "What are you doing up at this hour anyway?" she asked accusingly.

"Jus' waitin' for you," he replied simply. "I saw you leave, an' I figure you be back 'fore th' sun an' Gavin up. He in there, sleepin', I hope."

She realized then that he had come out of his own house to wait for her more for her protection than for any other reason, disapproving as he did and yet still willing to put himself between her and Gavin's wrath.

She touched his cheek, murmuring, "It's all horrible," her voice devoid of hope, and then she went inside, leaving him to stare sadly after her.

It finally dawned on Indian that Gavin had to be trapped in his own private hell to be so oblivious to the changes in Tessa, and he did not believe as she did that Gavin's blindness was caused by his love for Soledad. His determination not to interfere began to crumble in face of Gavin's misery, and he tricked him—something he would never have considered before.

It was pathetically simple because Gavin trusted him. Indian made genial noises about how much he looked forward to marrying Armenthia, even though it would mean a change in his habits. And he moved easily from that to inviting Gavin to go with him on a drinking bout for old times' sake. They went to the Golden Horse first because there there would be no trouble for Indian, and Indian made sure Gavin's glass was kept full and that his own seemed to be. And when he saw that the liquor was beginning to have its effect, he played the drunk himself and persuaded Gavin to accompany him back to his own house where the jugs waited. The ease with which it worked was an added sadness for Indian, because in all their years together he had never seen Gavin so drunk.

Normally he had a head like a rock and remained in complete control when other men would have long been under the table, but now in the kitchen of the frame house, Indian saw Gavin's eyes glaze and shift in and out of focus as his words rambled from one thing to another, and he saw too clearly how tired and thin he was. He didn't even have to broach the subject; Gavin did it for him, his face contorted with naked misery.

"I los' Tessa, never fin' her again. Wen' back to that whore Soledad an' me jus' th' same, not th' same as Tessa. Tessa doesn't love me any more, so I wen' back. But can't stop lovin' her, can't, an' I tell th' whore that, tell Soledad. She sends for her kid, litt'el girl, supposed to be mine. I don' know, maybe is, don' matter, Tessa'll believe it. Thas what Soledad goin' t'do, goin' to tell Tessa if I leave her. Soledad had a litt'el girl chil' an' Tessa los' hers. I know, I saw, an' I buried it in th' ground. My baby too." He hid his face in his arms, and his shoulders heaved silently while Indian stared in horror, the slurred words making far too much sense and showing everything to be so much worse than he had suspected.

When he found his voice, it was a savage bellow. "You fool! That blackmail, nothin' else, an' you got no choice 'ceptin' tell Tessa. She still your wife. You ain't no use to each other this way! An' you ain't got nothin' left to lose."

"Did thiz on purpose, didn't you?" Gavin accused him suddenly, half rising, and Indian caught his unconscious form before it hit the floor.

Gavin awakened long after the sun was up and long after Indian had watched from the window as Tessa slipped home in the shadows.

Gavin's head was splitting, his eyes bleary, and his skin pale, but he remembered. "You did do it on purpose, didn't you?" he croaked.

Indian nodded. "Figured you need tell somebody 'fore you go crazy."

Gavin stared at him for a moment longer before the grim set of his mouth eased. "Thank you, Indian. You're right. I feel god awful, but I also feel a damn sight better. Even if Tessa throws me out for good, at least it will be settled. A man ought to learn something from getting that drunk besides the fact that he never wants to feel like this again." He cradled his aching head in his hands. "It's been the waiting, waiting for Soledad to go to Tessa, not having the guts to talk to her myself, not being willing to bring it all out in the open and take my chances. But there's so much that just doesn't make any sense. I think Tessa knows about Soledad, but she hasn't said a thing, not a goddamn thing, and she looks happy. I guess I've just got to face the fact that maybe she really doesn't want to be married any more."

Indian's face remained impassive, though inwardly he marveled that Gavin still did not suspect the cause of Tessa's happiness. He was betting on only one thing, that what he had told Tessa was true, that she and Gavin had something special enough between them to survive anything, even Tessa's infidelity. That would be the final choice and Tessa's alone. "Reckon you jus' gotta take your chances like you say, like you always done," he said.

Gavin went home and felt nothing but relief to find Tessa had already left for the shop. He did not want her to see him in his present state, but by the time he'd washed and shaved he was actually humming, and he made himself an enormous breakfast and ate every bit of it.

And the first person he sought out was not Tessa but Jordan Ames.

Jordan's morning was a busy one, and the clients with set appointments gave him time to recover from the first shock of seeing Gavin waiting in the anteroom. He dealt with his clients as calmly as ever, but his mind was whirling with the implications of Gavin's visit. His first thought, that Tessa's fear of discovery had been realized, was quickly gone; Gavin did not look like a man who had come to challenge his wife's lover. In fact, he looked quite peaceful. Nor did Jordan think Gavin had come about the Land Act cases—everything that could be done was being done, and he knew it and knew how slow the process was. Jordan had seen Gavin only a couple of times by appointment and on purely business matters since his affair with Tessa had begun, and he was sure he had betrayed nothing. He had not risked visits to the house, but that was wholly explicable with the children gone and no specific invitations issued. But now he felt a light film of sweat break out on his skin at the thought that

Gavin might well have dropped in just as casually on an afternoon when Tessa was here. Even now she was only hours gone, her robe hanging in its place in the wardrobe, Kuanyin in his place, and a book with the marker halfway through the pages beside the bed. A poem of John Donne's Jordan had wanted her to hear, one he didn't know by memory, one beginning, "If yet I have not all thy love,/ Dear, I shall never have it all." He could see her pensive face, violet eyes far away in the words, arching dark eyebrows and every other delicate feature so still with her listening, the cloud of black hair falling over her breasts and down her back.

The burly man across the desk cleared his throat with annoyance and asked a question sharply.

Jordan wrenched his mind back and made the bland smile appear. "Forgive me, Mr. Thompkins, I was thinking of a minor point of law that might pertain to your case, but upon consideration, I don't think it does." He offered a few sentences of totally unnecessary legal jargon to confound his client, whose case entailed nothing more than collecting damages from broken mirrors and glassware, liquor spillage and general saloon mayhem from a man who was reluctant but able to pay. The words he could not understand mollified Mr. Thompkins, who left feeling that he'd hired a damn smart lawyer even if the man was a bit taken by some woman. Mr. Thompkins hadn't spent most of his life in saloons for nothing.

And then it was Gavin Ramsay greeting Jordan, apologizing for making no prior arrangement, both of them exchanging the expected pleasantries and explanations for not having gotten together socially for a long while. "The summer is nearly over, and the children will be home before long," Gavin said. "They'll not forgive your absence for long."

Jordan's face didn't change, but he shared Tessa's sense of impending disaster for the first time. When the children returned, the choice would be final. They could not continue the way they were. Tessa would have to decide between himself and Gavin, and facing Gavin now, he could almost see through Tessa's eyes and did not see much hope for himself.

Gavin gave him little warning, a rueful grin and then the

531

first bare words. "I never thought I would need to consult a lawyer for so personal a matter as this, but I find I must. And I know this might be difficult for you since you are not just my friend but a friend of my whole family." He paused, but Jordan assured him he had heard just about everything in the course of his professional life. "Listening is one of my best talents," he said, and he hoped his voice sounded natural. He saw no way he could refuse whatever sort of help Gavin was going to ask for without arousing his suspicions, but he knew they were now playing a very dangerous game, winner take all, winner take Tessa.

But as Gavin told the story, beginning clear back in Monterey and including Tessa's loss of the child, Jordan had to fight his insane impulse to scream at Gavin to shut up, that he couldn't listen any more, couldn't play his proper role of loyal attorney. He suddenly wanted it all out in the open, wanted to tell Gavin that he too loved Tessa, had been her lover these many days and nights and would fight anyone on earth to keep her. He wanted to tell Gavin to go back to his mistress and her bastard child and leave him in peace to love Tessa forever. But the rational voice that had been a part of him since childhood, the same uncompromising voice that had made his home an intolerable place, was no less insistent now.

"As I understand it, then, you are proposing to set up a fund for this child though you are not sure whether or not you fathered her. A fund that the mother will not be able to abuse. Is that correct?" Jordan was proud of the calm note.

"Yes. I know it must sound mad, but I also know what it's like to be raised an unwanted bastard, and perhaps this will make it easier for the child." He met the cold gray eyes without flinching. "I will, of course, tell Tessa."

"You're asking a deal of mercy from her," Jordan snapped, unable to keep his voice totally impartial.

"I'm asking more than mercy. I'm asking for our lives to begin together all over again. But I have nothing to lose by asking. I love Tessa more than my life, as unbelievable as that may seem."

The worst of it was, Jordan could believe it, and he could feel the power of the man. Gavin had made no ex-

532

cuses for his behavior, taking the full blame, but there was a strength and serenity about him that was absolute.

"I'll have the papers drawn up tomorrow," Jordan said stiffly, wanting the interview over.

"Thank you, Jordan," Gavin returned gravely. He almost said it aloud as he left the office—that he was so haunted by Tessa, even here he could smell her delicate scent of flowers and spice.

Jordan sat frozen at his desk for a long while after Gavin had gone, glad no other clients waited. Then, moving like a very old man, he went into his bedchamber and picked up Kuanyin, the jade so cool and beautiful in his hands. The sudden temptation to smash it was so strong, he trembled, but he made himself put it back on the table, safe from his need to destroy.

Gavin sought Tessa out at the shop and saw her immediate apprehension.

"Is something wrong? Has something happened to Indian, the children? Why are you here?"

Gavin smiled wryly. "That's a telling note, to be sure, that my appearance should spell disaster to my wife."

No smile answered his own, and the apprehension did not leave her face. She backed away instinctively. "What do you want?" she asked, her voice no colder than the chill that was beginning to invade her bones.

"I want to talk to you."

"Can't it wait until this evening?"

"No, it's very important." He didn't even mind that she wasn't giving an inch. He didn't expect her to. It was up to him to persuade her he still had something to offer her.

Tessa saw that Molly was within earshot now and Anne too, both looking puzzled, and she had no intention of putting on a show for them, besides the fact that Gavin's quiet insistence was obviously not going to cease until she did as he wished. Her office was too dangerously small a place to contain the trouble she felt brewing.

"Molly, I'll return later if I can; if not, please lock up for me, and I'll see you tomorrow," she ordered curtly, but Molly only smiled.

"Where are we going?" she asked Gavin when they were outside.

"Home," he said, and his voice still sounded that oddly gentle note.

She went with him because she did not know what else to do, and she refrained from saying that she did not know where home was any longer.

CHAPTER XLV

Once they were in the house, Tessa's agitation was so evident that Gavin finally trapped her hands in his own and drew her close for a moment. "Please, I'm not going to hurt you, for Christ's sake! I just want you to listen for a moment." Even though he had known this was going to be hard, he was dismayed to feel the fear in her, her hands cold, her body trembling and resistant.

He guided her to a chair and let her go only when he had settled her into it. Her face was so white, her eyes so enormous and staring, he was afraid she was going to faint. He poured a glass of brandy and held it to her lips. "Drink this, I think you need it."

"Sherry, so much more soothing to the nerves than brandy." She could hear Jordan saying that the first night. She took a sip of the brandy Gavin offered and felt its fire. She was so cold. She knew this was no business conference. This was one way or the other the end of her world as it had been for nearly three months.

"Will you hear me out?" Gavin asked, and she nodded wearily.

"You know I've been with Soledad again, don't you. You've known all along."

No quarter, she thought, *no quarter at all given in this*. The blue eyes compelled her to answer but her affirmation was only a tiny, dry rustle of sound.

Gavin voice was not hesitant. It cut the air as sharply as a lash. "I went back to Soledad that night, the night you refused me. That is no excuse, only proof that my pride is that of a boy hardly fledged. I've never loved Soledad, not then and not now. There's no polite way to say what

534

she is. She's more purely whore than any other woman I've ever known. The only part of her that lives is her sex. And with her I was no more than that either, no heart, no mind, no spirit. Only in loving you is everything asked and everything given from one to the other. And then, when I would have been entirely free of her, she told me she has a daughter, a daughter who is mine. She's seven years old, so it's possible. I haven't seen her. I don't know whether she's my child or not, but I can't forsake her. I have today seen Jordan to set up a fund for the child which her mother cannot take from her. Perhaps she'll have a chance to become something better than her mother and better than her father, myself or whoever he is. I let Soledad blackmail me with her threat to tell you about the child. But now I know I have to take the risk." He paused, and then he added very low, "Do you know, you are so much a part of me, even as I talked to Jordan, I could smell the scent of flowers that is only yours."

Tessa covered her face with her hands and willed her body to stop shaking. So close, so dangerously close.

The cowering withdrawal of her body turned his face ashen and his voice raw, but he knew if he didn't say it all now, he never would, and he would drown as surely as a man adrift in the sea a thousand miles from land.

"Dear God, Tessa, we can't go on this way! The children must come home soon, and they can't come home to us as we are now. Oh, hell, that's not what matters! And it is poor of me to try to sway you with them. If I could think of anything, even a lie, to make it better, I wouldn't hesitate to use it. But there is nothing. And I have nothing to offer that you don't already possess, including my love. If I were you, I would refuse, but still I ask. Is there any chance that we might begin again.?"

She raised her head, opened her eyes, and saw him, really saw him for the first time in months. She felt the beat of his heart; the turning of his mind, the agony of his soul, and his love. She tried in panic to block the sensations, knowing she was lost if he became part of her again, still unable to stop his rush back into her consciousness. The enormous irony of it all pressed against her until she wanted to scream and laugh hysterically though she could scarcely breathe. "I went back to Soledad that night,

535

the night you refused me." The words rang in her head. She did not doubt the truth of them for an instant, despite the fact she knew she had smelled Soledad's perfume that night. Whatever the reason for that, he had not made love to the woman until she herself had sent him away. And he did not, even now, suspect she had been having an affair with Jordan since then. Her scent, her signature in Jordan's world. The depth of trust that engendered Gavin's ignorance stunned.

Soledad had a daughter, or at least she claimed the child was hers. Soledad had had a daughter when Tessa had lost her own. She had never doubted the child had been a girl. A final irony, but more clearly than anything else, not Gavin's fault. Women like Soledad never had babies unless they wanted them. Tessa thought of that knowledge, and she thought of Belle. I need to know—she damned the terror rising. Soledad or herself, who had used Gavin most unfairly?

Unbidden and unwanted, desire flashed through her, desire for Gavin, for all of him, for the same unity he desired from her. She wanted it all back, not only him, but the children and Chong Sing and their lives together. The perfect asking from Gavin, and the perfect answer she could not give, not now. "Give me time to think, please, Gavin, give me time," she whispered.

It was the best he could hope for, but the obvious depth of her fear tore at his heart; anger and defiance he had expected, but not this. He cradled her face in his hands with infinite care and felt the violent pulse beating in her throat. Her eyes were as glazed as those of a bird trapped by a snake. "Tessa, my love, whatever time you need is yours. I will not press you further. There is no reason for you to fear me."

It was so swiftly done, he couldn't be sure it had happened at all, but he thought Tessa had turned her head slightly, her lips brushing one of his hands before she had wrenched free and was gone, running up the stairs, the slam of the bedroom door echoing through the house. He did not see her again until morning, and had he tried the door that night, he would have found it locked.

Nothing was to be easy in this ordeal, she realized when she came down in the morning to find him dawdling over breakfast, clearly waiting for her. She had not even been able to cry. She had lain dry-eyed with her heart pumping in terror until exhaustion overcame her, and she had no more of a solution now than before.

"You ought to eat something. You've lost weight," Gavin said abruptly, and she fought the hysterical surge of laughter rising in her again. If she didn't do something immediately, that would very shortly cease to be a problem. She regarded him suspiciously through her veiling lashes. Maybe he was just playing with her after all, maybe it already showed. But no, his expression was truly concerned, not accusing. The nausea she had been ignoring for so many mornings now rose stronger than ever.

"I'm not accustomed to seeing my husband at the breakfast table. It makes me nervous," she snapped, and she winced inwardly at the beaten look of accepted pain on his face, but to risk letting her guard down, letting him get too close now, was unthinkable.

She spent the morning at the shop, knowing it to be Jordan's busiest time, wanting the hours to go swiftly one moment, slowly the next, knowing they would follow their own set course no matter what she wanted. Molly and the others kept their distance once they determined Mrs. Ramsay's mood.

She knew the minute she saw Jordan's pale, taut face that he was waiting for her, had been waiting since Gavin's visit. All their days and nights together passed before her mind's eye with slow, terrible clarity; his nonsense, the books they had discussed, the poems and songs he had given to her in the languages he knew, the sensuous pleasure of velvet, of jade, and of his body, his smooth, strong body that loved her with such infinite care.

She felt it flutter. She knew it was too early. It was only guilt. But she could feel it, the hard lump of life beginning to kick inside of her. Jordan's child, not Gavin's.

Guilt, horrible guilt, not about Gavin, but about Jordan. Jordan had known from the beginning that she was married, but Jordan had loved her. He did love her. He would take her away now if she asked him to. She had used this man who was in his own fashion pure of heart and deserving of love. It was the worst thing she had ever done.

He had made no attempt to touch her, and she was the one who broke the deadly silence that stretched between them.

Even saying his name was difficult now, and she willed herself not to cry. "Jordan, you know that I am here only to tell you I cannot be here again. Such a strange thing to need this formal saying of it."

"I would like to know why. Is it because you fear he suspects? Is it the children? Or is it just him?" he asked softly.

"Just him. I've been terribly cruel. I've used you. You will never know how sorry I am."

"I love you, Tess. That is enough. I love you very much." Jordan's voice was still quiet, but hers was not.

"That's not enough! It must be both people. Don't you understand? I still love my husband. What I have given you is counterfeit."

"Then counterfeit will suffice. I knew what I was doing. I'm a grown man, my darling."

She sighed. "You knew I was married, but you didn't know how married, because I myself forgot. You're a lovely, lovely man. But I don't have room for anyone but Gavin. I never will. I haven't since the first day I saw him. All I've done is to hurt you by trying to pay him back. It will never work that way."

He was very still. "You really mean this. You know I would take you away, take your sons with us, anything. But you truly mean what you say."

"I do. Jordan, find someone who can love you, someone who can give you what you deserve." The next room, the bedchamber she knew so well now, she couldn't stop the clear image of the big soft bed, the lamplight, flowers, Kuanyin, Jordan.

His mouth twisted wryly and his bitterness spilled over. "I've gotten what I deserve. This is surely ample punishment for adultery. Never to touch you, never to love you again, yes, a remarkable example of just punishment."

The irony of his words knifed through her and strengthened her. He was hurt; she had no doubt of that, or of his love. But surely he was young and resilient enough to love again, while she was well and truly snared in the fact of her infidelity simply because she was a woman. Jordan

538

would soon bear only memories. She was bearing his child, and he must never know.

Her bleak, cold resolve reached him. He stared at her for one more long moment, and then he bowed his head in a brief gesture of submission. She knew his particular code of honor would force him to obey her dismissal.

She walked home blindly, not knowing how she had gotten there when she entered the empty house. She sank down in a chair, her knees no longer able to support her, and the harsh cries strangled in her throat. Jordan with his thick, silver-gold hair and golden-gray eyes. Jordan with his laughter and wit and loving. Jordan eclipsed by the image of Gavin. Gavin, lean, hard, and capable of terrifying rage.

She clasped her arms around her body and rocked back and forth in misery, as the full weight of her plight crushed her. Even were she now willing to seduce Gavin and claim the child as his, it was too late. For the first time, the child took on a horrifying reality. She had ignored its existence, but now she knew her body was not going to rid itself of this fetus as it had with so many conceived with Gavin. Just punishment. The words scrambled in her head until she wanted to scream and never stop.

The calm dropped over her panic quite suddenly, suffocating it completely. Of course, there was a way. Her mind had been skirting the idea since Gavin had spoken to her. It was just that women of her class were not expected to know or need the knowledge. Surely, it would never have occurred to María to teach her how to rid the womb of a child, if, in fact, she knew. But in this city there must be many who knew. Prostitutes, no matter how careful they were, must sometimes get more from men than they bargained for, and they did not, like Soledad, have children. She thought of Belle again and rejected her. Belle would be horrified, and she would undoubtedly go to Gavin; she was his friend too. She had an instant's insane image of going to Soledad.

She considered Belle again. Of course, it didn't have to be Belle herself. Her girls must be as well versed as the madam in such matters. Ginger, English Ginger, who owed her a favor and would be the last person on earth to make a moral judgment. Ginger, who never quite paid

539

her bill at the shop in full but was never refused a new gown because at least she did make some payment regularly and was popular enough never to be without a rich patron for long.

Tessa had something to do now, a way out. She felt at peace. The knowledge that she was going to rid herself of one life and perhaps lose her own in the process was no match for her terror that Gavin might find out before it was accomplished. Gavin, who was taking all the blame and was willing to begin all over. Their marriage had seemed irreparably shattered by indifference and infidelity, and now there was hope again; she would risk anything for that. She needed Gavin, the Gavin she had seen again, the one who loved and protected her; needed him so much she trembled with the wanting.

It took her three days to manage a meeting with Ginger. Where she had felt shielded, reckless yet magically safe from knowing eyes in the first days with Jordan, now she felt hideously exposed. Molly fussed over her at the shop, telling her she looked poorly, brewing cups of tea and offering home-baked tidbits that made Tessa's stomach heave and strained her patience until it was all she could do not to scream at Molly to leave her alone. And worst of all was Gavin. He hadn't been home this much in months, and now every time she turned around he was there, his eyes full of worry and love and patience.

The night before she saw Ginger, her nightmares were so grotesque, she awakened to the sound of her own screaming and heard Gavin pounding on the locked door, his voice frantic. "Tessa, let me in! Tessa, oh, God, what is it?"

She made her voice strong. "A nightmare, nothing more. I'm all right." She heard the door handle turn once more and then she heard his slow steps going back to his room, but she did not sleep again. She lay rigid, her body covered with sweat, her knuckles jammed against her teeth in her effort not to cry out for him. If he touched her now, she would be lost. She would tell him everything, beg him to protect her, help her, love her. The thought made her feel sick with shame for her cowardice.

When morning finally came, she knew there would be no way to avoid seeing him. After hearing her screaming in the night, he would never leave the house until he had seen that she was all right. But even her best efforts did little to improve her appearance.

He studied her pale face, grown so thin that it looked like a little skull surrounded by the luxuriant mockery of her raven hair. The shadows around her eyes were the color of her eyes and made them look huge and haunted.

"Sweetheart, whatever you want, I'll do. I can't bear to have you looking like this and know I've caused it. If it will make it easier for you, I'll stay across the way with Indian until you've made your decision. Surely Armenthia or someone else would stay here to keep you company." He reached out and touched her face before she could flinch away. "I think you might have a fever. Couldn't you stay home and rest today?"

"Not today, I have much to do, but tomorrow perhaps." She was proud of her steady voice. "I'm fine, and tonight I'll give you my answer." It was all she dared give him now.

"Tonight, then." The sad resignation in his voice reflected what he was sure her decision would be.

She left the room before he could say anything else, and she listened until she heard him leave. *Much to do indeed,* she thought. But tonight, one way or another, it would be finished. The trembling stopped and the icy calm filtered back. If it were to finish without her, she wanted the guilt to die with her. She left the sealed note for him on her bureau:

> Gavin, my love, we've been at fault, even as we are separate people. My sins are my own, and I couldn't be more sorry. You must carry your own without the added burden of mine. Despite everything which has come between us, believe that I love you, only you. Tonight my answer would have been yes, always yes to begin again with you. *Vaya con Dios.* Tessa

If all went well, she would destroy the note before he ever saw it. It would be today; she could wait no longer. If she didn't find Ginger, she would obtain the information some other way.

The house was so silent, and she thought of the noise of the children. *Dear God, whatever else, take care of them,* she prayed. Her concept of God did not allow for the same request for herself under these circumstances.

Though she would have been grateful to ride today, she walked. She had no intention of having Amordoro mark her trail with his golden gleam. Her reticule swung with its own weighted rhythm, perhaps payment for death. Never to ride or breathe or laugh or love again, never to see what the children became, never to know Gavin again. Just punishment, Jordan had said.

Ginger had a lot to think about—the new gown she wanted but couldn't afford now, the possibility that her newest regular just might set her up permanently as his exclusive property. She'd always had a yen for that kind of security, and the work of pleasing one man was less arduous than pleasing many. Belle wouldn't make a fuss over it; she wasn't like some madams, she knew a woman had to look out for the best chance, and she didn't keep her girls prisoners in the house. But try as she might, Ginger couldn't get Mrs. Ramsay off her mind. The woman had always been kind to her, extending credit though that was not the policy of the shop, and more important, she was a friend of Belle and Charles. The ways of the gentry, British or American, were strange in any case, and Mrs. Ramsay was surely gentry, even if she did have friends in other quarters and a business. Friends, her and the madam. Ginger contemplated that fact with even more unease than before. She thrust the cravats she was considering as a gift for her regular away from her.

"I can't decide yet," she told the clerk fretfully. "I'll be back later." She bustled out to the waiting barouche, ordering the coachman to return immediately to Belle's.

She was relieved to learn that her employer was up and dressed; she didn't think she could wait another minute to speak to her, and her words tumbled out in a frenzy when she confronted her. "Oh, ma'am, she said it were a housemaid in trouble, but I don't think so, I don't. An' I told her about Mother Patience, me lucky an' careful an' not needin' such just hearing of 'er, an' I don't think I ought
542

to have done, I think it's for herself, I do. If not, whyn't she come to you, you being friends an' all?"

"Ginger, who are you talking about?" Belle asked with exaggerated patience. She had a headache this morning, and she wasn't in any mood to listen to incoherent chatter.

Ginger's eyes went wide. "Oh, what a silly I am! I thought I told you that first thing. Mrs. Ramsay, that's who." With some satisfaction she saw she had Belle's complete attention.

"Repeat your story again, slowly please, Ginger." The tone was cold and deadly. Ginger's satisfaction died abruptly, and she wished she had had nothing to do with this, but she did as she was bid, beginning with Mrs. Ramsay being outside when she left the house.

"Now I understand. Indeed, I think I know which maid it is," Belle lied blandly. Her eyes held Ginger's. "You won't mention this to anyone else, will you?" Ginger shook her head vigorously in negation and fled at Belle's dismissal.

Belle said a few choice words that even easy-going Charley disliked her to use. She knew even more surely than Ginger did that Tessa wanted the information for herself. There were no housemaids at the Ramsay house, and neither Molly nor Anne at the shop would need someone like Mother Patience, but Tessa did. Surely even if Gavin were still carrying on with that woman, Tessa was not the kind of woman to rid herself of his child out of spite, and in any case, she had seemed to want more children. Just look at the way she had taken to the waif Gavin had brought home, and once she had said how very much she wanted a daughter.

Belle froze for an instant and swore again. The lover. It wasn't Gavin's child at all. "Never mind whose child it is," she told herself sharply. She had to decide what to do about it. There wasn't much time. Go after Tessa by herself. She rejected the idea immediately. She knew the force of a determined woman; she had been one all her life. Find Charley and have him go to Gavin? Despite the gravity of the situation, she almost laughed aloud at the ludicrous picture that presented. Charley, while capable of judging every player's skill and the way the cards were going to run within minutes of a game's beginning, was markedly lacking in the talent required for this kind of situation. And he was very fond of Tessa. Belle had no trouble at all imagining Charley descending to Ginger's level of uselessness. She refused to consider what she was going to do if she didn't find Gavin at the warehouse; to search the lumbermill and various other places where he might be would take far too much time.

Even though she had taken the covered carriage, far too many men recognized her and slowed her down with their clumsy efforts to pay court. It was all she could do to keep her smile fixed and her voice pleasant as she kept repeating, "Thanks, boys, but I'm in a hurry, if you'll just came around later . . ." The way things were going, she thought grimly, she'd have half the male population of San Francisco at her establishment before the day was over.

She swept into the offices of the Ramian warehouse wearing her most imperious expression, and when an officious clerk would have impeded her progress, she looked down her nose at him and snapped, "I have business with Mr. Ramsay, and I want to see him immediately." Then she raised her voice and called, "Gavin, come rescue me from your hireling!" The man flushed scarlet.

Gavin came out of his office and grinned when he saw Belle. "It's all right, Matheson." He nodded the young man away, and took Belle's hand. "To what do I owe this pleasure?" But his smile was already beginning to fade. Her hand was icy cold, and he could see the unfamiliar glitter in her eyes. "Charles?" he asked quietly.

Her own smile remained frozen in place. "Inside please, away from them," she whispered, a small jerk of her head indicating the curious clerks. "Is Indian here too?"

"No, he's at the mill," he said as he closed the door behind them, and the small knot of apprehension grew larger and pulled tighter inside of him.

"I don't know what the hell I'm doing here!" Belle burst out. "In my business, a happy marriage is money lost. And having a woman for a friend isn't exactly in my line either, though I'm rather fond of some of my girls." She paused, twisting her hands together nervously, and Gavin eyed her warily, suddenly sure this had something to do with Soledad. He didn't want any more lectures than
544

he had already given himself on the subject, but he was aware of his relief because instinctively he had thought it was something worse. His relief was short-lived.

"Do you know who Mother Patience is?" Belle asked, and could have cursed him for his blank look. Nothing was going to make this any easier, and at this moment she could have gladly thrown Gavin and every other man including Charley into the bay. "The name is a bitter jest. Mother Patience is a foul piece of hell who rids women of the babies they carry and often of their lives. Tessa got her name from one of my girls this morning. She said it was for a housemaid in trouble. It's for herself . . ." Her voice trailed away, and she swallowed convulsively. She saw the blue eyes darken until they were black without light; she saw shock and rage deepen the lines on his face, and she was momentarily afraid of this man she called friend. More afraid for Tessa's sake when Gavin said flatly, "The child isn't mine. We haven't been lovers for months." He did not question the fact of the child.

Belle was already tensing her muscles to spring up and flee the office, not caring what the clerks saw, thinking only that she must now find Tessa on her own after all and somehow hide her away from Gavin. It took her a confused instant to register the sense of his low, broken words. "I drove her to it. Poor Tessa, poor love. No wonder she was afraid."

Belle felt a great upsurge of hope; his rage was self-directed. She wanted to hug him for the beauty of his reaction, not a common one in her knowledge of men. But instead she said with forced brightness, "Come on, we've got to go find her," and Gavin found himself in her carriage.

"I believe in a woman's right to settle her own life, God knows I do, even in such matters as this, but Mother Patience is a devil. Surely Tessa will have had the sense to see that. We've probably gone through this madness for naught," Belle murmured, seeking to comfort herself as much as Gavin.

"You don't know her very well after all," Gavin commented grimly. "Once she's set on a course, it's damn near impossible to shift her from her purpose."

Neither of them mentioned the other person involved in this, the man who had fathered the child. Gavin concentrated on Tessa, willing her to be all right, willing his mind not to flash images of the men they knew, not to ask, *Was it this one, or this, or this?*

The atmosphere of filth, physical and spiritual, was so pervasive that Tessa had almost gotten not to mind it, like the stench of dead things so overpowering that the sense of smell is lost in protective insensitivity. The fat slug of a woman dangling and petting the emerald collar as if it were a live thing took on an aura approaching benevolence. After all, it was sly, dark work she did, no wonder it had made her odd. It was so good not to have her touching her shrinking flesh any longer, Tessa was beginning to believe perhaps it was not too hard and dangerous to rid herself of Jordan's seed after all. She had drunk the draught to the last dregs, a potion so foul and slimy there too she had ceased to mind. Herbs she didn't know. Toadstools glowing in the dark. "Do you pick them at night?" she asked Mother Patience and the little pig eyes watching her seemed answer enough. If the draught didn't work, Mother Patience had other ways.

Tessa tried to define how she felt. She had a great need to put a name to it. It was like being drunk. She remembered when her belongings had arrived in Monterey from Rancho Valle del Mar, and they had celebrated with wine and laughter as she sorted through her clothing. That was the first time she knew what it felt like to be giddy. How long ago that was, so long ago. No, this wasn't really like that. There were strange colors and shapes in the room now, things she knew could not be there even as she watched them whirl around her. She pondered the question idly and asked it. "What will you do if I die here?"

"Pay well to make sure no one knows. Pay well to make sure the body goes out to sea on the tide." The answer was prompt, and even the cackle of laughter that followed it didn't disturb Tessa.

"The body, not 'your' body, just the body, this is a fine way to state it. This has made me only body; I've never been only body before. Always there was a mind and a heart somewhere to go with it. I think only women can be made into only body." She knew it was profound. She wished her voice was not so slurred. She could hear them, all the edges missing from the words, but she couldn't say them.

She wondered how long she'd been here. She was suddenly sure she would not leave this place after all. Her body contracted into a tight fetal curl with the first burning spasm. She welcomed it even though it was ignominious to be sick in front of this creature. When she heard the thunder of Gavin's voice she was sure she was hallucinating again.

He had given Mother Patience no warning, creeping quietly up the stairs with the coachman and Belle at his heels, knocking the door in when he got to it. His eyes took in the whole sordid scene even as the fat woman shrieked and tried to back away from him. His fist shot out and caught her on the jaw, sending her crashing against the wall. Her head was at an impossible angle on her neck.

He picked up Tessa. Her eyelids fluttered, but then her head lolled limply on his shoulder.

In the coach it was Belle who took charge while Gavin held his wife and said her name over and over again hopelessly. Belle checked Tessa, noting the light racing pulse and the spasmodic heaving efforts of her body to rid itself of the poison.

"That woman gave her some medicine, she didn't cut the baby from her, there's no bleeding. Gavin, I know a doctor; he's a good man and no preacher. Should I send for him or do you want your own?" She made her voice brisk to get through to him.

He focused on her with great effort, sorting out the sense of what she was saying. Their own doctor, they had none. Tessa was the one who took care of them all. The irony of it choked him. "Send for your man," he managed. He didn't think it would do any good. The futility of it all was flowing from the limp form he cradled into his own bones. Her skin was clammy and cold, and even in the dim light he could see the blue-gray cast of it. And it came to him that he was feeling her surrender, not his own.

"Don't do it, Tessa, don't. We love each other, that's
547

all that matters, that's all. Nothing, no one else matters, just us, *mi vida*, just us. Don't leave me, don't."

The crooning, pleading repetition of his voice made Belle shiver, but she made no protest. If anyone on earth could get through to Tessa in her present state, it was Gavin.

As soon as they had stepped down and Gavin was carrying Tessa into the house, the carriage swung away at great speed, Belle's coachman willing to put it and himself at risk to find the doctor.

"Gavin, I don't really know enough, but I'm sure we should keep her warm," Belle said, knowing it wouldn't do any harm and at least it would give Gavin something to do to build a fire in the bedroom hearth. "Where are the extra linens?"

Gavin stared at her blankly for a moment, and then pulled himself together and gestured at a chest. "In there, I think."

Belle took linens, the ewer of water and bowl to the bed, and she kept up a steady stream of soft words as she ministered to Tessa. "That's it honey, that's it. Get rid of it all. Don't worry, sweetling, it'll be all right. Gavin loves you. We all love you." She was glad to hear Gavin's voice join her own and surprised at his tender skill when he began to assist her.

Tessa opened her eyes, and she nearly said his name aloud. Then she realized it was not Jordan but a stranger looking at her with anxious eyes. The same but not the same. Hair more sandy than golden, eyes more blue than gray, face squarish and features blunt, not like Jordan's sleek lines.

"There, are we feeling better?" the strange man asked.

"Are you feeling ill also?" Even though her voice was only a thin thread of sound, the tartness came through.

The man looked startled for a moment, and then he smiled, and his laughter was hearty. "I stand corrected, Mrs. Ramsay. I feel quite well, especially now that you're back with us. I'm Dr. Harland, John Harland. You're going to feel puny for a while, but you'll be all right with rest."

It didn't make sense, how could he be so kind? This man was a doctor, so surely he knew what she had done, tried to do?

"Not too long, Mr. Ramsay, she'll sleep naturally pretty soon. Give her a small amount of water if she wants it and broth as soon as she'll take it. Part of the problem is that she was already run down before she took the stuff," Tessa heard him say even as her hand moved across her belly. *No, God no! Not Gavin!* she wanted to scream, but she couldn't. She shut her eyes tightly and turned her head away, waiting for the stream of abuse that would surely come, that she surely deserved. She shivered and swallowed desperately as another wave of nausea swept over her.

Gavin's warm hands took possession of her cold ones, holding them gently, and his voice was as soft as his touch. "Look at me, please, *querida*, look at me."

She didn't understand. Had the whole world gone mad? She remembered now, Gavin finding her with that horrible woman, Gavin's voice pleading in the swaying world of the carriage. He knew; he had to know. Like the doctor, he was being kind, why was he being kind? She turned her head and opened her eyes.

Her face looked so pinched and ill, her eyes haunting in their huge depths of pain and despair. "It was poison, you drank poison! Sweet Jesus, Tessa, you nearly killed yourself! How you must despise me to risk so much!" His voice broke, he bent his head over their hands, and she felt his tears on her skin.

"Despise you? But it is I who have done this thing." She could not put a name to it. Surely she had rid herself of the child, and he must know. Perhaps they were never going to speak of it again, perhaps that was it.

But his head came up and his eyes glittered fiercely, dispelling that hope. "You haven't lost the child, Tessa, and you won't. It has a wild will to survive, and it will be born to both of us, *our child*." The emphasis was too distinct for her to mistake it, and then his voice changed to a low, savage note. "I could kill the man for leaving you like this."

"He didn't leave me. I left him. He doesn't know about the baby. I don't understand why you are being so kind."
549

Her voice was a dry, rasping whisper of effort, and Gavin carefully gave her a few sips of water before he answered. "I would be a brute indeed if I couldn't see that what you have done is no different from what I have done. We've both hurt each other and ourselves, but your pain is greater because your woman's body betrayed you. But before God, I would not have had you born a man." His attempted laugh failed in a sob, and he moaned, "Tessa, I love you so."

She wanted to comfort him and tell him how much his understanding meant, but her strength was spent and she slipped away in sleep.

He left her briefly to thank the doctor and Belle, who were finally taking their weary leave.

Dr. Harland cut short his thanks. "Mr. Ramsay, it's my business to cure the sick and my pleasure when I'm able to accomplish it. With care I judge that Mrs. Ramsay and the babe will be fine. I'll return to make sure all is going well."

The men shook hands, each liking what he saw, and then Dr. Harland went outside, leaving Belle to have a few moments of privacy with her friend.

She reached inside her reticule, and the emeralds sparkled in her hand as she gave the collar to Gavin. "That bitch dropped this when you hit her. She won't need them in hell. I couldn't leave them there."

"I know Tessa would be glad for you to have them," Gavin said, but Belle shook her head. "No, they belong around her neck, not mine. I know how she came to have them, and I've a good suspicion why she thought to use them as she did. Someday she'll wear them with pride again, and then you'll know she's fully healed."

Gavin stooped to brush her cheek with a gentle kiss. "You're one hell of a woman, Belle, and I'll never cease to be grateful for what you did."

She looked discomfited by the praise, but she smiled. "Even with my profession being what it is, I know a good deal about loving. Charley's seen to that. Give her time, Gavin."

Gavin stood a minute watching dawn seep over the city. Did he and Tessa still have something left? He shivered, thinking that in their blind, uncaring turning to other

lovers they had perhaps destroyed all they had build together. *Soledad*. The name had the power now to make
him want to retch as violently as Tessa had in the grip of
the noxious draught. And the missing name, the man who
had been Tessa's lover—someone he knew, one of his
friends or business acquaintances, or a stranger in this
city of men? He would not ask the name, and he did not
think she would tell him. Nor did he expect he would ever
be free of the pain of knowing she had given her body
willingly into the possession of another man. Finally he
understood her rage and grief over Soledad, and he cursed
himself for being so insensitive to it before. He could
see another man's hands roving Tessa's body, another
man's mouth teasing her, another's man's body moving
to take hers. Had the man pleased her more than he had?
Worst of all, beyond the physical joining, had Tessa loved
the man more than she loved him, did she still? He sighed
wearily, feeling twice his years. And then the first faint
hope began to steal into his heart like the sunlight flooding
the city. Tessa was alive.

He and Tessa, they had so much to live for, so much
to do together, and it would be the worst tragedy if they
went on with the bitterness of this ordeal. He forced himself to think of the child Tessa carried, and he found
himself amazed all over again at the tenacity with which
it had clung to life while Tessa had approached death. The
other beginnings that had ended in miscarriages these last
few years, they had lacked the strength of this one. Son
or daughter, the child would be cherished; he would see
to it.

Tessa was still asleep when he went back to her, and
only now did he see the note on the bureau. He hesitated,
thinking he ought to destroy it unread. But then he tore
it open. His throat constricted and his eyes burned as he
read it.

"I meant every word," Tessa said softly. "I don't know
if you can believe me, but it's true. I didn't love him. I
couldn't. You, it will always be you."

Gavin stood looking down at her. "I believe you. I
almost feel sorry for the man. The poor bastard." He
knelt so that his face was level with hers. "How do you
feel?" His hand hovered uncertainly near her head. He

wanted to stroke her hair back in the old gesture, but he didn't know whether he ought to touch her or not. Her hand came up and pulled his down until it rested on the black silk framing her face. "I feel better with you here, touching me. You are so weary. Lie beside me and sleep now."

He obeyed, lying down fully clothed on the coverlet beside her, moving carefully because he was conscious of her fragility. She moved to rest her head on his shoulder and their thoughts were not parallel, because she was conscious of her strength. Soon she would have to face the children, and she must begin to accept the fact that she was going to bear Jordan's baby. None of that was as important as having Gavin back again, here beside her. That was the key she had so nearly lost and must never misplace again. There were a thousand facets to their marriage, and certainly the mental and spiritual were not to be denigrated, but it was the physical bonding, the mutual possession that remained the central force of their lives and from which all other aspects radiated like rivers of light from the sun. She accepted the burden of being so earth rooted and sensual that the concept of heaven appeared not only ridiculous, but chillingly barren. To love this man, to know his warmth and to give him hers, that alone she would wish for eternity. She thought of death, so few hours ago an acceptable lover, now once more the implacable enemy. She pressed closer to Gavin who had sunk into an exhausted sleep. He murmured a name light as the wind, and she froze for an instant before she recognized it as her own. Not Soledad, and not Tess, but Tessa, Gavin's Tessa.

CHAPTER XLVI

Tessa felt as if she had died after all and had been reborn. Kindness continued to be offered to her by everyone around her. Sometimes she awakened to see Armenthia or Belle sitting quietly, waiting to see if she wanted company or anything else. And she finally convinced Indian that there was nothing he could have done even had he known what had happened that day, so that when he looked in on her, his face no longer wore the guilty look. But most often it was Gavin who was there, his patient love surrounding her like a protective cloak, keeping the world at bay. When she protested that all she needed was rest and food for a few days and not all his time besides, he told her gently that he had his own needs too, the greatest being to be with her.

He brought her tempting dishes though he admitted Armenthia, Molly, and a few others had more to do with the cooking than he, and he urged her to eat everything until she complained that she felt like one of the children. Gavin only smiled and kept on pampering her. With John Harland's assurances, he didn't really fear for her physical well-being now, but he knew better than she that it would take time for her mind and spirit to heal fully, no matter how sure she was that everything was all right now. Her reaction to the various bits of news he brought her were proof of the gauzy curtain that hung between herself and full consciousness. Molly and the other clerks had been told she had been taken ill by a fever caused by overwork, and they accepted this. Tessa was relieved they knew nothing more, but she was uncharacteristically incurious about how things were going at the shop. It was as though she had never poured her energy into making it a success. And her calm response when Gavin told her that Jordan Ames had left the city was no pretense; it was difficult for her to connect very much of anything to herself beyond the knowledge that Gavin had returned to her life.

She had been up for a few days, though she had not yet been to the shop when Gavin suggested they send for the children. "Indian and Armenthia want to get married before too much more time passes, and they'd like the children to be there. They'd be married at Rancho Magnífico if it weren't for Thia's loyalty to those Fitz-Williams people. I guess it's only understandable that they be at the wedding, because they are her only family, but Indian can't see hauling them out in the country."

Tessa laughed suddenly at the mental picture that produced, and Gavin loved the sweetness of the sound he had not heard for so long, but then her face grew thoughtful. "If you'll give me just a few more days, I will be ready to go, and then we can travel together to the *rancho* for the children and Chong Sing."

His refusal died unuttered. He saw the brightness in her eyes, the color in her cheeks at the idea, and he knew that it was a good one and would be even better with his additional plan. "We'll go as soon as you're strong enough, and first we'll go to Rancho Valle del Mar."

Her eyes shone with tears. "Sometimes you know me so much better than I know myself. I had not thought of it at all, and yet now I find with your words that I want very much to go."

He put his arms around her and held her as gently as if she were indeed a child, and a few days later they rode out of the city, leaving Molly in charge of the shop and Indian in charge of everything else.

Gavin watched over Tessa carefully, calling a halt long before she was tired, seeing to her needs, guarding her from harm and guarding the careful distance between them just as well. If she cried out at night, he was there instantly, holding her, soothing her from nightmare to dream, then withdrawing to himself again, going no further than comfort. And when she realized how deliberate it all was, she was grateful. The curtain would not separate her forever from everything she must face, and to be strong when it was gone was her only task.

They kept to themselves on the journey, not even stopping in Monterey, and they marveled at the spreading signs of civilization, the inns they avoided, the small farms and settlements that were gnawing at the edges of the vast *ranchos*.

But when they rode onto the land of Valle del Mar, it was as if time and progress had stopped, and Tessa's heart began to sing with the joy of this land, a soft faint note at first beginning to swell with power as she saw the acres sweeping down to the distant sea, the horses and cattle sleek and content as they grazed on grass still green despite summer's passage.

And then she was fast in María's arms and the people of the *rancho* were greeting the Ramsays with glad cries, and the fiesta began as if it had been planned for weeks.

Juan and Julio and their wives and children and countless others, but for Tessa most of all María and Ramón, both of them ever more earth-gnarled and comforting. She did not see the exchange between Gavin and María, María showing her worry plainly, Gavin telling her softly, "Here it will be all right. She needed to come home."

The feasting and dancing began before the sun was down, and Gavin watched Tessa carefully, saw the joy and the sorrow welling in her, and waited calmly for them to peak together. She ate little but danced feverishly, sometimes with him, sometimes with *vaqueros* proud of the honor. Gavin was glad that she danced because for her it was always an art without sham, a time when the passions of her mind and spirit were released in the fluid grace of her body moving to the music. In this too he understood her better than she understood herself.

"Let the fiesta continue after we have retired," he told María, and he moved to ask Tessa for the waltz before anyone else could.

They danced in perfect harmony, and the other dancers drifted to the sidelines under the flaring torches to watch the *patrón* and *patróna*. "Such love," one of the *vaquero*'s wives whispered. "It is like the night of their wedding."

"And more," her husband replied, taking her hand in his own.

Tessa looking up into Gavin's eyes was thinking the same thing. "Always you know what I need, how to comfort me," she said low, and she saw the flash of pain darken his eyes. "Not always, my love. Come, the dancing will continue without us."

There were clapping and cheers as they left, and the party sailed on smoothly under María's direction.

Gavin helped Tessa undress as he had that night years before, but this time she helped him in turn.

"Tessa, this must be what you want," Gavin managed, fighting to control his own desire. He had tried to judge and understand as well as he could, but he knew the final choice was hers, and even now he could feel the conflict raging in her, making her tremble as everything took on its full reality.

She leaned against him, and he held her tightly for a moment before he set her down gently on the bed. She

555

looked up at him with a thousand shadows moving in her eyes. But when he began to touch her softly, she pressed against his hands like a cat, body moving in slow, sinuous waves. His own tension eased, but when his hand moved down over her belly, she froze, and he felt the first cry welling deep inside her before she gave voice to it in a long, wrenching sob.

The words came out raggedly when she had the breath for them. "I can't let you take the blame," she began, and he heard her bitter tale of sending him back to Soledad, of letting his imagined infidelity be the excuse for her own.

He held her, and he let her weep, wanting her to rid herself of guilt and grief. And when he thought she could hear him again, he spoke to her, his voice low and even. He explained why Soledad's scent had clung to him.

"If there is blame, we share it. I would have told you about Soledad had not part of me been willing to go back to her poison. You and I had ceased to talk, ceased to share, and that is the only way what happened could have happened. And in that, I think the greater blame is mine. I offered you a grievous insult, wanting you to be less than you are while I asked more and more of your strength." Her hand stole up to press against his mouth, denying his censure of himself. He kissed her palm and held her hand prisoned in his own. "You see, blame and guilt are useless to both of us. It's over. We have nothing to do now but love each other and remember never to shut ourselves away from each other again."

"The child?" A trembling wisp of sound.

"Is part of you and therefore part of me. Sleep now, my love."

"You are my life."

He felt her go suddenly limp in exhausted sleep, and when he touched her face, it was still damp with tears.

He awakened to the pale light of dawn and something tickling his nose. Tessa was leaning over him, teasing him with the long braid of her hair, but when she saw his eyes opening, she scrambled out of his reach before he could grab her. "Come, sleepy one, I have plans for us today, but they cannot begin without you. Everything else is prepared."

556

She was still a little pale and heavy-eyed from the storm of tears, but she looked serene and really happy for the first time since their journey back to each other had begun. She was already dressed in an old blouse, skirt, and sash. An enormous well of tenderness closed his throat—she looked as she had the first day, and he knew without doubt where she was taking him.

Ramón smiled as he watched them ride away, and he was glad of the sweetness of María when she came to stand beside him. His arm went around her automatically. "I do not think we will see them again before the sun is fallen today," he said, and she agreed. "Let us hope we do not. Let us hope we do not see them until the sun has fallen and risen again. Our little one would have it so." She pressed closer to him. "Sometimes it is well, I think, not to know everything about those we love. I do not think I would care to know what has put the sadness in Tessa and Don Gavin's eyes."

"Nor I. It is only important that it is less today and will, God willing, be still less tomorrow."

They spoke little on the ride to the pool, letting the soft autumnal day weave its spell around them, but when Gavin felt the weight of the blanket rolls that had been secured to Diablo and Amordoro's saddles, he raised his eyebrow and inquired, "Am I to understand your plan includes our living here until spring comes?"

Tessa's eyes gleamed with mischief. "No, my plan includes loving here until morning comes, and I saw no reason we should be cold or hungry."

She saw the blue of his eyes deepen, and she grabbed her bundle and darted away despite its weight, laughing and calling, "See to the horses."

She disappeared up the path to the pool, and he hastened to complete the chores before he followed her.

His breath caught as he topped the rise and drank in the scene before him—the pool glimmering in the light and singing with its own life, the dark green of the pines and the spreading gold of other trees weaving a tapestried canopy and dappling the light on the ground and on Tessa, Tessa who lay on the blanket she had spread, her clothes folded in a neat pile, her hair loose and flowing around her, her body waiting for him.

The bundle he was carrying dropped from his hands unheeded and his clothes followed, his eyes never leaving Tessa, and then he was with her, taking her in his arms, drinking his fill of her, not knowing or caring whether it was his body or hers or both trembling, not with fear or sorrow now but with need. He loomed over her, watching her face as he entered her, feeling her body welcoming him, seeing the love in her eyes until they closed as she whimpered and arched her body against his, and he too was lost to any awareness beyond the pulsing rhythm.

They lay holding each other for a long wordless time in the after calm, and then Tessa began to quote softly, "Come live with me and be my love, And we will all the pleasures prove," but her voice stopped suddenly even as Gavin felt her body tense. "No, no old words, only new ones for us!" she said vehemently. She kissed him swiftly and was gone in a flash of long limbs, her hair spreading out behind her as she swam in the pool.

All the deadly little pieces of the puzzle finally fit perfectly.

He knew with no further doubt that Jordan had been her lover. Her admission last night that the scent of Soledad had begun it all had triggered a like memory in his own mind—the scent of Tessa's flowers in Jordan's office. And Jordan would have spiced the game of love-making with old and treasured lines. He had not wanted it to be Jordan, and so he had believed the message Jordan had left about urgent business in Sacramento, a chance to join an important firm there. He had accepted the man Jordan had turned their papers over to, a middle-aged attorney with a good reputation and humorous eyes. And Tessa had still been abed when he told her the news of losing a good friend and a good business colleague. She had met his eyes squarely, saying no more than, "Oh, dear, and I thought he was doing so well here. The children will be so disappointed when they find him gone." No betrayal of her own loss.

He watched her swimming with long, lazy strokes in the clear, cold water, and he felt the last of the jealousy he had been battling so hard against beginning to dissipate. Her lover had not been just anyone, but a man of culture, talent, wit, and enormous-intelligence, and she had given him up. Gavin realized now that Jordan had always looked at Tessa with love, but he himself had dismissed it in his arrogance. He would not make that mistake again. He pitied Jordan.

He dove into the pool in a shallow racing arc, and Tessa tried to elude him but then she started to giggle and had to give up as he pulled her back to the rocks. "Out with you, madam. I don't want to make love to a shriveled crone, and too much time in this cold water does even worse to me."

They lay warming themselves on the sunlit ledge, and Tessa laughed aloud in pure delight, her whole body humming with it. "It is so good to be alive!"

Gavin moved his hand gently over the small rounding of her belly. "It's good to have both of you alive."

She looked up into his eyes and let herself drift in the vast, safe blue.

There were so many perfections of the day that they spent much of it simply letting the magic of the place enchant them. Birds sang and fluttered in the trees. A yellow-and-black butterfly, late for the season, settled on a last clump of purple thistle. "I don't suppose we would know the difference if there was none, but isn't it grand of the world to have so much color?" Tessa whispered as if the butterfly might take fright at her voice. "If they built churches like this, I would go every day."

"You little pagan," Gavin teased. "I'd go with you."

They shared their memories of the pool without words, both thinking of the first meeting and the wedding beside the water.

At sundown a few deer came to drink and stayed for long moments before they caught the human scent and faded away swiftly.

Gavin left only once, to check on the horses and gather extra wood for the fire he had built while Tessa spread out the food María had provided for their picnic supper.

And replete with food and sun and love, they watched the night come down and the moon and stars filling the open space over the pool and rippling light on its surface. And Gavin loved Tessa slowly and deliberately now, reclaiming all that was his own until her cries were like the wild singing of a night bird.

559

He lay awake while she slept in his arms, and he sorted out the night sounds, hearing the faraway chorus of coyotes but no threatening sound of bear or lion. Then he settled Tessa more comfortably in his arms and let sleep take him, his last awareness the little nestling movement Tessa made against him.

The dawn awakened them, and they shared the sweet knowledge of the strength and peace they had been given by the earth in this hushing season before winter's dying.

María and Ramón needed only to see their faces to know that the blessing had been renewed. When she had a moment alone with Tessa, María said shyly, "Perhaps now the baby will be born already knowing of the mother's secret place by the water."

Tessa looked at her in amazement and smiled ruefully. "Since you know so much, perhaps you can make it a girl this time." For the first time she found herself looking forward to this child. And before they left, she put bouquets of late flowers on the graves of her parents and a small, delicate one for her baby brother. She did it without fear, thinking that as one had died, one would live.

Now they felt strong enough to face anyone, and they stopped on their way in Monterey before going on to Rancho Magnífico. It had been so long since they had seen Carmelita and Sam that all four of them, even taciturn Sam, were slightly hoarse after catching up on each other's news.

"Carmelita, I swear marriage does agree with you!" Tessa told her, and it was true, Carmelita was a little rounder, but merry, beautiful, and content.

"Marriage to Sam agrees with me," Carmelita corrected her. "It is foolish at my age, but I think I love him more every day. And you do not look as if it is a hardship to be married to Gavin."

Tessa found herself sharing the news of the coming child joyfully and scoffing at Carmelita's warnings to take care. The things Carmelita and Sam did not know were so much more terrifying than anything else.

They stayed in Monterey for only one night before traveling on, both of them in a fever now to see the children. "Perhaps they won't even want to come home with us, we have left them on their own so long," Tessa suggested nervously.

Gavin laughed at her fear. "I'd hardly call being with Chong Sing and everyone at Rancho Magnífico being on their own." And then he added gently, "We have much more to offer them now than when they left the city."

It certainly seemed to be true. Their arrival brought an explosion of children that made it difficult to believe they had only three sons. There was no doubt that the boys had missed them, but it was equally clear that their summer had been one of pure delight. Tessa was hard put to sort out the various adventures, since they were all being told at once in three voices. All three looked healthy; even Paul's pale skin had taken on a golden glow, and the frail look of the winter's illnesses was gone.

She knew she was crying, but could do nothing to stop the tears.

"Why are you sad, Mama?" Jefferson asked anxiously.

"I'm not sad, I'm happy!" Tessa protested, and Brand said, "That's a silly reason."

It was reassuring to find that though they had grown, they had changed little in their natures. Jefferson was still the one so attuned to other people's feelings, Brand quick and practical, Paul the shy one. And it was Paul who would always be the most vulnerable and insecure because his beginnings had been so harsh. She felt him trembling as he pressed against her.

"Did you think we'd left you here forever?" she asked softly.

"I 'oped"—He corrected himself quickly— "I *hoped* not. An' I did think you'd be back 'cuz of Brand an' Jefferson."

Gavin overheard and swung Paul up into his arms. "Enough of that, you're our son too, for always."

Tessa saw the look on Brand's face and sighed inwardly. The same indeed. The jealousy surfacing again now that he had his parents' affections to fight for again.

But nothing could dampen the joy of the reunion, and it was complete when Chong Sing appeared, obviously having deliberately given the family time alone.

"You've taken marvelous care of the children. Thank
561

you so much," Tessa said, but Chong Sing dismissed the praise and thanks with a small gesture of his hands. "Many, many people heah help take cale of children. We go back to de city now?"

Tessa had to smile. Chong Sing had had enough of his exile in the country. She was sure the first thing he would do when they arrived in San Francisco would be to re-supply his larder with the exotic foods he favored.

"Velly good see you an' Mista Lamsay so happy now," he said quietly, and padded away to make sure the meal being prepared for them was up to his standards.

They stayed only a few days, but it was time enough to ride the land and be glad of the fine care it showed. Pedro was justly proud.

They didn't want to have to travel too slowly, so they left instructions for a load of produce to be carted to San Francisco along with several horses. They had ever more horses to sell now that many of the foals born on the *rancho* were old and well trained enough to be good riding stock. These were not breeding animals, but rather the colts and some fillies driven off by the stallions of the *manadas* who would brook no rivals from males nor reluctance from females. They were still forming new *manadas* and would always continue the process, but only with the finest beasts.

Ramón and his sons would soon be sending like shipments to Monterey. Because there were more people now, it was a better market than in previous years, even if it did not rival San Francisco. Sam Collins would act as the agent there for a percentage, and so all were satisfied.

When Tessa saw how well the children now rode, she promised them that next summer each could choose a horse of his own. Their sadness about leaving the *rancho* was overshadowed by their excitement about Indian's wedding. Jefferson especially still thought of Thia as his special find. "Do they change the very minute the words are said?" he asked. "Did you?"

"Well, it's not like a magic spell from a story where a girl suddenly becomes a tree or anything like that, but . . ."

"But people do change when they are married," Gavin said gravely. "If they are very, very lucky, they grow to know each other better every day and to love each other more."

"Just like you and Mama," Jeff observed with a pleased smile.

"Just like us. And I am indeed glad your mother did not turn into a tree when I married her." Gavin grinned at Tessa, and a lovely, slow blush stained her cheeks.

CHAPTER XLVII

The house was filled with noise again, but the children got into less than their normal mischief and used much of their energy in the plans for Indian's wedding. When any of their ideas sounded a bit too outlandish, Tessa was careful not to hurt their feelings, even while she turned them in another direction.

Her own special project, with Molly's help, was Armenthia's wedding dress and trousseau. At first Thia balked at the gift, but Tessa gainsaid her. "It won't be you who looks at the clothes and the woman in them, it will be Indian, and plain has its place but not all the time." She had quickly discovered the way to obtain Thia's cooperation was to propose that something would be pleasing to Indian.

It was a challenge to design clothes for Armenthia because so many of the day's styles were too fussy for the woman's strong, exotic looks. But Tessa and Molly were well satisfied with the results they achieved. None of the colors they used were vapid; all were deep and vivid, setting off Thia's dark skin and eyes. And the expression on Indian's face when he beheld her in her wedding gown was the best thanks they could have received.

The deep wine velvet was trimmed in ivory satin, which glowed no more smoothly than Armenthia's skin. A circlet of small silk rosebuds from France adorned her head, and she carried a single hothouse rose. She came down the staircase of the Ramsay house alone, Indian met her at the bottom, and they walked together to stand in front of the preacher.

The preacher saved Tessa from making a sentimental fool of herself. He was one of the three or four black pastors who had flocks in San Francisco. The little experience Tessa had had with religion had been with rigid ceremony and chanted Latin, neither of which had anything to do with what she was witnessing now. God and the couple and everyone else were alternately praised and exhorted.

Gavin felt Tessa shaking at his side, and he risked one look at her face and no more. His own impulse to laugh aloud was too strong. But he realized even as she did that the joy bubbling around them was a good and glorious thing, fitting to the day. And if Indian's face looked a little rigid, Armenthia's beaming happiness made up for it. At the end of the ceremony, with a sheepish grin, Indian took his bride's hand and they jumped over the broom laid on the floor, to the cheers of the guests. It was not his tradition, but hers, and because it meant something to her, that was enough. He cupped her face in his hands and took his time kissing her before Gavin and other friends claimed the privilege.

Tessa felt a tug on her skirt and looked down into Jefferson's wide eyes. "Are all weddings like this one?" he asked.

"Not all. Different people have different ceremonies."

"Well, I don't think I'll ever get married probably, but if I do, I'd like it to be like this, all happy," he said.

"I'll remember that if I ever have to plan your wedding," Tessa told him. She hid her amusement until he had scampered back to his brothers, who like him had behaved very well and had helped mightily to decorate the house with ribbons and greenery, but now looked intent on the food table. She shrugged, thinking *Let it be "all happy" for them today even if they do get stomachaches,* and she went to hug the bride and groom.

The festivities continued until late in the evening, the hired musicians playing a variety of dance tunes that moved from the South to the North to the West and threw in a good deal of Europe for good measure. And indeed the guests were a cosmopolitan lot; Tessa was the only native-born Californian there. All the clerks from the shop and the warehouse and the mill were there, plus others who were simply friends Armenthia and Indian had made. Even the Fitz-Williamses looked less out of place when they began to enjoy the party despite themselves. Belle and Charles stayed as long as they could, and Mr. Peniston managed to drop by for a while before returning to his duties at the Golden Horse.

Tessa saw to it that the newlyweds were able to slip away to the frame house without interference when they were ready, but the rest of the guests stayed until very late.

When they were all finally gone, and Tessa had persuaded Chong Sing that sleep was more important than cleaning up the last of the debris, she sighed happily and let Gavin lead her up the stairs. "It was a good party, wasn't it?"

"It surely was. People of different races and professions coming together peacefully is always good." He chuckled. "I wonder if Mrs. Carlton Fitz-Williams knows what Belle does for a living."

He was almost asleep when Tessa sat up in bed, exclaiming, "Oh, my goodness! They're married, but what is Thia's name now, Mrs. what?"

"Mrs. Indian, of course," Gavin replied, and they giggled like children.

With the flurry of the wedding over, Tessa concentrated on her next project, which was to find a tutor for the children. Despite the initial high hopes for a state school system, it was slow in getting started and already Brand, Jefferson, and even Paul were too far advanced to be happy with the rudiments. Neither of their parents had sufficient time to teach them enough, and they were in accord that the boys should now be spending as much time studying as they did at play. They agreed too that the tutor should be someone who challenged their minds with ideas, not with a stick. Gavin and Tessa agreed, but the city seemed unable to produce this paragon.

They ran an advertisement in two of the most popular newspapers, and Tessa did most of the interviewing, seeing the applicants at the shop and planning to take the chosen one home to meet the children only when she was sure he would do. But he never materialized.

"You have no idea how many peculiar men present themselves as tutors," she complained to Gavin.

"Do you want to have them come to me at the warehouse or the mill?" he asked sympathetically.

"No, I don't. I think you might inflict some damage on a few of them just for their attitudes about children." She was still shocked at the prevalent idea that children could only learn by sound beatings and endless rote. It was so very different from the way she had been raised, and every time one of the would-be tutors expounded on his ideas of discipline, she saw the white scar on Gavin's cheek. There were a few who seemed qualified intellectually, but whom, for their own good, she could not hire. They were at the opposite extreme, men so prissy and full of delicate sensibilities she knew her sons would make short work of them, thinking of grand new mischief in the process.

She resented the thought as soon as it came to her, but she knew that Jordan would have been a great help in this situation. It was the lowest point of the search, to be unable to find a tutor and to think of Jordan besides.

The next day Mrs. Tubbs appeared. Her name was singularly inappropriate. She was a tiny desiccated stick of a woman who could have been anywhere from thirty-five to sixty. Her eyes were a luminous, ageless gray, young at one moment, ancient the next. Not quite the same as Jordan's eyes, but gray. Her brown hair was graying, and her dress was gray too, patched and turned with exquisite skill. Molly fluttered and Tessa assumed the woman had come for a job as a seamstress until Molly finally managed to inform her that "this person" had come to inquire about the tutoring position.

"Mrs. Ramsay, I am Mrs. Tubbs," the woman announced, holding out her hand. Her voice was clear and pleasing, with a trace of a British accent.

Tessa's good manners deserted her for a moment as she stared at the woman, before she extended her own hand. Mrs. Tubbs's handshake was cool and firm.

566

"I am sorry, perhaps it wasn't made clear in the newspapers but I have three sons, not three daughters," Tessa said, feeling that it was better to finish this as soon as possible.

The gray eyes studied her calmly. "The advertisement was quite explicit. It is true that I am not capable of teaching your sons how to shoot a gun or how to ride a horse as I cannot claim Californian excellence in either pursuit. I presume there are others to teach them those skills. Nor would I teach them to be girls. I would teach them mathematics, history, the classics, how to read and write clearly, how to think logically."

"How do you feel about discipline?" Tessa found herself asking.

"Discipline is an intrinsic part of an alert mind. Only the poorest of teachers needs a stick to produce it."

Tessa asked about her background, and her fascination about the woman increased. Her father had been the second son of a landed family and unusually fortunate to have inherited a comfortable living with none of the responsibilities of the heir. He had had good tutors and a scholarly turn of mind, and he had also had a yen for adventure. But he had fallen in love with a girl from the neighboring estate when they were both quite young. He had married her and settled down, planning to raise children, write a bit, and lead a quiet life. They had had one child. Tessa found it difficult to imagine Mrs. Tubbs as a child at all.

The pastoral life had ended abruptly with the death of her mother from a fever when the child was only two. Mrs. Tubbs had been left in the care of relatives for a few years and then sent to a boarding school until she was ten years old. During all this time her father corresponded with her faithfully, and spent as much time with her as he could whenever he was in England. So he was no stranger when he came to take her away with him on her tenth birthday, judging her ready to travel with him. He had already made quite a name for himself as an explorer; his lectures and essays were well received by many prestigious British societies. He took his daughter everywhere. They went to see strange mountains, alien

567

peoples, jungles, places of extraordinary flora and fauna. They traveled by any means available and mostly on foot. And her father taught her constantly.

"It was the most marvelous school," Mrs. Tubbs proclaimed. "For Father the whole world was a classroom. Perhaps he wanted a son, but I was never made to feel that. He claimed that the mind had no sex, and he deplored the famine inflicted on the intellects of most women.

"And then, when I was sixteen, we were in India, and Father hired Harvey Tubbs as his secretary. Harvey was a younger son whose circumstances were far less fortunate than Father's. The army had seemed the only place for him, but he had been wounded in one of the constant skirmishes fought in India and was being invalided out of the army. His assistance with Father's papers was welcome, and so was he. We were married two years later. I rather think Father had planned that from the beginning. Harvey was very much like him intellectually, and in his acceptance of my mind." The gray eyes were suddenly shining with faraway light, the whole face looked softer, and Tessa swiftly revised her first impressions—this woman had not always looked the part of a drab little mouse, any more than Molly Barker had.

"The three of us traveled together until father died five years later. We were in Switzerland. Father had always wanted to climb a certain peak. I saw the accident from a lower slope. The ropes gave way. Father pushed the guide to safety but lost his own life. It was tragic, but it was also fitting. Father was in his prime, still capable of believing he could do anything. And I was fortunate that the high altitude had limited Harvey's participation, because one of his wounds in India had been to the lung. Otherwise, he might well have died that day with Father." The brisk voice precluded any offering of sympathy for events long past.

"Harvey and I traveled about for a few more years, and our essays were received nearly as well as my father's had been. We earned enough to go where we pleased and to put enough by with the money Father had left to be able to open a school. We came to the United States ten years ago for that purpose. We built our school in a small town in the state of New York. And for the minds of the children we taught, I will always consider the school a success. But as a business venture it was a failure. Neither Harvey nor I could bear to turn away students simply because they couldn't afford the fees. Even so, we might have gone on." For the first time there was pain and anger in her voice. "But in the end it was very like a witchhunt. The friendships we had made seemed to count for nothing. The rumors grew more and more beastly. We were accused of blasphemy and idolatry because the only religious instruction we gave was a survey of the various systems of belief in the world. Our pupils were taken away from the school one by one. It broke my husband's heart. We decided to come to California, where perhaps the newness would allow us to begin again. We had enough for the passage and a bit besides. But Harvey's health failed him on the voyage. He contracted lung fever and was buried at sea. I have been in San Francisco for six months now. I have a few female pupils. I go to their homes and instruct them in subjects that bore me and undoubtedly them. They will know how to embroider a pretty pillow, how to paint an insipid watercolor, how to read a few notes of music, how to write a legible hand, and little more. I would very much like to truly teach again."

Only now did Tessa notice the white-knuckled knotting of the woman's hands, the betrayal of nervousness and need.

Mrs. Tubb's pale cheeks warmed with color. "It is not my habit to go on at length about myself. But if you give me the position of teaching your sons, I don't wish there to be any misunderstanding. I could not bear for what happened at our school to happen again."

If there had been a battle, Tessa thought, *Mrs. Tubbs had surely won.* "My husband must share approval," she said gently. "But the final decision really rests with the boys. Would you care to come home with me now to meet them?"

Mrs. Tubbs closed her eyes for a moment, and Tessa feared for a moment that she was going to faint, but then her face was lighted by a lovely smile. "I would very much like to meet your children, Mrs. Ramsay."

Gavin's greeting that night was a quick kiss and a babble of excitement from Tessa. "She's wonderful! She can give the children the world! She had them eating out of her hand in minutes. Brand can't wait until he's old enough to go to India. Jefferson wants to learn the name of every bird in the world. Paul is willing to talk about Australia for the first time; he's trying to remember everything about it because Mrs. Tubbs has never been there. She even tamed Chong Sing. She greeted him in Chinese, apologized for her accent, which she was sure was poor and explained to him that she has been trying to learn a few words and phrases ever since she arrived in San Francisco and would be grateful for any help from him when time permitted. And we're to call her Mrs. Tubbs because her given name is Natalia which she considers embarrassingly unsuitable."

Gavin let her go on, picking out what sense he could until she ran out of breath. He was smiling and his eyebrow was up. "Who are you trying to convince? If the woman is so well qualified, I have no objection. I did have a male tutor in my mind, but it seems we may not find a suitable one until the boys are grown men. Have you a prejudice against your own sex, madam, despite your own capabilities?"

"I must have," she admitted sheepishly, and then she threw her arms around him. "I do love you so, and you will love Mrs. Tubbs."

"Not like this," Gavin said, nuzzling her neck.

That night, the baby, which had made only small furtive movements before, kicked hard and long enough for Gavin to feel it against his hand. "We should tell the boys pretty soon."

Tessa agreed, adding, "I expect Mrs. Tubbs will prove helpful with that too."

Indeed, Mrs. Tubbs seemed equal to any occasion, and Gavin found himself as much impressed with her as Tessa was. She added her own strength and serenity to the household in the hours she spent there, and most miraculous of all, the children continued to look forward to every minute of their time with her.

When Tessa told her about the baby, Mrs. Tubbs said, "I offer my congratulations. Harvey and I always wanted a child of our own but never did have one. I expect you will want to tell the boys soon."

Tessa smiled. "Yes, I can't leave it for too much longer or else Jefferson will be sure to ask me why I am getting fat. Please, feel free to answer any questions they may ask."

Mrs. Tubbs smiled back at her. "I appreciate your attitude. I have seen prescribed ignorance regarding sexual matters cause so much heartbreak, I cannot think why such prudery has not died its deserved death. But you may rest assured I will answer as befitting the children's young ages. I think there will be little trouble; they have been raised where breeding and birth are not hidden."

The boys reacted characteristically. Brand took the news with seeming calm, but Tessa suspected he must feel even more jealous and displaced at the idea of yet another child in the family. Jefferson wondered if it was a girl, and if she would ever be any fun to play with; and he was fascinated by the idea that the little curled-up baby was inside his mother, growing until it was ready to be born. Paul blushed furiously, betraying the fact that he knew a good deal about where babies came from and wasn't sure he liked the knowledge.

Tessa found it immensely comforting to have Mrs. Tubbs backing up her own explanations of the process and the love involved. As Mrs. Tubbs put it, "The principle is the same, but the application and degree of emotional involvement in the case of human beings is far different from that of most other creatures as far as we know." It made Tessa very proud that her sons understood this level of thought because Mrs. Tubbs was already training them to it, and they were interested in pursuing the ramifications of her statement.

"We had a wolf, and I think he loved his wife," Jefferson said.

Mrs. Tubbs took it in stride. "Perhaps he did. You must remember that I said 'as far as we know.' "

Tessa left them, smiling to herself at the reasonableness the woman brought to any subject. "It makes perfect sense in our mad world," she told Gavin. "A man is in charge of the household duties and a woman is teaching our sons."

By Christmas, Tessa was in her seventh month and her condition showed plainly, and though she hated to admit it, it also sapped a great deal of her normal energy. She was more grateful than ever to have Chong Sing and Mrs.

Tubbs taking so much of the household burden from her shoulders. The clerks were ever more capable of doing the same at the shop, and were slightly scandalized that she continued to work at all.

She was pleased with all the gifts she had chosen for her family and friends, but nothing pleased her more than the one for Mrs. Tubbs. She and Gavin agreed that anyone who worked hard in their employ deserved good pay; they had long since raised Chong Sing's salary, and they had dealt generously with Mrs. Tubbs since the first day, though the lady had protested vigorously until she discovered that the Ramsays wouldn't listen. But Tessa had soon realized that Mrs. Tubbs would spend little on herself; so little that she worried she didn't get enough to eat, and made sure as subtly as she could that the woman ate as often as possible at the house. The idea of another school had obviously not been abandoned.

The blue dress was an irresistible idea. Mrs. Tubbs's clothes were never anything but clean, but they were all somber and repeatedly mended. And Tessa was sure even the disciplined teacher had enough vanity left to be happy with the deep soft blue wool.

Though she still had much to do at home, Tessa thought it only fair to spend at least a couple of hours at the shop on Christmas Eve day. It was one of their busiest days of the year, a day when dozens of men suddenly remembered that scent, gloves, a fan, or something more elaborate might be appreciated in certain quarters.

Tessa had done a good morning's work, and she was ready to go home. All the clerks had received their gifts and extra money, which she warned them was intended for frivolous use. Molly and George would make sure the shop was locked up an hour earlier than usual this evening.

She was folding the blue dress carefully to take with her, her mind on the pleasures ahead at home. It took her a minute to even recognize the woman who was glowering at her.

She straightened up slowly, bracing her back with her hands. She let the bulge of the baby jut out to its utmost. Molly hovered protectively. "Madam, Mrs. Ramsay is just on her way out. May I assist you?"

"It's all right, Molly," Tessa said quitely. "I have the

time. She is an old acquaintance." There was no pretense of warmth or friendship in her words, but Molly moved away obediently.

"Now, Soledad, what mischief brings you here?" she asked bluntly.

Soledad couldn't take her eyes away from Tessa's figure, and Tessa felt a vicious joy as she read the woman's changing expression. Soledad could count as well as anyone, and she took the baby to be Gavin's which meant he had been sleeping with his wife even as he had with her. In a horrible way, it was laughable; the whore felt betrayed.

Soledad licked her lips nervously and searched ineffectively for words.

And suddenly Tessa was tired of the game. She felt very strong. "I know about the child, the payments, and everything else. It is finished. Gavin and I are together again, and there is no room for you. I pity you, because I think perhaps you really love him in your fashion."

Soledad had come to taunt her, to find out if Gavin had really told his wife, to find some weakness, some way to return to her lover after these long months. But nothing had gone as she had planned. Her control snapped, and she sprang at Tessa, howling foul names in Spanish, her hands curved into claws.

Tessa had seen the sudden distortion of the voluptuous face, the sudden mad gleam in the dark eyes, but she was incapable of moving out of the way fast enough, and she cried out as long fingernails raked one cheek. And then George and Walter were there, holding Soledad fast with rage to match her own. "She belongs in jail," Walter said tightly.

"No, she belongs on the street," Tessa said. "Escort her out, please." She saw the fight drain from Soledad, her features suddenly small and crumpled, her face ashen with the enormity of what she had done. Tears welled in her eyes, and Tessa turned away from the sight, knowing how it felt to want Gavin so much.

Molly insisted on bathing the scratches, and Walter insisted on escorting her home, but no one asked why the woman had attacked her.

Chong Sing took one look at her white face with the vivid marks still oozing blood and immediately began plying her with strong tea. She smiled at him. "I'm really all right." She meant it. She knew she had gained the final victory simply because Soledad had lost control.

She told the children she had carelessly let a branch hit her. She tried to tell Gavin the same thing when he came home.

He held her chin and turned her head to see the scratches better. "A branch with talons? I'll kill her for this." His voice was calm and deadly.

She twisted her head from his grasp. "You'll do nothing, for me. If she had brought me a smile and a gift for the season, I would have killed her myself. But she did not. She brought me her rage and grief because I have you and she does not. Such a gift is priceless." She leaned against him and felt the heavy beat of his heart and the baby pillowed between them and his arms coming around to hold her.

Their Christmas celebration was riotously happy, with the children in high spirits and as excited about the gifts they'd made with Mrs. Tubbs's help as they were about things given to them. Tessa particularly liked the little sculpture of driftwood with birds which Jefferson had cleverly made of shell, wood, and seeds. But she was careful to exclaim equally over all the children's gifts.

Her gift from Gavin was the sweetest of all. It was a new cradle, lovingly built, carved, and polished in every detail. And though a baby would not be able to tell the difference, the delicate scrollwork, curving flowers, and birds were definitely feminine. She thanked him wordlessly with her eyes, not trusting her voice in front of the others, for their number was expanded not only by Thia, Indian, and Mrs. Tubbs, but by Belle, Charles, and Dr. Harland.

Mrs. Tubbs's reaction to the blue dress was infinitely touching. She had as much trouble finding words as Tessa had had over the cradle. She kept smoothing the fabric and saying, "It's quite, quite beautiful." And though it was usually Jefferson who noticed and commented on such things, this time it was Brand who looked from the dress to Mrs. Tubbs and said, "I think you will be beautiful in it." The matter-of-factness of his voice made it all the more a compliment, and Mrs. Tubbs glowed, her gray eyes so lovely that Belle murmured sotto voce to Tessa,

574

"A few years ago I could have found work for her," causing Tessa to sputter, "Belle, you're impossible!"

They were all made merry by the hot spiced wine Chong Sing had helped to serve though he found even the smell distasteful. They sang carols and persuaded Tessa to sing some of the old Spanish songs for them. Gavin got her guitar for her, and though she hadn't sung for a long time, she was glad to tonight, her voice soaring easily into the sweet, pure notes, seeking to banish her memories of singing with Jordan.

Because she herself had dismissed the scratches lightly with the branch story, everyone politely ignored them, though Belle's eyes had narrowed with understanding when she first saw them. But John Harland couldn't forbear mentioning them as he left. "Keep those very clean. Human nails are often as dirty as a cat's. I'd leave something for you, but I expect your herbs are just as cleansing. And I'll expect you to begin taking things pretty easy now."

"Always the doctor, even on Christmas," she teased, but he would not be charmed.

"Every day of the year, goes with the territory." He allowed himself the briefest of smiles. "Besides which anything my patients can do for themselves makes it easier for me. Merry Christmas and God bless."

She walked with him to the door, and she watched until he had ridden away into the darkness. Gavin came up behind her and drew her back from the damp December air. "He wouldn't approve if you caught a chill."

"He's a comforting sort of person. Though I never thought to need one at all, I'm glad he's my doctor."

Gavin was relieved Tessa couldn't see his face. The claws of fear that tore at him were as sharp as the ones that had raked her cheek.

But he showed nothing but pleasure and understanding when they were finally alone in a quiet house and Tessa cuddled against him, thanking him for the cradle, not caring now that her voice was unsteady. "It's so beautiful— even the baby will feel the love that went into the carving of the wood."

"Even our *daughter*," he corrected her. "Now sleep, my love, we must be wide awake to do justice to Armenthia's

Christmas dinner. Indian claims she's even got him help-ing."

CHAPTER XLVIII

With the advent of the new year Tessa took Dr. Har-land's advice. She had little choice. With the baby due in February, she was finally too big and clumsy to want to do anything very active, and that included going to the shop. Now one of the clerks came to the house a few times a week to give her an accounting. She was glad of the outside contact, because she couldn't help but chafe a little at her enforced inactivity; but most of the time she was wrapped in the serenity of waiting, not thinking of anything but the baby inside her so close to being born, deliberately letting her mind slip out of focus whenever it threatened to think about the baby's father.

On the advice of Mrs. Tubbs, all the boys had felt the baby kick. She was certain it was a harmless way of in-volving them in the whole process and making it an exciting reality for them. It seemed to have worked except in the case of Paul. At first the change in his behavior was not that noticeable. He had never gotten over being shy and sometimes afraid, though he tried hard to hide it. But finally it was undeniable that he was rapidly going back to the terrified urchin Gavin had rescued. His re-gression was particularly obvious when he was on an outing that took him away from the immediate vicinity of the house; now whenever he could, he made up some excuse not to go, even though they were things he would normally have loved to see and do.

They could not wheedle an answer from him; not even Brand's teasing, frequently harsh, about being a "fraidy-cat" brought any response. The only explanation Paul offered was that sometimes he couldn't help "remember-ing."

"Remembering, hell!" Gavin told Tessa in frustration.

"I've been trying to track down his father, but I can't find him. I think Paul's seen the son of a bitch."

When asked point blank, Paul denied it. "He's gone away, hasn't he? You gave him all that money and he went away." But the look in his eyes was strange.

It made them all nervous. Even Mrs. Tubbs admitted to looking over her shoulder when she had the boys with her, though she could never be sure whether or not they were being followed. And Gavin, the only one who could identify the man, never caught the barest glimpse of him, no matter how carefully his eyes searched the streets.

Tessa was saddened to feel Paul's withdrawal from her. It was as though he were deliberately removing himself from any love or comfort she could offer him. "Maybe it's all about the baby, maybe he's afraid he'll lose his place when it comes, just like Brand's feelings about him."

"It's possible," Gavin agreed. "And if it's true, we should be able to see a change for the good in him as soon as the baby's here and Paul realizes he hasn't lost anything. I just hope he adjusts better than our stubborn Brand."

But they did not have to wait that long after all. Tessa's only thought when she heard the thumping on the door downstairs was that she had heard no fire bells clanging and whatever other problem anyone had at the warehouse, the mill, or the Golden Horse was not important enough to awaken Gavin. He was sleeping exhaustedly, and his efforts to maintain a calm demeanor had not fooled her; she knew the major part of his burden was his worry about her.

She grabbed her wrapper and moved as swiftly as she could, which with the baby due any day now, was not very fast. She was halfway down the stairs when she saw Chong Sing padding toward the door. He opened it and all hell broke loose.

He was drunk and bellowing, but she knew who he was even before he shouted, "My son, Pauley, my son, yur da's come fer you." The heavy pistol he brandished swung with the words, knocking Chong Sing to the floor.

Tessa willed herself to move, and she had backed up two steps when she heard the sound above her. She glanced up and saw Paul's frozen, terrified face. She found her

577

voice then and screamed for Gavin, even as she heard Paul imploring, "Da, please Da, don't hurt her, don't hurt her!"

The man lurched toward the stairs, and Tessa sank down, closing her eyes and clinging to the banister, knowing she would surely kill herself or the baby or both if she tried to run.

She heard the roar of a gun, and for an instant she waited to feel the impact of the bullet, then opened her eyes and glanced fearfully up at Paul. He had not been hit either.

She looked at the man. The pistol had skidded across the floor, the man lay in a groaning heap. Even as she stared, she saw the final horrific act. Paul's father pushed himself up groggily to his knees, his shirt stained with blood, even as Chong Sing stirred, shaking his head as he got shakily to his feet.

It happened very fast, but Tessa saw it slowly, her brain making it seem almost as if Chong Sing were praying, his hands together for a moment and then one of them moving with swift grace under the man's chin, snapping the head back, snapping the neck, and continuing on as though nothing had impeded its progress.

There's a piece missing in this puzzle, Tessa thought with painstaking logic, and she looked upward again and saw Gavin. His face was rigidly carved with the killing urge, as spare and deadly as an eagle's head, and the gun was in his hand.

She fought back the sound, but she couldn't stop it; hysterical laughter burst from her so violently she could scarcely breathe. He had wanted to kill the man, but he had controlled himself enough to stop him without killing him. Chong Sing, frail little Chong Sing, had passed the final sentence with the graceful blade of his hand. And Gavin, so grim faced and dangerous, was dressed only in a gun, lean hard body stark naked. She couldn't stop laughing to save her soul. She clung to the railings, her body shaking with the sound.

Gavin pried her hands loose and gripped them tightly. "Stop it, Tessa! Stop it!" he shouted, and when he saw that she could not, he slapped her, flinching as he did it. The horrible sound stopped, and she drew deep breaths.
578

He gathered her into his arms and called down to Chong Sing, "Are you all right? Good—then go tell Indian and Thia we need them. And then find Dr. Harland and tell him it's an emergency."

Chong Sing was on his way out the door before Tessa spoke. "I'm fine. He didn't touch me. Paul—see to Paul, my poor little one."

Gavin saw what she meant when he glanced at Paul's face. The child looked as if he were in shock. "Paul, it's not your fault. But I've got to get your mother to bed. Do you understand?" The barest of nods reassured him, but even if the child had made no response, Gavin would not have tarried. He was terrified for Tessa, and could think of nothing but settling her in bed.

She was still protesting feebly that she was all right when he laid her down, but even as he gazed at her, holding her hand, she grimaced, her eyes tightly shut, her nails digging into his hand.

She took a deep breath and her face relaxed. "I'm sorry. It just took me by surprise. Perhaps it was just a warning. Paul, you really must——" but her words were cut off by a cry, and she turned her face away, her hands knotting into fists.

When she could speak again, she said, "For this one, not fair to you, you don't have to stay."

"Indeed I do. I have a deal to do with the child. Shame on you, my love, for thinking I would leave you now." He kept his face studiously calm and took her hands in his own again while terror shot through his veins in a blind lightning course. He was infinitely relieved when Thia glided into the room. She did not try to usurp his place. She lighted a few lamps in the room and then she came to the bed and touched Tessa's face gently. "Soon you gwine meet pretty new baby," she crooned softly, her face as tender as if Tessa were the child.

Quietly she asked Gavin what they could do to help. He dropped a light kiss on Tessa's forehead, murmuring that he would be right back. She let go of his hands instantly. He grabbed his pants and pulled them on though Armenthia had given no indication she even noticed he was nude.

"I want you to take the children to your house, if you will," he said when they were out of earshot.

"Sure, we do dat, but I gots to tell you, dat Paul, he in one shakin' fit. Indian drug de body outside, but dat chile, he shiverin' an' starin' likes he still sees it on de floor. Chong Sing say dat man de boy's real daddy. De other boys a little scairt, but not like Paul. I knows it's hard fo' Tessa, startin' so quick, but Dr. Harland, he be heah soon, an' he know what to do. Iffin you lets me, I set with Tessa an' you go talk to de childuns 'fore we takes dem."

He didn't want to leave Tessa at all, but he knew Thia was right about the boys' need for him.

He found Indian doing his best to cope with three overwrought children. Gavin didn't feel much better able to cope, but he pulled himself together. "Now, I want you all to be very brave tonight and go home with Indian and Armenthia." Christ, he thought, I'm asking them to do something I can't. "Your mother will be all right, but the baby is coming now, and that's hard work for the mother and the child. Your mother will have an easier time if she knows you're safe and sound asleep."

Paul was crouched against Indian. Gavin picked him up and held him very tightly for a moment. "Paul, we love you; you're our son. A terrible thing happened here tonight, but you're safe now, and when there's time, after the baby comes, we can talk about it."

The thin frame shivered in his arms, and he had to listen closely to understand the mumbled words. "I don't care about him. But it's my fault Mother's sick. She might die, and it'll be all my fault!"

The tears were damp on Gavin's neck, and he controlled his frantic urge to get back to Tessa. "That's not true! The baby was due any day; it's just chosen tonight to come. But I'm sorry you were too frightened to tell us. He's been following you for some time, hasn't he?"

He felt Paul's nod and then he heard the old, deadly hate in the young voice. "I'm glad you and Chong Sing killed him. I'm glad, glad, glad!"

Gavin did not contradict him; he knew better than most that the passions of a child were often wholly valid. And there was no time now for anything but Tessa.

He made himself take the time to hug his other sons
580

too. They had seen the body but not the killing, and they were more excited than anything else.

Brand asked, "Did Chong Sing really help? What did he do?"

Gavin told him that was neither here nor there right now, but he saw the sudden comprehension in Indian's eyes.

Jefferson was more worried about his mother than the facts of the killing. "God should plan things better," he insisted. "If I was God, I'd send the babies down from the mountains on mules and just let the mamas pick them up at the bottom."

"Oh, Jefferson," Gavin gasped. "I wish you *were* God. I think your plan is splendid. But if you were God, you couldn't be my son, and I wouldn't like that at all."

"Me either," Jefferson agreed, and he stood trustingly by Indian when Gavin put him down.

"You wait here while I go get Thia," Indian told the boys, and Gavin knew why he wanted to accompany him down the hall.

"Man's neck broke, don' think he done it hisself," Indian said.

"He didn't. Goddamnedest thing I've ever seen. Chong Sing was knocked cold, and when he came to it was like a dance, arm swinging around with perfect grace and the neck snapping with a sound you could hear. I'm more thankful than ever that he's a friend."

Indian gave him a long, measured look. "You don' miss. Why didn't you kill th' man?"

"Couldn't do it in front of Paul, glad that Chong Sing did," Gavin answered briefly, making his face calm again for Tessa as he went into the room.

Armenthia, alerted by the sound of the door, met him. "It bad. I knows Dr. Harland be heah soon, but you want me stay till den?"

"Thank you, but no, the children need you. I'll let you know when it's over." He gave her a hug, but already all his attention was focused back on Tessa.

The pain made her feel disoriented. She couldn't tell how little or how much time had passed. First Gavin's face looming over her, then Armenthia's, now Gavin's again. "Paul?" she whispered.

"He's all right. Indian and Thia have taken the children home with them. All you have to think of now is yourself and the baby."

She gathered herself to say it. "I love you." The effort pleased her. She knew her voice had been very strong. But she lost his response in the roaring wave.

This is how the world will end, Gavin thought. *Each second will be an eternity, and we will all just wait for the next terrible event, one following the other without ceasing.*

He had never been so glad to see anyone as he was to see John Harland.

"It's good you've had some experience in these matters; the only midwife I'd trust to assist me is off on a case of her own, one of your standard 'no-men-should-witness-such-a-thing' situations." The doctor grinned wryly and hoped he was getting through to Gavin. "As if men haven't anything at all to do with the process."

He'd been stripping off his coat and rolling up his shirt sleeves as he talked, and he washed his hands in the basin Chong Sing brought. Chong Sing slipped away into the far shadows, ready to provide anything needed.

John's voice was infinitely kind and reassuring as he examined Tessa. "Well, my dear, this one seems determined to make a quick entrance on the world, even though its mother might prefer a slower pace."

She almost managed to smile at him. "Thank you for not saying 'we,' John." She got the words out before her body convulsed again, and in the small respite that followed, she obediently drank the draught he offered.

He waited until he saw her relax a little, then motioned Gavin to follow him out of earshot. Gavin slipped his hands out of Tessa's once again.

"The baby's coming too fast. It's trying to leave the womb before the passage is ready to allow it. The medicine I gave her is slowing things down a bit, but not much and not for long. Anything strong enough to solve the problem would be strong enough to kill the child and possibly the mother."

The doctor's face was no longer calm and authoritative, despite his measured logic, and Gavin studied him for a moment before he said, "I know, it's hard to be impartial with Tessa. I haven't been since the first time I saw her. You know much about us and about this child, more than most people. But there is one thing you may not understand. I did not want Tessa to lose this child in the way she intended because that was not like her. And I know now, at this instant, whether she is conscious of it or not, Tessa would give the babe life at the cost of her own. But I would not. I made this decision with our first born, and it's not changed. Save her life even if you have to tear the child to bits."

Gavin's eyes held John's and the doctor nodded. "I'm relieved to learn it, but the risk of that is nearly as grave. I'll do my best, and that's damn good if I do say so, but you're the one who must remind her that she has a reason for fighting. Guilt isn't making it any easier for her."

Gavin realized the truth of the doctor's judgment ever more clearly in the next few hours. The easing effect of the drug was not long-lasting, but even when her grip on his hands and the renewed writhing of her body told Gavin the depth of her suffering, her mouth remained clamped tight and he wanted to scream in her place.

"Tessa, you're fighting as hard to keep silent as you are to have the baby. It won't do—concentrate on the baby and let everything else go," John urged her, and Gavin sent him a look of gratitude.

All of the things she had denied in the warmth of Gavin's love rushed back. It all had a terrible justice and nothing to do with medicine. She had committed adultery; she had sinned, and she was being punished for it, the brief stolen spaces of pleasure changed to interminable stretches of agony. The child had a new reality—it was an instrument of vengeance, tearing her body apart, stripping her of dignity and courage under the eyes of Gavin and the doctor, worthy of life while she no longer was. Nothing to do with Gavin, and he knew. How could he be so kind when he knew? She could see his face sometimes, and she had a renewed awareness that the comforting strength she clung to was him; it was his hands she was gripping, his flesh she was piercing with her nails to the warm wetness of blood. She tried to let go, but he would not allow it, and as the relentless blade sliced through her

583

again, she clenched her hands tightly on his once more. The last reality, the first and last reason to be, Gavin, not herself. Gavin.

She heard John Harland telling her to acknowledge the pain, and she wanted to explain that that would be the final indignity, that once she started, she would never be able to stop. She opened her mouth to form the words and heard her scream shattering the air around her, on and on and on until it felt good and dignity was something this sprawling creature of herself had never known. There was terrible sound, dark blood colors, and pain, and only the last vestige of herself knew Gavin was there.

The doctor's face was as tense as Gavin's when the baby was finally delivered. Chong Sing was on hand with warm water and sweet oil, competently evincing the fact that he counted care of the newborn among his many talents.

"You have a daughter," John said softly, and Gavin nodded, his throat tight, his hands stroking Tessa's still face. "We've always wanted a little girl. I hope she will be just like her mother." His heart pounded suddenly as he saw John's expression. "What is it, what's wrong?" he asked harshly.

"She's a lovely baby, she really is, but she's not perfect. Her right leg is deformed." John's voice was soft as a lullaby with regret as he handed the baby to Chong Sing, who held her as if she were an honored son rather than a crippled girl child. "But listen to the lungs she's just discovered, nothing wrong with those!"

Gavin was statue still, shock waves running through him, the convulsive working of his throat his only visible motion. Even his untrained eyes could see the tiny crooked twist of hip and leg. And he knew it was forever certain in the wet fuzz of pale hair, in a certain something about the eyes. Jordan's daughter.

He was surprised at his own reaction—not anger, not even now with the final proof, just overwhelming pity and love. Tessa had gone through so much, never once even in extreme pain betraying Jordan's name, and now this, the daughter she had longed for, a bastard and a cripple.

"I want to see her."

He started at the soft thread of words, wondering when she had regained consciousness, wondering how much she
584

had heard in the short rush of time since the birth. He leaned down and kissed her. "In a moment, sweetheart. Chong Sing is making her presentable while John cares for you."

"I heard." In the weak hollow of her voice, the words were flat, but then the helpless tears spilled over. "Poor baby, I caused it, I caused it by what I tried to do."

John's voice cut in sharply. "These things happen; there's no way to judge why, and she's a lovely child."

"Tell her that when she goes to her first dance." Tessa closed her eyes again, and Gavin wondered in horror what he would do if she refused to accept the baby, but when John finally handed him the child, now clean and wrapped in soft warm cloth, he swallowed his fear and placed the bundle beside Tessa, saying softly, "Meet our daughter, my darling."

Her eyes opened again, shimmering deep violet with tears. "Our daughter," she repeated slowly and she turned her head to stare at the child.

She saw Jordan's eyes, Jordan in a thousand ways. Never could she hope to see the ghost of Gavin in this child.

The baby mewed fretfully and moved her mouth, clean and pink as a kitten's, and her tiny fists and eyelids clenched as if she knew her welcome was in doubt.

Tessa felt the hard, painful knot of regret and rejection dissolve, felt the warm coursing joy begin until it flowed and filled her. She moved the baby slightly so she could look at her better and unwrapped the blanket to trace the crooked leg with gentle fingers. The baby cooed happily, her mouth curving into a smile that was reflected in Tessa's face.

"Unless you prefer otherwise, I'd like to name her Fiona, for my mother."

She was deeply touched. Fiona, a lovely sound, and she had not known his mother's name until this moment. She wanted to tell him she understood all the implications, but she could manage no more than a nod before the exhaustion she had been holding at bay overtook her.

"I'll stay with her for a while," the doctor said. "I think you have some chores to perform, including getting rid of that body on the doorstep."

Gavin glanced at him fearfully. "She's not bleeding any more?"

"No, she's not," John reassured him calmly. "She's fine and sleepy. But when it's been a difficult labor, I like to stay a while. Gives me time to rest along with the mother."

"Thank you, John," Gavin said gruffly.

He was more than a little tempted to simply dump the body somewhere on the beach and forget about it. The sun was up, but it was still early, and he didn't doubt that he could get away with it. But the man was, after all, Paul's father.

Chong Sing offered to come with him, willing to accept his share of the blame.

"No, that won't be necessary. He fell down the stairs after I shot him." Gavin understood a great deal more today than he had during the hectic night. The day Tessa had tried to defend Chong Sing from the bully was amusing in retrospect. Chong Sing could obviously have killed the man. But he was wise enough to know that there were few who would tolerate a Chinese killing a white man, no matter what the cause. He had risked a great deal for the Ramsays last night, more than he would risk to protect himself.

"I appreciate what you did," Gavin told him. "I couldn't bring myself to kill him in front of the boy."

"I know, velly bad see fadda die no matta how ewil, but Paul newa safe wid dat man still alive. Betta I kill him dan you." Chong Sing's bruised face was perfectly serene, and Gavin knew suddenly that the man's life had contained even more violence and death dealing than his own.

He had no problem with the sheriff. His explanation that the man had broken into the house and nearly caused Mrs. Ramsay's death was accepted without question. Self-defense and nothing more need be said about it. The man was obviously riffraff of the lowest order. Gavin offered to pay for the decent burial Christian duty demanded. He made no mention of the connection with Paul.

Indian, Armenthia, and the children were all delighted with the news that mother and child were doing well. Gavin minimized the baby's deformity, not wanting to spoil their joy. Even Paul's pinched face looked more lively and less tense after he had asked, "Are you sure, about

586

Mother?" and received Gavin's added reassurance and a promise that he could see her later on.

Controlling her own wish to see the baby, Thia told him they'd all be over toward sundown. "Gib de lamb some time fo' sleepin'."

He returned to the house to find it very peaceful and the last signs of anxiety gone from John's face. "They're both doing beautifully, and I expect they'll sleep the day."

They went downstairs, and Chong Sing who was as tired as anyone nonetheless insisted that the men eat, and they complied thankfully, beginning with steaming cups of coffee liberally laced with brandy.

"I sincerely hope I don't have to see any of my other patients for a few hours at least," John said, taking a good swallow of the brew. "The smell of this would make them damn nervous. Chong Sing, you ought to drink some too, that face of yours must ache like the devil today."

"Tea much betta dan dat," Chong Sing pronounced as he left them. Obviously, it was beneath the dignity of his manhood to even comment on his injury.

Gavin told John of his morning's activities, and then he repeated what Jefferson had said about how he thought babies ought to be delivered. But aside from a brief grin, he didn't get the reaction he expected from the doctor.

John's face sobered very quickly, and he nodded. "Bright boy, your Jefferson. I agree his plan would be much better. I know every profession has its worst complaint, and mine happens to be the ordeal of childbirth. You might guess that, since I specialize in the disorders of women. I do my best, but it's so often not good enough. The field hasn't emerged from the dark ages. Too many pious asses still believe it's all preordained, all exactly right as it's set down in the Bible—just punishment for women from the time they left the Garden to suffer and often die in child-bearing. They can't see it as a tale of ignorance then that hasn't changed much since. It's got to change someday, and I go on believing it will, that with increased knowledge more women and more infants will survive. But I won't live to see it, and my wife didn't either."

Gavin stared at him in shock, saying nothing, and John went on, his face suddenly much older than his years and worn with care. "Maudie didn't look like Tessa. She was
587

small and golden, golden hair and skin soft gold too, and eyes that were blue or green depending on what she was thinking." A sad smile curved his mouth. "I used to watch out for the green. She had a sweet temper, so I didn't see it often, but when I did, I minded my step. She was like Tessa in the essentials, a bright, quick, loving, and laughing human being. Our families were such good friends, Maudie and I grew up together, loving each other from the skinned knees to the first dance, absolutely certain we would have years and years to go on loving each other. We even played a game of describing what the other would look like in fifty years' time. We were married for three years. It was her first pregnancy, and I was worried because I knew she was very small for child-bearing, but she was sure everything would be all right. I had one of the best men in the field to assist because I knew my love might make me frantic and incapable when her time came. There was nothing either of us could do for her except watch her suffer. She and our son both died. The last thing she said to me was, 'What a terrible trick, I shan't ever see you old.' "

Gavin clenched his hands together in painful sympathy for the other man's suffering.

"You are kind to hear me out," John said quietly. "I came west as soon as I was capable of thinking again, and very few people know about this. I've told you for a specific reason. You don't have to be a physician to know that we nearly lost Tessa. I know it seems as if the hours were endless, but they were not long enough nor properly begun. Severe shock forced labor to begin and the child came too fast. The birth had caused damage." He saw the quick fear in Gavin's face and hastened to reassure him. "No, she's very tired, and she'll be sore for a time, but she'll recover. However, in my judgment, she'll never conceive another child. These are difficult words to say, particularly because you have been magnificent in your welcome of another man's child and in your acceptance of your own responsibility. I just trust you will go on being aware that you have Tessa when you might not, and that that will always be more important than the fact that you will have no more children."

Gavin didn't hesitate. "Good God, I will have no trouble with that at all! I cannot imagine our lives without the children now, but they are quite sufficient. I know she told you she'd had some problems with her pregnancies before, as if those problems were insignificant, but hell, I was terrified!" In a sharp staccato of words he told the doctor in detail what had happened in the other births, why he had had to face the prospect of killing Brand before birth, all that had followed and even about the first child lost. "Perhaps I should be condemned for this, but I am a husband first, a father long second. I feel only relief that she will not have to go through this again, and more for myself that I will not have her so at risk any more."

John's weary face showed his relief. "I could not have hoped for better from you. Obviously Tessa isn't built for childbearing in the first place; you are fortunate to have her and three children besides, not to mention Paul. But I must warn you that it is very doubtful Tessa will share this view. She may very well wish to have another child by you, a child without defect and with you for the father. I don't believe this is the time to tell her, but if her desire for another child is too strong, she will have to be told eventually."

"I'll tell her if the need arises," Gavin said, and then he asked. "Fiona . . . she really will be crippled, won't she? There's nothing to be done?"

"The honest answer is Yes, she will be lame, but it's a question of degree. With proper care and exercise, I don't think it need be that serious. She will walk with a limp, but she will walk, of that I'm certain."

After John had checked once more to see that Tessa still slept peacefully, Gavin saw him to the door. "Thank you for everything. She could not have had better care."

"I'll look in on her again tomorrow. I don't anticipate trouble, but send for me immediately if you think anything is wrong." He smiled suddenly, looking younger than he had since his arrival hours before. "Besides, my horse loves coming here. For some reason, the all powerful Chong Sing has elected to extend his beneficence to my lowly beast."

Gavin chuckled with him over the sight of the nag

warmly blanketed and munching contentedly from a feed bag. "The credit goes to Tessa. She discovered Chong Sing, or vice versa, I've never been sure which."

Gavin watched John out of sight and went back to Tessa.

CHAPTER XLIX

Though the idea was an obvious one, Gavin was glad he had thought of it, and happier still that Mrs. Tubbs proved not only agreeable but more than equal to it. She handled Fiona as if she'd spent years tending infants. So instead of an added burden for Chong Sing or a strange nursemaid for them all to adjust to, Mrs. Tubbs became a more permanent member of the household. She no longer had to give lessons in needlework and other "gentle" arts to survive, and she gave them up with great relief. Gavin helped her move from her boarding house room to the Ramsays', and Tessa was even more delighted with the new arrangement when he described Mrs. Tubbs's former living quarters.

"She'd done everything she could to make it cheerful, but nonetheless it was a dismal place. Her personal possessions took about ten minutes to pack. It was the books that took two hours. The smell of the landlady's cooking made me complete the task as quickly as possible. Mrs. Tubbs will be far better off with us."

They turned a guest room over to her and converted the small one beside it to a nursery, thankful the brick house had the space. Chong Sing had great respect for Mrs. Tubbs, and she was careful not to trespass on his areas of authority, so there were none of the problems there would surely have been had a stranger stepped into his realm. The boys were joyous to have more time with the teacher they adored, and they realized very quickly that she could spend time with the baby and still have plenty for them.

They seemed to have adjusted well to the additional

member of the family, though Tessa thought wryly that that was probably because Fiona had as yet made no demands on them. Jefferson came a little too close to the truth when he asked why the baby didn't look like the rest of them, but when Mrs. Tubbs explained that the looks of past generations often appeared suddenly in the new and asked him if all foals looked exactly like their sires and dams, he conceded they did not and lost interest in Fiona's blondness. If Mrs. Tubbs suspected anything else, she gave no sign. Brand's attitude was a sort of perpetual shrug that made it clear he was much too old and busy to be bothered with a squirming infant who could neither speak nor play sensibly. But Paul's reaction was infinitely touching.

His joy that Tessa and the baby were really all right despite what his natural father had done was boundless. He had been scared nearly witless by the reappearance of his father. His feeling of his own worth was so insubstantial that he had thought it quite likely that with the new baby coming, the Ramsays might give him back when his father demanded it, rather than pay more money. What Gavin had sensed was true. Paul had no regrets about his father's death. It was an ugly scene of blood and violence in his mind, but not of regret. For the first time in his life, he was truly free of all cause for terror. Even his continuing failure to be as close to Brand as he would have liked did not hurt as much now that that man could never come back for him again. He thought of him as "that man" now, not as his father. Gavin was his father, though Paul never called him anything but "sir." Because he had called that man "Father" and "Da," the words were tainted. "Gavin, my father," had a different sound in his head, private, unvoiced, and loving. Gavin suspected a great deal of this and never pressured Paul, though he sometimes winced inwardly at the formal address from this slight boy he had come to love so dearly.

It was as if his harsh first years had somehow engendered in Paul a deep capacity for gentleness, a vast longing to give and receive love, a shying away from things that hurt others. It gave him patience with Brand that few small boys would have had. Paul was well fed

591

and healthy now, and he knew enough tricks of fighting and violence to have bested Brand easily, but he kept the knowledge to himself and let Brand think otherwise.

He did not have to pretend anything about Fiona. He adored her from his first sight of her. He thought she was the most fascinating and perfect creature he had ever seen. Her vulnerability caught at his heart; he could not get over the miracle of her being so small and yet so complete. When Fiona clamped her tiny fingers with their miniature nails around one of Paul's fingers, and gazed at him vaguely through eyes now more lavender gray than blue, Tessa had to swallow hard and turn away from his expression of tenderness. It was very like the expression Gavin had had with all the children, including this one. Strange that while not related at all by blood, Gavin and Paul could be so alike. She was beginning to believe that only those who had known the lack of love could fully appreciate its presence.

Aside from Jefferson's observation, no one mentioned Fiona's coloring or her crooked leg. There was nothing to be done about either, and Tessa was grateful for the peace and love that surrounded her, for her recovery from Fiona's birth was far slower than it had been after the boys'. For once in her life, she found it acceptable to take things easy.

Molly and Anne came from the shop, oohed and aahed over Fiona, and presented her mother with finely stitched baby garments fit for a princess. And finally Belle came. Tessa sensed her nervousness instantly and waited warily, knowing it had something to do with her, but not sure what it was.

Fiona was with Tessa while Mrs. Tubbs gave the boys their lessons. Belle looked at the baby for a long moment. Fiona wiggled and seemed to smile. Belle smiled back and looked less nervous. "She's lovely."

She carried two packages, and she handed one of them to Tessa. "I wanted to finish these before I came, even though I know she won't wear them for some time."

Tessa gasped at the beauty of the little dresses. "They're exquisite! And it's so thoughtful of you to have made them for later. She has more clothes for now than any baby could possibly need."

"Well, I was a seamstress once," Belle reminded her, and then she offered her the other package, a narrow one heavily wrapped in bright cloth. "I haven't known what to do about this," she admitted quietly. "He left it up to me. I've had it all this time. He wanted you to have it, but he did not want it to cause you pain. If ever there will be a time, it must be now. This should belong to Fiona someday."

Tessa unwrapped it with shaking hands, knowing what it was now, feeling it, seeing it before the final fold was undone and Kuanyin was revealed, the jade glowing with its own life.

"It may seem betrayal, but he was distraught. He needed some last touch with you. He came to me because he knew I am your friend, and he knew I would not judge either of you harshly. Tessa, I knew there was someone. I am glad he was such a man as Jordan."

Tessa ran her hand over the cool smoothness. "It's all right. Fiona will have this when she's old enough to appreciate it." Her voice was tight. "Do you think Gavin knows?"

The question took Belle by surprise, and she stared at Tessa for a blank moment before she answered. "He has said nothing, asked nothing of anyone as far as I know."

"That's not what I asked," Tessa reminded her.

Belle looked from Fiona to her mother and back again to the baby. "He must know. If he did not before, he must know now. He knew Jordan too well not to see him in Fiona." She saw Tessa shiver, and her temper flared. "So he knows. What of it? He loves you, he loves Fiona. What else must he do before you learn that the past is past and your guilt is useless? The marks of Soledad's nails are gone. They have left no scars. Can't you let Soledad and Jordan both fade away as well? Fiona is not Jordan. She's your daughter, yours and Gavin's, because you will be the ones who raise her."

Belle's ample bosom rose and fell rapidly as she glared at Tessa, and Tessa glared back until laughter overcame her. "Oh, Belle, I'm sorry, but it's so funny to hear you defending the hearth and home!" She stretched out her hand, and unoffended, seeing the humor too, Belle took it. "But you defend it very well. What you say is true.

593

Gavin deserves the best of me and that is what he will have."

Kuanyin was wrapped carefully in his gay shroud and hidden away for the day when he would be a gift for Fiona. Tessa neither showed the jade to Gavin nor told him anything of Belle's words, but she wrapped him in the life and love Jordan had never had from her. Gavin felt the change without knowing why it had happened, and he didn't care why. He found himself humming snatches of Tessa's favorite songs during the day and going home to her at night as early as possible despite the fact that abstinence was still the rule and would continue to be for several more weeks, as it had been in the last weeks before Fiona's birth. He did not regret the loss of the young man of years ago who could not have imagined staying with a woman he could not possess at will. Nor did he have to make any effort to love Fiona. Most of the time now, he did not even consider the fact that Jordan, not he, was her father. She charmed him. To him she looked more like a tiny, ethereal, and sunlit version of Tessa every day, and already she was showing her own character, generally happy and content but capable of red-faced rage and stubborn perseverance when she felt neglected. And she had a definite preference for men. She cooed ecstatically when Gavin held her or Chong Sing or her brothers paid attention to her. Tessa accused them all of spoiling Fiona rotten, which made it only understandable she should prefer men.

"That's not it at all, she just has superb judgment," Gavin teased. "But God help us when she's old enough for courting. I can already see myself tossing poor young men out into the fog because they aren't worthy."

"It's a good thing we have three sons and only one daughter," Tessa retorted. "If it were the other way around, you'd go mad protecting the little princesses."

Fiona, having just been fed, fell asleep contentedly, and Gavin and Tessa were enjoying one of their quiet times together, rare in their busy household except late at night. And because Mrs. Tubbs recognized their need for these times and did not disturb them unless they called her, they were startled by her knock on the door and her agitated apology when she entered.

594

"Pardon me for intruding, but there is a problem I don't seem able to solve." The words were cool enough but not her rattled manner which was very uncharacteristic.

"Is something wrong with one of the children?" Tessa asked sharply.

"No, well, that is, not with one of yours. Oh, dear, the oddest thing has happened! Chong Sing has brought a baby home with him."

"Excuse me?" Gavin said politely, unable to believe he'd heard correctly.

"A baby, a poor starved mite who can't be much older than Fiona."

They stared at her speechlessly, and then they heard the thin wail from downstairs.

Gavin recovered first. "Is it his?" Chong Sing had had a few days off to celebrate the Chinese New Year, 4561, the year of the Cow, a few weeks ago, as he had for the major Chinese holidays throughout the year, but aside from these times, he seemed to lead the quietest of lives. Gavin remembered the killing and wondered if here was yet another dimension to the man, but Mrs. Tubbs set him straight.

"The child is not his." She paused, and her manner was much calmer as she slipped into the familiar role of teacher. "The child is a girl and Chinese, or at least part Chinese. Girls are not considered an asset in China. Boys carry on the family and provide a labor force. It's a wonder the race continues at all. In times of hardship, baby girls are the first to be abandoned to the elements and starvation. That seems to be what has happened in this case. Chong Sing found the baby on a pile of refuse. There were other people around, but they pretended not to notice, and no one would tell him where the child had come from. I think he's furious with himself for aiding the child at all. It is after all, a corruption of his background and a luxury of the West to value all children. And by his action, I suspect his beliefs hold him responsible from now on."

Gavin struggled to keep from laughing; even with this mad turn of events, Mrs. Tubbs was managing to give a succinct lecture on another civilization.

"There is every possibility the baby is the offspring of

one of the crib girls. The only other explanation is that she was born to a couple who are simply too poor to care for her." Mrs. Tubbs stated these suppositions without the pretense of outraged sensibilities fashion required if such things were mentioned at all. But not even her matter-of-factness could take the ugliness from the image of the crib girls. In the past year, the situation had radically changed from the times when San Francisco had only two or three Chinese women. Now there were hundreds. And most of them had been sold or had sold themselves into virtual slavery. Their boat passage costs were paid for out of the money received for them at auction or collected from the private fees some Chinese men paid for a concubine. They were the lucky ones. The others worked in "cribs," mostly tiny basement rooms, and they had no right to refuse any customer, no matter how loathsome or diseased, or to limit their hours of prostitution. They were the lowest of the whole profession, and it was unlikely that many of them would live to be very old. If the child had been born from a crib girl, it was impossible to fathom why she had gone through with it. Perhaps she had had the terrible misfortune to have fallen in love with one of her clients.

Some of her former nervousness crept back into Mrs. Tubbs's voice. "As I am sure you are aware, it is not my habit to interfere in Chong Sing's affairs, but in this case, I must protest his actions. He did not want you disturbed, but in an attempt to be kind, he is concocting a loathsome mixture that will surely make the baby even more wretched than she is."

Tessa finally understood. "Why, that's ridiculous! I have plenty of milk to feed another little one."

Mrs. Tubbs nodded gratefully but Gavin objected. "What if the child is diseased? She might infect you or Fiona."

"She looks quite healthy, just very hungry," Mrs. Tubbs ventured, and Tessa gave Gavin a piercing look. "Is it that you don't fancy me in the role of wet nurse?"

Gavin winced at her accurate shot. He understood and approved her wish to nurse her own children, though many women of her class hired wet nurses, but the idea of her taking a castoff bit of humanity to her breast was unsettling.

596

Chong Sing obviously felt the same way, but both men lost to the combined wills of Mrs. Tubbs and Tessa.

Tessa's first and overwhelming feeling was pity for the child. She was so emaciated, it did not seem possible she could live. For the first few days Tessa fed her often but did not let her take much at a time. It was miraculous that the child still had the urge to nurse at all in her weakened state. Even Gavin could not resist the pitiful frailty and watched as anxiously as everyone else for improvement.

And quite suddenly the change was visible. The cheeks filled out and took on faint color; the eyes were brighter; and the baby began moving and making the same sounds any contented infant makes.

Tessa, looking down at her, said in wonder to Gavin, "Why, she is going to be beautiful, as tall and beautiful as Ah Toy, I think." He was amused by the comparison with the famous Chinese madam, but he could see what she meant. There was a fineness to the baby's bones and features, a long slenderness to the tiny hands and feet, a glossy blackness to the cap of straight hair and to the brown almond-shaped eyes, everything promising that this child would grow to be an exotic-looking woman indeed.

But they were in an odd position concerning the child. They had not even given her a name. She was "the baby," as opposed to "Fiona," or she was "Chong Sing's baby." And she remained Chong Sing's. He made it quietly clear that he still held himself responsible for her.

Tessa and Gavin talked for long hours about it, trying to be as honest as they could. The baby was surely appealing, and the boys hadn't made any real objection to her presence, though that was probably because they considered her Chong Sing's property and not their sister. Fiona was enough of a sister in all their minds.

Tessa felt the strongest bond of all because the child at her breast had aroused all the same protective, maternal feelings Fiona did. And neither she nor Gavin would allow even Chong Sing to place the baby anywhere that did not promise her a happy life. But the harsh reality was that they already had four children and another of Fiona's age added more confusion and obligation at a time when Tessa was still not back to her normal level of energy.

597

Chong Sing solved the problem for them. "If you please, you come wid me tomollo an' we take baby to new palents. Dey fliends of mine ewen in China. Day hawe no children of dey own. He wait, an' wait, still tink baby come to dem. She know dat newa happen. He want a son. She be happy wid a daughta. Many days now we talk an' talk. Now dey say Yes. Be good fo' baby. She mostly Chinese, need Chinese palents."

Though they had misgivings, since the people hadn't even seen the baby yet, Tessa and Gavin agreed with his choice as soon as they met Chen Soon Lei and his wife, Chen Po Ling. Though the diminutive couple were surely approaching their forties if not already that old, both had bright kind faces. Chen Soon Lei was a merchant on a modest scale in Chinatown. His shop offered a variety of goods from the old country to his fellow immigrants. The living quarters were in the back and upstairs, and everything was scrupulously clean. They had prepared well for the baby's arrival, including having found a wet nurse for her, so that Tessa's duties were at an end.

Tessa's last misgivings vanished when she saw the softness in Chen Po Ling's face as she held the baby. Even Chen Soon Lei who wanted a son smiled at the tiny girl.

The Ramsays felt oversized and clumsy, but they did their best not to make any obvious blunders during their visit. They also avoided each other's eyes, lest they succumb to nervous laughter. Tea was served along with delicately flavored cakes, and even if it was all quiet and rather formal except for the slurping of the tea which Tessa couldn't bring herself to imitate, it was surely a celebration. The Chens were obviously very fond of Chong Sing, whom they addressed by his full name, Chong Sai Sing. They spoke English more slowly and carefully than Chong Sing, and Mrs. Chen often looked at her husband for approval or agreement, but Tessa gathered that despite her polite show of subservience, Mrs. Chen was an equal force in the marriage. That reassured her even further that the baby was in good hands. And she was totally charmed when Mrs. Chen informed her that they had met her sons when Chong Sing brought them to visit and that she had a right to be very proud of them.

"It's strange," she said later to Gavin. "I thought four

598

was a great number of children, but now with the fifth one gone, it seems quite reasonable."

Gavin made no comment; he only hoped she would go on feeling that way.

For the birthdays this year, Armenthia became one of them, for she was no more sure of her true birth date than the men were of theirs. They had a grand time, and Indian claimed the best gift of all which was Thia's news that he would be a father in the fall. "We start somethin' new," he said, "All Tessa's babies come in spring, even Paul born over in England in spring. Thia an' me, we take th' other side of th' year for this one at least."

Tessa was delighted with what Gavin had given her—a split riding skirt of the finest leather with a vest to match. They were so perfect for days on the *rancho*, she felt like putting them on and riding out immediately.

The party was over and they were alone when he gave her the heavy doeskin pouch. She put down her hairbrush, scolding, "Gavin, really! You should not have gotten anything else for me."

"It is not a gift. It's the return of something that belongs to you."

She opened the pouch and let the contents spill out into her hand, still not guessing what it was until she saw its gold and emerald fire. She stared at the collar and then at Gavin, saying nothing.

"Belle is responsible for its return. It was she who picked it up, and I know you would have given it to her. I offered in your stead, but she wouldn't take it. And she was right. It is yours and should some day perhaps be Fiona's. We will never know, but I think you were mistaken to think Don Esteban would have judged you so harshly. He was a man of discipline and honor, but he was also a man of passion and understanding." Gavin's voice held no doubt, and his eyes were without shadow.

He had given her time to accept, and more, time to fall under the spell of Fiona. And though her impressions of that day remained confused and terrible and they had never spoken of Mother Patience since then, she was sure now that Gavin had killed the woman. She was no more sorry than Paul had been at the death of his father.

She regarded Gavin gravely. This man so fierce that he

599

would kill for her and still so tender. "You are a wonder," she said softly, borrowing Jefferson's current favorite phrase, and a smile lighted her face. She put the collar down carefully. "I would put it on, but I think it more appropriate to take this off." She slipped out of her thin nightgown and into Gavin's arms. "It has been so long."

"That can be easily remedied," he replied.

By late spring Tessa was spending some time each day at the shop. Indian and Gavin had bought a milk cow, and now besides the eggs from the Rancho Magnífico chickens, both households had fresh cow's milk instead of the sometimes dubious product from the local goat herders. The mashed tidbits from the table supplemented by milk from the cow kept Fiona happy even when her mother was gone past feeding time, and Tessa, weaning Fiona gradually from her breast, had to return home only for her own discomfort rather than for the baby's need. And when Tessa did take Fiona with her the staff at the shop were delighted, especially Anne, who was expecting her own baby in October or November. Walter said he was practicing when he held Fiona. Tessa told Anne she could work as long as she cared to. "I cannot abide the notion that women must be hidden away when they are pregnant," she said. Even though Anne blushed, she agreed.

They sent the boys to Rancho Magnífico for the summer. It was no longer a question of getting them out of harm's way. They realized now that it was imperative that their sons learn both ways of life, because someday they would be responsible for businesses that encompassed both the city and the land.

Indian and Armenthia provided an escort because they wanted to go while Thia still could. And without consulting anyone else, Chong Sing and Mrs. Tubbs decided it was only sensible that she remain in San Francisco to care for Fiona and tend to household matters while he went with the boys. When Tessa protested that Mrs. Tubbs had not been hired as a cook or maid of all work, Mrs. Tubbs only smiled. "I shall enjoy the change, and so will the boys. No child should have to do lessons without ceasing. And in any case, they will go on with their studies because they are all very bright and curious. Paul especially remains unconvinced that he does not have years and years of lost knowledge to find. A few selected volumes will, of course, be included in their baggage."

Tessa found it much easier to say good-by to the children this time. All three were excited and happy to be going. The only lecture she gave them was on the choosing of their promised horses.

"You will choose, but Pedro will have the final decision. If he does not think your choice is suitable, you will not argue with him. If all goes well, your horses will serve you well for many years, so you must be careful in your selection. When you are older and stronger, you may choose stallions for your own if you wish, but this time you will select from the mares and the geldings. A mare can be as temperamental as a stallion, but she is usually easier to control because she is seldom as strong. And a gelding will serve you well because he does not waste his time thinking of the mares. Do not try to prove yourselves by choosing horses that frighten you, because it won't change, and the horse will win the battle of will." She directed this last remark more to Brand than to the other two, and he looked sheepish enough for her to know she had hit the mark.

"I'm glad of the advice you gave them," Gavin told her later, "but I'm surprised at it too. I thought the dictate of the old tradition was that all should ride stallions."

"So they will someday, and so they would now if all their time from the cradle had been spent in the saddle. But it hasn't been. They are part of the old and part of the new, and things must be cut to fit."

"Including the stallions," he teased, wincing ostentatiously, but he loved her for her sensible attitude. His own vision had run parallel to hers, and he had dreaded seeing Brand on a great prancing brute of a stallion, his sure choice if given a chance.

This time the quiet in the house, undisturbed by Mrs. Tubbs's smooth competence and only rarely broken by Fiona's fussing, was welcome, and had nothing in common with the previous year's deadly silence and separation.

Tessa and Gavin made every effort to enjoy the city's offerings together. They were hailed as old friends at the

French restaurant. They went to plays, musical reviews, and variety acts, ruling out only minstrel shows. Many good performers now made San Francisco a stop on their tours. Sometimes Belle and Charles went with them, and the Ramsays ignored the puzzled looks they received for being in the company of the notorious pair. It was enough that Belle and Charles were good and loyal friends, but in addition, they were enjoyable to be with. Belle's tart and shameless observations on everyone and everything usually left Tessa with sides aching from laughter at the evening's end.

More rarely they persuaded Thia and Indian to accompany them. There was no way around it—even in this supposedly free state, Negroes were made unwelcome, not only by unfriendly stares but by refusal of service. Indian and Thia were far more patient and philosophical about it than the Ramsays. Indian told Gavin bluntly, "You want share th' guilt, that fine, but don' get me in no fight over it. I pick my own time bust somebody's head. Time comin' soon enough." The only saving grace was that they were still in that blissful newly-wedded state most couples lose shortly after the ceremony—they still preferred each other's company to anyone else's and wanted few outside diversions.

Tessa and Gavin often attended the weekly masked balls and laughed together over the thin disguises. The "respectables" felt free to come to these dances though very few people remained incognito for the whole evening. The Ramsays went simply because they enjoyed the dancing.

Tessa found herself taking the time to visit the Chens quite often in the colorful and foreign atmosphere of Chinatown. At first it was only to reassure herself that the baby, now graced with the name Chen Chye Lin-Ao, Lin-Ao meaning Lotus, was all right. But that was readily apparent even from her first visit, and she went back because despite their disparate backgrounds, she and Mrs. Chen found common ground easily, and their friendship grew. In fact, the very things that made them alien to each other provided much to talk about. Mrs. Chen wanted to know everything about life in California, and Tessa was no less interested in memories of China. Chen Soon Lei seemed to regard these woman's talks with benevolent indifference, but Tessa was sure he questioned his wife closely for any useful bits of information.

The one subject Mrs. Chen did not talk about easily was Chong Sing. However, one thing was clear—the Chens had left China to better their lives; Chong Sing had left to save his. It always amazed Tessa that she and Mrs. Chen managed to exchange so much information with relatively short conversations carried on in an atmosphere of the utmost courtesy, not to mention the language barrier that often came between them on finer points.

But aside from the visits with Mrs. Chen, almost all Tessa's free time was spent with Gavin, and she would have had it no other way. One of their favorite diversions was to go to the horse races at the track that had been built beyond old Mission Dolores. Even the impossible road had been improved for this popular sport so the fashionable could come in their carriages.

Many of the race horses were imported from the swift stock of Australia, and when Gavin saw Tessa eyeing them with a speculative gleam in her eyes, he protested, "You wouldn't dare!"

"Once I would have," she retorted saucily, "but it would not be seemly for a mother of four. And in any case, I would not like our horses to be good for nothing but this mad pace."

He laughed aloud at her attempt at a demure expression.

It was a blissful summer, a time without guilt because they knew the boys were happy and safe even as they themselves rediscovered their endless delight in each other.

CHAPTER L

"Will they never stop talking about horses?" Gavin groaned in mock despair.

"Probably not until they discover women," Tessa replied. "And frankly, I prefer the horses for now.

"Brand, give him more rein. He's behaving well. He doesn't need his head tied to his chest!" she called, and Brand complied.

All three boys had been very good in the care and training of their horses since they had brought them back with them at the beginning of September. It was not only that they knew their mother would make good her threat to send any one of the horses back to the *rancho* if she saw signs of neglect, but also they were fond and proud of their beasts. And they knew that extra work was involved in keeping a horse fit in the confines of the city.

Their individual choices had amused their parents mightily. Brand had picked a big palomino gelding, a five-year-old that had just enough memory of being a young stallion to carry himself proudly though without malice. Paul had chosen a rather delicately built golden mare, a four-year-old with great dark eyes and a perfectly flaxen mane and tail. With Paul's own slender frame, there was something touchingly fitting about horse and rider. Tessa got a lump in her throat just watching them.

She was even more touched by Jefferson's choice, though when he had first shown her and Gavin the chestnut, they had had trouble believing he was in earnest, especially since there were titters of laughter from the other two boys. The chestnut gelding was not exactly ugly, but he was no beauty either. His coat was rough. His mane and tail were flaxen, heavily striped with chestnut, and looked incongruously gaudy. He might have had a white star on his forehead, but it seemed to have slipped so that it was partly over one eye. He would have brought a fair enough price in a run-of-the-mill sale, but Tessa could not credit that Jefferson had chosen him over the golden horses.

"Are you sure this is the one you want?" she finally managed to ask.

Jefferson slipped down out of the saddle. The horse nuzzled him gently and rested his head against Jeff. "This's why. I didn't choose him. He chose me. He followed me all over the place. And when I looked at other horses or patted them, he made awful sad noises. Maybe he won't mind if I have a palomino later on when he's old and tired," he finished hopefully.

Now watching the boys exercising their mounts in the

cool January air, the saddles they had received for Christmas still gleaming like new because they polished them endlessly, Tessa couldn't help but think that perhaps Jefferson's kind instincts had been rewarded. Gavin had laughingly called him Don Quixote, and though Jeff didn't fully understand the reference, he had named his horse "Quixote." The chestnut had good gaits, but more, he went out of his way to please his master, listening to the commands of voice, feeling the slightest touch of rein or knee, responding with nothing less than his best. Brand and Paul's mounts were good and more dependable with each day of training despite their youth, but they would never be as finely attuned to their owners as Quixote was to Jefferson.

Tessa heard Fiona screeching and left Gavin with the boys. But her daughter's protest was only, as Mrs. Tubbs pointed out, because everything was happening somewhere else. That a girl child and particularly a crippled girl child was supposed to be frail and quiet had nothing to do with Fiona. She did everything with energy, passion, and noise, and Tessa loved her for it even when it was hard to keep up with her. She knew Fiona would need all the gumption she could muster.

It amused her to watch Fiona's growing awareness of the world around her. Her temperament was far more like Brand's than Jefferson's. Fiona reached out and grabbed at life without caution. Tessa sometimes wondered if Jordan had been such a child. But the thought of him brought only a faint, elusive pain now. Though their child's appearance proclaimed it, it was hard for Tessa to believe that the interlude with Jordan had ever happened. She had never looked at the Kuanyin again since the day she had put the figure away.

Besides her immediate family, Fiona crowed and clapped when she saw Lin-Ao. It was a pretty sight to see the two of them together, one so blond and the other with coal black hair. But for Armenthia and Indian's baby boy, Dian, and Anne and Walter's Margaret, Fiona had not even a glance to spare. Mrs. Tubbs stoutly defended this indifference. "It is after all the only sensible course; those infants are no use to her."

Tessa wasn't quite sure why and thought perhaps it was
605

just the difference between being very young and being where she was now, twenty-six this year. She didn't want to think of herself as a too settled matron, but for whatever reason, she found herself enjoying her children, her role of mother to them and wife to Gavin, more than ever before. And always there was the soft inner sadness that made the time with the children more precious, always the little voice reminding her to remember how they looked, what they said, day by day, because they grew and changed so quickly.

By Chong Sing's calendar, it was the year of the Tiger, and the outside world did enough growling and nervous pacing to make Tessa think the description apt. She could no longer make herself believe that what happened in the rest of the United States had no effect on California, and she missed the comfort of that fantasy, especially when she discovered Indian and Gavin murmuring together, excluding both her and Thia.

"As if dey thinks we ain't got ears to hear de news an' brains to understand," Armenthia snorted, but her eyes were enormously sad, and she held Dian fiercely when she thought of the mounting battle over the slavery issue. With so much anger and so much hate, men were going to die, black men and white men.

The news came to them slowly but inexorably. A new political party had been formed. They called themselves the Republican party, and their members included men from all parties, bound together by antislavery sentiments. The lines between those for and those against slavery were being ever more clearly drawn. In May the Kansas-Nebraska Bill had passed, repealing the old Missouri Compromise that had been the beginning of balancing slave and free territories. Now the phrase "popular sovereignty," meaning a freedom of choice for all territories or states regarding slavery, was becoming the rallying cry for pro-slavers. Freedom of choice over slavery seemed the strangest contradiction in terms to Tessa. Already blood was being spilled in Kansas, and the capture and return of fugitive slaves was raising an ever greater howl of outrage from the abolitionists in the North, a swelling chorus of approval from the slavers in the South.

But the Ramsays didn't have to go afield for trouble;

there was enough of it at home, though it was of a different nature. There was no longer any doubt that easy gold was a thing of the past. Less was being produced, and the greatest part of that was being minded by groups of men formed into small companies. Indian and Gavin had taken one trip to watch a hydraulic mining venture, the process of using water under high pressure to get to the gold. They returned with grave doubts.

"It tears away great chunks of the mountains! The damage to the land and the amount of silt in the runoff is incredible," Gavin told Tessa. "That waste has to go somewhere. Just watching the work, I got a terrible feeling that every waterway in California will be filled with mud if it goes on."

They would have nothing to do with hydraulic mining operations, but they decided to go ahead with the investment that had interested them for years now—a quartz-mining operation in Grass Valley. Because of the high cost of mining quartz, crushing it, and extracting the gold, the money to be made was not as easy as that from a rich pure surface vein, and the process was slower and took much more capital. But in the long run there was the best of chances that a considerable amount of gold would be steadily produced.

The mine they were interested in was owned by the Brown brothers, Mark and Peter, from an undetermined eastern origin. They never talked about their pasts, and it was doubtful that their names were the ones they had started out with, but that was true of a lot of people in California. What did matter was that samples of quartz from the mine bore gold in good amounts, and the Browns were capable of answering technical questions more than adequately. And what mattered further was that the Browns needed capital to develop the mine—called the "Lucille," for sweetheart, wife, or mother, only the Browns knew—and were willing to sell shares. But even in their need, they were canny, offering only seven lots of seven shares each, so that their own interest remained the majority. There was to be a down payment plus additional operating costs to be paid quarterly for two years, after which time the investors were to receive steady repayment and profit. If a particularly rich yield was achieved, the repayment would begin earlier. No investor could purchase more than one lot of seven shares; even though it involved more people, the Browns preferred to have multiple sources of capital rather than one that might fail.

Tessa found herself liking the Browns much more than she did the investors. The brothers at least had a glint of humor and a gleam of vision in their faded blue eyes set in weathered and nearly identical faces. The six other parties, three of whom had wives with them, were decidedly dull, despite the risk involved in the mine.

Tessa and Gavin gave a dinner party for everyone involved and for the final signing of the papers. It took all her self-control not to yawn openly. Afterward she said in disgust, "I didn't know people could be so pompous! I'm glad Indian and Thia's part in this remains unknown. I think those people could be as rude as they are dull. It's difficult to credit that they would even consider investing in the mine."

"Times are changing," Gavin said. "Unfortunately, we're going to see more and more of these dullards. They're shrewd, pious, and endlessly greedy. And they always have the money to invest when nobody else does."

Tessa knew he was speaking of a world he had already seen back in the States. And by the end of the year, she saw the truth of his view. A law had been passed against prostitution and now there was one against gambling. Though she thought it unjust, Belle wasn't worried about the former; it was already proving to be nothing more than a way to harrass the nonwhite ladies of the profession. Belle was so confident, she was already making plans for building a more elaborate house in the new year. Charles wasn't much more worried about the antigambling law, though he thought it would probably be enforced, since gambling houses were a great deal easier for public officials to identify without the same degree of personal loss. Charles wasn't worried because private games were always to be found.

Gavin and Indian were not as easy about it. The Golden Horse brought in a steady and usually lavish share of their profits; to have the gambling shut down would be a severe blow. And Tessa knew it as well as they did because she still kept the accounts.

608

It was not that she particularly approved of either gambling or prostitution, though she had been involved in the former and couldn't see a city of men existing for long without the latter, but she thought it odd that laws could be passed against such private moral choices as whether one wanted to place a bet or buy a woman. After all, no one had to do either. There were abuses in both professions, particularly in the virtual enslavement of the Chinese and Chilean women, but she thought it ridiculous for the reformers to go after people like Belle and Charles.

"When times get hard, people find scapegoats," Gavin said. There was a new set to his mouth these days, a taut air of waiting about him, and Tessa's heart ached for him. He had even begun to move restlessly in his sleep and to mutter in the grip of nightmares. Tessa held and soothed him until he slept peacefully again, and she thought with longing of the peaceful days they had spent at both *ranchos* at the beginning of the summer.

They tried their best not to let their tension interfere with the children's pleasure of Christmas. Tessa slipped her hand into Gavin's as they watched Fiona scrambling about. Her progress was uneven when she pulled herself up and walked and she was still apt to surprise herself by sitting down suddenly, but she was determined. Gavin gave Tessa's hand a comforting squeeze.

By February the full weight of the financial panic had come down on them and the rest of the business community. "Honest Harry" Meiggs had sailed away on a ship he had bought. He had been a leader in civic affairs since the early days of the fifties. He had business assets all over the city including the longest wharf and a fine house on Signal Hill, now called Telegraph Hill, where the semaphore tower at the top received messages from a telegraph station on Point Lobos indicating which vessels were sailing into the bay. It was unfortunate that the same signals had not conveyed the news that Meiggs had outfitted the boat for far more than a pleasure cruise on the bay. He was even now purportedly in South America with his family, including the city's newly elected comptroller, his brother John. It was no wonder Meiggs had sailed away so precipitately; behind him he left not only hundreds of ruined investors, but a million dollars in personal debts,

609

$800,000 of which had belonged to the city before Meiggs embezzled it.

But Meiggs was only part of the disaster. There was graft and corruption on every level of officialdom. Too many banks had been too casual in their assaying of gold, and even had inadequate knowledge of the purity of the gold from different regions of California. Much of the gold they had accepted and even the gold that had been privately minted into coins had been weighted with brass filings before they received it. Speculation in land and other commodities had been rife and reckless. Many promissory notes were unsecured and worthless. Few people had recognized the signs of change in the economy and the decreasing amount of gold; life had gone on as before.

One major bank closed and nineteen others quickly followed, shutting down nearly half of San Francisco's financial houses.

They met in Indian's frame house beyond the noise of the children. Even Dian had been exiled to the Ramsay house under Mrs. Tubbs's care. They had all the figures. They had gone over them countless times. They had not trusted just one bank, but with twenty going under, they had sustained heavy losses. And now the Golden Horse was no more than a saloon, the tables closed down as they had been all over the city except for three establishments that were still said to be doing a lively business for inexplicable reasons. Mr. Peniston had smiled sadly and set about finding private games for survival in the style he was accustomed to. Running a saloon was not his business. Liquor sold well enough to be sure, but the flow of gold was minimal compared to that from gambling.

The rest of the businesses, the mill and wharf, the warehouse, and the shop were all intact, but aside from the shop, they were suffering the effects of the panic, doing just well enough now to pay expenses and not much more. The shop was the only one that was thriving, as if those who still had money were intent on spending it recklessly for luxury goods before they lost it in some other way.

There were horses to sell without touching the breeding stock, and there would be vegetables and other fresh produce to market later on at the extravagant prices such things still brought, even though beef prices had been going

610

steadily downward. But there was simply not enough to hold onto their seven percent of the mine in Grass Valley. Even their share of the payments was costly. The heavy equipment being installed at the mine was expensive, as were the wages the Brown brothers paid to the crew of experienced Cornish miners they had hired.

Gavin recounted it all briefly, Indian nodding in agreement, both of them thinking there was only one choice and they were lucky it wasn't worse. It took them both a minute to realize their wives weren't sharing their view.

Suddenly, even though he was not touching her, Gavin could feel Tessa's body humming with excitement. Her eyes were wide and glowing, her cheekbones traced with delicate color, the grim accepting look they had all worn lately gone from her face, but not in his wildest imaginings would he have guessed what she was going to say.

"I have found a way," she said. "All we must do is to sell the brick house. We will have enough then, and we will not lose our part of the mine or of anything else. I believe in the mine and in the Browns. I believe enough gold will come from it to be worth much more than our house. This is the least of our properties now, and already everything is beginning to change so that a home will soon be better placed elsewhere, further away from the crowded places of business. The children can go to the *rancho* for now, and Thia has said that unless Indian objects, we are welcome to stay with them until we have another house, as they must also have before too long."

Gavin started up and stared at her incredulously, his body rigid. "Sell our house, our home?"

Indian looked at Thia and wondered how such a sweet woman could have put him in this position of being unable to side with his friend.

"Yes, our house," Tessa said firmly. "Home is where we choose to make it, where we are together. It does not depend on bricks and beams. The house is what we can sell with the least loss."

"I suppose you're going to throw in Don Esteban's emeralds too?"

Her chin tilted up at the cut. "That's unkind, and they wouldn't bring enough anyway," she accused, and he had the grace to look abashed. But even as she spoke, she

611

understood where his pain was coming from. The unwanted, lonely, and abused little boy was never gone; he reappeared whenever the security he needed was threatened. And he needed the proof of walls and roof and a safe place he could touch more than she would ever need them. The land was her strength and Gavin was her safe place.

She realized they were alone, and she blessed Thia and Indian. She went to Gavin and put her arms around him. "My love, we have two homes at the *ranchos*, two places where the land is ours and goes on almost forever; two places where the herds and the crops grow strong under the sun. Here we have only a house that shelters us when the day is done. We can build such a shelter again when there is time."

She studied his face, the lines leaner than ever, the small scar showing plainly, the blue of his eyes so dark, all because his painful vulnerability had surfaced without his knowledge.

"My God, I love you so!" she whispered huskily, and she pressed her head against his shoulder and held on to him, wanting no distance between them, wanting him to be comforted by her as she was by his mere existence. And nothing could have made her happier than feeling him relax, feeling his cheek rubbing gently against her hair. "I'll get used to the idea, I promise. But right now why don't we go home and take advantage of the bedroom while we still own it."

On their way out, they met Indian who was returning with a sleeping Dian in his arms. "Figure you don' need no extra babies tonight," he said with a grin.

Once their plan was known, offers of help came not only from Belle and Charles but from Chong Sing and Mrs. Tubbs. All were politely refused. It simply seemed unethical to borrow from friends for the sake of a venture like the mine. But Gavin told Tessa he would like to find out how Mrs. Tubbs and Chong Sing had managed to stay solvent during the panic.

"Either they picked the right banks, or they've got money hidden under their beds," she replied.

Since it was her idea, Tessa was determined to accomplish it all with a minimum of fuss. She and Gavin escorted the children and Mrs. Tubbs to Rancho Magnífico, the boys excited about more space for their riding, Mrs. Tubbs serenely composed because, after all, these things did happen, she still had her job and the children, and she had quite enjoyed her first visit to the *rancho*. She sat her horse firmly, a no-nonsense wide-brimmed hat shading her face, gloves protecting her hands. A smile tugged at Gavin's mouth every time he glanced at her. He thought she would have looked no different even had she been riding across some foreign plain to face a host of hostile tribesmen.

The boys knew just enough of the truth to make them part of an adventure and to let them look forward to a new house. And everything seemed fine until it was time for Gavin and Tessa to return to San Francisco.

Brand sought out his mother, and his face was very earnest. "I've been thinkin' about it, Mama. It would be more fun if you'd stay here with us."

He looked so much like a small, young version of his father, her heart caught in her throat. She had been dreading and trying not to think about saying good-by to Fiona, but she found this worse.

"I'm needed in the city. I can't ask your father and Indian to run my shop and keep the accounts in addition to everything else they take care of," she explained gently.

His face was suddenly harder and much older. "You love Papa more than you love us, that's what it is! You just want to go where he goes. You've always loved him better!" he accused.

How accurate children could be with their angry blows, she thought. How to explain to him that love for a lover and love for a child were different. No way to explain because there was too much truth in his accusation. "If that's true, Brand, then you ought to feel very, very sorry for me," she said slowly. "You know how much I love you. Think of how hard it would be to love anyone even more than that."

His anger broke and he threw himself against her, sobbing, "I didn't mean to be hateful, I didn't mean to!"

"You're not, my little one. You're my wonderful Brand who is so quick and bright and can do so many things. There's something special I want you to do, and if you will, you can have your brothers help."

613

The sniffling stopped, and he pushed away so he could look at her, his expression changed to one of keen interest. "What do you want us to do?"

"It's sad, but Amordoro and Diablo are both getting older. Before too long, your father and I will need new mounts. So perhaps you can keep your eyes open for promising young colts we could train."

"Oh, I will!" Brand nodded enthusiastically. "They'll be the color of a new gold coin, their manes and tails will be sparkly white, and they'll have the biggest, darkest eyes of any palominos in all California! This time Papa will have a palomino too."

She hugged him, laughing. "There's no doubt that you know how to choose the best of them!"

Riding away from the *rancho* was hard this time, and it made everything else easier by comparison. The few pieces of furniture Tessa had chosen to keep were stored at the warehouse. All the lovely things that remained now would belong to the new owners and would hike the selling price considerably.

Good housing in the city was still at a premium, and the Ramsays didn't have long to wait for a buyer. The brick house would now belong to the Martinsons, to fat Mr. and round, overflounced Mrs. who both lacked confidence and taste despite the strong prop of fortune (a fortune Gavin suspected had been well fed by usury rates on loans that in past years had been as high as eighteen per cent a month). It didn't matter; the Martinsons had the money to buy the house and did not care who their neighbors were across the way.

As they were led on the final inspection tour, Mrs. Martinson kept sneaking sly glances at the Ramsays, and Gavin had a great desire to laugh aloud. Undoubtedly the woman was convinced she was viewing part of the wicked demimonde, and yet she was obviously envious at the unavoidable comparison between herself and the tall slender woman who was so calmly leaving all of this. Mr. Martinson's stare was so pathetically hungry, Gavin felt sorry for the man. He was suddenly very proud of Tessa.

Tessa was more aware of the woman's greedy glances at the things she would soon own than of anything else. *How awful to accept another's taste so easily*, she thought.
614

She would have been willing to bet that if she came back in a year, everything would be in the same places.

Shining rosewood and soft-hued brocade, velvet and crystal and brass, a luxurious house without being overwhelming or overdone. So much had happened to them in the years of living here. She knew she ought to be sad, but she was not. Their share in the mine was safe now; they had no debts; they would have another house in the city soon enough.

When she was lonesome for Fiona, she visited the Chens and played with Lin-Ao. Often Mrs. Chen discussed the child's future. Because the baby was of both races, she had every intention that Lin-Ao would learn not only Chinese ways, but the ways of America even if Mr. Chen was reluctant that it be so. Tessa agreed wholeheartedly with Mrs. Chen and proposed that Lin-Ao be taught by Mrs. Tubbs when she was old enough. She thought Chong Sing would approve. Though he tried to pretend indifference, he was very fond of the little girl and still felt much responsibility for her, playing the part of benevolent uncle to her. Tessa was sure that was why he had elected to stay in the city rather than go to the *rancho*.

At first the help he had insisted on giving Thia in her house had been hard for her to accept. "I'se—I'm used to doin' for people, don' feel right the other way 'round," she had protested, but later she confided to Tessa, "Still don' seem right, but I'm gettin' used to bein' spoilt now."

Thia was changing in other ways too, learning to read and write under Mrs. Tubbs's tutelage, and working diligently to change her speech. Though Tessa rather missed the old, softer sound, she understood. Indian could speak forever in the pattern of his youth and wandering days, but Thia's speech had been that of the slave quarters and was intolerable to herself. The drawl would probably never be completely gone, but the shape of her sentences was changing. "Don' want my son talkin' like a slave, an' he will if his mama do—does," she told Tessa bluntly.

Belle and her girls and Charles had moved into their new house in the spring as planned, and Belle was very proud of it. It was a two-story brick building on Pike Street with a private carriage entrance on Clay. It was opposite Ah Toy's house and was set a discreet distance back from the street with a pristine white picket fence and a flower garden in front. Belle's business hadn't suffered at all from the financial panic, and Charles was doing fine too, because he had an unerring instinct for finding high stake games.

"I think we chose the wrong businesses," Tessa told Gavin who replied that a mother of four was hardly fit material for a madam.

Gradually things were sorting themselves out, and though it would take years for the full adjustment to be made to a new economy, people were not as panicked as they had been at the beginning of the year. Tessa noted happily that all the account books were again showing a profit, including the figures of produce and livestock from both *ranchos*.

They made several trips to Rancho Magnífico during the summer, and though it was tiring to make the trek for so little time spent before going back to the city, it was worth it for the interludes with the children. On their very first visit, Brand had informed his mother that he and his brothers had picked out two colts, but they weren't going to tell which ones yet. "Going to watch 'em this summer and see how they do," he told her, very much the professional horseman. Tessa nodded gravely, controlling her smile.

Everything was progressing well except their search for a house. They had begun looking as soon as they were certain the worst of their own financial crisis was over. But they had had little luck so far. Each place they found was either outrageously priced or unsuitable for the size of their family. Even their willingness to buy an empty lot and start from scratch didn't seem to help in places that would be decent locations.

Then one day Belle sought Tessa out at the shop, her excitement evident even before she explained. "I think I've found, or rather Charley has found the perfect house for you. You know those elegant brick places at the base of Rincon Hill?"

Tessa started to laugh. "I certainly do! Who could help but know about South Park? All built around that flower garden and all enclosed with an iron fence. Only the residents have keys to the gate, my dear," she drawled
616

affectedly. "Honestly, Belle, we're not in the market for a house that costs as much as a palace."

"Ah, but it won't!" Belle said triumphantly. "This house is even bigger than the ones in that cage; it isn't part of South Park. Charley did some asking because he didn't think you'd want a place that restricted the children too much. This place has lots of space around it. And even people who live in palaces have their little vices. The man who owns this house has a bad habit of gambling too much. Charley says he owes far too much to far too many people. His life isn't going to be worth much around here if he doesn't start paying up. If you can raise the cash, it's a sure thing he'll sell it for far less than it's worth."

"That's horrid!" Tessa exclaimed. "Does he have a family?"

Belle shrugged. "I expect he must to be living in such a big house. That's his worry, not yours. The first rule in Charley's business is that if you can't pay, you don't play. In mine it's that I won't play unless the man can pay."

Tessa laughed even as she realized the truth of Belle's words—if the man had to sell the house, it would make no difference to him who bought it, any more than she had minded selling to the Martinsons.

CHAPTER LI

Even though they had had to go against their best instincts and borrow money at high interest, they knew they were lucky to have gotten the loan at all, and fortunate beyond words to have been able to buy the house for thousands less than it was worth.

It was a perfect house, three spacious stories that would allow the children to have their own rooms, plus quarters for Chong Sing, Mrs. Tubbs, and even guests. The previous owner had sold the furnishings separately, which was fine with Tessa, but she knew it would take a while before she and Gavin would be able to furnish the house properly. The pieces brought from the warehouse hardly made a dent. It didn't matter; the house was graceful in itself, from its shining wood floors, high-ceilinged first-floor rooms, and cozy upstairs chambers, to its sweeping main staircase and many fine-glassed windows. Even the kitchen had been designed as a large, well-lit, and comfortable place to work. Chong Sing fairly glowed when he saw his new domain.

And besides having room for Indian to build when he was ready, the ample grounds around the house were lovely in their own right. There was not only the rarity of some good-sized trees, but there had been some attempt at landscaping, including a rose garden that was well on its way to being firmly established. Tessa did not allow herself to dwell on the fact that another woman had obviously planned to be here for a long time, watching the blooms increase with the passing years.

They soon discovered there was less fog here than in other parts of the city, and the waters of the bay sparkled within their sight on sunny days. Not even the fact that it was quite a distance from the center of things caused any problem for the Ramsays. If they did not want to ride their horses in, there were horsecars every half-hour, a service begun the year before for the elite exiles of South Park. The unhappy restriction on the service was that Indian and Thia would not be allowed to ride the cars. There was little use in discussing it. Tessa and Gavin hated the discriminatory rule and that was all there was to say about it. Indian and Thia would have to ride horseback or maintain some kind of coach, and Thia already had plans for a pony cart when they moved out to Rincon.

They brought the children and Mrs. Tubbs home, and Mrs. Tubbs was less than her usual articulate self, repeating, "Well, oh, my, well, well," several times. The boys were in a frenzy to explore and claim both the inside and out for their own. Even Fiona looked around with wide eyes and babbled her excitement.

The first party Tessa gave was for Belle and Charles, who were toasted for having found the house.

"You're lucky it's so far out of town." Belle teased. "Otherwise I might have snapped it up myself." She was holding Fiona on her lap with complete disregard for what the baby might do to the gold satin of her dress, and Tessa

618

smiled inwardly at the contrasts in Belle's character—
(tough and practical, kind and gentle).

Tessa held on to the memory of Belle with Fiona for
years afterward. It was one of the last carefree times the
Ramsays had with Belle and Charles. She would remember
the night of the play forever, even to the date. It was a
Thursday evening, November 15, 1855. The Ramsays still
kept no carriage of their own, but Belle went so far as to
send her own out for them.

It was such a lovely evening, Tessa saw everything as if
it were cast in high relief. It did not even trouble her that
the continuing clarity of the weather probably fore-
shadowed a scarcity of rain for the next year's grazing.
She gazed at everything with the delight of a child and
pointed things out to Gavin with such enthusiasm that he
laughed.

There were gas lights on the corners downtown now;
several streets had cobblestones in place of the old, rough
planking; and because of the ordinance passed the year
before requiring all new commercial building to be done
in brick or stone, the city now boasted hundreds of these
new, more fireproof structures, many of them quite im-
posing.

"I can hardly remember what it looked like when we
first came here," Tessa said.

"Yes, I've heard even the wharf rats are required to
wear waistcoats now," Gavin replied.

"Ugh! You must be determined to ruin my romantic
mood!"

"Not all of it, I hope," he protested, running his hand
playfully over her neck and shoulders. She moved close
enough to hug him, quite a feat in her wide skirts.

Belle and Charles were waiting for them at the American
Theatre with the tickets for *Nicodemus: or the Unfortunate Fisherman*. The Ravel family troupe was
presenting it for the first time anywhere, and the air
hummed with the excitement of the event and civic pride
that San Francisco would get to see it first.

Red velvet and gilt abounded in the theater, and Belle
quipped, "I feel right at home here. Surely a madam
designed this place."

619

The custom adopted from the East was for the demimondaines and their men friends to sit in the curtained stalls behind the pit, which was right in front of the stage and offered the cheapest seats. But there was no set rule, and Belle and Charles always sat in the first balcony, which contained some of the highest-priced seats.

The stage curtain had a terrible, bloated painting of George Washington on it. When the play began, Tessa was still giggling over Belle's scandalous remark that she wouldn't ask any of her girls to take that man for a client because he obviously had something catching.

The play was quite enjoyable. And when the lights went up for the intermission, Tessa had even more fun watching some of the men in the pit paying court to Belle with smiles, waves, and conversation among themselves. Belle smiled back and inclined her head graciously, accustomed to such tributes to her beauty and fame. Charles watched her fondly and with pride.

It happened so quickly, it took them all by surprise. The man of the couple sitting in front of them barged past them after his wife had hissed something in his ear. Gavin recognized them as U.S. Marshal Richardson and his wife. They were less than popular; he was more often drunk than not, and she was forever a self-righteous and insufferably boring prig. They saw him reappear in the pit, gesticulating angrily as he talked to the men who had noticed Belle.

And then suddenly he was back, demanding that Belle and Charles leave. "People like you have no right in this section," he growled. "You have caused my wife great embarrassment."

Belle simply stared at him. Charles said very quietly, "We bought the tickets, just as you did. We'll leave when the play is over. As for your wife, I believe we're talking about jealousy rather than embarrassment."

The man turned beet red and sputtered with rage, which was not mitigated by Gavin's coldly polite, "Evening, Marshal Richardson," a reminder to the man that he was insulting the Ramsays too.

Richardson's mouth worked furiously for a moment, and then he was gone but only to return with the manager. He demanded that Belle and Charles be thrown out. The manager refused on the same grounds Charles had. It was the Richardsons who left, Mrs. Richardson's face a rigid mask.

"Looking at her could turn a man to stone," Gavin muttered.

"Guess a lot of men feel that way," Belle said. "I didn't do it on purpose, but I hear she gave a party the same night I had my last soirée, and most of the men came to my party instead of hers even though it cost them plenty at my house. I guess she thought those men were talking about her tonight. As if they'd bother!" Belle didn't respect the woman enough to be insulted; she found it all a little amusing.

But Gavin wasn't so sure Charles felt the same way. "That man is a bad drunk," he warned. "Best to give his kind a wide berth."

"I won't seek him out," Charles said, but Tessa saw the same chill gleam in his eyes that she had seen in Gavin's —it was the look of a man who could only be pushed so far before he became a lethal weapon.

The confrontation had been so ugly and unsettling to her, the evening lost its glamour for Tessa and she was glad when it was over. And on Saturday night when Indian arrived at the house in wild-eyed haste, she knew instinctively that it had something to do with Belle and Charles.

"Charles, he shot Marshal Richardson dead. Had good reason from what I hear, but they goin' hang him less they stopped. Fire bells ringin'," Indian panted.

The peaceful calm of the evening with the children was shattered. Gavin was already grabbing his gun, his hat, and his coat as he implored Tessa, "Please, stay here! I'll send you news as soon as there is any."

"But Belle might need me!"

"Belle will be all right. If she isn't, I'll send for you. Please make it easy! I don't want to worry about you too." He had visions of a mob killing everything in its path.

She gave up and nodded curtly. "Take care. But if you're not back in twenty-four hours, I'll come to find you."

It was the best he could hope for. He kissed her and was gone.

She saw the questions beginning in the boys' wide, shocked eyes, and she spoke as calmly as she could. "I do not know any more than what you just heard. We must all hope and pray that Mr. Cora will be safe."

"But he killed someone," Brand insisted, and his voice quavered.

She closed her eyes for a moment, wishing she were more adequate to this task, wondering if any parent ever was, knowing this was her domain for the moment, and Mrs. Tubbs would not interfere. "Taking a life is a terrible thing," she said slowly. "But sometimes it is a choice between your own life and another's. And then you must make that choice, as it was made in our house on the night Fiona was born. I wish I could make it simple for you to understand, but life and death are not simple things. I know it doesn't help much, but you will grow to understand it better as you grow older." That's the way it ought to be, even if it is not always so, she thought, realizing that parents specialized in "ought to be." "The only thing I can tell you for certain is that Charles Cora is your friend as he is mine. And knowing him, you must know he would never go out to kill a man without reason. Surely the other man came after him."

That made sense to them and gave them comfort as no abstract theory could. She only wished she could be as comforted. Long after the children were asleep, she was still awake, and when she gave up and went downstairs again, she found Chong Sing and Mrs. Tubbs sitting in quiet companionship, sipping tea, no less worried than she about Gavin, Indian, and Charles.

Tessa reached a hand out to each, reserved as they were, and was touched by the warm response. "Thank you," she said huskily. "It would be difficult to be alone now."

Gavin rode in on Sunday evening to find Amordoro saddled, Tessa ready to ride into the city.

"Is Charles still alive?" she asked.

"He is," Gavin said, and he hugged her so tightly, she could feel the little tremors of exhaustion running through him.

When he told her what had happened, she could understand why. He and Indian and several others had joined the official guard that had kept Charles safe from the mob for the night. They had numbered around fifty. Fifty against a surging, bloodthirsty mob. Sheriff Scannell had nowhere near the force to effectively resist the actions of many, but Sam Brannan had been promptly arrested for inciting violence, and without his bellowing, the mob had lacked direction. It didn't matter that Brannan was released later on his own recognizance; removing the match of his personality from the beginning tinderbox had, by the time morning came, proved effective.

The mob had reassembled at ten o'clock to hear the verdict of the coroner's jury. The jury had heard sixteen witnesses and examined the evidence, which consisted of three derringers. Their verdict was that "said act was premeditated, and that there was nothing to mitigate the same."

At least there had been no further attempts to hang Charles on the spot. The matter was now in the hands of the Grand Jury, which would meet in several days.

"How did it happen? Do you believe it was premeditated?" Tessa asked hoarsely.

"No, I don't believe it. Avoidable maybe, but not premeditated. It started Friday. Richardson and Charles passed on the street, and I guess Charles made some remark. They both ended up at the Cosmopolitan Saloon Friday evening, and a man who knows both of them, a Dr. Mills, thought he might prevent a disaster if he introduced them formally. It seemed to work for a while—they had a couple of amiable drinks together—but when they went outside, the insults started again, ending with Richardson threatening to slap Charles's face. Charles went back inside and told Dr. Mills because he really didn't want trouble at that point. Richardson followed him in and was going to make good his threat, but several men talked him out of it and nothing more happened. But yesterday afternoon Richardson started looking for Charles at around four o'clock. He babbled vengeance everywhere he went and drank a good deal on the way. Yet when he passed Charles in the street, everything was fine, probably because Charles had a friend with him. But I think Richardson was insane in any case. He and Charles visited two bars together before they separated again. It was like some mad cat-and-mouse game, and Richardson wasn't sobering up any. Then around six-thirty when Charles was in the Blue Wing Saloon on Montgomery Street, a messenger found him and told him a friend was waiting outside to see him. I expect Charles thought it was word of a game somewhere. But it was Richardson. Apparently they talked together peacefully enough before walking down Clay Street until they got to Leidesdorff. That's where everything went wrong, and Charles shot Richardson. There are two completely different versions of how it happened. One is that Charles pinned the man to the wall with one arm and shot him in cold blood, and the other is that Richardson started his trouble-making again, and Charles tried to grab him by the collar and stop the whole thing before it got out of hand, but Richardson drew on him and Charles was faster."

"Shooting a man in cold blood doesn't sound like Charles at all!" Tessa exclaimed. "I'm sure it was self-defense. If only they had stayed away from each other!"

"That's hard to do when someone is after you; the world never seems big enough. The trouble is that you and I and other people who call Charles friend know he would not kill in cold blood, but there are many others who are sure he would simply because he is a gambler and his woman is a prostitute. They're saying all three derringers are his, that Richardson was unarmed. They're saying that even though now a knife has been found under a grating near where Richardson fell and it appears to be his. A gun and a knife, you can't be much better armed than that."

"It's preposterous to think Charles would have had three guns! He always has his two derringers and Richardson is always armed too."

"One of Charles's derringers had been fired, the other was loaded but not cocked. Richardson's was loaded and cocked. His supporters can hardly prove he was innocent and unarmed with that evidence, so they'll have to load it on Charles's back," Gavin pointed out cynically.

"Belle—what about her? She must be wild."

"She is, but wild with a purpose. She's already going after the best attorneys she can find. I told her you would visit her tomorrow."

"What do you think will happen?" She had to ask it.

"I don't know. The fire bells ringing tonight were really for a fire, but there's still talk of the committee assembling

624

again. Things are still unsettled financially for most people; they want a scapegoat, and Charles is handy."

Belle was pacing with controlled fury, her eyes gleaming savagely. "I'd spring him from that jail, but I won't have us sneaking out of this town like beaten dogs. Charley didn't do anything wrong. It was self-defense—that ass Richardson should have been dead a long time ago, drunken, murderous bastard!"

All Belle's energy was concentrated on Charles. She arranged for fresh clothing, linen, and good meals to be taken to him in jail. Even before the coroner's jury had met, she had hired two prominent lawyers, and she asked Colonel E.D. Baker to head the defense. He was well known for his skills as a criminal lawyer and a great orator. Only the best would do for Charles. Belle paid Baker $15,000, half of the fee he asked, in gold before he left her parlor and promised him the other half as soon as she could raise it.

The Ramsays could do little to help besides subscribing to the fund being raised for Charles's defense. City Supervisor James P. Casey and some other friends of Charles, including Gavin, managed to raise $40,000 in a few days. But then the press attacked Baker so viciously that he announced his withdrawal from the case. It was a measure of Belle's persuasive powers that she could prove stronger than Baker's care for his standing in the community, but the Ramsays, knowing the force of her will to save Charles, thought it would take a much stronger man than Baker to refuse her.

The press was revolting. Day after day they printed salacious stories of Belle and Charles and righteous yowlings against them and their kind. It was sickeningly apparent that Charles would be on trial for being a gambler and for loving Belle more than for shooting Richardson. And Belle was obviously also on trial.

Tessa felt terribly frustrated to be able to offer so little, but she did persuade Belle to come out to the house a few times just to get away from everything. "If you're careful, no one will know where you are, and you can have a few moments of peace. Come in a carriage no one will recognize."

Belle accepted gratefully, but she never stayed for long, always afraid she might miss some word of Charles. The children were wonderful, understanding now that Charles was in trouble though it wasn't his fault because the other man would have killed him, understanding that Belle was very sad and worried. They drew close to her when she came out to the house, telling her little incidents of their days, showing her the treehouse Gavin had built for them, using every way they knew to make her smile, and Belle did seem comforted by them.

They tried to persuade her to spend Christmas with them, but it was a futile request. "I expect all I'd do is cry," she admitted.

It was a relief to Tessa that all the staff at the shop liked Belle and remained sympathetic to her and Charles despite the scurrilous newspaper attacks. But Tessa shared their shock when Molly told her the latest news one day. The clerks were all looking alarmed and stopped talking the minute Tessa walked in. Then Molly burst out, "Do you think it's true? Do you think she did it?"

"Who did what?" Tessa asked, completely at sea.

She heard Molly out with a sinking heart and went immediately to see Belle.

"Oh, Belle, is it true? Did you threaten that witness, Mrs. Knight?"

Belle's eyes were pure green; the softening brown lights had vanished. She shrugged. "I didn't do it the way the bitch reported it. I didn't try to poison her or threaten to have her killed, though now I wish I had. I did offer her money to change her story. She's lying anyway."

"Good God! You have given them another weapon to use against you and Charles," Tessa burst out.

Belle's face was suddenly very cold. "I'd bribe the devil himself if I thought it would help Charley. Don't meddle, Tessa, this game's too rough for you."

Tessa knew she could say no more without risking their friendship.

Charles had been arraigned on December 1. His trial began on January 3, 1856. The first week was spent in selecting the jury, and on the eighth day one of the jurors swore out an affadavit that Belle had attempted to bribe him. Neither of the Ramsays said anything about it to her, but they both despaired over what her activities would do to Charles.

On Baker's advice, Belle did not attend the court sessions, but there was no doubt she was on trial. Tessa went as often as she could and reported to Belle afterward. There were dozens of character witnesses on both sides. Gavin testified for Charles which made the prosecutor's claim that all of the witnesses for the defense were Belle's customers all the more galling. But the defense pointed out that the same could be said for the prosecutor's witnesses.

Mrs. Knight's testimony was hard to dispute. She had certainly seen the interior of Belle's house; she remembered the back parlor down to the last detail of a silver tray with a small decanter and two little glasses. But her claim that she had been tricked into going there rang false, and her description of Belle's threats sounded like a bad melodrama. Tessa judged her a woman always on the borderline of hysterics and one who would welcome anything that might give her significance, even a scandal. And perhaps she had wanted more money than Belle was willing to pay.

The defense didn't try to break her testimony, because she was the one who said that Richardson's arm was raised, which meant that he had been free to shoot and not helplessly pinned by Charles. It was one of the more bizarre aspects of the case that Mrs. Knight should have been the one to offer that piece of information. But despite her testimony and that of the character witnesses, the defense had only two things in its favor—the extra derringer and Baker's powers as a speaker. On Tuesday, January 15, he rose to speak.

Tessa glanced at Charles, as she often had during the trial, trying to send him her encouragement. Though the tension of the murder trial had caused bursts of nervous laughter throughout, Charles never smiled. The only sign of his nervousness was the quick movement of his jaws as he chewed a quid of tobacco. Because of Belle's arrangements, he was always well dressed. Today he wore a suit complete with pleated shirt, gloves, and a figured velvet vest, much the same as he had the first night he

627

had come to the Golden Horse. Somehow it made him look very vulnerable to Tessa. His eyes met hers for an instant, and she managed to smile. He acknowledged her with the barest of nods. Gavin was sitting beside her, and she gripped his hand.

Baker's eloquent voice filled the courtroom. His hair was gray, a fairly rare shade since most of the immigrants to California had been so young. Baker was only forty-five, but the papers described him as "old." There was a reassuringly paternal air about him, a kindliness and dignity about his face. Tessa didn't know whether it was true or all an act for the courtroom, and she didn't care as long as he got Charles freed.

Baker didn't thunder at the crowd. He spoke at length on the fairness of the laws and the courts in the American system. The crowd stirred restlessly in their boredom, and some of their snide remarks about Baker were audible. Obviously they had expected fireworks, not a lecture.

"What is he doing?" Tessa whispered worriedly to Gavin.

"I'm not quite sure, but I hope it's all part of a good plan."

Next Baker praised the jury, the judge, and the prosecution for their integrity, and then he admitted that he too was moved by the plight of the tearful widow and the orphan, the blood and the loss.

"I don't complain of these things; I don't shrink from their being mentioned; I feel them; my heart quivers while I think of them. But"—Baker paused long enough to capture everyone's attention—"there is another aspect of this case to be thought of."

He had them now. Everyone was sitting up straighter, listening intensely. He had woven a spell of deceptive calmness and subtle voice changes. He had brought the pathos of the Richardson family out into the open. And now he spoke about Charles.

He admitted that Charles was not perfect; he admitted that Charles was "cared for by a woman of very bad relations in life, whose name, indeed, is a reproach." And then in a brilliant shift, he had Charles as the victim, Charles and Belle attacked by a vicious and lying press.

"Against this we have but one defense—against this we have but one resource, but one hope. It is to be found

628

in time, which tempers all things—it is to be found in human sympathy and the justice of this tribunal—in the merciful condition of human infirmity—and at last is stern, naked, and irresistible truth."

Was Charles Cora all bad and Richardson all good? Baker thought not. He began to carve away at Richardson's image with sharp, deadly words. Even Richardson's friends had called him a drunk, so much so that one of their claims was that he was too drunk to defend himself. He was known for his bad temper and his drunkenness as much as for his role of husband and father. Baker quoted witness after witness, until he had everyone in the courtroom nodding each time he said, "Richardson was a violent, quarrelsome drunk."

He digressed for a moment, giving his audience time to catch their breath before his next blow, defending the ethics of the legal profession, saying that every man had the right to good counsel and that he himself would never cease to offer it, no matter how public opinion raged against him. He seemed to have forgotten that he had tried to back out of the case.

He switched back to the case again, holding up his arm. Mrs. Knight had seen Richardson's arm upraised, though two other witnesses for the prosecution had seen differently. Mrs. Knight was to be believed. A cocked pistol and a knife were found nearby. There was no possibility other than the fact that Richardson had drawn first and Charles Cora had shot in self-defense.

He discussed a few other aspects of the case, and Tessa held her breath, sensing he was getting ready to deliver another jolt to the courtroom. But even she was surprised by the directness of it. Baker had seemed to want to ease Belle out of the picture, and he had alluded only briefly to her. There was a collective gasp as he launched his next attack.

"I will now proceed to grapple with the great bugbear of the case. The complaint, on their side, is that Belle Cora has tampered with the witnesses. In plain English, Belle Cora is helping her friend as much as she can. In the Lord's name who else should help him? Who else is there whose duty it is to help him? If it were not for her, he would not have a friend on earth. It is a woman of base

629

profession, of more than easy virtue, of malign fame, of a degraded cast—it is one poor, weak, feeble, and if you like it, wicked woman—to her alone he owes his ability to employ counsel to present his defense.

"What we want to know is, What have they against that? What we want to know is, Why don't they admire it?

"The history of this case is, I suppose, that this man and this woman have formed a mutual attraction, not sanctioned, if you like, by the usages of society—if you like, not sanctioned by the rites of the Church. It is but a trust in each other, a devotion to the last, amid all the dangers of the dungeon and and all the terrors of the scaffold."

There was a dead silence in the courtroom as everyone strained to hear what Baker would say next.

"They were bound together by a tie which angels might not blush to approve."

Though his voice was soft, it carried to the furthest corner to everyone in his stunned audience.

And his closing words floated over the audience like a prayer. He asked for mercy in the name of humanity, in the name of "Him who died for that humanity." He invoked the memory of parents, the respect and admiration for beloved women, the knowledge of one's own imperfections. "And so may you answer for your judgment on that great day when you and the prisoner at the bar shall alike stand up to answer for all the deeds done in the body," he finished, and no church could have been so still.

The prosecution bumbled and raged through its rebuttal, only too aware that no one was paying attention. Forty one hours later the jury came in to admit they couldn't reach a verdict. The newspapers reported that in the final balloting four had stood for murder, six for manslaughter, and two for acquittal.

Charles was remanded to the county jail until there could be a second trial. Given the nature of people and their tendency to forget and go on to something else, there was every chance that Charles would be freed at the new trial.

The release from the long tension hit Tessa, and she began to giggle helplessly, gasping. "It was bad enough to hear that we, his friends, had all fled away and left him alone, but to hear Belle married to him in a word and described as poor, weak, feeble, and wicked, my God, that is too much!"

"It worked," Gavin said, and then he was laughing with her.

CHAPTER LII

The newspapers continued to print stories of corruption and graft in the city, some true and some false, and to rage against the undesirable elements while they touted the perfectly respectable society as the goal, a society which had more adherents now that the railroad across the Isthmus of Panama had been completed for a year and allowed for more settled and timid types to reach California. And there was still a great deal of unrest financially and otherwise; it would take years for a full recovery from the effects of the Fifty-five panic.

But for Gavin and Tessa everything seemed marvelously calm with the trial over and Charles's chances for release so good. They saw the same peace and hopefulness in Belle and were glad of it. Their business prospered despite the continued low in beef prices and the glut on the market due to the drought sale of excess animals. They spent as much time as they could with the children, and found life very good.

Armenthia was pregnant again, and Indian was so proud, it was difficult not to tease him. Thia claimed that he wouldn't notice if she gave birth to a hoot owl as long as it learned to say Papa someday.

Whenever they got together, Tessa and Thia spent the first few minutes discussing the coming event and babies in general. Though he tried to hide it, this was something that made Gavin acutely uncomfortable. And finally the reason dawned on Tessa.

Indian, Thia, and Dian had been to the house for dinner, the latter now having enough personality to interest Fiona so that the youngsters had played together quite well.

Tessa finished brushing her hair and slipped into bed beside Gavin. "I wonder how Dian will react to the new baby," she said casually and felt Gavin's start of alarm.

"You mustn't fret whenever I speak of a baby," she said firmly. "You and Dr. Harland, you are both so kind, but also so much like children with a secret everyone knows. You both seem to forget that I was present at Fiona's birth, to be sure I was. I know I won't have any more children. Part of me is sorry for that, but the greater part knows that four living children are a gift of plenty and to be alive with them and with you is yet another blessing. It would have been so much easier for you if you had spoken to me before,"—she added in gentle reproach.

Gavin felt like laughing and crying at the same time with the release of the burden, but instead he kissed her, murmuring, "My lovely witch, we poor, stupid men haven't a chance."

"It depends on what kind of chance you're looking for," she answered softly, and she moved against him, enticing him slowly at first, then quickening the pace until he was shuddering with the pleasure of her hands and mouth claiming the fierce beat of his pulse, the heat of his flesh. He cried aloud when she changed the rhythm again, straddling him, sinking down on him with voluptuous enjoyment.

They were lovers more often than ever, somehow made more aware of each other now that there would be no further issue from their flesh, love and pleasure the sole purpose of their joining.

But their idyll ended on May 14 when City Supervisor James P. Casey shot down the *Bulletin*'s editor, James King of William. The editor was king of nothing; he had rearranged his name to give it significance. He was a bitter man who had lost his job and his reputation during the bank crisis, having assured depositors that everything was fine when it was not, having been accused of faithlessness and fraud when the truth was out. He had risen again with the *Daily Evening Bulletin*, and his voice was never kinder than a snarl. The public enjoyed the brief, brisk attacks King employed as his medium. He attacked officials of the state, county, and city with equal virulence,

632

and sometimes he was right about the corruption. But his venom knew no bounds. He used the paper for personal spite just as frequently as he did for public good. His had been the loudest voice in the condemnation of Belle and Charles on moral grounds rather than on the facts of the case. And he disliked Southerners, Catholics, and various other groups as much as he did gamblers and prostitutes.

On May 14, he published an editorial about James P. Casey, revealing Casey's prison record from Sing Sing without giving the reason for the incarceration. (It was later revealed to be of the most pathetic and embarrassing nature. An unfaithful mistress had driven Casey to retaliate by stripping her apartment of the furniture he had bought in the first place and selling it—the woman had brought charges of theft and Casey had been sentenced to eighteen months.) And he accused Casey of stuffing the ballot box to win his position as supervisor. The paper hit the streets around three in the afternoon.

Casey had a quick temper and no column for reply, but the editor had already been challenged by many people and had made it clear he would fight no duels, including the one Casey had in mind. The issue was further clouded by the words James King of William had written previously in reference to another threat from another source: "God have mercy on my assailant." It was not intended as a kindly remark and he was known to be armed despite his refusal to duel.

But the fact remained that whether or not Casey had called out a warning for King to defend himself, King had not done so, and had been shot down in cold blood. King was the hero of the hour. By evening there was a newspaper notice calling a meeting of the Committee of Vigilance at 105½ Sacramento Street at nine o'clock the next morning. The bells of the California and Monumental fire companies tolled ominously, and this time it was not for a fire.

Tessa and Gavin's terror was all for Charles. He was helpless in jail, and with the committee meeting again, was a sure victim, especially since Casey was a friend of his.

Gavin rode out to tell Mrs. Tubbs and Chong Sing what had happened, but he and Tessa spent the night at Indian's house to be closer to what was happening.

When they went to see Belle the next day even as the committee was meeting, they knew their fears were justified. She had obviously not slept. Though her exceptional beauty would always shine through, she looked years older than twenty-nine, and for the first time, the Ramsays saw her break down. She sobbed wildly and choked on her words. "Do . . . do you . . . know . . . that, that Charley heard the bells, he heard them! And when . . . when they brought Casey in and, and put . . . put him in the cell next to Charley's, Charley said———" She stopped, making a visible effort to pull herself together, and when she spoke again, her voice was a steady, eerie facsimile of Charles's. "He said, 'You have put the noose about the necks of both of us.' He's right, isn't he? Those damn fire bells, those damn Vigilantes! They're going to hang him, aren't they? I should have gotten him out while there was still time. There's no time now, is there?"

"We'll do the best we can. And King isn't dead yet. If he lives, everything will be much better," Gavin said. Tessa hoped Belle could not judge his voice as well as she could.

When they were alone, Tessa asked, "Is there any hope at all?"

"Not if they want him, and I expect they will. The jail is undefendable. There are higher points all around in other buildings that will give gunmen an easy target. There's no wall or fence even as a first barrier. Sheriff Scannell hasn't a chance of securing his prisoners against the committee. Just pray that King lives."

They rode out to check on the household and to pick up a few personal articles for the stay at Indian's house. They arrived to find Mrs. Tubbs packing for the children. "Indian has already been here," she told them. "He feels as I do, that the children's summer on the *rancho* should begin early. He'll escort us if it meets with your approval. Chong Sing will mind the house."

They agreed completely and were infinitely grateful for Indian's tact and understanding. He knew there was little chance that he could do anything for Charles Cora,

634

but he could help the Ramsays by taking the children to the peace of the *rancho*. Gavin was a prominent business-man and had been a member of the 1851 Committee. He would not be popular now when his refusal to join the new one became common knowledge, but his was still a voice that might be listened to.

The children knew something was afoot, but when they saw the sober faces of their parents, they asked fewer questions than they would have liked. Only Fiona howled at the change in plans, but once she realized that Mrs. Tubbs and Paul were going to be with her, she was all right.

They asked Indian if he was going to take Thia and Dian out too, but he shook his head. "I like to, but she say no an' mean it, so that's that, stubborn as 'nother lady I know."

By Friday the sixteenth, the Vigilance Committee was drilling large numbers of men, and their ranks were swelling by the hour. Already there were some three thousand of them, and they were confident the number would double before too long. The city was rapidly taking on the aspects of a siege.

Sheriff Scannell appealed desperately for a posse to defend the jail. And though he knew it was useless, Gavin felt obliged to volunteer. He thus allied himself openly with the faction now being called "The Law and Order Party" in direct opposition to the Committee of Vigilance. The man who headed it solely by virtue of his office was William T. Sherman, major-general of the state militia. Gavin didn't envy him. Sherman had been in the army until he resigned his commission the year before to be able to give full time to his job with a banking firm in San Francisco. He had only accepted the post of major-general out of a sense of duty because of his superior military training, which had included graduation from West Point.

Tessa was frantic with worry about Gavin, but she knew she could not ask him to do less than his conscience demanded. She had to content herself with repeated pleas that he take care of himself. She was grateful for Armenthia's calm strength as they waited for news.

Gavin returned late Friday night for a quick wash and

something to eat. "Things are quiet because Governor Johnson has come down on the boat from Sacramento. He's meeting with Vigilance leaders right now."

"Do you think he can do anything?" Tessa asked.

"I don't think anyone can. And Johnson is young and hasn't any force to match the numbers of the Vigilantes. Even if he did, he could easily precipitate an active civil war. But at least his being here should give us some breathing space." He paused, rubbing his neck wearily. "I saw Charles, talked to him for a couple minutes. He's calm and resigned, so much so that it's almost as if he isn't there at all any more. I don't think he has any hope left."

Tessa went outside with him when he was ready to leave again. The night was a mockery of brilliant moonlight and tranquility.

Gavin put his arm around her. "They're well-meaning, you know, or at least many of them are. The committee has its share of scoundrels and cowards who simply want to be on the strongest side. But the leaders, Coleman and the rest, they're men of good faith, bankers, merchants, professionals. They're so sure they're right, they can't see the forest for the trees. They judge themselves pure of heart and thus they judge what they are doing in the same light. They can't see that they're choosing an easy and violent answer to a lot of problems, everything from business losses to political corruption. It's true there's been some ballot stuffing and too much power has rested in the hands of the Southern Democrats, but this isn't the way to change that. There haven't been more than a few good men running against the professional politicians, no more than a few who are willing to let their businesses suffer while they serve in public office. Hell, I'm not willing. And a lot of the committee leaders are the same ones who pay the fines rather than serving on juries and then scream about the verdicts the low-life juries bring in. Considering all the problems, I think our courts and judges have been doing a fair job."

He stopped, and Tessa said nothing, just pressed close to him, knowing he wasn't finished, knowing he needed to say it aloud, not only to explain to her, but to clarify and reinforce the choice he had made.

"I didn't approve when I was part of it in Fifty-one, but

this time it's much worse. There are thousands of men involved, and they're virtually setting up another government. They're only willing to believe in our system of law when the verdict goes as they wish. They've forgotten the whole point, that a man must be proven guilty beyond a reasonable doubt. That wasn't true in Charles's case, but because of what he is, they won't accept anything less than a guilty verdict and an execution. And with Casey, there's every chance he would indeed be found guilty in a court of law, but the committee won't wait for that. They're blind fools! They're so certain of the safety of their own virtue, they can't see that the rule of law is the only thing that protects them from the depredations of other men. They're choosing the illusion of security by force over their own rights to freedom. It's a terrible choice!"

"You would think just one of them would have read of the excesses of the French Revolution, wouldn't you!" Tessa said, and her voice was steady. *"Vaya con Dios,* Gavin."

"Keep safe, my love," Gavin replied. He kissed her deeply and was gone.

She saw him again briefly on Saturday night. All day long the Committee of Vigilance had been moving into its quarters on Sacramento Street, piling up sand-filled gunnysacks in a barrier in front and reinforcing the interior also so that already it had been nicknamed "Fort Gunnybags" in place of "Fort Vigilance." It was another ominous sign of preparation for an outright war. And the governor had most certainly failed to impress his authority on the committee—he had agreed to allow ten of their men into the jail. Major-General Sherman was meanwhile trying desperately to get arms and men, with little success.

Gavin looked so tired, Tessa could not forbear asking him if he could not sleep for a few hours at least. He refused, ate a little, and drank a great deal of black coffee before he left again.

"Don' you fret, Tessa," Thia told her. "He's strong, but when nature tells him lie down, sleep now, he'll do it. He'll be fine." Tessa clung to her for a moment.

Sunday began as calmly as Saturday had, but by midday everything was changed. Suddenly there were people everywhere, jamming the streets, blackening Telegraph Hill.

"He want you here an' safe!" Thia wailed, but she knew it was useless to try to stop Tessa's wild-eyed flight from the house. If she hadn't had Dian to tend to, she would have gone with her.

"If he comes back here before I do, tell him I'm being careful. But I can't wait here when he might be staring down thousands of committee guns!"

"What you goin' to do if he is?" Armenthia asked in a last attempt to stop her.

"Die with him!" Tessa snapped.

There was no doubt that everyone was headed for the jail, and it didn't take Tessa long to understand why. Everyone was talking about it. The committee had withdrawn their ten men from the jail as an official notice that they were breaking their truce with the governor. It was all preplanned. The army of the committee was assembling to take Casey and Cora.

Tessa plodded patiently with the slow flow of the massed bodies for as long as she could bear it, but finally the image of Gavin in danger was overwhelming. She kicked the man blocking her way. She kicked him hard in the back of his leg. He swung around with his fist clenched, but when he saw her face, he pressed back, clearing a space for her, mumbling, "All right, lady, all right."

She kicked, clawed, and pushed her way through, and she knew she was making horrible angry growling noises deep in her throat. She couldn't stop any of it, and she realized dimly that that was why people were letting her through; no one liked dealing with insanity. It was at the least embarrassing, at the worst perhaps catching.

She froze in horror at the sight that greeted her at the jail. Not only were there thousands of spectators; there were thousands of committee members fully armed with muskets and rifles, thousands more arm in arm and silent, walls of men in neat military formation. They even had a fieldpiece, a small cannon aimed at the main entrance to the jail. And every high point and window overlooking the jail was manned by a rifleman. There were surely ten thousand or more people within rifleshot of the jail.

Tessa's heart pounded furiously. She was quite a distance away still, but she caught sight of Gavin, his tall frame making him an easy target. *Dear God, do not resist, do not fire that first shot,* she thought between curse and prayer. One shot and the streets would be awash in blood.

There was an eerie, waiting silence. Then a man rode by on a white horse. A carriage followed in his wake. They stopped at the jail door. A murmur went through the crowd. Sheriff Scannell was surrendering Casey. He had no choice. The carriage rolled away with Casey inside. Two platoons of about eighty men with bright muskets preceded it, and there were two files of armed men on each side of it. A now boisterous crowd followed it as it headed down Kearny to Pacific whence it would go to Montgomery Street and then to the committe headquarters on Sacramento Street.

It wasn't over. An hour passed. The remaining Vigilantes and spectators waited as Tessa waited. The carriage returned. This time Sheriff Scannell refused. In a precise maneuver, men moved to either side, leaving an open path between the cannon and the door. The fieldpiece was readied for action.

Tessa closed her eyes. Her body was bathed in cold sweat; her ears were prepared to hear the roar of the gun. There was nothing she could do.

Then the word passed through the spectators like a swift wind. Scannell had agreed to give Cora up, but he asked that the man have a chance to write his will and a few letters and to say good-by to a few friends. Within minutes Tessa saw Belle arrive and go inside. She hoped everyone would be kind enough to give them this time alone.

Shortly after four o'clock they brought Charles out in irons. Belle was with him. Tessa had worked her way closer, and now she covered the last distance by using her most imperious manner. When the Vigilantes would have stopped her, she drew herself up to her full height and stared them down. "They are my friends and one of the guards is my husband," she repeated over and over.

She heard Belle say, "Good-by, Charley. I've done all I could to get you clear."

Charles looked calm and distant.

The firepiece was rolled in front of the carriage, and slowly the procession moved away.

Tessa had gotten to Belle as the carriage door was closed, but Belle was beyond comforting. Her eyes were dull and blank. "Leave me alone. I've got to go home now," she murmured, and twisted away.

Gavin had seen Tessa, and when he reached her, he burst out, "Jesus! What the hell——" but then he buried his face against her hair and his shoulders shook convulsively. Tessa made no effort to wipe away the tears rolling down her own cheeks.

The city was quiet in the iron grip of the committee, with no force to oppose it.

Gavin slept exhaustedly for twenty-four hours, and then he went with Tessa to see Belle on Monday night. They were turned away at the door. Belle wanted to see no one.

"It's probably just as well," Tessa admitted sadly. "I expect I would have done nothing but weep."

On Tuesday afternoon James King of William died. It made no difference that the medical treatment he had received, including a sponge left in the wound, had had as much to do with his death as the gunshot.

The committee had already made plans to try the two men; King's death just added to their belief in the organization's virtue. The same witnesses who had testified against Charles in his civil trial testified against him again. Mrs. Knight had presented herself as not only available to testify against Charles but she also just happened to have been an eyewitness to the shooting of King. Tessa wished Belle had poisoned her after all.

King's death was announced during Charles's trial, but Charles had no chance anyway. His counsel was provided by two Vigilantes; the jury was the Executive Committee. The Committee of Vigilance had elected itself judge, jury, defense, and prosecution all at once. Indeed, Charles's previous counsel, Baker, had fled the city when he heard the committee had issued a warrant for his arrest. Charles was beyond the help of independent counsel, friendly witnesses, and Belle's money. But the worst irony was that not even the committee could agree on a verdict, and in a true court of law where a unanimous verdict is needed to convict a man of murder, Charles could not have been sentenced. The committee took care of that by requiring no more than a simple majority.

Casey met the normal requirements; the ballot was unanimous. Both men were sentenced to death by hanging.

The proceedings were secret, in keeping with the way the committee conducted all of its business, even down to the numbers its members used in place of their names, but the Ramsays knew most of what was going on because Gavin had contacts among the membership, men who were not quite sure they were doing the right thing and who knew Gavin was a friend of Cora's. They admired the courage of his stance, and it eased their consciences to do him a favor by keeping him informed.

At least the committee allowed Belle to visit Charles a few times. Tessa could not even imagine the depth of strain and grief that must accompany those meetings.

At first Gavin heard that the hanging would take place on Friday, but then he learned it had been moved up to Thursday, May 22, to coincide with King's funeral.

Belle was allowed to be with Charles until his execution. The Ramsays heard later that a Catholic priest had come in not only to give Charles absolution but to marry Belle and Charles as a condition of that absolution. To Tessa it seemed a final insult that a union that had been so loving and so freely chosen should need approval by anyone, even the Church.

Gavin did not want Tessa to go to the hanging, but he gave up trying to dissuade her when she told him her reasons. "I don't want to go. But it is the last thing I can do for Charles. Maybe he will be able to feel that there is someone who loves him in the crowd. I shall will that he knows it, that he knows not all are hungry for his death."

She clung to Gavin as they made their way through the crowd. Word had traveled swiftly, and though many people were following King's funeral cortège as it wound toward Lone Mountain Cemetery, there were many more who didn't want to miss the hanging. Some had children with them. There were smiles and jokes all around and a nervous animal tension rippled almost tangibly through the spectators. Tessa wanted to curse them all for their barbarism. She clamped her jaw shut and pressed closer to Gavin.

Charles, you are not alone, you are not alone—she repeated it silently in her mind over and over again.

Two beams with nooses extended from the upper windows of Fort Vigilance, and there were two platforms that would drop when ropes were pulled. A piece of white paper fluttered down from a window in signal. The guard below presented arms. Charles was guided out on the platform, helpless because his hands were tied to his sides, his feet were bound together, and his face was masked by a white handkerchief.

Casey was not bound yet because he had asked to address the crowd. He was nearly incoherent with fear and anger, alternately begging and blaming, but his main point seemed to be that he didn't want his mother in New York to hear of his end. He implored the press not to print the story. It was horrible. Charles remained silent.

The noose was finally placed around Casey's neck. Tessa dug her nails into Gavin's arm without knowing she did so, and he didn't notice either. Part of Tessa's mind refused to believe what she was seeing, and she felt strangely numb and removed.

The church bells began to ring for James King of William. The platforms were pulled. The bodies fell, jerking sharply as the ropes ran out. Casey writhed, hands clutching at the noose until he went limp. Charles's body jerked and was still.

It was real, terribly, terribly real, no protective numbness now. "Oh, God, they knew, they knew how they were dying! I thought they would die instantly," she sobbed. Gavin picked her up and pushed his way forcefully through the crowd, putting her down when she struggled, holding her head comfortingly while she retched. Even after he got her back to the house, she shivered for hours despite his and Thia's efforts to warm her. He remembered the other time this had happened. Finally Thia said, "Cold on the spirit is the worst kind of cold, jus' got to let it pass on its own time."

Gavin held her for hours until his warmth became hers and she slept in his arms.

Indian was home the next day, mute and sorrow-filled with what he had learned on his return, and the Ramsays went back out to their own house and Chong Sing.

On Saturday they attended Charles's funeral, riding with others in one of the four coaches provided for friends that followed behind Belle's own coach and that of her servants. The quiet privacy of it was in marked contrast to Casey's enormous and very Irish ceremony. His remains were

642

escorted to the cemetery by eighty-four carriages, eight horsemen, and some four hundred people on foot.

Two days after Charles's funeral a letter addressed to the Vigilance Committee appeared in the *Bulletin*. It lauded the actions of the committee but informed them that the job would not be fully done until Belle Cora was banished from the city. It contained cloying phrases about the request being without bitterness but needed simply as an example and to protect virtuous women from contamination. It was signed "Many Women of San Francisco."

It was quickly answered by another letter:

> A woman is always a woman's persecutor. In my humble opinion I think that Belle Cora has suffered enough to expiate many faults, in having been torn from her bosom friend, executed by a powerful association. It was just and right that Cora should die, but I contend that by his death the public is avenged. She has shown herself a true-hearted woman to him, and such a heart covers a multitude of sins. This very circumstance of expulsion might be the means of utter desolation of heart. The effects of the tragedy may be the means of improving her moral character and making her socially a good woman.
>
> Adelia

It did not matter that the second was kinder than the first; the damage had been done. Tessa discovered that as soon as she saw Belle. Aside from a brief meeting at the funeral, she had been unable to gain access to her friend. She realized Belle must surely need time to herself, but this continuing distance was disquieting. It was reassuring to see her again, and then, not reassuring at all.

Even after what she had been through, Belle was more beautiful than any woman had a right to be—her skin so white, her dark hair lit by burnished copper strands, her hazel eyes huge. But there was an enormous change in her. It touched Tessa until she felt the chill as deeply as she had on the day of Charles's hanging. The warm gaiety in Belle had turned to pure ice.

"Have you been reading the papers?" she asked abruptly, and Tessa nodded.

"I won't leave, you know. The Vigilantes won't be able to make me go." The light, conversational tone was eerie.

"If there's anything we can do . . ." Tessa mumbled.

"There is," Belle said in the same pleasant tone. "You can hear me out, and then you can do as I say. Charley was the only man I'm ever going to love in my life, and now he's dead. But the bastards who hung him are still alive. One way or another, I'm going to ruin them, as many of the leaders as I can. It's something to live for. I know what's been going on, you and Gavin have been collecting trouble here and there for being friends to me and Charley. That'll stop sooner than later once it gets around that the Ramsays don't have anything to do with the infamous Belle any more. That goes for Indian and Armenthia too.

"Let me finish!" she snapped, when Tessa gasped in outrage and would have spoken. "It's the way I want it anyway. I told you once before that the game was too rough. Well, this one's going to be a lot rougher. It's my game, and I don't want any of you involved. And seeing you reminds me of Charley and the good times we had. I don't want to be reminded of that. I want to remember them taking him away from me, pulling him out of my arms, and hanging him. That is what I need to remember." The words were cool, smooth stones.

Tessa stared at Belle's implacable face, and bowed her head. "Nothing anyone can say about us can hurt as much as losing you as a friend. I owe my life to you! Always remember that. You are always welcome in our home, in our lives should you choose it to be so. I think Charles would be sad to know you wish to forget the good times."

"Charley is dead," Belle said flatly. Her eyes were jade green.

CHAPTER LIII

The committee continued on its course without interference. The Vigilantes terrified many into fleeing the city; banished others, and imprisoned still others. One of their prisoners, a man named Yankee Sullivan, committed suicide at committee headquarters. The rumor was that one of his guards had frightened him into it with threats of a hanging the next day.

On June 3, Governor Johnson issued a proclamation declaring San Francisco to be "in a state of insurrection." Members of a conciliation committee carried messages between the Vigilantes and Sherman, hoping to manage a peaceful settlement. Sherman continued to try to get arms, particularly from the federal arsenal at Benicia, which was under the command of General Wool. General Wool kept delaying his answer until finally he refused on the grounds that only the president could grant arms or munitions to a state in the case of an insurrection. Sherman, who had been desperately trying to keep the lack of arms a secret and had been hoping that his pretense of a shipment due to arrive any day would prove true, resigned his commission.

Gavin kept track of it all with growing and malicious amusement. "If the city doesn't get burnt to the ground or blown into the bay, this might all be worth it. They tried to say that the Law and Order Party was just a bunch of rowdies, but now they're looking to their own. With the governor's proclamation and the possibility that he might appeal directly to the president for help, the committee is rapidly taking on a very bad light. They could well be held responsible for civil war by the federal authorities. They've set the beast on the prowl, and they don't know how to stop it."

But he and Tessa had clearer reasons for rejoicing. Belle's knowledge had been correct. They had lost some business at the warehouse (though Tessa's shop had done even better with loyal support from the demimondaines), and there had been some vile references to them in the press, but they were left alone now and there was little chance anyone would come to arrest Gavin on trumped-up charges, something they had feared for a time. Tessa tried not to contemplate the fact that Belle's curtailment of their friendship had probably helped.

The best news was from the Brown brothers. The Lucille was beginning to yield very rich gold-bearing quartz, and payments to the investors were forthcoming.

Tessa gave another dinner party. Two of the original investors had been unable to make their payments during

645

the bank crisis, but two more, as dull as the others had been, had taken their places.

At first everything went well. The group was exhilarated by the knowledge of the investments paying off, and the Brown brothers were very engaging. Peter said it was a lot safer out in Grass Valley right now than it was in the city. "Dusted off my gun an' trimmed my hair a bit jus' so's I'd look respectable."

"Safe out there as long as you ain't Cornish," his brother remarked. "Best durn miners I ever did see, an' you need a few more, you jus' ask an' everyone got a 'Cousin Jack.' We call 'em all Cousin Jacks. But they's more full of superstition than any I ever knowed before. Cain't whistle underground 'cause you might start the earth movin'. Cain't start a new tunnel on a Friday or let a woman go underground. Hell—er, 'scuse me, heck—it's a plain wonder there's room for th' miners down there with all th' other folks. There's jabberwocks, which I collect is little gremlins, an' Tommyknockers, which is the spirits of dead miners who tap warnings on th' walls when trouble's comin', an' lord knows what else."

"I don't think I shall try to break the rule about women in the mines," Tessa said with an elaborate shiver. "I should not want to be in the dark with all those creatures." She pressed him to tell more. She was enjoying his stories and feeling truly relaxed and happy despite the other guests at the table.

Both of the Browns were appreciative of the Cornish miners' skills and knowledge, and they fairly beamed at the intelligent questions Gavin asked about the Cornish pump and various other systems.

Tessa didn't know how the conversation had shifted, but suddenly it had, and with it went her peaceful mood. The Browns were noncommittal on the subject of the Vigilantes, but Peter's comment about coming to the city gave Tessa the idea that they shared the Ramsays' view. They were the only ones.

Praise for the Vigilantes' actions, for "showing those rascals they can't get away with it," the "it" remaining unspecified, swirled around the table. Gavin's face was cold, his eyes dark and glittering, but he said nothing.

Tessa would have kept silent too had it not been for
646

Mrs. Beecham, the wife of one of the original investors. She had disliked the woman since their first meeting. Her fat body was strapped in a corset and a gown of purple satin trimmed within an inch of its life. Her face looked like a pudding with two little currant eyes, and yet the way she patted her hair, arched her fat-ringed throat, and laughed behind her fan indicated she found herself an attractive woman.

Her voice ran on and on about how good it would be for a lady of quality to be safe on the streets once again. "I was thrilled to see them hang that Cora. I clapped when it was done. But they must get rid of his harlot. I have children, you know, and it's intolerable they and I should have to be subjected to the presence of such a woman."

Tessa saw the beady little eyes watching her with vicious amusement, and she knew it was all deliberate.

"You unspeakable bitch," she said quietly. The room went dead still except for Mrs. Beecham's gasp. "You fat vulture picking on the bones of the dead. Charles Cora would have crossed the street to stay away from your kind, and Belle would pity any woman who is so ugly inside and out. Charles was a good, kind friend, and Belle once saved my life. And you knew they were our friends when you spoke of them. You are no longer welcome in this house, Mrs. Beecham. Get out!"

The calm, steady flow of words had stunned Mrs. Beecham and everyone else, but now her cheeks matched her dress. She started up and turned on Gavin. "You heard what your wife said! How dare she!"

Gavin smiled wickedly. "I couldn't have said it better myself, but I would have tried had she not. May I add my voice to hers? You are not welcome here." He looked at Mr. Beecham. "I'm sorry for the inconvenience to you, sir, but if you insist on taking your wife out in public, you ought to muzzle that poisonous mouth of hers."

There were ample grounds for Mr. Beecham to demand satisfaction for the insults to his wife, and though it was against the law, dueling was no rarity in California. But Mr. Beecham had no intention of going against Gavin; in fact he had no desire to. Though he could not show it openly, he thought his wife had gotten just what she deserved and inwardly he applauded Mrs. Ramsay for calling the shrew to account; so few ever did.

"Come, my dear," he said, offering his arm to his wife.

"You mean you're not going to——" she sputtered.

"Die for you? I should hope not!" For the barest instant, his eyes met Gavin's, and Gavin saw the rueful amusement in them. He nearly laughed aloud.

"To let that greaser——" Mrs. Beecham began as her husband pulled her with him.

"Shut up, my dear," Mr. Beecham said.

Tension still filled everyone, and the rest left shortly after, the other wives eyeing Tessa nervously as if fearful she would pounce on them too. The Brown brothers made their polite farewells, but their eyes gleamed, and the Ramsays heard them burst into whoops of laughter as soon as they were outside.

"Oh, Gavin, it was sweet of you to support me, but I was awful!" She looked at Gavin, and suddenly they were laughing as hard as the Browns.

"She looked like a ripe plum," Gavin choked, and even Chong Sing couldn't hide his smile as he cleared away the last of the dishes and glasses.

"I think, my dear Mrs. Ramsay, that it's time we go visit our offspring for a while. Things seem a good deal less than sane around here."

"And perhaps there will be no Vigilance Committee left at all when we return," Tessa ventured hopefully.

It was not to be. The interlude with the children on the land restored them both, but when they returned to the city in July, they found the situation worse than ever. A schooner on the way to the city with over a hundred muskets aboard had been pirated by another small vessel manned by Vigilantes. The arms were taken, but the three crewmen from the schooner were released. They promptly went before the United States District Court and filed a complaint for piracy on the waters of the bay. The committee suddenly found themselves about to be embroiled with the United States government, their worst fear from the beginning. They conveniently found that one of the schooner's crew, a man named Maloney, was surely a criminal, being a ballot-box stuffer, among other things. They issued a warrant for his arrest, and a prominent committee member, Hopkins, went looking for him. He found him with Judge Terry of the Supreme Court and several others. They threw Hopkins out. Judge Terry was one of the most violent opposers of the committee.

Terry, Maloney, and the others armed themselves as best they could and headed for one of the armories used by one of the state volunteer companies. But they were followed by Hopkins and other Vigilantes. The Vigilantes tried to grab Maloney but Terry and his friends prevented it and had almost reached the armory when Hopkins seized the gun in Terry's hands. A gun went off, and Terry commanded the peace as a judge of the Supreme Court, trying all the while to loose himself from Hopkins who held his gun with his left hand and was using his right to hold onto Terry's hair. Terry drew his knife, showed it to Hopkins, and stabbed him in the left shoulder.

Hopkins ran down the street screaming, and in the confusion Terry and the others made it into the armory.

Indian shook his head as he described the ensuing bedlam. "Th' bell rang wild an' men all over th' place yellin', 'hang him, hang him.' Streets fill up with men carryin' muskets, swords, pistols, any kind of killin' piece. Terry an' them others, they got no choice an' they surrender, Hopkins still alive an' everybody waitin' to see if he stays that way."

Even as the men had surrendered so had all the armories of the state volunteers, giving their arms to the Vigilantes. It was the final proof that California had ceased to have the power to protect men in defense of her own sovereignty.

The Vigilantes were everywhere, drilling, marching, some even in uniforms and with bands playing as if they meant to establish their military power forever. Governor Johnson had written to the president and received his reply—on the grounds of constitutional law, the president declined to interfere. The arrests went on.

But against all the visible evidence, Gavin remained optimistic, his view confirmed by his contacts among the Vigilantes. "The rank and file are ignorant, but the leaders know what they've done. They have a Supreme Court judge in custody, and he happens to have a good many friends, particularly in the Great Valley. The committee

649

can't be sure for a minute that those friends won't march in from the interior to free Terry if they think his life is truly in jeopardy. It doesn't matter who would win; there would be blood everywhere. And beyond that, the execution of a high court official would be as serious in this country as beheading kings elsewhere. You may do it, but the violent consequences are certain. If you execute one of the supreme guardians of the law, what's left to protect you from the complete lawlessness of your fellows and the vengeance of all the other forces that must maintain the law to survive? If Judge Terry is executed, there is little doubt President Pierce will change his mind and send in federal troops."

Tessa clung to Gavin's convincing arguments even when the committee hung two more men toward the end of July, and her faith was confirmed when Judge Terry was released on August 7. To the relief of the Committee of Vigilance leaders, Hopkins was going to live. The glory had flown, and they had lived in terror these last weeks for the very reasons Gavin had given Tessa. The visions of staring down the barrels of guns held by federal soldiers or feeling the noose around their own necks had gotten clearer by the day.

However, they would not go out without one last self-congratulatory gesture. They held their final parade on August 18, filling the streets with their ranks, buttons and weapons shining, bands playing as they marched in military formation. Indian, Thia, and the Ramsays stayed away, gathered together in the frame house to drink a toast to the demise of the committee.

"I've been wonderin', but now I know this chile goin' to be born in freedom. It's late, jus' waitin' round for that to be so," Thia said, patting the bulge of her stomach.

Two days later, Julie was born, with very little help from Dr. Harland. Tessa was very flattered because the name was from the Julieta in her own name. Armenthia insisted that Julie carry the second name Jefferson, and she bestowed the same on Dian. "Everybody else has two names. Maybe you don' need it an' I don' either, but my babies goin' have it case they want it," she told Indian.

The time was deceptively peaceful for them. Business prospered and their families did also. In 1858 Thia had another boy, Joshua Jefferson, and Anne and Walter Long kept pace, Anne no longer working at the shop but devoting herself to her family. Lin-Ao began to take lessons with Fiona, much to Chong Sing's pride and surely due to Mrs. Chen's will despite what Mr. Chen thought about it. Lin-Ao seemed as comfortable at the Ramsay house as she was in her own in Chinatown, and she spoke English and Chinese interchangeably as Fiona did Spanish and English. There were the visits to both *ranchos* and more time with Carmelita and Sam than there had been in the early, hectic years of the Ramsays establishing themselves in San Francisco.

But one continuing sadness was Belle's absence from their lives. They read about her sometimes in the papers. It appeared her sister Anne was with her now, but they did not know that for sure since Belle made no effort to reestablish contact with them, nor did she respond to the messages Tessa sent periodically. She no longer visited the shop, and once when Tessa caught a glimpse of her driving with her girls in an open barouche, Belle's eyes slid away, and she acknowledged Tessa with only the briefest of nods. And yet, exquisite baby clothes had arrived for Julie and Joshua shortly after each of the births, and Fiona's birthdays did not pass without a lovely and suitable garment being delivered. There were never any cards, but Tessa knew the work was Belle's. She missed her sorely.

It was Gavin who finally guessed the course of Belle's revenge on the committee. In 1856 two scandal sheets had appeared, *Varieties*, published in San Francisco, and *Phoenix*, published in Sacramento but dealing mostly with San Francisco and arriving there by boat in time for weekend sales. The proprietor and most certainly the main editor of the former was a man named Walsh, and McGowan was the owner of the latter. Walsh seemed to hate almost everyone; McGowan, having been chased out of San Francisco by the Committee of Vigilance, hated many but none so much as former Vigilantes. Because of them he was not even safe in Sacramento but had to change his lodgings frequently, and wouldn't have had a chance in San Francisco. Despite the disbanding of the committee, former members still often identified themselves with pieces of white cloth in their buttonholes, and the feelings between them and those who had opposed them, while they might be quieted, did not die. McGowan was too handy a target to risk the city.

Both publications were of the lowest order. They reported the sexual doings of every prominent name they dared mention, needing only the slightest excuse to print full-blown tales. They intimated that so and so had been seen doing such and such here and there. They were racy, slanderous, and hate filled. "Pimp," "Jew," and hints that bloodlines were less than white were favorite attacks, along with hints that so-and-so suffered from various venereal diseases, always clearly catalogued.

The scandal sheets were as addictive as they were disgusting, and Gavin and Tessa confessed mutual guilt in wanting to read the latest issues. The bigotry appalled them as did almost everything else in their pages, but they couldn't help but share a fiendish delight as one after another of the Vigilantes was held up to be far less than perfect, with dates, times, and places given.

"If I catch one of my sons reading something like this, he'll be very sorry," Gavin said as he pored over the newest issues one weekend, allowing Tessa to read over his shoulder. He found yet another reference to Belle even as Tessa saw it. It reported the misconduct of an ex-Vigilante at Belle's house, but Belle herself was referred to quite mildly and as "Lady Belle." It was not the first time such a reference had been made.

Gavin folded the paper suddenly. "Do you suppose . . ." His voice drifted off as he followed his train of thought, and then it quickened. "*Varieties* and *Phoenix* both attack madams and prostitutes viciously, but not Belle, they don't attack her that way at all! References to her are downright kind! And a lot of the information these papers get must come from her, or at least it could."

Tessa saw it as clearly as he did. "So she found a way to revenge Charles! My God, what a way! Always just enough truth to ruin a man."

Gavin was suddenly very grim. "I can't blame her. They hung Charles. But I'm damn glad she counts us friends!"

Phoenix was finished after less than a year, but *Varieties* went on. Finally Tessa was attacked. She had hired more clerks and expanded the store, and the windows were now larger and contained larger displays of goods. One week she dressed a window with gossamer lingerie, admittedly a daring thing to do, but the work was exquisite and the materials so fine, she felt no guilt. To class such garments as "unmentionable" when every woman and every man who had ever been with a woman had seen them seemed ludicrous to Tessa.

Varieties did not share her view. The paper accused the shop of displaying garments that would be worn against the skin of a white woman so openly that "buck niggers" might touch them before they were sold. It also hinted that the proprietress was intimate with just such a buck. Tessa's fury knew no bounds, but before she could decide what to do about it, an envelope was delivered to the shop by a paid messenger. It contained the clipping and a brief note: "It won't happen again. Love, Belle." It was so little and so much, Tessa wept when she showed it to Gavin.

Her shop was not mentioned again, and whenever she was tempted to feel pity for an ex-Vigilante who was attacked in print she remembered Charles dying at the end of the rope.

Belle must have felt ultimate triumph when *The Bulletin* closed its doors forever in January of Fifty-nine. Tom King, brother of James King of William, was driven away by relentless attacks in *Varieties*. It was true that his ex-wife was a madam in the nation's capital; it was doubtful that she had agreed to come and set up a house in San Francisco. But the threat of her arrival and the endless campaign against him in *Varieties* was enough to convince Tom King that things must surely be better elsewhere. The Ramsays knew Belle would feel no pity. Tom King had been as harsh as his brother in his condemnation of her and Charles. Tessa and Gavin felt no kinder toward him. He was one of the editors who had labeled them friends of "the harlot and her pimp."

CHAPTER LIV

Think of it all, just think of it all! she cautioned herself continually. *Think of the children growing and watch them grow, see them change. Look at the businesses, they're all doing so well. Why, people even come now and request the privilege of purchasing a Ramsay palomino. And they are so beautiful, the golden horses are so very beautiful. More and more of them trained each year and sold; more and more of them proving themselves more worthy than any others of the color. Think of it. Gold coming in now steadily from the Browns' mine. We were right to trust the Browns; we were right to sell the other house. Think of it. Think of it all. We began with so much less, and we are doing so well. Even the court cases settled now when so many are not. Yes, we have lost some acres at Rancho Valle del Mar, but Rancho Magnífico is still whole, and both are very large pieces of the earth. How far Gavin and I have come, how very far.*

Think even of the bad things. Think of Fiona's limp showing more as she has grown more active though she never seems to let it trouble her. Think of earthquakes and bad beef prices. Think of Charles dead and Belle still so distant, surely never intending to be a friend again, not after all this time. Think of her wild and hard as she never was when she was with Charles, flaunting her beauty and taking her revenge. Think of Thomas Larkin to whom we owe much though our lives have gone separate ways for a long time, think of Thomas now dead of a fever, leaving Rachel and his children to cope with an empire only he truly knew how to manage. Think of the bad things.

The other voice was so much stronger. *Yes, think of all those things good and bad ringing round your life in California—they are all so very small.*

It was getting much, much closer. Every year it got closer. She watched it coming on the horizon of their lives as if it were a terrible thunderstorm, and the feeling was the same. The distant sound getting closer until the roar would be louder than anything else; the dark heavy clouds building visibly with no way to get out of their path. California was losing her isolation step by step. Now there was an overland mail service taking little more than three weeks to St. Louis and from there by rail, and room for six hardy passengers each way depending on the mail load. And since this April of 1860 there had been the Pony Express; if you were willing to pay the price the mad riders would take your letter from Sacramento to St. Joseph, Missouri in just ten days! Another link, another way to being closer to those states, that nation Tessa had never seen. Soon, much too soon there would surely be a telegraph line clear across the country, coupling East and West so immediately. And someday a railroad. Tessa had never seen one until Gavin had taken her to view the line from Sacramento to Folsom, built in 1856, the first in California. It had terrified her, and she had not truly believed the monster of wood and metal chugging down the shining tracks. But she knew it was true. And someday those rails would make the distance between California and the East so much less. Not even the mountains would stop them. Already the distance was far too little.

The news came to them. No matter how delayed, it came inexorably. The thunderheads building, purple black as bruised flesh. War was coming. There was no doubt about it. The sectional differences got worse and worse, flaring hotly, banked down by yet another compromise for a moment, but never going out, never really dying. Only now, after too many bloody years, was Kansas establishing herself as free soil, but she had not been admitted as a state yet. Two others had, Minnesota and Oregon, becoming the thirty-second and thirty-third states of the Union and both free. But they weren't going to make any difference if the vast block of the South left the Union.

Harriet Beecher Stowe's *Uncle Tom's Cabin* was still the abolitionist bible, and William Lloyd Garrison's fiery speeches against slavery rang like the voice of Jeremiah. They used even the most terrible setback such as the ruling in the Dred Scott case to bolster their cause. Dred Scott was a slave who had been taken to a free territory

657

by his master and had lived there for some years. When he was taken back to Missouri, he, with the help of an antislavery group, sued for his freedom on the grounds that his residence in a free state had freed him. The court ruled that a slave was not a citizen and had no right to sue in court. The abolitionists had staggered under the blow and then straightened up screaming at the injustice of it, at the mockery it made of calling any state or territory "free." Tessa had thought of it on a much more personal level, for surely it meant that if the Fitz-Williamses had chosen to do so, they could have taken Armenthia back to the South, and she would have become a slave once more. Thank God she was under Indian's protection.

And last year the abolitionists had gained a new martyr. John Brown had had a vast and fanatic vision of establishing an abolitionist republic in the Appalachian mountains with fugitive slaves and abolitionist whites for its citizenry and raids into the South to free slaves as its purpose. In October he made an abortive attempt to start a slave uprising and seize the arsenal at Harpers Ferry, Virginia. He was hanged at Charlestown, Virginia on December 2, condemned as a murderer and traitor in the South, hailed as a hero in the North.

Frémont had lost his bid for the presidency in 1856 because there had not yet been enough support for his antislavery stance and the chaos it would bring. That was all changed now. The Republican party had been growing steadily in strength, men from different parties bound ever more closely together by antislavery and pro-Union sentiments. And the man they were putting forth for president this year was no longer an unknown backwoods lawyer. Even when Abraham Lincoln had lost his race for a Senate seat in 1858, his words had remained like a banner in thousands of minds. "A house divided against itself cannot stand," he had said, and this year he had proclaimed his belief that no compromise on slavery was possible.

The war was not going to be over slavery, though that was surely the rallying cry each side would use. The war was going to be fought over power, over whether it rested with the individual states or with the Union they all formed together. Were the parts greater than the whole or the other way around?

Tessa tried not to think about it, and thought about it until she felt as if she had a frantic rat living in her brain. If the Union won, slaves would surely be freed, but if it lost, the last illusion of one country would be shattered into many. It had taken her so long to feel the reality of being part of the United States, she did not know how she would feel to lose that reality. What she did know was that she did not want Gavin or Indian to go to war.

They were at it again, more now than ever. They talked softly together; they stopped talking when their wives were too close. And Tessa knew she didn't make it any easier for Gavin. She thought about it, but she refused to talk about it with him, becoming cold and distant every time he mentioned some new development, until now he did not try to involve her. She knew it was childish and futile, but she kept hoping that by some miracle of silent neglect, the danger would go away. She didn't think Thia was being much easier on Indian. They lived in their own house across the way now, and Tessa and Armenthia saw much of each other, their friendship deepening with the years. Whenever Thia held her children or worked in her kitchen these days, she sang songs so hauntingly full of pain and loss, they had nothing to do with the "happy darky" songs that were supposed to be the common anthems of plantation slaves. And Armenthia's voice was as rich and dark as her eyes so that she could make ice and fire run up your spine at the same time. "Ain't Gwine Study War No More, No More," was one of her favorites. Only in her singing did she allow her past to show.

Tessa tried to shake off her melancholy. She caught herself too often these days doing what she was now, holding a book she wasn't reading, staring off into space. She was tempted to spend more time at the shop than was necessary simply to avoid this. But she was home by midafternoon most days and could make it earlier if she wished—the shop was so well established now, it demanded less of her. And at least she had more time with the children. She could hear them shrieking and laughing outside, and she smiled. Mrs. Tubbs did not believe in endless lessons.

She bolted up at the terrified scream that cut through the soft fall day, and then she was running, not even conscious that Mrs. Tubbs and Chong Sing were right behind her.

Their faces identically bleached by fear, the children were climbing down out of the big oak, except for Paul who lay crumpled on the ground. Tessa bit back her own scream and knelt beside the still figure. He was alive. She took his hand and rubbed it gently, calling his name.

His eyelids fluttered and then lifted. His brown eyes were dark with pain and shock, but he tried to smile at her. "I'm all right, Mama. I can feel everything, some of it too much. Guess sixteen is too old for climbing trees." The deep voice he had acquired in the last couple of years still surprised her.

He could feel; his neck wasn't broken. She had an instant of giddy relief. "Where do you hurt?" she asked.

"It's my right leg mostly. I landed on it when I fell. I felt it break."

She willed her hands to steadiness as she exposed the break. It was a bad one between knee and ankle, bone gleaming whitely through the skin and blood. Paul closed his eyes again and stifled a groan. Tessa had no intention of setting the bone herself.

"Chong Sing, Mrs. Tubbs, we'll need blankets and materials for a splint. We can't leave him here until the doctor comes; the ground's too damp. Brand, you ride into town for Dr. Harland. Jefferson, you go with him and find your father." She rapped the orders out, but her voice softened when she saw the tears rolling down Fiona's cheeks as she stared in anguish at her beloved Paul. "Fiona, you go make sure Paul's bed is ready for him." She didn't want the child to have to see Paul in such pain any more than she could help.

Chong Sing and Mrs. Tubbs were already hurrying into the house, but Tessa found the boys still standing behind her. "Move, God damn it!" she screeched at them, and they did, jerkily like marionettes. The look Jeff gave Brand was strange, but Tessa had no time to think of anything but Paul.

"Love, I'm going to have to splint your leg so it won't get any worse when we carry you in."

His eyes remained closed but he gave a small nod to show her he understood. His skin was beaded with sweat.
660

Tessa cut the pants leg away and Chong Sing and Mrs. Tubbs held Paul down as gently as they could while Tessa worked. She felt nothing but gratitude when his body arched suddenly and went limp.

Though still slender, Paul was now just under six feet and no light burden to carry. It made no difference; fear and concern made them all strong, and together they got him onto a blanket and carried him upstairs. He came to at intervals only to pass out again. Tessa wanted desperately to give him something for the pain, but she was afraid to before the doctor saw him, especially because there was a bruise already beginning to show on his forehead. If he had a head injury, she knew the worst thing of all would be to drug him into deeper unconsciousness. Long ago María had told her patients could easily die that way.

She sat by the bed, sponging his face with a cool cloth, holding his hand and crooning to him. Her impulse had been to send Fiona out of the room, but she hadn't the heart to. Knowing the bond between Paul and his sister was so strong, she thought perhaps Fiona was as capable of comforting him as she herself was. Fiona sat on the other side of the bed, her delicate frame trembling with the intensity of her caring, but her small face was surprisingly calm and her voice steady when she patted Paul's face gently and said, "You'll be all right because I love you best in the world."

Paul struggled up through the layers of pain again and saw Tessa's face swimming into focus. He remembered that look in her eyes, the same sound in her voice, the knowing and the love that made you feel she would fight any adversary and win and keep you safe forever. "I remember," he murmured. "Just like then when I was seven." He drifted off again, feeling Tessa's soft kiss on his forehead as strongly as the fire in his leg.

The next touch he knew was not his mother's but Dr. Harland's, which hurt a good deal more. "Hurts like hell, doesn't it?" Dr. Harland said sympathetically, even though his hands went on poking. "For a while, it's going to hurt a whole lot worse, but then it'll be a damn sight better."

Outside in the hall, Jeff held Fiona, who had been banished with the advent of Dr. Harland. He held her

661

close against him as Paul's scream echoed around them. In the ensuing silence, he squatted down on his heels to be on her level and brushed the tears from her cheeks. "It'll be over very soon now. I promise. They've had to put the bone back into place and put everything else back together so it will heal properly, and that hurts him. But he'll feel much better." He swallowed hard as another muffled cry came from the room.

"I hate him and I'm going to tell!" Fiona cried passionately, and Jeff flinched. "Hating's no good, Fiona, no good at all. It just makes things worse. And if Paul doesn't want to tell, how can we?"

"I need to go be by myself," she said, confusion sounding in her voice, as she squirmed against the restraining hands. Jeff let her go, and he couldn't blame her when he heard the slam of the door as loud as a gunshot. He felt like slamming something too. The smack of his fist hitting his open palm coincided with the sound of Paul's door opening.

"Obviously Brand found John. Did you find your father?" his mother asked.

His eyes slid away from hers. "He was expected back within the hour at the warehouse. He and Indian were both gone. I left a message, but I just had to get back to make sure Paul was all right."

Tessa studied him thoughtfully. At thirteen he was no longer a child but surely not a man. In the past few months his voice had begun to quaver and crack, going up and down without his volition. He was hoping to need a shave in the near future. He wasn't even as tall as his mother yet, but his body was suddenly showing odd angles and a gangliness till now foreign to him, so much so that Tessa often thought in amusement that if he didn't start shooting up soon, he was going to spread out horizontally like some strange plant, all spindly joints and reaching limbs.

A wave of tenderness washed through her, but she held it in check. He was still the one who always told the truth, the one most uncomfortable with anything less than the truth. He looked nearly as ill as Paul right now. The signs she had not had time to consider before came back to her —the children, so white-faced and restrained, not looking

662

at each other, something beyond their fear for Paul, the look Jefferson had given Brand.

"How is he?" Jeff asked, and Tessa heard the tremor in his voice.

"He's more comfortable now the bone is set. Dr. Harland doesn't think the bruise on his forehead is anything serious. Apparently Paul bumped his head on a branch as he fell." She paused, searching Jefferson's face intently. "What happened out there? It was not just an accident, is that it? Is that why Brand is not here with you?"

Jeff's face crumpled. Had she guessed anything else, he would have been able to keep it a secret. It was so typical; she knew the truth the first time. Her eyes seemed as big as the world, leaving him no avenue of escape. He swallowed convulsively. Paul hadn't told, but now he was going to. "Brand pushed him. He did it on purpose."

"Dear God!" Tessa gasped. It hurt unbearably to have her suspicion confirmed.

"It happened so fast, Mama. We were talking about lots of things, and Paul said something about being glad you were his mother, and Brand just sorta went crazy. We were all up in the treehouse, and he pushed him out, just pushed him."

The beastliness of it filled Tessa's mind. "It's not your fault," she managed to say, and she touched Jeff's cheek briefly before she turned and went back into Paul's room.

When Gavin arrived at the house he was breathing as hard as his ill-used mount. When he saw Tessa's face, he knew there was something beyond her terse assurance that Paul would heal—the fact that Dr. Harland had already left confirmed that beyond a doubt. The boy was asleep under a careful dose of laudanum.

Gavin said little to Tessa until he persuaded her to leave Paul under the watchful eyes of Mrs. Tubbs. He took her to the study and handed her a glass of brandy. "Drink this, all of it," he commanded. "You need it."

She thought of how brandy always tasted of disaster. Her eyes filled with tears. "It was deliberate. Brand pushed him. I made Jefferson tell me. I can't bear it! How could a child of ours do that? He could have killed him! Paul might have broken his neck!"

663

"Have you spoken to Brand since?"

"No, He has made himself invisible. I'm glad. I might do something horrible. I'm ashamed he's my child."

"Stop it, Tessa! I don't feel any better about it than you do, but maybe I can understand it better. Brand is our first born. He loves you very much, and he's terribly jealous."

"I don't care, jealousy, whatever reason. You can't kill people because you are jealous." She stopped abruptly and Gavin's skin crawled as he watched her face change. She really did look like a witch, not his loving tease of the name, but ageless and knowing, the skin stretched so tightly over the bones of her face, it looked like a skull. And her voice was a low yet piercing chant. "This is how it will be, not as it was in Fifty-six with faction against faction, not that at all, but this. Brother against brother. Mother against child. Father divided by sons. This is what it will be, blood against blood and pain everywhere, death and guilt everywhere. The war will be this, will it not?"

He was hypnotized by her steady gaze, compelled to answer, and he felt a sudden relief that the forbidden subject was out in the open. "Yes, it will be like this. There's no other way it can be. And both sides are going to need compassion—beginning with Brand right now. I think I'm the one who'd better talk to him."

"I'm going back to Paul. You can let me know what happens later. I don't want to see Brand just yet."

Gavin nodded. He wanted to comfort her, but he himself was appalled by what his son had done. He had known all along that feelings between Brand and Paul really hadn't improved despite the truce of years and had probably been worsened by the fact that Jefferson and Paul got along so well and with Fiona seemed to make up a group of three which excluded Brand. But part of that he knew was Brand's fault; he wanted to dominate too much, and none of the others were such weaklings as to allow that.

He sighed and sat a few moments longer before he went in search of his son. The pain of this multiplied by thousands, by millions. That was what it was going to be, just as Tessa had said.

He found Brand outside hunched down at the base of the oak tree. The chill of night had come down, but the moonlight was white on Brand's face.

There wasn't any reason to beat around the bush. "You could have killed your brother," Gavin said quietly.

"He's not my brother! He's just some boy you brought home," Brand flashed.

Gavin's own anger rose. "He is your brother. By all rights he is your brother now. Your mother and I have chosen it to be so." Then he saw it again, the fear and hurt behind his son's defiance, and he had the eerie sense of looking into a younger version of his own face. At fourteen Brand was already just over six feet, taller than Paul and nearly as mature. The planes of his face Gavin knew were his own, only slightly finer from Tessa's blood, and Brand's eyes were nearly as dark a blue as his own, his hair as black.

His voice gentled. "Brand, haven't you learned yet that there's enough love in this house for all of you? You've never accepted Paul, not from the day he came here. You ought to feel glad you have another brother. Instead you fight him. And he did not, by the way, tell what happened."

Brand looked away and his voice trembled. "It was awful. Part of me knew what I was doing and was glad, really glad, feeling hateful and strong, but another part of me was watching and felt sick and really scared." He buried his head on his knees.

Gavin squatted down and gripped his shoulders. "You'll be all right if you let that second part become the strongest. You're nearly full grown now, and you've got to watch your temper. If you don't, you're liable to meet up with someone who has one to match it. We all want to protect what's ours, but you've got to be damn sure what belongs to you and what doesn't. You don't own Paul's place in this family any more than he owns yours."

"You going to punish me?" Brand asked after a pause.

Gavin almost smiled at the hopeful note. "You mean make it easier for you? What do you suggest, that I throw you from the treehouse? I think from the look of you that you're punishing yourself enough. If you weren't, I'd be worried. But I'm asking you to go tell Paul you're sorry.

And I'm asking you to mean it. Don't do it until you do. Empty words have no place here."

"You know the hardest part?" Brand said suddenly. "The hardest part is that Paul is really a nice fellow. He's smart, and he's kind and patient. He's never a bully; he never tattles on anyone. He's never greedy. He never tries to get out of any of his chores. He makes us all laugh a lot. And he's not goody-goody about it; it's just the way he is. And Jeff's a lot like that too."

"Pretty goddamn hard to live with, isn't it?" Gavin remarked, and after a stunned instant, Brand laughed with his father.

It wasn't something he'd ever done easily, and it was harder now, but he hugged his father and mumbled, "Thanks, Papa. I love you."

Gavin walked back to the house with him. He felt a great tenderness for him. But fear still moved inside him. He wondered whether Brand would really ever be able to control his temper and his jealousy. Brand was going to be a big man and his reflexes were quick. He sighed, thinking the episodes could surely be worse as Brand got older. He wondered whether it was an inborn trait or whether all the spoiling Brand had received as a baby had more to do with it. Brand certainly had been aware of his status as first born to have attached such importance to his position from a very early age. Gavin supposed all parents faced problems like this when they had more than one child, and he could only hope they would be able to cope with each problem as it came.

When Tessa heard the soft knock on Paul's door, she knew it was Brand, and she had to steel herself against turning on him. She made her face calm and waiting.

He came in timidly, and his eyes were downcast. "I'm sorry for what I did, Mama, I'm very sorry. Is Paul okay?"

Tessa's heart melted. Poor Brand, such a burden, even though it had been his fault. And he looked so much like Gavin. "We've given him something to help him sleep. He won't be very comfortable for a while, but he'll be all right. Come here, love."

He came to her in a rush, and she put her arms around him and cradled him close despite his size. "Brand, my foolish one, you must not ever, ever doubt that I have

666

enough love for you and for the others, for all of you forever. Love is not like other things; it's magical. The more you give, the more you have, endlessly, giving and receiving. It goes on and on and on. Do you understand?"

"I'm not sure I understand it all, but I'm trying," he admitted honestly.

"That will surely do," Tessa assured him, but she shared Gavin's thought and wondered if this would really be the last of this kind of behavior. Hate too could feed on itself, on and on.

Paul was glad of anything that would make things better between himself and Brand. He knew Brand was truly sorry, and it almost made the discomfort of his broken leg worth it. He had feared coming to blows with Brand for a long time, and he couldn't think of anything he'd rather not do.

He was patient and uncomplaining because to be otherwise was contrary to his nature. There was still a deep core of him that accepted pain and disaster as the nature of his life. And everything was made easier by the fact that Fiona came often to sit with him, showing him leaves, pebbles, feathers, and anything else she found that suited her standards of the beautiful or interesting. She amused him mightily with her chatter. Her observations were often wise for a seven-year-old, and she saw nothing odd in skipping from one subject to another with no warning.

Paul couldn't really explain it, the deep protective love he felt for the little girl, but she enchanted him with her pale, elfin looks. For years when Tessa had told them a tale or read one, no matter what the description, he imagined the little girl or the princess of the hero's wife to be Fiona, sometimes a quite grown-up Fiona. For him, Bulfinch's *Age of Fable* still contained more stories about Fiona than anything else. He knew brothers ought to feel embarrassed about being affectionate toward a little sister, and sometimes he did, but in his love for beautiful things, Fiona was the most beautiful of all, looking so different from everyone else. Now that his leg was broken, she informed him gravely, he was more like her, and he smiled at the comparison. Quick, light little Fiona; sometimes he imagined she could even fly like the airy magical creatures that even now, at sixteen, he hoped might live in some enchanted wood. Maybe that was why she had been born with a crippled leg, because earth things are not supposed to fly. He chided himself for his fantasies, but they didn't cease. And it moved in him often, never quite going away, the vague dread of what would happen to her when he was fully grown and took a wife and a life separate from Fiona. He wanted to love someone and to be loved as Tessa and Gavin loved each other, but whenever he tried to picture the woman, she was no more than a shadowy form with hair the color of Fiona's, almost white at first, but now a rich silver gold.

The only other thing he knew about this shadow woman was that he wanted her to have a mind like his mother's. To his delight, she too spent a good deal of time with him while he was recuperating. Never before had he so fully understood how much Gavin must enjoy having a wife who could think as well as Mrs. Tubbs but looked like Tessa. Since they agreed on too many things, they made a game of choosing sides on various subjects, drawing straws to see who would have to argue "yes," who "no," and then proceeded to have rousing debates.

Tessa drew the short, the "no," on Mr. Darwin's *Theory of The Origin of Species*, which had been published the year before and had immediately become a favorite of Mrs. Tubbs, who had been infinitely relieved to find the book readily accepted in the Ramsay household.

Tessa threw herself into her objecting role with great fervor, arguing that it was the worst of insults to be descended from monkeys and that it was a sacrilege besides, sheer heresy. She stopped suddenly and burst into giggles, saying, "I can't, Paul, I simply can't do this! I have never believed that such a complicated, glorious and nasty beast as man could have been formed in an instant from the mud of a swamp. Perhaps monkeys have bad habits and beautiful thoughts too that they acquired from odd ancestors over many years. It makes much better sense."

Paul made a face that he hoped was simian, and they dissolved in laughter.

But he was too sensitive to her feelings to be fooled by the gay front she always tried to present in the sickroom. Often in the first days after the fall, he had awakened to find her staring off into some unseeable place, her expression one of ineffable sadness, though as soon as she felt his eyes on her, she would smile and her face would show nothing beyond concern for him. But lying in bed, he had a lot of time to consider the contrast, and he was never more conscious of it than the day they got the news that Abraham Lincoln had won the presidential election.

They had been reading *A Tale of Two Cities*, taking turns reading parts of it aloud, though they had both read it before. Gavin had given it to Tessa as one of her birthday gifts, and Paul knew by heart what was written in the flyleaf: "To my Tessa who was sixteen and liked Dickens. My love, always, Gavin." It intrigued him to think that his father had loved Tessa even then and to think that his mother had been only sixteen, his own age. It intrigued him more that she was now twice that age, and he knew she loved Gavin more now than you could ever love anyone when you were sixteen. Somehow he knew that was true. He didn't know much about how they had met and married, and he didn't think the others knew much more than he did—just the barest facts of a Yankee riding through and meeting a Californio girl.

Her voice wasn't quite steady as she read, and he could see the book trembling slightly in her hands. He was sure Lincoln was a good man, and yet she . . .

Suddenly all the pieces fit together, and he knew, but still he approached it obliquely, feeling instinctively that she needed to let go even while he felt inadequate, though willing, for the role of listener.

"Why aren't you happy that Lincoln is president? He seems to believe what we believe," he ventured softly even though she was just getting to the exciting part of the exchange in the book.

The book slammed shut and slipped from her nerveless hands, landing on the floor with a thud.

She fought violently for control and lost because Paul was no longer a child; his brown eyes were old and enduring. She bowed her head on the counterpane of his bed and wept.

"It's true. This man Lincoln has come when he is needed and when there is no other answer. There is no time left. But Gavin will go now, he will go to fight in this war, and he may never come back. I would not have it

669

be so for anyone, but I have no belief, not even the hope for my own soul, that is as strong as my love for him. I can't bear for him to go and die in that foreign place."

With infinite patience, Paul sorted the words out of the sobbing that rushed, stopped, and broke them into strange patterns. He reached out and patted her hair very gently.

"It won't be the same, I know, but we'll be with you, all of us, and we'll do the best we can to make it easier for you, even Fiona will," he promised gravely.

Tessa was comforted because he offered no falsehood, no claim that Gavin would not go, perhaps forever—just the best of himself and the other children.

She straightened her spine and sat up again, wiping her eyes unashamedly. "That is far more than most women will have," she said.

CHAPTER LV

Before the year was over, South Carolina had seceded from the Union, and as 1861 began, others followed: Mississippi, Florida, Alabama, Georgia, and Louisiana. They formed their own government of the Confederate States of America and elected Jefferson Davis of Mississippi as their president. Texas joined them next.

By the time Lincoln was inaugurated in March, he could surely not be called president of the United States. It was a further irony that Kansas should finally be admitted as a free state after years of struggle, admitted on the eve of even worse conflict than she had already seen in her "bleeding" years.

On April 12, the Confederates fired on Fort Sumter, a federal fort, at Charleston, South Carolina, when Major Anderson, who was in command, refused to surrender. But by the next day, he was forced to give up because the fort was not stocked for a siege. He and his men were allowed to return north.

President Lincoln declared the existence of an "insurrection" and called for the first lot of volunteer troops. He wanted 75,000 men for three months' service.

"More like 750,000 for thirty years," Gavin told Indian grimly.

They had not stated their intention openly yet, but it was obvious. They fired the foreman at the lumbermill and hired a man they trusted more. They worked tirelessly to make sure everything would run smoothly without them with the least effort from Tessa. The birthday party this year was a farce of badly acted joy.

Tessa moved in a cloud of fear all her waking hours, clung frantically to Gavin at night, and prayed desperately that the war would be over before it was fully begun.

In May, Virginia, Arkansas, and North Carolina joined the Confederacy, and there was little doubt Tennessee would follow soon. The battle lines were drawn; it would be the eleven states of the Confederacy against the twenty-three that remained in the Union. The South was going to pit her staple export of cotton plus other agricultural commodities that might entice foreign governments, particularly England, to help her against the power of the North that rested in factories, in gold from California and Oregon, and in silver from the Comstock Lode in the Nevada Territory.

"We're going to be on our way soon, but I'd like to see the children off for the *rancho* first." Gavin said it softly, love and regret drifting through the words and beyond to a place unfathomable miles away.

Not even the golden lamplight could soften the rigid planes of Tessa's face reflected in the mirror, her hands clutching her hairbrush, the nightly ritual cut short by his words. His hands rested gently on her shoulders as he stood behind her.

There was nothing gentle about her reaction. She whirled up and out of his reach, the black curtain of her hair and the gossamer and lace of her robe swirling around her. He could see the frenzied pumping of her heart as she faced him.

She drew a deep, shuddering breath. "I have not even *seen* your country! I've tried, but it does not seem like mine, and I can't imagine what it's truly like. What makes you think I'm going to smile politely and kiss you and send you off to die?" she spat. "You're wrong, and you're too old! So is Indian. You are forty-three, and he is nearly fifty. You are both too damn old to go play soldier! Let someone else do it. You have a job to do here. Both of you left that country. You came here. You found a new life."

Her eyes were deep purple, fierce and angry, all from love for him and fear of loss. His voice remained quiet. "Though it hurts my pride to admit it, you are probably right about Indian and me. But I've never liked the idea that wars are fought by boys while old men plan them. Tessa, we have to go back. It's where we both began; it's what we both believe in despite the time away. It's what we've talked about all these years. And if we aren't one nation, we'll be prey to many."

"I don't care what we have talked about all these years. I don't care about the Union. I care about you. We have a life together. What am I to do when you are gone?"

The low sadness of her question was harder for him to bear than her anger, but he answered evenly. "What you have always done. What I expect you to do now. You will carry on. You will do everything you do very well. That's the least of my worries."

She turned away so he could not read her expression. "I'm not ready to leave the city right now. You take the children to Rancho Magnífico. You explain to them why you are leaving them. It is the least you can give them, some last time with you."

"All right, if that's the way you want it," he agreed patiently, but when he tried to take her in his arms to comfort her, she pulled away.

Long after he was asleep, she still lay awake. "I will not wait. I will not wait to see you go from me," she whispered aloud in the darkness.

He arrived back in the city bone weary. Saying good-by to the children had been a grueling experience. They had listened to his arguments, agreed that he had to do what was right, and all the while four pairs of young eyes had told him they knew they were being abandoned. He almost wished they weren't so bright and well educated; it would have been such a relief even if one of them had
672

thought of war as a grand and glorious adventure. Mrs. Tubbs had left it to him, venturing no opinion, wrapped in her boundless reserve.

He was in a foul mood. He hoped Tessa would have relented at least a little; he needed her comfort desperately. He found her gone, having left five days ago, leaving behind a very agitated Chong Sing who knew nothing beyond the fact that she had ridden off alone, forbidding him on his honor to accompany her or to tell Indian and Thia, saying only that she was going home. The note she had left for him held the words she had spoken when he slept and no more.

"God damn that woman!" he roared, and he sought out Indian and Armenthia. They were less surprised by what Tessa had done than he was. Indian shook his head dolefully, but Thia's silence lasted a very short time.

She turned on Gavin, her normally shy manner completely changed. "I was born a slave, nothin' my own, nothin' till Tessa she looks round an' says, here, Armenthia, here's my frien' Indian, man who needs a woman, needs you, here you take him. So I do. But all th' time, I know Devil goin' come 'round 'gain an' strip me naked jus' like always. I be thankful now if jus' th' children lef' to me, jus' them, please Jesus.

"So I know, I'm used to it. You two goin' go get kilt an' nothin' I can do to stop it. Tessa, she don' know. She used to havin' an' fightin' to keep. An' you she loves more 'n all, mebbe more 'n God Himself. She's spittin' at her own death in yoahs. You 'spect her tell you go right on, put death on her own heart? You 'spect that? You crazy man, Gavin Ramsay, same as my Indian. An' Tessa's right, you both too damn ol' be goin' off to that place I know too good an' Tessa knows no better 'n th' back side of th' moon." She glared at him, and Indian smiled sheepishly.

"You been thinkin' Thia take this better 'n Tessa? My Thia, she tell me I lose anythin' belong to her, I better send her one whole buck take my place." Indian reached out, and Armenthia came into the curve of his arm, muttering, "You, you big fool, you," making it sound like an endearment. The ache for Tessa grew in Gavin until he was afraid he was going to cry.

" 'Spect you want be on your way. Take my horse; yours sure worn out," Indian offered.

Tessa felt no fear of traveling alone. She wore the same garb that had protected her on the trail before and kept her hat pulled down low on her face when she encountered anyone. The tense form with the rifle so ready to hand gave warning that this rider was dangerous and not to be challenged.

She spent one night with Carmelita and Sam in Monterey. They welcomed her and tried to offer comfort, though they themselves were stunned, particularly Carmelita, who had thought she knew Indian and Gavin well but would never have foreseen this action from them.

Tessa herself made it easier. She didn't want fussing; she wanted a place with a real bed, a place to rest for the night and the quiet comfort of friends who loved her without having to make a point of it.

Nor did they try to dissuade her from going on, though Carmelita's eyes met hers in a long, knowing look as she prepared to leave. Tessa shrugged. "It's not the same this time. Gavin decided to run away first, and we're going in opposite directions."

Within minutes of her arrival at Valle del Mar, the word had spread that the *patrón* was going away to a Yankee war and the *patróna* was better left alone. Even Ramón and María could not get close to her.

She spent the days riding until her body trembled with fatigue and she knew she could sleep. The one place she avoided was the pool; she could not bear to go there now.

She drank in the smell of the salt air on rolling meadows. She rode to the edge of the earth meeting the sea. She listened to the gulls and seals and wondered why they sounded different here, stronger, more sure of their purpose than those further north. She searched the sky for hawks and eagles and wished she could soar into oblivion with them. She did not allow herself to think; the endless worry and thinking had helped nothing. She filled her head with a manic, minor-key humming, an endless dirge.

And she was sure she had gone mad when she awakened in the middle of one night to candlelight and Gavin staring down at her. She stared back, seeing the stubble of his beard and the travel stains on his clothes. "Dreams do not smell of horse and sweat," she said, beginning to laugh and cry at the same time.

He sat on the bed and gathered her close, and she savored the warm strength of him and even the travel scent and the roughness of his face.

"Carmelita wondered what took me so long to follow. Did you really think I'd leave with no more than that damn note?" he asked, more in wonder than anger now.

She nodded her head against him.

He spoke very slowly. "Somehow I didn't make it clear. Even though I must go, there is nothing that could be harder than leaving you."

Her defiance was broken. She bowed to the inevitable. Nothing would stop him in his course. And now she had a little more time with him, a wholly unexpected gift despite her own behavior. A little more time before she again felt as she had these past days. "How long?" she whispered.

"I must start back the day after tomorrow."

"Then we shall live very hard and very much before then."

He was deeply touched that she had not yet gone to the pool. They rode out early the next morning. It was difficult to believe the earth could be so fresh, young, and giving when men were preparing to slaughter each other, for surely the seasons were turning on the wheel there as they were here. Tessa tried desperately to picture the country where Gavin would soon be, but it was impossible, and she strove instead to feel nothing but the immediacy of this day.

Late spring had given the foliage around the pool bright leaves, and hollows and sweeps of blossoms grew to the edge of the rocks and in the very fissures of stone, anywhere they had the slightest chance of rooting. And the intricate melodies woven by birds and insects were as rich as the fabric of leaves and flowers. Far away they could see the sparkle of the sea.

They tried to pretend this was the first of many days instead of the last, but the truth never left them. It showed in the way Gavin had watched Tessa riding Amordoro's

675

successor, El Rayo, named "El Rayo de Sol" because his coat was as shining and deep a gold as the rays of the sun on rising. It was a sight Gavin had seen countless times before—this raven-haired wife on a golden horse—but now he watched as though he feared to miss the slightest detail for the image in his mind. And at the pool, he reached out to trace the shape of her face often, wanting the knowledge even when sight was gone. And Tessa found herself simply gazing at him or gripping his hands with force enough to feel the steel of the muscles and bones beneath her own.

It showed in the way they talked, saying, "Do you remember when . . . ?" too many times because they had a sudden fierce need to establish a joint memory, another way of being together when they were separated in the flesh. And it showed more in what they did not say; Gavin careful not to give instructions; Tessa avoiding all the questions of "What should I do if . . . ?" It sounded in the songs Tessa sang and more when Gavin joined her, love and sorrow shaping every note because music was so much closer to the bone than mere words.

And it showed most plainly in the way they made love. They had never taught their bodies to lie to each other— anger, hurt, and most of all love had always been translated directly from their hearts through their flesh, and never more so than now. Their union was violent, as though for them the war began with each other. Even when his bones pressed hard against hers, Gavin wanted to go deeper, be closer, make her part of himself, take her away with him, and Tessa wanted no less to keep him with her. Filled with him, her body still pleaded for more and her voice begged, "Gavin, please, *mi corazón*, please . . ."

Though she wished for a miracle this once, time had no care for them. The sun allowed the too brief night and rose again. Tessa steeled herself to do as Gavin wished. His journey back to the city would be frantic, and he and Indian would leave immediately by stage coach, which would take them south again by the route that avoided the impossible crossing of the Sierra Nevadas. Gavin did not want her to go north with him. He did not even want her to accompany him to the boundaries of the *rancho*. When she had protested, thinking he meant to spare her, he had grinned wryly. "It's a selfish wish, nothing else. It is my talisman to leave you here in this special place and to believe you will both be waiting to shelter me when I return." It was as if their sanctuary was a separate and equally loving spirit.

The time was upon them, and there was only one thing left to say. Gavin kissed her and held her against him for a moment. She felt as if her life were draining from herself into him, but in the last instant, she found the words. *"Vaya con Dios,* Gavin, *mi vida."*

He turned back to look at her briefly from the top of the rise, and then he was gone.

Her knees buckled and she sank down, hugging herself, rocking her body in tight misery, voice finding the words, adult singing to the child of herself who could not comprehend the depth of this grief.

> Hushaby,
> Don't you cry,
> Go to sleepy, little baby.
> When you wake, you shall have
> All the pretty little horses—
> Blacks and bays,
> Dapples and grays,
> Coach and six-a little horses.
>
> Way down yonder, in de medder
> There's a po' lil lambie,
> De bees an' de butterflies
> Peckin' out its eyes,
> De po' lil thing cried, "Mammy!"
> Hushaby,
> Don't you cry,
> Go to sleepy, little baby.

She sang it over and over, as Armenthia sang her babies to sleep. She heard the sad, haunting melody as something separate from herself. She wanted to cry, but she was beyond anything so civilized. When she finally let go, she howled and screamed and pounded her fists on the ground until she had scraped them raw, and the pain was welcome.

677

CHAPTER LVI

Christmas was over, and it was still raining. The city was a river of mud despite the improved paving, and Tessa didn't even want to consider what the Great Valley must be like; she could imagine only too clearly the *vaqueros* huddled in their houses and the palominos stained brown with mud.

She prowled the room restlessly, straining for sounds of the children but not wanting to be with them. When the Ramsay four, Armenthia's two eldest, Dian and Julie, and Lin-Ao were all in the house, it was a lively place, even when they were all more or less concentrating on Mrs. Tubbs's lessons. Mrs. Tubbs did not believe that all learning was a silent process.

She picked up a book and put it down without opening it. Night would come too quickly; it always did now. Nights without Gavin. She envied Armenthia and her condition as she had never thought to again. Thia's baby was due in February. Tessa thought how comforting it would be to have Gavin's child growing inside her, kicking and moving in proof that she and Gavin had loved each other, in proof that Gavin existed.

Lately she had had terrifying moments of panic when she could not remember what he looked like. She had a photograph, an ambrotype of him, but it was somehow only superficially like him. Its grainy tones did not allow for the contrast of his black hair and blue, blue eyes. And she had his two sons who looked so much like him, more than the photograph did, Brand most of all. But that was not the same either. She was not looking for the general image but for that essential presence that seemed too vital to trap fully for long, even in adoring memory.

She and Thia had heard from their men, but little good it did them beyond knowing they had still been alive when they wrote the letters. In October the Pony Express had been made obsolete after a short life by the completion of the transcontinental telegraph line, and President Lincoln had received the first telegram in Washington, D.C. They received only long-delayed letters from their husbands, and were never sure if and when their replies would reach them.

Gavin and Indian had not been content with any halfway measures. They had gone clear east and were engaged in the campaign with the Army of the Potomac. With the Army of the West at least they would have been a few states closer to California. Gavin's letters were full of love for her, and little information. Only by painstaking reading between the lines and putting it together with the patchy stories in the press could Tessa guess what was going on. At least the men had not arrived in time to take part in the July battle of Bull Run. It was the first major engagement, and the Union lost. The Confederacy was already showing it possessed some fine generals, while the Union's leadership was doubtful. Gavin had written in disgust, "It is my profound hope that our military will soon discover this is a real war and not a matter of a few days' maneuvers." It was a wonder the letter had not been censored.

They were well and hadn't seen much action yet. Every letter said that, and neither woman would believe it until the men were safe at home again. They did not speak of it directly, but Tessa was sure Thia had come to the same conclusion she herself had. No matter what lip service the cause of freeing slaves received, there was hardly less prejudice against Negroes in the flesh in the North than there was in the South. Gavin and Indian had obviously met pressure because of their determination to stay together and Gavin's refusal to allow his friend to be put in a subservient position. Neither of them wrote specifically about it, but there were enough angry comments in Gavin's letters for Tessa to guess it. And she suspected the men were now attached to some unit as scouts. There was little difference between that and spies if one crossed the enemy lines. She remembered the story of Gavin and Indian's first meeting. *They could do it*, she thought, *they could pass as a loyal son of the Confederacy and his slave.* Her flesh crawled when she thought of the danger.

No letters for two months now. It made horrible sense.

Even if the authorities by some chance discovered the death or capture, did they notify the wives of spies, or did they just pretend the men had never existed?

She almost wished the men had not left everything in such good order; it left too much time on her hands. Gavin had left a letter for her, too. The days right after he had left were a blur. She knew she had done what he asked in taking a *vaquero* escort with her when she left Rancho Valle del Mar and again when she left Rancho Magnífico and returned to the city. The papers Gavin had left had drawn everything into sharp, painful focus. His will had been neatly made and included specific bequests to each of the children and orders for the payments they had made all these years to a San Francisco bank account for Soledad's child to continue until the girl would be twenty-one in 1866; the rest of the Ramsay share in Ramian Enterprises was Tessa's. The letter was brief:

> I could not bring myself to say it by the pool nor can I leave it unsaid. You are young and beautiful. If I should not return, don't waste your days in mourning. Make a new life for yourself, my darling.

It did not matter that the letter was put away with the will; the words were burned on her brain. "Never!" she said aloud, her reaction no less fierce now than when she had first read it.

She changed her mind and sought out the children, suddenly needing the reassurance of their vitality. There was time for tea and cakes before Chong Sing took Lin-Ao back to Chinatown and Thia's children went back to their own house. Tessa made her face serene.

She and her sons made one trip to Rancho Magnífico in January. It was a miserably cold, wet journey, and the depth of the mud they often had to ride through was frightening. It took them three times as long as it normally did but at least they found Pedro and the others coping as well as could be expected, and better than most. Every stream and river was over its banks, but the *vaqueros* worked ceaselessly to move the animals to higher ground, especially the horses, which didn't seem to have the cattle's acute sense of survival.

680

"At least there will be fine grass when the sun shines again," Pedro said, offering the only comfort he could.

It had rained steadily for thirty days before the sun finally came out again. Brand said he was disappointed—he had already begun plans for his ark. Mrs. Tubbs told him it was just as well since from what she'd read, rather a lot of spiritual help was necessary to complete such a project.

Tessa loved them all for the effort they made to make life easy and cheerful in Gavin's absence. Even Brand and Paul were getting along better than they ever had before. But February came and along with it Thia's new daughter, Indiana Jefferson, and still no news from the men. Indian didn't even know he was a father again because Armenthia had elected not to tell him of her pregnancy until the baby was safely born. "No use him frettin' when he can't do anything 'bout it," she had declared.

In the same month, Tessa had her own much sadder news, but she did not even consider putting it in a letter to Gavin. He could do nothing about it either, and it would only add sorrow to his distant burden. At thirty-five, Belle was dead of pneumonia and buried beside Charles. She had died with very little of her prior wealth left. Surely it had gone to help support the scandal sheets and her revenge on the Committee of Vigilance. Tessa's sorrow and regret were compounded by the fact that Belle had never allowed their friendship to blossom again; the only way Tessa had known of her death was by a brief notice in the newspapers. She wondered if she could have helped had she known of Belle's illness and need, but she suspected Belle had simply grown tired of revenge and everything else without Charles.

Finally, in March, they heard from their husbands. The minimal information was enough. Gavin wrote that he and Indian had been "out of contact, unable to write" due to various things, but that they were both all right. They had found the announcement of Indiana's birth waiting for them. Indian hoped his daughter would be just like her mother.

Christmas presents arrived in April and birthday gifts in June, and the women wept together both times for the sweetness of their men. And there was wry laughter too, because they had received frivolous things, though they had sent only the useful to their husbands—socks, shirts, boots and blankets, and San Francisco newspapers—as if the East were the wilderness instead of the West. But the gifts that got through were gratefully acknowledged, and they could only hope that the packages that ended up somewhere else were being put to good use.

Through the months, they read the war news, one confrontation after another, a few major ones—Pea Ridge in March, Shiloh in April, Seven Pines at the end of May, and the "Seven Days Battle" ending at Malvern Hill on July 1. It was possible their men had been involved in some of the battles fought in the eastern campaign, but impossible to tell for sure; Gavin and Indian seemed to have made a pact not to distress their wives with war news. Tessa could see why, but it drove her mad because it made it even harder to imagine where they were and what they were doing. A Washington, D.C. post office box was the only address they had.

The Federal forces won some of the battles, but not enough to turn the war in the Union's favor. They were routed too often by ferocious Confederate troops and their own generals' indecisiveness at crucial times. It was becoming very clear that despite their lack of factories and their smaller population, the Southerners had some real advantages. Their military leaders showed themselves ever more capable products of a chivalrous tradition that included the best of training at West Point for some, such as General Robert E. Lee; their troops were most often fighting on home soil and fought harder because of it; and there was still the possibility that France and more probably England would come in decisively on the side of the Confederacy. Already there were reports of arms shipments from England, and Confederate ships that managed to run the Union blockade were welcome in English ports where they took on supplies for their army.

In August, the Union forces were defeated at Cedar Mountain, Virginia, and again in the Second Battle of Bull Run. In September they lost to "Stonewall" Jackson at Harpers Ferry, and only with a tremendous loss of life on both sides was General Lee's northward invasion stopped at the battle of Antietam in Maryland. President

Lincoln had had to issue calls for more and more troops; there was now even an organized troop of Negroes.

"Wonder if they'll let Gavin join," Armenthia said with uncharacteristic sarcasm. They breathed again when they heard from the men.

It was only gradually that Tessa realized there was a war beginning in California. It had nothing to do with arms and men, but with nature and man. As Pedro had said, the grass had grown rich and long after the thirty days of rain of last winter, so much so that beef prices had taken another serious fall with the glut of fat animals on the market. That alone would be enough to ruin many ranchers who had suffered a falling market for years now, but Tessa had the prized palominos to balance the beef losses. But no livestock could live without water or the grazing it provided.

No rain at all had fallen since the flooding storms. The summer had seen the Great Valley even more seared than ever, the long reaching blades of the lush spring burnt brown. With the fall came what should have been the start of the rainy season, but there was none—no large storms, scant rain, and endlessly clear days that began to get on every rancher's nerves.

A letter from Gavin in January confirmed the winter cold in the East. He and Indian were in camp with thousands of other soldiers waiting until spring, when the roads would dry out enough for horses and caissons to move without bogging down. "We're safe for the moment as long as we don't freeze our asses to the ground," he wrote inelegantly. "I'd forgotten how cold it can get back here. I long for California and my warm woman." He went into such detail about what he longed for that Tessa blushed and laughed through her tears as she read the letter. And for the first time, Gavin wrote about other soldiers by name, describing most of them with grave compassion. "So many are so young. I think of our sons and find it hard to bear."

In his next letter, he spoke angrily of the Emancipation Proclamation Lincoln had issued January 1. "Hell, I concede that it's a start, but why not go all the way? We're in this thing up to our necks, and I would we could achieve one great triumph."

683

Tessa understood his anger. The proclamation was nothing if not political, aimed mostly at keeping foreign countries from entering the war on the Confederacy's side, because that could now be construed as direct support for slavery. The proclamation did not cover those slave states which had remained in the Union—Missouri, Delaware, Kentucky, and Maryland—and there was nothing in it to prevent the South from reinstituting slavery if and when its states were readmitted to the Union.

It was disheartening to realize that President Lincoln felt as badgered as his soldiers, struggling as hard as anyone to find the right course, changing generals, plans, and policies. In March the first national conscription act was passed requiring all male citizens, including aliens who had declared their intention to become citizens, to enroll if they were between the ages of twenty and forty-five. But conscripts could get out of it by finding a substitute or paying a fine of three hundred dollars. It was tantamount to saying the poor would go while the rich stayed home. Tessa didn't care about the injustice; all she could think of was that Paul would be nineteen this year, far too close to twenty. She was selfishly glad that the term "national conscription" did not include California, but she knew that might change, and in any case, Paul could sign up if he wanted to. She'd have something to say about that if he ever appeared to be heading that way.

Though Gavin and Indian were missing the fair weather of California, it was becoming ever more a threat. Tessa could scarcely believe that the season when rain should have fallen had ended as drily as it had begun. Her attention turned more and more to the land. They had enough land and had never been so greedy as to overstock it, but a dead land would support nothing. The spring growth was minimal, and Tessa prayed that 1863 would see an unseasonably wet summer. But it did not; it saw blazing heat and the land slipping from the brown of winter to the brown of summer, the negligible green between lasting no time at all. There was little they could do besides selling off some horses they would have preferred to keep and train for a higher selling price later and selling beef cattle for paltry sums.

"If we can just manage until the fall, surely the rains
684

will come again," Tessa told Pedro and Ramón, but her thoughts were as grim as theirs. Valle del Mar had a slightly easier time because its closeness to the sea allowed for more moisture than the inland valleys received. It was one thing to be thankful for.

Tessa felt her life disintegrating, drying up and breaking off in small pieces like the drought-stricken foliage on the land. She suddenly felt unable to cope adequately with anything. When she was in the city, she wanted to be on the land, and when she was on one of the *rancho*s, she worried about things in the city. She knew the problem was within herself; the businesses in the city were doing well and her sons were taking increasingly active roles. Even Jefferson, the youngest at sixteen, had little of the child left in him. He was best at handling people, gentle and patient. Paul, though as thoughtful, was much more shy, but he was superbly confident at working out business details and figures. And Brand was the one who hit on new ideas, constantly finding ways to make everything work more smoothly, blessedly capable of putting the fire of his ideas to work rather than leaving a trail of sparks for others to save or stamp out. All three had responded beautifully and matured swiftly in face of their father's absence. Tessa was enormously proud of them, but she would have given them years more of childhood to have had Gavin with her.

The only child she had left was Fiona, and sometimes she wondered if even her daughter, though only ten years old, could be considered a child. There were times when she felt very close to her, times when Fiona seemed very much a little girl, though her interests were evenly divided between dolls and tomboyish pursuits, which Tessa considered very good for her physical handicap. But there were other times when Fiona seemed strangely removed from those around her. She didn't brood for attention; she simply went away to some unseen place that made her eyes sad, thoughtful, and old. When that happened, Tessa couldn't help seeing Jordan in her daughter. She knew she would have been better able to suppress the knowledge of the resemblance had Gavin been there.

She was at the shop, as she always was at least part of the time while she was in the city. Molly and the others (now expanded by six from the early days, four of them, to Tessa's secret delight, every bit as competent as the men) didn't need her for the daily routine of the store. But she was still the decision-maker and the drawing card; clients were always flattered when Mrs. Ramsay herself helped them with their selections.

Tessa was doing her best to concentrate on Molly's problem that concerned a green silk gown for a woman who should never wear green in the first place. "She insisted, and I just couldn't talk her out of it!" Molly declared in distress. "And not only that, she wants the widest of hoops, and there is no way to lace her tightly enough to make the effect elegant. She will look like a large green barrel."

In other days, Tessa would have laughed at Molly's apt description, but the best she could manage now was a wan smile. She had a sudden desire to scream. It started with the thought that the increasingly popular contraptions of metal hoops and horsehair, "artificial crinolines," and all the other garbage of wide skirts and corsets she herself would never torture her body into were insanely devised to conceal every true curve of a woman's body. Gavin had told her if he ever had to open her clothing like a tin of oysters, he'd probably die of apoplexy on the spot. Long ago, Jordan had said he couldn't stand women who creaked. The green silk would have looked lovely on Belle. Belle was dead. Charles was dead. Who knew where Jordan was? Who knew where Gavin and Indian were? It was obscene to be talking about hoops and green silk while men were dying.

A sudden chill engulfed her, as deep and real as if she had been hurled into a snowdrift. She shivered, and her face was suddenly so pale, Molly asked in alarm what was wrong.

"I expect I'm . . . just tired, it's nothing . . . I——" Tessa stammered, and she fled.

She sought out Armenthia, not even going to her own house first. Thia took one look at her and gathered her close. "I don' know, swear I don', but I feel somethin'— not th' cold like you, but somethin'."

It's Gavin then, not Indian, Tessa thought, but she did
686

not say it aloud. She held onto Thia for a moment and then turned and left without a word.

They heard about the battle at Gettysburg, Pennsylvania, and Tessa no longer wondered how it was possible to feel cold in a hot, dry July. General Robert E. Lee had tried to go north again, and for a time, it seemed possible that he would break through. At the end of the long days of battle, he had been defeated. But at what cost, so many dead on both sides.

Tessa endured the month blankly. She could not understand how she felt. She could not believe Gavin was dead, and yet at first she felt as if he were further gone from her than ever. Then there were a few days when she knew if she could turn around quickly enough she would catch a glimpse of him.

Indian's letter reached them in the first week of August. Gavin had suffered a bullet crease in the head at Gettysburg, worrisome for a while but truly getting better now. Gavin himself would be writing shortly.

To her chagrin Tessa saw black dots, then nothing, and came to to find Thia ministering to her and crooning, "There now, he's all right, he's jus' fine."

"I knew, Thia, I knew! I just didn't understand exactly what it meant," Tessa whispered.

"Course you did," Thia said matter-of-factly. "Don' jus' love a man when he's close by."

The men showed no signs of coming home.

In November President Lincoln dedicated a national cemetery at Gettysburg. He spoke for only two minutes. His address was widely reprinted. When Tessa read it, she knew it was of rare eloquence, but all she could think of was that "these dead" had very nearly included Gavin. And she found it difficult to summon the necessary spirit to celebrate Thanksgiving Day, which the president had previously declared as a national holiday to be observed on the last Thursday of November.

Her children were healthy; Gavin and Indian were, as far as she knew, alive. She tried to find things to be thankful for. But the land was dying. The rainy season in California was failing to materialize this year as it had in the last, even while the East knew a bitterly cold, wet winter, the worst in years. Indian wrote that if he didn't freeze and turn white this year, he never would. Thia sent him another parcel of warm underwear and a warning to keep his hide just the color it was because she wasn't ever going to love a lily.

She knew he would laugh at that, but she confessed to Tessa, "Sometimes, I'm jus' sorry I learnt to read. Them newspapers say too much, an' our men say too little."

Tessa heartily agreed, but she found herself writing to Gavin the same way. She did not tell him the seriousness of the drought, and she sent him no newspapers that mentioned it.

One or another of her sons provided an escort, and they went often to the *ranchos*. The toll on the beasts was, as she had foreseen, beginning to show most plainly at Rancho Magnífico. Bones were beginning to protrude even on some of the younger horses, and the luster was gone from their coats. That was the most painful of all for her —to see the gold of the palominos tarnishing, turning slowly to dry straw.

She had never felt so helpless in her life. The horses were her talisman, her proof of life and hope, her tie with her past and her hope for the future, beauty in a world that had separated Gavin from her.

The new year of 1864 dawned. January, February, and March passed without appreciable rain. It had been more than two years now. There was no spring in California. In the East the season came on schedule to thaw the earth and make it bloom while the armies waited for the roads to dry enough so that they could go at each other's throats again. Strangely, as Tessa's optimism failed, Gavin's seemed to increase. Spring was so beautiful, he wrote, he longed for her to see it. General Ulysses S. Grant had been named commander-in-chief of the Federal armies; he was a great soldier and hopes were high among the troops that he would succeed where others had failed. And Gettysburg, bloody as it had been, had surely marked a turning of the war in the Union's favor. For the first time, Gavin could see the end in sight.

Tessa grew more frantic by the day. Ramian Lumber was nearly shut down because, without sufficient water power, the equipment would not work. Her sons worried about this, but Tessa was obsessed with the horses. She had the same nightmare over and over. She saw them shining gold in the sun for an instant and then there was nothing but bleached white bones glowing sickeningly in the night. She awakened shivering and whimpering so many times, she forgot what it was like to sleep peacefully through a whole night.

And it was on one of these nights when she could still see the bones in the darkness though she was awake, that the idea came to her. It was mad, but it was something to do, the only thing.

She did not ask the family, she told them. "I should have considered this before. It's very late to do it now. But I will. The best of the herds at Rancho Magnífico must be driven to Valle del Mar. There they will have at least a little better chance of living."

Her sons stared at her wordlessly for a moment, then Jefferson smiled ruefully. Tessa's heart skipped a beat, because of the familiar slant of his eyebrow. "Well, you'd have thought one of us could have thought of that instead of leaving it all up to you. When do we go?"

"I hoped you would ask that," she admitted breathlessly. "I'll need all three of you."

"Sorry we can't give you the fight you obviously expected," Brand said kindly. "It's the only thing to do. The horses can't all survive the summer at Rancho Magnífico. Maybe this way they'll all have at least a chance."

The only problem was Fiona.

"I ride as well as the boys," she insisted defiantly.

"My dear, I know, but you just can't go. We won't be able to move any faster than the slowest in the herd, and we won't have shelter for hours, maybe days at a time. You are too fair. I'll not risk having you seriously burned by the sun. You may come to Valle del Mar later, when we are settled in."

Fiona's pale skin was stained by red patches of anger, her delicate features drawn into a scowl, but she knew she couldn't persuade her mother. "Why couldn't you have made me like my brothers?" she shrieked, beyond caution because they were all going away on an adventure without

689

her, even Paul. "Why did I get yellow hair and white skin when they didn't? Why don't I have good strong legs like theirs?"

Tessa felt the color drain from her own skin, leaving it nearly as pale as Fiona's. "I wanted an especially beautiful daughter, and that is what I have," she got out, but she knew she had not been quick enough to cover her reaction; her perceptive child had seen her panic, and it made Tessa uneasy enough to protest still further.

"I love you very much," she said, and she had never thought the words so futile. She blessed Paul for being even kinder than he usually was to his little sister that evening, and when she could slip away, she went to Thia and told her what had happened.

"You lettin' guilt get in the way," Thia said bluntly. "Seems like girls come to knowin' different ways an' need bein' important early on. She's jus' mad 'cuz her brothers aren't goin' be here to spoil her. But she got Mrs. Tubbs, Chong Sing, Lin-Ao, an' all of us to spoil her some."

Tessa put her arms around her and rested her head against the strong shoulder. "Oh, Thia, I don't know what I would do without you. When I do not have the strength, you give it to me. I am frightened about this drive. I don't know what else to do, but maybe this is wrong, maybe we will lose more this way."

Armenthia patted her back gently. "I know, honey, I know. It's missin' those men so bad like to die of it. Makes everythin' damn hard. But you're strong too. I can't push those beasts to th' sea, but you can, an' you will, an' I don' see no other way. You take good care of yourself now. That ol' Indian an' Gavin, they're goin' need their women when they get home."

Neither of them voiced the other possibility.

Both households turned out at daybreak to wish the travelers Godspeed, and Fiona came out to hug her mother and her brothers. Her face no longer wore its mutinous expression, and she even managed to look quite grown up and maternal when Tessa assured her she trusted her to take her mother's place and help Armenthia too.

"Thia and I will do fine," she said and she admonished her brothers, "Take care of Mother. Don't let her get too tired." Tessa had to hide a grin. Fiona was behaving as if she were in her twenties instead of eleven years old and her mother a good ninety or so.

They knew the full effects of the disaster as soon as they left the sea-touched air. It was only April, but the heat in the interior was intense, and the air was so dry, they could feel the moisture being drawn from their bodies.

Cattle and horses stood with their heads down though many no longer made the effort to graze on the little grass there was and were too weary even to swish their tails at the flies that settled on their scabrous hides stretched over bony frames.

"My God, it's like a graveyard!" Paul exclaimed, and Tessa muttered, "Worse than my nightmare."

CHAPTER LVII

The horses spread in a golden sea before them, shadowed with the dark fire of the chestnuts. The stallions shrilled orders to their own *manadas*, and the mares and colts answered in nervous whinnies. But despite their excitement, the effects of the drought showed. Most were so much thinner than they should be, and they settled down much more quickly than their hot blood would normally allow. The force of her love for them and her will that they survive kept Tessa going through the next terrible days.

Pedro had made no protest to her idea. He had broken down and wept for the tragedy that had come to the land and to his beloved charges. He had helped make sure they took the best of the stock with them, and he had bowed his head in agreement with Tessa's order that any animals that were suffering too much were to be shot. He had wanted to go with them but had stayed with his sad duties at Rancho Magnífico, sending instead four of his best *vaqueros*.

The heat was so oppressive and the dust so constant, she feared they would all suffocate. She found herself panting and clutching her chest several times and when she saw others doing the same, she gave strict orders that all riders would take shifts, leaving the dusty wake of the herd at intervals to ride outside the churning cloud. They had little choice in their route; they had to drive the horses through the mountains at Pacheco Pass. Much of the land on their way was now settled, and no one had escaped the punishing effects of the drought. The valley was a great dead plain, and Tessa's horses were not a welcome sight to the ranchers and farmers trapped there watching their own livestock slowly perish for lack of water and grazing, their fields and orchards withering. She begged, she bargained, she paid in money and in golden horses that would probably die, though now they sparked an avaricious gleam in men's eyes. It was agonizing each time to part with the horses and the ache inside her pulsed with a relentless life of its own. But her will to save what she could grew apace. And it was this more than the greed for payment or the inevitability of the crossing when the landowners were faced with this woman and her herd that made them give way to her even to the point of suggesting where water might sometimes be found. They recognized a survivor and applauded her for it. They might be giving up and going under, but one of their kind was fighting tooth and nail against all odds. "Next time you see ol' Mother Nature, spit in 'er eye fa me," said one rawboned farmer.

"I will do so indeed," Tessa replied, and the man blinked at the sudden beauty he saw in her tired face. He had no way of knowing that the tart sound of New England in his voice reminded her of Gavin, even though Gavin's voice held only its faintest trace.

Their slow pace stretched the journey to nearly two weeks. Their lips and knuckles split and bled. Their noses bled too, without warning. Their hair was as dry and mussed as straw. The dust had given them second skins and their voices were hoarse from raw throats. A score of the horses had to be shot when the journey proved too much for them. Tessa made no attempt to hide her weeping, and she knew the final toll of being as desiccated as the land, so that her body had little water to spare for the luxury of tears.

One thing sustained her above all else, and that was the

beauty of her sons. They never complained, nor did they question her orders. They did their full share of work and more. They rode like young centaurs; sometimes she could hardly bear to look at Brand because he looked so much like his father. Even Jeff, who when he was younger had carried more of her own image, now appeared very like Gavin to her longing eyes. She knew it was foolish, but she fancied she could even see Ramsay blood in Paul.

She realized early that one of the gifts her young men were giving her was their sense of adventure. They knew the gravity of the situation, but nothing was greater than their excitement.

Though it was cooler at night, the horses could only be moved during the daylight for fear of injury in the darkness. Tessa looked forward to sundown as an absolute godsend for her aching bones, but her sons didn't seem to share her feeling. She smiled in the darkness beyond the circle of their carefully laid fire one night, listening to them.

"This wouldn't be a bad life for a while," Jeff said dreamily.

"I'd add some waterholes and more grazing, and I'd remove some *rancheros*, then I'd agree with you," Brand offered.

"I think you're both in the wrong state," Paul said. "You'd have to go to wilder country than this. California's getting awfully civilized. I'd go with you, except I'll bet Mother's the only boss who'd hire a fellow with books falling out of his saddlebags."

Jefferson hooted with laughter. "I can just see it! You'd have to take a pack mule loaded with your library. I swear, you're as bad as those old men in the opium dens, only you crave paper and print."

"It's true," Paul agreed with mock sadness. "I get too far away from a book and strange symptoms appear." He made a horrible face in the fire's glow, squinted his eyes slyly, and did a pantomime of searching for invisible books.

Tessa joined in their laughter, loving the gentle moment with them, loving the differences in them. She could still see Paul clearly on the day she had found him holding a volume of Shakespeare, tears of frustration in his eyes because he couldn't read it and didn't believe he would ever be able to. Strange to think that though he was not
693

related by blood, he carried the same hunger for books that she had had since she was a small child.

Long-suppressed guilt moved in her, and she decided there would never be a better time to release it. "Even before you were born, Brand, I dreaded the idea of sending my children away to school as the Larkins and many others did. I think perhaps I have been very wrong. You're all very intelligent. And even though it is beginning now, there is still not enough in California to challenge a fine mind in the pursuit of higher studies." Though she had spoken softly, she had their undivided attention.

Her voice grew stronger. "If any of you want to enlist in the army, I will fight with everything I have to keep you from it." She eyed Paul steadily; he would be twenty this year. "But if any of you wish to go East to a university to prepare for a profession or simply to study those things in which you delight, I will do anything necessary to help you go. Things will settle down again. The war will not last forever; it can't last forever!"

Paul broke the silence, speaking confidently for all three. "It's a generous offer, Mother, but you mustn't feel guilty. No school could offer a finer education than the one we've received from Mrs. Tubbs, from you, from Gavin, from Chong Sing, Indian, Armenthia, and all the other people in our lives. We've been surrounded by wisdom, love, and laughter, and by an appreciation for everything that's beautiful. No one can ask for a better education than that." He was very firm about it. "I've already made my journey from England to Australia to California. That's far enough for me." It was a measure of his love for her that he mentioned his background at all, and he finished with the same assurance. "It will end, Mother, and soon. Gettysburg was the beginning of the Union's victory."

"Amen," Brand said without sarcasm, encompassing school and the war in one word, and Jefferson echoed him.

"Thank you all, but I'll not hold you to it if you change your minds," Tessa said, her voice unsteady with emotion, love, pride, and relief equally mixed.

The night was suddenly filled with the high, wild laughter of a coyote. Others joined him, and after listening intently to be sure the horses were not alarmed by the familiar sound, Tessa let the sensuous pleasure of the eerie voices flood through her. Surely this shivery, half-mad singing was more the music of California than any other. She thought of all the times she and Gavin had paused to listen to it together, the times when the notes had risen moonward in chorus around their love-making. Did Gavin stop and listen in the far distant nights where he was—did he miss the sound that was certainly no part of that alien land? Did he think of her as she thought of him, his beautiful body, the white heat of joining? She saw him with startling clarity, and desire moved in the depths of her body, want heating the blood, nerves and flesh stirring, opening, waiting for him. She wanted to scream aloud for the frustration, the dying land waiting for rain, she waiting for Gavin. She was thirty-six years old and in this instant she wanted him more than she ever had. She had been without him for nearly three years. Did it ever end, this hunger? Did it ever grow more gentle? Or did it continue to soar upward and upward until oblivion came and this and all else was nothing?

She started a little at Jeff's soft voice, realizing that the others had moved off for a final check on the horses before they would begin on their rounds of sleeping, someone always keeping watch.

"He'll come back, Mother, he will, you'll see."

"How did you know?" she asked softly, and he did not pretend to misunderstand.

"You were with us and then suddenly you weren't," he said simply, though it was anything but simple. He couldn't admit what he had seen as he kicked the fire to its final glow and banked the embers. The flaring light had illuminated her face, the wide eyes and fine bones, familiar and yet not familiar because he had seen beyond to her fierce woman's hunger for her man in the way her mouth had looked suddenly fuller, ready, in the way the light had moved in her eyes. He had wished for a split second that he was too young to understand, but it was too late for that. Though he had always known it in some way, it would take getting used to, this clearer knowledge of Tessa's role as a woman quite apart from her comforting role as his mother. And right now, he didn't want to think about it too deeply aside from understanding better how much she missed his father.

Tessa did not press him for further explanation. She gave his hand a squeeze as she said, "You're a very good sort of person to have for a son, if I do say so myself," adding silently, "myself being your wanton mother." She had a sudden wicked impulse to giggle at the irony of feeling uneasy lest her son had detected her lustful thoughts, when he owed his very existence to the same.

She smelled the sea far from the sight of it, and she knew the instant they were on Valle del Mar land. It too was deeply wounded by the drought, but the faint green on the rolling hills looked like the Garden of Eden compared to the interior.

"We're home," she announced huskily, but her body was too dry for any tears at all.

Ramón and his sons were no less wise than Pedro, and they wanted to save the best animals as much as Tessa did. They set about the grim task of culling out inferior animals so that the finest would live. They slaughtered cattle and horses, dragging some of the carcasses to the wildest parts of the *rancho* for the predators that were left to feast on, burning others in noxious smelling pyres, throwing some into the sea because Tessa would not allow rotting carcasses to be left anywhere near where people lived. "The flies and maggots alone profit from this!" she said furiously, the sick taste of death in her mouth as it always was these days.

The only exceptions were the three special horses Tessa had brought from Rancho Magnífico—Amordoro, Diablo, and Tesoro. They would always ride fine horses, but none would ever be loved and used as much as these had been in their mutual youth. They had given faithful service, and when their replacements, well chosen by Brand and his brothers, had been fully trained, Amordoro and Diablo had been taken to the *rancho* to live out the rest of their lives in pampered laziness, joined shortly after by Indian's Tesoro. The drought had changed all that. Tessa had not been able to bear leaving them there to die and had risked them on the journey. They had all made it through, but Amordoro was failing.

She brought him the best fodder she could find and even grain from the scant supply, but at the end of the first week at Valle del Mar she knew it was useless, even before Ramón came to tell her that the horse was down.

She settled beside him on the ground and took the hard golden sculpture of his head onto her lap. One deep brown eye looked at her for a moment before the long-lashed lid closed over it, and his labored breathing grew more audible. She stroked the whorls of hair on his bony forehead, the age hollows over his eyes, and the still soft velvet of his ears. Her courage gave way and she wept, having the tears now, knowing Ramón would keep even her sons away until it was over.

A gift from Don Esteban, the link with her youth and the first day of knowing Gavin. This beast who had carried her so willingly through so many years and so many changes. He had been part of her life for over half of it. He was old, but the drought was what had finished him.

"It's all over now, Amordoro. Go from here with God on your last journey," she sobbed.

He raised his head suddenly and his legs thrashed for an instant before he settled back. Tessa heard the old stallion's challenge clearly, though there was nothing but silence.

"Gavin, Gavin come home, please, please come home! I am so weary of being alone! I love you, Gavin, I need you!"

Ramón stood guard over her private keening, knowing how much she needed to let herself go after being too strong for so long, and he was not ashamed of the tears coursing down his own leathery cheeks. And when the silence came, he put his arms around her, drew her up, and led her to María.

"Poor little one, she is so tired," he said. María helped Tessa to bed. It did not occur to either of the Ramirezes that they were old and their "little one" scarcely young any more—the need for comfort was still the same.

Tessa awakened in terror during the night. The chill was deeper this time than the last. "Hold on, Gavin, don't die. Hold on, my love, I am with you," she cried. She saw the murky light of a place webbed with trees and vines, smelled the dank swamp place. Her chest hurt so, she could hardly breathe. She staggered out of bed, and the next thing she

697

knew, she was in her mother's rose garden where the flowers bloomed because María refused to let them die and every day brought them the used water from the household.

The rose scent engulfed Tessa, but still she sensed the last trace of dark, oozing mud and rotting vegetation. She had never felt this disoriented. She knew where she was but it seemed to take forever to sort nightmare from reality. Nightmare. She did not think so. She shivered uncontrollably even as she willed herself to feel the warmth of the night.

She stayed in the garden until just before dawn, and when her sons were up, they were greeted by her announcement that she had to go back to San Francisco. They did not question her decision. Her face was set, but her eyes were wild.

"I don't even want to know why," Jeff murmured to his brothers as they prepared to leave.

"It's Gavin," Paul said quietly. "It has to be." And neither of the other two gainsaid him.

Tessa allowed no unnecessary stops, not even to see the Collinses in Monterey. The only reason to halt was when the horses were weary. They passed other riders and stages, but Tessa hardly noticed them.

She went straight to Armenthia, not even pausing to greet Fiona, Chong Sing, or Mrs. Tubbs.

Thia nodded slowly. "Word's been comin' for days now on th' telegraph. Big battle in Virginnie, in th' woods."

"And the swamp," Tessa said.

"Jus' so. Indian too. I knew like you 'fore th' wire brought th' news. But I don' know if they're dead or not. I jus' go on believin' I goin' to hold my man again."

The terrible details of the Battle of Wilderness continued to be revealed. It had begun on May 5. It had been fought near the old battlefields of Chancellorsville and Fredericksburg in woods so dense with stunted trees and underbrush it was nearly impenetrable. More often than not, the opposing forces had fought blindly, unable to see each other at all. Horses sank in the mud and thrashed in the foliage, rendering the cavalry useless and leaving only the cannon dragged by hand for heavy artillery. Forest fires broke out further endangering the troops who were fighting, burning to death the wounded who couldn't get away.

The battle had commenced when Grant had found General Lee and the Army of Northern Virginia blocking his way, and the Federal commanders who had preceded him would surely have given way, but not Grant. The savage fighting went on for days, and the Union suffered tremendous losses that were hard to defend even in light of the fact that at the end of it, Grant seemed closer to his objective of taking Richmond.

Tessa didn't care if Grant never got there and Richmond stood forever. She ceased to pay attention to the war news. She was absolutely sure Gavin and Indian were out of the fighting, had been out of it since her wilderness nightmare. And she tried to go on believing they were alive. But nothing since had been as clear as the image of trees, swamp, and pain. Nor had it been for Thia. They considered sending a telegram to the capital, using the power of the encroaching wires for their own benefit, but they could not imagine any official who would care enough in the general carnage to answer their faraway fear.

June came and there was still no word.

"I can't stay here," Tessa announced suddenly, and she was as firm in her cowardice as she had been in her courage. She made no pretense that she was needed at either of the *ranchos* now, but she was returning to Valle del Mar. She apologized to her sons for leaving them with the burden of the city enterprises. This time she offered Fiona a chance to go with her. Fiona was no fool, and she declined. She knew a retreat when she saw one, and the tenseness of her mother made her uneasy. She offered the excuse that Paul had promised to take her sometime later in the summer.

Tessa knew she could trust Chong Sing and Mrs. Tubbs to run the household, though their eyes were grave and worried over her decision. Molly could run the shop; she'd done it often enough, especially during these last months.

It was Armenthia Tessa felt the greatest guilt for leaving, but Thia understood. "Jus' got to look for him where you think you'll find him. Nothin' wrong with that long as you go on lookin'. An' I'll be fine."

Brand escorted his mother southward, and when they stopped in Monterey, he and Sam found all sorts of things to talk about so that Carmelita and Tessa could have their own chat. But there was only one subject on Tessa's mind, and Carmelita read her easily.

"Must be goddamn hard having that son of yours around," she remarked.

"Yes, it is," Tessa admitted honestly. "He looks so much like his father. Gavin was only seven years older than Brand is when I met him. Most of the time I have the sense to be thankful his image is being carried on, but then I have terrible minutes of wanting to cast a spell, almost like being willing to give up the son in exchange for the father."

Carmelita took her hand and patted it comfortingly. "Fortunately, you do not have to make that choice. I must confess, I have blessed every year of Sam's life that made him too old to go to the war.

"If you are still at Rancho Valle del Mar when word comes from Gavin, one of the boys can send a telegram here and Sam and I will make sure you get it as quickly as possible."

Tessa was infinitely grateful for Carmelita's firm "when word comes"; it sounded so much better than "if."

CHAPTER LVIII

Tessa went often to the pool. It was more than ever a symbol of her life. Even here the drought had finally taken its toll. The barest trickle of water ran into the pool now, so little it made no sound, slipping into the murky, stagnant water that gave itself up to the sun so quickly, only the tiny incoming stream kept it from drying out completely.

The pool smelled of death, yet more slimy, more shelled, and more many-legged monstrosities moved in and around the sludge than had ever inhabited the cold, clean swiftness. Tessa tried to think of it as reassuring proof of life out of death, but ugly life out of ugly death was more apt.

And still she came because day by day she had trained her will to see the pool as it had been when the earth was green, water flowed, and Gavin loved Tessa.

July now and soon August. Heat and endless sun and no word.

She closed her eyes and wished the heat drowse would take her into the blank stupor she could see in the thin horses all over the *rancho*. They had shot ten more this week. Ten of the finest, because only the best were left now.

Her mind jumped and would not settle. She felt vaguely uneasy at first, and then the feeling grew stronger. She sat up, listening intently. Insects, no more than that. Then the whinny of a horse. El Rayo being answered. A long wait until the shuffling on the path. If it were Ramón or any of the *vaqueros*, he would call out to her.

She stood up, her rifle ready.

She was not overly alarmed by the figure of the man who came over the rise. She was only angry because some stranger had found her last sanctuary. He was moving at such a slow, fragile pace, she reckoned him to be an old man and no match for her. There were still mountain men and trappers left, though they were as rare as the animals they had once hunted in plenty before their world had passed away. They were odd, old men. This one carried no rifle, and if he reached for a sidearm or a knife, she would . . .

The breath left her lungs as if she'd been kicked, and her heart slammed into her ribs so hard, she dropped the rifle. His name was no more than a gasp as he said hers in the same moment.

He stood staring at her. The strength poured back into her limbs, and she ran. "Gavin, my love, oh, Gavin, Gavin!" She couldn't stop saying his name, but other words screamed in her head. "Dear God, he is old, old and weary, and weak. So little is left of the man I knew!"

Even when his arms came around her, it was not the same, not as strong, but when his mouth came down on hers, it was more than memory of the essential and desire shot through her from the hard, demanding kisses, her mouth opening to his searching tongue. She wanted him to take her right here, right now. Over three years without

701

him, it was an eternity, and the fire was in flame again. But he broke the kiss and had to lean against her, he was trembling so violently and struggling for breath. Her hands moved of their own frantic desire to affirm his existence, finding hollows and bones that had turned him from a lean man into an emaciated one, feeling him flinch when she touched his right side, sensing the clammy fever sheen on his skin. The sickly gray showed even through his tan, his eyes were murky blue, and her lust died as abruptly as it had risen, tenderness flooding through her, filling her eyes with tears.

"Don't weep, Tessa," he said low, and she knew he was having trouble controlling his own emotions. "Christ! I've been crazy to find you, went to the city first and you weren't there." His voice stopped abruptly as it grew too ragged for him to control.

She would never know everything he was feeling, but she heard the same kind of panic she had heard in the children's voices when they were small. "Mama, I couldn't find you!" terrified reproach for an empty universe. But so much worse for this man who had been so self-sufficient.

She had been his goal, his reason for staying alive. The closer they had gotten to California, the more frantic he had become to see her, to touch her, waking up at night in a cold sweat for fear it would not be accomplished. Now it was done. He put his arms around her again with an inarticulate cry.

She knew there were changes in herself too, and wondered if he had seen them. She had been fined down, hardened by these months, and the drought caused aging to show no matter what you did. Her hair was dry and fly-away, her skin rough. She almost laughed. Her vanity had come back with him. He was so ill he could barely stand upright, and she was wondering if she could still spark desire in him on the clear sight.

She pulled away. "Come, we must go home. A clean, soft bed and María's cooking awaits you." She said it so easily, he knew it was natural for her, but it gave him a strange feeling. So this was home now, home again. Perhaps he had always known it despite her protests. He was too weary to puzzle it out. He felt her tension even before she asked the abrupt question, "Indian, did he come back with you? Is he all right?"

He swallowed hard, cursing the waves of weakness which seemed to make his emotions so quick and exposed that he wanted to weep as she had. "He's alive, and we came home together. And he is as well as a man can be who has only one arm left to hold his woman."

She gazed at him, her eyes swimming in tears again, so deep a violet he saw his night fantasies of their color had been less, not more than the truth. Her chin came up, and her voice was steady. "It won't make any difference. Armenthia has two strong arms to hold him."

He knew what she was saying. She too had the strength to hold him, strength that had grown with the tasks she had had to perform in his absence. He accepted his need for her strength and acknowledged it by putting his arm around her shoulders, leaning heavily, murmuring, "The bed sounds best of all."

She supported him down the path and helped him mount his horse, one from the *rancho* where he had left his own weary mount to rest. That focused her thoughts immediately on the practical. Obviously everyone at the *rancho* knew he was home, and that would mean plans for talk and celebration. But there was going to be none of that; she had to see that he was not troubled, no matter how well-meaning the people were. She could see him growing weaker by the minute. If she had her way, she would make him stop right now and she would come back with Ramón, Juan, and Julio and a cart, but she could not do that to his pride and the last of his will. She could not avoid *déjà vu* —that first day twenty years ago she had brought the man she had nearly killed home. Twenty years ago, a lifetime. A small wave of comfort stole through her. She had saved him then, she would again.

She had managed for three years without him, but it didn't matter, life was untenable without him.

She made her voice falsely strong and cheerful whenever she saw him sway in the saddle. "I've just realized," she said at one point. "You must have seen all the children."

He straightened his spine and turned his head, focusing on her with effort. "Yes, I saw them all. They insisted that

703

one ride with me and delegated Jefferson. He's at the house." He managed a small grin, "They've all grown quite out of mind. It was all I could do not to tell them I remembered them when they were knee high to a grasshopper."

Her reply was soft, warm, and without bitterness. "They have indeed grown up; they were all a marvelous comfort while you were gone and a great help besides." She thought of how kind and right it had been for Jefferson to let his father go without him to her, recognizing need over sense.

But by the time they reached home, Tessa had given up all pretense of conversation, because Gavin was no longer capable of answering.

"Hold on, love, hold on, we're almost there, just a little more." She wondered how long she'd been saying that when the life and noise of the *rancho* suddenly engulfed them. There was, after all, no need to make excuses, just Gavin slipping down from the saddle into Jefferson's strong, young arms, Jefferson ignoring his father's mumbled protests and accepting Julio's help to carry him in. Tessa led the way briskly to cover the swell of emotion she felt at the sight of Jefferson holding his father.

She and María undressed him, María's struggle with tears making it easier for Tessa to control her own. She was used to his scarred back and had forgotten that María did not know about the lash marks until she heard her gasp. "Luis, a long time past," she said shortly, but her own calm faltered when she saw the reason he had flinched when she pressed his side. Where the ribs should still curve outward there was a cavity, an ugly, badly healed wound of smashed bone and muscle as if he had been battered with a club across his ribs and part of his chest. The discoloration was ominous; the heat from the infection tangible.

He opened his eyes when she touched him, and saw María's tears spilling over. "Poor María, just like the first time, yes? More trouble for you." He spoke in Spanish, trying to make her smile, but it was too much for her, and she hid her face in her apron to smother a sob before she regained control.

As gentle as she was being, when Tessa touched another spot, his body stiffened. "I need to know what did this."

704

His eyebrow went up. "The Confederate army, with the help of an exploding shell. An army surgeon did his best, but he didn't have enviable working conditions. Please, sweetheart, don't look so scared. I've come all this way back to you, I haven't any intention of leaving again just yet." She could hear the effort the words cost him.

She knew then how rigid her face had been, and she tried to relax, but already his eyes were closed again, and she had to resist her impulse to shake him awake because he looked so still and dead.

Instead she gave herself a mental shake and went into action. She found Jefferson and the others anxiously awaiting news, and she did not dissemble.

"Jeff, your father is ill, very ill. He has a chest wound that must still have metal and bone fragments embedded in it. There's infection and fever, and he's very weak."

"We never should have let him make the journey, but he didn't even want any message sent. He wanted to surprise you. He hardly said a thing all the way here—just did his best to hang on," Jeff said miserably.

Tessa smiled bleakly. "You had no choice in the matter. I'm just glad you rode with him. This was something he had to do, and his problems have not been caused by the last lap of his journey, but by all of it and the war together. The only thing we have to concern ourselves with now is making him well again. María and I are quite competent about the sicknesses we know, even about gunshot wounds, but this is something beyond our ken. We will do our best, but I want you to ride to Monterey, ask Carmelita if there is a really good doctor she would trust to help us, and if there is not, telegraph John Harland. He can come by stage to Monterey and then you can bring him back with you. Take as many men and extra horses as you need. Go as fast as you can, but do not kill yourself; that would not help your father or me."

He bent from the height that was equal to his father's now and kissed her cheek. "Don't worry. He came all this way just to be with you. He'll be all right."

"That is what he told me. With both of you saying it, I must believe it. *Vaya con Dios*, Jefferson."

Tessa was devoutly thankful she had María to help her nurse Gavin; without the old woman's advice and assistance, she would have doubted she was doing the right thing, because for days Gavin got worse, not better. He had used all his strength to come home before he collapsed, and he had precious little left to fight with. The burning waves of fever made him so falsely strong in delirium, they had to tie him down to prevent him from injuring himself while his pain-racked voice conjured horrific battlefields with blood, bodies, and loss everywhere. Tessa shuddered and sobbed when his raving voice kept pleading with Indian to stay alive. The disjointed phrases gave all too clear a picture. They had been together when they were both hit, and they had lain for hours in the mud before they received any medical attention. "God, oh, Jesus, I'm all right, but you can't take his arm off without giving him something, the pain will kill him! Indian, God damn it, Indian—don't die!"

And he called to her constantly, not even believing she was there or knowing where he was when his eyes recognized her for brief interludes, his fevered brain sure she was his familiar phantom of the battlefield. She held onto him, murmuring reassurances until her voice was hoarse, praying some part of him would understand she was with him.

She and María soon realized that the cycle of fever and chills, while made worse by the septic wounds, was a thing apart, malaria or some other disease, God only knew. The stuporous chills were worse than the fever, for then Gavin lay still, his only movement the involuntary trembling rippling through his body. His eyes were closed and sunken in bruised sockets, his face so thin his cheekbones were cast in high relief; and his skin was the color of lead. There were heavy strands of gray at his temples now, and near one temple ran the scar of the bullet that had nearly killed him at Gettysburg.

They made his life even more miserable with the hot poultices they strapped to his injured side and chest. His body twisted and strained, trying to escape the blistering heat, and when his hands were freed even for an instant, he clawed at the wrappings. But they had no choice; they had to do their best to bring the poison out rather than to let it filter ever deeper into his body. And Tessa did not even think it odd to find beauty in two ugly swellings that she lanced, finding small, sharp shards of metal in the putrid effusion. And as she cleansed the wounds with strong spirits, Gavin's eyes opened, and she knew he was lucid for the first time since he had gone into the fever cycle.

"I'm sorry, darling, I know I'm hurting you, almost finished." She could hardly speak above a whisper for fear her voice would fail her, but he heard her and croaked, "Feel better," before he drifted away again.

She held to that memory all through the next days. Carmelita and Sam arrived to confirm her fear that Jefferson had had to send for Dr. Harland. "Oh, my dear, I'm so sorry, but Sam and I just don't know anyone we'd trust to handle this. We're too healthy to have done much testing of our local medicos."

Carmelita made no comment at all about the obvious fact that she and Sam had left their home and business to come and offer their assistance to the Ramsays, and Tessa's throat closed when she tried to thank them. All she could do was hug first one, then the other wordlessly.

Carmelita had been there for a day before she asked hesitantly, "My friend, Indian?" and Tessa managed to give her the few hard facts she knew. Carmelita closed her eyes for a moment before she said very quietly, "But he is alive." And she was suddenly very brisk with Tessa. "You look dreadful and soon you will be no use to Gavin at all. Now that I am here you will rest at least a little."

Tessa could not bear to be away from Gavin for more than short periods of time, but she found she was able to sleep deeply during these brief spells because she trusted Carmelita to share the burden with María. The former proved herself competent and strong-stomached in the duties of nursing the sick man.

If Gavin did not seem much improved, at least his condition no longer seemed to worsen, but no arrival could have been greeted with more joyous relief than John Harland's when he rode in with Jefferson and Brand, who had insisted on coming down with him. "Paul was crazy to come too, but he's sticking it out in the city to keep everything running and Fiona out of your hair," Brand explained.

Tessa's control slipped so that all she could do was sob, making her description of Gavin's condition unintelligible.

707

John put his arm around her and held her comfortingly while Carmelita explained the situation.

John's presence had a steadying effect on everyone. While he agreed that Gavin's condition was grave, he praised the women for what they'd done so far and agreed with their diagnosis of a separate fever. "Battlefields, and worse, field hospitals are always fraught with epidemics and fevers. I don't think he has malaria, some of the symptoms are missing, but he has a cyclical fever very like it, and the best we can do is keep him warm and as comfortable as possible. The greatest dangers are the infection and his general debility now, but even so, he has always been a strong, healthy man, and he has a great deal to live for. That gives him an enormous advantage."

Even María approved of the doctor and was glad to relinquish her responsibility to him, especially when she saw the skill of his blade in cleaning out one of the worst patches. He had never held with the bleeding and purging so many practiced, and María believed it only further weakened the sick.

Gavin started to improve subtly after that. Restraint was no longer necessary because he was resting so much more peacefully, though John warned there would be ups and downs and the fever might plague him intermittently for the rest of his life. But nothing could lessen Tessa's joy when Gavin opened his eyes and recognized her and where he was for the first day since he had told her he felt better. This time he did not fade out of consciousness again, but came quickly back to full alertness even after he'd been sleeping.

"Welcome back, *mi vida*," Tessa said softly, and Gavin smiled. She leaned down to kiss him and then buried her face against his neck, her tears warm against his skin. "I always cry when there is every reason not to," she choked.

"I know," he whispered, and he turned his head so that his mouth rested in gentle benediction against her cheek.

He spoke little of the war, but he often muttered and moved restlessly while he slept. Tessa was sure the day would come when he would need to talk about it openly. She dreaded it and did not press him. But at least she understood now why he and Indian had come back to California with no warning. Stunned, their wounds far from healed, and completely against doctor's orders though they had been honorably discharged, they had had one desire, and that was to go home. But they both had their doubts they would make it. The task had become the world. By train part of the way, by jarring stagecoach the rest, to survive became all.

Tessa panicked sometimes when she realized how separate their lives of the past years had been, making the memories of one alien to the other. Gavin had had no idea of the devastation of the drought, and he was stunned by the decisions Tessa had had to make, the horses that had been destroyed. He was further shocked when he asked after people in San Francisco, including Belle. "Has she decided she can allow respectable friendships again?" he asked, but his smile faded at Tessa's expression.

"She died of pneumonia two years ago. She and Charles are buried side by side."

"Why didn't you tell me all of this?" he demanded angrily.

"Why didn't you write the truth to me?" she returned calmly.

"You're right, of course," he said, his anger gone. "I have something to give you which I wish I didn't have. It's been bothering me, but I realize there won't ever be a good time."

She got the leather pouch from his belongings as he asked and gave it to him. He drew something out and handed it to her.

She stared at it with a puzzled frown. It was a faded piece of purple velvet. "I don't understand."

"Jordan Ames gave it to me. He died at Gettysburg a couple of days before I was hit. I saw him go down and I went looking for him when the fighting had quieted down for the night. He was still alive, but he knew he was dying. He'd been taken to one of the field hospitals, but the doctors couldn't do anything for him, and they couldn't even find shelter for him in one of the tents: War makes the world so small and the familiar so precious. When I saw that silvery hair like Fiona's I knew without doubt it was him. He was honestly glad to see me, and I wept like a baby when he died. He wasn't fully conscious most of the time, but I told him about Fiona and he understood. I
709

didn't tell him about her leg, only that she was a beautiful child who looked like him and like you, and that we love her very much. Jordan was still Jordan for a moment, his mind grasping all the ironies. He said what would otherwise have been an unbearable burden of guilt became a miracle of his own life going on even as he died. He gave me the velvet to give you, wanted you to know he had carried it always. He never married. He sent you his love. He thanked me, and he died." There was nothing but the deepest grief in Gavin's voice.

The lovely robe she had worn in Jordan's rooms, the memory of it in an old scrap of velvet.

"Poor Jordan," she said softly when she could trust her voice. "What a dreadful choice for him, but I am glad he chose the Union."

Gavin's eyes held hers. "He was a good man, and you must never think that because he left San Francisco because of you that that had anything to do with his dying at Gettysburg. The choice was made for him long before the war began, just as it was for Indian and me."

"You are very kind," Tessa said, and she held his hand against her cheek.

CHAPTER LIX

Tessa had so longed for the crisis of Gavin's illness to pass, she had been thinking of nothing else, and so the new and total confusion in the pattern of her life came as a shock. She had kept the many facets of their empire under control in his absence, but now the chain of command was in doubt. She did not want to overburden him with business affairs until he was fully recovered, but he was restless, fretful, and determined to ignore the terrible weakness that overwhelmed him so frequently. He was not always kind. He felt helpless, and worse, old for the first time in his life, and the unfamiliar fear made him bad-tempered, the brunt most often falling on Tessa because she was so constantly with him.

While Gavin was still very ill, Brand had gone back to the city and Paul had arrived, bringing Fiona with him. "I don't think I could have held out much longer without seeing him," Paul admitted. "Indian said he'd been having severe attacks of fever ever since he was wounded. And he looked so ill when I saw him. I should have——"

Tessa cut him off, reminding him as she had the others that there was nothing they could have done to prevent Gavin from going his own way. She changed the subject back to Indian, asking how he was doing, still unable to accept his mutilation.

Paul saw the horror in her expression, and he shook his head. "Mother, it isn't like that. Oh, it would be better if it had never happened, but you mustn't fret about him. Indian is—well, Indian. When I left he was devising a system for carving wood with only one hand, said he was training his knees to work like fingers and hold the wood. He was lucky, and he knows it. He didn't get the fever like Gavin and the amputation healed cleanly without infection, which is a wonder. He was just damn glad to get back to Armenthia and their children. You know they both send love. If Thia had not put her foot down and insisted that he needed rest even if he is the strongest one-armed man on earth, they would have come with us."

Tessa had been cheered and strengthened by the presence of the children during the dark hours, but now their presence added complications, and it was easy to see it was all part of the same new pattern. They had grown and matured so much in Gavin's absence, both he and they were uneasy about their new roles. Only Fiona could still be considered a child at all, and even she was more responsible than her years would warrant. Gavin objected to the fact that Paul had brought Fiona alone from San Francisco, and though Paul explained quietly that he had taken very good care of his little sister, Tessa could see the hurt in his eyes because the man he worshiped had so little trust in his abilities. And it was the same with Brand and Jefferson; Gavin questioned everything they had done with the mill and the wharf, the warehouse, the Golden Horse, and the land, until both young men were looking as cold-eyed and tight-jawed as their father.

She tried to explain before she sent them back to the

city, but Brand, in one of his rare displays of affection, hugged her and said, "It's all right, Mother, we understand. We've talked about it. He's not well, and he hates that, and it makes it harder to find us wielding the power that used to be his. After all, we're pretty much strangers to him now. It'll work out when we've all had time to adjust and to get reacquainted."

Gavin was disagreeable about this turn of events too, especially about Fiona, and Tessa's frayed temper snapped. "Fiona is perfectly safe in the care of her brothers, and she'll be much better off in the city now with her friends and with Chong Sing and Mrs. Tubbs to look after her. And I'm going out riding right this instant before I say something I shouldn't."

"You do that," Gavin snapped back. "You've become even more a hoyden than when I first met you. You look like a goddamn scarecrow."

She stood frozen for an instant, and then she was gone, running, not hearing him call her back. He stood up to go after her and cursed the swimming world as he sank down in the chair again, cold sweat beading his skin.

Tessa wished desperately that Sam, Carmelita, and John had not returned to their respective homes. She hated herself for the thought, but she wanted one of them here, any one of them, to hold her and tell her it would be all right, someone who wasn't as close and hurt by all of it as María was. John had warned her that if she didn't start getting more rest and taking better care of herself, she wasn't going to be much better off than Gavin, and now Gavin's words confirmed it and hurt most of all. She did look like a scarecrow, hair and skin dry, body so bony she might have been a boy instead of a middle-aged woman with children. Not a soft curve left to attract her husband, not much softness left inside either after having to deal in a man's world without his support for over three years.

She cried until she felt ill, and then she spent the rest of the time by the pool, trying not to cry any more so she could go home without the telltale traces.

She avoided María and kept her face turned from Gavin when she went to check on him on her return, but he was not fooled. "Come here, *querida*," he said gently, and she hesitated only briefly before she went and curled up
712

wearily in his lap, taking care not to lean against his still tender side.

His hand stroked her hair, and his voice was contrite. "I'm so sorry. I didn't mean to go at you like that. I've been a miserable bastard ever since I got home. I can't even stand to live with myself. I wouldn't blame you if you wished me back in the war."

"Never that!" she said, clinging to him, but then her voice quavered. "I *do* look like a scarecrow. I've never looked worse in my life. It didn't matter when you were gone, but it matters now." She tried to stifle a sob, but it came out anyway, a pathetic hiccoughing sound that twisted his heart.

"I said the meanest thing I could think of, but it isn't true. You're the most beautiful woman I've ever known, the only woman for me. I'll never cease to bless the strange fate that brought me to you."

"A strange fate named Don Esteban," she murmured, relaxing against him, comforted even while she accepted the sadness. They were clinging to each other as though they were lost children, the survivors of a terrible disaster, stunned and unsure of what to do next. She mourned the loss of the lovers, and wondered if their time would ever come again. She thought she understood how Gavin felt, because at this moment she was too tired to even imagine they would ever have the energy to make love again.

It was worse when they returned to the city. She knew it was far too early for Gavin to make the journey and knew as well that he would not be gainsaid, so she spent the whole time on nervous edge watching him covertly for signs of another collapse. Even when they stopped for the night, she could not sleep deeply, because she had discovered that when nightmares of the war came, if she began to speak to him calmly as soon as the restless moving and whimpering began, he would sink back into peaceful sleep. Even having him in bed beside her, something she had longed for for so long, had turned out to be one more thing requiring adjustment. She awakened at his slightest movement and had nearly screamed aloud a few times when she had been startled by the touch of his flesh on hers because she had grown so accustomed to sleeping alone.

On the night they stayed with Carmelita and Sam on their way north, Carmelita maneuvered her aside and asked bluntly, "Is there anything I can do?" Her expression said plainer than words what she thought of Tessa's state.

"No, my dear, you and Sam have already done so much for us. Don't worry, Gavin's gone through a hard time, and he's been gone so long, it's just taking us a while to put the pieces back together again."

"Take care you don't break too," Carmelita warned, but then she let it drop, frustrated and distressed because she knew she couldn't help her friends any more than she could stop worrying about them.

The city clutched at them from the moment they arrived. There were some merchandise problems at the shop that needed Tessa's attention because a good deal of money was involved. The lumbermill was still in trouble due to the drought, but business at the warehouse was good, gold was still coming in steadily from the Browns in Grass Valley, and the Golden Horse ran smoothly and was one of the more popular saloons in town. Even when loosened restrictions would have allowed them to open gaming tables again, they had decided not to. The laws changed too quickly. However, there was never any lack of private games in the back, often presided over by Mr. Peniston for old times' sake, and the house took its share.

Much of the credit for how well things were going belonged to the boys, but there were always decisions to be made, and Tessa's sons often deferred to her, not only out of habit but because now they did not want to clash with Gavin. She sorted everything through, trying to give Gavin enough to do without overtiring him with myriad small problems.

Indian's determined attitude to his handicap and the countless signs of his joy at being with Armenthia again did much to ease Tessa's initial horror of the maiming of his great strong body. His directness helped too.

"Ain't nothin' Thia cain't do without," he said. "so I ain't goin' fret. Other things. if I lost 'em back there, she'd not take me back. Head, heart, an' a few more." It had
714

been wonderful to laugh with him and Thia. It was not so easy with Gavin.

Finally one night he said, "This edited version of our enterprises is interesting, but I'd prefer the standard text if you don't mind. I'm quite well—you needn't coddle me any longer."

His voice was kind; his eyebrow was up, and a small smile curved his mouth. He was in fact acknowledging what she'd done, paying tribute, and taking the burden back in the same breath. Indeed, he did look much improved and had even begun to gain back weight. She just didn't know; she felt less and less able to cope. Among the squads of visitors they had had since their return, John Harland had come frequently and had professed himself very pleased with Gavin's recovery, far less pleased with the look of her. She had shrugged off his concern, but now she suspected his dire predictions might prove accurate. She felt terrible.

But her voice was sweet and even as she got up and handed him the ledger she'd been working on. "I'm relieved to hear how well you are, my love, because now I can hand this over to you. As if there aren't enough problems at the mill as it is, the raw lumber coming in and the board feet going out are just enough off to be driving me mad. I'm only too pleased to leave you with the problem while I take myself off to bed." She kissed him lightly and headed for the door. His voice stopped her, sharp and anxious, "Tessa, are you all right?"

"Absolutely fine, just tired," she assured him and blew him another kiss before she slipped out of the room and up the stairs. She almost believed it herself except for the strange feeling she had of her body floating away at odd intervals. She almost gave in and called Mrs. Tubbs to help her undress, but then she set her teeth and did it herself, her hands shaking as she worked at the hooks.

She was curled tight and sound asleep when Gavin came to bed. He regarded her intently for a moment, but she did not stir, not even when he slipped into bed beside her. He had a boyish impulse to wake her and tell her of his triumph in solving the faulty mill accounting, that was not faulty at all if one had the luck to find the minuscule but precise

715

note left by Paul which in translation read: "Purchased this load from T. Bennet, admits much dead and less than sound but good price will give profit even low yield plus other use. Lucky to get it at all."

Gavin tapped her shoulder lightly, unable to resist, but he got no response. He knew she was very tired, had good reason to be, and had even admitted she was, but still he slept uneasily. The only times when she had slept so completely apart, so curled in on herself, had been in times of deep crisis. He wondered if it was because they had not been lovers since he came home. He was willing to accept full blame for that. Desire had begun to quicken his blood again lately, and he was profoundly grateful. In the morning he would talk to Tessa honestly about it.

But in the morning, all pretense had vanished. Tessa's normal early hour for rising came, and an hour later she had still not awakened. Gavin bent over her, unable to wait any longer. "Darling, are you all right? It's growing late."

He saw her then, more clearly than he had since the day he had ended his quest by the pool. He had come home to what he knew and had refused to see anything else until now. His cruel taunt of scarecrow was horribly apt. The disguise of her spirit was lost in sleep, and the truth showed. She was as bruised-eyed and hollowed as the dirt farmers' wives he had seen in the South.

When Tessa opened her eyes, she saw tears on Gavin's cheeks. "I'm sorry," she whispered. "I don't know what's wrong, but I can't get up. Maybe in an hour or so." She closed her eyes again, and he touched her forehead, feeling faint heat, enough to indicate a fever but nothing catastrophic. When he found her pulse, it was light and racing. He was appalled by her mysterious symptoms and could not send for Dr. Harland fast enough.

It seemed a very short space to her, but the next time she identified the face hanging over her, it was John's. "I don't expect this is social. Am I sick?"

"I hope your sense of humor never fails," John said, smiling, though his eyes were grave, and she saw Gavin standing behind him. "You're the best judge of whether you're sick or not, but I rather suspect you are. Can you give me any useful hints?"

716

"I'm not sure," she murmured. "I feel decidedly odd. My joints ache as if I've been riding a bad horse, but I know I have not. I don't raise bad horses. Most of all, I just feel as if my body is trying to float away from the rest of me. If you could convince it all to go back together again, I think the problem would be solved." She was trying to reassure them, but the slow slurring of her words was totally unlike her normal way of speaking.

"She has a fever, and it seems to be affecting not only her joints but her heart and just about everything else," John said later to Gavin. "You needn't look so guilty; it's not the one you brought back with you, and I think it's only a complication of her major problem. She's exhausted, absolutely worn out to the point that while she'd like to go on at her normal fast pace, her body is refusing." He sighed in frustration. "There's nothing I know to do except ask that she has complete rest and no worries, and we'll see how she does. Can you manage that for her?"

"I certainly can." The determined note in his voice was enough to make John sure no one was going to get a chance to bother Tessa.

The aching came and went and was bearable, even welcome proof that she was still living in her body. That was the worst feeling, the sensation of living on the fringes of herself. She had never known anything quite like it, the fearful lassitude and weakness that made even lifting her head require enormous concentration and effort and made her heart pound wildly. She felt as if she had never been young and strong.

It took her some days before she realized that what she had lost, Gavin had gained. He was totally in command again. He moved with renewed sureness, not hunching over his battered chest any more. His face looked years younger. His voice was calm and authoritative. He seemed perfectly able to cope with the children and business and still spend hours with her.

She knew his body and his soul would carry the scars of the terrible war forever, but now when she looked at him, she found his eyes clear deep blue without shadows, without the terrible inward-looking blankness she had seen before—eyes filled with his overwhelming concern for her.

"You didn't know you married such a quitter, did you?"

717

she asked once, awakening to find him reading beside the bed.

"Don't say nasty things about my wife, ma'am," he teased. "I won't listen, especially when they're lies." His face sobered. "God, what a long war it's been, for both of us."

"For the land too. I wonder if it will ever truly rain again," she said sadly.

"It will, sweetheart. Someday we'll be up to our necks in mud again, cursing the rain." But he wondered; there had not been beneficent rain in California for over two years, an incredible time for the earth to go without nourishment. The more he learned about the drought and the terrible hardship it was wreaking on the farmers and ranchers, the more impressed he was by what Tessa had been able to save of their herds.

Though he had proposed sleeping elsewhere for fear of disturbing her, Tessa had refused the suggestion, thinking of readjusting yet again to an empty bed after just getting used to him once more, assuring him it was the best medicine in the world to have him with her, and so he slept beside her, often holding her all through the night. And finally one night, he smiled in the darkness at his discovery that he could feel the soft curves again covering the fine bones which had been so painfully obvious. The changes were apparent in other ways too. Now she moved of her own accord to settle herself comfortably against him, no longer trapped by the dreadful lethargy that had made her as limp as a rag doll. New color in her cheeks, new brightness in her eyes, and the beginnings of restlessness. She wanted to see more of the children, and when Jefferson came to visit her, he told her it was about time the Chinese dragon was chained.

Tessa giggled, surprising even herself with the sound. "Poor Chong Sing, I expect you've all been driving him mad."

"We've tried, but you know him, nobody drives Chong Sing to anything or anywhere. 'Velly solly, Misee Lamsay need velly quiet, you not velly quiet.' It's been his standard line, velly much more Chinese than his usual style." Jeff was beaming at her but when he stooped suddenly to kiss her, his voice was as uneven as if he were going through
718

adolescence again. "Lord, Mother, you scared us to death! Good thing I'm already grown, a fright like that could stunt a man's growth for sure!"

Brand and Paul brought her a huge bouquet of hot-house flowers. "Fit for the toast of the town," Brand proclaimed, his eyes gleaming with mischief and looking very like Gavin's. "And don't ask how I know about such things. Mothers must be protected," he added piously. Tessa was far more pleased by the fact that he and Paul continued to show that they had finally grown to not only toleration of each other but genuine liking than she was by the transitory beauty of the flowers.

Fiona brought herself and a new book Gavin had helped her select. "He helped me pay for it too," she declared with her usual directness. "My, you do look better, Mama. You weren't pretty at all for a while."

Tessa fell asleep with her mouth still curved in amusement. When she awakened again, she blinked and said, "Honestly, Carmelita, you and Sam have been making a full-time job out of taking care of the Ramsays lately. You'll have to sell the store to pay your travel expenses."

"The store is doing very well, thank you. I'm using you as an excuse to get my good Sam to spend some time in the city. Monterey is as lovely as can be, but damn quiet. As a matter of fact I've got a little plan concerning just that fact, but you'll have to be up and about before I tell you."

"What very special friends you are," Tessa said, causing Carmelita to tut-tut and become overly busy with rearranging pillows and straightening books. And later when she asked Gavin about it, she learned that Carmelita had sent word that she and Sam were worried about her just after she had fallen ill, and they had kept in touch since, not coming until Gavin thought Carmelita could be of use as company.

"I wonder how she knew so precisely?" Tessa mused, and Gavin said, "Love makes it easy to know," as if it were an ordinary occurrence. That he should say such a thing so matter-of-factly was even more interesting than Carmelita's near magic sense, and Tessa hoped she'd find out someday how he knew.

All sorts of things stirred her interest once more, and

719

her first tottering moments out of bed stretched to longer and stronger spaces until she felt human again, capable of spending the day doing more than sleeping. She had never thought to feel such triumph in such a mundane accomplishment, but she knew Gavin understood without words, because he had felt the same. They shared now more than ever the knowledge of how frail the tie was between flesh and spirit, how terrifyingly simple it was to lose even the best-loved other in one's life. She and Gavin were perhaps twice cursed because neither of them had any real belief in a life after and beyond the flesh. She would be quite willing to go if the place were tailored more to her liking, if they were still allowed to . . .

With a guilty start, she looked up, feeling Gavin's eyes on her. She also felt the blush spreading warm on her skin.

"That's a thought I'd pay well for," he chuckled.

"Well, you can't buy it. I'm ashamed of it myself." She laughed with him and found it natural to go to him, standing behind him to knead the sinews of his neck. He gave a little murmur of pleasure and dropped his head forward lazily. *How separate are the beauties in the one I love,* she thought, *all part of the same, but oh, so very separate: this strong sculpture of his neck and the thick, so soft texture of his black hair and the coarser strands of silver at the temples, the cheekbones I can't see now and can see anyway forever, and the little white scar of the lonely child, part of him which will always pull at my heart, his long lean flanks and the hard strength of his manhood which will stir my blood, invade my body, and possess my soul for as long as I live.*

A smile he couldn't see curved her mouth. *So it begins again, the first spark, and soon, surely soon, the leaping flames. I wonder if he feels it from my hands. I think he does, but he knows, I know, that we are beginning, really beginning again, like any courting couple, finding the first pattern. Surely we will find it.*

The sudden fear stilled her hands, and silence filled the room except for the separate life of the fire.

Gavin pulled her around, and she sank down against him, content just to feel the hard muscled reality of his body against her own. *Surely we will find it.*

The next day, Carmelita, smiling a cat's cream smile

for sensing the change, proposed her plan to Tessa. Except as Gavin said when he heard, it was not so much a suggestion as marching orders.

"Sam and I have decided that you and Gavin, just the two of you, must go to Monterey for a short visit. You will use our house, and we will continue here." She saw the protest rising in Tessa. "Your businesses, every one of them, can do without you both for a short time; if they cannot, they aren't very well managed. I don't think your very capable sons would like to hear that. And as their adopted aunt and uncle, Sam and I get along fine with the children and have far too little opportunity to be with them. I know Mrs. Tubbs will approve, and I can work out some kind of peace treaty with Chong Sing. Look you, this is terribly important. You and Gavin haven't had anything but illness and people all around you since he came home; you haven't had any chance to be alone together. There isn't any use in being married, is there, if you forget what that's like?" she finished softly.

Tessa's hands twisted nervously in her lap, and she fought desperately against the sudden threat of tears. "Carmelita, I would like to say you are wrong, but it's so obvious, isn't it? We are coming close again, we truly are, but I think we're both afraid that it won't ever be the same again, afraid to really find out that it is going to be different, less from now on."

"Mother of God!" Carmelita exploded. "I knew it was bad, but not like this! Fools, both of you. What you and Gavin have cannot be broken and thrown away like that. Not years or children or even war end such love. We should all be dead of despair at birth if it were so. You are both frightened and tired from bearing so much without each other. It is time you learn again why you married." She swept her hand in a gesture which encompassed the house, the children, and all the symbols of wealth. "It was not for any of this, was it?"

"No, it was not," Tessa conceded softly.

CHAPTER LX

They arrived in Monterey to find the Collins house neat and welcoming; surely evidence of preplanning. Gavin had proposed they travel by stagecoach, something Tessa had never done, but after hearing Carmelita's description of the dusty, jarring ride she and Sam had endured going north, Tessa had no desire to share the experience, and she was still too much a Californio to think it anything but odd to travel without one's own fine horses.

They had taken their time and had avoided other travelers and their stopping places. They had talked surprisingly little, but neither of them felt the lack. They were communicating in other ways, remembering other journeys, hoping the path back to each other was still open.

The great sadness they could not ignore was the blight on the land and the fear that rain would not fall again this year. They were into the season now, and it had not come, But on the afternoon they arrived in Monterey, there was at least a smudging of clouds on the rim of the sea.

Tessa prepared an ample dinner with a good deal of help from Gavin. "Indian and I earned a pretty fair reputation for our campfire fare, but then anything would be better than what army cooks produce," he joked.

"While your skills were improving, mine were disappearing. Chong Sing doesn't like to share his kitchen," Tessa returned with a smile. It was good to hear him speak so easily of the army, up to now a nearly unmentionable subject and certainly no jest. The rest would come soon she was sure. She felt a renewed intimacy with him, and she blessed Carmelita for her wisdom. It was true; they had needed so badly to be alone. And if their new way was to be indeed different and less passionate than the old, this was the time to learn and accept it.

Neither of them pressed the issue because neither wanted to demand too much of the other. And despite the

722

leisurely pace of the trip, they were both tired enough to succumb easily to the softness of a real bed.

But a few hours later, Tessa awakened with a gasp of terror, her heart pounding painfully. She reached for Gavin, recognizing the answer even as she asked, "What is it?"

She sprang from the bed and ran to the open window, still not quite believing it. But then her voice rang out. "It's raining, raining hard! Gavin, the drought is broken!"

He came to stand behind her, pulling her against him, wrapping his arms around her, feeling what she was feeling, filled with pleasure near pain because the healing of the earth was beginning at last after more than thirty months without measurable rain.

She laughed aloud, whirling out of his arms only to grab his hand and pull him with her. The night had begun warmly, and neither wore anything, but Tessa just laughed harder at Gavin's sputtering protests. "I do not care what the neighbors think! They are not our neighbors, and they can't see into the patio anyway."

They stood outside in the downpour, overwhelmed by the roaring power of the storm, the slashes of lightning and the explosion of thunder, the huge masses of clouds boiling with the wind from the sea, surely enough to move inland. The rain fell on the dry earth and the rich smell of the new dampness was the sweetest of perfumes.

Tessa's emotions swung around as swiftly as the clouds had come in from the sea. "What a long, long time it has been!" she murmured brokenly, and Gavin knew she was not only speaking of the land, but of their personal struggle to find the mutual space of loving they had once known. The most deadly thing of all had been the growing conviction in both of them that what they had been through, and simply growing older, had taken away their ability to feel as they once had with each other. The falsehood was exposed now in the excitement flowing through both of them, in their mutual perception of the storm and each other, neither knowing where one's senses ended and the other's began.

Gavin sought her mouth hungrily, and she trembled with the exquisite shocks rippling through her as he ran

723

his hands over her rain-slick body, cupping her breasts, moving his mouth to tease the taut peaks while his hands caressed the soft curve of her buttocks and ran strongly down the flat plane of her belly to delve in the warm darkness between her legs. She sighed his name on a long, shuddering breath, locking her hands behind his strong neck as her knees gave way, and he swung her up into his arms as easily as he ever had, laughing, "We shall be arrested for lewd behavior. And you shiver. Sweetheart, I have a way to warm you."

She pressed against him in the bed, wanting him right now, feeling the beautiful readiness of his manhood against her flesh, urging with her hands, then her whole body while still he teased until she was clawing at his scarred back and moaning aloud.

When he entered her, strong thrusting, his loins fitting hard against hers, he heard her gasp of delight, and then even this boundary was lost. They were the same sound, the same flesh, nerves, blood, and bone, the same wild rhythm and wild hunger. And they reached the same high place and whirled in the exploding light before they drifted down together to perfect peace, where stillness was the only answer and their bodies were drowsily replete.

"My God, I love you," Gavin murmured when he was capable of rediscovering the self separate from her.

She lay nestled against him, and her hand began to trace soft, idle patterns on his battered chest. Her voice was the slow, lazy echo of her pleasure-laden body. "While you were gone, I hated going to bed at night. In that loneliness was all the pain of being without you. But for this night it is almost worth it." She paused before she added, "I have to ask—did you miss the sound of the coyotes?"

Even before he spoke, she knew by the small shock that ran through him that the seeming non sequitur made perfect sense to him. "It really was you then! Indian understood it from the first with Thia. It was harder for me; I only fully believe it now. It wasn't that I ever stopped thinking of you, missing you, but sometimes it was so strong, I could understand why some soldiers deserted not because they were cowards, but because they couldn't bear to be away from their women any longer. And when it was the worst, you would be there suddenly. I couldn't
724

put out my hand and touch you, but I knew you were there. I never knew until then how much California meant to me and how much California meant you. There's no difference in my mind any more—my home, my woman, they're the same." He traced the angle of her jaw. "You tried to tell me that so many times, didn't you?"

She was glad when he went on in the same musing voice; she could not have answered had her life depended on it, the lump in her throat was so large and the tears so near.

"It's strange how minutely the senses record what they know and love. I don't think anyone can know how deep it runs until the mind conjures the familiar in strange places. Nightfall is the final battleground for a man and from your words, for a woman also. When I am with you, in my home with my love, it is the safest time of all, but in the war it was the most terrifying time. There was seldom any action after the sun was gone. There was just being bone tired—just yourself and night noises and a solitude that not even your best friend or a camp full of soldiers could ease. Jesus, Tessa, the night noises!"

He took her hand in his own, and she didn't wince at the brief, fierce pressure. "The pickets called back and forth some nights, Union and Confederate troops, enemies by day, but in darkness just lonely men, all the same. Some one usually had a mouth organ and some men liked to sing. The horses chewed and stamped and snorted all night long, and the sounds from the field hospitals were constant too—I'll never be able to think of those easily. So many were scarcely more than children, lying there dying, screaming in agony." Now it was her hand pressing his, slender, strong, and comforting.

"But often it was just the earth for Indian and me, some places so swampy that the dark could make you deaf with its sounds, mumbling, scraping, humming and howling until you almost believed there was one huge beast out there instead of millions of small ones, and you wished the enemy would find you because at least they were your own kind." He stopped abruptly.

"It cannot distress me now; you are safely home," Tessa said gently. "Thia and I knew that you and Indian must have been working behind enemy lines much of the time."

725

"Strange, even though I knew it was necessary and we were good at it, I have dreaded having you know I was a spy for more than half the time. And now I find you have no feeling about it beyond being glad that I didn't get caught. Does your love have no limit?"

"I hope not, for then it could not match the full measure of yours."

He struggled for control for a few moments before he went on. "I'd been in country like that before, but not in a war and not when I had you waiting for me. Some nights I would have given my life to hear the sharp, separate sounds of California, to see forever. And it was you, all of it was. One night everything I knew was real just vanished, and I heard coyotes, and I could see your face in firelight. I could even smell your scent—in the middle of the goddamn swamp muck and blood, I could smell the flowers." His voice trailed away again for a time, and Tessa hid her face against his neck, trembling for the beauty of her man.

Gavin stroked her damp hair, smoothing out the tangles of their love-making with gentle fingers as he finished his story. "I told Indian I thought I was going mad. I knew I hadn't been asleep, hadn't been dreaming all of that. Indian just grinned. 'Thia come visitin' all th' time,' he said. 'But I know that an' I ready any ol' time. Reckon Tessa has a bigger job gettin' through to you. White men ain't no damn good at magickin.' He accepted it absolutely, and I tried after that; at least I figured if it was madness, we both had it. But it wasn't ever as clear again until we were hit, and I never heard the coyotes again at all."

He could feel Tessa's tears on his neck, but she had her voice under control, and there was a current of joy and wonder in it. "I know what night that was, I know for certain. It was while we were driving the horses to the coast. We had made camp, the coyotes began to sing, and I saw you and wanted you so much, I could have died of it. And Thia and I both knew when you and Indian were hurt. We both knew."

"I know. Now I know. I heard you telling me to hold on. The Wilderness was the worst place of all, a place to die in roots and mud and darkness. But I heard your voice."

726

"If only you and I had really known such a thing was possible, really known it!" she breathed in awe.

"Well, we won't have occasion to practice that any more, will we?" he said. "But this, this we will practice forever." He could see her face in the eerie storm glow and the lightning flashes. He kissed the last tears away.

"Nothing is as magic as this, nothing on earth," she murmured. "Welcome home, my love, my life."

"Rain and love for my lovely witch," he whispered. He kissed her willing mouth and pulled her body against his own.

It rained on and off for five days, and the promise of other storms showed on the horizon.

The rain made Tessa feel as giddy as champagne. Her skin and hair felt softer and cleaner than they had since the drought had begun. And even better, the well of love, energy, and enthusiasm was renewed within her so that she felt it bubbling and overflowing endlessly.

They sought no one out; they didn't even bother to visit old haunts. They went out only for foodstuffs, and they laughed about what people were undoubtedly thinking about them. At least the neighbors believed that they were guests of the Collinses, since no one came to evict them.

They made love and slept, laughed and sang and talked, all the things they had not been able to do together for so long. Gavin assured Tessa that the war was over. "It will drag on, because there are many brave men in the South who know their way of life will be finished when the war ends. But the Confederates have lost too many men and too much equipment they can ill afford. Substantial help from abroad would have made a difference, but that dream is finished. Grant will never give up until the South is beaten, and General Sherman will go all the way to the sea. He's a tough, capable soldier; I learned that in Fifty-six when he tried so diligently to establish a force to stop the Committee of Vigilance.

"But God only knows how long it's going to take to put this country back together. At least with Lincoln in for four more years, we have a chance. He's a man of great compassion, in addition to his political shrewdness."

They spoke of the children too, and Gavin apologized

727

outright for his attitude when he had first gotten home. "I don't know what I expected them to do while I was gone, cease to change and grow until I got back, I guess. You've done a beautiful job with them."

"I had a great deal of help, and they themselves did most of it. But I confess, I'm glad they have their father back again. There are certain subjects they feel are not suitable for their poor, innocent mother."

"As in young girls?" Gavin inquired with a grin.

"Just so, only in the case of Brand, I suspect 'women' is a better term. I don't know for sure, but I've heard Jefferson cautioning his brother, and Brand has never introduced me to any special girls." She laughed suddenly. "Neither have the other two, for that matter. They do everything very properly. I have been introduced to several young ladies whom Paul and Jefferson have taken to sweet shops and plays and various other harmless diversions. I've even played reluctant *dueña* a few times. But one could not accuse any of those young women of being special, and I don't think our sons were any more impressed than I."

"Are you trying to marry them off?" he teased.

"I am not! I expect I shall be unbearable and refuse to accept any woman as good enough for any one of my sons. But it will be even more difficult if they choose those empty-faced porcelain dolls."

"How could they, with you for their mother?"

"That might be reason enough," she replied tartly, and he laughed.

Strangely, it was Fiona she found most difficult to talk about. It was not because she was Jordan's child; Gavin had never treated her as anything but his own daughter. It was the developing complexity of Fiona herself that dazzled and often dismayed her mother. The child had as many facets as a piece of finely cut crystal, and they seemed to be increasing by the day now that Fiona was on the verge of womanhood. She was bright, nearly as book-oriented as Paul, and kind, and these characteristics reassured Tessa enormously. But she could be very practical one minute and lost in a dream world the next. The same erratic pattern characterized her dressing and behavior, one minute appearing in her oldest and most comfortable
728

clothes for a good romp, the next so prissily dressed that Tessa often felt like mussing her hair just for the hell of it. Sometimes she was all giggles and then she would be so solemn that it was impossible to draw a smile from her, except for Paul, who could usually coax her out of any moodiness. Her feelings were injured by some inexplicable thing, and then she'd turn right around and take a hard bit of teasing without being offended.

Tessa realized that most of this was surely part of the coming of age of girl to woman, though she had trouble remembering herself as ever having been so flighty. But realizing it didn't seem to make it much easier to cope with. She was deeply thankful that, after all, she had but one daughter. It was the old, wise look that she saw in Fiona's eyes sometimes that disconcerted her most of all.

Another storm came in, and the Ramsays could not resist going south before they returned to the city. It was the final healing to see water beginning to run into the pool again at Valle del Mar, and to find the people of the *rancho* as delirious as they.

"María says that God is good," Ramón confided out of the hearing of his wife. "I agree, but I say he is also forgetful. I hope that his memory does not fail us again for so long a time. Even now it will take much more rain and much snow on the high mountains to make the earth safe again."

They didn't even mind the mud that slowed the journey back to San Francisco and still ran in the streets there despite many improvements.

It was a joyous Christmas, even though the war dragged on. And even there, there was hope. General Sherman had taken Savannah, Georgia, at last, devastating the land on the way. The South could not hold out much longer.

Only through Jefferson did Tessa learn that Gavin and Indian had been officially commended for bravery not once but twice. "How did you find out about that?" she asked curiously.

"I kept asking until I tricked him into telling about Father. It was easy from there on, but I sort of wished I hadn't started the whole thing at all. He said he didn't think prizes ought to be given for fighting and killing; it was bad enough they happened at all. Made me think."

729

It made Tessa think too, though she didn't say anything to Gavin; she just tried to show him all the more how much she loved him. And she held his hand tightly when they read Lincoln's second Inaugural Address together. He held the paper, but they each read silently because the words meant too much, were too hard to speak aloud:

> With malice toward none; with charity for all; with firmness in on the right, as God gives us to see the right, let us strive on to finish the work we are in; to bind up the nation's wounds; to care for him who shall have borne the battle, and for his widow, and his orphan—to do all which may achieve and cherish a just and lasting peace among ourselves, and with all nations.

On April 9, General Lee surrendered to General Grant, and on April 15, President Lincoln was dead.

The shock waves ran through the nation, no less strong in the West than in the rest of the country. It was inconceivable that a United States president could be assassinated, and yet it had happened. For many, many thousands it was as if someone close and dear had died, and they wept.

Gavin and Indian were grim-faced, but neither shed any tears. They had seen so much death too short a time ago, and their response was what it had been in the times of greatest danger and carnage; an indrawing aloofness while they grappled with acceptance.

Gavin actually felt pity for Andrew Johnson, who was immediately inaugurated as the seventeenth president of the United States. "He is inadequate to the task, and he has none of Lincoln's vision nor his heart. God help us, it is going to be so much harder to heal this country now."

CHAPTER LXI

By 1868 all but four of the once Confederate states had limped back into the Union after complying with the Reconstruction Acts. The four would be readmitted as soon as they complied with the Acts and in addition ratified the Fifteenth Amendment to the Constitution, the amendment preventing suffrage from being denied on the basis of race, color, or previous condition of servitude.

"I notice it doesn't mention women," Tessa remarked acidly to Armenthia.

"Mebbe our daughters vote someday," Thia replied peaceably. "I'm jus' glad they let me ride on horsecars here. Been ridin' four years now an' that's somethin'."

Tessa regarded her friend in wonder. "I don't know where you find the patience."

"Born to it, raised up in it, learnt it jus' like you learnt to ride them horses. An' th' thing I've been scairt of ever since I got here is that some ol' slave catcher goin' come 'round an' steal me back, mebbe even take Indian. Don' have to fret 'bout that no more, an' I'm thankful."

Tessa wanted to tell Thia how humble and grateful she made her feel sometimes, but she knew it would only distress her friend. It was true; some very good things had come out of the terrible war. The Thirteenth Amendment abolished slavery. The Fourteenth was on its way to being passed and would give citizenship to Negroes. With the Fifteenth, basic rights would have been granted.

But in spite of these advances, the federal government was in turmoil. President Johnson had been impeached, the action failing by only one vote, and Tessa could almost pity him. Gavin's assessment of the man had been accurate. The president had tried to do what was best, but he was a man pulled too many ways, lacking in the vision and magnetic power that had even charmed some of Lincoln's enemies, and he was solidly opposed by the Radicals in

732

Congress, who judged everything he did as insufficient. Unfortunately, it often was.

Tessa had never been more thankful that she lived in the Far West than she was now. The great drought had damaged the land and proved the final ruin of most of the old landowners whose coffers had already been stripped by legal defense of their claims to their land. Tessa recognized her own savage will to survive in her guiltless joy that that had not happened to the Ramsays, and more, the land itself had healed far more quickly than the devastated acreage of the South possibly could. To have seen California so burnt, trampled, and abandoned as descriptions of the South ran would have been unbearable. And not even the worst of California's political scandals could match the tragedy of the current chaos in the South, where the most reasonable and experienced voices, black and white, were ignored in favor of their less qualified brothers. "With malice toward none"—the dream had died with the man.

It was a good thing she wasn't in charge of reuniting the country, Tessa thought wryly; she was having enough difficulty keeping her own family together. There were so many different currents, she sometimes felt as if she lived in a very treacherous part of the ocean rather than on land at all.

Some were obvious and the changes they brought were understandable, such as Mrs. Tubbs's gradual departure from the family. Her school had been in existence for a year, and though it had begun slowly, it was well on its way to being established now. There were no longer young children in the Ramsay household, and if she were ever to have her school it must be now. Indian and Thia's children would, of course, attend it.

Gavin claimed that if Mrs. Tubbs had been put in charge of the Union armies, the war wouldn't have lasted any time at all. He helped her find a place to rent, but she was the prime mover. Her school was surely radical. Both boys and girls were welcome, nor was any student barred because of race or creed. At first there had been a real question in everyone's mind, except for Mrs. Tubbs's, as to whether or not enough parents would be willing to send their children to such a place and pay fees to do so. Mrs.

Tubbs's faith in the open spirit of the West was rewarded; in fact, it was rewarded far beyond her hopes. It began with a small group of children from free-thinking parents, and now there was a waiting list. Sending one's children to school was rapidly becoming a chic thing to do and a mark of being an intellectual bohemian. Even when Mrs. Tubbs did not like some of the parents who were thus motivated, she always had hope for the children. The school would need larger quarters very soon, and then Tessa knew Mrs. Tubbs would move out of the Ramsay house, where she had remained only on their insistence since the school was opened. Tessa dreaded the day, even while she was enormously pleased for her friend.

The Ramsays, Indian, and Armenthia had much to do with the school. Already they had paid the fees for several children whose parents could not afford them (Mrs. Tubbs had an uncanny talent for finding such children), and they would pay most of the cost of the new building. There had been quite a struggle over all this help, but finally Gavin took Mrs. Tubbs in hand.

"To put it bluntly," he said, "we have made a great deal of money in this state. We give regularly to several charities, and some of them are worthy enough, but none as worthy as your school. You have enriched our children's lives beyond measure, and think how good it makes us feel to help other children have the same experience. The school is obviously going to be larger than you ever imagined, and it would be foolish for you to use all your savings and go into debt when we can manage that side of it so easily. But we can't do what you do, we can't teach the children to see the world so clearly. If you refuse our money, you will not be able to teach as many children, you won't be able to hire enough other worthy teachers, and I think that would be very selfish of you."

"Winning a battle with Mrs. Tubbs is wickedly satisfying," he confessed to Tessa, "even if I did have to use the weapon of children against her."

Fiona and Lin-Ao both went to the school, and Mrs. Tubbs, totally ignoring the training she herself had given them, claimed they were born teachers and of great assistance with the other students. The girls seemed to enjoy it, and Tessa was glad of the contact with additional young people that the school allowed them.

Fiona seemed much calmer and more predictable now, for which Tessa was grateful. She still had great swings in mood, but Tessa was becoming accustomed to them with the realization that her daughter simply had no middle ground; she was either totally happy or very low in spirit, and while it certainly wasn't the easiest way to be, it did make Fiona a tremendously vibrant person. She was growing to be a real beauty besides. Her hair remained silvery gold, framing a delicate face dominated by large eyes. Her eyelashes and brows were several shades darker than her hair, and her eyes were remarkable for the range of color; depending on her mood they could be almost pure gray, sometimes a gray-lavender and then again very blue. She would always be small and slender, several inches shorter than her mother, but now soft curves were beginning to blur the angles of childhood. She was in all so appealing to the eye that people often forgot that her crippled leg marred the perfection.

And Tessa could not have been more pleased than she was by the friendship between Fiona and Lotus. Brand had started the calling of Lin-Ao by the English equivalent of her name, and at first, Tessa had been worried lest the girl be offended by it. But nothing seemed to offend Lotus, and she was capable of dealing with her life in Chinatown and her life outside of it with equal serenity. Serenity was so strong a force in her, people were drawn to her instinctively, knowing that they would find rest if only for a moment and despite the fact that Lotus, like Fiona, was only fifteen.

"Only fifteen" had little to do with Lotus, far less than it had to do with Fiona. If Lotus felt the self-doubt and insecurity that normally came with being fifteen, she did not show it. She did everything quietly, competently. There was a fluid grace about her that Tessa wondered if any Western child could ever acquire. Mrs. Chen had made sure that Lotus had every advantage she would need to live in a Western world, but Tessa knew that Mr. Chen had had his way too. Lotus had long attended classes in a Chinatown school in addition to her lessons with Mrs.

Tubbs. And from the school and her father, she had learned self-discipline and a deep knowledge and appreciation for her Chinese heritage. But it was the strength of the girl herself that had allowed her to assimilate the two divergent cultures so smoothly.

And the physical promise Tessa had glimpsed in the starving infant so long ago had more than been fulfilled. The ivory skin was flawless, the features perfectly symmetrical, from the winged brows and almond eyes to the perfect rosebud mouth. Her nose was straight, her cheekbones delicate curves of bone. A subtle blend of East and West, Lotus was drawn on long and slender lines as pleasing to the eye as an exquisite statue. She was more than a head taller than her adoptive mother, and Tessa was eternally thankful that her feet had not been bound to make her appear more aristocratic. That Lotus's grace might have been impaired purposely while Fiona had suffered from a crippled leg since birth was an untenable thought. Even the way Lotus spoke English was part of her charm. She made no mistakes in pronunciation or grammar; her command of the language was as wide and sure as any who spoke it as a native tongue. But the cadence of her voice came from the Chinese she spoke at home and heard all around her there, so that her English had an exotic lilt.

Lately Tessa had often heard that voice intermixed with the deep notes of Brand's. It was in fact her sons who were causing much of Tessa's unease. She tried not to, but she resented it. Just when she would have judged them to be the least of her worries, they had become the greater part.

They got along better with their father now and he with them, and for that she was thankful. They all did their share of work and were fairly paid for it. But Paul and Jefferson, now twenty-four and twenty-one respectively, seemed to get more broody by the day. They both continued to escort the empty-faced beauties Tessa so detested, and neither of them seemed capable of being happy any more except in brief flashes. She had given up trying to find out from them what was wrong; they closed up and became wary and distant the minute any conversation got too personal. Gavin was no help, because he considered it

736

nothing unusual. "Men take a long time to grow up," he said with a smile. "And some never do. But I wouldn't worry about them. They seem to be doing fine to me."

His attitude exasperated her, but she suspected that mothers were simply more finely attuned to the intangibles in their children, and she knew that neither of the boys was happy. If they went on this way, there was every danger they were both going to be morose old men before too long; Paul with his endless reading and Jefferson with his endless silent staring off into the distance. She did not want to smother them with her maternal concern, but she did ask them again if they might want to change their minds and go east to school. She had never entirely lost her guilt about this and thought perhaps it would be a solution now. But her sons did not agree. Neither showed the slightest interest in the idea.

Brand was the only one of the three boys who was happy, and perversely, Tessa was as disturbed by this as she was by the melancholy of the other two. Brand lived at an ever more frenzied pace. His work never suffered, but he played as hard as he labored. Though only a year older than Jefferson, Brand was the man of the world where his brothers were not. He took no great pains to disguise his activities, though he made it very clear that he considered his life his own business. The pattern Tessa saw was an alarming one. Brand gambled and usually won; he was too bright to be taken in by a crooked game. And it seemed that he had a mistress, or at least there was a woman he saw more or less regularly. These things in themselves his mother could have accepted as normal, but it was Brand's preference for the most vice-ridden section of the city that frightened her.

Its victims had christened it the "Barbary Coast." It had grown out of the alleys that had been infested with the Sydney Ducks. It was a place of cheap shops, gambling dens, booze parlors, bawdy houses, and obscene entertainment. There were so-called "lodging" houses where the madams drugged their victims or had them beaten senseless before they had them crimped, or "shanghaied" as it was now being called, since many of the men sold to ships ended up in even so remote a place. At best a man could

737

expect to lose his money to pickpockets or crooked gamblers and whores; at worst and too frequently, he could expect to lose his life.

Tessa tried to ignore it, praying the danger there would lose its attraction for Brand before he was hurt, but her patience snapped one early morning. She and Chong Sing were the only ones up and she was savoring the peaceful feeling of the house when Brand came in.

For once he looked sheepish, though it took his mother a moment to realize that because his face was such a mess. He had a black eye, a split lip, and various other bruises.

"My God! What happened?" she gasped. "Are you all right? Can you see, can you hear?"

He started to grin, and winced instead. "I have all my faculties. I didn't even lose any teeth, though I think a couple are looser than they were. Don't look like that. You should see the others."

Tessa would not be charmed, and Chong Sing, seeing her expression, took himself elsewhere. Brand wished he could do the same, but he faced her defiantly.

"Why?" she demanded harshly. "Why must you go to those terrible places? You will be killed there or sold away to a sea captain or dead of the pox. For no sensible reason! Why?"

Brand was not sure he himself knew exactly, but he tried to explain. "It's so alive there. It's a whole other world. It's fast and hard and never dull." He touched his mouth. "I got this because I was too cocky, won too much, and didn't pay attention. It won't happen again. I take care of myself just fine there. They know I can handle my fists, a gun, a knife, cards, and women as well as the next man, and better than many."

The pride in his voice made Tessa feel wholly inadequate. It was as if he were talking about an ancient coming-of-age ceremony for males, one she could not possibly understand.

The peace of the morning was shattered. "You'd better wash and put cold water on those bruises. Chong Sing will give you raw meat for the eye," she said wearily after she had inspected him closely enough to know that nothing needed her care.

"Really, Mother, you mustn't worry about me. I'll be
738

okay," Brand offered gently, but there was no answering softness in Tessa's face. "You'll be all right the day you quit the Barbary Coast," she replied grimly.

She had one hope and that was Lotus. Lately whenever the girl was in the house, Brand paid her marked attention. He seemed to have claimed her as his special friend. His attitude toward her was protective but not exactly fraternal, and though he teased her sometimes, it was never unkind. They always seemed to find plenty to talk about, and only with Lotus, did Brand ever wear a look of quiet contentment. She was still too young yet, but if only Brand could stay out of serious trouble for a few more years, surely he would take a close look and be lost. Or at least his mother hoped he would. Mr. Chen might object, but Tessa was sure the combined force of Lotus and her mother could overcome that obstacle.

Gavin was much calmer than she about Brand's escapades. "After all, he's over twenty-one, and he'd be hard put to do anything I hadn't done already by that age."

"Ohhhhh, you!" Tessa yowled in disgust, rolling over and beating her fists against his chest. "You're all alike, you men. You sound as prideful about your sins as your son did. This house full of men is driving me to madness! Even Chong Sing has been acting strangely lately."

"Good for him," Gavin laughed. He pinioned her flailing arms with ease and pulled her close. "Sins, you say. Would you have had me a blushing virgin, then, with everything yet to learn when I married you?"

She couldn't resist; she giggled at the absurd picture of Gavin not knowing how to make love. "I expect you were born knowing, and you just had to wait for everything to grow. Which it most certainly did.

"You do comfort me, my love," she murmured on an entirely different note as his mouth savored the curve of her breast, his last chuckle of laughter vibrating against her skin.

"Comfort is a soft word for this." His voice rasped with his sudden hunger for her.

But what Tessa had said was true; part of the love Gavin gave her was comfort no one else could bring her, and she needed it in plenty in the following days. She had a terrible sense of impending disaster, and because it had to do with

Chong Sing, she was reluctant to talk to anyone about it. Her passing comment to Gavin was the last reference she made. But she watched Chong Sing with growing puzzlement. He was such an orderly, controlled person, it seemed inconceivable that anything could upset him for long. But something was doing just that. In subtle but myriad ways, his normally calm pattern of life was changing.

He had always kept close ties with his friends and his culture in Chinatown, but now he spent more time there than at the house, and when he was home with the Ramsays, he wasn't really home at all. He asked politely for things to be repeated. His hands fidgeted nervously. His eyes were curiously opaque.

Tessa wondered how she could be conscious of all of this when no one else seemed to be, but then she realized that in the running of the household, she had always been closer to him than the others were. And it went beyond that, to the first day when she had kicked the bully in the shin in defense of Chong Sing.

She tried to consider the possibilities. Gambling was very popular in Chinatown, especially the game of *fan-tan*, where bets were made on the odd or even of how many coins or other small objects would remain after all that could be had been counted off in twos or fours. Many games were in process at almost any time, and the bets were usually small. But there were sometimes high-stake bets in this, as there were in any form of gambling. But it didn't tally with Chong Sing's character. She was sure risking money on a game was not his style. He had always seemed disapproving of the Golden Horse when it had been a full-scale gambling house.

And a compulsive involvement with a "joy" girl hardly seemed more likely.

Perhaps Chong Sing had noticed Brand's growing interest in Lotus and disapproved of it because he knew of Brand's other activities. Maybe his trips to Chinatown involved meeting with the Chens, or even with a marriage broker to plan Lotus's future.

She was so distressed by this possibility that she finally mustered her courage enough to question him directly, something she would ordinarily never have considered in reference to his personal affairs.

"You . . . you have seemed uneasy recently. Is it . . . has it to do with Brand?" She wished she didn't sound so hesitant, but Chong Sing only looked at her blankly.

"Bland? Something wong wid him? His eye all fix, can't be dat."

Tessa was thrown off stride. Brand had nothing to do with it. She tried again. "It was just a guess. It's you I'm worried about. If there's anything I can do, please tell me."

"No'ting wong. But tank you fo' asking, Missee Lamsay." It was the first time Tessa had known him to lie to her. She had no doubt he was lying; his agitation was evident. She only hoped he would come to her if he really needed help.

A few days later she cursed herself for her arrogance in having thought she could solve any problem he might bring.

She came home in the afternoon, and she thought she was alone in the house because Chong Sing did not come out to greet her. She was tempted to go over to visit Thia, but she knew once they started to talk, neither one of them would accomplish anything more this day, and she had come home specifically to work on the ledgers, a never-ending task.

She had the figures marching in neat columns when she heard the sound. At first it wasn't alarming, just curious, a pathetic mewling as if there was a lost kitten in the house. She went to investigate, and when she neared Chong Sing's rooms, the sound was no longer indistinct. She listened incredulously as it rose in pitch and volume. A woman crying, sobbing hysterically, a woman in Chong Sing's quarters.

Not knowing what else to do, she called his name. He appeared, looking guilty and harassed and totally unlike himself. The wailing rose behind him.

"Bad I bling gil heah, solly, solly, don' know what else to do."

His near incoherence steadied Tessa. "It's all right. Whatever reason you have I am sure is a good one. But your friend, she is in such distress, perhaps another woman could help her."

Chong Sing accepted her offer with alacrity, clearly not knowing how to cope with the weeping girl. She was

741

scarcely a woman. She was tiny, and so terrified that when Tessa first approached her, she drew back until she was huddled against the wall like a cornered beast.

Tessa didn't know whether she spoke English or not, but it didn't seem to matter, her gentle flow of words reached the girl until she allowed Tessa to put her arms around her. "There, little one, there, you're safe now," she crooned, and when the sobs had subsided to little gulps, she led the girl to the kitchen, where Chong Sing hastily set about making tea.

But though the crying had stopped, the tension had not, and Tessa shared it without knowing the cause. Chong Sing hesitated for a moment when she asked him, but once he started to explain, it was all she could do to understand. The girl obviously understood some English after all because she nodded vigorously now and then in agreement as Chong Sing told the story.

It was a very complicated one, and Tessa soon grew tired of hearing her own voice asking him to repeat this and explain that. But at least she thought she had it sorted out. The girl was the promised wife of the younger brother of a man Chong Sing had known in China. But another man had desired her and had stolen her away from her family's home in Chinatown. Chong Sing and others had taken her back. There had been some fighting, but so far no one had been killed. Chong Sing had reluctantly brought the girl out to the Ramsays' house because he could think of no other place where she would be as safe. But he was not sure he had been successful. Perhaps they had been followed.

It dawned on her suddenly, and she did not want it to be true even though she knew it was. "This is not just a fight over a woman, is it?" she asked. "She is the trigger, I expect, but this is between two tongs, isn't it?"

He hesitated, then nodded, and she detected relief on his face that the truth was out. He explained it painstakingly. The families in the tong he belonged to had been rebels against the ruling dynasty; the tong that was their particular enemy was composed of families who had supported the imperial rule.

"That is the most foolish thing I have ever heard!"

Tessa exploded. "I understand family loyalty and the bonds of honor—a Californio is raised from the cradle to respect them—but this is beyond all reason! You have all come so many miles, could you not leave the burden of an old war behind you?"

Chong Sing smiled sadly. "Man cally all he is wid him, de good an' de bad. Is no way put down spilit an' walk 'way flom it. Fo' same Mista Lamsay an' Indian go fa' way fo' wa' not heah."

She was beaten, and she knew it. And her practical side knew there was no way out for Chong Sing in any case. Even if he was willing to forget old grudges, others were not. "How many will follow you here if they know?" she asked.

"One. One *boo how doy.*"

She knew the meaning. *Boo how doys* were hired killers. Some called them hatchet men because of their penchant for carrying various kinds of blades in their full, concealing sleeves. They were reputed to be good at their job.

"I'll send for Gavin, and we'll take you and"—she looked at the girl, who offered her name willingly—"you and Lee Bow Kim far away from San Francisco as quickly as possible.

Chong Sing was very calm again. "Is too late an' make do difflent anyway. He follow. Betta end heah. He not hult you. Don' wan tlouble wid white people."

"That's just fine! I'll watch him kill you and take Bow Kim. I'll know I'm safe. I may even applaud," she said sarcastically.

"Not so easy kill Chong Sai Sing." Pride was evident in his voice.

"Maybe not, but I'm going to go warn Armenthia and have her go for Gavin," she snapped, angry because she had already wasted so much time, had nearly been drawn into his patient net of waiting.

He made no useless protest; indeed, he looked as indulgent as he was wont to look when one of the children wanted to do something silly but harmless.

Never had the distance between the two houses seemed so vast. Tessa made herself walk though her impulse was to run headlong. She saw nothing, but she felt a thousand

743

pair of eyes watching her, and every rustle in the shrubbery was another enemy. She even damned the roses for their profuse, concealing beauty.

Her skin was clammy, her breath coming in short gasps by the time she knocked on the door. Thia's pleasant greeting died unspoken at the look on Tessa's face, and Tessa explained rapidly before Armenthia could panic over the possibility of some harm to one of their husbands or the children. "I would go, but I fear to leave them. I doubt Chong Sing would use a gun to defend himself, but I'd use one if it's necessary."

"I'd go, but I don' think it'd do much good." Thia's face was suddenly rigid.

They were still standing in the doorway. Tessa whirled around and screamed a warning at the top of her lungs. "Chong Sing, bolt the door!" Even as the words rasped out of her throat she knew that he would surely not hear them distinctly, if indeed he heard any sound at all.

The man advancing toward the Ramsay house checked only briefly at her scream, casting one disdainful glance at the two women. He obviously knew Chong Sing was the only man on the premises, and he equally obviously held women of no account.

Armenthia sprang from Tessa's side and was back with a rifle, but the battle had already been joined by Chong Sing. He had come out boldly, advancing on the man, and now the two circled each other with wary grace.

Tessa made up her mind with terror pounding in her ears. "It's his fight. Go no closer. If the man bolts, we won't know how soon he will return. But you keep them covered from here. I must get back to the girl. One way or another, Chong Sing is going to win."

Thia nodded grimly, not suggesting that Tessa stay, believing as she did that the two men were not going to bother any but each other.

She started back to the house, never taking her eyes off them, biting back further outcry that might distract Chong Sing even when she saw the bright, short sword appear as if by magic in his assailant's hand. She could not help but feel she was watching an alien piece of theater, the players with matching pigtails, wide-sleeved coats, and loosely fitting pants, moving in an intricate dance. They were in deadly earnest, and yet they both wore expressions of intense enjoyment. They whirled and spun, arms and legs swinging in extreme arcs which defied gravity.

Tessa flinched each time one or the other went down, but even her untrained eye could see that none of the falls had damaged either man. They scarcely touched the ground before their bodies flexed them out of harm's way. They were evenly matched save for the blade Chong Sing's opponent had. She could hear it cut the air, and she kept expecting it to slice into Chong Sing's body, but no blood had yet been drawn.

She reached the safety of the house, and for an instant her knees threatened to buckle, but she fled inside only long enough to see that Bow Kim watched from the shadows; whether from shock or complete resignation, the girl was calm. Tessa grabbed her rifle and went back to the doorway.

She had heard no outcry, but now Chong Sing's left sleeve was torn and blood dripped from his arm, splattering everywhere as he moved. She held the rifle tightly, filled with a fierce urge to kill the man before Chong Sing fell dead under his blade. But she couldn't get a clear shot.

She saw Chong Sing falter and go suddenly still; she heard the enemy's cry of triumph in the same instant, and she raised the rifle again.

Chong Sing's body tautened, whirled and leaped in a movement so rapid Tessa gasped aloud. He landed neatly with no new cuts showing. She blinked, wondering stupidly for several seconds why the other man was flat on the ground. And finally her mind supplied the missing link in the death chain, the tremendous force of Chong Sing's feet smashing into the man's neck. She put the rifle down and moved like a sleepwalker to the fallen form. His throat was a pulpy mess of smashed flesh.

"Solly you see dat, Missee Lamsay," Chong Sing apologized, but his eyes shone with victory.

By the time Gavin and Indian arrived, having been found by Thia at the warehouse, Tessa had Chong Sing's arm neatly stitched and bandaged. She had wanted to summon Dr. Harland, but he wouldn't hear of it.

They were all conscious of the time passing swiftly. Soon the rest of both families would be home. Though

Chong Sing was perfectly willing to take all the consequences for what he had done, Tessa and Gavin made a
joint decision, and though it made them guilty of concealing a crime and worse, everyone helped, even tiny Bow
Kim. They buried the hatchet man with great haste and
no ceremony not far from the rose garden, taking care to
trample leaves and grass and sticks into the earth to cover
the fresh scar.

It had not been a hard decision to make. At this moment all the rival tong knew was that they had sent a *boo
how doy* after Chong Sing. They did not know that the
fight had been joined and lost by their man. Gavin and
Indian checked meticulously and found no sign that more
than one man had come. All of this gave Chong Sing time
to get Bow Kim safely away again and surely some time
after that before his enemies realized their man had failed.
And there was no way now for them to know for sure that
their man was dead unless one of the conspirators told.
Tessa knew none of them would; even Bow Kim, the most
vulnerable, was as resolute as any of them, and looked at
Chong Sing with respect bordering on adoration.

CHAPTER LXII

Chong Sing and Bow Kim were gone by the time the
children had filtered home, and they were told that Chong
Sing had been summoned to the bedside of a sick friend in
Chinatown. Jeff asked anxiously if it were one of the
Chens and was relieved to find it was not. But Tessa knew
he suspected something, picking up her tension as easily
as if it were a large object dropped at his feet. He didn't
ask any further questions, however, and she offered no
further explanations.

She was so happy to see Chong Sing return alive, she
nearly kissed him, but she could not fail to notice that he
did not share her joy. He said little, taking up his duties
busily, leaving Tessa to wonder if perhaps Lee Bow Kim
had meant more to him than she thought.

She hadn't long to wonder. A few nights later as she was brushing her hair, Gavin told her. He had never wanted to do anything less than he wanted to relay this news, but he knew delay was impossible now and would not make it any less painful.

"Tessa, Chong Sing is leaving. He's going back to China. I've already booked passage for him."

"Oh, how nice!" she said. "I expect there are still people he would like to visit there. I'm ashamed I haven't suggested it. Surely it would be safe enough now."

"I'm not talking about a visit. He's going home. He's not coming back," Gavin's voice was infinitely gentle.

The brush clattered on the dressing table as Tessa whirled around to stare at him. "Not coming back? What do you mean? His home is here. You can't be serious!"

"I am, or rather he is. My darling, it's no easier for me than it is for you. I'll hate to see him go. He was afraid to tell you, that's how much he cares for you. But he has come to California; he has seen the Golden Mountain. He has raised our children, and he's ready to go home. He says the old war is over in China, and he will be safer there than he is here now. I wish I didn't have to tell you this, but there is a *chin hung* out for him in Chinatown. That's a public notice offering a reward for his death. And there's no way we can protect him forever. You know as well as I do that the Chinese are a law unto themselves. They govern themselves, in however harsh a way, and leave everyone else alone. They've had to do it with so little help and so little justice from the legitimate government here. And even without another hatchet man looking for Chong Sing, things are getting steadily worse for the Chinese— new fines, new laws, more hate and more blame are being heaped on them each day. The railroad will be finished soon, and all those thousands of Chinese who have been working on it will need jobs and will get them because they are willing to work so hard for so little. Few will remember that; most will simply blame them for taking jobs from 'deserving' white men."

He paused, watching as Tessa prowled the room nervously, but he knew she was still listening. "Chong Sing and I talked for a long time. He knows all of this, and beyond that, he always meant to go back. It is not as if he really wanted to stay here forever like the Chens. It's not the same. His devotion to us, to you, to Lotus, delayed his plan, but it never changed. I expect he's saved almost everything he's earned. He'll be wealthy in China, and his standing will be good. Before the wars interrupted everything, he was a man of some substance, his family having been merchants and small landowners. He told me that, and he said that he will find himself a young wife, and before he dies, he hopes he will have sons and perhaps a daughter, because here he has learned to appreciate girl children."

Tessa hardly heard the placating note in his voice. She could scarcely imagine life without Chong Sing. She could not believe he was truly going to do this, even with all the reasons presented by Gavin. "But he has everything here! And surely we could guard him until this trouble is over," she protested, her voice thin with shock.

Gavin stopped her pacing, holding her by the shoulders. "This trouble will not be over until long after we are all gone. And what does he have here? He has nothing. Oh, yes, he loves us and he loves our children. But there are no children now. Others may come, grandchildren, but even so, they will not be his. He has no life of his own here at all. He's a strong man. If he'd wanted to find a wife and settle forever in California, he would have done so. He doesn't want to do that. He wants to go home. You, of all people, should understand that."

He put his arms around her and she sobbed heartbrokenly against him.

The few remaining days passed too quickly. Tessa could not have borne it if they had been filled with silent tension. When she had been able to do so without breaking down, she had gone to Chong Sing and offered him every good wish for the future. It had been his mouth which had quivered suddenly, he who had turned away to busy himself with needless tasks.

Chong Sing's diligent work to leave the household in smooth running order made everything harder to bear, even while the Ramsays were grateful. Through Lotus he got in touch with a young man who bore the slightly Anglicized name Kam Lee and would take his place. "Good Chinaboy," Chong Sing called him, and Tessa and

Gavin agreed with his choice, but both of them knew it would never be the same. Chong Sing drilled Kam Lee relentlessly in the brief time he had, and Kam Lee learned quickly. But he would never be the friend the older man had been.

The Chens and other friends from Chinatown came out to the house to bid farewell to their friend, all conscious of the fact that it was no longer safe for Chong Sing in Chinatown.

The family was as stunned as Tessa, but only Jefferson came close to the truth. "Does it have something to do with the grave near the rose garden?" he asked his mother without warning.

She gasped and met his eyes. "Do they all know?" she asked, making no attempt to deny it.

"No, or if they do they haven't said, which isn't likely. Pretty good job. I just happened on it myself and some odd things began to make sense."

"Well, it does not matter now," Tessa said heavily. "There is one less hatchet man and tomorrow Chong Sing will be gone too."

Only Gavin and Tessa went with him to the ship. The other farewells were said at home. They did not want to cause any extra attention to be focused on Chong Sing by having a large group see him off. Gavin knew and trusted the captain of the ship, but they would not feel easy until Chong Sing was safely away.

Suddenly there was no more time. Chong Sing thanked Gavin courteously for everything and turned to Tessa.

"Velly happy heah wid you an' all de Lamsays. Now I go back to China. Be big man in dat place. Be able say I see Golden Mountain. Velly glad I come heah, velly glad I meet you, velly glad you kick dat man." Chong Sing's voice grew unsteady at the end, and Tessa abandoned reticence to throw her arms around him.

"Life without you will seem so strange. Thank you, thank you for all the help for all the years. *Vaya con Dios*, my friend."

"Mebbe alla spilits, alla gods same afta all. Some go wid me, some stay wid you, all happy, all safe," Chong Sing said, and then he was gone.

They watched the launch reach the ship. They watched

749

until the ship had sailed out of sight, taking with it the tiny figure that waved once from the deck.

"I am very tired of saying good-by," Tessa whispered finally, her voice quavering.

Gavin drew her close. "Tessa, you love so hard. It's why I love you so much. But there is no answer. If the plan were more to our liking, once we found someone we love, we would never, never have to say good-by. But somehow the plan is very faulty, and so we are always saying it. And you live every moment so fiercely, you are better able to survive than most. You have countless memories of Chong Sing. They are yours. Now you will never have to see him grow old and die. You will have only the best memories of him. That's all we ever have of people. My love, you must just go on as you are and enjoy every moment you live."

She looked up at him. "You are not talking about Chong Sing at all, are you? You are talking about us."

He flinched away from the question. "I'm talking about everyone, anyone who ever loves someone else in whatever way. It was you who told me years ago that there is never enough time, that not even eternity would be enough."

Tessa heard from Chong Sing only once. In the new year a gift came to her from China. The box was of purple sandalwood inlaid with silver wire and inside were two fans, two because to give one of anything was inharmonious and impolite. They were old and precious, with delicate scenes painted on one side and a poem in Chinese on the reverse of each. The sticks were of ivory and rare woods inlaid with amber and malachite.

Tessa did not need Lotus to tell her that Chong Sing had sent a gift fit for an empress no matter what his feelings were about royalty. But she needed the comfort Lotus offered so continually. Lotus understood that when Tessa wept over the gift, it was not only because Chong Sing was gone, it was most of all because of Jefferson.

Jeff had ridden away on the first day of the new year. He would, he had told his parents, have left long before that had it not been for the earthquake in October. It was the first time Tessa had been thankful for that disaster. It had been a severe one, costing lives and over three million
750

dollars' worth of property damage in the city. Every bit of glassware at the Golden Horse had been smashed, and there had been damage at the warehouse, the shop, and at Mrs. Tubbs's school. They were all glad to be alive, but they had all had an enormous amount of work to do to rebuild and resupply.

By Christmas they had accomplished most of it, and that was when Jefferson had spoken to them. He hadn't asked them; he had simply informed them.

"I don't understand. Where are you going, for how long, why?" Tessa asked in quick panic. She looked so like a frightened, confused child, Jeff couldn't bear to look at her, and fixed his attention on his father.

"I'm not sure where I'm going, and I don't know for how long, but I promise, I'll be back. I don't have a much better explanation for why I'm going, at least not one that's easy to say. I feel smothered and spoilt. Just drifting along, almost as if I don't exist as a separate person at all." He heard his mother's hurt whimper, and he winced. "I've said it badly just as I knew I would. It's not anybody's fault but my own. But I need time away . . . away from having things too easy."

Gavin's kind understanding had made it harder for Tessa. He wasn't happy about Jeff's leaving, but he understood everything Jefferson had said and felt, and he made no protest beyond asking his son if he would consider waiting until the holidays were over. Though she knew it was for her benefit, Tessa didn't know whether it had been a good idea after all. Every day had been an agony of self-control and covert watching—he walks just so, he talks just so, his eyebrow slants up just like his father's, his hands are so long and lean and expressive—remembering everything about him. But the time did bring a certain resignation. Jefferson was much too thin and taut; not even the days he had spent on Rancho Magnífico this summer had healed him. If he could only be happy by going away, then it must be so. Not even to herself could Tessa admit the full extent of her love and her dependence on this one of all her children.

"We've been very fortunate to have remained a family this long," Gavin told her, and she fought down the urge to scream that she wished one of the others was leaving, not Jefferson. The penalties for having a favorite were severe.

She worked harder than ever and clung fiercely to Gavin's supportive love, but she found Lotus the most comforting of all. The girl had a way of talking about Jefferson as if he had just stepped out for a moment, and more, she had a talent for conjuring him before Tessa's eyes with a perfectly imitated gesture or a story.

They heard from him infrequently, but when a letter did arrive, it was always full of interesting descriptions of the places he had seen. He said little about himself beyond assurances that he was well, but his growing confidence and enthusiasm were evident, and his mother had to be content with that while she tried not to dwell on the fact that he was traveling further away—southern California, Texas, and now he thought he would be joining a cattle drive to Abilene. Even the herds in California could not match the vast numbers of cattle being driven to the railhead at Abilene for shipment to Kansas City, he wrote. The only way they could write back to him was to send letters to the towns he mentioned he might visit.

Life did go on, Tessa discovered, and she listened less often now for his voice and his footsteps. He was all right; he would be home someday, and in the meantime there was no lack of things to keep her occupied.

When Gavin had told Mrs. Tubbs that they had made a good deal of money in the state, he had not been exaggerating. They had invested in neither the Comstock Lode, which had crowned the silver kings nor in the railroad, which was even now creating a new and ruthless aristocracy of wealth. But they had done very well in their diverse ventures, so well that now Gavin felt strongly about investing yet more of their capital which, even after earthquake repair costs, was considerable, because they had undertaken no large new projects in years.

Tessa blessed him and Indian for the care they took in consulting Brand and Paul about their ideas, though it would surely add confusion to the process. But her sons proved splendidly adequate to the task. They asked for two weeks and made two trips out of the city before they presented their idea.

"A winery?" Gavin said, his eyebrow at an extreme angle.

"We've found a grand place in the Napa Valley," Brand announced enthusiastically. "More and more California wines are being made and sold with new stock from Europe to improve the old Mission grapes. If we can produce some truly fine wine, the market is endless."

"Only it wouldn't really be us," Paul broke in. "It would take a lifetime to learn as much as the Vincentis already know. They're the family who have started the winery we want."

"We've talked to them," Brand assured their audience before anyone could protest. "They've got the knowledge but very little money. If we provide that, they can expand, take in more of the acreage around them, plant more vines, and in about five years things ought to start happening. They're willing to have Ramian as a partner; they're willing to do almost anything so that they can make good wine."

"If these two ain't pure Ramsay," Indian chuckled, and Paul was warm with pleasure at being included in the tribute.

Gavin and Tessa went with their sons to view the reality, and their last doubts vanished. The Vincenti family kept Tessa in a continual blush with their compliments, but business was not neglected. Their English was broken with the patterns of their Italian homeland, but they communicated very well. They spoke of the vines as if they were precious children, and the Ramsays knew they would never have been willing to take help and sell a share to anyone outside of the family had that love not been present. Gavin was especially proud that his sons had obviously charmed the Vincentis, and Tessa had been the final touch.

That they had managed to immigrate at all and to do so with such joy and hope was a reassuring promise for the future. There was the grandfather and grandmother, their three sons and two daughters, all with spouses and most with children, and they were hopeful that a wave of cousins would follow soon. There would be no lack of Vincentis to tend the vines in this place where they found the sun and soil near perfection.

Gavin noticed with amusement that there were two ripening daughters who looked at Brand and Paul as if they'd like to tend them as well as the grapes. Both girls had shining black hair, huge dark eyes, and smooth olive skin turned tawny by their field work in the sun. He thought his observation private until Tessa admitted, "It is most odd to see young women hungering for my sons. I wonder if I shall ever grow accustomed to it."

They were standing on a lower slope of the hills that backed the winery. The small house and storage areas that would soon be expanded lay below them and the acres that would one day be bright green with new leaves spread out toward the valley floor. It was a spectacular yet peaceful view, and Gavin was glad they were alone when his laughter broke the stillness.

"You are the most observant creature! Here I thought I was the only one who noticed."

"One would have to be blind to miss it," Tessa replied. "They are beautiful, and they seem to be sweet girls, I think they would be kind to our sons." She sighed. "But it makes no difference. Brand is flattered but not interested, and Paul is the blind one. I honestly do not think he even knows how that girl Francesca gazes at him. Sometimes I worry about him."

"Well, you shouldn't. I'm sure his appetites are quite normal, even if they are not sharp." Gavin said firmly. "He's growing more sure of himself and that's what it takes." There was more on his mind, but he wasn't going to offer it.

She gazed up at him, a soft smile curving her mouth. "I'm glad you grew so sure so early."

He succumbed easily and kissed her. "I, for one, am too old and sure miss a hungry look from a certain lady."

She pushed at him playfully. "We are old, but you don't have to say it. And I for one do not feel old, even though my body betrays me." She smoothed the hair at her temples. "You see, for months now I have seen the gray beginning. I had thought to pluck them out, but I don't think you would like a bald woman."

"You have a good way to go to catch up with me," he pointed out, which was true. The silver at his temples was thick now.

"Yes, but men grow to be distinguished while women only grow old."

"Not this one, never this one," he murmured, and he kissed first one light streak and then the other in her silken hair and ran his hands hard and possessively down her body. "It is magic. You feel as you always have to me, not one day changed."

Tessa giggled. "If we are not careful, we are going to be in trouble right here on the hillside. The Vincentis might think twice about taking such abandoned people for their partners."

"They would probably cheer. Judging from the number of children," he said, laughing with her and pulling her hand to lead her down the hillside.

But she stopped suddenly, her mood completely changed. "Gavin, perhaps you don't know either. I was afraid to ask him. But do you think Jefferson's leaving had anything to do with a woman?"

Gavin regarded her gravely. "I did ask. It seems to be the sort of question expected from a father. The reasons he gave both us for leaving were indeed the most important. But there was a woman. He told me little about her beyond assuring me that he had done nothing dishonorable." He gazed out over the valley for a moment before he continued. "I don't know this for sure, it's only conjecture on my part, but I think Jefferson is in love with Lotus."

Tessa stiffened and gripped his hand hard, but she waited for him to finish.

"It's the only thing that makes sense. It wouldn't be like Jeff to fall in love with a married woman or anything like that; he's just too sensible. And there's no reason why he shouldn't be able to court just about any available girl he wants. But in his eyes Lotus would not be available, not while Brand wants her. I'm less convinced of that than Jeff apparently was; I can't tell whether Brand is waiting for Lotus to grow up sufficiently before he marries her and settles down or whether he just takes her for granted as a beautiful woman of whom he is fond but no more. Tessa, I just don't know, perhaps I'm way off track. And I never had any brothers to worry about, but I can't imagine it would have made any difference about you. It would have made it harder, but I still would have had you. Jefferson is going to have to decide the same thing if he really loves Lotus, if it's not just a childhood infatuation. But if Brand marries Lotus before Jefferson gets back, that will be the end of it. Damn complicated, isn't it? I hope I'm wrong."

"You are not wrong," Tessa said flatly. "And I spoke of blindness! It's all so clear now. The way Jefferson looked at Lotus when he thought no one was watching him. And the way Lotus speaks so easily of him, and so often. I have been an idiot, but they are worse! If they love, it's up to them to do something about it, Brand or no Brand."

"You're right, and it should be some comfort to know that it's out of our hands." He felt her relax a little, and he was glad she had not brought the subject of their children's romances back to Paul.

Their new projects only began with the winery. There was much to be done in the city. Tessa's shop was fine enough even to compete with such a store as the City of Paris, which had had its beginnings in 1850 when a Frenchman, Felix Verdier, stepped off the *Ville de Paris* and began immediately to sell the goods he had brought from France. Tessa never wanted her shop to lose its personal touch, but she had planned its expansion at a steady rate even while she continued to sell only the finest goods. She and Molly Barker and the staff they had trained over the years worked diligently to ferret out the latest trends in fashion and to be ready for them, paying particular attention to the designs from the House of Worth in Paris, which wielded ever more power in setting the styles of haute couture. Gowns were becoming ever more luxurious, but with the increasing numbers of the newly rich, Tessa never lacked customers.

"It seems the shape of fashion is changing," she informed Gavin solemnly. "The round fullness is moving toward the back."

"I'd like to get my hands on whoever decided the shape of a woman's ass isn't perfect just the way it is," Gavin said, sighing gustily. He grabbed Tessa, who was sputtering helplessly with laughter. "On second thought, not all are as perfect as this one, and I'd just as soon keep it a secret."

The Golden Horse received its share of their attention also. It was doubtful that it would ever bring in the same wealth it had as a gambling house, but liquor was thought to be a necessity by enough of the city's population for the Golden Horse to make a handsome profit despite the heavy expenditures on the free lunch it offered. The free lunch was rapidly becoming one of the most popular traditions of San Francisco, and there were few places where one could partake of a better one than at the Golden Horse. From late afternoon until midnight, drinkers could help themselves to seafood ranging from caviar, clams, oysters, and smoked salmon to terrapin stew, to assorted meats from all cuts of pork including pigs' heads (which Tessa thought disgusting) to beef to venison, and to cheeses, fruits, and nuts. And even though the feast was always large and tempting due to the fact that the chef was a talented Frenchman, it was seldom that any patron took unfair advantage of it. It was considered dishonorable to be an obvious glutton.

The one area where Tessa had grave doubts was in Gavin and Indian's determination to invest in more lots in the city. She knew they had selected them carefully, and their plan was to buy a few at a time in a continual process. What she could not understand was the quality of the land. One piece on Fern Hill was barely reasonable, a lovely spot with a magnificent view of the bay, but even so, the hill was so steep that little had been built on it. It was impossible for a carriage to negotiate the incline, and even a strong horse would have a hard pull. (Gavin and Indian were serenely confident that something would be done about that, perhaps a cut-in, curving road to lessen the angle.) The other acres they wanted were even more inexplicable choices to Tessa—for the most part barren sand dunes. But she kept quiet about her doubts, especially because her sons were as enthusiastic as the men, and she struggled to see whatever vision they shared.

Gavin was too sensitive to her moods to be fooled by her silence. "You don't approve, do you?" he asked one night after another conference during which Tessa alone had been still and withdrawn.

"It is not that I don't approve, I don't understand," she confessed, and in struggling to explain, she began to see things more clearly. "Land that will grow something in my sight is something I know well and love. But much of

757

this in the city will not . . ." She stopped and drew a shaky breath. "You and Indian, you have known all along! We will not live to see anything built or planted on most of this land."

"Perhaps not. But our children will, or their children," Gavin said calmly. "There is no end to what this city will be. We ourselves have seen the changes just twenty years have brought. And the railroad is complete now. The last barrier is gone. California is no longer a separate world."

She did not share his peaceful acceptance of the passage of the barriers of safety, of time and generations. She was suffocatingly aware of the years slipping away from them, Gavin being taken from her.

He felt the sudden chill on her skin as she shivered, and he pressed his own warmth against her. "Now, we have now, sweetheart!"

"I want forever!" Tessa cried, and even when he was deep inside of her, she ground her bones against his in endless need.

CHAPTER LXIII

In many ways, Gavin still understood Tessa better than she did herself. He had tried to be a good father, but his role had had limits, especially in the years he had been away. Tessa, despite the doubts she had always had about her fitness as a mother, had been, he knew, a very good one, and she was closely bound to the children. But whether she liked it or not, those ties were changing, stretching, breaking. The children, even Fiona, were adults now. Even believing that Jefferson loved Lotus and Brand perhaps loved her not enough, there was nothing Tessa could do about it, any more than she could bring Paul out of his shell or make sure Fiona never came to harm. And Gavin could see that there could be nothing more calculated to remind Tessa of the passage of time than this passage of her babies into adulthood.

He too was sometimes saddened by it, but a part of him

rejoiced, because it meant he had more of Tessa. And he had every intention of taking full advantage of it. He wooed her away from the city at every opportunity, taking her back to the winery, to both *ranchos* under the guise of business but making sure they played as much as they worked, and to Monterey and the Collinses. Carmelita found herself smiling with satisfaction the whole time the Ramsays visited, and Sam was no less pleased, though he was less obvious about it. And at Valle del Mar, María and Ramón blessed anew the good fortune of their little one.

Indian's dream was to plant more wheat at Rancho Magnífico and to improve the cattle by bringing in Herefords to cross with the range cattle they had now. The cross was being done in more and more places and in greater numbers every year because it improved the quantity and quality of beef. They had agreed with his plans and included them in their new investment plans, but as they rode out to check the horses (increased from the great drought year by stock returned gradually from Valle del Mar and by prize animals purchased to improve the bloodlines), Gavin teased Tessa for the bright, eager look on her face. "You're never really going to care about wheat and beef as much as you do about your horses, are you? Poor Indian, I hope you haven't hurt his feelings."

"Indian is glad," she said smugly. "He would not like my interference in his plans. He has seen how particular I am in the breeding of horses. It would take too much work before I could find beauty in a cow, though a sheaf of wheat is easier to admire." Her hand swept the scene before them. "There are no more beautiful palominos anywhere except on Rancho Valle del Mar."

Her pride was justified. Year by year the horses had been improved. There were stallions at both *ranchos* which sired colts of their own golden color every time, despite the odds against it. And as much attention had been given to conformation as to color, so that Tessa's palominos were big enough but had the slender grace, the large, wideset eyes and shapely heads, from the blood of fine Arabian horses. Tessa was particularly proud of this when she saw some of the horses from other lines—horses gold to perfection but built on chunky, ungraceful lines with boxy

759

heads. And the chestnuts, which would never be anything but a side product to Tessa, were necessarily as fine.

Jefferson had ridden away on a golden horse. She hoped they would both come back safely. The thought rose unbidden, but she felt much quieter about it now. "I would know if something had happened to him, just as I knew about you," she said.

Gavin understood. "I'm quite sure you would," he agreed, and the serenity of her face pleased him.

The last trip they took that year was in the autumn and Gavin did not even pretend it was for business. "We'll stop and see the Browns in Grass Valley, but just for the hell of it. They know their business. Otherwise, glory be, we'll be surrounded by strangers."

Tessa widened her eyes and simpered. "Sir, you have been courting me for months now, but I think it only fair to tell you, I'm a married woman."

Gavin beat his brow dramatically. "It can't be! But surely, he's short, fat, old, and bald, and bores you to distraction. Come away with me!"

"You misjudge him," she accused. Her voice changed, all playfulness leaving it, and her eyes were vast violet pools for him to drown in. "He is tall and beautiful and as bright as the sun. Never for an instant has he bored me. I would not leave him for the world and heaven too."

Gavin gathered her into his arms, holding her against his heart which beat with a suddenly jagged rhythm.

"You two are certainly foolish," said a voice from the study doorway, which they had neglected to close. They both jumped, and Fiona giggled. "Honestly, it's no secret that you love each other. We've all known for years." Her eyes twinkled with fond approval, and Tessa felt as if she were the youngster and Fiona the adult.

"I'm glad you approve," Gavin said, grinning at her, "since there doesn't seem to be much we can do about it now."

Fiona insisted on helping her mother pack for the trip, choosing the finest garments until Tessa protested, "We are not going by wagon or stage, you know. We'll be riding. I can't take all of this."

"You'll be taking a pack horse, so you can take more

than usual. And Papa says you'll be staying in inns and hotels. You do want him to be proud of you, don't you?"

They compromised, Tessa taking twice as much as she would have packed herself, half as much as Fiona wanted her to take.

They did stop to see the Browns, and Gavin went underground to get a firsthand look at the mine while Tessa stayed in the sun counting the minutes until he reappeared. He looked pale, and later he admitted he'd felt as anxious as she had.

"Miners must be the rarest breed on earth to be able to tolerate that day after day. The darkness is astounding, gives the word a whole new meaning. The blackest night up here doesn't compare with it. There's a cold damp that seeps into your bones so quickly I'm surprised the miners don't shake the tunnels apart. And worst of all was suddenly feeling as if every ton of rock and dirt above me was beginning to press down hard enough to collapse the tunnels. I nearly jumped out of my skin every time the timbers creaked until I realized that the men down there would be the first to know if something was going wrong."

Tessa shivered just listening to him. "This is one time when I have found a right denied women to be much to my advantage. It was probably a Cornish woman who started that superstition."

Despite the fact that the Browns were very rich men now, they seldom ventured far from the mine, making few trips to the city, preferring their old and rugged way of life to the soft style their gold could have provided. Yet they were remarkably well informed, particularly regarding factors that affected the gold market.

They discussed the "Black Friday" gold conspiracy which had recently rocked the administration of Ulysses S. Grant when two unscrupulous speculators, Jay Gould and Jim Fisk, had devised a scheme to make millions of dollars by cornering the nation's gold supply. They had nearly succeeded, and during the crisis, the price of gold had been driven up radically, and that in turn had driven many to bankruptcy when they could not get gold for legitimate business transactions, especially those involving international loans or contracts. Grant had finally realized

761

what was happening and had ordered the Treasury to sell gold, thereby pricking the speculative bubble, but for thousands it was too late.

"Grant is proving himself to be a less able president than he was a soldier, though his difficulties come, I think, more from naïveté and bad judgment than malice," Gavin observed. "He failed as a businessman, everybody knows that, and perhaps that's why he trusts those who have succeeded too much."

Even while they felt sympathy for those who had been ruined, it was difficult for the Ramsays and the Browns to suppress the awareness of their own good fortune. California's gold reserves had been good since the rush began and the paper greenbacks issued by the federal government in 1862 to help finance the war had never been circulated in the state, so the currency was far sounder here than in the East. And when gold prices had soared, it had not hurt the Browns or their investors.

"Damn good luck, 'scuse me, m'am, comin' to California," one Brown said, and his brother offered fervent agreement.

The journey was not without sadness. So much of the wild fastness of the Sierras had been invaded, and the scars of hydraulic mining were hard for Tessa to credit. Huge wounds showed on hillsides where the high pressured water had eaten away the plants and soil to jagged rock. The silt from this butchery choked streams and had filtered so far down that even the bays of the ocean were being contaminated with it. As Gavin and Indian had foreseen, laws were finally being passed to limit it and would surely soon end it, but the scars would remain for generations, if not forever.

And even having loved the serenity of the untouched wilderness, it was sad to see where people had once settled to seek their fortunes only to lose and leave behind them the crumbling remains of the houses and stores raised with such hope. Saddest of all were the neglected graveyards, where the wooden markers and the occasional painstakingly carved stones weathered and slanted and succumbed to the weeds and twining vines.

As they rode past one on an early morning, Tessa reined in. The sun cut through the surrounding trees and spilled on the last tangled flowers and the rusting leaves of autumn. Once there had been a fence with a tidy gate, but it had sagged and long since fallen. The earth had shifted and settled, not one marker stood straight any more, and most of the graves were grass-covered depressions.

"It is so silent, I can almost hear them speaking," Tessa whispered. "It's a way to make mankind small, this pitiful place far below the great peaks of the mountains.

Gavin resisted his impulse to make the obvious response, to laugh and tell her that if someone here did speak it would scare them both out of several years, to make light of the eerie death place.

"It's not so bad a spot," he said instead. "It's quiet and beautiful, though I doubt very much that that makes much difference to those who lie here. Some of them loved, some of them hated, and some of them cared very little one way or another, but they all had life for however long or short a time, and that is something no mountain ever has no matter how large and enduring."

The sunlight was suddenly part of her, and birdsong she had not noticed before filled the silence. "You are life," she said. She was so full of love for him, only the barest words were possible.

It was the reason Gavin had brought her on this trip, and it colored all their days—to take time away from their normal routine just to love and to know they loved. It strengthened the bond between them, and it reminded Tessa that her role as Gavin's lover was unchanged, no matter how altered her position in the children's lives.

Gavin's delight in his wife was endless, and he marveled that it could still be so. She was such a blend of knowledge and wonder, he never knew quite what her reaction to something new would be. In the old days, they had never had any need to stay in a hotel, and would not have done so under any circumstance since most of the establishments had offered nothing more than cramped quarters, bad food, and lice and fleas which were guaranteed to make life miserable. But now there were many places that offered fine accommodations, and though they still could have made camp every night, Gavin had planned this trip to include a good many nights in soft beds. It had not really occurred to him until now that this was something wholly

763

foreign to Tessa's experience. A campsite immediately became familiar and convenient through her work even as their various dwelling places had. But hotels where strangers bedded down in adjoining rooms were totally new to her, and Gavin had difficulty controlling his mirth as he noted her reactions.

She was very much on her dignity, not wanting to shame herself or him, but alert as a deer in a suspicious clearing, and as wide-eyed as a child. She could not overcome the oddness of being waited on by complete strangers in surroundings rich with plush and polished wood chosen by some unseen person. The only place she had ever seen like these had been Belle's parlor house. She was glad after all that she had brought some of the clothes Fiona had chosen. Being well dressed gave her confidence, and she knew Gavin was proud of her.

Her favorite hotel was the National Exchange in Nevada City. Deer Creek Diggings had long since become a thriving town, the center of commerce of the northern mines. It had a habit of burning down with fair regularity, but it was always quickly rebuilt. It was set on several hills against a backdrop of higher, tree-covered slopes, and it boasted some grand houses, a few of them outlandish, all proclaiming the wealth that had come out of the area. The streets ran in steep, haphazard patterns, having grown up from the pack trails leading out to various diggings. Early settlers had planted maples, and the leaves flamed red and bronze while the tall poplars were shimmering yellow in this fall season. The vivid colors set against the deep green of the pine and fir trees were breathtaking, and Tessa persuaded Gavin to take her for a long stroll that made them both hungry for supper.

The National Exchange had enough sights of its own to fascinate Tessa. In its lobby were the rattling sounders of the telegraph office, and there also were the headquarters of the stage lines and the Wells Fargo Express. There was a continuous stream of people coming in and out. Tessa, her hunger forgotten, could have watched them for hours had Gavin not insisted that they eat.

There seemed to be very few women at the hotel, and many of the men followed Tessa with admiring stares.

"They're wondering what an old man is doing with such

a young woman on his arm," Gavin said good-naturedly. "And I'm trying not to strut like a peacock."

Tessa touched the silver in her own hair. "What do you suppose they think of this?"

"Moonlight and stardust of course, my dear," he replied promptly.

"What a romantic you have become," Tessa sighed happily, and they rushed through their meal, leaving most of it, finding they were hungrier for other things after all.

Gavin left the lamps burning when Tessa would have extinguished them. "No, love," he murmured, "I want to see you."

Their clothes lay in a heap, and she leaned against him as he unpinned her hair and ran his hands through its heavy length. He could feel her trembling and knew it was not for cold. Her mouth opened under his, and the deep probing kiss was the small dance of what their bodies would do. Yet when they lay on the bed, Gavin knew something was amiss. Tessa lay so still and silent under his caresses. He teased one taut nipple with his tongue and she moved the tiniest bit but kept silent, her jaw a tight line.

He raised his head. "What is it? What's wrong?" His own passion was cooling with worry.

Her eyes flew open. "The bed, it creaks so, and these walls are very thin. Someone will hear."

He tried to stop it, but could not. His laughter jarred the bed and filled the room. "My sweet lord, Tessa, we've been married for twenty-five years! What in the hell does it matter what anyone hears or thinks?" he gasped.

"Twenty-five years, has it really been so long as that? Is it not a wonder we can still do this?" she asked innocently, and then she was laughing with him and the bed creaked merrily far into the night, and when it was silent at dawn, Tessa bounced on it until Gavin woke up.

"I have grown to like the sound. Let us stay here for the next twenty-five years."

Gavin studied her at his leisure as she knelt on the bed. Her body was still so supple and slender. Her skin was rosy in the light that filtered through the curtains, and her hair gleamed in wild disarray, the long tendrils trailing on the bed. Her eyes sparkled with love and mischief.

765

"I would perish of overwork, but what a way to go," he said, pulling her down on top of him.

It was hard to accept that the trip was over and they had to return to the city to take up their duties, but they carried with them an almost tangible aura of joy. Tessa found herself humming all day long and smiling at nothing, and the nicest part was that it seemed to be contagious—people smiled back. Even Paul's mood was light around his parents.

And her happiness was increased when a long letter arrived from Jefferson. He admitted he missed everyone, but as Gavin pointed out, there was no doubt that he was having the time of his life. He had acquired two good friends, Smokey and Shanks; God only knew what their real names were, Jefferson certainly didn't. Abilene had to be the wildest place on earth, maybe even wilder than San Francisco in the old days though not as sophisticated. Life on a trail drive could be monotonous, but just when you thought nothing was ever going to happen again, something did—a stampede, a flash flood, rustlers.

"He writes as if he enjoys such disasters!" Tessa exclaimed, and Gavin chuckled. "At his age, I would have too."

Afterward Tessa remembered bitterly that fate never allowed one to be too happy for too long, and she should have known something terrible was going to happen. But she was totally unprepared when it did.

Christmas was drawing closer, and she was busy both at the shop and at home. Brand, Paul, and Fiona, even at their ages, made a game of ferreting out the surprises she planned, and so she'd taken to outwitting them by spending at least part of the afternoon at home doing her Christmas work while they were all busy elsewhere.

She was wrapping a fine set of leatherbound volumes of Shakespeare for Paul when Fiona burst into the room, and her first reaction was only relief that Paul hadn't caught her. But her relief turned swiftly to dismay when she saw the expression on her daughter's face.

Fiona was pale as death except for two angry spots of color on her cheeks. She was breathing hard and her eyes were a murky gray, as wild as a storm at sea.

Tessa started up in alarm. "My dear, what is the matter?"

"Was my father crippled too, or is this just the mark of bastards?" Fiona hissed, and when her mother would have reached out to her, she backed away. "Don't touch me! I couldn't bear it!"

A fit of trembling seized Tessa, and she held onto a chair back to keep from falling. She felt stunned and helpless. It was too late to deny it, and yet she couldn't imagine how Fiona had discovered it. She found her voice with difficulty, and then the words poured out.

"I am sorry, Fiona, so terribly sorry! Whoever told you could have done so for no reason except malice. I thought of telling you; I thought of it quite often. But then I could see no reason save to ease my own burden of guilt. I wanted a daughter desperately. You are that daughter. And Gavin is your father. He's your father in every single sense except the beginning. The man who . . . who was the beginning of you was a lovely man, a marvelous human being. He would have loved you, and dearly too. He died at Gettysburg. Gavin saw him there and told him about you. He was proud and glad to know that something of his spirit would continue in the world though he could not." Her voice trailed away at the look of revulsion on Fiona's face.

"You may think of it any way you care to and tell pretty tales," she snarled, "but the truth is that you were a whore and my father—Gavin was a cuckold, and your friends were prostitutes and pimps."

Tessa's head snapped up and her eyes flashed dangerously, "You may call me any filthy name you wish, but you keep your foul mouth off of Gavin and the Coras, or I will make you regret it!"

Fiona cowered away in real fear; she had never known her mother so angry with her.

Tessa buried her face in her hands with a little moan. "Oh, God, Fiona, don't look like that! I would not hurt you for the world! It is just that I can't bear to hear cruel things said about people who have given me so much love and kindness." She saw a sudden ray of hope, and her voice quickened. "Will you stay here for just a moment, please, Fiona? I have something to show you."

Fiona said nothing but she nodded, and Tessa fled the room, returning with the bundle cradled in her arms. With infinite care she unwrapped it.

"I meant to give you this later, but there is no reason now to delay. I would have told you that an old friend wanted you to have it. But I think the truth is, after all, better. His name was Jordan Ames. He loved beautiful things, and he had a beautiful mind and spirit. He could speak several languages, and he had read and understood more than anyone else I have ever known." Her words were as soft as the gentle motion of her hands stroking the cool jade. "This was a gift from him. I know he would have liked very much for you to have it."

Fiona took the Kuanyin and stared at it for a moment. Then, before Tessa could stop her, she hurled it against the wall. It shattered with a terrible, sharp sound.

Tessa gazed at Fiona in horror. "That was a very lovely, very valuable piece. How could you have destroyed it?" Her voice was slow and hollow. She was appalled not only by what her daughter had done but by her own mistaken judgment in thinking Fiona's curiosity had been the beginning of understanding. A sick sadness filled her. She thought of all the years Kuanyin had been hidden away waiting to be a gift for Fiona. And now there was nothing more than shards of stone in the place of the tranquil perfection of the statue.

"He paid you well," Fiona said, and she slammed out of the room.

Mrs. Tubbs found Tessa slumped in a chair, her eyes wide and distant, a cut finger dripping blood on her dress, her hands still clutching what looked like pieces of green glass.

"I am so sorry," Mrs. Tubbs said. "I came as soon as I could leave the school, but I see I'm too late."

"Sorry does not seem to be an adequate word today," Tessa replied tonelessly, "but I know whatever happened, it wasn't your fault."

Mrs. Tubbs took out a clean handkerchief, glad of something to do while she explained. "There's no sense in bleeding to death," she chided, not asking what the fragments were as she pried open Tessa's hands and bound the cut.

768

Tessa made one half-hearted attempt to hold onto the jade, but then she let it fall.

"What happened was not only terrible, it was inexplicable. Fiona is much more teacher than pupil now, as you know, and she is very patient with the children and well liked. And the little girl who behaved so horribly is not generally like that. Cissy is a trifle slow in some subjects, but she tries and is well mannered, almost too polite. I think she is less than happy at home. She is three years younger than Fiona, and she will never be an attractive girl. So perhaps she is jealous of Fiona's beauty, but she's never done anything like this before. Fiona was trying to explain a problem in arithmetic to her, and Cissy suddenly looked very sly, and then she told Fiona that she didn't have to listen to her because she was a . . . " Mrs. Tubbs swallowed and went on, "a bastard. She said quite a few other nasty things besides, and I am sure someone put her up to it."

"What is Cissy's surname?" Tessa asked.

"Beecham," Mrs. Tubbs offered, and she recoiled at the sudden change in Tessa's face and the humorless wail of laughter.

"That fat insufferable bitch! Obviously you don't remember the incident, but I threw her out of this house years ago. I should have cut her tongue out. And do you want to know the final irony? She and her husband were simply investors in the Lucille mine. They were never friends of ours, never moved in the same circles. There is no way Mrs. Beecham could possibly know the truth. She asked her daughter about her school; she heard about Fiona, perhaps even saw her. She guessed and twisted the words with her hate and fed them to her child. What sweet revenge she has taken, some truth, some lies, and no way now to undo it." Her face was so bleak, Mrs. Tubbs looked away.

The harmony of the house was destroyed. Even Kam Lee, who had kept himself aloof from the first, muttered constantly, darkly and in Chinese, over the state of things. Inadvertently, all the Ramsay men made the situation worse.

When Gavin came home to Tessa's grief, he went to

Fiona, knocking on her door and speaking gently until she let him in. And he remained calm until Fiona attacked her mother. Then he lost his temper, even as Tessa had in the mirror image.

"It was a long time ago, and it's over now. But it was a hard time for both of us, and both of us were at fault. Your mother goddamn near died giving birth to you, but there's no one on earth who could love you more than she does. If you ever become half of what she is, you'll be one hell of a woman!" he thundered, and the only thing he could give himself credit for when he cooled down was that he had not told her that she had nearly not been born at all and it might have been better that way.

Brand's reaction was no more satisfying to Fiona. He was stunned, but he remembered far enough back to have more than a little understanding and to realize that it was surely something he had always known, at least subconsciously. He had known and liked Jordan Ames, and Fiona looked so much like him. In a strange way, it made him love his parents more because now he knew that they had weathered a rough time and the love they shared had not come without hazard. "For Christ's sake, you're getting to be a prime shrew," he told his sister. "You sound like you'd like the pedigree of a good horse." And he had no more interest in the subject.

Paul had always been Fiona's fierce protector and dearest brother, and his defection to the enemy camp was hardest for her to bear. "So," he said quietly, "what do you want? What's done is done. You were born, and you've grown up to be a beautiful woman, even though Gavin is not your natural father. Would you prefer not to exist at all? I expect I'm a bastard too. I doubt very much that my parents were ever married. Does that make you think less of me? And whatever happened before or after, you can be sure that Mother and Jordan Ames shared something very special, something they both needed at the time. You're the result of that, and you ought to be proud."

Fiona's palms itched with the urge to slap him. But her hurt was far deeper than her anger. They were all, even Lotus and Mrs. Tubbs, bound together in a way they scarcely realized, and she saw too clearly—they all loved Tessa so much, nothing on earth could alter that love.

Fiona had never felt so lonesome in her life. And worse, she lost the image of her own beauty and wholeness. Fears she had never fully faced surfaced and possessed her. She was lame and pale and small—a bitch, a shrew, a bastard. She was jealous of them all for their tall, dark, and perfect beauty; even Paul, who was not related by blood, looked more a Ramsay to her eyes than she did. And most of all she was jealous of her mother.

It was satisfying at least to know she had effectively ruined the joy of the holidays for the family. That much power she had.

CHAPTER LXIV

Tessa watched her daughter with growing sorrow in the following months. Gone was the loving girl who had laughed tenderly at her parents' clowning. Fiona seldom laughed these days, and when she did it was almost always at someone else's expense. Her face wore a perpetually guarded look as if she were peering out at the world from protective shutters, giving nothing of herself in return. Her spirit was becoming more crippled than her leg had ever been. And every attempt to reach her failed. Even her friendship with Lotus seemed at an end. Lotus had only spoken the truth when she said, "I am the child of the Chens but not by blood. I will never know who my mother or my father was, and I do not find that I care greatly. It would not change me to know."

Now when Lotus came to the house, she came to see Tessa or Brand or Paul, anyone except Fiona.

The one area of Fiona's life that remained as it had been was her involvement in the school. Tessa and Mrs. Tubbs discussed it at length, but neither of them could be sure of Fiona's motives. The only one that made any sense at all was that this was where she focused all that remained of the old Fiona. For whatever reason, she continued to teach with the same sweet spirit she had had before. Even Cissy Beecham was not neglected or punished. Tessa hoped that

that stuck in Mrs. Beecham's craw like poisoned grain—the woman had caused so much hurt, but there was nothing to do to her that would not make it harder for Fiona.

Tessa's worst fear was confirmed when Franklin Lauder escorted Fiona home from the school one late afternoon. He was in his late twenties, a handsome man. His features were finely cut without being feminine. His hair was a rich chestnut brown, much the same color as Paul's, and his eyes were deep brown, almost black. He was well dressed in the subtle style of a man with money and taste. His speech was cultured and hinted of an East Coast origin. He was honest about having made his money only by luck and the Comstock Lode. He had great plans for his ranch in southern California, not far from Los Angeles. He was only visiting San Francisco for pleasure; the theaters were so much better here, not to mention the book shops and other attractions.

Including Fiona, Tessa thought. His courtesy was flawless. He explained his first sight of Fiona and his subsequent boldness guilelessly. He had been so struck by her beauty, nothing would do but that he introduce himself, escort her home, and meet her parents. He was sorry Mr. Ramsay was not at home; he hoped to meet him soon, and Fiona's brothers too.

Tessa's long training in hospitality failed her. She was so cold in her reception of the visitor, even her movements were stiff and jerky. She saw Fiona's delight fade, angry defiance taking its place, and still she could not do as her daughter wanted and welcome the man.

She hated him on sight. His eyes could have been so warm, but no soft light moved in the brown depths. They were the eyes of Luis, flat, dark, glittering on the surface like a reptile's eyes. Tessa's revulsion was so great, she nearly gagged. And she failed utterly to hide her reaction, stammering that she was not receiving visitors this afternoon. His apologies for inconveniencing her were eloquent and his promise to Fiona that he would certainly be seeing more of her and looked forward to meeting the rest of her family was silky smooth. But his eyes watched Tessa with cruel enjoyment and managed at the same time to strip her naked.

Fiona's mute and drooping pose lasted only until he had
772

left. Then she turned on her mother. "How could you? How *could* you be so rude? Haven't you done enough to ruin my life?"

Tessa listened dully to the quick, uneven rhythm of Fiona's flight and the now familiar slam of her door.

Tessa was so irrational about Franklin Lauder, Gavin had little choice but to take the calm role. He found it ironic that Fiona was perfectly willing to claim him as her father when she introduced Mr. Lauder to him.

Gavin did not have Tessa's visceral reaction to the man. Nor did he particularly like him, and this inability to make a clear judgment disturbed him. Normally, it did not take long for him to know how he felt about someone; he would have been dead long since had his senses been less acute in this. But Franklin Lauder remained an enigma. Sometimes Gavin felt his polite manners and respectful courtship of Fiona were wholly genuine, but at other times, for no reason he could name, he felt the man was playing them all for fools. He would have been relieved to have caught him being disrespectful to Tessa or too bold with Fiona, but he knew it wasn't going to be that easy, just as he knew that Tessa was driven to a nervous frenzy by Lauder's courtesy to her, a courtesy she continued to damn as false.

Gavin was in a quandary, and he could not see any way to resolve it to Tessa's satisfaction. There was no doubt that Lauder was courting Fiona, and she blossomed under his attention as she did under no one else's. And she moped and brooded endlessly while the man was away tending to his business in the south, though that was not as often as one would have thought. Frank seemed to think nothing of the distance between Los Angeles and San Francisco and seemed to have his properties running smoothly to be able to spend so much time in the north. Gavin made discreet inquiries through one of his banks and found that Lauder's wealth was genuine and extensive, so at least he was not after Fiona's money.

Tessa pleaded desperately for Gavin's help in sending Fiona away, anywhere away from Lauder.

Gavin regarded her compassionately. "Do you really think that would do anything except make her more sure than ever that he is her only champion? And do you think with his money and her determination there is any place where she could be safely hidden? I wouldn't even bet on a convent."

Tessa frowned at his attempted humor, and he held her for a moment. "Ah, sweetheart, there's always the possibility that we just aren't ready for our only little girl to grow up. But she's a year older than you were when you married me."

"Franklin Lauder is not you, and Fiona is not as old now as I was then, no matter how many years she has," Tessa said firmly. But she knew he was right about the limitations of their power over Fiona, and she did not spurn the comfort he offered.

It was almost a relief when in October Frank asked permission to marry Fiona. Gavin had to give him credit; he played by the rules—not once had he failed to do things properly. Whether he believed in the game was another matter.

Gavin pointed out that Fiona was very young and Los Angeles was nearly five hundred miles away. Lauder countered with his claim that many girls married when they were younger, as Mrs. Ramsay had (Fiona had obviously given him every weapon she had), and that Fiona was remarkably mature for seventeen. As for the distance, he himself had proved it was no barrier. Fiona could visit via ship from San Pedro or by stage, and undoubtedly before too long, by rail. He admired Fiona and loved her dearly; he would do everything to make her life a happy one.

Gavin gave his consent, knowing he had no other course except to risk having a raging and more rebellious Fiona on his hands; a Fiona who perhaps after all knew better than her parents what would make her happy.

Tessa made one last appeal to her daughter. She knew she couldn't tell her the whole story of Luis; Fiona would twist that until it became her mother's fault and further proof of her immorality. But she came as close to the truth as she dared.

"Please, listen, my dear," she begged. "You are intelligent and very beautiful. If you wish to marry you will have countless chances. But please, refuse Mr. Lauder. You can still do that; it's not too late!" She paused, trying to steady her voice. "I almost had to marry a man like Mr. Lauder.

774

I was nearly witless with terror by the time your father"—she said the word firmly—" rescued me. I can't tell you how I know, but I do. Franklin Lauder is a vicious man. You will come to hurt through him."

"That's the most ridiculous and slanderous thing I've ever heard," Fiona sneered. "Frank adores me. You just hate to admit you have a daughter who is old enough to marry because it reminds you of how old you are. You're impossible, and I shall be glad to leave this house." She turned her back on her mother and walked away.

The wedding was set for early December, and Tessa began to plan it with a lavish hand and deadly precision; she would not disgrace Fiona for her own grief. Even Fiona could see that everything was being taken care of. There were two things Tessa would not do, but they mattered to herself and would not have occurred to her daughter in any case. She would not invite Ramón and María or their sons to the wedding. They did not in any case, know Fiona that well, but they would know about Lauder; they would see the ghost of Luis as clearly as Tessa did, she was sure of it. She would send word afterward, making some excuse for not telling them before. Her other decision was that the emerald collar from Don Esteban would remain in her possession. She had intended it for a bridal gift to Fiona from the day Belle had returned it to her; now she could not bear to bless the unholy union with it.

Carmelita and Sam did come north, arriving several days before the wedding. They stayed with Armenthia and Indian, since the Ramsay household was in such an uproar.

Carmelita regarded Tessa gravely before she embraced her. "I have seen you look happier," she said, and Tessa clung to her convulsively for an instant. "I suspect all mothers of brides are a little nervous," she offered.

Tessa drew back and managed to smile. "I have never seen you looking so lovely." She meant it; there was a new fineness to Carmelita's figure and features and a strange radiance that made Tessa feel as if she could put her hands out and feel them warmed.

Carmelita blushed at the compliment and gave all the credit to her loving husband. Tessa missed Sam's worried frown, but she saw Carmelita's complete comprehension when she met Mr. Lauder. She was no less perceptive than the Ramirezes. She would not speak of it to Tessa or Gavin, beyond admitting that the man was a little too flashy for her taste, but she sought out Indian.

"So, the dead do come back," she said softly. "You should know perhaps even better than Tessa does."

He didn't try to evade her meaning. They looked at each other from the depths of their friendship and love that would tolerate no lies. Indian nodded. "Seem so, at least th' evil ones. Ain't never seen th' good come back. I jus' been keepin' out of th' way. It's good as done. Fiona will have her way. I get too close to that man, I jus' might make her widow 'fore she a wife. Thank God ain't one of my daughters marryin' him. At least Tessa, she got Gavin help her through this."

Tessa did have Gavin, and she was constantly thankful for his support. When she woke screaming in the night from renewed nightmares of Luis, Gavin held her and soothed her back into sleep. When she thought she just couldn't accomplish one more task, he was there, persuading her to stop for a while, holding her curled in his lap until he felt the tension draining away.

It was all he could do, and he wished there was more. Tessa's eyes were shadowed, and she had grown thin and pale as if she were grieving for a dead child rather than sending her daughter off to a new life. He spent much more time at home than usual simply to be there when she needed him.

He heard a sound in the library and checked automatically to see who was home in the in-and-out madhouse of the past week. He found Paul, surrounded by half-a-dozen books open but discarded, obviously inadequate to the task of comforting. He guessed the half-empty snifter of brandy wasn't doing the job any better. Paul wasn't flushed with drink; he was pale, tight-lipped, and hollow-eyed. He looked worse than Tessa. And it took him a moment to even notice that Gavin had come into the room. When he did, he sprang to his feet with a guilty start.

"Hello, sir. I quit work early," he stammered.

Even after all these years, Gavin still wanted to smile at Paul's form of address—Tessa was "Mother" but he was "sir," always sir. He no longer winced in discomfort at it;
776

as Tessa had explained once, it was the same way Paul would address God if he had anything to say to him. He scolded her for the comparison, but he knew what she meant. He felt a deep welling of tenderness for this young man as dear to him as his blood sons. And he felt Paul's pain as if it were his own. He had observed and considered for a long time. He had hoped he was mistaken, but he knew now he was not, and he attacked the subject directly.

"Goddamn awful to watch the woman you love marrying another man, isn't it? I came near to having to do the same thing with your mother."

Paul went even whiter, then flushed, but made no attempt at denial. "I thought I had hidden it so well, but it's getting impossible now. How long have you known?"

"Not as long as I should have. Looking back it all fits. You've adored and protected Fiona ever since she was born."

"Just as any brother should." Paul said dully.

"Well, that's what I thought and what Tessa still thinks, and I expect Fiona too. But it hasn't been like that for years, has it?" He saw the haunted look in Paul's eyes and gave him no time to answer. "You can stop feeling guilty right now. In every way that matters you are a son to me and to Tessa. We could not love you more had I sired you and she delivered you from her womb. But you are not Fiona's brother; there is no blood shared between you. What you feel is incestuous only if you allow yourself to think it is. Neither Brand nor Jefferson love her the way you do. If they did, then I would worry." Not even now did Gavin make any reference to the fact that Fiona was only half-sister to his sons, and Paul wondered anew at the strength of this man he loved and respected so deeply.

Gavin was silent for a long thoughtful moment, and when he spoke again, his voice was grave. "If my own life had been different, I could tell you, that you'll get over it and everything will turn out for the best eventually. But in all honesty, I can't say that. I loved Tessa from the instant I saw her. We've had hard, even hating times, but what I felt for her then and what I still feel for her now, I could never have felt for another woman. If that's the way you feel about Fiona, and I think it is, then all I can hope for

777

you is that the pain will become more bearable with time. And for the present, I'm damn sorry I have to send you away on business right now, damn sorry you'll miss the wedding."

Paul's face was suddenly bright with hope, but it was quickly dimmed. "What will Mother say? What with Jefferson gone and all?"

"There're two things I can do about that. I can lie to her and tell her it's absolutely essential you accomplish this imaginary task, or I can tell her the truth and give everyone else the lie."

Paul managed a credible grin. "I think you'd better tell her the truth. You don't seem very good at lying to her."

Gavin smiled back. "You're right about that." His smile faded abruptly. "She's trying to be very civilized about it because she has no choice, but our plan will be greatly assisted by the fact that she hates Franklin Lauder more than I can tell you, more than you and I can possibly hate him." He was speaking almost to himself, looking back to the days of Luis, and his face was suddenly so dangerous looking, Paul banished all thought of asking for further explanations.

"Thank you, sir," Paul said simply when they had finished discussing plans and details of Paul's nebulous errand, and Gavin grinned wryly. "You are most welcome. I only wish I were going with you."

Paul was folding the last shirt into his bag when he heard the uneven footsteps approaching his door, which he wished to God he'd closed, locked, anything to avoid her. Cold sweat beaded his skin and his hands couldn't seem to remember the easy task of folding a shirt.

"Paul, what are you doing?" she asked from the doorway, but he didn't turn around. She came to his side.

"For goodness' sakes, you should have called me or Kam Lee to do this. You're a terrible packer." She took the shirt from him and folded it with competent hands, which stilled suddenly. "The wedding isn't until day after tomorrow, and surely you can't be going anywhere until afterward, so why are you packing now? And where are you going, anyway?" The beginning of suspicion and panic edged her voice.

He was drowning in the soft fragrance of her, as soft as the cloud of silvery-gold hair and gray-blue eyes and pale skin. It was mad to love so much, so much that her voice and even the sound of her crippled walk were a private kind of music for him. The horrible image he had been fighting for so long rose up to blind him—Frank Lauder looming over her, sinking into her. *God, don't let me think of it any more, God, let me find the words, don't let her know!* It was a screaming prayer in his head, and with detached wonder, he heard his own voice explaining calmly that he was awfully sorry, but he was going to miss the wedding because of important business in Monterey.

Fiona was stunned. Despite their recent estrangement, she counted so much on Paul; he had always been there to protect and support her. "It's them, isn't it? He and my mother are sending you away because they don't approve of Frank and they want to make it harder for me!"

It was good to feel a spark of anger against her, anything to get him through this. "Your mother and father, my mother and father," he corrected her sharply. "When are you going to stop punishing them and yourself? You're going to be a nasty, twisted old woman long before your time if you don't watch it."

She disarmed him easily, pulling him around to face her, her eyes filling with tears. "I'm sorry, I don't mean to be hateful, I'm just so confused. Please, please don't be angry with me. I can't bear it. I need you so, you're my favorite brother. Don't go away!"

He wanted to yell at her that he was not her brother, that he loved her as a man, not as a brother; he wanted to command her to banish Lauder forever. Instead, he felt the deliverance of icy calm descending. "I have to go, it's very important, but you have my best wishes for tomorrow and forever. I hope you will always be very, very happy. And it's not really me, you're the one who is leaving." He stooped from his slender height to kiss her gently on the forehead. "God bless you, Fiona. Now run along and let me get on with this." Just the right degree of brotherliness, but he saw the first faint and puzzled awareness dawning in her eyes and he was doubly glad to be leaving.

But his ordeal was not over. First Brand appeared, coming in with his usual quick stride to regard Paul without surprise. "Wondered how long you could stand it. Wish I were going with you, though my reasons aren't the same."

779

"What reasons?" Paul asked stiffly, regarding Brand warily. And then he was touched and pleased as he realized that Brand, always elegant and in command, was actually going awkward and gruff-voiced with emotion. "Nobody needed to tell me. Hell, Paul, she's a fool not to know, and maybe you're a fool for not telling her. No one's ever going to love her like you do. But as it is, I'm glad you're not going to have to suffer through the ceremony. Ride swiftly and get your ass out of town, brother mine," he finished with a crooked grin.

Different as they were from each other, they had grown closer over the years, even more so after Jefferson had left, but this was the closest they had ever been, and Paul had a sudden strong temptation to use it to plead with Brand to take care with the wild company he was keeping, to take good care of himself, since he would be the only son for their parents to rely on for a while. But he knew what Brand's reaction to that would be, so instead he held out his hand, and all he said was, "Thanks, Brand. I'll be seeing you. Don't let Kam Lee poison you. His idea of a wedding feast smells pretty strange so far, probably starts off with chopped pickled priest on rice." Safe ground, the endless variations on the old jokes that had begun with Chong Sing's exquisite cooking.

When Tessa came in search of him, he was glad all over again that she was who she was, her love and compassion showing plainly; never any holding back with her, never. "My poor darling," she murmured, putting her arms around him as though he were a little boy again. He dropped his head to her shoulder for a moment, breathing in her delicate scent, drawing comfort from her before he stepped back. "I picked a fine dramatic time to give myself away, didn't I?" he said ruefully.

She would have none of his self-reproach. "We have all come unraveled. It is horrible to feel this way about a wedding, as if we were planning a funeral. Listen," she commanded, cocking her head, and he heard the wind; it had been blowing so constantly since December began that he had ceased to notice it, but now the roar was loud and ugly. "I feel as if even the earth disapproves. The wind has felled the old semaphore station on Telegraph Hill. When

I learned that, I wished for a moment it would cause enough havoc here so that we need not have this wedding. But it will be, and I can only pray that Fiona is right about the man and all of us are wrong." She regarded him solemnly for a moment, her beautiful eyes the color of the amethysts he had tried to steal so long ago. He felt a helpless flash of pity and understanding for Fiona, so lovely in her own way, but a pale shadow next to her mother. Then, now, the years simply adding grace.

"Parents can be so blind about their children. I should have seen long before this how you feel about Fiona. I should have known the reason for your quiet sadness. Now all I can do is give you my blessing for this trip. If you need extra time away, take it. Carmelita and Sam, though they may stay for a couple of days after the wedding, will be back at their own home soon enough. I have already spoken to them. They asked for no explanations. They love you dearly. Their house is yours, they said, and they hope you will use it. I think it might be better for a while than either of the *ranchos*, where you would have to explain too much. *Vaya con Dios*, my son." One more swift hug and a kiss, and she was gone, before her tears came to make it harder for both of them.

The only person Paul managed to avoid was Kam Lee. His relief far outweighed his guilt. Kam Lee would never allow himself to be as close to the family as Chong Sing had been, but he did have a firm idea of what was proper in a family, and he would frown and mutter at the older brother's desertion. Riding away, Paul almost smiled. A hopeless idiot for loving Fiona he might be, but at least he wasn't a joss house sacrifice for the day.

He savored the quiet of Monterey, doing his best to ignore the images of Fiona. He decided to take his mother's advice and wait there for the Collinses to return. He liked both of them very much, and they were easy to be with and comforting in their love for each other.

It wasn't to be. They still weren't back when the messenger from the telegraph office found him.

He could hear his own voice howling, "Oh, God, oh, God, no!" over and over, and he wished it would stop. The next thing he knew he was down at the waterfront

781

been drinking, but he wasn't drunk, and Gavin's feeling of apprehension grew swiftly. He glanced back into the room distractedly.

"I don't want Mother to hear," Brand whispered.

Gavin abandoned all thought of telling his son that whatever it was, it could wait until morning. Normally very little disturbed Brand; whatever it was now, it was serious. Gavin checked to make sure Tessa was still asleep, and then he and Brand went quietly down the softly lighted hall and downstairs to the study.

Gavin declined one but made no objection when Brand poured himself a generous drink. Brand's hands were shaking, and his voice wasn't much steadier. "She was right. She's been right all along."

"Who's right about what?" Gavin asked patiently.

Brand took a quick gulp and choked a little. "Mother, about Frank Lauder." His eyes slid away from his father's. "I know it sounds farfetched, but there's a kind of honor code on the Barbary Coast. If you can survive, most people will keep your secrets. I knew Frank wasn't any stranger there, but who am I to judge a man for pleasure-seeking—I do enough of it myself. But I asked around anyway. Tonight was the first time I learned anything about him." He buried his face in his hands, and his voice was muffled. "I would to God I hadn't!" He shook himself like a dog coming out of icy water, got up, and began to pace the room, still avoiding Gavin's eyes.

"Hell, I expect everybody knows I've had a Barbary Coast whore for years. I pay and she delivers whatever I want—talk, drink, sex. It's honest on both sides, and Dorie's a grand woman in her way. I'd trust her a lot further than I would many so-called honest citizens I know."

"You don't have to defend her to me," Gavin said quietly. "Your mother was the first and will be the last woman I ever love, but she was a long way from the first I ever had."

Brand nodded his head in quick thanks. "I guess I knew that. I'm having trouble getting to the point." He stood stock still and met his father's eyes squarely. "My appetites may be too keen, but they're normal. Frank's aren't. Dorie asked around for me too, and she heard from an woman today. Dorie's seen a lot, and she's no innocent, but even she was repelled by what she told me tonight. Lauder has been known to pay outrageous sums for his pleasures. And his pleasures all have one thing in common; they're all crippled or disfigured in some way. They have twisted or missing limbs or they have birthmarks or scars. They haven't all been female—young boys seem adequate for him as long as they aren't perfect. Madams have had to go to a lot of trouble to find what Frank Lauder wants. But now he won't even have to pay for it, will he? He's marrying Fiona." Brand's face was suddenly an unnatural shade of green; he clapped a hand over his mouth and staggered out of the room, mumbling that he'd be back.

Gavin would have gone after him to make sure he was all right had he not felt so sick himself. He changed his mind about the drink, but not even the taste of good brandy could wash the bile from his mouth.

Brand came back, still ashen-faced, but more in control. "I've never been much of a brother to Fiona; somehow we've just never been very close, maybe because poor Paul was always there for her. But I could kill that man easily now for her."

Gavin shook his head. "Surely we can find some other way." His father's calm acceptance of murder as one alternative comforted Brand as nothing else could. "First, could we obtain proof of this and quickly?"

Brand thought for a moment. "No," he admitted slowly. "I believe every word of it, but proof would be impossible. As soon as anyone got wind of it being official and important, they'd scuttle off like crabs to protect their own. After all, Lauder did pay."

"Then there's only one thing to do, and I'm the one to do it," Gavin said. "I'll speak to Fiona in the morning." He raised his glass. "To Dorie, and to you, Brand."

Brand slept peacefully through the hours left before dawn, relieved of the burden his father now carried. Gavin did not sleep at all.

"You look dreadful," Tessa said remorsefully. "I am so sorry to have given you such a bad night."

"Not bad at all," Gavin lied, planting a tender kiss on her forehead. "I'm just suffering from father-of-the-bride nerves." His light words had nothing to do with the ice inside, and he sought out Fiona before she had even arisen. She looked very small and young lying in her bed with the coverlet up to her chin.

He learned quickly how woefully misleading that image was, and he knew with a growing sense of despair that somehow he was failing in his mission. It began badly.

Fiona's voice was small, silvery, and cold as Gavin felt. "It is a trifle late for us to have a father-daughter chat about the realities of life, don't you think?" she asked. "And I can't think of any other reason you would be here, unless my mother has sent you for a last useless argument."

He stumbled through his reason for being there, trying to soften the blow because she was, after all, so young, and because his own revulsion for what Brand had told him was so great, he had to temper it somehow. He managed only to sound unsure.

"He told me," Fiona returned coldly, and Gavin was completely taken aback. "He tol' . . . told you?" he stammered.

"Yes, he did. Frank and I have no secrets. Of course, the truth from him sounded different than these lies from you. He is no virgin, and I prefer it that way. One of us fumbling around in ignorance will be adequate."

He gazed at her for one shocked instant. "That's disgusting," he said, and coming from her in the way she said it, it was, though her mother had long since told him the same thing.

"We all grow up sometime. Don't try to prevent this marriage, Gavin Ramsay. I will make you sorry forever if you do." The venomous words followed him as he lurched out of her room.

He had never felt so defeated, and Brand made him feel worse when he collared him, looking distraught. "Everything's going ahead! For God's sake, didn't you talk to her?"

"I did," Gavin answered tightly. "But Lauder had already covered that ground, just in case. I thought of talking to him, Brand, warning him off, but I fear he might take it out on Fiona. And I know him well enough now to know he'll have some explanation smooth as glass. And your sister is the most determined of all. I think she will destroy herself if we get in the way of her will. She has some of her

785

mother's strength, all to the wrong purpose." His shoulders sagged wearily. Brand looked at him without sympathy, shaken to the core by his father's failure. "Well, then, I'll go put on my finest to play the loving brother in this farce," he snarled.

The day was even more nightmare for Gavin than it was for Tessa, who drifted through it in frozen blankness. Gavin gave his daughter in marriage through a red mist of helpless rage, but he said the words. Fiona looked exquisite, Lauder the prince of every girl's dreams, and Gavin swallowed the bitterness rising in his throat. There was such travesty in this day. It was Fiona who had insisted there be music and dancing after the ceremony, and Gavin wanted to look away but could not when her new husband led her out for the first waltz. He heard the indrawn breaths of pity from the guests, and it took him a moment to realize that the pain in his hand came from the bite of Tessa's nails. He had to give Frank credit; he managed the dance by holding Fiona so that her feet scarcely touched the floor, but it was still a pitiful and awkward thing to behold.

"I cannot bear to dance with him," Tessa muttered so that only Gavin could hear, and when there was a slight pause during which he should have partnered Fiona while Lauder danced with Tessa, Gavin looked straight at him and shook his head just once in negation before he led his wife out on the floor.

His greatest worry was Brand, and he tried nervously to keep track of him. Mrs. Tubbs and the Chens were among the guests, and he hoped they would have some effect on his son, especially Lotus. He did spot her talking earnestly to Brand at one point, but Brand's face did not look receptive. He was drinking heavily, not the champagne the guests were enjoying, but raw whiskey, from the odor Gavin picked up when he got close enough. "Go easy," he warned, and it was a shock to see his own eyes looking back at him with an expression as dangerously tense as he himself felt.

"Why should I go easy?" Brand asked with a sardonic smile. "It's time to celebrate, isn't it?" His words were sharp, untouched as yet by the alcohol, and that reassured Gavin a little. He searched the crowd for Tessa and saw

786

her pressed back in the shadows against one wall. He went to her, slipping an arm around her waist. "You look like the proverbial ghost at the feast."

She pressed against him. "I cannot wait until this is over. I wish everyone would leave. The wind is my own voice wailing."

Even over the chatter and music, the wind was audible as it gathered strength in the growing darkness. And then there was a new sound that stopped every other except the wind. Brand's voice, loud and frighteningly distinct.

"Drink a toast one and all. It is not often you can witness a fairy tale come true. We have before us Beauty and the Beast. But no, not quite the same. In the old tale they were both kind of heart and full of love. The Beast was no beast at all inside his fearsome form. Ah, but here you have a man beauteous to behold on the outside, true beast inside. He lusts after the lame, the halt, the blind. He fondles them as the sweetest of all flesh. Male or female, it matters not, his cock will rise and crow on any occasion of imperfection. I give you my new brother and my sister, the poor idiot who married him."

Everyone had been pretending that all was well, and Brand had exploded the myth in their faces, his voice rolling over them eloquently in the lewd litany. They stood frozen for an instant. Lauder broke first, going for Brand, but Brand's fists were already knotted and his voice was savage now. "Just try it. I'd love to break your neck."

Lauder backed off, standing at bay, his face beet red, and then the rest of the trance shattered. Fiona screamed and went on screaming and noise rose in every corner until Gavin's voice thundered over the Babel. "Enough! Brand, get out! Go somewhere and sober up before you set foot in this house again." He knew it was unjust—part of him had relished every word of Brand's outburst—but although neither Brand nor Lauder was armed, there was so much violence boiling in the room, it had to be stopped before someone was hurt or killed.

Brand faced his father and spoke very slowly. "Glad to oblige you, father. Cowardice has a vile stench." He turned on his heel and didn't look back.

Tessa had seen it all, heard it all as if it were happening a very great distance from her, but everything snapped back into focus with Brand's exit. She didn't know why, she only knew it was very important that she go to him. She fought off the kindly friends who tried to impede her progress, seeing Carmelita, Armenthia, and Mrs. Tubbs as little more than obstacles in the path to her son.

He had already thrown the saddle over his horse when Tessa got to him. The wind whined around them, and the palomino skittered nervously.

"Don't leave like this!" she cried desperately.

"You heard the man," he said, swinging up into the saddle and controlling the prancing horse with skillful hands.

"Not like this, don't leave like this! Go to Indian's house. Rest there until morning."

He leaned from the saddle and dropped a kiss on her cheek. "Don't fret, Mother. I'll be fine."

She watched and listened until the darkness swallowed him and the thunder of the horse's hoofs blended with the wind. When she turned back toward the house, she saw Gavin's tall form silhouetted in the doorway.

"What he said, is it true?" she asked.

"I don't know for sure, but I expect it is. I tried to tell Fiona, but she wouldn't listen," Gavin replied wearily. The rage that had spent itself in him glowed in her face. The skin was stretched tightly over her cheekbones, her mouth was a thin line, her nostrils were arched and distended, and her eyes were wild. But her anger was not directed against him. She swept past him into the house before he thought to stop her.

"This farce is finished! All of you, go home, go home now!" she cried. Even the people who knew and loved her well backed away from her. She moved like a stalking cat until she stood before Frank and Fiona. "Fiona, you are a blind, stubborn fool, but you have married this creature of your own will. Both of you, get out! You have brought nothing but sorrow on this house." It was some satisfaction to know that the one thing Fiona wanted to say could not be said without revealing her true parentage to her husband. That it would make no difference to him was inconceivable to her.

It was no satisfaction that Frank Lauder had, in spite of the unpleasant scene, gotten what he had come for. He

788

made an elaborate bow before he took Fiona's arm and led her outside to the hired carriage whose driver had been waiting long enough to know that something very odd was happening. Fiona moved like a badly made wooden doll.

Tessa stood as still as a statue, her face as cold and white as alabaster. She made no move to call anyone back and not even Carmelita dared to stay to try to comfort her. Kam Lee disappeared to his quarters.

Gavin crossed to her, hearing every squeak of the floorboards as if it were deadly silent outside instead of blowing a gale, not at all sure of what his reception would be.

He touched her, saying her name softly, cautiously. She burrowed against him without hesitation. "Not your fault, not yours! Good is not always stronger than evil, and he is evil, evil, evil!" She stopped the chant of the word with a wrenching effort. "Brand—I am worried about Brand."

"He can take care of himself. He'll be back," he said, and he felt her sagging against him, both of them trembling with weariness and reaction.

She woke up screaming before dawn had broken, but she didn't know why, only that it had been no nightmare of Luis this time.

Gavin could not believe she intended to go to the shop this day. Neither of them mentioned the newlyweds, whose plan had been to stay overnight at the St. Francis Hotel and take a private schooner in the morning, sailing to the port of San Pedro and from there to the ranch by coach. It was as if the young couple had been swallowed up forever by the wind. But the toll of their passage showed on Gavin's face and on Tessa's.

"There's no reason for you to go to the shop today," Gavin protested.

"There is. Tales of last night will be all over the city by now. I would rather be there to face them than here wondering." And I cannot bear to do nothing while I wait to see Brand again, she added silently. Gavin had no intention of taking the day easy either, she noticed. She left a note with Kam Lee to be delivered next door inviting the Collinses, Indian, and Armenthia to dinner that evening. By then she was sure she should be better able to face their love.

All the clerks at the shop were nervous and subdued;

789

most of them had been at the wedding. But the tension eased when Tessa announced firmly, "It is over and done with, and there is work to do here."

Mrs. Chen found her there. Tessa had never seen her look so distraught, and icy fear gripped her heart.

"I come fo' you. Husband go fo' docta an' Mista Lamsay. Lin-Ao wid Bland. He velly bad. You come quick!"

Tessa heard Molly's cry and then she heard nothing else until Brand's jagged breathing assaulted her ears.

He lay on a mat, his head cradled in Lotus's lap. He was covered with blood, and there were dark stains all over the fine silk of Lotus's clothing. He had been stabbed several times. Lotus explained briefly. He had gone from one Barbary Coast dive to another. He had gotten very drunk in the process. In the early hours of the morning there had been a fight. Word had gone around, and someone had started mouthing obscenities about Lauder and his new bride. Brand had given as good as he got for a while, but he had been far outnumbered. They had dumped him in an alley. Two men had found him there a short time ago. He had asked to be taken to the Chens.

Tessa thought he was unconscious, but now she found that he was drifting in and out of knowing. " 'Shamed to go home. Father right, tell him sorry." He got the words out with great effort, and blood trickled out of the corner of his mouth.

"You tell him, my darling. He will be there and Dr. Harland too. You will be all right." Tessa was amazed at the strength of her voice. Her heart wanted to believe her words; her eyes saw the lie. His skin was gray, blue ringed his mouth, and he had surely lost too much blood to live. Lotus had done her best to stanch the flow, but it was impossible. It seeped and pooled, draining away life.

Lotus moved as if to give her place to Tessa. Tessa shook her head. With infinite care she took one of his cold hands in her own, rubbing it gently. "I love you, my son, I love you dearly." His voice gained strength for a moment, rambling around in another time, mixing everything together except for the reality of the present. "Jeff, I've got something to show you. . . . Sure, Paul can come too. He's okay for a brother. . . . Oh, boy, I think Chong Sing's angry! . . . Pedro taught me how to do it. . . .

790

Do you think Mrs. Tubbs knows everything in the world? . . . That colt, that's the one for Mama. . . . Listen, listen, Jeff, Sombra's singing, makes me warm and cold at the same time."

He stopped, and his eyes opened, the deep blue glazing over. But he focused on Tessa's face. "It doesn't hurt now. Say it, Mother, so I may go safely," he whispered.

She leaned over and kissed him. *"Vaya con Dios*, Brand. *Duerme bien, mi hijo."*

His breath stopped on a long sigh. Tessa shuddered as she felt him leave. Lotus closed the lids gently over the sightless eyes.

As he entered the house, Gavin heard a woman crying, not Tessa. He could feel the hairs rising on the back of his neck. In a small careful voice, Tessa was singing.

> Hushaby,
> Don't you cry,
> Go to sleepy, little baby.
> When you wake, you shall have
> All the pretty little horses. . . .

CHAPTER LXVI

Brand's palomino was found tethered near the warehouse. They never knew who had returned the stallion.

They took Brand to Rancho Valle del Mar on a miserable last journey of rain and mud. Paul waited for them in Monterey as the second telegram from Sam Collins had instructed him, and he travelled south with them from there. Tessa hardly noticed that he had joined them. She noticed very little of anything; Ramón's attempts to comfort her, María's tears, the loving presence of Carmelita, Sam, Indian, Armenthia, and Mrs. Tubbs all went unmarked. But she felt every shovelful of heavy wet earth crashing down on her as Brand's grave was filled. Her need to weep grew to an agonizing physical pain, but no tears would come. The "Hushaby" song swirled ceaselessly in her brain until she was half mad with it, always the cruel plaintive lines of the second verse:

> De bees an' de butterflies
> Peckin' out its eyes,
> De po' lil thing cried, "Mammy!"
> Hushaby,
> Don't you cry,
> Go to sleepy, little baby.

Blue eyes, he has such beautiful blue eyes. That's it, that's it, she would try to tell herself, he's just sleeping, little baby sleeping. Grown man, bleeding, bleeding, senselessly dead, never, never to do it all over again, her mind reminded her savagely. My son, my son.

They returned to the city. Tessa made herself blind and deaf to the obscene colors and sounds of the Christmas season.

Neither Tessa nor Gavin had ever thought to do it, but Mrs. Tubbs had sent word to Fiona of Brand's death. Even she was shocked by the coldly formal little note Fiona sent in return. Tessa threw it in the fire.

Gavin made the first attempt to move away from his guilt and grief. They had hardly spoken since Brand's death and had slept little, their bodies kept carefully separate, but Gavin's need to comfort Tessa and to draw comfort in turn from her grew so intense, he had to risk her rejection.

He watched her one night as she brushed her hair. It was an intimate ritual he loved. There had always been something erotic in the movement of her slender arms, in the sibilant whisper of the brush through the silky black hair. But even that was changed now. Her arms moved in short bursts as she jerked the brush through her hair without pleasure, her only motive to get the tangles out.

He stood behind her and smoothed a heavy tress in his hand, but she pulled it out of his grasp, standing up suddenly, turning to face him. "What is it all for, what?" she snarled. "Jefferson is gone. Fiona is married to that slime. Paul is miserable. And Brand is dead!"

He tried to put his arms around her, but she backed away from him, fingers curved in rigid claws, eyes glittering. "No, our love must be cursed to have come to this.
792

We fucked in darkness and in light and produced nothing but misery."

He had never heard her say that word in English, and in Spanish she had always spoken it as a love word. He was stunned with the shock of the raw, hateful sound she made of it.

Her voice rose to a shrill keening. "It must be me! I am the cause. Fiona is my child, not yours, and she's like the others. Mother to Paul I am too. Yes, it is my fault!" She looked quite mad, and he was lost, his own raging grief paralyzing him. His outstretched arms dropped to his sides as though puppet strings had been cut. Her eyes were closed now, her head turned away from him. Moving very carefully, he left her. She did not call him back. He crossed the landing to the room that had been Brand's.

Neither questioned how Carmelita and Sam happened to be back in San Francisco and staying with them, nor why Indian, Armenthia, and Mrs. Tubbs were so often in the house. Gavin acknowledged them politely and spent his time either in the upstairs room or secluded in the study going over the business ledgers Tessa kept so neatly as if he could find some sensible pattern for life in the dry figures. Tessa ignored everyone. She ate little and slept less. They could hear her prowling the house at night. Carmelita and Indian shared the memory of how their friends had been during the time of Luis, but this was worse. There was no revenge to be taken and nothing to be said to comfort. Their attempts were met with blind graciousness by Gavin, while Tessa ignored them, as she did everything and everyone else. It was unnerving to talk to her, impossible to touch her. Her eyes and her still face denied the existence of her friends and threw an impenetrable wall around her.

Paul had returned to slip into silent guilt, helpless to comfort her or his father.

And then with the dawn of the new year, Jefferson was home. Mrs. Tubbs had sent letters to all the possible addresses mentioned in his last letter. But none of them had reached him. He had seen the announcement of Brand's death only because he had made it a habit to read San Francisco newspapers whenever he was lucky enough to find a copy carried by some traveler or abandoned here

793

and there in barber shops and saloons. It was sheer chance that he had seen the little black-bordered box and read it. His journey home had been a nightmare.

When Carmelita saw him, she flew into his arms and burst into tears. Indian's huge form trembled, and he could find no words except, "Thank God, you come, Jefferson, thank God!"

Jeff had known it was going to be bad, but the picture they gave him of his parents and Paul was worse than anything he could have imagined. That they had been so violently separated by Brand's death was unbearable. Ruthlessly he controlled the rising tide of his own guilt for his long absence, knowing it would only add useless complications; his grief was not to be thought of at all right now. And he knew suddenly that whether his parents were aware of it or not, their guilt must be equal if not more than their grief. Carmelita's description of his father ordering Brand out of his sight was all too vivid. Gavin's last words to his son, angry words, enough guilt there for a lifetime. And he thought of his mother, who had lived with such force and energy, who had fought her whole life to live as an independent human being outside of the carefully measured box, the early coffin of the mind and spirit and body offered to "respectable" women. How easy it would be for her to see the burden of Brand's death as the cost of her freedom. He had thought a great deal about them in his years away from them, had seen them for the first time as people, not just parents. He had glimpsed the woman in Tessa by the campfire on the horse drive, but he had flinched away from it. No longer. But to have his theories, conceived in the quiet of lonesome nights far away, put to this severe test was terrifying. If he had misjudged, he feared he would make it worse. The only comfort he could grasp was that Carmelita and Indian did not think it could be worse than it was. He was glad Paul was not in the house right now—one problem that could be dealt with later.

He made himself take deep breaths and slow steps as he climbed the stairs, but his mind was skittering and bucking like a green colt. Seeing the physical separation of the two wings of the second story brought home Carmelita's distracted words. This too he had come to know, that his parents were lovers, first and last, as an overwhelming bond. He remembered the shock he had felt when as an adolescent, his heightened awareness of his own sexuality had led him inexorably to the knowledge that in order to have children, his parents had to make love. Despite having been raised with livestock breeding at the appropriate seasons on the *rancho*, despite his parents' calm, frank answers to his and the other children's questions and their open affection for each other, despite Mrs. Tubbs's sensible approach to the subject, he had felt disbelief amounting to disgust and had shied away from the image of his mother opening her legs, his father entering her, the two of them grappling and groaning in the dark. It was impossible and unsettling. Parents were there to make life secure for their children; that was their sole function. Tessa by firelight.

Jeff grinned wryly to himself. All the signs had been there since he could remember—the times he had resented his mother leaving to be with his father, even while he had somehow accepted that Gavin had to be away; the special feeling he had sensed even as a small child when his parents were together, something that changed immediately even when one of them left the room.

He sought out his father first, and he hoped his incredulous shock didn't show on his face. Gavin looked like a very old man. Even when Jeff said, "Papa, I came as quickly as I could," Gavin continued to peer at him as if he did not recognize his own son, until something snapped inside of him and his broad shoulders heaved. Jeff put his arms around him and felt the wonder of being even more parent than child.

"I'm all right now," Gavin mumbled, his voice hollow, drained of all strength. "Your mother, have you seen her yet?"

He shook his head.

"You must go to her. Thank you for coming home, Jefferson." The words were as politely spoken as if Jeff were a not-too-well-known guest to be greeted, but he saw the agonized depths of the welcome in his father's eyes, and his own throat closed.

He stood on the landing for long moments before he had a strong enough hold on himself to face his mother.

795

How different the tolls of grief, his father looking so aged, his mother looking so pathetically young even with the silver in her hair. It was the first thought that slammed into his brain when he saw her. She had always seemed tall and strong to him. Now she looked tiny and very frail, bones showing through skin gone strangely transparent, eyes enormous and shadowed in her small face. Her unfocused gaze looked past him, swept back, sharpened, and then she screamed his name, and he was holding her in his arms. He sat down with her in his lap as the dry sobs shook her. He held her and comforted her as if she were his child, and all the while he was gathering his strength for the task ahead.

"Mother, you can make a pet of grief." He spoke the hard words very softly. "You can keep it on a leash, close beside you, snarling at anyone who comes too close. You can stroke it and feed it and think no one else has ever owned so splendid or so terrible a beast." He felt the outraged stiffening of her body, and he held her tighter. "You can even set it on Father and let it kill him. And it will, because he is not as strong as you are." Again, he felt the change in her; his assertion that Gavin was not as strong as she had stunned her into giving him her complete attention. "It's true. The only reason Papa has to believe in love, in anything soft or beautiful, is you, and that makes you stronger than he because you can take all of it away from him. Do you understand what I'm saying?" He put her away from him gently so that he could see her face.

She wanted to deny it, refuse to accept its burden, but looking at Jefferson was strangely like looking in a mirror reflecting both herself and Gavin in one image, and she couldn't conjure the image of the lie. Hadn't she always known? She had been raised as an adored child, love flowing all around her, no matter what had followed after. Gavin had been loathed, abused, and intolerably lonely from the beginning of his memory. No matter the coping of years, the cloak of maturity; the difference moved forever just beneath the surface, waiting to open old wounds or inflict new ones whenever his guard was down. In the emotional crises of their life together, he had always suffered the deeper hurt. And she had abandoned him to grief and guilt surely the equal if not greater than her own. "My poor darling," she moaned, and Jeff knew she was not speaking to him.

"Go to him now," he commanded gently, and her eyes looked at him from a face still thin and drawn but softer somehow, and luminous. "Yes, I will. Bless you, Jefferson. It is humbling to have so wise a man for my son." It was the first time she had said the words aloud since Brand's death. *My son.* She hugged him with spontaneous welling joy. "Nothing else on earth could gladden my heart as much as your homecoming has."

He ducked his head in an echo of a childhood gesture, more touched than he could say.

It would be all right between them now. He had a deep, sure sense of it. His mother was going to his father with an open heart; Gavin had never been able to resist that.

But Jeff's feeling was not one of triumph; he still had to deal with Paul. He felt let down, betrayed in a subtle way. He and Paul were more alike than he and Brand had been. He could scarcely believe that Paul had so failed when his parents had needed him, had left the whole mess untouched, left it for someone else to sort out, as if he had known Jeff would be home.

The more Jefferson thought about it, the angrier he became, so that by the time Paul came in, he was ready to knock him down. And it didn't help matters any that everyone else was keeping out of the way, also letting good old Jefferson handle it.

His anger died as abruptly as a candle flame pinched out when he was finally face to face with Paul. The silence stretched between them, both frozen in place and making no move to bridge the distance, and Jeff could not credit the change in his brother. It was worse than the lost waif look of Tessa or the haggard lines in his father's face. Paul's clothes hung on him as if his body was trying to shrink itself out of existence. His eyes were dull, and after one brief glance at Jeff, they remained fixed on the floor. His hands pleated the brim of his hat in uncharacteristic nervousness. The skin that had never darkened much in the sun was a sickly gray now.

The new image and very old ones jumbled and doubled

in Jeff's mind, and then suddenly, they coalesced into one stark and shocking whole. Paul was just an older, taller version of that beaten and starving little boy Jeff had felt so sorry for when Gavin had first brought him home. All the years of love and security had entombed but not killed the harsh beginning, and somehow Brand's death had smashed the walls. The parallel with Gavin was inescapable. Jeff was groping for something to say when Paul confirmed it.

"It should have been me." His voice was so low, Jefferson had to strain to hear. "They've lost their real son, and I'm still alive. It should have been me. Or at least I should have warned him. I had a chance, but I was a coward, I didn't want him to be angry with me. I shouldn't have gone away when I did. It should have been me!"

Jeff's paralysis lasted an instant more and then he sprang at Paul, thanking God for the return of anger. He grabbed him by the shoulders and shook him furiously. "You stupid son of a bitch! All your fault, is it? When did you become God, when did you become Brand's keeper? But you're right, you're damn clever to figure out the Ramsay's game; it's a wonder it took you so long. Father bought you so we'd have an extra body to offer Death when he came around, so he wouldn't take any of us true bloods. We've all just pretended to love you to keep the human sacrifice happy."

Paul's head came up, his eyes wide and startled. "I didn't mean that!" he cried in anguish. "They've given me everything!"

"And you've never understood, have you?" Jeff's voice was quiet now, but he didn't let go of Paul. "Too much gratitude can be a dangerous thing. Sure, they've given you a lot, but you've given in return. They didn't pour their love down the gutter; they poured it into a human being who has given it back to them a thousand fold. You are their son and my brother, my only brother now."

Suddenly they were clinging to each other, and the weeping of one was the weeping of the other until Jeff managed a strangled, "I need a drink," and they went arm in arm to find one.

Kam Lee presented them with an elaborate meal that

night, but no one minded that Gavin and Tessa did not come downstairs to share it with them.

The short distance across the landing seemed a long journey to Tessa. She wondered with each step what she should say, what she should do. But when she was in Gavin's presence, all indecision vanished. He looked so old and defeated, she felt the last of the ice which had settled around her heart shatter, melted away in an instant by the white heat of her love.

She ran to him, putting her arms around him, pressing her body hard against him. *"Mi vida,* my dearest only love, what a cold, empty waste of time this has been! Forgive me for adding to your hurt."

"Tessa!" was a wrenching cry in his throat, and they stared at each other until his mouth came down on hers, and he kissed her savagely, the aged, hesitant way of the past weeks vanishing. He picked her up and her head was swimming, and then they were in their bedroom, undressing with frantic hands, hers not quick enough, Gavin's easily tearing the lacy fabric of her undergarments, stripping her, running over her body with feverish urgency, pressing her down on the bed. He thrust into her with hard readiness and she welcomed him, her bones turned to liquid fire, her whole being centered in the place of their joining, her sharp panting cries not seeming to come from her at all.

She knew she had only slept a few hours, yet she felt more rested than she had since Brand's death. Her mouth, her body, everything felt heavily, lazily voluptuous. A slow blush stained her skin as she met Gavin's eyes. He was propped on one elbow so he could look down at her, and he bent his head swiftly to plant a soft kiss on the edge of the blush where it met her breasts.

"Oh, Gavin, oughtn't we be ashamed to act like this?" she asked with a troubled frown.

"No, madam, we ought to be damn proud we can at our ages," he replied promptly, winning an involuntary smile from his wife. But then he sobered and held her eyes with his own. "It's the best way I know to spit in Death's face."

She thought it over carefully, knowing he was not just
799

trying to make her feel better about it, and with a growing sense of wonder, she realized the truth of his words. So much of death's victory was in the secondary wreckage: the dark panoply of mourning, the stifling of light and joy, the guilt and remorse of the living for things done and not done, the fearful reluctance to let love and life flow in the blood again. And all the while the initial corpse mixing inexorably with the earth. Brand, first born and the nearest image of his father, Brand dispersed by the elements, seeping into the earth, carried on the wind, dissolving in the air, transparent irridescent rainbow, sunlight catching, and then nothing.

She was too earth-rooted, too bound in the beauty of the senses to ponder or draw comfort from the idea of a spirit flown to other regions. Brand as she had borne him and loved him had ceased to exist except in memory. The pain might lose its intensity with time's passing, but she could accept it now as an essential part of her, no more or less than remembered joy.

The present was in her other sons, and most of all in this man who lay beside her watching her with such quiet, kind patience. "Here's to life, my love," she whispered and the shared tears came at last, as healing as first rain on earth.

CHAPTER LXVII

Laughter filled the house again as Jeff entertained them with his stories. He made light of everything, though Paul knew there were some scars that hadn't been any fun to acquire. He was like a great bright spill of sunlight in their lives.

Many of the changes in him were visible. His skin was deeply tanned, making his eyes appear more vivid than before. He was still thin, but now it was a whipcord leanness that gave all his movements a strong, agile grace, as if the gangly figure of the past had never been. Sometimes when his eyebrow tilted up like his father's, Tessa thought she would drown in the tenderness that washed over her.

He sang ridiculous songs about little doggies and long lonesome trails and girls left all over the place; he claimed that these were the tunes every cow on the trail went to sleep by.

"You ain't never goin' sing to my cows," Indian said. "They jump on th' train an' never come back."

Jefferson's ready humor and easy smile, his deep, sure voice, the way he looked and the way he moved, were all outward signs of the inner changes. He knew who he was and he found the man not only livable, but likable. He had no more confusion about his identity separate from everyone else's. And in being comfortable with himself, he had discovered people were comfortable with him and he with them. His only regret was that it had taken so long to learn such a basic thing.

He had always been sensitive to others, but now there was nothing of himself that needed to stand in the way for self-protection, and so it was even easier. He felt the tension in his mother even before she asked with elaborate casualness, "Those two men who were your friends, the ones with the strange names, will you be seeing them again?"

"Shanks and Smokey? A long shot, but maybe. They're drifters who might show up any place." He was in the middle of a careless shrug when he guessed what she was driving at. "They'll have to show up here to see me," he said firmly. He took her hand in his own and rubbed the knuckles gently. "I'm home, Mother, really home. I'm sorry I didn't realize before that you've been worrying about me leaving again. Brand—"he said the name and neither of them flinched—"Brand was a hard worker. There's plenty for me to do, and I want to do it. And Paul needs a brother. I wouldn't leave him now for the world. Poor fellow, I'm not sure he'll ever get over Fiona."

He paused, and his eyes were far away and dreamy. "I'd like to tell you something about Shanks and Smokey. They're grand men in their way, the best friends anyone could have. They saved my neck more than once. But they belong to a new, special breed of men. They all talk about

801

having a little spread of their own someday, and some of them even pick out the exact spot. But not one in a hundred will ever settle down. They complain about the food, the coffee, the hours, the heat, the cold, the cattle, the horses, and they love it all. They'll go on working for a dollar a day and found until they're too stiff to climb into a saddle any more, and then they'll spend the rest of their days doing chores around a bunkhouse and dreaming of the time when they rode the trail from dawn to dusk and bedded down on the hard ground. And deep down, in spite of all the complaining, they'll know their lives were good and full of sky and space and exactly what they wanted all along." His eyes came back to the present and to her face. "I'm not one of them. They taught me much I needed to know, and I'm grateful, but that's all. I'm a root person, like my mother." His smile flashed and broadened with her next question.

"Did you have a name other than your own?"

"Your fault again." He laughed aloud. "I'm embarrassed to tell you. Shanks earned his name from the expression 'shanks' mare,' meaning on foot. It's the way he got to Texas from Ohio, and I don't think he's walked more than a few feet on his own since. He's damn near glued to his saddle. We used to swear that if a saloon was built with too broad a plank walk in front, Shanks wouldn't go in. And Smokey is never without his foul-smelling pipe. And I, well, they called me 'Wildflower.' Part of it was because I took too many baths for their taste. As far as they were concerned, streams were for watering livestock and baths only happened when you hit a good-sized town. They said I not only smelled like flowers, I had eyes just the right color. The sense of humor on the trail is broad to say the least, and the same jokes have to last a long time. Somebody always got a good laugh out of my nickname." He laughed harder at Tessa's outraged expression. "You don't have to defend my honor, it was all in good fun. And I doubt anyone here will call me Wildflower unless my mother tells them."

She smiled then, but her fingers played nervously with the cuff of her sleeve, and Jeff looked at her inquiringly.

"Have you been to see Lotus yet?" she asked bluntly.

The question took him completely by surprise, but he regarded her steadily. "No, I haven't. How did you know?"

"Your father figured it out, just as he did about Paul. I was as blind as a bat in both cases. I would like to remedy that if I could. About all I can offer is the suggestion that you go see her, if you are still interested. She hasn't been here since Brand died. I think she too has her share of guilt, and for no reason at all."

Jeff sighed. "I'm still interested, but I don't see any point in it. I kept hoping I'd meet a woman I liked as well; I spent a lot of time looking in every town I visited. I never found her. But Brand died in her arms. I expect she's had just about enough of the Ramsays."

"Perhaps there will be nothing between you, perhaps you will be like strangers, but you shouldn't let the ghost of your brother make it so." A gentle smile curved her mouth. "He wouldn't like that. And I can't tell you for certain, but I don't think he loved Lotus enough nor she him to move beyond friendship."

He called on Lotus the next day, seeing her parents first. Though Mr. Chen looked disapproving, Mrs. Chen looked pleased and welcomed him back excitedly, so Jefferson counted himself lucky so far.

Mrs. Chen led him to Lotus's room and did a very unusual thing. She knocked on the door, called softly in Chinese, including Jefferson's name in the rush of words, and left him there.

A soft voice bade him enter.

She was even more beautiful than he remembered. In his absence the final transition had been made from girl to woman. Her ebony hair was drawn back in a smooth style that softly framed the oval ivory of her face. Her features were perfect, the long brown eyes enhanced by the arching brows and thick lashes, the straight nose, the soft pink symmetry of her full mouth—so perfect that it took Jefferson a moment to notice that there was uncharacteristic color on the crescent cheekbones and that her mouth was trembling just the slightest bit, despite the stillness of her slender body and folded hands. She was dressed in a long rose silk tunic over trousers, in the style she had always preferred in the home of her parents; her way of being both Chinese and American had obviously not changed. He knew his feelings were beginning to show, and he steeled himself against them, knowing how kind she was, not wanting to put her in a position where she would know she caused hurt.

Because he was conscious of that, his greeting was stiff. "Lotus, I am sorry my family's sadness involved you," he said, and the chill of his own words made him want to shiver.

Lotus did. He saw the movement of her slight frame before her discipline made all still again. She had been kneeling on the floor in the posture he would never be able to bear for long and she found so comfortable. There was an open book, an empty tea cup, pen, ink, and paper around her, not randomly scattered, but each in its place. She had not gotten up when he entered the room, and now her head was bowed so that he could no longer see her face. He was noticing everything. He felt as if his senses were sharper than they had ever been, even sharper than they had been on the trail when his life had depended on them minute to minute.

Lotus raised her head to look at him, and her voice was very calm. "It is my sadness also that my friend, your brother Brand died. It is not my sadness that he died in my arms. It is my hope that I gave him some comfort because he knew of the love I had for him. But it is finished now. You do not need to trouble yourself for me. It is good that you are safely home; your family needs you."

Why is it, he wondered, *that her English, each word so correctly spoken, still sounds Chinese? It's the cadence, the lilt unlike any other, that lovely, exotic sound that gives each word its own value.* Even as he answered his own question, he became aware of time suspended between them, of the glittering brightness in her eyes. He had never seen her cry in all the years he had known her, but he knew the light for tears, and his own control began to falter. He heard again but this time with more clarity the way she had said, "He knew of the love I had for him."

"How did you love him?" His voice was gentle but insistent. He had to ask despite her reserve.

She clenched her hands together so tightly, her knuckles gleamed against her pale skin. A few tears escaped and
804

rolled down her cheeks. "I loved Brand very much as a friend loves a friend, not as a woman loves a man. Is that what you wish to know?"

He could feel the flinching nakedness in her voice. He had nothing left to lose, everything to gain, and surely he would not hurt her after all. "Yes, that's what I wished to know. He was my older brother. I couldn't take from him. But I'll fight anyone else for you. Is there anyone else? Damn, I'm making a mess of this! I love you, Lotus, I should have told you that first of all. I've loved you for years."

She saw him through her tears. She remembered her despairing hopelessness when he had left, her conviction that she would never see him again, that her world would never be whole and beautiful again, that he had never cared for her and never would. Just for an instant she was tempted to share her pain, to tell him of the marriage plans her father had begun to consider for her, to tell him that he could not simply walk back into her life and expect to find her waiting. But it would never be her way to hurt him, not even now, not even for an instant. He had gone away still much a boy; now he was a lean, hard-muscled man, but the beautiful blue-violet eyes were still Jefferson's. Jefferson, always.

"There is no one else. I love you, Jefferson Ramsay. I love you as a woman loves a man." Her voice was low but very sure.

She came up into his arms with fluid grace, and they touched for the first time ever with love admitted between them. Jefferson cupped her face in his hands and kissed the tear tracks and traced the fine pattern of her features before his mouth claimed hers. She pressed against him with an inarticulate murmur of delight, but then suddenly she tensed and pulled away. "Your parents, what will they say? I do not think they believed Brand and I would ever . . . "

"Marry?" Jeff supplied cheerfully.

"Yes, marry. And now that Brand is gone, they will care even more about what becomes of you. There is much feeling here against the Chinese. Few will approve of a marriage between a white and a Chinese, even though I am perhaps partly white also."

"My lovely fool, I hate to admit it, it sounds so unmanly, but my father guessed and my mother sent me." He drew her close again, and they were still standing like that, just holding each other, when Mrs. Chen knocked to offer tea and cakes more elaborate than she would have provided on a routine day.

Jefferson and Lotus decided on a very small and quiet wedding because of the recent death which had touched them all. But nothing could lessen the joy of the day. They were so obviously in love with each other and the world, Tessa's eyes misted every time she looked at them, and Gavin's voice was husky. Jeff was no more loyal to an organized church than his parents were, nor was Lotus. Her mother had been at least a nominal Roman Catholic convert in China, but her father had never followed. He had continued to worship the familiar gods of his family's tradition, and Mrs. Chen prayed to a blend of old and new, making no great point of it because she considered matters of worship a private business despite what the missionaries had told her. She had, in any case, no intention of wasting energy and her persuasive powers in bending her husband to her will over unseen spirits when there were always so many more practical things to think of. It was victory enough that he was not trying to forbid the marriage.

The wedding was unique. Lotus wore a flowing gown with wide sleeves that she and Tessa had designed. It was made of bright red silk, red, the Chinese color for luck and celebration, red to please her father, who still considered white the color of mourning. To please her mother, she wore a sheer white veil under a crown of tiny white flowers, and she carried a bouquet of white roses. White, the Christian color of purity. And to please herself and Jefferson, to keep dissension from the day, a justice of the peace, an acquaintance of the Ramsays, performed the ceremony. Lotus knew all she had to do to please the Ramsays was to love Jefferson, and that required no effort at all.

The only guests outside of the immediate families were Indian, Armenthia, and their children, and Mrs. Tubbs.

Jefferson wondered if he could find his voice to speak the vows. It was not that he didn't want to; he had never wanted anything as much in his life. But his heart was picking out an erratic rhythm, and he had trouble breath-
806

ing just from looking at Lotus as she came toward him. He could see her face through the veil. Never had there been so beautiful, kind, and wise a woman. For a panicked moment, he wondered if he'd announced those words aloud. But then there was nothing except her hand in his, warm and fearless, and their two voices were firm and audible.

Everyone toasted them joyfully, including Paul, who was enormously pleased for them despite his own heartache. Gavin's toast touched Jefferson most of all. "If you have but half the happiness Tessa and I have had, you will be happy indeed." The private words from his father meant a great deal too, and made him smile. "Be patient with her," Gavin cautioned him. "You have a lifetime together ahead of you." His eyes twinkled. "And if you get as far as Nevada City, the National Exchange has beds that creak splendidly."

Jefferson finally understood fully the expression that changed the stern lines of Gavin's face every time he thought of anything dealing with Tessa; he knew his underwent the same transformation now because of Lotus.

Their honeymoon journey would take them to Monterey to visit the Collinses and to both *ranchos* and then wherever fancy led them. It did not disturb Lotus that they would not have all the time alone. Jeff had been gone for a long time, he had many old friends to see, and they were now to be a very important part of her life too.

They rode away together on golden horses, Jeff's the same one that had carried him away from San Francisco and back again, Lotus's a wedding gift from the Ramsays. She thought the palomino magnificent, but the gift that had moved her most of all was the necklace of California gold and Chinese jade. Chong Sing had left it with her parents to be given to her on her wedding day with his blessings for a tranquil and fruitful life. She wondered if he had known it would be Jefferson.

"What a perfect day it has been!" Tessa sighed as she and Gavin got ready for bed. "A day of rejoicing, just as it should have been. Poor Fiona, what a dreadful day that was!"

Gavin drew her close. "Neither one of us will forget it.

807

But she did make a choice, and she knows where we are if she needs us."

Tessa had to admit that Fiona showed no signs of needing them at all. Another stilted note, this one congratulating Jefferson and Lotus on their marriage plans. No other communication. Of course, the way had hardly been left open for easy visits back and forth, and Tessa accepted a good deal of the blame for that. What was done was done, but it was impossible not to worry about one's child, no matter how wayward or adult.

She nestled against Gavin, feeling his warmth, conscious of his every bone and muscle, and she thought, *Just let this go on forever, and I can face anything.*

She clung to him when the telegram came. Gavin had had some warning because when Jeff and Lotus had returned from their trip, Jeff had sought his father out, and he looked so troubled, Gavin's face immediately reflected it.

"No, it's not that," Jeff said quickly with a smile. "We had a marvelous time. Lotus is . . . well, I don't see how the years can improve her though I expect they will. I just hope I can keep pace. And the bed did creak." His face sobered again. "It's Carmelita. I don't think she's well at all. When I asked her, she smiled and said it was only old age catching up with her, but the way Sam looks at her—ah, hell, maybe it's because I want everyone to be as happy as I am, but I'd swear he's scared to death. And Carmelita doesn't look as I remember her. She's almost too glowing, like a flame burning out."

Though Gavin didn't want to believe it, he knew how acute Jeff's senses were in regard to other people. "Have you told your mother?" he asked quietly.

Jeff shook his head. "I came to you. I'm a coward."

"A wise one. If it's true, she'll know soon enough. I hope she has a little longer to enjoy the happiness you and Lotus are giving her before sorrow comes again. She lives so hard." His voice was very soft.

"I know, that's what makes it so easy to love her," Jefferson said. He added, without any rancor, "She loves you better than anyone on earth. She can bear anything as long as you're beside her."

Without arrogance, Gavin knew it was true, though it had taken him years to learn it. He felt the same way
808

about her; the only times he had lost the way since he had married her had been when he thought he had lost her. But the force of her love frightened him because he knew in his bones, quite literally, that sooner or later, she was going to have to go on without him.

He mentioned nothing to Tessa about his conversation with Jefferson. She was happily busy helping Lotus make a small house on Stockton Street into a home and being so careful not to be an obnoxious mother-in-law in the process that Gavin had to hide his amusement. He knew she was doing a good job. From the first she had made it clear that Jefferson and Lotus were welcome in Rincon house, but that she thought they would be more content in a home of their own. Only Gavin knew how much it cost her to do that with her beloved Jefferson so recently returned.

The message came when spring was nearly finished. It read: "Carmelita very ill. Don't tell Indian. Please come. Sam."

At her first sight of her friend, Tessa knew it was already over. The fine bright beauty she had first noticed in Carmelita at Fiona's wedding had not been beauty at all, but Death honing his knife on her flesh. Now she was emaciated, all softness gone, her hair nearly snow white, her lips thin and blue; all the life that was left in her was pooled in the dark eyes.

Tessa closed her own eyes for an instant. "Carmelita— oh, why didn't you send for me sooner?" she gasped.

Carmelita's voice was a pale echo of her old liveliness, but it was firm. "I would not have sent for you now. It was Sam who did that. You have had enough, Tessa. To watch a friend die is not kind, and I would give you only kindness."

Tessa bowed her head and wept.

"Please, do not, my dear. You'll have me weeping with you, and that will do so little good. There is so much weeping in this world. Can't you see? It is going quickly, and for that I'm very thankful. And there is something I can tell you and you will understand, though I can't tell Sam. I am so glad to be going before he does. My life has been full and good, but I have no wish to be here without Sam. If he went first, I do not know what I would do. We have no children, no nephews or nieces or cousins, no

809

family at all to see each other in. We have shared your children, and we love them, but it is not the same. I hope Sam is braver than I am. If you would really do something for me, make it as easy for him as you can." She paused for a long moment, and then she added. "That is why I would not have Indian here now. We were too close as a man and a woman, and he is too gentle."

Carmelita's request and the men's helplessness made it easier for Tessa to be strong. Gavin was no more use than Sam; he looked as lost and terrified at seeing his old friend slipping away as Sam did.

Tessa had one last hope, but that too was lost when she asked Carmelita if she could send for Dr. Harland. "John's awfully good. Perhaps he has an answer."

Carmelita smiled without bitterness. "He does indeed. I saw him when I was in San Francisco last. It is he who prescribed the laudanum, and told me to do anything that makes it easier."

The drug did help. Carmelita slept much of the time, drifted in and out of the time and the place where her body really was. When she was conscious, she and Tessa talked of the old days in Monterey, laughing over some of the memories that emerged as clear and bright as though the days when they were young were just beginning.

Tessa did not cry again in front of Carmelita, but often when they were alone, she wept in Gavin's arms, and he wept with her.

Two weeks became an eternity, and Tessa began to long for the end as much as Carmelita did. Even with the drug there was pain that was never gone and often all-engulfing as the wasting disease gnawed at her. Finally one evening she said very clearly, "Tessa, it is time." Her frail hand took the full bottle of laudanum, and she drank it all, grimacing slightly at the taste. Tessa made no attempt to stop her; she herself had made sure the bottle was always full and within reach. She felt no guilt. It was little enough to do for someone so loved.

"Please get Gavin and then Sam for me. I would like them to know it is all right, though not about this." She handed the bottle to Tessa. "Thank you, my dear. It was my choice."

"My friend, I love you so, I will miss you forever," Tessa
810

whispered, and she kissed Carmelita. *"Vaya con Dios."* When she went out to summon the men, the bottle was hidden in her sleeve.

Sam emerged only once and beckoned to Gavin, and when Gavin came out again, he was weeping unashamedly. He held Tessa hard against him. "One of the things she wanted me to know was that my choice of a wife was a good one," he choked. And suddenly there was laughter mixed with their tears, a last gift from Carmelita.

They buried her in her beloved Monterey, but the sorrow was not over. Sam told them that he would find another agent for them before he left, but that he was going to sell out his own business and go back East.

They were both stunned by his decision.

"Sam, you were never going to go back there again. You may come live with us if you want to, anything, but don't go back!" Tessa begged passionately, and Gavin added his own words of welcome.

But Sam did not waver. "I can't stay now. If things were otherwise, maybe I could, but not now. I came lookin' for the golden land and the sun, and I found both, but I also found Carmelita, and she became everything that's California. Now she's gone. And I'd just as soon not stay where the sun shines so much and the land's so fair, because all it'll do is remind me of her. I think it's about time I go back to where it's rocky all the time and cold most of the year. That's pretty much how I feel now myself. I'll come back if I change my mind." His eyes held Gavin's, and Gavin nodded in understanding.

"Good-by Sam, and good luck," he said gravely.

Tessa kissed Sam on both cheeks while tears ran down her own. "You made Carmelita very, very happy. Go with God."

When they told Indian, he broke down and sobbed uncontrollably.

"She wanted to spare you," Tessa murmured. Her heart ached. Never had Indian looked so maimed as he did now, with only one hand to cover the pain in his face.

"You go on an' cry, let it all out," Armenthia said compassionately, putting her arms around him. "She was one good woman."

"You are one good woman too," Gavin told Tessa that night.

She studied the steady approval in his eyes. "How did you know?"

"I saw the pupils of her eyes growing wider and darker even though the light was the same, and her breathing was strange, and then I noticed the bottle was gone."

"Did Sam know too?" she asked fearfully.

"No," Gavin replied without hesitation. "Sam saw only that Carmelita's suffering was over. One good woman," he repeated, and he gazed at her for a long moment before he kissed her.

CHAPTER LXVIII

Sam Collins died in a small town in Connecticut at the end of October, so said the polite, dry letter from a law firm there. Mr. Collins had left his estate to be divided fifty percent to the children of Gavin and Tessa Ramsay, fifty percent to the children of Indian and Armenthia, sometimes known as Indian and Armenthia Jefferson. The money was to be dispensed by the parents. The letter Sam had left to be sent to the parents wasn't much longer than the announcement, but it was anything but dry:

> My dear friends,
> It's a good time here now. The trees are more red and more gold than I remembered. A good time, much better than winter. What I am leaving to your children is not enough to change their lives. If it was, I'd ask that they spend it wisely. As it is, I ask that they use it only for things which will pleasure them. Duty is easy to learn. To be joyful is a much harder lesson. Carmelita was a good teacher.
> Love,
> Sam

It was difficult for Tessa to believe Sam was dead. In spite of the letter and the bequests, it had happened too far away. She missed Carmelita in a thousand ways; it was therefore unacceptable that Sam wasn't going to drift back to California and into their lives someday. She knew it was illogical and the truth inescapable, but it made no difference.

Her reaction was the same when Julio Ramirez came to the city with the news that his parents were dead, María within four hours of her husband. They had died of pneumonia with the onslaught of the rain and cold of winter, a common enough way, but Tessa could not accept it.

"They cannot be dead! They cannot be! There has been too much death. It will be spring again and warm, and then they will be all right!" she screamed at him.

His eyes were deep, sad, and knowing as the earth itself. He looked like his father. "Doña Tessa, they are dead. They were old, and they were weary. And there could be no more blessing than that one did not have to go without the other. My mother followed so shortly after, surely she found my father, and they are together."

His precise Spanish, his absolute belief, defeated her. He saw the progression to eternity as measurable in time and space as the pace of a good horse. Ramón and María were dead. Dead and already deep in the ground. There was not even time for her to see them buried. Part of her was glad of that, and knew that was why she had not received word earlier. Brand, Carmelita—she had seen the earth covering them. She did not know if she could have found the strength to bear it again so soon, and now there would be no need.

"Thank you for coming to me, Julio Ramirez," she said finally, using their old and common tongue even as he had, her voice quavering as if she were a very old woman. "You and your brother and your families are to continue as before at Valle del Mar if you will. You have kept it safe. You have made it prosper, and for that I am grateful. I was not their child, but I loved them as they loved me."

Gavin found her in their bedroom. She had been crying for so long already, her eyes were nearly swollen shut, her face was blotched, and her body was wrenched by dry heaves. Julio had come to him, and then having delivered his message formally to both the *patrón* and the *patróna* he had headed home again. Nothing could persuade him to rest in the city.

Gavin knew Tessa was making herself ill with the force of her weeping, but he made no attempt to stop her. He had seen her control grief too harshly too often. He knew she wept not only for the passage of Ramón and María from her life, but for the others, all lost within a year, Death giving no quarter, attacking too many too swiftly.

He held her, offering the comfort of his presence and his gentle words until she had cried herself into numb exhaustion. Her face was flushed and feverish, but enough of her grief had been washed away so that she fell asleep and did not awaken for more than twelve hours.

"Have you been here the whole time?" she asked drowsily when she discovered how much time had passed.

"I slept some too," he assured her.

It was such an inescapable fact, she was shamed by the length of time it had taken her to achieve any acceptance of it at all and by her continued resistance to it. The longer one lived, the more inevitable was the pattern of sorrow following joy. At times like these it was difficult to remember that the reverse seemed equally true. Gavin's loving reminded her, and the happiness of Jefferson and Lotus helped enormously. They were just beginning their journey together. Journeys beginning and ending and beginning again. She clung to that thought and tried not to think of where Fiona's journey was taking her.

Paul worked hard and played little. Tessa teased him, gently telling him that the money from Sam, which had amounted to nearly five thousand dollars for each child, would take him years to spend unless he learned to indulge himself more. Paul smiled tolerantly and continued on his own way, which included most meals and most of his time away from the house now. Tessa had a brief period of hope when he seemed to be seeing a good deal of a young woman named Janet Maury. He even brought her home to dinner a few times. Janet was small, dark-haired, dark-eyed, and vivacious. She was fairly well educated, had a good sense of humor, and obviously adored Paul. But before 1872 was very old, it was clear that while Paul was fond of her, he was not in love with her. He saw less

814

of her, and though it was too delicate a subject for Tessa to question him about, she was certain he was purposely nipping the affair in the bud before the girl could be too badly hurt.

By March, Janet Maury was completely forgotten not only by Paul, but by his parents, in their growing concern over Fiona. The worry started tamely enough. Gavin had sent a bank draft for the amount due Fiona from Sam's estate, and now the bank manager felt it his duty to inform Gavin that the draft had never been collected. It wasn't a fortune, but after all, it was nearly five thousand dollars. And there were, of course, business delays too often, but hardly for four months. Would Mr. Ramsay care to get in touch with his daughter to determine whether or not she had received the draft?

Under any other circumstances, Gavin would have done just that, but in this case he decided to do nothing until he had discussed it with Tessa. He told her over dinner, even though Paul was there that night.

"I know she's a rich woman now," Tessa said slowly. "But this is not like her, or at least, not like the daughter I knew before Franklin Lauder came along. Fiona has never been careless with money. She can keep accounts as well as I can. Before she left she'd taken over much of the bookkeeping for Mrs. Tubbs at the school."

"There's something wrong!" Paul interjected with sudden violence. "I don't care how rich she is or how out of touch with us, there's a practical streak in Fiona that I don't think anything or anyone including Frank Lauder could ever change. And everyone likes money of their own, money they can do absolutely anything they want to with." He looked at Gavin. "You did make Sam's wishes clear?"

"I did indeed."

Paul swallowed nervously, realizing that Tessa and Gavin were both watching him intently, willing to follow his lead. "This may be too much to ask," he admitted, "but if you would, Mother, I think you ought to write Fiona a friendly letter asking about the draft only in passing." Their faces showed neither acceptance nor rejection, and he blessed them for their patient consideration. "You see, I think if you, sir, write about the draft, there will be
815

an answer one way or another, but I don't think it will come from Fiona. I don't think she's been free to communicate with us since she left. I think those duty notes were carefully dictated."

For a moment, the only sound that broke the silence was Kam Lee bustling in the kitchen.

Paul ignored the compassion in both faces. He knew what he knew from his loving of Fiona for so many years. "Will you write the letter, Mother?" he asked softly.

"I will," she said, and he heard the unspoken words, "for you."

She let him read it before she sent it, and he could not have been more pleased had he himself had a part in composing it. It was a loving, chatty letter that said, directly and indirectly, that old bitterness was better left to perish and any news of Fiona's new life would be welcomed. The money from Sam was mentioned between a description of Jeff and Lotus's house and a glowing report of how well the vines seemed to be doing at the Vincenti winery.

They all awaited the reply anxiously, and when it came, Tessa and Gavin moved a step closer to believing Paul's theory. The draft was not mentioned at all nor was much of anything else. It was a short, dutiful letter saying that Fiona was well and happy. It could have been written by a child. Even Fiona's handwriting looked younger, much less neat than her writing was wont to be, though it was surely hers.

"I'm going to see her," Paul announced flatly. "I'm her brother." His mouth twisted bitterly with the words. "And if I need an excuse beyond that, I'll use the business of the draft."

Tessa felt a rush of fear so tangible it was as if a cold hand had touched the back of her neck. Her eyes flew to Gavin, and she willed him to know what to do.

He studied Paul for a moment before he spoke. "You have the strongest right of all. I trust you will do nothing rash. We have had enough sorrow."

"Thank you, sir," Paul murmured, and Tessa bowed her head; she had left the decision to Gavin, and he had made it.

As soon as Jefferson heard of Paul's plan, he wanted to go with him, but he too bowed to Paul's special right and had to content himself with adding his own warnings to take care. Paul traveled by stage, the quickest way, and planned to hire or buy a horse once he got there.

Six weeks after he had left, he was back, with Fiona. For over a month, they had had little word from him except that he had seen her and was trying to sort things out. And then they received a telegram: "Bringing Fiona home." And that was all they knew until the stage arrived.

Tessa nearly screamed at her first sight of her daughter, she looked so tiny, gray-faced, and ill. But worst of all was the expression in her eyes. They seemed strangely colorless, like dirty pieces of mirror glass, and she peered from them like a frightened and slow-witted child.

She stared at Tessa and then asked the question very softly. "Mama?"

"Yes, darling, you're home now," Tessa breathed, and she put her arms around her.

Fiona made no response of any kind. They took her home, and Tessa undressed her and put her to bed in her old room. Dr. Harland confirmed Tessa's suspicion. "She's pregnant, over four months, I'd say. She's undernourished and exhausted. Good food and rest will correct those maladies, but as for her mental condition, I just don't know. Her mind seems to have taken her back to her childhood, I suppose to a time when she was safe and happy. That man should have been . . . But then, you knew that from the first, didn't you?"

When John had left, Tessa, Gavin, and Paul met together in the study.

Paul looked nearly as terrible as Fiona, gaunt and sallow-skinned.

"What happened?" Gavin asked quietly. "All of it, if you can bear it tell it."

Paul looked at them from bruised eyes. "I didn't think the news would be printed up here. Lauder is dead. I killed him." He trembled uncontrollably. "I never thought I'd do anything like that, but when I got there, I just didn't think it was going to do any good to walk in and ask to see her. I didn't know whether I'd be able to find anything out. So I played the goddamned spy. I collected all the information I could. God, Los Angeles is one hell of a rough town! But you can find out almost anything

817

about anyone if you're willing to pay. The Lauder ranch isn't too far away. Well, the more I heard, the sicker I got. Fiona was a virtual prisoner there. The stories about him —they'll never leave my mind. He wasn't . . . wasn't natural." He gave a harsh, ugly croak that could have been laughter or a cry of grief. "The understatement of the age. What Brand told you was true. Lauder had a penchant for the crippled, male and female, adult and child, and he enjoyed inflicting pain. I watched him a lot, scouted everything else, saw the pattern of his days. Sometimes he rode with a bodyguard, but not always. On his own place, he felt pretty damn safe. I caught only a couple of glimpses of Fiona. She didn't go any distance at all from the house, and there was always someone following her. Once she stumbled near some bushes, just stumbled, but the guard must have thought she was trying to run away. He dragged her back, and then Lauder was there. She screamed. He hit her and pulled her into the house. I heard her scream again and again, but there were too many people around the place. I couldn't get to her or to him. That decided everything. I stationed myself where I knew Lauder was going to ride by. I hid there for two days, and when I had a clear shot, I took it. I killed him. I would have preferred man to man, but I couldn't risk it. Too many people around, and if I'd lost, I didn't know what would have happened to Fiona. Oh, Christ! I shot him in cold blood from ambush!"

Tessa put her arms around his shuddering body, and Gavin poured a glass of brandy for him.

"Paul, it was all you could do," he said firmly. "It feels much better if you can face your enemy and have it out. Of course, that is the code. But not at the expense of Fiona's life. And from the state she's in, she wouldn't have lasted much longer. It's serious enough now as it is. But how did you get her out after that?"

"That was the hardest part. I waited for two weeks after that. And then I just rode in and said that a friend had notified us in San Francisco that Fiona's husband had met with an accident and that the family had sent me to take my sister home. I figured maybe I'd get away with it because they wouldn't think I'd come in like that. I went unarmed too, and well . . . they believed me. I think
818

they were glad to get rid of her. There was total chaos there. I don't know for sure, but I don't think anyone who worked for him could stand the man. I don't think the foreman knew what the hell to do. And Fiona was . . . incapable of deciding anything, or doing anything. I expect the foremen and the others might strip the place and leave. I don't know. I told them to send all papers to us. I didn't even stay to see if there might be a will. I just got her out of there. She barely recognized me." He buried his face in his hands.

"Thank God for your courage," Tessa murmured. "There is only one person who might make you feel easier about what you did." Her eyes met Gavin's, and his gleamed with understanding. He nodded. "I'll find him." He left them, knowing Tessa could give Paul more comfort now than he could.

Paul was so locked in his own misery, he didn't even have any idea of how much time had passed when he looked up and saw Gavin come back with Indian. He didn't understand at all.

Tessa went to Gavin's side. "Paul, I think it will be easier for both of you if your father and I leave you alone with Indian." She looked up at Indian's troubled face. "Tell him everything," she said. "I would not have had any of my other children know, but Paul needs to know, all of it, from the night of Luis to the night you came back to our camp in the foothills."

Indian nodded. "All right. That th' way it be then."

When Indian found Tessa and Gavin later, he said, "Guess it was th' right thing, tellin' him. Don' think he's slept for one long time, but he sleepin' now, all curled up in a chair."

Paul was still sleeping when night fell and Tessa tiptoed in with a blanket, but he opened his eyes when she came near. "Thank you. You survived and so will Fiona," he said simply.

Tessa ruffled his soft chestnut hair. "I am glad you are here to help her."

But she wondered in the following days whether even Paul's love was going to be enough. She took care of Fiona as if she were a baby, and her stomach churned at the marks still on Fiona's flesh. There were fading bruises

819

and long stripes that could have been caused by a belt or a whip; but awful as they were, they were healing. Her mind seemed mortally wounded. Mrs. Tubbs, Jeff, and Lotus came to see her, and she gazed at them all with no discernible interest or recognition.

She had something to tell Brand, he would know what she meant. If she didn't sign the draft maybe they would know she needed help. She refused to sign it. Frank couldn't make her, no matter what he did. Those terrible letters he made her write.

Tessa didn't know which was worse, the long periods of silence or the rambling, disconnected, and terrified words. She learned much of what had happened to her daughter, some so graphically she flinched from fully picturing what Fiona described. Franklin Lauder had been an expert in physical abuse as well as mental cruelty. It was a miracle that Fiona still carried the child. Luis all over again and worse.

Paul, Gavin, and Tessa took turns watching over her, wanting her to have someone familiar with her rather than a strange nurse. But both Tessa and Gavin were sure that if anyone held the key, it was Paul.

Paul knew it too, and he waited until food and sleep had made a visible difference in her. He knew he was not imagining it—behind the blank childlike stare he had seen it move, a vast and painful awareness with nothing of the child in it. And now when he saw it again, he took the risk.

"Fiona, you cannot go on pretending forever," he said firmly. "You are a grown woman. Soon you will be having a child. I promise, you will be happy if you allow yourself to be."

He saw the deliberate attempt she was making to withdraw, but her hand had moved involuntarily over the coverlet to the small curve of her belly.

Paul put his own hand over hers, holding it there when she would have snatched it back. "You see, you do know. A child should not have a child. Only a woman is fit for that."

It began with a small whimper but then it erupted from her in a high-pitched shriek. "I am not fit for anything. And I don't want this child. It's his, oh, God, it's his!"

He pulled her against him roughly, wanting to establish every contact before she could retreat again. "Yours too, Fiona, the child will be yours too! You know how to love, and I can tell you from experience that can make a world of miracles in a child's life. Your baby needn't be at all like Frank Lauder."

He said the name deliberately, and she flinched violently.

"He's dead, he can never hurt you again. You made a mistake, but it's over." He stroked her hair, and his voice was as gentle as his touch. "I've waited so long, much too long. I should have told you years ago. I love you. I've loved you since you were born, and it's never been the love of a brother for a sister. You are not my sister. Will you be my wife? I don't want to wait any longer."

She struggled so hard, he had to let her go, and she pulled as far away from him as she could. "Marry you! Are you mad? You used to make me feel like a fairy princess. And I used to believe I was. Don't you understand, that's over, not what I've become. That goes on and on! I've learned things and done things, and had things done to me that make me lower than the lowest whore in the city. I could teach them things on the Barbary Coast. Brand is dead because of me. Mother and Father have been through hell because of me. If I can't rid myself of it, the creature of Frank's seed is going to be born because of me. And you love me. What a fool you are!"

He listened patiently to the snarling words, but the ones he dreaded had not been spoken. She had not said she didn't love him—only that he should not love her.

She blinked in surprise at the smile illuminating his face.

"You see, you have not forgotten how to love," he said. "You would protect me from this horrible woman only you can see. I don't need protection. I need you. You judge me more frail than I am." He held her eyes with his own. "I killed your husband in cold blood. Now shall we talk about who is evil and who is not?"

It was the first she knew of it, but it made so much sense she was amazed that even in her distraught state, she had not considered it. She stared at Paul, seeing all of the things she had held so dear for so long and things she had never noticed before.

821

"You have not said that you don't love me. If that's true, then I must accept it, and we won't discuss it again. Say it, Fiona," he commanded harshly.

She opened her mouth and closed it again. Her hands knotted into fists.

"Say it!"

She shook her head, and tears overflowed and ran down her cheeks. "I can't," she gasped. "I want to, to keep you safe, but I can't say it. I've loved you for so long, depended on you for so long, I didn't know how much until the day you left, before my wedding." She choked on the word. "I felt as if the world had gone away with you, but I was too proud and stubborn to admit it. And I knew I didn't love you like a brother, but . . ." Her voice was lost in sobs.

Paul drew her close again, crooning, "I know, I know, it all seemed so complicated when in fact it is so simple. I love you, Fiona Ramsay, and there's not a drop of shared blood between us. And I don't give a damn about what's been except that you've been hurt by it. We'll start again, when you're ready. I'll teach you that love can be as fierce as it is gentle without ever being cruel. With all you say you've learned, the most important lesson was missing. But the one thing I will not tolerate is any more talk of ridding yourself of the baby. John Harland told me you raved about it, and we discussed it. It has nothing now to do with the choice. You are too far along. The risk to your life is not one I will allow."

It came out more as hiccough than giggle, but Paul could not mistake the humor in her muffled voice. "You have the good doctor and everyone else dumping Fiona in your lap, and what's more you're happy about it. There's no doubt at all that I'm marrying a fool." Her voice changed, drifting soft and slow. "My gentle heart, that you should have to kill for me!"

He tilted her face up, meaning to give her only a brief kiss, but they had gone through too much in their separate hells, had waited too long to be able to come together without fire.

Her mouth opened to his, tongue darting, retreating, teasing, promising with exquisite skill while her body pressed against his, moving in slow voluptuous patterns.

He realized suddenly what she was doing. Her need and

822

her love were real, and yet she was still giving him explicit warning, showing him how long past was her sexual innocence.

He broke the kiss and held her by the shoulders. "I'm twenty-eight years old, full grown, my love. And I want it all when it is time." His voice was rough with his need to make her understand.

Only now did he know how tense she had been; he could feel it leaving her, the last doubt, the last resistance. She smiled and he saw a Fiona even more beautiful than the one he had known.

"All for you, forever," she said, and this time she kissed him with sweet solemnity, sealing a vow.

CHAPTER LXIX

The wedding had been as quiet and as much a family affair as Jeff's, and it had been as joyful. Fiona had murmured audibly to Paul, "Ramsay is a lovely name," and he had answered, "I'm the last one you'll have to convince of that." Tessa hadn't had to say a word to Gavin to tell him how she felt about it. And the emerald collar, encircling Fiona's frail neck, made its own statement.

Both the elder Ramsays knew without doubt that the marriage had not been consummated. There was an eager, waiting quality about them that exists only between those who love but have not yet been lovers. They knew too it was Paul's choice—Fiona so obviously wanted to give him everything of herself, physically and spiritually.

"He's a wise man," Tessa said. "When a woman is with child for the first time, it's difficult for her to know what she wants beyond the birth and health of that baby. And for Fiona, it is so much harder."

He saw it so clearly, the time of Tessa's first pregnancy when she had so little known what she wanted and he had so little known what she needed, and it had all ended so badly—it was impossible to believe it had been nearly thirty years ago.

"If only we had had Paul's wisdom," he said gravely, and he heard the birdsong as clearly as he had in that dawn when he had known death had passed over Tessa.

"We have learned together. It is enough," she murmured. She leaned against him in perfect peace, and he wondered if any other man and woman had ever fit so well together.

The one thing that didn't fit in Paul and Fiona's life was the baby, and that was something Paul did discuss with his parents. The problem was not with him. His own adoption would always be vivid in his mind; Fiona's baby would receive nothing but a loving welcome from him. The welcome from the mother was much more in doubt.

Fiona ate and slept well as Dr. Harland had ordered, and she made no more mention of ridding herself of the baby. She did not mention the child at all. She didn't speculate on whether it would be a boy or a girl, nor did she express any preference. She made no preparations for its arrival. It was Gavin who got out the cradle and refinished it; Tessa who made sure the baby would have plenty of soft garments to wear.

They all clung to the hope that when the baby came, Fiona would be unable to resist loving it; especially Tessa who knew what that was like from Fiona's own birth.

Fiona's labor began on July 3, and the baby was delivered on the fourth while the city celebrated Independence Day with speeches, bands, and fireworks. Paul had been with his wife for most of the time, taking turns with Tessa in giving Fiona loving hands to cling to. Fiona's labor had been hard. She was small and it was her first, but it was not only that. Tessa read the signs clearly—the patient agony in her daughter's eyes, the acceptance of pain as punishment for marrying Frank Lauder.

Let her be all right, let everything be all right when the baby is finally born, Tessa had prayed inwardly, not even conscious of Fiona's nails digging into her flesh.

It was a boy, a perfectly formed child with a pale fuzz of hair and the bluish eyes of the newborn.

"You have a fine son," Dr. Harland announced to Fiona, and the tension in the room was palpable when Tessa put the clean and tenderly wrapped baby beside his mother.

824

Fiona had lain in silent exhaustion, her fair hair plastered to her skull in wet strands, but now she turned her head and stared at the baby. "It looks like its father. I would rather it had a crippled leg than its father's crippled nature. I don't want it!" Her voice was savage with rejection. She didn't touch the baby.

They were all helpless. Fiona's pain, fear, and grief were real. The baby linked her to the vicious man who had nearly killed her, and she was sure he lived on in his son, though no one else could see the slightest resemblance to Lauder in the child. It was as if even her body joined in the rejection, producing so little milk that even had she been willing to at least feed the child, it would not have been enough. The baby didn't seem to mind. He thrived on condensed milk and fresh cow's milk when they could get it, and that the woman who held him was his grandmother and not his mother made no difference to him.

Paul and Fiona had the wing of the house that contained what had been their rooms and their brothers' rooms. Fiona had not been well enough to have the strength to set up her own household, though she and Paul planned to move as soon as possible after the baby's birth. Tessa wondered how Fiona could bear to be in the same house with the baby, to hear him crying sometimes and never ask to see him. She had hoped every day would be the day that Fiona changed her mind, but when two weeks had passed, so had her hope.

Gavin watched her as she rocked the baby in her arms, and he felt a pleasurable sense of the past. He could see Tessa mothering their own children. It was hard to believe she was a grandmother.

She looked up at him and smiled wistfully. "This poor little mite, he has no mother and no name."

Gavin studied the child thoughtfully. "It shows more and more every day. He doesn't look like Frank Lauder. He looks like his grandfather. He looks like Jordan Ames. That's the name I'd give him, and I'd hope he'd grow up to be like his namesake."

"He'll be a better man," Tessa said firmly. "He will not have another place calling him home to sorrow and war."

"And perhaps he will have some woman as near to you as possible to love as a man loves a woman only once if

825

he is very fortunate." His words were full of tenderness and compassion.

"What a beautiful man you are," Tessa said softly, and in her mind she saw the beauty of his mind, his spirit, his heart, and even the scars on his flesh, all part of this singular man.

When Paul and Fiona moved out, Jordan Ames Ramsay stayed behind. Paul's pain at leaving the child was acute, but he knew it was imperative that Jordan be with people who loved him, and though he was willing, Fiona was not. He doubted that she would ever be. He did not condemn her for it; he saw it as the final wound Lauder had inflicted. He steeled himself to fight each battle as it came. The matter of the Lauder ranch and the rest of the estate hung around his neck like a lead weight. It was ironic that a man as unnaturally twisted as Franklin Lauder should have left such a conventional and current will. Everything was now Fiona's. She refused to discuss it at all, but Paul knew he could not put off going south to settle everything indefinitely. If nothing else, it was little Jordan's patrimony. Gavin or Jefferson would go in his stead, but that was something he would not consider. Fiona's problems were his even as her love was his. He tried to dismiss the thought that Lauder's generosity beyond the grave was the final revenge.

Within short months, Jordan Ramsay began to prove himself an exceptional child, and not only in his grandmother's eyes. His good humor seldom failed, and his alertness and curiosity were extraordinary. As soon as he could focus his eyes and recognize a world outside his own immediacy, he reacted with unlimited delight. Bright colors charmed him. Buttons, shiny objects, anything moving and everything else fascinated him. And his other senses kept pace. He was alert to every sound, and he reached out constantly to savor every texture, including that of his food. He was even easy to feed, objecting to new food very seldom and then only by a puzzled look as if questioning why anyone would feed him something so unpalatable. But his chief joy in the world was people. He crowed exuberantly for Gavin, Paul, Jefferson, and Indian; he smiled continually while Lotus talked to him; he gazed with perfect contentment and trust at Armenthia and Mrs. Tubbs; he chortled at Kam Lee, who so forgot his aloofness as to make faces and funny noises guaranteed to amuse; and he wiggled and cooed and simply beamed whenever Tessa was within his sight or hearing.

She knew it was foolish, but she saw part of all of her children in Jordan. He was bright and fearless like Brand, gentle like Jefferson, elfin like Fiona, reflective like Paul, though he wasn't even related to the latter. He was like the original Jordan Ames, too, with a sure inheritance of charming ways. And he was also his own version of Jordan, a unique combination of the old and a totally new human being.

Tessa continued to search, but she saw no evidence of his father's nature in the child. Franklin Lauder might even have been a normal child until some terrible abuse deformed him, she thought. That at least was something she could prevent from ever happening to Jordan.

Gavin, who in the beginning had had inner reservations as to their fitness to raise another child at their ages, could no longer recall his doubts. He was comforted and renewed by the presence of Jordan. He couldn't help thinking they had been given another chance, another son, not to replace Brand because no one could ever do that, but to ease the void in their hearts. He had forgotten how comical the antics of a baby could be, and he roared with amusement while he watched Jordan discover such interesting things as the possession of hands and feet.

"I think we should have named him Sherry," Gavin said one day, looking down at Jordan, who was staring back and grinning while he tested his fierce grip on one of Gavin's fingers.

Sherry, so much more soothing to the nerves than brandy. Tessa nearly jumped at the startling clarity of Jordan's voice in her memory, but there was no pain left. Fiona and this beautiful manchild, Jordan's legacy.

"The color is surely right, but I think Jordan will do," she said, smiling at both of them. The new born blue of Jordan's eyes had changed to a strangely compelling color that was like sherry, amber and brown and gold all at once, luminous with light that seemed to come from deep within the eyes themselves instead of from without. His hair was growing to be a silky brown gold. Even his little hands were unique with long fingers and an expressive grace odd for a baby. His grandfather had had the same kind of hands, as indeed Gavin had. Jordan Ramsay was going to be a handsome man.

They had thought to hire a nursemaid for the baby, but Kam Lee took over the duties without the slightest hesitation. It was gratifying that Kam Lee's weakness should prove so useful. He was a changed man around the baby, indulgent and endlessly patient. Gavin claimed that Jordan's first language was sure to be Chinese, and Tessa replied that that could only be useful in California.

The family gathered for the first joyful Christmas they had had in years. Even the fact that Fiona was there and hardly glanced at her child did not dampen their spirits. They had grown accustomed to her choice. She and Paul now lived not far from Jefferson and Lotus, but Fiona visited her parents often, needing a certain comfort and support only they could give. She was deliriously happy with Paul. It showed in the way she looked at him, and it sounded in her voice when she spoke to him. She was radiantly beautiful, very much the silver-haired princess again. And Paul was a changed man, all trace of the old melancholy gone. He laughed often and infectiously; his face was so alive it almost hurt to look at him; and there was no doubt now that he and Fiona were lovers in every sense.

"I would say your long-suffering patience has been rewarded," Gavin observed softly as he and Paul watched Fiona and Lotus, who were giggling girlishly over some private joke.

"It certainly has!" Paul agreed, and blushed—his mind was suddenly filled with images of Fiona, her body perfect to him despite her handicap, which did not exist in bed; Fiona and the things she knew, the sensations she could arouse in him, the silky hair running through his fingers, her hands, her mouth, the way she moved . . .

"You may find this difficult to believe, but I still must be careful when I think about Tessa in public," Gavin said kindly, and they laughed together.

Paul waited until 1873 had dawned before he traveled south to check on the Lauder estate. He knew he simply could not put it off any longer, and though Fiona hated the very idea of the trip, she made no protest.

When he returned he sought out his father. He explained that he had found the ranch in surprisingly good shape. Many of the men had stayed on, waiting to see what would happen, being paid by the bank out of the estate. It was not the job they hated, but their employer.

"I don't know whether I've done the right thing or not. There's a great deal of land speculation going on down there, and I expect I could have sold the place for a fairly respectable price. But it's good land, and I somehow just couldn't bring myself to sell it. I wish Jordan were old enough to make the decision. But in the meantime, I've appointed one of the men as foreman. Lauder's foreman was one of those who left. Carlos, the new foreman, seems competent, and besides, he's one of the few who expressed concern for Fiona. Someday I expect they'll have to know I'm not only her brother but her husband. I just didn't want to explain that this time around."

"Sounds to me like you've done a fine job," Gavin said. "But then, you know I'd much rather have money working than sitting in a bank. It can be a damn dangerous place for sitting."

Tessa found herself humming through the days, waking each morning feeling thankful all her children were so happy. Not only were Jefferson and Paul busy, but Fiona and Lotus both had the full status of teachers at Mrs. Tubbs's school. Mrs. Tubbs thought the rule against allowing married women to teach, a rule prevalent in most places, was ridiculous. Any rule that prevented qualified people from teaching was greeted with her contempt. She knew the two Mrs. Ramsays would probably take time out to have their own families, but in the meantime, she was pleased to have their bright young minds helping her with the students.

Though Lotus spent some time at the shop and had a good eye for color and style, Tessa made no attempt to influence either her or Fiona to take over. If they wished to continue the shop after she was gone, that would be their choice. For the present, she and her staff were quite capable, though Molly and George Barker would retire within the year.

Even with her full days and Jordan's presence, Tessa found more time than ever to spend with Gavin. It was as if they were beginning all over again as lovers, finding new delight in each other. She thought of how often these subtle changes had occurred, not one journey, but many in the same.

"Watching your face is better than reading a good novel," Gavin said. "I don't think I miss a word either." He reached out and delicately traced the curve of her breasts. "You know, we could manage the time to go East for a visit," he suggested idly. "We could go by rail, and I could show you . . ." His voice trailed off, and he stared at her in consternation. There was no mistaking the fear in her suddenly pale face and wide eyes.

"Sweetheart, what is it?" he asked urgently.

"I have always been afraid that you would want to go back someday, and that . . . that more civilized people, women . . ."

Gavin gave an exultant whoop and hugged her fiercely. "My love, that you should worry after all these years! You flatter me. I left nothing I ever want to see again back there. Everything is here, and here, and here." He marked the places with kisses that warmed her skin. "To hell with going East, there's enough traveling to do at home."

It was late spring when Indian and Armenthia announced their plan. They wanted to leave the city to live at Rancho Magnífico. Dian, their eldest son, would be twenty this year. He was courting a girl named Freedom Brown, and he liked his work in the city and would remain here. The other three children would move with their parents. It made good sense. Indian was ever more involved in his beef and wheat projects, and Dian got on well with the Ramsay sons and had taken over much of his father's work in the various Ramian enterprises. With Jefferson back, it could no longer be said they were shorthanded.

But it was hard to imagine not having Indian and Armenthia right next door and close to their daily lives.

"Ain't like we leavin' th' state," Indian reminded them gruffly, his arm tightly around Thia. "Jus' movin' out to th' country." But they all knew it would be forever different. Tessa and Thia found a thousand things they had to
830

say to each other before moving day came, and there were often tears not hidden in time.

Tessa felt the lonely chill of the house across the way. It made no difference that they would undoubtedly be able to rent or sell it if they wished; it would not be the same. Nor was it the same in the Ramsay house with so few of them left in it. And Rincon Hill itself was changing, had been changing since 1866 and the first new road cut through it. New grading projects, new streets, more houses year by year by year.

She recited it all very quickly, not looking at Gavin, wanting to say it all before his doubt could infect her. "So, I think we ought to seriously consider moving." She stopped, out of breath because she was so nervous, peeking at him now to see his reaction.

His eyebrow was at its most absurd angle. "Are you finished, or have you another twenty things to say in half a second?"

Incredulously she saw that he really was amused. "You have already considered it!" she accused.

"I have indeed, even to having discussed it with Indian. He thinks it is a fine plan. For a while longer at least, we need a home in the city. What would you think of a house on Fern Hill? With Halliday's gripper cable cars going in, or rather, up, we won't have any trouble getting to our lot."

"I suppose you have plans of the house to show me?"

"No, I thought I'd let you have a say in that."

"How kind of you," she managed to say before relief overwhelmed her and she began to laugh helplessly.

CHAPTER LXX

In the fall there was yet another financial panic, that began in Europe and had its counterpart in America, due mostly to overexpansion in railroad building and in the businesses that had sprung up following the war. In addition, Congress passed a bill that discontinued the purchase and coinage of silver while nature added her own ironic footnote by suddenly yielding more silver, thus causing the price of it to drop just as coinage of it was stopped. Those with fortunes in the metal yowled in outrage.

There were additional and specific problems in California. Silver was not gold. It did not provide nuggets that could be picked up or dug out and presented in exchange for commodities. Silver had to be extracted from ore with complex machinery, and many people who had invested in operations purported to be doing just this had yet to see the results. These investors owned nothing more than paper linking them to nebulous claims, yet they traded on the paper and traded well, and the majority of them, whatever their origins, were Californians now. Having avoided the greenback problem, California now had her own in the credit extended for worthless silver stocks. People like Franklin Lauder who had actually made money on the Comstock Lode were in the minority in the inflated ranks of dreamers who were sure tomorrow or the next day silver would pour out of their claims that they had never seen, enough to make them wealthy in spite of the drop in prices.

The railroad too was proving as much a curse as a blessing. Rather than bringing the boom that had been predicted, it brought cheap manufactured goods with which local products could not compete, and it brought working men and their families who dreamed of better conditions and pay in California, but who arrived to find jobs scarce and the labor market flooded with thousands of Chinese whose stints on the railroad were over and who were willing to work very hard for very little. Even as Chong Sing and Gavin had known, the Chinese were fast becoming the number one scapegoat for the frustrations of the working class.

In the early days of the gold rush there had been a feeling of the common lot, common chances, one class. Now society was becoming dangerously stratified into the poor and the rich, with few in the middle.

Anything that hurt business affected the Ramsays, but their holdings were too diversified and too well financed for them to go down as others had. They had never believed in living on credit. The warehouse suffered the most, but even it continued to show a small profit. The Golden Horse was evidence that the last thing men were going to give up was their drinking rounds. There was no doubt the wines from the Vincenti vineyard would receive the same welcome. Lumber was always needed, and that need continued to insure the success of the mill. And because Tessa's shop had always dealt in goods of the finest quality, she found they were selling more, not less. It seemed a strange paradox that the more nervous the economy became the more the rich spent on luxury goods.

The produce from the *ranchos* showed far more fluctuation in profits, with beef prices the most precarious. But even here they were better off than most because, barring a great natural disaster like drought, they could afford to withhold their animals when the prices dropped too low, while the produce from the orchards and the wheat continued to sell well. Tessa's palominos were like the silks and satins she sold at the shop; they were luxury items sold to the rich. Even when the value of horses on the open market dropped, the golden horses continued to fetch high prices. They never flooded the market with them, but took care to sell only the best trained and most finely bred. They sold them in San Francisco and Monterey, but buyers came from as far away as Los Angeles, San Diego, and even Texas.

Sometimes Tessa felt almost guilty for their prosperity, but she knew that was foolish. They had worked hard and planned wisely and never indulged in wild speculation.

So while many were already calling the decade the "Terrible Seventies," the Ramsays went on with building their house on Fern Hill. They spent one more Christmas in the Rincon house, and by the spring of 1874 had moved.

Tessa felt no sorrow at leaving the house. It had grown too big for them, and there were too many ghosts haunting it now. Chong Sing and Brand gone, and the hatchet man buried near the roses. Mrs. Beecham's fury swirling in the dining room, waiting all those years to take revenge by hurting Fiona. Both houses and the grounds were being purchased by a developer who would undoubtedly build too many houses and tear out the rose garden. He had gotten a bargain and he knew it, because real estate prices had fallen drastically. The Ramsays and Indian accepted that philosophically; it helped them as much as hurt them because they were continuing to buy lots in the city.

If ever one needed proof of what sudden wealth could do to people, it could be found in some of the mansions going up on Fern Hill. Tessa was stunned by the grotesqueness of some, which imitated everything from Greek temples to European palaces. Railroad and silver money was perching on the hill, and many of the people who had money had neither the education nor taste to go with it. Some admitted openly that that was true by importing whole rooms complete in every detail from European estates. Tessa was appalled by the idea, as she had been when they had sold the Happy Valley house with most of the contents.

"To be surrounded by things others have chosen, it's, why, it is indecent, like wearing someone else's undergarments," she told Gavin, who laughed heartily in perfect agreement.

He was as pleased as she was by the house they had built. It was in the two-storied Yankee-influenced Monterey style, with a tiled roof and rooms made airy by large deep windows. It was big enough for them and for guests without being overwhelming, and its white walls and polished wooden floors gave it a quiet dignity. There were a few Oriental rugs laid on the floors to give color and warmth, though much of the wood was left bare. Tessa had never quite gotten over her early training, which labeled rugs as unsanitary hiding places for dirt and fleas. There was enough space around them to plant a terraced garden, but they put only a low brick wall around their property line rather than the high, forbidding iron fences many favored. The view of the Bay from the house was even more spectacular than it had been from Rincon Hill.

Kam Lee immediately assumed control, and Jordan, now a very active two-year-old, was perfectly happy in his new quarters. The cable cars that made the hill accessible were his special delight. He loved the clanging bells and showed no fear at all when he was taken for a ride. It took Tessa a lot longer to be able to breathe normally while trusting her life to the machine. She had far too clear a vision of plunging right down into the Bay should the grippers fail to hold the cable. It was just possible to ride a horse up the hill to their house, but it was a hard pull, and so they kept

their beasts at a livery stable in town. The stableboys soon
learned that Mr. and Mrs. Ramsay knew more about horses
than they did and were kind as could be when the horses
were well looked after, but would raise Cain if anything
was amiss.

Tolerance rather than real liking seemed to be the rule
on Fern Hill unless one's business associate lived in the
next mansion, and sometimes tolerance was the kindest
description in these cases too. Privacy was respected. It
suited the Ramsays just fine. They hadn't any desire to be
particularly friendly with the people on Fern Hill. They
had little in common with most except financial success,
and that hardly seemed enough to provide the foundation
for friendship. They exchanged pleasantly vague nods and
very few social visits with their neighbors. They had enough
commitments with their family and Ramian enterprises,
including the *ranchos*.

Tessa had dreaded going back to Valle del Mar after the
deaths of Ramón and María, but she had found her dread
to be needless. If their ghosts were there, they were kindly
ones. The couple lived on in their descendants and in the
care they had lavished on the *rancho* for so long. She felt
the pull of the place more strongly than she had in years.
It was home again, and given the choice, she would spend
her last years there. She did not mention it to Gavin, wanting it to be a mutual decision someday, but she suspected
he knew anyway. The time they spent there was more
loving than it had ever been, and she could feel him relax
as soon as they arrived. And Jordan, with his laughing
sherry eyes, enjoyed going there too, as well he should
since everyone on the place spoiled him.

Rancho Magnífico belonged ever more to Indian and
Armenthia. When she had first realized it, Tessa had
searched her heart honestly, looking for jealousy. She
found none. She found only relief that they had their home
land to settle on, just as she and Gavin had Valle del Mar.
There was a vast agricultural fiefdom being built by two
men, Miller and Lux, in the Great Central Valley, and the
edges of it already licked at Rancho Magnífico's boundaries, but the Ramsays agreed completely with Indian's
refusal to even consider offers being made for their
acres. Indian was gradually turning Rancho Magnífico

835

into supremely productive land, much more than it had been before.

Since they had begun their family later, they were only now having to yield their children to adulthood, as the Ramsays had already done. Dian married Freedom Brown, a lovely, shy slip of a girl whose parents had been fugitive slaves who had escaped to Canada in time to have their first baby born beyond the yoke of slavery. They had returned to the United States after the war but had then come West, finding the South too full of painful memories and new troubles. Thia and Indian were fond of Dian's wife and so there were few problems there, aside from Thia's poorly hidden desire to hold a grandchild in her arms.

Julie, who would be eighteen this year, had surprised them all. She was as tall and impressively beautiful as her mother, but her nature was much like her father's, quiet and unlikely to betray innermost feelings except under duress. She had made no protest about moving out to the *rancho*, and indeed, she seemed to enjoy life there very much. No one expected the man named John Williams to follow her out into the country, but he did, making the journey as often as he could. He was twenty-three, a thin young man whose habitually serious expression was transformed when he looked at Julie. He was versatile in his interests, having some education and enjoying working with his mind and his hands equally well. Indian and Thia had met him in San Francisco, had liked him, but had not singled him out as being any more favored than Julie's other beaus.

"Did this come on all of a moment?" Thia asked her daughter when she saw how the wind blew.

"No, Mama, you know things never come on all of a moment for me. I just had some thinking to do, and I figured John might need to do some too. There probably won't ever be another marriage as happy as yours and Papa's, but I want to come as close as I can, and I think I will with John. We're going to get married before the year's out; all this traveling is wearing John down, and he's skinny enough already. Reckon Papa could use another hand around here?"

Armenthia's smile was suddenly as wide as her daughter's. "Reckon he could but more like another son."
836

Joshua and Indiana teased their older sister unmercifully, and John, who was an only child, sometimes looked acutely uncomfortable, but Julie paid them no heed. John's parents had died of yellow fever when he was twelve, and Julie was determined that before she was through with him, he was going to know what having a family meant.

It was her two youngest who worried Thia the most. Joshua was a dreamer and enormously bright, a combination that frightened his mother. He'd stop in the middle of some chore, going off in his mind, totally forgetting what he was supposed to be doing. If she didn't keep a close eye on him, he'd forget to eat too, and since he seemed to get taller every day and was thinner than John Williams, Thia tended to fuss. Built on a much slighter scale, still Josh had his father's coppery skin and strong bones. He was as sweet natured as anyone could wish, but his mother sensed the fire in him too keenly for comfort. There was an inevitability about it that terrified her. The fire would burn brighter and hotter as he got older. He might forget to eat, but he never forgot something he read or an idea that interested him. Sometimes Armenthia could feel the heat of his mind spinning out flames. Such men attracted danger. The thought occurred to her far too often. If only he would stay where it was safe and never wander far. But already his vision was of distant places. He asked her continually to tell him what it had been like to be a slave, and when she refused to talk about it any more he turned to other sources, reading every account he could get his hands on plus long treatises on the economic and philosophic problems of the South before and after the war. It was as if the origins of his parents drew him back like a strong rope.

Indiana, twelve this year, presented her own set of problems. She was quick-tempered, feisty, and amazingly stubborn when she judged she'd been wronged. But she was as swift to love as to anger, and Indian thought maybe she fought so hard for everything because she wasn't only the youngest, but also the smallest. She was short and slender, built totally unlike her parents or her siblings, and Armenthia didn't think she was going to grow much. Her face was pointy and long-eyed and the liveliest of them all, one expression chasing after another like quicksilver.

Her hands were her most beautiful feature, exquisitely shaped and long-fingered for her stature, and though they looked frail, they were strong hands and what they could produce was her chief delight. They were never still, always drawing, or painting, or carving something from wood, molding something from muddy clay or stitching some bright intricate pattern. There was no doubt that her eye for color and line and her ability to transcribe them from her mind was amazingly fine. Mrs. Tubbs had remarked on it long since. There was also no doubt that all Indiana wanted to be was an artist. She never said, "When I get married," or "When I have children"; "When I paint better than this," "When I know how to make the inside of the wood shine out," were typical of her ambitions. Not even her stitchery showed any inclination to small prettiness. Everything she did was uniquely marked by strong colors and curves and a pulsing energy. Birds exploded out of tangled bushes in one painting, and the drawing done before it showed the same thing, though in an odd pulsing arch of curves and brief spirals. The wood she carved showed rough and smooth figures that looked as if they'd grown naturally out of the piece. The small heads she'd made of her family in clay caught the essence of each, although you couldn't say the pieces looked exactly like their models.

Thia knew that power moved in this child as it did in Joshua, though for different purpose, and it frightened her no less in her daughter than it did in her son. It was hard enough to be an artist when you were a man; to succeed as a woman seemed impossible. Indian wasn't much use for comfort, for though he feared for the difficulties his daughter would face, he knew the joy of creating something with your hands and he knew Indiana created things of great beauty. That in Indian's mind went a long way toward banishing other problems. And the fact was that Indiana need never go hungry.

Tessa understood Thia's anxieties very well because she had suffered through the like with her own brood. "But you would have to go far to find anyone less qualified than I to give advice on the raising of children," she pointed out ruefully. "I made mistakes or misunderstood at every turn. I can only hope that I have learned enough to do a better job with Jordan!"

"We both did the best we could," Armenthia said slowly. "It's jus' lettin' them go after borning them that's so hard."

It was partially that shared feeling that made the women object so strenuously when their husbands first proposed the legal division of Ramian enterprises. They all got along so well, including the second generation, adding legal boundaries to the situation seemed like declaring an end to their innocence and love for each other. But the men were adamant. Dissension could come between the best of friends. They had been very fortunate so far. But all it would take was one serious battle within the ranks and everything would be put at risk. And their children had as much right to know what they were working for as they themselves had known when they first began. It was probable that one or more of the children would eventually want to start some business in which the others had no interest, and if that were to be possible, each of them was going to need to know what his or her private assets were. In fact, it was a measure of how fine the older children were that they had not demanded such security before, but had worked hard for the common good of the company and had been content with the shares of the profit they received.

The logic was irrefutable, but Tessa was glad when Thia brought her own dread out in the open. "One of you plannin' to die soon?" she asked sharply.

"Ain't in my plans for next week," Indian replied, "but I expect we all get 'round to it someday."

"Only way I've heard of to avoid it is to sell your soul to the devil," Gavin said, "and I haven't had any offers that I know of."

Despite the men's attempts to pass over the subject lightly, the cold flooded into Tessa's veins until it was a physical effort not to shiver, but she, like Armenthia, agreed to every provision when the papers were drawn.

Both families would continue to share in the proceeds from the warehouse, the Golden Horse, the lumbermill and wharf, the winery, the mine, and various lots in San Francisco. Each family had fifty percent and any decision to sell or buy with the joint capital required a two-thirds majority vote so that when the second or even third generation was in charge, neither family could dictate to the other. The money from the Rincon houses and land went to Indian and Armenthia in exchange for the Ramsays' ownership of the Fern Hill property, which was a much smaller property and purchased for less in the beginning. Tessa's shop, the palominos, and Rancho Valle del Mar were henceforth owned solely by the Ramsays. Rancho Magnífico now belonged solely to Indian, Armenthia, and their heirs.

In the late spring of 1875, the prime palominos and chestnuts of Rancho Magnífico were driven home to Valle del Mar to join the larger number there. The drive was much easier this time, because there was verdant grazing all the way and plenty of water. At some farms and ranches, golden horses gleamed in the sunlight, and Tessa wondered how many were the same horses she had bargained with in the horrible journey during the great drought, or their descendants. They met two ranchers on the way who remembered her, and one was the spare New Englander who hadn't changed at all in the years. "You spat right nicely in 'er eye," he said, as if Tessa had passed through only the day before. "Been hankerin' to see this river of gold and red goin' by again."

"We found water right where you said it would be, and I am still grateful," Tessa replied. It took her some time, on the border between laughter and tears, to tell the whole story to Gavin.

"Just when I think I understand what it must have been like, I hear something else, from Jefferson or Paul or a strange farmer, and I know I'll never really see it all clearly. But I can still hear the coyotes," Gavin said softly.

Tessa had a strange double view of the journey. Gavin was with her now, as she had wished so desperately that he was then, but of the children, only Paul rode with them. Lotus was too close to the birth of her first child for Jefferson to leave her unless it was absolutely necessary; Fiona, who had been forbidden to go the last time, had lost her desire to go now, although she was, as she put it, only a little pregnant; Brand's journeys were over. Jeff and Lotus were happily in charge of Jordan while his grandparents were gone. Tessa suspected that Paul had come with them only as a gift of memory to her. There was no panic now, and plenty of *vaqueros* to help. Her throat closed with the thought of Paul's enduring love. Indeed, she was proud of all of her children. Though they had spent much of their youth at Rancho Magnífico, not one of them thought it anything but just that Indian and his family should own it.

They had left Rancho Magnífico before, when they had gone to the city to try their fortune. But this was the final severing. No matter how friendly the welcome, they would be only visitors there from now on. Pedro and the others of the old guard had cried openly, even though they and their families loved Indian and Armenthia and were more than willing to work for them. And the changes extended to Valle del Mar. The days of range cattle were fast ending, and special breeding was taking over everywhere, as it was on Rancho Magnífico. Valle del Mar would see no more vast herds of cattle; the grass would belong to the horses now, and only enough cattle would be kept to provide beef and leather for the *rancho's* own needs.

Tessa was forty-seven this year, Gavin ten years older, yet they both could sit erect in the saddle for long hours. She was quietly proud of that fact, and further delighted that they still cared intensely enough for each other and the world to spend long moments before they slept simply holding each other, gazing at the stars and listening to the night sounds.

Life was very good, but it was also much too swift. She was ever more conscious of the days spinning away at a fearsome rate. She stirred restlessly, and Gavin's mouth found the pulse at the base of her throat and his hands began to rove under her loosened garments.

"They'll hear!" she whispered, stifling a giggle.

"They won't," he retorted. "They've all settled a polite distance away. Damn buckskins!"

This time she did laugh aloud, and moved obligingly to help him. *Only this makes the hours stand still forever*, she thought, *only this*, and she awakened at dawn with the thought still in her mind and Gavin's body keeping her warm as she lay tightly against him, the curve of her back and buttocks perfectly sculpted to his chest and lean stomach. "Too bad the sun is rising," she murmured drowsily.

"We should be home in a real bed by tonight, my lecherous woman," Gavin said, nipping her ear playfully. Tessa rejoiced to hear him call Valle del Mar home so easily.

CHAPTER LXXI

Toward the end of August, there was a week of financial chaos that was sure to leave scars on California's economy for decades. William C. Ralston's Bank of California finally closed its doors, despite Ralston's frantic last-minute attempts to save it. He had overextended himself and the bank by using more than twelve million dollars of his depositors' money to finance various mining and water-supply schemes. There had been rumors of trouble all summer long, and many had quietly withdrawn their funds, but the culmination was the end of August run on the bank. When the Bank of California closed its doors, the angry and frightened crowd of depositors moved on to other banks, withdrawing everything they could, which while it wouldn't ruin all of these banks, certainly put a strain on them. The market for mining stocks had been glutted and ruined in the same week, causing thousands to realize they were holding worthless paper and further increasing the general panic. After Ralston ordered his bank closed, he went down for his daily swim in the bay, and his body was recovered sometime later.

The Ramsays could not help feeling some guilt. They had paid close attention to the rumors and had withdrawn what money that had in the Bank of California early in the summer, thereby contributing to the situation that brought about its final ruin. But it was a way of survival, and it had worked. They were still solvent, and they were happy.

Lotus had given birth to a son, Brand Soon Ramsay, and by Christmas, Fiona had produced a daughter, Teresa, for Tessa, but already bearing her own nickname, "Resa."

Though Jefferson had been nearly out of his mind with worry, Lotus had had her son with the same calm lack of fuss with which she accomplished everything else. Fiona had had a more difficult time, as Dr. Harland said she always would, but at least it had been easier than the birth of Jordan.

Tessa was very touched by the naming of both children, especially the continuance of Brand's name. It had an entirely different significance now from the first meaning, but that was fit and proper. That Brand should live on in the name of this vital new human being rather than solely in memory was a gift beyond price.

Armenthia and Indian too had their first grandchild, from Dian and Freedom, and were no less besotted with little Thia than the Ramsays were with theirs, their only lament being that they didn't get to see her often enough. It would be better when Julie and John started their family, since they were living at Rancho Magnífico.

Gavin was even more indulgent with his grandchildren than he had been with his children. He maintained that that was the sole function of grandfathers—discipline and saying No were the province of parents. He had endless patience with them and had taken to carrying everything from string for hand tricks to sweets in his pockets, even though Jordan was the only one old enough to appreciate them.

Tessa tried not to worry about Jordan, and worried anyway. He regarded Fiona as an unfriendly aunt married to Uncle Paul, who was very nice indeed. But someday he would have to be told. Gavin and Tessa had realized from the first that it would be both foolish and futile to pretend to be his parents. There could have been no clearer example of the wages of lying even by omission than the bitter time with Fiona. They had labeled themselves as Jordan's grandparents from the beginning. The problem was that he was too young thus far for that to make any difference. They were simply the people who loved him and kept him safe, but the day wasn't far off when he would ask why other children had mothers and fathers instead of grandparents.

The year 1876 dawned with great fanfare as the centennial of the country with innumerable exhibits, fairs, parades, and speeches planned from one coast to the other and culminating on July 4. It was a great relief to Tessa that they spent July at Valle del Mar. She reckoned that was the difference between being a mother and a grandmother—as the former, she had been willing to plunge into the noise and excitement of such a day; as the latter she was relieved not to have to face the crowd. Jordan thoroughly enjoyed his birthday at the *rancho*.

It was ironic that such a landmark year should end with a presidential election that was so disputed that Rutherford B. Hayes would not be declared the winner until early in the new year. Federal troops had to be called out to control angry mobs in various cities, and President Grant felt obliged to make a speech of apology to the Congress before he left office because of the scandals of his administration. The speech was widely reprinted. His troubles had arisen from inexperience, and his mistakes were, he claimed, "errors of judgment, not of intent."

"I used to feel sorry for him, but he had enough time and practice but too little ability to get it right in the end," Gavin said unsympathetically, and his two sons were in such complete agreement, Tessa had to resist the impulse to jump in on Grant's side just for the sake of defending the underdog.

"I dare you," Gavin murmured softly, watching her face and grinning. She had to smile back, especially because she had just seen his and Jefferson's eyebrows tilted at the same angle.

But there was nothing to smile about in California's political situation in the new year. Discontent was growing toward outright violence in the white laboring class, which had been swollen by the influx of Irish workers from the eastern crew of the transcontinental railway, and the Chinese were clearly marked as their target. There was no question but that the problem was real. It had been worsened by the recent ups and downs in the state's economy; the fact was that there were too few jobs and a considerable number of the jobs there were were held by Chinese. It all had the simplistic arrogance Tessa had so hated for years: they do not look, talk or think as we do; therefore they are foreigners; therefore whatever they have should be ours. And it was worse now, not only because there was so much less easy wealth to be had, but because the Chinese were visually so easy to pick out.

It made Tessa fear for Kam Lee, the Chens, and most of all for Lotus. Even with her height and her obvious mixed parentage, she was Chinese. Though Jefferson said little about it, worry haunted his eyes and made his face haggard and old beyond his thirty years. Guilt showed there too because he had not insisted that Lotus and little Brand go to Rancho Valle del Mar, and now in June, though it looked as if the summer would bring more trouble, it was too late for her to travel, because their second child was due in July.

Lotus alone was serene, sailing through her days with that contented inner smile Tessa recognized. Nothing was as real or important as the child within. When Lotus thought of the situation in the city at all, she thought that she would not be cast out by these louts. Some were only recently arrived in America, and many, like her, were only first-generation citizens, most of their families having come from Ireland in the forties and fifties. She belonged here, she would stay, and that was all there was to it. She granted her parents the dignity they deserved by respecting their wish to do the same.

Gavin said little, but the lines around his mouth were taut these days, and he kept track of every rumor and gauged the temper of the knots of men who gathered on the street corners and harangued crowds on the sand lots as carefully as he would have judged a rattlesnake coiling to strike. Personally he wished all the women and children were at Valle del Mar, and he wouldn't have minded his sons being there also. But since that was an impossibility, he planned the next best things. Jefferson and Paul agreed with him; when the trouble began they were to bring their wives and children and the Chens, if they would come, to Fern Hill, which was at least safer than most other sections of town.

Tessa listened gravely when he explained the plan to her. "You are not saying 'if' but 'when.'" Her voice was not as steady as she wished it to be.

"There's no way around it," Gavin said grimly. "It's like putting a blind army on the march; they won't stop until they hit a wall. And there's no wall for them to hit right now. News of the labor strikes back East is giving them a sense of power, and there's no force here that's strong enough to stop them when they turn to violence, as they surely will. Too many angry words and too many angry men turn into angry mobs."

She pressed against him, suddenly needing the comforting contact, her hands kneading his shoulders convulsively, her voice muffled.

"Those goddamn bells! They will ring again for violence and hangings! And this time not only you but my sons will be part of it."

He patted her back comfortingly, but he did not deny her words, and his eyes were bleak.

It was almost a relief when it finally began, toward the end of July. The threats of violence were being openly made now, thousands of firearms had been purchased by unknown persons, and the combined force of 1200 members of the militia and 150 city police were woefully inadequate.

This time it was called the Committee of Safety and William T. Coleman was chairman again. But though there was little difference in the name, there was a vast difference in the purpose of the organization. This time the committee met at the request of the civil authorities for help, and there was no division between its members and the government. There were soon nearly ten thousand members, and Tessa's men were among them. Gavin, Paul, and Jefferson all had the identifying badges, their sidearms, and hickory pick handles that had been shortened to make clubs. Tessa felt sick every time she saw the clubs, and that was fairly often since the Fern Hill house was now the Ramsay clan's headquarters according to Gavin's plan. Even though the house was a trifle crowded, there was comfort in being together. Only the Chens had not joined them. There had already been minor battles between white workingmen and Chinese; two men had been murdered, and several Chinese laundries had been burned. The Chens refused to leave their shop, contending that it would be harder to destroy it if they were there to defend it. Lotus could understand their feelings even though she was concerned for her parents, and she was grateful that not only Jeff but his brother and father had promised to check on them frequently.

When the morning of the twenty-eighth dawned, five nights had passed since the committee had been formed. The threat of fire had been constant, small skirmishes had been fought every night, and everyone's nerves were on edge. Lotus thought at first that was why she felt so uncomfortable when she awakened. But when the pain twisted sinuously around her back and belly, she knew the newest Ramsay had finally decided to be born. She waited for a long time, but no new pain followed the first.

She heard the men come in and knew how Jeff's face would look even before he opened the door and poked his head in cautiously to see if she were awake. He had had so little sleep this week, his eyes were ringed by dark circles, but he smiled when he saw she wasn't asleep, and came over to kiss her. "How are you?"

"As enormously pregnant as I was yesterday, but obviously better than you are." She traced the tired line of his mouth, feeling guilty now—if she had allowed herself to be persuaded to leave the city, perhaps he would be out of it too. "If you'll help me get out of bed, I'll go down and help Kam Lee and your mother fix breakfast for the army. I assume you're all still intact?"

"Not a scratch on us, and your parents are fine too. We checked before we came here."

She laughed at her own ungainly progress out of bed. "I don't think I could have gotten up at all today without your help."

Jeff looked at her closely, his face even paler than it had been. "You're not, it's not——" he sputtered.

"No, it's not, though it is surely past due," she assured him smoothly. Though only brief moments had passed, it seemed as if she had decided on the lie hours before. It was partially true, since there was certainly no regular pattern of labor yet. It would undoubtedly be hours. And she didn't want to add to his burdens, even though it was tempting to keep him safely by her side. He would be torn between wondering what was happening to his father and brother and concern for her, and he had already proved to be less than his calm self during her first labor.

847

The look she gave him was so tender, Jefferson felt a lot less weary than he had.

Tessa was not so easily fooled. She had let Lotus help prepare the meal only because she could see the girl wanted to be doing something; that Tessa could understand, since she felt the same way herself, even though she knew the women in his kitchen were driving Kam Lee crazy. But she watched Lotus carefully and thought she looked even paler than usual. And while everyone else ate hungrily, Lotus, who had only taken a little bit of food to begin with, merely pretended to eat, rearranging her food on the plate but hardly tasting it.

Tessa saw the flash of pain on her face and the quick concealment and she nearly exclaimed aloud, but the slight shake of Lotus's head and the look in her eyes stopped her. The men were oblivious, strung high on the possibility of a real confrontation in the coming night because of a rumor that an attack was to be made against the Pacific Mail Steamship Company's properties due to their connection with Chinese immigration. Tessa was sure if they weren't so battle hungry, they'd notice all was not well with Lotus.

They had only a few hours before they were due back, and they spent them trying to sleep. Lotus didn't go upstairs with Jeff, and Tessa finally managed to get her alone.

"How far apart are your pains?" she asked bluntly.

"Too far apart to count the minutes," Lotus answered calmly. "Really, it has hardly begun. You mustn't think Jefferson is blind. He asked me, but I didn't tell him, and I thank you for not telling him either. This is no time to trouble him."

Tessa had to laugh. "You might tell that to the baby!"

Lotus was still able to smile when it was time for the men to leave again. Her hands resting on the mound of her stomach, she ordered, "You take care of yourself, all of you. I want this one to have a father, an uncle, and a grandfather."

As soon as the men were out of sight, Tessa sent Fiona for Dr. Harland. She knew they didn't need him yet, but with all the confusion she wanted him to be ready. When she told Fiona what was happening, Fiona shook her head.

"Honestly, she amazes me! I love Paul dearly, but I don't think I could be so unselfish."

"Nor I. Gavin delivered Brand and helped with you and Jeff."

She saw Fiona off, knowing she would be safer on the errand than Kam Lee, and since Kam Lee with Jordan's help seemed to be keeping Resa and little Brand amused, Tessa went to keep Lotus company.

Lotus had gone back to bed. The pains were slightly more regular now, but she was still unruffled and happy to have Tessa with her.

"Should I send word to your mother?" Tessa asked, but Lotus declined. "Father needs her more right now, I think, and you have always been so good to me, it's like having my mother here anyway."

"Ah, my dear, we are bound together by a thousand lovely things, and surely your love for my son and his for you is the loveliest of all." She looked at Lotus tenderly and held her hand tightly when another pain hit, and she thought how strange and beautiful it was that she had nursed the baby who had become this exquisite woman at her own breast.

Fiona arrived back with the news that John Harland was alerted and would come in due time. The city was street after street of nervous men, she reported, even more chaos close up than what they could see from Fern Hill, and the doctor had sent word that he would much rather deliver a baby than be involved in a brawl.

Tessa smiled at the message, but then her face sobered again, and she gazed at her daughter. "Under other circumstances, I would send the children to another house at this time so that they would not be distressed by the sounds of birth. But that's impossible today. Kam Lee is going to need help with them, and I hope you will offer it."

"Of course I will!" Fiona exclaimed, insulted by her mother's tone of voice.

"That includes Jordan," Tessa said quietly. "He's trying to be very grown up, and he's doing his best to help, but he needs as much comforting as the younger ones."

"I won't bite his head off!" Fiona protested, but not long after she found herself coming close to it.

Night came down and Dr. Harland still hadn't arrived. The babies were restless, and there had been a few audible cries from Lotus when especially hard contractions had taken her by surprise.

Fiona was tired, worried about Paul, and more nervous than usual around Jordan. He made her feel too many things at once—anger at him for existing, guilt for abandoning him, and a steadily increasing sense of loss for having rejected this small, shining boy. Kam Lee was busy in the kitchen, making sure that whenever anyone wanted to eat there would be plenty of good food available, so Fiona did not even have him as a buffer between herself and her child.

Jordan for his part was frightened, and the more he tried not to be, the larger the fear grew until it was a living thing inside him. Everything about the day had been askew, but this was the worst—to have Aunt Lotus whom he adored upstairs crying out as if she were hurt, while Uncle Paul's wife who had always scared him glared at him as if it were his fault. He knew it wasn't. Little boys couldn't do much to big people, it was the other way around. He had never received anything but love and kindness in this house, but he sensed the violence in Fiona. He pinched himself surreptitiously to see if maybe being left alone with her was a nightmare, but he felt the pinch and everything remained as it was.

He winced at another sound from upstairs. "Is she going to get well?" he asked, and wished his voice didn't sound like one of the frogs at the *rancho*.

"She's not sick!" Fiona snapped. "She's having a baby and that always hurts, at least some." The big, scared eyes touched her for a moment. "Look, as soon as the baby comes, she'll forget all about the hurting—it just isn't as important as the baby; it's just part of the work that goes into having one."

Jordan was glad she was talking to him, and her voice hadn't sounded so nasty at the end. Maybe if they kept talking, she'd forget she didn't like him. He searched around for something else to say, and when he found it, he offered it eagerly. "It's nice that you have hair like the tails on grandma's horses. Mine is sorta like that but not 'zackly." He crossed the small space to where his cousins lay sleep-

850

ing. "Resa has it too." The little girl stirred fretfully, and Jordan reached down.

The hissing snarl of Fiona's voice lashed him like a whip. "Don't you dare hurt my baby!"

"Didn't hurt Resa, wouldn't!" he gasped, backing away. "She's all tangled up."

One glance at Resa showed her what Jordan had seen—Resa's little gown was snarled around her legs, making her move uncomfortably.

Jordan's eyes filled with tears that overflowed and dripped down his white cheeks. His hands were clenched into fists at his sides, his whole body shaking, as he pressed himself against the wall, too terrified to make a run for the door, and he had wet his pants, something he hadn't done since he was an infant.

Fiona had never loathed herself as she did now. There wasn't a sign of Frank in this child, only in herself, and to have reduced this sturdy little boy to mindless terror with the force of her hate was utterly depraved. She had dammed up and denied the tide for so long, it broke through and washed over her with the force of the birth pangs Lotus was enduring. She wanted Jordan; she needed him; and she loved him. He was a singularly beautiful child, like an exquisite flower that had taken hold and bloomed perfectly among the rocks.

She went to him, and he closed his eyes, cringing, but the blow didn't fall. Instead she was using a voice he had only heard her use for Resa and Uncle Paul. "Oh, my poor baby, Jordan, sweet Jordan, I'm so sorry, so very, very sorry, can you ever forgive me? My love, my love, I'll never hurt you again." The broken words fell around him like a fine web of music, and her arms came around him gently, not hurting at all. When he dared to peek at her face so close to his own, he saw she was crying too.

The babies, awakened by the noise, began to fuss, and Kam Lee appeared.

"Take care of them, please," Fiona said, not letting go of Jordan. Jordan couldn't understand half of what was happening, but it was enough to know that she liked him now and was holding him even though he had disgraced himself and his tears had done further damage by making a big wet splotch on her dress.

851

"We'll clean you up, and then if you'll listen, I have a story to tell you," she said gently. Jordan was quite prepared to listen.

When John Harland arrived, one of the first sights that greeted his eyes was Fiona with Jordan on her lap. Their fair skins showed that they had both been crying, but they looked blissfully happy now, Jordan sleeping with a little smile curving his mouth. Fiona looked luminous and as beautiful as her mother for the first time in her life.

The doctor wondered as he hurried upstairs if the Ramsays had the slightest idea what a normal household was like.

He apologized for his lateness, explaining that he'd had to repair a cracked head, then wished he hadn't explained at all, since Tessa and Lotus thought immediately of their men.

"There is some fighting," he admitted, "but I wouldn't worry if I were you. The committee seems to be out in force, and three Ramsays are more than anyone should tackle. And now, my dear, how are *you* doing?" He eased the tension in the room by emphasizing the "you" and adding, "Your mother-in-law taught me long ago not to say 'we' in such situations."

Lotus smiled at him. "I'm doing very well. This one's taking a little longer than Brand, but it's definitely coming."

John agreed with her, and when Lotus had dozed off, he reassured Tessa. "She's a little tired, but everything's fine. It'll be some time yet; her labor's still pretty irregular, but I think you'll have another grandchild before dawn. This baby is overdue, and I suspect a good bit larger than Brand was, so it's giving her more discomfort, but she's handling it well."

He started to tell her about the amazing sight of Fiona and Jordan together, but a commotion downstairs stopped him, and Tessa was already at the door saying, "Stay with her, please. I'll be back."

She stifled a scream when she saw them. There was blood on all three of them, and it took a moment to understand that it was mostly Jeff's. Gavin had a grazed cheek and Paul a scratched hand, but it was Jefferson who lay on the sofa looking dead. His face was devoid of color, and his left arm was wrapped in a bloody makeshift bandage.

"He'll live," Gavin said firmly. "He's lost some blood and the arm needs setting and stitching, but the rest of him is intact. We brought him straight here. I'll go for John."

"You won't have to. He's upstairs. Lotus is in labor," she said, kneeling by Jeff as Fiona came into the room.

"I'll get him and I'll stay with Lotus," Fiona said with a calm that matched Gavin's. "Kam Lee is with the children, and they're all asleep now." Only Paul, who was so attuned to her moods had time at that instant to mark the change in her. She blew him a kiss from the doorway.

Jeff's eyelids fluttered, and then his eyes opened wide, focusing with difficulty on his mother. "Did you say . . . Lotus?"

"She's fine, I promise she is," Tessa answered, smoothing his hair back from his forehead, but Jeff struggled in panic to sit up, groaning and falling back as the movement awakened new agony in his arm.

Gavin was there instantly, holding him down. "Pretty lively, isn't it? You're not going anywhere until John has a look at that arm. If Lotus saw you now, you'd scare her to death."

"Wouldn't see me at all, wasn't for you. Thanks, Papa," Jeff muttered thickly. He wished he could pass out again as he had a couple of times on the way home, but when Dr. Harland wanted to give him something, he refused. "Want to see Lotus, not sleep," he insisted stubbornly.

Tessa swiftly gathered everything the doctor asked for while Gavin cut splints, and then the men lifted Jeff as carefully as they could and carried him to the dining room, laying him down on the table.

Paul and Gavin held him still, their faces now as white as his, and Tessa bent over him, cradling his head against her breast, his face turned away from the doctor.

"What in the hell did this?" John asked angrily when he saw the long deep gash and felt the broken bones in Jeff's forearm.

"A hatchet aimed at his head," Gavin said through stiff lips.

The doctor asked one more time about drugging him, but Jeff mumbled, "Just get it over with, want to see Lotus."

They could all hear the bones grinding back into place and the horrible half-uttered cry, and they could feel Jeff's body arching against the pain and slumping into stillness. John worked as swiftly as he could, muttering, "Hard to believe, but he's lucky. There's some muscle damage, but I think he'll have full use of his hand and arm in time."

Tessa knew when Jeff came to again. His eyes and mouth were clamped tight, and he flinched involuntarily every time the needle pierced the edges of the wound. She thought she had never heard such wonderful words as John's satisfied, "Well, that's finished."

There was a collective sigh of relief, and then Jefferson said very clearly, "This is a strange place, the rain has salt in it."

Tessa leaned down and kissed him on the forehead, thereby raining even more tears on him. When she looked up she saw that Gavin and Paul's eyes were as bright as hers.

"I've got another patient upstairs," John said briskly. "Pour something down this one and have some yourselves while you're at it. And don't let him get up by himself because he'll keel over and ruin my fancywork."

Tessa stayed just long enough to take a hearty choking gulp from Gavin's glass before she followed the doctor upstairs, thinking on the way, *Brandy and disaster, how sweet never to taste either again.* Fiona met her at the door.

"Not long now," she told her mother. "Everything's better because Dr. Harland has convinced her that Jeff's really all right. Is he?"

Tessa nodded. "I'll stay here. Go on down and see for yourself. You've been a great help." It was beginning to dawn on her, as it had earlier on Paul, that Fiona was somehow changed, but there was no time to think about it now.

Jeff was there when his second son was born before dawn had broken. He sat white-faced and enduring beside the bed. When it was all over, he tottered out into the hall, told his father and brother the news, and fainted.

"Glad we were there to catch him," said Paul as they carried him to bed.

"I'm surprised he held out this long," Gavin replied, and there was pride in his voice.

John stayed long enough to have breakfast with them because Tessa threatened to prevent his leaving by force if he refused. "The least you can do is eat and rest for a minute after all we've put you through."

"Don't apologize," he retorted. "My life would be dull were it not for the Ramsays stirring it up now and again."

And finally the doctor, Fiona, and Tessa got to hear what had happened. Just as expected, the confrontation had come at the docks of the Pacific Mail Steamship Company, where a ship newly arrived from China with 138 immigrants aboard lay at anchor. At first the committee's so-called "Pick-handle Brigade" had had a rough time of it, but then reinforcements had come to turn the tide. A nearby lumberyard went up in flames, but the attempt to burn the docks failed. The fighting had been bloody, with a few killed and many wounded from what Gavin had heard as they headed home. Fire alarms had gone off in other quarters, there had been other skirmishes going on, and it was a wonder more had not been killed with all the bullets flying around. But Gavin was quite sure the committee had dealt a death blow to the rioters.

Jeff had been battling hand to hand with one man when another had swung the hatchet at him. Gavin yelled a warning, and Jeff just had time to swing around and protect his head with his free arm. That's the way Gavin told it, and his embarrassment was plain when Paul insisted on adding the finer details.

"Jeff would have been killed, crushed to death if nothing else, when he went down, except that Gavin roared like a hound out of hell and got to him so fast nobody had time to trample him. The men he didn't throw out of his way ran, and nobody tried to stop us when we carried Jeff off."

Jordan wandered in, blinking sleepily, and asking if Aunt Lotus and Uncle Jeff were all right and would someone tell him the rest of the story that went with the ending he had just heard?

"I'll tell you," Fiona said softly. Jordan hesitated for the briefest instant, realizing that it was all true and not something he'd dreamed, before he gave her a sunny smile and climbed up into her lap. "Well, you see, your grandfather was very brave last night and saved Jeff's life while Lotus was having her baby, which is another little boy," she began. She looked up and met the stunned eyes of her parents and her husband and Dr. Harland's smile.

"A lot happened to all of us last night, and when you've all had a good rest, I'll tell you about it," she said, and she went on with the story for Jordan.

Gavin gave a groan of relief as he sank down on the bed and Tessa settled against him. "I'm getting too old for nights like this last one."

"I should hope so!" she snorted, but then she murmured very low, "Thank you for my son. I could not bear to lose another."

"My son too, and sweetheart, I feel obliged to confess. It wasn't bravery as Paul saw it. I wasn't thinking at all. I was in a blind rage to get to Jefferson."

"*Mi corazón*, it is the same thing," she whispered, and they slept.

CHAPTER LXXII

Gavin's judgment had been correct. The Pick-handle Brigade had triumphed, and a few days later the Committee of Safety disbanded its army, which was replaced by a much smaller force of special police. The Workingmen's Party of California, as it was now called, was by no means silent, finding an especially loud voice in Denis Kearney who had, oddly enough, been a member of the Pick-handle Brigade. Perhaps he had needed a new club when the old one disbanded, but whatever his reasons, his voice screeching, "The Chinese must go!" was the loudest in the continued sandlot meetings of the summer and fall. He was arrested once for inciting to riot, but there was none. The dockside battle had shown the workers that there were too many who would rally against them in any physical confrontation, and they were turning their attention to political action.

The Ramsays were united in their hatred for the rallying cry, but they were equally agreed that political action was not only acceptable but infinitely preferable to mob violence.

Their own changes from the dockside battle were enough to contend with. Jeff's recovery was slow and painful, but he worked doggedly until he could move his arm and all the fingers in his hand. "The better to hold my sons," he said.

The new baby's name was Gavin Soon Ramsay, and his eyes were very blue. Any boys they had would bear the middle name "Soon" to remind them of their Chinese heritage, but only this one would bear Gavin's name. Even the Chens insisted on honoring Gavin for saving their son-in-law, as if the fact that Jefferson was his own son had nothing to do with it.

But the greatest change was between Fiona and Jordan. She had told him the truth that night, sparing herself little. She had told him she was his mother but that she had been ill when she had him, sick in mind and body, and that she had known his grandparents would be kind to him as she could not be because she had not felt kind even to herself. She had told him how much Paul had wanted him even when she had not. She had told him how grand a person she thought he was and how proud she was he was part of her, the best part. She had not asked that he give up anything of his life as it was now; she had only asked that he understand she loved him. The only part of the truth she had omitted was his father's true character and how he had died. She did not want him to grow up to remember bitter words and to begin to question his own nature.

There was no doubt about it—Fiona had finally grown up. The last defiant insecurity was gone, and the wounds of the past were part of her maturity now, no longer locking her into the petulance of an overgrown child. She had taken responsibility for herself, and she wasn't overburdened by it. Even Paul, who had loved her just as she was, was astounded by her new beauty.

It was what Tessa had wanted from the beginning and

857

still wanted with the best of herself, but there was another part of her that mourned the loss of Jordan as if another of her children had died. Fiona did nothing except welcome Jordan with love, and a lesser child would surely have been confused by the strong pull from two quarters, but love was something Jordan could handle. "Aunt Fiona" became "Mama" and Paul was shortly after "Papa" because as Jordan himself explained, there was a sort of rule which made the man married to your mother your papa whether he really was or not, and he thought it a good rule since he liked Paul an awful lot. He was undismayed to have discovered his mother when he was five years old, and Tessa knew she and Gavin could take a good deal of the credit for that because they had given him the security of those first years.

But now he spent more and more time with Fiona and Paul, and slowly the confidential bond between mother and child, the bond of small secrets shared and woven into the fabric of a day, the trust that an answer would be forthcoming for nearly every question, the myriad ways of touching for mutual reassurance, all shifted and became the shared world of Jordan and Fiona rather than Jordan and Tessa. And it was only natural that he should move in permanently with his mother, stepfather, and half-sister.

"I'll still see you lots," he told Tessa and Gavin gravely as they helped him pack the last of his belongings. "And you'll always be my best friends besides my grandparents."

"We're glad of that," Gavin said. He knew Tessa was going to cry if she had to talk. Tessa hugged Jordan fiercely and managed a smile for him, not crying until he had left the house with Paul.

"I know how you feel," Gavin said, stroking her back gently in familiar comfort as he held her. "It's going to be goddamn lonesome not having him living here."

She felt the slight tremor run through him, and it strengthened her. "Ah, but we still have each other, and that's the important thing, always. I'm selfish to weep. Jordan needs the youth of Fiona and Paul, and they need him. The way I'm behaving, you'd think they had taken him out of the country." She wiped her eyes and smiled up at him. "Let's go somewhere very elegant for dinner tonight, and who knows what will happen afterwards?"

"The Cobweb Palace?"

"Certainly not! Those are real spiderwebs, you know, with real spiders in them and sometimes in the soup."

"Delmonico's then?" he said, laughing—that had been his plan all along.

Not only did they have a lobster dinner at Delmonico's, but they spent the night at the elegant Palace Hotel, where every room had its own fireplace and plumbing facilities and everything was done on a grand and opulent scale. It was seven stories high and filled with imported crystal, china, linen, and richer fabrics, plus rare woods and European marbles. Hundreds of gas-fueled flares lighted the marble-columned Grand Court, which was domed over with glass and boasted such things as a tropical garden, statues, jetting fountains, and music from an orchestra playing nearby in its own pavilion.

"Kam Lee will have the police out looking for us," Tessa protested when Gavin told her where they were going.

"He won't—I told him we wouldn't be back tonight."

"What will they think at the hotel when we arrive without luggage?"

"Something suitably salacious, no doubt," he replied with a grin, and she gave up trying to be sensible.

The desk clerk couldn't quite hide his smirk in time, but Tessa found herself feeling wickedly flattered rather than insulted. It was nice to think they still looked like lovers capable of indulging in an affair—at their ages and after so many years of marriage! Her face was suddenly so beautiful the desk clerk blinked and wrenched his eyes away with an effort.

They danced for a little while before they went up to their room, and again, the delicious pride and pleasure flowed through Tessa as she saw the other women in the room casting envious, hungry, feline glances her way.

"What are you thinking about?" Gavin whispered as he led her gracefully in a waltz.

"You. How handsome you are. How all the other women in this room wish you were holding them instead of me."

859

"Not to mention the men who would like to have my place with you," he retorted. "Talk like this has lost you the next dance, ma'am. I find I'm overly ready to go upstairs."

"No more than I," she murmured, pressing against him quite indecently as the dance ended.

It was a night she would remember for the rest of her life. It was as though they were very young again, without the hesitancy or doubt of youth, as if they had distilled the best essence of youth and age and mixed them together in a magic potion.

They toasted each other from the bottle of Vincenti wine Gavin had had sent to the room, and Tessa read "Bottled and distributed by Ramian" from the label with mocking solemnity. She felt as if they owned the world tonight, or at the very least, the entire city of San Francisco.

"This is decadent," she murmured when Gavin set her down on the thick carpet in front of the fireplace and began to make love to her in the glinting flame light.

"Isn't it though, just like the cabin in the rain," he agreed, nuzzling her breasts and sending exquisite shocks through her with flicks of his tongue, moving his mouth lower and lower yet, until she was writhing and crying out in utter abandon.

And later when they lay on the bed, she bounced on it, and laughed, "I wish this bed creaked. Tonight I would love to hear it."

"If we try hard enough, maybe it will," Gavin said, pulling her down until she collapsed against him.

Memories of that night made it easier for Tessa to refocus her life. It was time she and Gavin were free in their shared solitude again. It was not as if they didn't see their family: they did, both children and grandchildren, often taking care of the latter when their parents had something to do. But with Jordan no longer living with them, they were free to go where they pleased when they pleased, and they took advantage of it, visiting the Vincentis, returning to Nevada City (and the beds that still creaked), visiting Indian and Armenthia now and then, and spending more time at Valle del Mar.

It was increasingly clear that Jordan was very precious

to Fiona and Paul. Lotus gave birth to a girl, Chena Chye Ramsay, in 1880 and another boy, Lin Soon, two years later, but Fiona followed Tessa's own sad pattern of miscarriages and was not able to carry another baby to full term until she gave birth to Natalia, named for Mrs. Tubbs, in 1883. John Harland was quite sure she would not be able to have another child after Natalia, and that left Jordan as their only son.

Tessa knew how lucky she and Gavin were to have their family close in both heart and actuality. Joshua had left the state, and Armenthia mourned him as dead, though Indian continued to believe they would see him again someday. He had not gone rambling as Jefferson had. He had left with his savings, and he had gone back to his mother's origins, back to Mississippi. He had gone with all his will, brilliance, and energy aimed at a single dream —to teach black adults and children wherever he could. For every new federal law passed to insure Negroes of their rights as citizens, local and state regulations, particularly though not exclusively in the South, had been instituted to circumvent them. Joshua believed passionately that the ability to read and write were weapons that never lost their killing edge against those who preyed on ignorance. He was willing to die for his dream, but his mother was not willing that he should, and every time she received a letter from him, every one of them filled with glowing reports of progress and little mention of trouble, her joy was tempered by the thought that he might have been killed between the time he had sent the letter and she had received it. It was very much like the time of having Indian away at war.

Tessa had no easy comfort to offer, only her own knowledge of what it was to lose a son. The situation was further complicated for her by her ability to know how Thia felt while at the same time understanding Josh and admiring him for what he was doing.

Everything was more complicated than what she now knew to have been much simpler days, though they hadn't always seemed so at the time. Now in the eighties everything seemed to move at the same swift pace, changes for good, for evil, and for everything in between, all swift changes. There were many new rail lines in the state, including a major southern route, and that made transportation and shipping much easier, but almost all the railroads were controlled by a small group of men, and deserved the terrible image they had of an octopus engulfing everything. They abused the land privileges they had been given, letting farmers settle and build and then reneging on their promises and confiscating the improved land. Freight rates fluctuated wildly depending on whom the railroad was punishing and whom they were rewarding or bribing. Rancho Magnífico was hard hit, but Indian fought doggedly and managed to show a profit while continuing his fight against the extravagant rates for shipping wheat and beef to the best markets.

The Workingmen's Party of California faded away, but not before it had made its political clout felt. They had had much to do with the new, enormous, and unwieldy California Constitution of 1879 and with the Chinese Exclusion Act of 1882, which was so severe that even had someone like Chong Sing wished to return, it would not have been legally possible, despite his years of work and residence in California. The act had led immediately to the new trade of smuggling in Chinese. Kam Lee left the Ramsays to go into the restaurant business with a cousin, and the man he chose to replace him just happened to be another cousin, who just happened to be named Kam Lee also. It was possible, since Chinese nomenclature was different and seemed limited in its choices, but the new Kam Lee spoke very little English at first though he learned quickly, and neither Tessa nor Gavin ever asked him exactly how he came to be related to the first Kam Lee nor how long he had been in California. Privately they called him "Kam Lee Two."

Daily life, and even the face of the land, were changed by the accoutrements of the new age. The days of open range were over; there was barbed wire everywhere, even on sections of Rancho Valle del Mar where natural barriers were not enough any more.

Tessa hated the growing power of the railroads and the laws against the Chinese; she thought the constitution Gavin had helped write in 1849 was far more just and comprehensible than the new one; she loathed the damage barbed wire could inflict on an animal even while she saw

862

the necessity for cheap fencing. She was delighted, though, by the sequential frame photographic exhibit of a horse in motion, even while she could scarcely believe what the pictures showed: San Francisco had a small exchange, but Tessa was appalled by the idea of the telephone which was spreading like a disease—she had absolutely no desire to speak to anyone whose face she could not see. She approved of the more efficient sewing machines that facilitated work at the shop even while she mourned the passing of fine handiwork, used only for details now; and she was enthusiastic about the new fashions for women, despite Gavin's teasing about the bustle.

There were now two distinct ways for a woman to dress —frivolously or in the tailormade look—and the same women wore both on different occasions, with a clear understanding of their separate functions. Gone was the time when a woman had been laced into yards of material and rendered as helpless as a china doll. Women were holding far more jobs now—they were telegraph operators, journalists, teachers, clerks—and they were active in sports. The new angular look with the fitted bodice, narrower skirt, and jaunty bustle in the back made its own statement about the new woman—brisk and businesslike—and left her the option of putting on softer, flowing garments for her alter image at other hours. Tessa did not go so far as to adopt the closely frizzled hair that went so well with the new hats, which were shaped like inverted flowerpots, but Fiona did and looked utterly charming, so gamin-faced it was difficult to believe she was the mother of three. Jefferson became so panicky at the idea of Lotus's doing anything to her long silken hair that she dismissed the whole idea. "He knows the way around me," she confided to Tessa. "He didn't forbid it, he just looked worried and sad at the idea."

Tessa approved and disapproved just as she always had, but now she knew it made no difference. Surely that was age. Whatever she thought, it all went on. The sense of power she had had in her youth was gone. Then she had believed she could change things by the sheer force of her will, and now she knew she could not.

But her sense of purpose had not changed. It had begun as a half-realized will to be herself and to participate in life

863

around her, and she knew she had fulfilled that early determination with a vengeance. She gave California a full share of the credit for her success, for women had continued to have more freedom and power here than elsewhere simply because of the unique status they had had since the Gold Rush. But everything in her life had been inextricably bound up with the fierce business of loving Gavin since that spring day when she had marked the tall Yankee with her knife. And now the loving took more energy than it ever had before.

Gavin was growing old before her eyes, and the change was quite sudden. It began as a chill and slight fever in the winter of 1884. Gavin tried to ignore it and nearly died as a result, spending pain-racked days in a high fever with pneumonia. Tessa was like a tigress, hovering over him, only letting Fiona and Lotus help when she herself was ready to drop.

It was spring of the new year before Gavin had any energy at all, and the change in him was drastic. His hair was nearly snow white, his face pale and lined. He moved slowly and tired easily and had no patience at all with himself.

When Tessa came to see him, John Harland's heart ached for the fatigue and fear he saw on her face, and most of all in her eyes.

"He nearly died," she said bluntly. "John, tell me, what can I do? I don't want to lose him."

"My dear, you've done everything you could do. It's a miracle he survived. But you must know, this isn't something that's just happening now. His chest was weakened by his wounds, and I'm sure the fever is part of the same thing. I'm amazed it hasn't happened before this. His body is wearing out, and we don't have the knowledge to halt that or even to cure so prevalent a disease as pneumonia." He hated having to say the harsh words.

She gazed at him without seeing him at all for a long time, and he watched the shadows moving in the violet eyes. Finally she said very low, "It will happen again and again until it kills him. I'm going to take him home. Perhaps there where it is quiet and so very beautiful, we will gain a little more time."

John knew where she meant by home.

She talked to the children first and then she went to Gavin.

"I want to go home," she announced firmly.

"For a visit?" he asked carefully.

"Call it a long one if you like."

"What about the shop and everything else here?"

"We have trained the children well. Paul, Jeff, and Dian are all capable and John Williams adds to their number fairly often when he and Julie come to the city. And Fiona and Lotus are perfectly able to make any decisions at the shop that the staff can't make. The shop runs like a good machine anyway, and only needs a little oil now and then. I have talked to them all already." She met his eyes steadily. "Jeff and Lotus will move into this house. They need the extra room. Kam Lee Two will stay with them."

"All this for me, Tessa? What will you do, cast a magic spell around the *rancho* forbidding Death to enter?" So gently said, so starkly out in the open now, just as Carmelita had done.

"If I could cast such a spell, I would, even were I to lose my soul for it!" she cried passionately. "Not just for you, for myself. Whatever happens to you happens to me. I want to go home to the land that heals as nothing else can. I want you to myself for whatever time we have left. We have done enough here. I want to rest where the only sounds are sounds from the earth, and I can watch the golden horses growing fine and strong."

Even when she had stopped speaking, the air vibrated with her words, and suddenly Gavin ached with the same need to go back to her root place, which had become his own.

They were home by the early summer. Tessa began to see the changes she had hoped for in Gavin's face, and knew they were reflected in her own—the easing of the lines of tension, the healthy color in his cheeks, the tranquility in his eyes. They slept and ate, read and talked and rode out on the land, enjoying all as if they were newly discovered pleasures, even as they had when the drought had ended. They went often to the pool, and they made love with a new and quiet tenderness.

The children kept them informed by letters, but though Tessa missed her grandchildren particularly, she felt no

865

desire to return to the city. She found Gavin felt the same when he remarked with some surprise, "I have surely succumbed to the spell. I haven't the slightest wish to be working, making decisions, or anything else except what I'm doing here. Perhaps it is not so terrible to grow old after all, my love." He drew her close for a moment, and she murmured, "Anything, as long as we are together."

Armenthia and Indian came for a visit in the fall, and those were happy days full of shared memories and visions so that it was almost possible to forget that Indian too was showing his age in the white of his hair, though Thia's tight black curls looked as if they would never concede age. But Indian's body still looked as huge and strong as ever, and Tessa knew by the anxious glances he cast at Gavin when he thought no one was looking that the change in Gavin was obvious despite the gains of the summer.

They exchanged news of their families, and the Ramsays were relieved to learn there had been a recent letter from Joshua, but the most startling news was about Indiana. She was living in San Francisco, and not alone.

"I like th' man fine, an' he loves Indiana, but she says she isn't goin' marry any man 'cuz she's already married to paintin' an' such. Isn't doin' too bad with it either. She's sold a couple of paintings, signed jus' I.J. Most people think that's a man an' wonder who he is. 'Course she has money enough of her own so she won't starve." Thia paused and looked at Indian, and both of them were smiling. "Isn't exactly what we'd of picked for her, but she's happy, my, is she happy! And that's really what we want for her."

"You're very wise," Tessa said. "There isn't anything more bitter than estrangement from one of your children—I know that from experience."

But that problem certainly no longer existed. The Ramsay clan came en masse to spend Christmas with Gavin and Tessa. The house was full of children and laughter, and Tessa marveled at how much they all seemed to have grown since she saw them last, especially Jordan, who at thirteen was the oldest and beginning to go through the stage where it seemed that he grew an inch a day and his voice shifted unpredictably from a squeak to a growl.

In February, with very little warning, Gavin was ill

again. It was not as serious as it had been the year before, but again it took him a long time to recover. Tessa sat by his bed for hours, reading to him sometimes, sometimes just sitting quietly, sponging him off when his fever rose, giving him draughts of the best herbal brews she knew, watching over him with so much anxious love that sometimes it was painful for Gavin to look at her.

He was much stronger by late spring and out riding by summer, and they were lovers again. But now their loving had a piercing edge as if in the physical truth of their joining, the lie that they would go on forever in the flesh was revealed. It was a lie. Tessa could feel it in the new skeletal leanness of her man, could see it in the bare sculpted bones of his face, where the eyes alone remained young and fiercely blue.

They had one more Christmas with the family, but scarcely had the children returned to the city than they received Tessa's summons to return.

It had hit so hard and so fast, Tessa knew this was the last time she would watch over Gavin; she knew it as clearly as she had known in all the other times of sickness since the first day that he would not leave her. Not with fire, war, the crack of a rifle or the swift thrust of a knife, just this inexorable drifting away.

She sat stony-faced beside the bed, paying no attention to any of the family except Jefferson, hearing no one's words except his. Jeff was more like Gavin than any of them, and finally when the two of them were alone one day with Gavin, Tessa turned to her son. "I am being selfish about him. I have always been since the first time I saw him. Will you forgive me if I ask you to leave us alone?"

There was complete understanding in the eyes, which were like her own and Gavin's too. He took his father's hand and held it for a brief moment. "Good-by, Papa," he said quietly. Then he kissed his mother and left the room.

Gavin had been in a stupor for the last twenty-four hours, his only movement the labored rising and falling of his chest, but Tessa had felt the change and she saw the miracle of the deep blue eyes once more as they opened

867

and gazed at her. "I like you better with no clothes," he whispered. "How old are you?"

"I am sixteen today, and I do not know your name," she answered, her mouth trembling.

"Gavin, Gavin Ramsay."

"Now I know, the builder of empires."

"No, the lover of Teresa María Julieta Margarita Macleod Amarista de Ramsay." A smile lightened his drawn face for remembering the long train of names.

"Just Tessa, Tessa Ramsay," she reminded him brokenly, and she could bear it no longer. She got into bed beside him, holding him, sobbing in Spanish, "I will hold you until the sunrise and again until the sunrise following after and still until the last of the earth. I will hold you from darkness, from death. *Mi vida*, Gavin, please, please, my beloved, there will never be another sunrise for me without you, no light, only darkness."

In some strange way their roles were reversed, and it was he who gave comfort, the thin thread of his voice yet holding the spirit of the strong man she had slept beside for over forty years.

"Tessa, my darling, you know I would stay if I could, I would never leave you. But I'm too tired this time. And you'll see the sun again, because you are full of life, yours and mine now."

She shuddered in the last struggle against the inevitable and surrendered. "I know, my love, I know you are weary. Go in peace. *Vaya con Dios*."

His head turned, and his mouth brushed hers in the lightest of kisses.

Tessa held the great empty stillness of him, her anguish beyond tears now.

CHAPTER LXXIII

Nobody else knew, but Tessa did. The world had stopped. It had no sound or light or movement. It was strange to be the only one who knew.

868

They buried Gavin beside the pool because that was where he belonged, not in the family graveyard, Tessa told them calmly. She did everything calmly, slowly.

Jefferson and Paul said the simple service of words they had chosen. None of them could imagine a strange priest chanting over a man he had never known.

Tessa listened to the words and to the sobbing without hearing them. Indian's shoulders heaved with grief, and he leaned on Armenthia, but even that image failed to touch Tessa, who remained dry-eyed. It was all so foolish, puppets pretending to move against a vast still space.

Jefferson was delegated to approach her a few days after the burial. "Mother, we think you ought to come back to the city with us for a time," he said gently.

"Why? Will it be better there? Will he be there?" She stared at him impassively, and he shook his head. He was undone by her frozen reasonableness. He felt young and awkward and not nearly wise enough to handle this properly, especially because his own sorrow kept rising up to choke him. This was worse than when Brand had died. He was afraid to imagine the full depth of her loss, and he realized suddenly that perhaps it was for the best that she be layered for a while in what he could only judge to be protective shock.

In the end, Fiona and Jordan stayed at Valle del Mar when the others returned to their homes. Though no one told Jordan, it was an obvious ploy. No one, not even Indian or Thia, had been able to get through to Tessa. But given time, surely the presence of Jordan would reach her. She had, after all, half raised him, and the bond between them was a special one.

But Fiona began to have her doubts about the plan. Jordan seemed as tightly locked into his grief as his grandmother, though at least he ate and slept more than she because his young body demanded it.

Tessa had developed an elaborate game for sleeping—she did as little of it as possible. She paced her room or read or went for long walks outside, anything to fulfill the cardinal rule that she not touch the bed until she was nearly unconscious with exhaustion because then she wouldn't know that he wasn't . . . *Don't even think of it, not true, doesn't matter anyway with the world a dark dead plain.*

She listened to the inner madness as if it were the voice of God.

But tonight the outer stillness was broken. She was wandering outside under a cold white moon that turned the barren trees and shrubs into bleached bones when she heard it. It came to her clearly as nothing had since Gavin's death. For a moment, she tried desperately to deny it, but it engulfed her, penetrating to the bone with its pain. She followed the sound.

She found him slumped on the wooden bench in the garden where everything looked dead because spring had not begun. But there was nothing but wild grieving life in Jordan. He would be fifteen this year, and he was already six feet tall; his voice had dropped for good; and he was mature for his age. He alone of the family had been as tearless as Tessa. And he was not now shedding the tears of a child soon comforted. He was wrenched by the deep, hopeless sobs of a man in terrible pain.

"Oh, Jordan, my dear," Tessa breathed softly, touching his shoulder, and his head jerked up. Neither was there anything dead in the moon on Jordan. His hair gleamed a strange copper and his eyes were filled with tears and light. "I'm sorry, I didn't know you were out," he gasped. "I've been pretending, but I finally know. He's never going to come riding in again. I don't know how you'll bear it; he loved you so much, the world must feel even colder to you than it does to me."

She didn't know where the words came from, but she heard herself saying them as she cradled Jordan's head against her breast. "This garden looks so bare now, but soon there will be flowers again. Season following season. It's hard to believe in spring when winter is on the land, but spring always comes whether we believe in it or not. Gavin believed in life, and he believed in living it to its fullest, and for us to do less now would be to offer him the worst insult." She waited, feeling the frozen layer that had separated her from the world splintering and falling away, and she welcomed the pain of life flowing back into her body and her spirit. She bowed her head against Jordan's, and they wept together.

The sun did shine, eagles and hawks screamed their triumph and softer birds sang, flowers bloomed, new colts

870

were born, and Tessa saw, heard, and felt it all. Sometimes the beauty was indistinguishable from pain because Gavin was not beside her to experience it too, but gradually she began to feel that he was, not in the same way as before and not in the same way as others lost, but in his possession of so much of her that there was always the double image of them standing together, watching the world together. "Life, yours and mine now." And it went beyond that to a sudden warmth she would feel, a swift conviction that if she looked quickly she would see him, or something he had said would echo in her mind. She had felt like this when he had been away at war. He had come back. Perhaps it was the same.

She learned to live with the particular loneliness of going to bed without him. They had been such fierce lovers, she understood why this would be the hardest to accept, as it had been when he had gone to war. She grew accustomed to finding she had been stretching an arm or a leg so far that it cramped and awakened her in the search for Gavin in the cold half of the bed, and often she woke up smiling in the morning until she realized it was a pillow she held so tightly. She tried to make herself sleep in the middle of the bed, but always found herself to one side by morning. This too she would learn in time.

Step by step she learned to walk in the world again. She went to the city but refused Jeff and Lotus's offer to move out of the Fern Hill house (which was now more recognizably the "Nob Hill" house, the location having been renamed by the populace for the wealth that centered there). She told them honestly that if they could stand it, she would rather just visit them or Paul and Fiona without having a house of her own any more in the city. Home was now and forever at Valle del Mar. She spent some time at the shop, spoiled her grandchildren, saw a lot of Mrs. Tubbs who had managed to grow old without losing any of her liveliness, and spent many evenings having dinner or going to the theater with John Harland. Delmonico's and the Palace Hotel were two places she would not go, and John accepted that without question. And when she tired of the city. She went home.

The world had not stopped after all. A year after Gavin's death, Jordan headed East to attend Harvard University.

871

There was still so little higher education offered in California, it was inevitable that one of the brood would go East eventually, and though it was hard to see Jordan off, Tessa knew it was something he needed and wanted to do. He was the most intellectual of all the grandchildren, and he had his stepfather's love for books and learning.

"Take care of yourself for me, Grandma," he said gravely before he boarded the train. "I'll be back before you know it."

"I'll see you then," she replied firmly.

He loved his studies, but he soon knew beyond any doubt that he was Californian to the bone. "Some days I'd give my life to see forever with only green hills and golden horses between me and the sea," he wrote. "It's too damn crowded back here. But I'll pack my brain with what they have to offer here and be home soon enough."

He completed his studies in three years, working hard even during the summers, and came home in 1891, ironically the same year that Stanford University, purported to be designed on the basis of the best eastern schools, opened in California.

He had grown to be such a handsome and debonair man that his family was a little taken aback, but he soon set them straight on the matter and let them know that the old Jordan was alive and well under the spit and polish.

Tessa clung to him for a moment, looking up into his laughing sherry eyes, unable to say more than his name.

"Told you I'd be back, Grandma, and am I ever glad to be!"

He regaled them with stories of the people he had met. When his mother asked if he'd met any special girls, he rolled his eyes and gave them an imitation first of the simpering misses and next of the most radical feminists.

"I kept looking for something in between like the Ramsay women, but I couldn't seem to find one. Guess I'll have to marry Grandma."

"I think someone else has his eye on her," Fiona quipped, and Tessa blushed in annoyance and changed the subject.

She had received several offers of marriage in the years since Gavin's death, and after her initial surprise, she had realized that almost all of them were motivated as much, if not more, by greed for her wealth as for any personal

872

attraction to her. They had been easy to dismiss. But her current problem was not easy at all.

John Harland had been such a steadfast friend for so long, it had never occurred to her that he thought of her as anything more than that in turn. But when she had arrived in the city to await Jordan's homecoming, John had appeared almost immediately, and a few nights ago, after a lovely dinner, he had quietly asked her to marry him. She had not seen him since. He had wanted to give her time to think about it. She had promised to give him her answer tonight.

"I want to visit Valle del Mar pretty soon, and then I have to go on down to Los Angeles to check on my inheritance; Paul says it's time I had the decision-making power, and he's right, I guess. Want to run away with me?" Jordan whispered under the cover of the continued chatter.

"I wish I could! But I have to give my answer tonight. Oh, Jordan, it's not funny at all. It's Dr. Harland."

"My God!" he said, sobering instantly. "That is touchy. I can't blame him for asking, but I feel sorry for him."

She gripped his hand. "Thank you for understanding."

It amused and annoyed her at the same time that her own children treated her like a valuable porcelain antique, even including John's courtship in the same light, approving of it, she well knew, because they saw the suitability of two antiques on the same shelf and wanted her to have any comfort that might ease the pain of Gavin's loss.

It was true that physical tasks took more effort and often left her slightly breathless and overly weary, but since there was less to do now, she considered the balance acceptable.

She had a wicked impulse sometimes to tell them how she really felt. Her exterior might be showing some signs of weathering, as might be expected at sixty-three, though she would have been blind not to have known that she could still turn men's heads, but inside she was exactly the same as the day she and Gavin had first met. There had been that middle time of her life when she had felt each year's passage, had known she was getting older. But now it was as if that had never been. She was a young woman trapped in an aging body. The first realization of that after Gavin's death had brought claustrophobic panic and outrage. But she had learned to live with it and finally to enjoy it, the sly young girl hidden so safely, peeking out through the honored façade of age.

She nearly laughed aloud thinking about it. Lotus especially was so prone to grant her the status of a near deity that sometimes Tessa was tempted to tell her that what she would most like was a long night of love-making.

That finally was why she must refuse John's offer. In her youth, she had been as guilty as any of assuming that desire drifted away and died quietly with the years. It was untrue. The blood still quickened, the body still wanted. But for her, the want would always be for Gavin. She could abide no substitute, and she had no need for less, for a gentle companion to hold without fire. And John was only a few years older than she and still a fine figure of a man, to make him less than that would be a dreadful sin.

Jefferson. He of all of them came closest to understanding, perhaps even catching glimpses of the young girl his father had loved. Jeff and Jordan knew.

She broached the subject that evening as soon as she managed to maneuver Jeff out of earshot of the others.

"It will be difficult enough to explain to John. Do you suppose you could manage the rest? I know everyone suspects he's asked me."

He showed no surprise, not even a lift of his eyebrow at the news she would not be marrying John.

"Of course, I'll explain. There might be some disappointment. Everybody likes Dr. Harland very much, and it would be so neat, wouldn't it, just like a paper parcel perfectly tied, taken care of in one motion? Only it isn't like that, is it?" He paused, and now the eyebrow did slant and the shadow of Gavin regarded her with grave compassion. "I could not love Lotus more nor she me, but even so I don't believe our love is what you and father had." He saw the protest rising in her and forestalled it. "No, darling, don't mistake me. I couldn't be happier, and I'm not in the least envious. I don't think either Lotus or I could bear the intensity with which you and Father lived. And it hasn't left you yet, has it?"

She shook her head, loving him enormously for knowing.

"You give me hope. Perhaps I have enough of you and of Father in me to age with some measure of grace and
874

more blood than brittle." He flashed a sudden wicked grin that caught at her heart. "It wouldn't be fair to John. He would probably die of too much excitement on the wedding night."

Her laughter caused heads to turn, and she only had a brief second to squeeze Jeff's hand and whisper, "Bless you," before the rest of the family engulfed them asking to share the joke.

"I was just telling Jefferson that I want you all warned against telling me how well preserved I am for my age. I've thought about it and I've decided I don't like it at all. Preserved for what? You make me sound like something packed in a barrel or a jar against the winter."

Paul smiled mischievously. "All right. Henceforth we'll say, 'Good day, Mama, how old you look!'" They all joined in comfortable laughter, though they knew Jeff had something to tell them and would do so in his own good time.

The actual task of telling John turned out to be surprisingly easy. Tessa realized that it was not only because she had Jefferson's understanding and support, but because she was dealing in the truth, even as she had dealt with Jordan Ames long ago. Hard, even unkind, but still the truth.

"John, even at my age, I'm as honored as any blushing young maid could be by your offer. You are such a trusted and close friend."

"But you're not going to marry me," he cut in, and she was shocked by the harsh pain in his voice. She took a deep breath and abandoned the polite for the essential.

"No, I'm not going to. I can't. I was wrong not to tell you immediately. You are such a comfort, such an important part of my life, perhaps I feared losing that completely. But I can't marry you. I don't quite know how it happened, to this day I don't, but I loved Gavin Ramsay from the day I met him, and even during our worst times, even when I felt hatred toward him, I never stopped loving him, not for a minute." She held his eyes with her own, and her voice did not waver. "That's why I made such a mess of adultery—I could not even stop loving Gavin long enough to have a successful affair. And it would be adultery now, and badly done again. I still love him. I always will.

875

No man will ever mean the same to me, and I can't pretend to be happy with less."

There was a deadly silence between them, and then suddenly John smiled, really meaning it. "God above, I've just realized I'm relieved. I saw Gavin all at once as you must see him always, and the thought of competing with him was enough to make me reconsider. He was one hell of a man, and you are a perfect match for him. There need be no embarrassment over this. It's not every man who can claim to have asked the most beautiful woman in California to marry him. And I'll expect to retain the privilege of taking you out when you are in the city."

"You are one hell of a man too, John Harland," Tessa said unsteadily, and she kissed him very gently on both cheeks.

Jordan did accompany her to Valle del Mar and tarried a few days before he went on to Los Angeles. Tessa enjoyed his company enormously, and was glad to find he had lost none of his interest in the palominos or the land. He had read literature and a smattering of law at Harvard, and he had taken more than a few science and mathematics courses. "To be able to figure the accounts, plan what is scientifically best for the land and livestock, know enough law to keep the land, and read for pleasure—what better training could I have to be a *ranchero*?" he asked cheerfully, and she knew there was every hope that he might eventually take over Valle del Mar.

She did not visit the city again for several months, but when she received letters from various members of the family, including Jordan himself, with the news that Jordan was in love, she went north. Jordan had met Brígida Farraday in Golden Gate Park, which after nearly twenty years really did look like a green haven and was becoming increasingly popular for pedestrians, cyclists, fashionable carriages, and dog carts. Brígida had fallen into the second category and into Jordan's arms because she had been going too fast for her limited skill. It had been, according to all reports, love at first sight, with a good sprinkling of hilarity due to the circumstances of the meeting and the fact that Jordan had soon discovered that Bridie, as she was nicknamed, had been East to finishing school and was as apt at imitating the young gentlemen she had met as Jordan was on the subject of the opposite sex. She too was Californian to the bone, and that was only the beginning of the things they had in common, including an engagement to be married. The family was enchanted with her.

So much Tessa knew before she met the girl, and Jordan's shining eyes told her all she really wanted to know. But when she was face to face with her, her heart pounded so hard, she could scarcely breathe.

Bridie was a head shorter than she, with a trim, round figure and golden skin. Her hair was shining black, her eyes large and dark with the slightest tilt. Her nose and cheekbones gave her face a strong beauty which hinted at an exotic touch of Indian blood somewhere in her background, and her mouth was full and rosy. Younger, slightly altered, and still dreadfully familiar. Soledad. Soledad was as visible in this girl as she herself was in her own descendants.

She blinked, and the rest of the room came into focus. Everybody was looking at her oddly, Jordan with the beginning of anger in his expression. And she saw it in Bridie's eyes now, terrible disappointment and apprehension because Jordan cared about his grandmother's opinion, and his grandmother was obviously prepared to hate her on sight.

Tessa smiled and let it reach her eyes. "I apologize. For a moment it was like seeing a ghost. Beauty like yours is unforgettable, and I once knew a woman, many years ago now, who was nearly as lovely as you are. I'm glad that Jordan had the good fortune to catch you, as it were."

Relieved laughter filled the room, and Bridie beamed. Tessa heard her whisper to Jordan, "She's gorgeous!" and Jordan whispered back, "I know—I asked her first."

Brígida Farraday, the name made no difference. Tessa smiled and chatted and listened and didn't betray herself when Soledad's name was finally mentioned. Soledad, Bridie's grandmother, the woman who had raised her after her parents had died.

It was the most natural thing in the world to tell Bridie that surely grandmothers had much in common, and to suggest that she herself call on Bridie's grandmother as soon as convenient. Bridie was so pleased with the suggestion, she could hardly wait to arrange it.

Only Jefferson wasn't fooled. "First question, what happened tonight, and second, what are you up to?"

She shook her head. "It's too complicated to explain, and it all happened a long time ago. What I said about the ghost was true. I promise, I like Bridie, I'm happy for Jordan, and there's nothing more to be said about it."

"Think I'm too young to handle your lurid past?" he teased, coming very near the truth as usual.

"That's exactly it," she replied, reaching up to pat him on the head as if he were a foot and a half shorter and forty years younger.

She was sure Soledad would not refuse the meeting, and she dressed with care when she made the visit, wearing a beautifully cut skirt and jacket in the newest style, the jacket sleeves puffed at the shoulders and fitted to the wrist, the jacket edges scalloped and open over a blouse of the finest white lawn, the skirt fitting smoothly about the hips and flaring at the bottom for easy walking. The skirt and jacket were lavender trimmed in black and a jaunty matching hat with a plume sat on her upswept hair. She was dressed to kill, but her purpose began to shift beneath her from the moment she walked into Soledad's parlor.

The years had dealt unkindly with Soledad. She was grossly fat, not even attempting to heave herself out of the chair when Tessa came into the room. Tessa saw the walking stick beside the chair. She saw the round old-young face, the fat keeping the skin strangely smooth but the whole countenance sagging just enough so that it was as if the wax head of a doll had been held too close to the heat. Her hair was thin and gray. There was something pathetic about the scrupulous cleanliness of the room and the woman's dress, as if she too had scrubbed and steeled herself for this meeting. Only the eyes held the old spark, crafty, dark, and watchful.

The knowledge of the late prison of the flesh rose in Tessa again and with it overwhelming pity for this woman who had so bedeviled the early years of her marriage.

"Hello, Soledad, it has been many years," she said, and her voice was gentle. Bridie was looking nervously from one to the other, confused because they knew each other, sensing something amiss, and Tessa smiled at her. "Why don't you run along, dear? Your grandmother and I have just discovered we are not strangers after all. We met years ago, and undoubtedly we can find old and boring stories to exchange."

Bridie fled in relief and still Soledad said nothing, not even challenging Tessa's taking of authority in her house.

"Is Bridie Gavin's granddaughter?" Tessa asked abruptly. Pleasantries would be the worst sham between them.

Soledad regarded her a few minutes longer before she answered with a question of her own. "Why would it matter? Though I did not suspect it at the time, from what I've seen and things I've heard, Jordan's mother is no kin to Gavin. Now I would guess he knew that and it made no difference."

"You heard correctly. Fiona is not Gavin's daughter," Tessa answered calmly. "It would not matter even if Bridie and Jordan did share the same grandfather; the blood would still not be too dangerously close. I just want to know."

"Bridie is a good child, and so was her mother. I raised her to be a lady, and she was. She married a respectable man and when they died of cholera down south, I took Bridie and raised her to be as fine as her mother, not like me. We moved back to San Francisco ten years ago, and I sent Bridie to a good school back East for many of those years.

"You needn't worry about a whore's taint. And it's foolish anyway; she and Jordan are very young, Bridie a year younger than he. Perhaps they will not marry, perhaps they will have forgotten all about each other in a few years' time."

"No, Soledad, I don't believe they will, and you do not either. Sometimes when love begins, it never ends. I do not think it will end for them."

The silence stretched between them and was broken by Soledad's sudden harsh cackle of laughter. "Look at us, both old women—old but not dry, are we, wife of Gavin? It took me long to understand, but looking at you now, my understanding is confirmed. You have a whore's body, a whore's lust, but it was all for him. That is the only difference between us. And it's the best a woman can ever give a man. He knew that, he always knew. Yes, you gave him your high breeding, your education, you gave him children, but most of all you gave him the hunger to possess you, and his hunger never eased." Her features were suddenly sharper, less round and blurred, and her eyes were narrow and glittering. "You were a fool, you are still a fool to think I took anything from your life. He was the only man I ever loved for so long a time. But he never loved me, never, do you hear? He came to me because of you, not for myself. He came when his burden of loving you was too great for him to carry. He came to be with a woman he did not have to love. But always he picked up the burden again and returned to you. My daughter was not his get. A tall, dark Yankee, like and not like at all. But I loved him for a while, long enough to wait too long to lose the child. I used the lie and took the money because I knew you would suffer, and I hoped you would leave him. You were not the only fool. When I discovered who Bridie's boy was, it was a final bitterness. Fate has punished us both. You are right. Bridie will belong before long to Jordan and to you. I love the child, as I loved her mother once I held her in my arms. I could not take Bridie's joy from her for old spite." Her voice died away, aged and hollow.

. Tessa did not dispute the other woman's judgments; the truth rang all too clearly. "Oh, Soledad, what an age we have lived through!" she heard herself say, and after a startled moment, Soledad's laughter sounded again, without bitterness now, really amused. "We have, we have indeed. I try to tell myself that each generation has its own fun, but life seems a dull proposition now compared to the days of our youth. I give you another gift, to finish all your doubts. My daughter was barely six, not seven at all, when I showed her to Gavin."

When Bridie returned to check on the women, she did so with trepidation, still fearful of the combination without knowing why, but to her relief she found them embarked on a sea of memories of California's early days and San Francisco's beginnings. She found it fascinating, though she was sure the tales had been brightly colored by time. She would have been astonished had she known how her grandmother and Tessa had, in deference to her innocence, toned down their recollections once she'd joined them.

Only as she was taking her leave did the strangeness of it all strike Tessa anew. Pity and compassion filled her for

Soledad, for herself, for the futility of learning each painful lesson of love just in time to lose the object. The agonizingly sharp pang of missing Gavin stabbed at her with edges unblunted by time. She could see her whole life stretching behind her in a ceaseless series of farewells, always another one to bless on the journey away from her. Perhaps death was no more than the final one, a leave-taking from self.

There was no reason now not to see Soledad again; shared memories could provide reason for future visits, but both of them knew it would not be so. They would nod pleasantly to each other at the wedding, and that would be all.

"*Vaya con Dios*, Soledad," Tessa said softly.

"And you also, go with God, wife of Gavin," Soledad replied.

Rancho Valle del Mar
New Year's Eve, 1899

They were all here, and she was immensely flattered that they were. When she had ceased to go to the city for the holidays and seldom for anything else, they had instituted a new tradition and they had traveled down en masse for New Year's Eve, as they once had for the last Christmases with Gavin. There was no rule that they all must come— even the grandchildren had been told that once they were sixteen, if they had a reliable friend with family in the city and preferred to stay there, it would be allowed. But they never did, and often the friends came with them. The house overflowed with people, and the younger ones thought it a great adventure to sleep in the tents set up near the house.

Jordan and Bridie didn't have any distance to travel at all. They had been living at the *rancho* for four years now, and had brought new life to the house and land. Jordan still had to make the trip to the *rancho* near Los Angeles to make sure things were running smoothly, more often now with most of the wealth blooming seasonally in citrus crops and other exotic produce rather than in cattle, but his home was at Valle del Mar, and he loved it nearly as much as Tessa did and knew fully as much about the horses. Bridie loved it too, but then she would love anything anywhere where Jordan was, and she thought it a fine place to raise children. They had three already, two girls and a boy, and hopes for more.

The years had suddenly run out like the last grains of sand in an hourglass, which always seemed to pour down more quickly than the first. They had not flowed smoothly or without marking some of the faces around Tessa with their passage. There had been a worldwide financial panic in 1893, and it had taken four years for the signs of recovery to be clear. Everyone had worked hard to keep the Ramian empire intact, and had done a good job. And even now the land was recovering from another drought, which
884

even though it had been worse in southern California, had had its effects in the north too. And there had been personal tragedies that no amount of work or planning could circumvent or soften.

She knew that Indian and Armenthia were gathered with many of their own family tonight. They would never see Joshua again. The letter had come several years before from a woman in Mississippi. She had told them in strong, eloquently simple terms that Joshua had been a great man and that many had learned enough from him to carry on his work with others. Joshua had been lynched by night riders. Though Indian had taken it hard, Armenthia had confessed that it was almost kind to have it confirmed because she had known deep in her heart for so long. Tessa suspected Thia knew now, and she could almost feel the blessing clear from Rancho Magnífico. She rejoiced that Indian and Armenthia even at eighty-six and seventy-three were still strong and enduring, and she hoped they would live for many more years to give their wisdom to their descendants and to hers.

They had lost their Joshua, but they had their other children, grandchildren, and now a first great-grandchild. And they had special pride in Indiana who continued merrily on in her bohemian life, still with the same man but never having married him nor had a child by him, and still known to few as the IJ who painted the pictures that earned a little more each year. Most people thought IJ was a male artist from the avant-garde French world of painting.

Tessa held them all in her mind for an instant and wished them Godspeed in the new century.

The faces of her own family showed what they had lost and what they had gained.

Before she had had her first child, Bridie had lost Soledad and had mourned her deeply, because she had known the soft and loving side of the woman. But she had had Jordan to cling to for comfort, and her shining confidence in him showed every time she looked at him.

Fiona, in a sea-green gown with Don Esteban's emerald collar around her neck, looked breathtakingly beautiful. These had been good years for her and Paul, perhaps in return for the bad ones at the beginning. Their two

885

daughters were as much a delight to them as Jordan and Bridie were. With her red-gold hair and gray-green eyes, Resa was fire and sweetness mixed in an intriguing combination. It was she who ran the shop now, with a keen eye for fabric, color, and style. She wasn't married, but a grave young lawyer named Mark Carrington had been courting her for some time, was with her tonight, and looked as if he had every intention of winning her by sheer perseverance. Resa's younger sister, Natalia, who had Paul's eyes and her mother's gilt hair, was the studious one of the two. She was determined to be a teacher at the school, which now that Mrs. Tubbs was so old and frail though still spry mentally, was run jointly by Fiona and Lotus and would be theirs some day.

The rites of passage were clearly marked on Lotus in a deeper serenity and the shadow of sorrow in her eyes, a shadow that vanished when Jefferson was near. Lotus had lost both of her parents, but they had been quite old, and that was more acceptable than the loss of her oldest son, Brand. Tessa wondered, were they all required to make some sacrifice of a child, to give up the most precious thing they produced, in order to earn the right of existence? Thinking of those who had not yet lost any offspring, she prayed that no sacrifice would be asked of them.

She would never say it because it sounded so superstitious and foolish, but she now hoped no future son would be named Brand. Perhaps there was a wild spirit in the name itself. The second Brand's death had been as senseless as the loss of her own son. Lotus and Jefferson had sent him to her before he left, and she had tried desperately to dissuade him from joining the army bound for Cuba. She could still hear her arguments. "Spain has been pushed out everywhere else, she will leave Cuba soon enough. It is none of our affair; certainly it is none of yours. Civil wars belong where they begin, inside the country without outside interference. Your grandfather might never have come home at all had England helped the South in the sixties, and I hate to think of what might have happened here had she helped earlier in California's troubles. For God's sake, Brand, no one even knows who blew up that ship! It might not have been the Spanish at all. Can't you at least wait to find out?"

886

She had known her failure before the last words were spoken. The same glitter of excitement and lust for adventure she had seen in her son's eyes had lit the eyes of her grandson. He had gone, and he had died as most of the five thousand had, not by bullets, which had killed a scant four hundred, but by disease.

Tessa knew it was a sorrow that would never leave Lotus and Jefferson, but there was joy in their other three children. Gavin with the deep blue eyes had a blue-eyed wife whose maiden name had been O'Shay. They had met at Stanford University, and it had taken a full measure of courageous defiance of her parents for Maggie to marry Gavin. Her parents had wanted her to better herself and taking a part-Chinese husband did not fit with their plans, no matter how progressive their ideas were about education for women. Maggie claimed with a determined smile that it was the only way for the Chinese and the Irish to come together peacefully, and her parents were beginning to develop a reluctant liking for Gavin even though he had stolen their daughter from church and race.

The third child, Chena, was as beautiful as her mother. As Jefferson fervently put it, "God help the men!" And the youngest, Lin, had long gray eyes, the lanky leanness of his father, and the same penetrating sense of humor. Tessa suspected Lotus was hard put not to treat him as the favorite. Three fine children spared; she wondered how often Lotus and Jefferson had to remind themselves of that, and knew that they surely must at gatherings such as this one.

Jefferson held up his hand, and there was an instant hush. The grandfather clock that had once graced the Fern Hill house chimed the twelve strokes of midnight, and the voices rose with the old and perfect words.

> Should auld acquaintance be forgot
> And never brought to mind?
> Should auld acquaintance be forgot,
> And days o' auld lang syne?
>
> And for auld lang syne, my jo,
> For auld lang syne,
> We'll take a cup o' kindness yet,
> For auld lang syne.

She watched them as they sang. Part of her, part of Gavin, and in Jefferson the blend of both showed, even in Lotus and Jeff's children whose finely drawn features gave her a special pride she would never admit for fear of making the others jealous. The native born, the conqueror, the immigrant, their blood had run together to produce these children of bright and blessed countenance as Indian and Armenthia had produced the strong, dark beauty of their children. She prayed the future would not fail their promise.

The twentieth century, newly born, only minutes old. It was for them with their constant flow of new ideas and new projects. Even if she were not so tired, she would want no part of it. Light without flame, machines that clanked and chugged ever faster, leaving man and horse behind, even machines that her grandsons assured her would soon take to the sky where only eagles had held sway, new states carved briskly out of the territories and admitted to the Union so that there would surely be people strung clear across the country before too long—these were problems and wonders for the young.

She had gone out from this land and come home to it. Her life had come full circle. Her family was a flourishing and affectionate clan, yet each member was an individual of strength and purpose, not even the youngest lacked personality or will. She had given them all she had to give. She was finished with the years without Gavin and glad to be.

She had last seen John Harland several years ago, as a patient. He had told her then that if she were careful and took it very easy, she would have years and years yet. "Thank you, John," she had said, and she had meant it. It was like being given a final option, final control of her life. "I trust this will go no further."

"As you wish, my dear."

She hoped his eyes were no longer as sad as they had been then.

There was a sudden stillness as she rose to her feet. She smiled and raised her glass. "My darlings, may it be a glorious new century for all of you. I thank you for coming to celebrate its beginning with me."

"To Tessa!" they responded, giving her name, herself,

a significance beyond whatever relationship of blood or friendship she had to them.

There was the soft chime of crystal on crystal and then the *vaquero* musicians swept into the strains of a waltz, and the floor cleared as Jeff led her in the dance.

She was as light as a young girl in his arms, and it was not the two white wings in the ebony of her hair that betrayed her age. It was the glowing violet of her eyes, infinitely compassionate, loving and knowing as no young girl's could ever be. The curious sense of seeing her through his father's eyes engulfed him more strongly than it ever had before, and he would not have been surprised had Gavin cut in to finish the dance with Tessa.

"Yes, he feels very close tonight, doesn't he? It's lovely," she whispered, and Jeff just managed not to miss a step.

There was applause when the waltz was finished, and Tessa swept the crowd a graceful curtsy and announced that it was time for old women to be abed, as the children were. She gasped in protest and then laughed as Jeff picked her up in his arms. "This is not a very dignified way for an old lady to take her leave."

"Anyone who calls you an old lady will have me to reckon with, ma'am," Jeff replied, his eyebrow slanting up. She was so small and weightless in his arms, he marveled at it. All his life he had thought of her as a tall woman of commanding stature. He remembered suddenly how she had looked after Brand's death, after Gavin's death. And he knew. He had to clamp his jaw against crying out as he carried her to her room.

She reached up to touch the tense lines as he put her down carefully on her bed. Of all of them, she didn't mind his knowing.

"Jefferson, my dear, it is all right. It becomes a matter of will, and tasks yet to be completed. And now my tasks are finished, and my will is as weary as my body. Don't grieve. You make it much easier. I am so proud of you, my son, so proud of you all. Tell Jordan that season follows season. He will understand and know that even living in this house with me, he and Bridie could not change that. Go now before we have a pack of concerned females to contend with."

For an instant he was a very small child again, and he

wanted to scream at her not to abandon him, but he could not deny the strength and maturity of the man she had raised. He drew a deep, shuddering breath and looked down at her, etching the clear lines of her beauty in his mind for all time. Then he stooped and kissed her gently in benediction. *"Vaya con Dios,* Mama."

"And you, my son."

He would face it in a few hours' time, when he had to. His face gave nothing away when he rejoined the others, but Lotus came to his side immediately, slim and graceful, her slender hand gripping his with reassuring strength and warmth, her eyes soft pools of love. He wanted her suddenly with a burst of passion that startled him.

"I am growing a little sleepy, soon may we retire?" she asked, her false yawn convincing to everyone except Jeff who was receiving another message entirely. *How do they know?* he wondered. *Why are women so much closer to the pulse of life and death and the passion in between? Is it because their wombs bear the burden of the future, or are the knowledge and the deep earth root earlier than that, the reasons for being able to bear the burden?*

His mind ceased to worry the unanswerable in face of Lotus's diverting mischief. Her calm face betrayed nothing as she smiled and chattered with those around them, but one of her long nails traced intricate erotic patterns ever so delicately on the palm of his hand. *Mother would approve of this,* he thought with great tenderness, and rather abruptly, he began their good-nights.

Tessa welcomed the wild fluttering in her chest, wilder than it had ever been before. "Soon, very soon I'll set you free," she murmured. There was one flash of pain and no more.

She gazed on a sea of magnificent palominos, each one perfect, their coats as bright as newly minted gold, their manes and tails fine spun silver, the lovely golden horses. She heard the full-throated howl of a wolf. "Sombra," she said, and warm contentment flooded through her.

It was not in the least strange that she could see them all, so many who had been so beloved, so many even back to her mother, her father before his spirit had died, and Don Esteban. But she searched still, and then he was there, the same, the essence of the first day by the water's edge and all the years after.

"Gavin, *mi vida*. Was it done well, then?"

"Well and truly done, my love. It is finished. It is beginning. Come with me now."

She heard his voice so clearly, and she answered, "Always, anywhere."

She felt her joy expanding until it dissolved the limits of herself forever.

Historical Romance

Sparkling novels of love and conquest against the colorful background of historical England. Here are books you will savor word by word, page by spellbinding page.

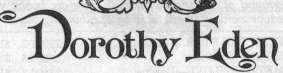

Dorothy Eden

One of today's outstanding novelists writes tales about love, intrigue, wealth, power—and, of course, romance. Here are romantic novels of suspense at their best.

Mary Stewart

"Mary Stewart is magic" is the way Anthony Boucher puts it. Each and every one of her novels is a kind of enchantment, a spellbinding experience that has won acclaim from the critics, millions of fans, and a permanent place at the top.

☐ AIRS ABOVE THE GROUND	23868-7	$1.95
☐ THE CRYSTAL CAVE	23315-4	$1.95
☐ THE GABRIEL HOUNDS	23946-2	$1.95
☐ THE HOLLOW HILLS	23316-2	$1.95
☐ THE IVY TREE	23976-4	$1.95
☐ MADAM, WILL YOU TALK	23250-6	$1.75
☐ THE MOON-SPINNERS	23941-4	$1.95
☐ MY BROTHER MICHAEL	22974-2	$1.75
☐ NINE COACHES WAITING	23988-8	$1.95
☐ THIS ROUGH MAGIC	22846-0	$1.75
☐ THUNDER ON THE RIGHT	23940-3	$1.95
☐ TOUCH NOT THE CAT	23201-8	$1.95

Buy them at your local bookstores or use this handy coupon for ordering:

FAWCETT BOOKS GROUP
P.O. Box C730, 524 Myrtle Ave., Pratt Station, Brooklyn, N.Y. 11205

Please send me the books I have checked above. Orders for less than 5 books must include 75¢ for the first book and 25¢ for each additional book to cover mailing and handling. I enclose $_____ in check or money order.

Name_____

Address_____

City_____ State/Zip_____

Please allow 4 to 5 weeks for delivery.

W0102-W

Victoria Holt

Here are the stories you love best. Tales about love, intrigue, wealth, power and of course romance. Books that will keep you turning the pages deep into the night.

☐ BRIDE OF PENDORRIC	23280-8	$1.95
☐ THE CURSE OF THE KINGS	23284-0	$1.95
☐ THE HOUSE OF A THOUSAND. LANTERNS	23685-4	$1.95
☐ THE KING OF THE CASTLE	23587-4	$1.95
☐ KIRKLAND REVELS	23920-9	$1.95
☐ LEGEND OF THE SEVENTH VIRGIN	23281-6	$1.95
☐ LORD OF THE FAR ISLAND	22874-6	$1.95
☐ MENFREYA IN THE MORNING	23757-5	$1.95
☐ MISTRESS OF MELLYN	23924-1	$1.95
☐ ON THE NIGHT OF THE SEVENTH MOON	23568-0	$1.95
☐ THE PRIDE OF THE PEACOCK	23198-4	$1.95
☐ THE QUEEN'S CONFESSION	23213-1	$1.95
☐ THE SECRET WOMAN	23283-2	$1.95
☐ SHADOW OF THE LYNX	23278-6	$1.95
☐ THE SHIVERING SANDS	23282-4	$1.95

Buy them at your local bookstores or use this handy coupon for ordering: